# Garrett
# Investigates

# Garrett Investigates

## Deadly Quicksilver Lies
## Petty Pewter Gods
## Faded Steel Heat

# Glen Cook

50 YEARS SFBC FANTASY

# Garrett Investigates

# Contents

# Deadly Quicksilver Lies

# 1

There ain't no justice, I guarantee absodamnlutely. There I was, comfy as could be, feet on my desk, a pint of Weider's porter in my hand, Espinosa's latest potboiler in my other hand, and Eleanor reading over my shoulder. She understood Espinosa better than I did. For once the Goddamn Parrot wasn't squawking. I sucked up that sweet silence more enthusiastically than I did the beer.

Some fool went to hammering on my door.

His pounding had an arrogant, impatient edge. Meant it would be somebody I didn't want to see. "Dean! See who that is! Tell him to go away. I'm out of town. On a secret mission for the king. Won't be back for years. And I wouldn't buy what he's selling anyway, if I *was* home."

Nobody moved. My cook-slash-housekeeper-slash-factotum was the one who was out of town. I was at the mercy of wannabe clients and the Goddamn Parrot.

Dean had gone to TemisVar. One of his herd of homely nieces was going to get married. He wanted to make sure her fool fiance didn't wake up before it was too late.

The pounding continued bruising my door. I'd just installed it, replacing one broken down by a villain who couldn't take a hint. "Damned insensitive jerk!" I muttered. Hollering and threats backed the hammering. The neighbors were going to get upset. Again.

Sleepy, puzzled noises came from the small front room between my office and the door. "I'll kill him if he wakes that talking chicken." I glanced at Eleanor. She offered no advice. She just hung there, baffled by Espinosa.

"Guess I better dent a head before I got to deal with another citizens' committee." Or had to put up a new door. Doors aren't only not cheap, they're hard to come by.

I dropped my feet, stretched my six feet two, got going. The Goddamn Parrot made a noise. I peeked into his room.

The little buzzard was only talking in his sleep. Excellent! He was one pretty monster. He had a yellow head, blue neck ruff, red and green body and wings. His tail feathers were long enough I could maybe someday cash in with a band of gnomes who needed decorations for their hats. But a monster he was, for sure. Somewhere sometime somebody put a curse on that foul-beaked vulture so he's got the vocabulary of a stevedore. He lives to be obnoxious.

He was a gift from my "friend" Morley Dotes. Made me wonder about the nature of friendship.

The Goddamn Parrot—dba Mr. Big—stirred. I got out of there before he took a notion to wake up.

I have a peephole in my front door. I peeped. I muttered, "Winger. Wouldn't you know?" My luck and water have plenty in common, especially always heading downhill. Winger was a natural disaster looking for a place to happen. A stubborn disaster, too. I knew she'd pound away till hunger got her. She didn't look underfed.

She wouldn't worry about what the neighbors thought, either. She noticed the opinions of others the way a mastodon noticed undergrowth in the woods.

I opened up. Winger moved forward without being invited in. I stayed put and almost got trampled. She is big and beautiful, but her candle doesn't burn too bright. "Need to talk to you, Garrett," she said. "I need some help. Business."

I should have known better. Hell. I *did* know better. But times were dull. Dean wasn't around to nag me. The Dead Man had been asleep for weeks. I had nobody but the Goddamn Parrot for company. All my friends were beset by lady friends, a trial that hadn't befallen me during any recent epoch. "All right. I know I'm gonna be sorry, but all right. I'll give you a listen. Promising nothing."

"Hows about a brew while we're jawing?" Winger shy? I don't think so. She headed for the kitchen. I took a look around outside before I shut the door. You never knew what might be tagging after Winger. She didn't have sense enough to look back. She survived on luck, not skill.

"Awk! Holy hooters! Garrett! Check them gazoombies."

Damn! What I got for not closing the door to the small front room.

The street showed me only a clutter of people and animals and dwarves and elves and a squadron of centaur immigrants. The usual.

I shut the door. I went to the small front room and closed that door, ignoring outraged allegations of neglect. "Stow it, bird. Unless you want to get neglected right into some ratman's dinner pot."

He laughed. He mocked.

He was right. I have no use for ratmen, but I wouldn't do that to them.

Then he yelled rape. I didn't worry. Winger had heard it before.

"Help yourself, why don't you?" I said when I hit the kitchen, like she hadn't helped herself already. She'd glommed the biggest mug in the house, too.

She winked. "Here's to ya, big guy." She knew exactly what she was doing but didn't have the grace to be embarrassed. "You and your sidekick in there."

"Yeah? You want a parrot?" I drew myself a mug, settled at the kitchen table.

"That crow in a clown suit? What would I do with him?" She planted herself opposite me, beyond dunes of dirty dishes.

"How about get yourself an eyepatch, get into the pirate business?"

"Don't know if I could dance with a pegleg. It ever say 'Shiver me timbers' or 'Argh, matey'?"

"What?"

"What I thought. You're trying to stick me with a substandard bird."

"Huh?"

"That's no sailor bird, Garrett. That critter is pure city. Knows more gutter talk than me."

"So teach him some sea chanties."

"Yo ho ho. Dean finally croak?" She stared at the dishes.

"He's out of town. Got a niece that's getting married. Looking for a part-time job?"

Winger had met some of Dean's nieces, all of whom brought new meaning to the word homely. She controlled her astonishment, though, and pretended to miss my hint about the dishes. "I was married once."

Oh, boy. I hoped she didn't get started.

She was still married but didn't let legal trivia encumber her. "Don't go misty on me, Winger."

"Misty? You shitting me? After that, Hell is gonna look good."

Winger is a tad unusual, case you haven't noticed. She is twenty-six, as tall as I am, and built like the proverbial masonry privy—on an epic scale. Also, she has what some guys think is an attitude problem. Just can't figure out how to stay in her place.

"You want my help," I reminded. Just a poke. My keg wasn't bottomless. I smirked. Maybe she was desperate enough to take the Goddamn Parrot off my hands.

"Uhm." She would get to the point only after she had mooched her fill. That quantity would clue me as to the state of her fortunes.

"You're looking good, Winger." Even Winger likes to hear that. "Must be doing all right."

She assumed I meant her outfit. That was new and, as always, remarkable. "Where I work, they want you should dress snappy."

I kept a straight face. "Unusual" is only the most cautious, gentlest way to characterize Winger's taste. Let's say you couldn't lose her in a crowd. If she went around with the Goddamn Parrot on her shoulder, nobody would notice the bird. "That outfit *is* pretty timid. When you worked for that fat freak Lubbock . . ."

"It's the territory. These guys want you should blend in."

Again I kept my face straight. Being amused by Winger when Winger isn't amused can be hazardous to your health—especially if you're dim enough to, say, crack wise about her blending in.

"Old-timer's gone, eh? What about the ugly thing?" She meant my partner, the Dead Man, so-called because he hasn't run any footraces since somebody stuck a knife in him four hundred years ago. "Ugly thing" is apt. He isn't human. He's a Loghyr, which explains why he's still hanging around so long after he was murdered. Loghyr are slow and stubborn, especially when it comes to sloughing off the old mortal clay. They're deliberate, he would say.

"Asleep. Been weeks since he bugged me. I'm in heaven."

Winger sneered, flipped blond hair out of her face. "Likely to wake up?"

"Maybe if the house catches on fire. Got something to hide?" The Dead Man's big trick is mind reading.

"No more than usual. I was just thinking, it's been a dry spell. Way I hear, weather ain't been so hot for you, neither."

That was my pal Winger, so shy and demure. Somehow, with her, the romance and adventure were absent. "Thought you had desperate business."

"Desperate?"

"You like to tore the door down. You woke up the Goddamn Parrot with your whooping and hollering." That about-to-become-roasted squab was holding forth up front. "I figured you had killer elves slavering on your trail."

"I just wish. I told you how my luck's been. I was just trying to get your attention." She refilled her mug, did mine, headed for my office. "All right, Garrett. Business first."

She paused, listened. T.G. Parrot was on a roll. She shrugged, slipped into my office. I followed quickly. Sometimes things fall into Winger's pockets if you're not there to keep an eye on them.

I wriggled into my chair, safe behind my desk. Eleanor guarded my back. Winger scowled at the painting, then eyed my book. "Espinosa? Ain't that a little heavy for you?"

"It's a real thriller." Espinosa *was* beyond me, mostly. He tended to make a big deal out of questions that wouldn't have occurred to anybody who worked for a living.

I'd gone to visit a lady friend at the Royal Library. The book was all I got.

"Philosophy is thrilling? Like a hemorrhoid. The man should've got a hobby."

"He did. Philosophy. Since when can you read?"

"You don't need to act so surprised. I been learning. Got to do something with my ill-gotten gains, don't I? I thought maybe some learning might come in handy someday. But mostly what I've learned is studying don't make you no smarter about people."

I started to agree. I know some pretty dim academics, people who live in another world. Winger cut me off. "Enough chit-chat. Here's the gig. This old broad name of Maggie Jenn is maybe gonna come see you. I don't know what's up, but my boss is willing to pay a shitload of money to find out. This Jenn crone knows me so I can't get close to her. What I figured was, why don't I get you to let her hire you, then you let me know what she's up to and I can take that to my boss."

Vintage Winger.

"Maggie Jenn?"

"That's the name."

"Seems like it ought to ring a bell. Who is she?"

"You got me. Just some old broad off the Hill."

"The Hill?" I leaned back, just a harried man of affairs taking a moment out to relax with an old friend. "I have a case."

"What is it this time? A stray lizard?" She laughed. Her laughter sounded like geese headed north for the winter. "Meow, meow."

A few days earlier, I'd gotten stung by an old biddy who'd hired me to look for her beloved missing Moggie. Never mind the details. It's embarrassing enough just *me* knowing. "That's on the street?"

Winger swung her feet onto my desk. "All over it."

Dean was in it deep. *I* hadn't told a soul.

"Best Garrett story I heard in a while, too. Thousand marks for a cat? Come on."

"You know how some old ladies are about their cats." The cat hadn't been the problem, really. The problems started when I found a real animal that was a ringer for the imaginary, red herring beast. "Who would suspect a sweet old lady of wanting to set him up for a fall guy in a scam?"

Honk honk, har har. "I would've got suspicious when she wouldn't come to my house."

What saved me was finding that cat. I caught on when I tried to take him home. "Yeah."

The Dead Man might have saved me all the embarrassment. Had he been awake.

Part of the discomfort of the mess was knowing he'd never stop reminding me about it. "Never mind that. Since we're talking about old ladies, tell me what this Maggie Jenn is going to want."

"I figure she's gonna ask you to kill somebody."

"Say what?" That wasn't what I expected. "Hey! You know—"

# 2

Somebody else was trying out my front door. This somebody had a fist of stone bigger than a ham. "I have a bad feeling about this," I muttered. "Whenever platoons of people start thumping the door . . ."

Winger stowed her leer. "I'll disappear."

"Don't wake the Dead Man."

"You kidding?" She pointed toward the ceiling. "I'll be up there. Find me when you're done."

I was afraid of that.

Having a no-strings, no-complications friendship can have its own complications.

The small front room had grown quiet. I paused to eavesdrop. Not one obscenity marred the precious silence. T.G. Parrot was asleep again.

I thought about making it that jungle pigeon's last nap, the beginning of the big sleep, the longest voyage, the . . .

Boom boom boom.

I peeked through the peephole. By-the-numbers Garrett, that's me. Fixing to live a thousand years.

All I saw was a smallish redhead facing three-quarters away, staring at something. That little bit did all that pounding? She was stronger than she looked. I opened the door. She continued staring up the street. I leaned forward cautiously.

The neighborhood pixie teens were chucking rotten fruits off the cornices and gutters of an ugly old three-story half a block up Macunado. A band of gnomes below dodged and cursed and shook their walking sticks. They were all old, clad in the usual drab gray, with whiskers. Not beards, whiskers, like you see in paintings of old-time generals and princes and merchant captains. All gnomes seem to be old and out of fashion. I've never seen a young one or a female one.

One spry little codger, chanting a colorful warsong about discount rates and yam futures, pegged a broken cobblestone hard enough to actually hit a pixie. It did a somersault off a gargoyle's head. The gnomes pranced around and waved their sticks in glee and sent up an ave to the Great Arbitrager. Then the pixie brat opened his wings and soared. His laughter was a mocking squeak.

I told the redhead, "An exercise in futility. All sound and fury. Been going on all month. Nobody's gotten hurt yet. Probably all die of shame if anybody did." Gnomes are that way. Gladly make fortunes financing wars but don't want to watch the bloodshed.

I spied a sedan chair at streetside down toward Macunado's intersection with Wizard's Reach. Beside it stood something half man and half gorilla with hands that fit the prescription for whatever it was that had tried to demolish my door. "That thing tame?"

"Mugwump? He's a sweetheart. And as human as you are." The redhead's tone suggested she might be, unwittingly, insulting friend Mugwump.

"Can I help you?" Boy, would I like to help her. Mugwump was old news.

I make a point of being nice to redheads, at least till they're not nice to me. Redhead was always my favorite color, barely edging blonde and brunette.

The woman turned to me. "Mr. Garrett?" Her voice was low, husky, sexy.

I didn't owe any money. "Guilty." Surprise, surprise. She was a good decade older than my first guess. But time had stolen nothing. She was proof on the hoof that aging produces fine wines. Second-guessing, I put her over thirty-five but under forty. Me, I'm a tender, innocent thirty and don't usually look for them quite so ripe.

"You're staring, Mr. Garrett. I thought that was impolite."

"Huh? Oh. Yeah. Excuse me."

The Goddamn Parrot started muttering in his sleep. Something about interspecies necrophilia. That got me back to the real world. "What can I do for you, madam?" Other than the obvious, if you're looking for volunteers. Hoo.

I was amazed. Yeah, female of the species is my soft spot, my blind side, but the mature type didn't usually get me. Whatever, something about this one totally distracted me. And she knew it.

Businesslike, Garrett. Businesslike.

"Ma'am, Mr. Garrett? Am I that far past it?"

I sputtered. I stumbled around and tripped over my tongue till it was black with footprints. She finally had mercy and smiled. "Can we get in out of the weather?"

"Sure." I stepped aside, held the door. What was wrong with the weather? It couldn't have been nicer. There were barely enough clouds to keep you from falling into a sky as blue as you will ever hope to see.

She brushed past without tricks, just close because she had to. I shut my eyes. I ground my teeth. I babbled, "My office is the second door on the left. I can't offer much but beer or brandy. My man Dean is away." The woman had to be a witch. Or I was out of practice. Bad.

"Brandy would be perfect, Mr. Garrett."

Of course. Pure class. "Coming right up. Make yourself at home." I dove into the kitchen. Dig dig dig till I found some brandy. A bit of a tippler, Dean hides the stuff all over so I won't know how much he has bought. I poured from a bottle that I hoped contained good stuff. What did I know about brandy? Beer is *my* favorite food. I zipped to the office. The seasoned redhead had set up camp in the client's chair. She frowned as she studied Eleanor. "Here you go."

"Thank you. An interesting painting. There's a lot there if you look long enough."

I glanced at my honey as I settled. She was a lovely blonde, terrified, fleeing something only hinted at in the painting's background. If you looked at that painting right, though, you could read the whole evil story. There was magic in it, though much of that had gone once I got the man who murdered Eleanor.

I told the story. My visitor was a good listener. I managed to avoid getting totally lost in my own chemistry. I observed carefully. I suggested, "You might introduce yourself before we go any further. I'm never comfortable calling a woman 'Hey You'."

Her smile softened the enamel on my teeth. "My name is Maggie Jenn. Margat Jenn, actually, but I've never been called anything but Maggie."

Ah, the monster of the prophecy. Winger's old crone. Must have lost her walker. I blurted, "Maggie doesn't sound like a redhead."

Her smile warmed up. Incredible! "Surely you're not that naive, Mr. Garrett."

"Garrett is fine. Mr. Garrett was my grandpop. No. It hasn't escaped me that some women miraculously transform overnight."

"This is just a tint, really. A little more red than my natural shade. Just vanity. One more rearguard skirmish in my war against time."

Yeah. The poor toothless hag. "Looks to me like you've got it on the run."

"You're sweet." She smiled again, turning up the heat. She leaned forward. . . .

# 3

Maggie Jenn caught my left hand, squeezed. "Some women enjoy being looked at that way, Garrett. Sometimes they want to look back." She tickled my palm. I stifled an urge to pant. She was working me and I didn't care. "But I'm here on business and it's important, so we'd better get to it." She took her hand back.

I was supposed to melt, going through withdrawal.

I went through withdrawal.

"I like this room, Garrett. Tells me a lot. Confirms what I've heard about you."

I waited. Clients go through this. They're desperate when they arrive. They wouldn't come to me if they weren't. But they stall around before admitting that their lives have gone out of control. Most end up telling me how they chose me. Maggie Jenn did that.

Some change their minds before they get to the point. Maggie Jenn did not.

"I didn't realize I was so well known. That's scary." Apparently my name was common coin among the ruling class, to which Maggie Jenn clearly belonged, though she had not revealed where she fit. I should avoid the flashy cases. I don't like being noticed.

"You're on everyone's list of specialists, Garrett. If you want a coach built, you go to Linden Atwood. You want unique flatware, you commission Rickman Plax and Sons. You want the best shoes, you buy Tate. You need prying and spying, you hire Garrett."

"Speaking of prying and spying."

"You want me to get to the point."

"I'm used to people circling in on their troubles."

She reflected a moment. "I see where they might. It's hard. All right. To the point. I need you to find my daughter."

"Huh?" She blindsided me. I was all tensed for her to ask me to kill somebody and all she wanted was the basic Garrett service.

"I need you to find my daughter. She's been missing for six days. I'm worried. What's the matter? You have the funniest look."

"I get like this when I think about working."

"You have that reputation. What will it take to get you out of the house?"

"More information. And the fee settled." There. I could be proud of me. I was taking command, being businesslike, handling my weakness.

So how come I was practically agreeing to take a case blind?

Actually, despite my reputation and past habit of laziness, I had been working steady, minor stuff, grabbing a few marks while I avoided the house and Dean, the Dead Man and the Goddamn Parrot. The former suffer from the delusion that it will be a better world if I work myself to death. T.G.P. just nags.

"Her name is Justina, Garrett. She's an adult, though just barely. I don't hang over her shoulder."

"An adult? What were you, ten years old? . . ."

"Flattery will get you everywhere. I was eighteen. She turned eighteen three months ago. Never mind the math."

"Hell, you're a spring chicken. Twenty-one with a few years' experience. You don't need to stop counting yet. I bet plenty of people take you for Justina's sister."

"Aren't you the sweet talker."

"Actually, I'm only being honest. I'm way too distracted to . . ."

"I'll bet the girls love you, Garrett."

"Yeah. You hear them chanting in the street. You saw them climbing the walls so they can get in through a second-story window." TunFaire being TunFaire, my house has only one ground floor window, in the kitchen. Iron bars cover it.

Maggie Jenn's eyes sparkled. "I have a feeling I'm going to wish I'd met you sooner, Garrett." Those eyes promised. Maybe I was going to wish that, too.

A redhead will knock me for a loop every time.

She continued. "To the point. Again. Justina's been running with bad companions. Nothing I can put my finger on, no. Just youngsters I don't like. I got the feeling they were up to something wicked. No, I never saw anything to confirm that."

One thing you notice about parents who are looking for strayed children. They never liked anyone the kid liked. The kid is gone because he or she fell in with evil companions. Even when they strain to be nonjudgmental, there's this basic assumption that the friends are no good. If any of the friends are of another sex, boy, howdy!

"I expect you'll want to know all about her before you start, right?"

We had us a built-in assumption I'd be working for Momma Jenn. Momma Jenn was used to getting her own way. "Best way to do it. I knew a guy in my line whose whole thing was to get right inside the head of whoever he was hunting. He'd ignore everything but the character of that one guy. He'd almost become that guy. 'Course, lots of times he could've got his man quicker by looking at the big picture."

"You'll have to tell me about some of your cases. It's not a side of life I see. Must be exciting. Suppose you come to my house for an early supper? You can examine Justina's room and her things and ask your questions. Then you can decide whether or not you want the case." She smiled a smile that put her earlier efforts to shame. She was confident. I was getting roasted, toasted, manipulated, and I loved every second of it.

I said, "It happens I'm free tonight."

"Perfect." She rose, began donning flesh-colored gloves I hadn't noticed before. She considered Eleanor. Her face darkened. She shuddered. Eleanor can have that effect. "Fifth hour?" Maggie asked.

"I'll be there. But you'll have to tell me where."

Her face did darken then. Big mistake, Garrett. I was supposed to know without being told. Unfortunately, I knew so little about Maggie Jenn I didn't know that she would be irked because I didn't know who she was or where she lived.

The lady was a trooper. She carried on. She dallied only a moment before offering an address.

I got real nervous real sudden.

We were talking way up the Hill, where the richest and most powerful of the rich and powerful live, up where the altitude itself is the best indicator of wealth and might. Blue Crescent Street was in the realm of fairy tale as far as I was concerned.

Maggie Jenn was a lady with big connections, but I still could not recall why I thought I should know her name.

It would come when it was really inconvenient.

I escorted the lovely lady to my front door. The lovely lady continued to smolder and invite. Would the evening have *anything* to do with a missing daughter?

# 4

I stood bemused by Maggie Jenn swaying toward her litter. She knew I was watching. She made it a good show.

That killer stump Mugwump watched me watch. I didn't get the impression that he wished me well.

"You never stop foaming at the mouth, do you?"

I realized that I *had* settled down to savor every second of Maggie's departure. I tore my gaze away, turned to see which of my busybody neighbors was going to permit me to bask in the chill of her disapproval. I discovered, instead, a very attractive little brunette. She had approached from the other direction.

"Linda Lee!" This was my friend from the Royal Library, about whom I'd been thinking while holding Espinosa's book instead. "This is the nicest surprise I've had in a while." I went down to meet her. "I'm glad you changed your mind." Linda Lee, barely five feet tall, with beautiful big brown puppy eyes, was just about the cutest bit of a librarian I could imagine.

"Down, boy. This is a public place."

"Come into my parlor."

"If I do that, I'll forget all about why I came here." She plopped herself down on a step sideways. She locked her ankles together, pulled her knees up under her chin, wrapped her arms around them, and looked at me with a little girl innocence she knew would turn me into a love zombie.

It was my day to be a plaything.

I could handle it. I'd been born for that role.

Linda Lee Luther was no innocent, whatever impression you got at first glance. But she did try hard to be the icemaiden some folks thought a librarian should be. She tried but failed. Real ice wasn't in her nature. I just stood there, wearing my winningest grin, confident that she would talk herself into leaving the public eye.

"Stop that!"

"What?" I asked.

"Looking at me like that. I know what you're thinking. . . ."

"I can't help that."

"Yes, well, you're going to make me forget why I came here."

I didn't believe that for a second, but I'm a good guy. I can go along with a gag. "All right. Tell me about it."

"Huh?"

"What brought you here if not my irresistable charm?"

"I need your help. Professionally."

Why me?

I didn't believe it. Librarians don't get into fixes where they need guys like me to get them unfixed. Not cute little bits like Linda Lee Luther.

I'd begun moving toward my door. Preoccupied, Linda Lee rose and followed. I had her inside. I had the front door closed and bolted. I tried sneaking her past the open door of the small front room. The Goddamn Parrot mumbled obscenities in his sleep. Lovely Linda Lee did not take exception. I began to recall why I was so fond of this girl. I asked her, "What's got you so distracted?"

This was her big chance to come back with something clever and suggestive, an opportunity she wouldn't have wasted usually. But she just moaned, "I'm going to get fired. I just know it."

"That doesn't seem likely." Really.

"You don't understand. I lost a book, Garrett. A rare book. One that can't be replaced. It may have been stolen."

I eased into my office. Linda Lee followed me. Where was this attraction when I wanted to use it most?

"I have to get it back before they find out," Linda Lee continued. "There's no excuse for me having let this happen."

I told her, "Calm down. Take a deep breath. Hold it. Then tell me all about it, from the beginning. I'm already tied up in a job that's going to keep me busy for a while, but there's still a chance I can suggest something."

I took her by the shoulders, maneuvered her over to the client's seat. She settled.

"Tell me from the beginning," I reminded.

Aargh! The best laid plans, and so forth. Instead of spinning her sad tale of woe, she started sputtering and gesturing, original mission completely forgotten.

Uh-oh.

The Espinosa. Right there on my desk.

I hadn't quite observed all the formalities when I'd borrowed it. The library powers that be don't trust ordinary folks with books, anyway. Books might give us ideas.

I gobbled something placatory that got lost in the uproar, totally failed to steer her back to that matter of the loss that had brought her to me. "How could you do this to me, Garrett? I'm already in trouble. . . . If they miss this book too, I'm dead. How could you?"

Well, the how had been easy. It wasn't a very big book and the old veteran guarding the door had been napping. He'd had only one leg, anyway.

Words continued to vomit from my lovely Linda Lee. An awesome performance. She got a grip on the Espinosa like it was her firstborn about to be reposed by a dwarf with a polysyllabic name.

How do you argue with panic? I didn't.

Linda Lee suddenly made a run for it. I didn't get around the desk fast enough. She squawked every step to the front door.

Wa-hoo! said the Goddamn Parrot. What a great excuse for raising hell. He went to work.

A moment later, I was watching Linda Lee scamper up Macunado, her anger so palpable eight-foot ogres scooted out of her way.

Her visit lasted so briefly I caught a last glimpse of Maggie Jenn's litter before it, too, got lost in traffic. Mugwump sent me a scowl to remember him by.

What a day. What next?

One thing seemed certain. There were no more lovelies headed my way. Sigh.

Time to take a minute to see what Eleanor thought about Maggie Jenn.

# 5

I settled behind my desk, stared at Eleanor. "What did you think of Maggie, darling? Should I be your basic opportunist? Go for it even if she is older than me?"

Eleanor doesn't say much but I manage by putting words in her mouth. "Yeah, I know. I went for you. A ghost." Picture that. I've been infatuated a few thousand times but hopelessly in love only twice, most recently with a woman who died when I was four. "So what's the big deal she's a few years older, eh?"

Weird things happen to me. Vampires. Dead gods trying to resurrect themselves. Killer zombies. Serial murderers who keep right on killing after you find them and send them off to the happy hunting ground. So why consider a love affair with a ghost outrageous?

"Yeah. I know. It would be cynical of me. What? Sure, she plans to use me, too. I know. But what a way to be used."

From the hall, I heard, "Yo, Garrett. I'm getting gray hairs hanging around up here."

Winger. Damn! I can't remember everything, can I? I rose slowly, still distracted. Maggie Jenn had cast a spell on me, no doubt about it. I'd almost forgotten my disappointment over Linda Lee.

I found Winger sitting on the stairs. "What are you doing, Garrett? The old broad left fifteen minutes ago." She didn't mention Linda Lee's hollering.

"I've been thinking."

"That's dangerous for a guy in your condition."

"Huh?" I didn't have a comeback. For only about the ten thousandth time in my life. The perfect response would spawn sometime as I lay tossing and turning an hour before dawn.

Winger strode to the Dead Man's door, stuck her nose in. His room takes up half the ground floor. I looked over her shoulder. All 450 pounds of him remained planted in his chair, still as death. The Loghyr's elephantlike snout dangled down a foot to his chest. Dust had begun to collect on him, but the vermin hadn't found him yet. No point cleaning until they did. Maybe Dean would come home first and save me the trouble.

Winger backed out of there, grabbed my elbow. "He's out of it." She knew because he hadn't reacted to her. He has no use for females in general and less use for Winger. Once, I threatened to boot Dean out and move her in.

"What did she say?" Winger asked as we headed upstairs. "Who's the target?"

"You don't know?"

"I don't know squat. All I know is I'm getting paid a shitpot full to find out."

Money was important to Winger. It is to all of us, in a palsy sort of way: nice to have around, fun to be with. But for Winger, it was like a patron saint.

"She wants me to find her daughter. The girl's been missing for six days."

"Say what? I'll be damned. I was sure it was going to be a hit."

"Why?"

"No special reason. I guess I added the cues up wrong. Looking for her kid? You take the job?"

"I'm thinking about it. I'm supposed to go up to her place, check out the kid's stuff, before I decide."

"But you'll take it, right? Make yourself some of that old double money?"

"An intriguing idea. Only I haven't seen single money from anybody yet."

"You sly bastard. You're thinking about topping the old broad. You're here with me and you're thinking about that. You're a regular villain."

"Winger! The woman is old enough to be my mother."

"Then you or mom is lying about their age."

"You're the one that went on about what an old hag she was."

"What's that got to do with anything? Hell. I forgive you, Garrett. Like I said, you're here. And she's not."

Arguing with Winger is like spitting into a whirlwind. Not much profit in it.

Only through a supreme effort did I get away in time to join Maggie Jenn for dinner.

# 6

"Ta-ta," I told the Dead Man—softly, so the Goddamn Parrot wouldn't hear. "I spent the day with a beautiful blonde. In penance, I'm going to spend the evening with a gorgeous redhead."

He did not respond. He sure would have had he been awake. Winger had a special place in his heart. He had half believed my threat to marry her.

Laughing gently, still unforgiven, I tiptoed toward the front door. Before his departure, at incredible expense (to me), Dean had had a key lock installed in the new door, like I hadn't survived before he was there to slam bolts and bars into place behind me. Dean placed his trust in the wrong things. A key lock never stops anybody but the honest people. Our real protection is the Dead Man.

Loghyr have many talents, dead or alive.

I strutted away smiling at one and all, deaf to their squabbles. We were getting a lot of nonhumans in the neighborhood, mostly rough type refugees from the Cantard, never shy about expressing opinions. There was always a fuss among them.

Worse, though, were the proto-revolutionaries. Those crowded every loft and sleeping room. They overflowed the taverns, where they chattered foolishly about ever less workable dogmas. I understood what moved them. I didn't think much of the Crown, either. But I did know that none of us, them or me, was ready to try on the king's shoes.

A real revolution would make things worse. These days no two revolutionaries agree whither the Karentine state, anyway. So they would have to murder one another wholesale before . . .

Revolution had been tried already, anyway, but so ineptly that hardly anybody but the secret police knew.

I ignored the hairy-faced, black-clad agents of chaos on the corners, scowling paranoiacally while they debated doctrinal trivia. The Crown was not in much danger. I have contacts in the new city police, the Guard. They say half the revolutionaries are really spies.

I waved to people. I whistled. It was a glorious day.

I was on the job, however. Though I was whistling my way to dinner with a beautiful woman, I observed my surroundings. I noticed the guy following me.

I roamed. I dawdled. I ambled. I strolled. I tried to get an estimate of the clown's intent. He wasn't very good. I pondered my options.

Turning the tables appealed to me. I could shake him, then follow him when he ran to report.

I do have enemies, sad to admit. In the course of my labors, occasionally I inconvenience some unpleasant people. Some might want to even scores.

I hate a bad loser.

My friend Morley Dotes, a professional killer who masquerades as a vegetarian gourmet, claims it's my own fault for leaving them alive behind me.

I studied my tail till I was sure I could handle him, then hurried along to keep my date with Maggie Jenn.

# 7

The Jenn place was a fifty-room hovel on the edge of the inner-most circle of the Hill. No mere tradesman, however rich, however powerful, would reach that final ring.

Funny. Maggie Jenn had not struck me as the aristo type.

The name still nagged. I still did not recall why I ought to know it.

That part of the Hill was all stone, vertical and horizontal. No yards, no gardens, no sidewalks, no green anywhere unless on the rare third-story balcony. No brick. Red or brown brick was what the mob used to build. Forget that. Use stone that was quarried in another country and had to be barged for hundreds of miles.

I'd never been to the area so I got disoriented.

There weren't any spaces between buildings. The street was so narrow two carriages couldn't pass without climbing the side-walks. It was cleaner than the rest of the city, but the gray stone pavements and buildings made the view seem dingy anyway. Walking that street was like walking the bottom of a dismal limestone canyon.

The Jenn address was in the middle of a featureless block. The door was more like a postern gate than an entrance to a home. Not one window faced the street, just an unbroken cliff of stone. The wall even lacked ornament, unusual for the Hill. Hill folk build to outdo their neighbors in displays of bad taste.

Some slick architect must have sold some otherwise shrewd character the notion that starkness was the way to shine. No doubt storehouses of wealth changed hands, the ascetic look being more costly than mere gingerbread.

Me, I like cheap. Gimme a herd of double-ugly gargoyles and some little boys peeing off the gutter corners.

The knocker was so discreet you almost had to hunt for it. It wasn't even brass, just some gray metal like pewter or tin. It made a restrained *tick tick* so feeble I'd have thought nobody inside could hear it.

The plain teak door opened immediately. I found myself face-to-face with a guy who looked like he got stuck with the name Ichabod by malicious parents back around the turn of the century. He looked like he had spent the numerous intervening decades living down to the image that kind of name conjures. He was long and bony and bent. His eyes were red and his hair was white and his skin was oh so pale. I muttered, "So this is what they do when they get old. Hang up their black swords and turn into butlers." He had an Adam's apple that looked like he was choking on a grapefruit. He didn't say a word, he just stood there staring like a buzzard waiting for a snack to cool.

He had the biggest bony arches over his eyes I ever saw. They were forested with white jungles.

Spooky guy.

"Dr. Death, I presume?" Dr. Death was a character in the Punch and Judy shows going around. Ichabod and the bad doctor had a lot in common, but the puppet was six feet shorter.

Some people have no sense of humor. We had us one of those here. Ichabod neither cracked a smile nor twitched one of those woodlots camped over his eyes. He did speak, though. Fair Karentine, too. "You have some cause for disturbing this household?"

"Sure." I didn't like his tone. I never like the tone of Hill servants. It's filled with the defensive snobbishness you find in the tone of a turncoat. "I wanted to see if you guys really do shrivel in the sunlight." I had the advantage in this dumb game because I was expected and he'd been given my description. And he'd recognized me.

If he hadn't recognized me, he would've slammed the door against my nose. Word would have gone out to the thugs who defend the rich and mighty from nuisances like me. A band would be hastening hither to deal me an exemplary drubbing.

Come to think of it, they could be hastening anyway, if Ichabod had a confederate with no better sense of humor. "Name's Garrett," I announced. "Maggie Jenn asked me to come for dinner."

The old spook stepped back. He never said a word, but it was plain he doubted his boss's wisdom. He didn't approve of letting my kind in the house. No telling what might have to be dragged back out of my pockets before they let me go. Or maybe I'd scratch off some fleas and leave them to colonize the rugs.

I glanced back to see how my tail was making out. Poor sod was playing hell staying inconspicuous.

"Nice door," I observed as I caught it edge-on. It was four inches thick. "Expecting a debt collector with a battering ram?" Hill people are rich enough to have those kinds of problems. Nobody would loan me enough for me to get in trouble.

"Follow me." Ichabod turned.

"That should be 'follow me, sir.'" I don't know why the guy made me antagonistic. "I'm a guest. You're a flunky." I began having second thoughts about revolutions. When I go over to the Royal Library to see Linda Lee, I poke around in the books, too. Once I read one about rebellions. Seems like the servants of the overthrown get it worse than their masters do—unless they are perceptive enough to be agents of the rebels.

"Indeed."

"Ah. A comment. Lead on, Ichabod."

"The name is Zeke, sir." The sir dripped sarcasm.

"Zeke?" That was as bad as Ichabod. Almost.

"Yes, sir. Are you coming? The mistress doesn't like to be kept waiting."

"Do lead on, then. The thousand and one gods of TunFaire forfend that we distress Her Redheadedness."

Zeke elected not to respond. He'd concluded that I had an attitude problem. He was right, of course, but for the wrong reasons. And I was a little ashamed. He was probably a nice old man with a herd of grandkids, forced to work into his dotage in order to support ungrateful descendants who were the offspring of sons killed in the Cantard.

I didn't believe that for a minute, though.

The interior of that place bore no resemblance to the outside. It was pretty dusty now, but it had started out as the daydream of some wharfside loser who imagined himself a great potentate. Or a great potentate with the tastes of a wharfside loser. I'll get some of these and a bunch of those and . . . And the only thing missing was a troop of houris.

The place was lousy with tasteless billows of wealth. Plush everything and way too much of it, and even more of everything as we moved nearer the center of the pit. Actually, we seemed to advance from zone to zone, each another expression of bad taste.

"Whoa!" said I, unable to restrain myself. "There it is." *It* being a mammoth's-foot cane and brolly stand. "You don't see a lot of those."

Zeke gave me a look, read my reaction to that bit of down-home chic. His stone face relaxed for a moment. He agreed. In that instant, we concluded a shaky armistice.

No doubt it would survive no longer than Karenta's armistice with Venageta, which had lasted a whole six and a half hours.

"Sometimes we cannot relinquish our pasts, sir."

"Maggie Jenn used to be a mammoth hunter?"

The peace was over. Just like that. He hunked along sullenly. I think that was because I'd admitted I didn't have the faintest idea what Maggie Jenn used to be.

How come everyone thought I should know who she was? Including me? My famous memory was doing famously today.

Zeke ushered me into the worst room yet. "Madame will join you here." I looked around, shading my eyes, began to wonder if Madame didn't used to be a madam. The place was for sure done up in whorehouse modern, probably by the same nancy boys who did the high-fly joints down in the Tenderloin.

I turned to ask a question.

Ichabod had abandoned me.

I almost squeaked for him to come back. "Oh, Zeke! Bring me a blindfold." I didn't think I could stand the sensory assault otherwise.

# 8

It got to me. I stood around like I'd just made eye contact with a medusa. I'd never seen so much red. Everything was a red of the reddest reds, overwhelmingly red. Ubiquitous gold leaf highlights only heightened the impact.

"Garrett."

Maggie Jenn. I didn't have the strength to turn. I was scared she'd be wearing scarlet and lip rouge of a shade that would make her look like a vampire at snack time.

"You alive?"

"Just stunned." I waved a hand. "This is a bit overpowering."

"Kind of sucks, don't it? But Teddy loved it, the gods know why. This place was Teddy's gift, so I keep this part the way he liked it."

I did turn then. No, she hadn't worn red. She wore a peasanty sort of thing that was mostly light brown and white lace and a silly white dairymaid's hat that set off her hair. She also wore a heavy-weight smile that said she was amusing herself at my expense but I was free to join in the fun. I told her, "I'm missing something. I don't get the joke."

Her smile faded. "What do you know about me?"

"Not much. Your name. That you're the sexiest woman I've run into in an age. Various self-evident characteristics. That you live in a classy neighborhood. And that's about it."

She shook her head. Red curls flew around. "Notoriety isn't worth much anymore. Come on. We don't stay here. You'd go blind."

Nice to have somebody crack wise for me. Saved me the trouble of thinking them up and pissing her off.

She led me through several memorable rooms which weren't important enough to note. Then we roared out into the real world, bam! A dining room set for two. "Like a night in Elf Hill," I muttered.

She hadn't lost her hearing. "I used to feel that way. Those rooms can be intimidating. Go ahead. Plant it."

I took a chair opposite her at the end of a table long enough to seat two dozen people. "This is a love nest?"

"Smallest dining room I've got." Hint of a smile.

"You and Teddy?"

"Sigh. How fleeting infamy. Nobody remembers except the family. That's all right, though. They're bitter enough for everybody. Teddy was Teodoric, Prince of Kamark. He became Teodoric IV and lasted a whole year."

"The king?" Bells began to ring. Finally. "It's starting to come."

"Good. I won't have to put myself through a bunch of explanations."

"I don't know a lot. That all happened when I was in the Marines. In the Cantard, we didn't pay much attention to royal scandals."

"Didn't know who was king and didn't care. I've heard that one." Maggie Jenn smiled her best smile. "I bet you still don't follow royal scandals."

"They don't affect my life much."

"It wouldn't affect your work for me, either, you knowing or not knowing all the dirt."

A woman came in. Like Zeke, she was as old as original sin. She was tiny, the size of a child about to lunge into adolescence. She wore spectacles. Maggie Jenn took good care of her help. Spectacles are *expensive*. The old woman posed, hands clasped in front of her. She neither moved nor spoke.

Maggie Jenn said, "We'll start whenever you're ready, Laurie."

The old woman inclined her head and left.

Maggie said, "I will tell you some of it, though, to soothe that famous curiosity of yours. So you do what I'm paying you to do instead of rooting around in my past."

I grunted.

Laurie and Zeke brought in a soup course. I began salivating. I'd eaten my own cooking too long.

That was the only way I missed Dean, though! You bet.

"I was the king's mistress, Garrett."

"I remember." Finally. It was the scandal of its day, a crown prince falling for a commoner so hard he set her up on the Hill. His wife had not been thrilled. Old Teddy had made no pretense of discretion. He'd been in love and didn't care if the whole world knew. A worrisome attitude in a man who might be king.

It suggested character flaws.

For sure. King Teodoric IV turned out to be an arrogant, narrow-minded, self-indulgent jerk who got himself snuffed within a year.

We aren't tolerant of royal foibles. That is, our royals and nobles aren't tolerant. Nobody else would consider assassination. It just isn't done outside the family. Even our mad dog revolutionaries never suggest offing the royals.

I said, "I do wonder, though, about this daughter."

"Not Teddy's."

I slurped my soup. It was broth and garlic somebody tossed a chicken across. I liked it. Empty bowls went away. An appetizer course appeared. I didn't say anything. Maggie might talk just to extinguish the silence.

"I've made my dumb mistakes, Garrett. My daughter was the result of a lulu."

I chomped something made of chicken liver, bacon, and a giant nutmeat. "This's good."

"I was sixteen. My father married me off to a virgin-obsessed animal who had daughters old enough to be my mother. It was good for business. Since nobody ever told me how you don't get pregnant, I got. My husband had fits. I wasn't supposed to whelp brats, I was supposed to warm his bed and tell him he was the greatest there ever was. He went buggo when I had a daughter. Another daughter. He had no sons. It was all a female plot. We were out to get him. I never had the nerve to tell him what would happen if us women really gave him what he deserved. He got a taste, though." Nasty smile. For one second, a darker Maggie shone through.

She nibbled some food and left me room to comment. I nodded and kept chomping.

"The old bastard never stopped using me, whatever he thought about me. His daughters took pity and showed me what I needed to know. They hated him more than I did. I bided my time. Then my father got killed by robbers who got twelve copper sceats and a pair of junk boots more than a year old."

"That's TunFaire."

She nodded. That *was* TunFaire.

I nudged, "Your dad died."

"So I no longer had any reason to please my husband."

"You walked."

"After I caught him sleeping and beat the living shit out of him with a poker."

"I'll take that to heart."

"Good idea." There was mischief in her eye. I decided I was going to like Maggie Jenn. Anybody who could live through what she had and have a little mischief left . . .

It was an interesting meal. I got to hear all about how she met Teddy without hearing word one about what she did between her shoeleather divorce and that first explosive encounter with the future king. I suspected she had loved Teddy as much as he'd loved her. You wouldn't keep something as ugly as those red rooms in memory of somebody you disliked.

"This place is a prison," she told me, a little misty.

"You got out to visit me." Maybe they let her out on a tease release program.

"Not that kind of prison."

I stuffed my face and let that old vacuum suck more words out of her. I don't deal well with metaphor.

"I can leave any time I want, Garrett. I've been encouraged to leave. Often. But if I do, I lose everything. It's not really mine. I just get to use it." She gestured around her. "As long as I don't abandon it."

"I see." And I did. She was a prisoner of circumstance. She had to stay. She was an unmarried woman with a child. She had known poverty and knew rich was better. Poverty was a prison, too. "I think I'm going to like you, Maggie Jenn."

She raised an eyebrow. What an endearing skill! Few of us have sufficient native talent. Only the very best people can do the eyebrow thing.

I said, "I don't like most of my clients."

"I guess likable people don't get into situations where they need somebody like you."

"Not often, that's a fact."

# 9

The way things started, I became convinced that a certain eventuality had been foredoomed from the moment I'd opened my front door. I'm not a first date kind of guy, but I've never strained too hard against the whims of fate. I especially don't struggle to avoid that particular fate.

Dinner ended. I was unsettled. Maggie Jenn had been doing these things with her eyes. The kind of things that cause a bishop's brain to curdle and even a saint's devotion to monasticism to go down for a third time in those limpid pools. The kind of things that send a fundamentalist reverend's imagination racing off into realms so far removed that there is no getting back without doing something stupid.

I was too distracted to tell if the front of me was soaked with drool.

There had been banter and word games during dinner. She was good. Really good. I was ready to grab a trumpet and race around blowing *Charge*!

She sat there silently, appraising me, probably trying to decide if I was medium or medium well.

I made a heroic effort to concentrate. I managed to croak, "Tell me something, Maggie Jenn? Who would be interested in your affairs?"

She said nothing but did the eyebrow trick. She was surprised. That wasn't what she'd expected me to say. She had to buy time.

"Don't try to work your wiles on me, woman. You don't get out of answering that easily."

She laughed throatily, exaggerating that huskiness she had,

wriggled just to let me know she was capable of distracting me as much as she wanted. I considered distracting myself by getting up and stomping around to study some of the artwork decorating the dining chamber but discovered that rising would be uncomfortable and embarrassing. I half turned in my chair and studied the ceiling as though seeking clues amongst the fauns and cherubs.

She asked, "What do you mean about people interested in my affairs?"

I did pause to reflect before I gave away the store. "Let's back up some first. Did anybody know you were coming to see me?" Of course somebody did. Else Winger wouldn't have come to me first. But I needed Maggie's perspective.

"It wasn't a secret, if that's what you mean. I did ask around once I decided I needed a man of your sort."

Hmm. What *was* a man of my sort?

This was not an unfamiliar phenomenon. Sometimes the unfriendlies get the jump because they hear about my client asking after someone who can help. "Next step, then. Who would be bothered if you started looking for your daughter?"

"Nobody." She was getting suspicious.

"Yeah. It would seem like nobody ought to care. Unless maybe they were to give you a little support."

"You're scaring me, Garrett."

She didn't look scared. I said, "Might be a good idea to be scared. See, I knew you were coming."

"What?" She was troubled for sure now. She didn't like that at all.

"Just before you showed up, a friend who's in my racket stopped by to warn me you'd be coming." Saying Winger and I are in the same business is stretching a point, maybe. Winger is into anything likely to put money in Winger's purse, preferably fast and easy. "He thought you were coming to buy a hit. That's why he warned me." Catch that clever misdirection. Not even a dead Loghyr often mistakes Winger for male.

"A hit? Me?" She knew the argot. She was off balance but coming back fast.

"He was sure of it." But I wondered. Winger took shortcuts. Big, slow, lovable, goofy, crafty, bigoted, and lazy Winger. She was confident that anybody she couldn't sweeten with reason she could bring around with a good old-fashioned ass-kicking. She was just a big old simple country girl with simple country ways—if you accepted her the way she wanted to be taken.

I was going to have words with Winger about Maggie Jenn. If I could find her. I didn't think that would be tough. The big goof was bound to turn up on her own, soon. Probably before I was ready.

I said, "Then somebody followed me here."

"What? Who? Why?"

"Got me. I only mention it to show you that somebody out there is interested."

Maggie shook her head. It was a fine head. I was starting to lose my focus again. I concentrated on describing the villain who'd followed me.

Maggie smiled wickedly. "Garrett! Don't you ever think about anything else?"

"Lots of times." I thought about starting a little contest in which we would see who could run the fastest.

"Garrett!"

"You started it."

Unlike many women, she did not deny her complicity. "Yeah, but . . ."

"Put yourself in my place. You're a red-blooded young man who's suddenly alone here with you."

"Flattery will get you everywhere." She chuckled. Ouch! This was getting painful. "You do dish up a ration of shit, don't you?"

I chuckled right back and put myself into my own place, assuming she meant to put herself into her own place and things would proceed to proceed. But after a painful pilgrimage to her side of the table all proceedings proceeded to grind to a halt. Reluctantly—it seemed—she slipped away from me. I muttered, "We can't keep on like this if you want to sell me on looking for your daughter."

"You're right. This is a business arrangement. We can't let nature get in the way."

I was willing to let nature play havoc, but I said, "Durn tootin'. I don't sell that way, anyway. I sell on logic and facts. That's me. Just-the-facts-ma'am Garrett. How about you start giving me some of those instead of using all your energy on those come-hither eyes?"

"Don't be cruel, Garrett. This is as difficult for me as it is for you."

# 10

So, eventually, we reached the suite belonging to Maggie's daughter Emerald. "Emerald?" I asked. "What happened to Justina?" Emerald. Wouldn't you know? Where are all the lovely Patricias and Bettys?

"I named her Justina. Emerald is what she uses. She picked it, so don't give me that look."

"What look?"

"The one that says you're shitting me. *She* picked it. She was fourteen. Everyone else went along, so I use Emerald sometimes myself."

"Right. Emerald. She insisted." Of course. That's what became of Patricia and Betty. They started calling themselves Amber and Brandi and Fawn. "But she might be going by Justina. When life gets serious, they fall back on their roots. Anything I need to know about the suite before I start digging?"

"What do you mean?"

"Am I going to find something you think needs excusing ahead of time?"

Wonder of wonders, she understood. "You might. Only I never go in there, so I don't know what it might be. Yet." She gave me a strange look. "Are you looking for a fight?"

"No." Though maybe, unconsciously, I didn't want her hanging over my shoulder. "Back to that name. Might as well go after this by the numbers, find out everything you can tell me before I start looking for things you don't know."

She gave me that look again. I *was* a bit testy. Had I developed that strong a dislike for work? Or was it because I knew she would lie and distort and whatever else it took to shape reality to her own vision? They all do, even when there's no hope they won't get found out. People. They do make you wonder.

"Justina was after my grandmother."

I understood from her tone. Never was a kid who did not resent hearing how he or she was named after some old fart they never met and couldn't care less about. My mom played that game with me and my brother. I never figured out why it meant anything to her. "Any special reason?"

"The name's been in the family forever. And Granny would have been hurt if . . ."

The usual. Never made sense to me. You sentence a kid to a lifetime of misery on account of somebody might get his feelings hurt if you don't. Three rousing oriental cheers, say I: foo-ee, foo-ee, foo-ee. Who is going to be upset the longest?

You entered Emerald's suite through a small sitting room. There you found a small writing desk with its chair, in blond wood. There was an oil lamp on the desk. There was one more chair, a storage chest with a cushion on top, and a small set of shelves. The room was squeaky clean and more spartan than it sounds. It did not look promising.

I hate it when they clean for company. "Your daughter ever take a powder before?"

Maggie hesitated. "No."

"Why did you hesitate?"

"Trying to decide. Her father kidnapped her when she was four. Some friends convinced him that a child is better off with her mother."

"Would he try something like that today?"

"Probably not. He's been dead eight years."

"Chances are he wouldn't." As a rule, the dead don't get involved in custody disputes.

"She got a boyfriend?"

"A girl from the Hill?"

"Especially a girl from the Hill. How many does she have?"

"What?"

"Look, believe it or not, it's easier for Hill girls to slip around than it is for downtown girls." I offered examples from my own cases, one of which had featured a bevy of Hill girls working the Tenderloin just for the thrills.

That stunned my Maggie Jenn. She had a blind area, an inability to believe her baby could be anything less than the absolute image of what she desired. It hadn't occurred to her that Emerald was going to break her heart. Plainly, she didn't understand that people sometimes did the wicked stuff for other than survival reasons. Whoring as an amusement was a concept too alien to encompass.

Only the classes in between don't believe in whoring.

"You didn't grow up on the Hill."

"I admit that, Garrett."

I had the suspicion that my pretty Maggie had maybe had to make ends meet to make ends meet during the hiatus between husband and crown prince. I didn't need to know about that, though. Not yet, anyway. Maybe later, if it began to look like the past had some bearing. "Plant yourself on a chair. Talk to me about Emerald while I work."

I prowled.

# 11

Maggie said, "To my knowledge she has no boyfriends. Our circumstances don't let us meet many people. We aren't socially acceptable. We form a class unto ourselves."

A very classy class it was, though Maggie Jenn and her kid weren't its only members. The sisterhood of mistresses is quite large. At these rarified heights, a man is expected to have a mistress. It demonstrates his manhood. Two is better than one.

"Any friends at all?"

"Not many. Girls she grew up with, maybe. Maybe somebody she studied with. At her time of life, kids are real status conscious. I doubt anybody would let her make any strong connections."

"What's she look like?"

"Me, twenty years less shopworn. And wipe that silly grin off your mug."

"I was thinking how looking for you twenty years younger would have me hunting somebody barely out of diapers."

"And don't forget that. I want my baby found, not—"

"Right. Right. Right. Any special stress between you before she disappeared?"

"What?"

"Did you have a fight? Did she stomp out yelling about how she was never coming back in ten thousand years?"

"No." Maggie chuckled. "I had a few of those with *my* mother. Probably why she didn't squawk when my father sold me. No. Not Emerald. This kid is different, Garrett. She never cared about anything enough to fight. Really, honestly, swear to whatever god,

I wasn't a pushy mother. She was happy just to go along. Far as she was concerned, life is a river and she was driftwood."

"I maybe lost something in all the excitement. Or maybe I've started remembering things that never happened. I could have sworn you were going on about her having fallen in with bad companions."

Maggie chuckled. She snorted. She looked uncomfortable. She did it all fetchingly. I tried to imagine her as she might have been in Teodoric's day. I was awed by the possibilities.

She stopped wriggling. "I fibbed a little. I heard about you having a relationship with the Sisters of Doom and figured you were a sucker for a kid in trouble." The Sisters of Doom is an all-girl street gang. The girls were all abused before they fled to the street.

"It was a relationship with one Sister. Who left the street."

"I'm sorry. I overstepped."

"What?"

"It's obvious I just stomped on some tender feelings."

"Oh. Yeah. Maya was a pretty special kid. I messed up a good thing because I didn't take her serious enough. I lost a friend because I didn't listen."

"Sorry. I was just trying to find a sure hook."

"Did Emerald see anybody regularly?" Business would take me away from memories. Maya was not one of my great loves, but she was pretty special. And both Dean and the Dead Man had approved of her. There had been no separation, she just didn't come around anymore and mutual friends all hinted that she wouldn't unless I grew up a little.

That don't punch your ego up, considering it traced back to a girl just eighteen.

Emerald's writing desk had numerous cubbies and tiny drawers. I searched them as we talked. I didn't find much. Most spaces were empty.

"She does have friends but making friends doesn't come easy."

That wasn't the story as it was told a few minutes ago. I suspected Emerald had troubles that had nothing to do with social status. Chances were she was lost in her mother's shadow. "Friends are where I'll find her trail. I'll need names. I'll need to know where I can find the people who go with them."

She nodded. "Of course." I slammed a drawer, turned away from her. I had to keep my mind on business. The woman was a witch. Then I sneaked a peek. Did I really want to leave all that, to go hunting somebody who probably didn't want to be found?

Ha! Here was something. A silver pendant. "What's this?" Purely rhetorical. I knew what I had. It was an amulet consisting of a silver pentagram on a dark background with a goat's head inside the star. The real question was, what was it doing where I had found it?

Maggie took it, studied it while I watched for a reaction. I didn't see one. She said, "I wonder where that came from?"

"Emerald into the occult?"

"Not that I know of. But you can't know everything about your children."

I grunted, resumed my search. Maggie chattered like the fabled magpie, mostly about her daughter, more in the way of reminiscences than useful facts. I listened with half an ear.

I found nothing else in the desk. I moved to the shelves. The presence of several books brought home how much wealth Maggie stood to lose. Because a book takes forever to copy, it is about the most expensive toy you can give a child.

I grunted as I picked up the third book. It was a small, leatherbound, time-worn thing with a goat's head tooled into its cover. The leather was badly foxed. The pages were barely readable. It was one old book.

My first clue was that it was not written in modern Karentine.

Those damned things never are, are they? Nobody would take them seriously if any schnook could pick one up and decipher the secrets of the ages.

"Check this out." I tossed the book to Maggie. I kept one eye on her as I resumed my search.

"Curiouser and curiouser, Garrett. My baby is full of surprises."

"Yeah." Maybe. That whole visit was full of surprises. Including those tree-sized fingers pointing at witchcraft of the demonic sort.

The bedroom and its attached bath yielded more occult treasures.

Much later I asked, "Is Emerald especially neat?" Neat would not describe any teen I knew.

"Only as much as she has to be. Why?"

I didn't tell her. I had gone into full investigator mode. We crack first-line investigators never answer questions about our questions, especially if those are posed by our employers, lawmen, or anybody else who might help keep us out of the deep stink. Fact was, though, that Emerald's apartment was way too neat. Compulsively so. Or nobody lived there. My impression was of a stage set. I was wondering if it might not be exactly that, carefully primed with clues.

All right, I told me. Get busy deducting. Clues are clues to something even when they're artificial or false.

I was not that sure. What I had was some inconsistent indications of witchcraft—which did little to amaze, dismay, alarm, or otherwise excite my new employer.

Maybe I was going at this from the wrong end.

Tap on the shoulder. "Anybody in there?"

"Huh?"

"You just froze up and went away."

"Happens when I try to think and do something at the same time."

She did her eyebrow trick. I distracted her by flashing her back. I told her, "I've got enough to start. You give me that list of names. As soon as we settle the finances."

We had no problems there till I insisted on half my fee up front. "It's an inflexible rule, Maggie. On account of human fallibility. Too many people get tempted to stiff me once they've gotten what they want." But that was not the only reason I pressed.

The less a client argues the deeper his desperation.

My pretty Maggie Jenn argued way too long. Finally, she huffed, "I'll have Mugwump bring you that list as soon as I can."

I was thrilled. I really wanted to see Mugwump again. Maybe I could tip him a talking parrot.

# 12

I stood in the shadows down the street from Maggie's, just staying out of sight while I thought.

Like most folks, I don't get any kick out of being played for a patsy. But people do try. It's an occupational hazard. I'm used to it. I expect it. But I don't like it.

Something was going on. I was being used. None too subtly, either. Unless Maggie my sweet was a lot less worldly than I suspected, I didn't see how she could think I would buy everything.

I'd sure enjoyed the job interview, though. As far as it had gone.

The thing to do now was what she had said she didn't want me to do: investigate Maggie Jenn. For my own safety. In my line, what you don't know can get you killed as fast as what you do know. Once I could guess where I really stood, maybe I'd do something about Emerald.

I glanced at the sky. It was dark but still early. I could touch some contacts, take a few steps along the path to enlightenment. Right after I dropped Maggie's retainer off at home. Only a fool carries a load like that longer than he must. TunFaire teems with villains who can count the change in your pocket at a hundred yards.

I could imagine no explanation of recent events more convincing than what Maggie purported. Nevertheless, there was Winger. I shook my head. The cobwebs did not go away. They never do. All part of the service. All part of my naive charm.

I looked for my tail. No sign. Maybe he got tired and went home. Maybe the Hill's security thugs whispered sweet nothings in his ear, like, "Get lost pronto or you'll crawl home with two broken legs." Or maybe his job had been done once he'd found out where I was going.

I shoved off. All that thinking was giving me shin splints of the brain.

Good thing I exercise. I had oomph enough to vacate the area steps ahead of an unpleasant interview with the goon squad, who did not seem to care if I had legitimate business on the Hill. They had been summoned by Ichabod, no doubt, in a vain hope that my attitude could be improved.

I zigged and zagged and backtracked and used all my tricks. I didn't spot a tail so I went home, got rid of Maggie's retainer, drew myself a long draught, then sat down for a cold beer and a chat with Eleanor, who seemed concerned about the state of my soul.

"Yeah," I confessed, "I'm getting more flexible when it comes to taking money." I spoke in a whisper. I did not want to waken the Goddamn Parrot. I'd even tiptoed in and filled his seed tray.

If I remembered to feed him more often, he might have a higher opinion of me. Maybe.

"So what? If they're villains, they deserve to be done out of their money." She had taught me that money has no provenance. "If they aren't villains, I'll see that they get their money's worth."

More or less. Sometimes I don't exactly deliver what the client has in mind. One such case resulted in Eleanor coming to live with me.

It had taken me a while to outgrow the notion that taking a man's money meant having to go for the results he wanted. I must be getting old and judgmental. These days, I try to give people what they deserve instead.

Which yields mixed results for sure. Even so, I get more offers than I want. But a lot of fat jobs go elsewhere because some folks have decided to avoid me. Most especially the kind who rob people with paper instead of a blade. Lawyers and slicks. I have embarrassed my share of those.

Actually, I mostly avoid working. I don't think anybody ought to work more than it takes to get by. Sure, I wish I could afford my own harem and fifty-room palace, but if I worked hard enough to get the money, I'd have to work as hard to keep it. I wouldn't get a chance to enjoy it.

After a few beers, I developed a whole new attitude. I told

Eleanor, "Think I'll go down to the Joy House, hang out with the guys."

She smirked.

"It's just to pick up street talk about Maggie Jenn."

Eleanor didn't believe one word.

I had to find me a new girlfriend.

# 13

Morley Dotes never changes but his neighborhood can. Once upon a time, that was the worst. You weren't alert, you could get killed for the price of a bowl of soup. For reasons to do with Morley's intolerance of squabbles and his sometime role as arbitrater of underworld disputes, the neighborhood grew almost reputable and came to be called the Safety Zone. Those who worked the shadow side met and did business there, with every expectation of suffering none of the embarrassment, unpleasantness, or disappointment one faced at the hands of lone wolf socialists in other neighborhoods.

Every city needs some quiet area where business can get done.

"Waa-hoo!" shrieked the guy who came sailing out the door as I walked up to Morley's place. I ducked. That fellow touched down halfway across the street. He made a valiant effort to land running and did a laudable job till a watering trough slunk into his path. Slimy green water fountained.

Another man came out sprawled like a starfish, spinning and howling. He was one of Morley's thugs-turned-waiter.

This was backwards. The way these things go is Morley's people toss troublemakers. They don't get dribbled along the cobblestones themselves.

The howling waiter went across the street like a skipping stone. He crashed into the guy trying not to drown in the horse trough. If you ask me, putting those things around was a grave mistake. Horse troughs are sure to draw horses. TunFaire is infested by enough evils.

On hands and knees, I peeped around the edge of the door frame and discovered true pandemonium.

A behemoth of a black man, who beat my six feet two by a good three feet, and who had to slouch so he wouldn't split his noggin on the ceiling, was having himself a grand time cleaning house. He snarled and roared and tossed people and furniture. Those few men accidentally exiting through the front door were lucky. They were out of the action. Those who tried to leave under their own power got grabbed and dragged back for the fun.

The feet of the walls were littered with casualties. The big man had a fire in his eye. No mere mortal was going to quiet him down. Some very skilled mortals had tried and had found places among the fallen.

I knew the berserk. His name was Playmate. He was one of my oldest friends, a blacksmith and stable operator, a religious man who was as gentle a being as ever lived. He went out of his way to avoid stepping on bugs. I had seen him weep for a mutt run down by a carriage. Like all of us, he had done his time in the Cantard, but I was sure that even there he had offered violence to no one.

I thought about trying to talk him down. I left it at a thought. We were good friends, but Playmate had equally good friends among the fallen. Everybody loved Playmate.

And I had learned about being a hero doing my five years as a Royal Marine.

No way could Playmate have gone this mad.

Morley Dotes himself, dapper and exasperated, watched from the stair to his office. He was a darkly handsome little character, dressed way too slick for my taste. Anything he put on looked like it was baked onto him. Anything I put on looks slept-in after ten minutes.

Morley was so distressed he was wringing his hands.

Guess I'd have been upset myself if someone was busting up my place. The Joy House started as a front—Morley was an assassin and bonebreaker—but it had grown on Dotes.

A short, slim form snaked through the crowd and leapt onto Playmate's back. The big man roared and spun. He did not dislodge his rider, Morley's nephew Spud, whose mother had passed him to his uncle because she could not manage him anymore.

For a while, Spud just held on. Once he was confident of his seat, though, he let go with one hand and fumbled at his belt. Playmate kept spinning. The idea gradually got into his head: spinning and prancing and roaring would not get the weight off his back.

He stopped, got his bearings by consulting stars only he could see. He decided to run backwards and squish Spud against a wall.

Spud had his own plan, though.

Spud was set on being a hero in his uncle's eyes.

The kid wasn't stupid, he just suffered from natural elvish overconfidence.

His hand came up from his belt clutching a black cloth sack. He tried popping that over Playmate's head. Guess who did not cooperate?

That sack was a mark of the esteem in which Playmate was held. The guy was set on destroying the world, but nobody wanted to stop him badly enough to kill him. Not one soul inside the Joy House wanted to do anything but get him under control. Not your true TunFairen attitude, I guarantee. Life is the cheapest commodity of all.

Morley moved as soon as he understood what the kid was doing. He didn't run or appear to hurry, but he got there right on time, a moment after Spud did get his bag into place, a moment after Playmate started his all-out plunge toward the nearest wall. Morley hooked a foot behind the big man's heel.

Boom!

Playmate sprawled. Spud separated just in time to keep from being sandwiched. He was a lucky kid. Instead of getting squashed and collecting some broken bones, he just got coldcocked.

Not so Playmate. My old pal tried to get up. Morley popped him a bunch of times, so fast you barely saw him move. Playmate didn't like that. He figured maybe he ought to take that sack off and see who was aggravating him. Morley hit him a bunch more times, in all those places where blows are supposed to incapacitate.

There came a day when Playmate, buried under a dozen people, finally stopped struggling.

# 14

Morley looked down at Playmate. He was breathing hard. I strode inside, chirped, "Congrats. You wore him down."

Morley checked me from glazed eyes, failed to recognize me for a moment, then wailed, "Oh, damn! You. On top of everything else."

I looked behind me to find out who was causing my best pal so much distress. I'd fix him! But the guy was too fast for me. The doorway was empty.

I put on my best hurt face. I get to practice a lot around the Joy House. Morley's guys are always riding me. Naturally, I play along.

I righted a table, selected a chair, made myself comfortable. I eyeballed Playmate. "What happened? You have to pump that guy up on weed to get him to swat flies."

Morley took several controlled breaths, picked up a chair, and joined me. "Excellent question, Garrett." Playmate wasn't doing anything now. In fact, the roars from beneath the flesh pile sounded suspiciously like snores.

Morley Dotes is a bit short for a grown man but isn't entirely human. He has dark-elf forebears. But he never lets the human in him get in his way.

Maybe the mix is responsible. He is a mass of contrasts, especially in his profession as opposed to his hobby. His health food haven has become a hangout for half the villains of TunFaire. Contrast again: the clientele is half those double-nasties and half the kind of clown you *expect* to find gnoshing tubers of uncertain provenance.

"Boy did pretty well," Morley observed, glancing at Spud. The kid's real name was Narcisio. Only his mother used that.

"Pretty good," I admitted. "More balls than brains."

"Runs in the family."

"What happened?"

Morley glowered. Instead of answering me, he shocked the house by bellowing, "Eggwhite! Get your heathen ass out here!"

I was amazed, too. Morley employs vulgarity only rarely. He fancies himself a gentleman rogue. Gentlemen rogues are slick like they're covered with lard. But a villain is a villain, and Morley is one of the worst because he gets away with everything. I should try to take him down. I don't because he's my friend.

A thug ambled out of the kitchen. He wore cook's garb but carried his professional resume scarred on his face. He was old and looked as stupid as a stump, which answered a question: what becomes of hard boys if they live long enough to get old? They become waiters. I didn't see how this goon had survived to get there, though. He looked like a guy who needed a major run of luck to get through any given day.

Maybe the gods do love the incapacitated.

Morley beckoned.

Eggwhite edged our way. His gaze kept darting toward Playmate. Playmate had begun to reappear as guys climbed off and went to set the bones of their buddies.

"Big mess, huh?" Morley said.

"Yeah, boss. Big ole mess."

"You have any idea why I would entertain the notion that you might have been at fault? Can you tell me why your face popped into mind the moment my friend asked me what happened?"

Will wonders never cease? He never called me friend before.

Eggwhite muttered, "I guess on account of I got a weakness for doing jokes."

Morley grunted. "That one of your pranks?" Playmate was sleeping like a baby now, but he was going to be hurting when he woke up. "That big ha-ha there?" Morley's tone was hard, the street leaking through. He was angry. Eggwhite was petrified.

Morley asked, "What did you do?"

"Put angelweed in his salad?" Eggwhite made it a question, like a kid caught in a lie experimenting with a new tactic.

"How much?"

Excellent question. Angelweed didn't earn its heavenly name because it will boost your mind into paradise but because it will send you off to hallelujah land if you aren't careful. Slipping it into a salad would be a clever way to dose somebody. The leaves look like spinach that's gone a little bluish.

"Half a dozen leaves." Eggwhite looked everywhere but straight at Morley.

"Half a dozen. Enough to kill most people."

"He's humongous, chief. A goddamn mountain. I thought it would take—"

"And there's the problem." Morley's voice dropped way down, to a level of softness that meant he was in a killing mood. Egg-white started shaking. Morley continued, "I told you when I hired you I didn't want any thinking. I wanted you cutting vegetables. Get out."

"Chief, look, I can—"

"You're gone, Eggwhite. Out the door. Walking or carried. Up to you."

Eggwhite gulped. "Uh . . . Yeah." He headed for the door.

I observed, "He's making off with your cook outfit."

"Let it go. I don't want to make a scene."

I gave him an encore look at my eyebrow trick.

"I hate firing people, Garrett."

I added the fish-eye to the raised eyebrow. This was the most feared hired knife in town? Was he putting me on?

He kept plugging. "I do it only because you have to if you want to be successful in business. Besides, I owe him eight days pay." Before I could comment, he eyed me directly. "What is it this time, Garrett?"

"How about a platter of that stuff with the black mushrooms, pea pods and whatnot, on the wild rice?" I dropped money onto the table.

Morley gave me my fish-eye back with interest. He gathered my coins, examined them as though he suspected they were counterfeit. "You want to eat? Here? And you're willing to pay for it?" He sank his fangs into a coin, the classic hardness test.

"I wouldn't go so far as to employ the concept of privilege, but it is an age of wonders. You've converted me. I'm born again. I'm never going to eat anything but swamp tubers, bark, and gravel ever again."

# 15

Morley stirred Playmate's fingers with his toe. "He's alive, but I couldn't tell you why." He came back to where I was wolfing the mushroom stuff. It contained more garlic than mushrooms. "Trying to keep the girls away?"

"I don't need garlic for that. I have natural talent."

He wasn't in the mood for banter. Guess I wouldn't have been either had my place just gotten trashed. "What are you into now, Garrett? What do you need?"

"I'm doing a missing person caper." Love that word. I told him the story, leaving out only those parts a gentleman leaves out. "I want to know whatever you know about Maggie Jenn. Felt like she was running a game on me."

"Somebody must be running a game on somebody. I don't think you saw the real Maggie Jenn."

"Huh?"

"Never mind the witty remarks. I'm thinking you must have been chosen for your ignorance."

"Thanks. How about shoving a stick in the spokes of the scheme by lighting a torch in the darkness?"

"That wouldn't be right. Not quite. You not being up on the adventures of the royals *could* be part of it, but . . ."

"All right. I don't know what you know, Morley. That's why I'm here."

"It isn't impossible that you spent the afternoon with a king's lover, but I'd call it wildly improbable. Maggie Jenn exiled herself to the Isle of Paise after her Teddy boy died. If there was a daughter I never heard. Kind of thing that would be kept quiet, though.

On the other hand, that place on the Hill sounds like the one where Teodoric stashed his doxy. Curious."

That was an understatement. "I'm lost, Morley. None of this makes sense."

"Only because you don't have the key."

"I'm missing the key, the lock, the damned door, and all the hardware. Somebody ran a game on me? I'll buy that. Happens all the time. But the woman also paid me to look for her daughter."

"How well?" Was that smile a smirk?

"Handsomely, shall we say? Enough so I'm sure she expected something in return. Even top of the Hill don't throw money away."

"Good point."

"*If* Maggie Jenn came back," I mused, "what would she do?"

"She has no reason to come back. She lives like a queen out there. She'd find nothing but trouble here." Morley eyed Playmate. "Pity you didn't get here earlier. He always kept track of the royals."

"He won't be doing anything but whine about his headache for a week."

"You in a hurry?"

I wondered. "Maybe not. No apparent jeopardy. Just a puzzle. Maggie didn't seem in any hurry, just worried."

"You buy the woman's story?"

I never take a client's story at face value. Some natural law compels them to lie part of the time. "Maybe. Some. It feels like the truth being used for something else."

"I'll put out feelers. Meantime, you ought to corner Winger."

"That occurred to me." I didn't relish trying to get anything out of her, though. "It's not an appetizing idea."

Morley chuckled. "She's a handful. The trick is get her thinking what you want is her idea."

"Ingenious. How?"

"With great difficulty."

"I can get advice like that from my parrot and save the price of this fish food."

"Way I hear, Dean is out of town and the Dead Man is asleep. You being hard up for company, I just wanted you to feel at home. Crumbs! You try to be a pal." He grinned a diabolical dark-elf grin.

"You want to be a pal, find out about Maggie Jenn."

His grin dwindled. "Try to be a pal." He shook his head.

He would check around because he thought he owed me. And I agreed. I collect like a loanshark.

"Bed is starting to sound good," I thought aloud. "It's been a hard day."

Morley grunted. His nephew came to the table. Getting no hint that he ought to take his big ears elsewhere, he spun a chair around and straddled it. Around us, Morley's people, moving slowly and muttering about their aches and pains, put things together again. Spud asked, "How is Mr. Big, Mr. Garrett?"

I cursed.

Morley had sent me the Goddamn Parrot when he was in an Eggwhite mood. That was far enough out of character that I suspected Sarge and Puddle had a hand in developing the scam. The bird came guaranteed to have a major hatred for cats and a habit of attacking them from above. I accepted him because Dean had a habit of accumulating strays.

Spud gave me a dirty look. He was the only one in the world with any use for that foul-mouthed jungle chicken. Make that any love. The Dead Man had a use. Wherever I went, he could send Mr. Big after, nagging.

I had tried to give the beast away. There were no takers. I gave it every chance to fly away. It wouldn't escape. I was getting near taking heroic measures. "Spud, you're so worried about Mr. Big why don't you come get him? He needs a home where he's appreciated."

"No, you don't," Morley sneered. "That there is *your* bird, Garrett."

I scowled. This was a squabble I couldn't win.

Dotes showed all those pointy teeth again. "I hear some parrots live a hundred years."

"Some, maybe. In the wild." I could donate Mr. Big to a charity. Like some hungry ratman. "I'm out of here, friend."

Morley laughed.

# 16

It was dark out. That did not help.

Neither did the fact that I didn't see them coming. I had no chance to get ready.

I put up a fight, though. I dented some heads good with the weighted oak head-buster I carry when I go out. I tossed one guy through the only glass window in the street. But I just never got rolling. I had no chance to use the tricks I had stashed up my sleeves.

Somebody whapped me up side the head with a house. I think it was a house. Had to be a house. No mere man could hit me that hard. The lights went out—with me still trying to figure out who and why.

Ordinarily, I come around slowly if I've had my conk bopped. Not so this time. One minute I was in dreamland, the next I was bouncing along face downward, wrapped in something soggy, staring at a floor sliding past inches from my nose. Four guys were carrying me. I was leaking red stuff. I couldn't recall drinking any wine. I had the worst headache anyone ever had since the dawn of time.

A fine pair of female legs strode along practically in nibbling range. I really wanted to appreciate those. In other circumstances, I would have devoted hours to those legs. But a guy does have to keep some perspective.

Things were not going well. This sort of thing was not a normal part of my life. I tried to shove the pain away long enough to think.

Aha! They had me wrapped in a wet blanket. I didn't want to poop somebody's party, but that didn't make me happy. I roared and twisted and flopped and wriggled and bellowed. I failed to make any impression. I did get a gander at what went with the gorgeous gams. The wealth was piled on all the way to the top. I could have fallen in love. But this was not the time or place. Beside a fire, maybe on a bearskin rug, maybe just her and me and some TunFaire Gold wine. . . .

I didn't like the looks of the guys. They weren't the brunos I danced with earlier. Those had been standard lowlife, out for the price of a drink. These clowns wore dirty, ragged uniforms.

That failed to cheer me up.

They were unreasonable. They wouldn't answer questions. Nobody responded at all, except Miss Legs. She just seemed sad. I hollered and flopped some more. They kept on lugging me down a long hall.

Long hall, huh? And what was that smell?

Everybody stopped but me. I thrashed some more. I was serious about it now. I knew where I was. This was the crazy floor of the Bledsoe, the imperial charity hospital.

The empire is long gone, but its works and the imperial family linger, the latter hoping for a recall. They sustain the hospital, which serves the indigent poorly.

The cackle factory is a bad place. They stick you in there you could be gone forever. Wouldn't matter that somebody made a mistake.

"Hey! Put me down! What the hell is this? What am I doing in here? Do I look like I'm crazy?"

That was the wrong question. I had to look like a prime specimen. And the way things work, they would assume that they wouldn't have me if I didn't belong.

Man, this was the dirtiest trick anybody ever played on me.

A door crashed open. It was oak and iron and about nine inches thick. I glimpsed my destiny.

One of my guides bellowed. Somebody scuttled away. The boys tossed me through the doorway without missing the frame. I landed hard. The Legs gazed at me pityingly. The door closed before I convinced her this was all a horrible mistake.

I unwrapped myself by rolling around, stumbled over and wasted energy pounding on the door. I exercised the full range of situationally specialized vocabulary, but without the enthusiasm I might have managed had my head not hurt so much. You do these things even when you're wasting your time. The rituals must be observed.

I heard noises behind me. I spun around.

At least a dozen men stood staring at me. I checked the ward beyond them. There were lots more men back there. Plenty were wondering about the new guy. Some studied my outfit. Plainly, there had been no general clothing issued in years. Nor had anyone taken a bath during the modern era. Here was the source of the odor I'd caught in the hall. A glance told me the welcoming committee all belonged inside. It was obvious in their eyes.

I pounded and yelled some more. Service did not improve.

At least they hadn't dumped me into the violent ward. Maybe I stood a chance.

An old character who looked like he weighed about fifty pounds stumbled toward me. "How are you doing? I'm Ivy."

"I was doing great till about five minutes ago, Ivy."

"How are you doing? I'm Ivy."

"He don't say nothing else, Ace."

Right. I'm a quick study. Ivy never even looked at me. "Gotcha."

A guy about nine feet tall guffawed. "You don't pay Ivy no nevermind, boy. He's crazy."

"How are you doing? I'm Ivy."

This was the tip of the iceberg. The part that would be easy. It was sure to get weird.

After thinking a while, somebody yelled at the big guy, "You got so much room to talk, muddlebrain?"

"Yeah? What do you know? I don't belong in here. I was set up. Somebody drugged me or something. I woke up in here."

Oh, my. A fellow traveler as bad off as I. I had a lot of sympathy for him—till some grinning idiot shrieked, "Powziffle! Powziffle pheez!" Or something like that.

The big guy hunched up, stooped, made gurgling noises, and started running around the ward like a gorilla, howling. His howls would have chilled the spine of a banshee.

"How are you doing? I'm Ivy."

The big man's racket started some other guy screaming. His cries were a species I'd heard in the islands, coming from a guy caught out in no-man's land with a bad gut wound, begging for somebody to kill him. Soldiers from both sides would have done so gladly after a while. But nobody was dumb enough to go out there and let the other side snipe. So we'd all just laid low and listened, ground our teeth, and maybe thanked our personal gods it wasn't us.

I glared at that door. Maybe I could chew my way through.

Or maybe . . . My pockets hadn't been cleaned. They must've been in an awful hurry to get me put away. A real bunch of screwup charlies.

Patients came to check me out—those who still had a foot in our world. Many were timid as mice. A look sent them scurrying. Others . . . Some might have been there as accidentally as I, only instead they belonged in the ward for the dangerous.

I wished everybody would back off.

Any doubts I had about the irregularity of my commitment disappeared when I discovered that they hadn't cleaned my pockets. Had I been brought in legitimately, all my possessions would have been taken from me and would never have surfaced again.

I was encouraged. About a roach-weight worth.

The physical plant wasn't encouraging. The ward was a hundred feet wide, three hundred feet long, and two storys high. There were rows and rows and rows of sleeping pallets but not nearly enough to go around.

The ceiling was way up there, a good twenty feet. Windows peeked through the wall opposite the door, way high, too small for a man to get out even after he cut the bars. I supposed they passed light during the day. What little light was available now leaked through windows high on the door side wall, there so the ward could be observed by hospital staff.

"How are you doing? I'm Ivy."

"I'm doing just fine, Ivy. What say you and me bust out of this toilet?"

Ivy looked at me directly, startled, then scampered away.

"*Anybody* want to break out?"

# 17

My suggestion drew an underwhelming response. I gathered that half the patients could not be dragged out and the other half thought I was crazy. There? Forsooth!

The big man who had cautioned me about Ivy's lack of capacity recapacitated himself. He came over. "Ain't no way out, Slick. They was, half these guys would be long gone."

I glanced around again. The prospects seemed ever less promising. "They feed us?"

The big guy grinned that grin the old salts put on when they see a chance to teach a greenhorn. "Twice a day, you're hungry or not. Through them bars down there."

I looked. I shrugged. Them bars was hopeless. "Things are that bad I might as well get me some shut-eye before I start my serious worrying." I looked for an empty pallet. I had some thinking to do. Especially about why I found myself in such straits.

I wanted to scream as loud as any of the whacks in there with me.

"You get in line for a bed," the big guy cautioned me. "You make friends, maybe somebody will share. Otherwise, you just wait till enough guys die to leave you your own." His casual manner told me this was one of the capital laws of the ward. Amazing. You'd expect it to be *total* survival of the strongest.

"My kind of flophouse." I settled near the door. That didn't seem to be a popular area. Plenty of elbow room there. I pretended to fall asleep.

There were no corpses in the ward and no smell of death. That suggested that staff removed the dead quickly. So, how to use that in a scam the staff hadn't seen before?

I gave the notion of a riot a look. Feeble. If I was the Bledsoe staff, I'd just let everybody starve till the fuss stopped.

"How are you doing? I'm Ivy."

My act wasn't fooling Ivy. I considered putting him out of his misery.

Which gave me an idea. A twist on the riot scheme. I went looking for the big guy. I found him seated against the far wall. I planted the reverse side of my lap on the hardwood, grunted. "I got about enough splinters."

"Send out for a chair."

A wise guy. "How come it's so quiet?"

"Maybe on account of it's the middle of the goddamn night." Eloquent verbal stylings, too.

"I mean, we only had one screamer." Not counting him. Nobody was yelling at the moment. "I heard there was lots of screamers. Mostly guys who can't handle what they remember about the Cantard."

His face darkened. "Yeah. There's some of them. They get drugged if they get too bad. Like they get each other going."

Interesting. "Know any way to set one of them off now?"

He studied me narrowly. "What you up to, Slick?" He thought there had better be a damned good reason for pulling a stunt like that.

"Up to getting out of here."

"Can't do that."

"Maybe not. But they didn't empty out my pockets before they dumped me in here. You game to try?"

He thought about that. His face grew darker. "Yeah. Yeah! I got business out there. Yeah. You get the damned door open, I'll go."

"You figure any of these guys would help?"

"Plenty would go if the walls fell down. I don't know how many would help make them fall."

"So could you get some guy screaming as the first step?"

"Sure." He got up, strolled to the far end, messed with somebody a minute, headed back. Plenty of inmates watched him. The man he'd visited started screaming. Chills slithered all over me. He was one of the lost souls.

The big man asked, "Good enough?"

"Perfect. Now try to round up some guys willing to help out."

He went away again.

I went into my act. "Shut up down there! I'm trying to sleep."

The guy didn't stop screaming. I'd been afraid he would. I glanced at the observation windows. Someone was up there, but the racket didn't interest him. Were they that indifferent? I needed to be seen.

I yelled at the screamer. Somebody yelled back at me. I yelled at him. Some genius yelled at both of us like that would shut us up. The racket picked up. We were like a troop of monkeys. Some of the men started moving around, just shuffling numbly, without purpose.

The uproar finally caught the ear of whoever was on duty. He looked down but didn't seem concerned.

I screamed louder than the screamer, threatening mayhem if he didn't shut it up.

"How are you doing? I'm Ivy."

"Pack your trunk, Ivy. We're checking out of this cuckoo inn."

The big guy came by. "I got a dozen guys willing, Slick. You want more?"

"That's plenty. Now I need everybody back away from the door. It's going to get nasty there when they come in." I hoped. If I hadn't been suckered too bad.

"They'll figure we're up to something, Slick. They only look dumb."

"I don't care. That won't matter. I just need the door open."

He sneered, confident I was on a fool's quest.

I screamed some more at the screamers.

There were several people at the observation windows now— including she of the glorious gams.

I chuckled, sure I was on my way out. No woman would work the Bledsoe unless she had a giant soft spot. I roared, bounded over pallets, started strangling the loudest screamer.

The big guy came by and pretended to drag me off. I gave him further instructions, then ran him off. He wasn't a bad actor.

Me, I was a master. I made it look real good. To my surprise, none of my fellow patients tried to stop me.

I only strangled my victim a little, enough to cause unconsciousness.

I galloped to the other end of the room, went to work on another screamer.

Soon there were guys flying all over the place. The majority got into the spirit. It wasn't exactly a riot, though. Real violence was almost nonexistent. But the pandemonium was not pretend.

I glimpsed the woman arguing with the men. She wanted to do something. They didn't.

Excellent.

A little goblin breed three feet tall scrunched himself into a ball near the door.

Upstairs, charity apparently overcame common sense.

I kept the show rolling. People did get hurt, but *I* wasn't in a charitable mood, to put it mildly. If I stayed a nice guy, I wasn't ever going to get out. If I didn't get out, I'd never get the chance to crack the heads of the clowns who'd put me in.

The big guy came around again. He bounced me around some. "They're coming," I told him. "And you don't have to be so enthusiastic here."

He seemed scornful. I don't know about what.

# 18

I glanced at the door, then cautioned the big guy, "Take it easy. We don't have to convince them now." No one was near the door but the little breed. He would be sorry he had volunteered. "How many will come?"

The big man shrugged. "Depends on how worried they are. Least eight or ten. You better watch out." He tripped me. I tripped him back. We rolled around and punched each other. He was having a great time. "They have a policy of kicking the living shit out of troublemakers."

"I kind of figured that was part of the program. Hell, I've stopped bleeding. I'm ready for anything." I wasn't looking forward to the kicking part. You lays your bets and takes your chances, but I was hoping things would go well and I would not have to deal with any boots.

You have to believe you're going to win.

I did have to win. Nobody knew where I was. It could be weeks before anybody even missed me, what with Dean out of town and the Dead Man sleeping. It might be weeks after that before anybody tracked me down. If anybody bothered to try.

I didn't have weeks. I didn't feel I could waste the time I'd spent inside already. The Dead Man might chuckle and tell me to consider it a learning experience, which is what he does when I have a bad day.

If I didn't break out, it was going to be the all-time bad day to start a long string of bad days.

The woman stayed at the observation window. I kept howling

my head off and throwing people around and strangling other guys making noise.

The thing that got me, down deep, was that almost half the guys in the ward didn't get involved. Most of those never opened their eyes. They just laid there, indifferent.

Man, that was scary. That could be me in twenty years if I blew this.

Fear provided the inspiration I needed to keep howling and foaming at the mouth. I tried speaking in tongues. That came to me naturally. A little something for when I got too old to make it on the street. A good howl and roll man can start his own church.

The door opened.

Wonder of wonders, miracle of miracles, those dopes actually opened the door.

It swung outward. Attendants boiled inside. They knew something was up. They were ready for bear. They had clubs and small shields. They all looked about twelve feet tall. They formed in a tight knot before they started forward.

A few months earlier, in a moment of weakness brought on by engulfing an inland sea of beer, I'd bought some stuff from a third-rate wizard who'd called himself Dread but whose name was really Milton. You don't never trust the skills of a wizard named Milton—as I'd learned to my sorrow on trying to use one of his charms. His stuff came with a warranty, but he wasn't around to make good on it.

In my pockets were several tiny bottles, the last of my purchase. According to Dread, they constituted the ideal means of dealing with unfriendly crowds. I didn't know, never having tested them. I wasn't sure I even recalled Dread's instructions. It was real drunk out that night.

I told me I had another good reason for wanting out. I had to find old Milt and register a consumer complaint.

As I recalled, all I had to do was throw a bottle against a hard surface, then stand back.

I did the throwing part. My bottle missed all the boys and bounced off the wall. It skittered back into the midst of the attendants. Guys walked all over it, but it didn't break.

My guardian angel was on the job. Cursing him, I tried again.

The second bottle broke. Gray mist boiled off the wall. It reached the attendants. They started cussing. Cussing turned to howling fast.

Meantime, my little breed volunteer slithered into the doorway so it couldn't be closed. His job was going to get nasty if the staff got determined.

The attendants in the ward lost all interest in quieting people down. They were too busy scratching and rubbing and yelling.

Maybe Dread wasn't a complete fraud.

I inhaled a bushel of clean air and charged. I was ashamed of me for pulling such a dirty trick. Almost. I wouldn't take it back. If I spent much time hanging out with Ivy and the boys, I'd end up singing in the same choir.

The mist didn't bother me much. I did start itching a little. Since I had a major headache and an acre of bruises, an itch seemed pretty trivial.

Somebody was hollering in the corridor. They'd left somebody to cover the door. He was aggravated at my breed doorstop.

Who wasn't doing so good. The mist tended to settle. He'd gotten more than the attendants had.

Nonetheless, he fulfilled his mission.

I smashed into the door so hard I feared I'd dislocated my shoulder. Oh, damn, did that hurt! And that damned door only gave barely enough to let me skip over the whining breed.

"Surprise!" I popped the guard outside. A whole herd of patients stampeded out behind me. Those that didn't have scores to settle with particular attendants still inside.

Naturally, luck would have another squad of staffers arriving just then. I did my banshee routine and charged. Boy, was I going to have a sore throat when all the hollering was over.

These attendants were bigger and meaner than the first bunch. There were eight of them. That put the odds in my favor because I was mad enough to whip a whole battalion. "Nothing personal, guys." Then I recognized two of the clowns who had carried me in the wet blanket. "Like hell!"

I didn't get a lot of help at first. Surprise did for a couple of attendants, but then the others got going. They played a game using me for a shuttlecock. My companions had been beaten too often. They held back till my nine-foot buddy jumped in.

"Oomph!" I said, breaking some guy's knuckles with my forehead. "Took you long enough."

It turned into a real brawl. Fists and feet and bodies flew. I skinned my knuckles to the elbow pounding handy chins and jaws. I got my own chin and jaw liberally pasted. My nose avoided rearrangement.

All that thumping was just the thing for a headache.

I had opportunities to be thankful that I have good teeth as I sank them into people who didn't have my continued good health foremost in mind.

When the fur stopped flying and the dust settled, me and the big guy were the only ones standing. And I needed the help of a wall.

I stumbled to the door at the end of the hall, beyond the vanquished attendants. It was locked. It looked every bit as massive as the door to the ward. Well, all that work for nothing. I exchanged glances with the big guy. He grinned, said, "I told you." He wiped blood off his face, grinned some more. "They going to have a time cleaning this one up, though. We got most of the night staff in here."

"Fine. We're a step closer. Let's drag these guys into the ward." Maybe we could use them as hostages.

All of a sudden, we had plenty of helpers. Guys turned brave, thumped heads soundly whenever an attendant threatened to wake up.

I checked the end of the hall I hadn't checked before. Another locked oaken vault door. Of course. "I guess this just isn't my day." It had had its moments earlier, but the downs were starting to outweigh the ups. "Anybody want to guess how long it'll be before they come after us again?"

The big guy shrugged. Now that the active part was over he seemed to be losing interest.

I produced two tiny folding knives that hadn't been taken, reflected that this incident was going to generate strident calls for an investigation of how blades and sorcerous gook and whatnot had gotten to the inmates. Like there'd ever been a doubt that any inmate who could flash the cash couldn't buy any damned thing he wanted.

An investigation might mean hope. If it was serious, it would require my testimony. That would mean the pointing of fingers at the kind of people who'd take bribes for falsely imprisoning heroes like me. Ugh! They'd be villains who'd be aware of the distress my testimony could cause their careers. Surely they'd take steps to assure a paucity of witnesses likely to testify.

I gave the big guy a knife. "Carve me some kindling out of anything wooden. If we get a decent fire going, we can burn our way through those doors."

He grinned but without the wild eagerness he'd shown before. He was winding down.

The notion of arson did excite some of the others. We all got to work ripping the stuffing out of pallets and whittling on the ward door.

Then I suffered another brainstorm, way late, unlike the hero of an adventure story. I claim genius only because nobody else thought of the obvious first. The adventure boys would have planned it from the start. It's one of their old tricks.

The Bledsoe staff wore uniforms, scruffy though those were.

I got my fires burning at both ends of the hall. Ivy tended them. His vocabulary didn't improve, but he became more animated. He liked fires. He even paid attention when I said, "Use plenty of horsehair. We want plenty of smoke." The horsehair came out of the pallets.

Ivy grinned from ear to ear. He was one fulfilled lunatic.

The people outside would *have* to make a move. They couldn't wait us out once we had fires burning. Fires had to be fought.

I had to have a guy follow Ivy and make sure his fires didn't grow too fast. Already they seemed likely to burn through the floor before they ate through the doors.

Once the smoke was thick enough, I picked an attendant my size and started trading clothes. He got the best of the deal.

My companions caught on. Soon they were squabbling over the available uniforms. I made sure Ivy and the big guy got theirs. I wanted one for the little breed who'd body-blocked the ward door, but he'd have gotten lost in a shirt.

Interesting that I had so many supporters now that it looked like I had prospects.

The smoke almost got too thick before somebody outside decided action had to be taken *now*.

# 19

They brought almost every warm body they had left. They burst
through both doors at once, behind thrown buckets of water. They
concentrated on the fires to begin, taking what lumps they must
until those were extinguished, then they started whipping on anybody in arm's reach. When they got into the ward, they started
hauling fallen comrades away.

It was real exciting for a while. The issue was definitely in
doubt.

The smoke got to me more than I expected. After they dragged
me out and I decided it was time I made a run for it, I found that
my legs were saying no way.

"Don't. You aren't ready yet."

I didn't look up and give myself away. Around me, impelled
by the cunning of madness, my buddies did the same. What a
team!

There were better than twelve men scattered along the hallway, many from the ward. The rest had gone down in the current
invasion.

The speaker was a woman, the owner of the legs. She added,
"Get the smoke out before you do anything."

I coughed and made noises and kept my face hidden. She
moved on, evidently to tend someone else who was stirring. A female doctor? How about that? I never heard of such a thing, but
why not?

I scooted back till my spine found a wall, raised myself up
against that, lifted my head to scope out an escape route. I kept
seeing two of things when I could see through the water in my

eyes. I got my feet under me again and practiced standing up till I could do it with no hands.

My chosen escape route did not become overgrown while I was catching my breath. I shoved off the wall and started staggering. There was a stairwell door straight ahead, out in the remote distance, on the far horizon, about twenty feet away. All kinds of racket came from behind it, as though thunder-lizards were mating in the stairwell. I didn't pay the racket any mind. I didn't have any mind left over. What I had was busy thinking "out."

I was chugging right along, hardly ever falling down, when she of the glorious gams intercepted me. "What are you trying to do? I told you . . . Oh!"

I grinned my winningest grin. "Oh-oh."

"Oh, my god!"

"Hey, no. I'm just a regular guy."

Maybe she had trouble hearing over the racket from the stairwell. Or maybe she had trouble hearing over the uproar from the hall and ward. She sure didn't get my message. She whooped and hollered like she thought she was going to get carried off by a lunatic or something.

I grabbed a wrist, mostly to keep from falling down. I noticed that she was blond and recalled that that was one of my favorites but I didn't have oomph enough to let her know. The bleeding had stopped a long time ago, but my head wasn't much better. The smoke hadn't done me any good, either.

I hacked out, "Pipe down! We're going for a walk, sister. I don't want anybody should get hurt, but that ain't my top priority. You get the drift? You keep on wailing. . . ."

She shut up. Blue eyes big and beautiful, she bobbed her head.

"I'll cut you loose at the front door. Maybe. If you're good and I don't get no more trouble." Snappy rhetoric, Garrett. Your roots are showing.

I was getting the edge on the smoke, though. I was ready to bet myself she would be good. A figure like that, it burned. No. Forget fire. Fire means smoke. I just swallowed enough smoke to last forever.

I leaned on the lady like she was my sweetie. "I need your help." Rotten to the heart, I am. But this would be our only date.

She nodded again.

Then she tripped me, the naughty girl.

And *then* my friend Winger blasted through that stairwell door, flinging battered orderlies ahead of her. "Goddamn, Garrett!

I bust in here fixing to save your ass and what do I find? You trying to bop some bimbo in front of the whole damned world." She
grabbed my collar, hoisted me away from my latest daydream,
who had gone down when I had. Winger set me on my feet, then
proceeded to whip the pudding out of a burly, hirsute attendant
who meant to object to the irregularity of the way she was checking me out. Between punches she grunted, "You got to get your
priorities straight, Garrett."

No point mentioning who tripped who. You don't explain to
Winger. She creates her own realities.

While she was amusing herself with the hairy orderly, I asked
the lady doctor, "What's a nice girl like you doing in a place like
this?"

She wouldn't answer even after I apologized for playing so
rough.

"For heaven's sake, Garrett, give it a rest," Winger snapped.
"And come on."

I went along because she grabbed hold and took off. I grabbed
the blonde as we went past. Down those stairs we went, stepping
over the occasional moaning attendant. Winger had come through
like a natural disaster. I bubbled, "I do hope I haven't been too
much trouble. Unfortunately, I can't hang around just because
somebody out there wants me in here instead of stomping on his
toes." I put on my grim face. "When I catch up with him, I'll make
sure he gives you a big donation. Big enough to cover damages."

Winger rolled her eyes. She didn't slow down and she didn't
let go.

The lady of the legs said, "You're serious, aren't you?"

Winger grumbled, "As serious as he can get when he's in rut."

My new friend and I ignored her. I said, "That's right. I find
things for people. Just this morning, a lady from the Hill asked me
to find her daughter. I'd barely started looking when a band of ruf-
fians set upon me. Next thing I knew, I was coming to and there
you were and I thought I'd died and gone to one of those afterlives
where they have angels, only my head hurt too much."

"I risked life and limb for this," Winger muttered. "Your head
is about to hurt a whole lot more."

The lady doc looked at me like she really wanted to believe.
She said, "He does spread it thick, doesn't he?"

"With a manure rake," Winger growled, reverting to uncul-
tured country ways. You can take the girl out of the sticks, and so
forth.

I said, "You ever feel the need to get in touch, just go up Macunado Street. When you get to Wizard's Reach, start asking around for where the Dead Man stays."

The lady offered a weak smile. "I might do that. I just might. Just to see what happens."

"Fireworks. For sure."

Winger suggested, "Save yourself for marriage, honey. If there's anything left."

The lady's smile vanished.

You can't win them all. You especially can't when you have friends intent on throwing the game.

We'd reached the street in front of the Bledsoe. I tried to sprint off into the night at a fast shamble. I figured I ought to make tracks before some avenging orderly appeared.

After I'd gone a few steps, Winger observed, "That was the most disgusting display I've seen yet, Garrett. Don't you ever stop?"

"We have to get out of here." I glanced over my shoulder at the Bledsoe. A glimpse of the place nearly panicked me. That had been close. "We got to disappear before they send somebody after us."

"You think they're not going to know where to look? You all but gave that bimbo your address."

"Hey! You're talking about the love of my life. She won't give me away." I didn't let her see my crossed fingers.

Winger shifted ground. "Why would they bother, anyway? Really?"

At this point, they probably wouldn't. Anything they did now was likely to draw more attention than they could stand.

I shrugged. That's always a useful, noncommital device.

# 20

I waited till we had a good head start, just in case the hospital gang did decide to come after me. Then I grabbed Winger's hand in a comealong grip.

"Hey! What the hell you doing, Garrett?"

"You and me are going to sit here on these steps like young lovers and you're going to whisper sweet nothings about what the hell is going on. Got it?"

"No."

I added some muscle to the hold.

"Ouch! Ain't that just like a man? No gratitude. Save his ass and—"

"Looked to me like I was doing an adequate job of saving it on my own. Sit."

Winger sat, but she kept grumbling. I didn't let go. I wouldn't get any answers if I did.

"Tell me about it, Winger."

"About what?" She can turn into the dumbest country girl that ever lived.

"I know you. Don't waste stupid on me. Tell me about Maggie Jenn and her missing daughter and how come as soon as I take this job I get jumped, coldcocked, and shoved into the cackle factory in such a big hurry the fools don't bother to empty my pockets? All the time I'm in there, I'm wondering how this could happen to me when only my pal Winger knows what I'm doing. And now I'm wondering how my pal Winger knew I needed help getting sprung from the Bledsoe. Stuff like that."

"Oh. That." She thought a while, making something up.

"Come on, Winger. Give truth a try. Just for the novelty."

She offered me a Winger-sized dirty look. "I was working for this pansy name of Grange Cleaver. . . ."

"Grange Cleaver? What kind of name is that? Come on. Tell me there ain't nobody named Grange Cleaver."

"Who's going to tell this? You or me? You want to sit there and listen to the echo of your lips clacking, that's all right with me. Only don't expect me to hang around listening, too. I know how corny you get when you're up on your high horse."

"Me? Corny?"

"Like some holy joe Revanchist roll in the aisles preacher."

"You wound me."

"I'd like to, sometimes."

"Promises, promises. You were working for a character with a name even a dwarf wouldn't tolerate."

"Yeah. His mom and dad were probably named Trevor and Nigel." She gave me another dirty look, thought about getting stubborn. "I was working for him, you like his name or not. He had me watching Maggie Jenn. Because he expected her to try to kill him, he said."

"Why?"

"He didn't say. I didn't ask. The kind of mood he was in most times, it didn't seem like a bright idea to nag."

"Not even a guess?"

"What's with you, Garrett? I get three marks a day if I mind my own business and do my job. I maybe get kneecapped if I don't."

Thus did we head for an argument about moral responsibility. We'd had it about fifty times before. The way Winger saw it, if you covered your own ass you were doing your part.

She was trying to divert me.

"Guess it don't matter, Winger. Go on. Explain how you ended up here."

"That's easy. I'm a big dummy. I figured you for a pal. Somebody what didn't deserve that raw a deal."

"How come I feel like there are some details shy here? You think you could put a little flesh on those bones?"

"You can be a real pain in the butt, Garrett. Know what I mean?"

"I've heard that rumor." I waited. I did not relax my grip on her hand.

"All right. All right. So I was working for this Cleaver. Mostly on watching the Jenn bimbo, but on other stuff sometimes, too. It was like regular work, Garrett. Top pay and always something needed doing. Tonight I figured out why. Cleaver was putting me out front. People watched me while him and his nancy boys pulled stunts in the shadows."

I grunted but provided no sympathy. I can't find much of that for somebody who won't learn. Winger had gotten herself used before. She was big and good-looking and a woman, and because she was a woman hardly anyone took her seriously. This Grange Cleaver probably just thought she was a handy freak, though he was a freak himself.

"I know, Garrett. I know. You heard this one before. Probably you'll hear it again. Sometimes it works out profitable."

Meaning she took advantage of those who used her, playing dumb country girl while she pocketed their silver candlesticks.

I gave her a shot at my famous raised eyebrow.

"I know. I know. But I got to get by while I build my reputation."

"I suppose." Getting a nasty rep was an obsession with her.

"Thanks for the passionate support. At least I caught on before it was too late to get out."

"Did you?"

"Get out? Damned right I did. See, this Cleaver told me, yeah, Winger, that's a great idea, putting somebody next to Maggie Jenn. Somebody else on account of she'd recognize me. But when I told him it was you I got to cover it, he got a face looked like he was about to have a shit hemorrhage. You'd a thought one of his buddies sneaked up and showed him he loved him by surprise. He got me out so fast I got suspicious. I sneaked around to where I could listen in on him."

I suspected Winger had done plenty of eavesdropping. "I've never heard of Cleaver. How come he's shook up about me?"

She spat. "How the hell should I know? You do got your rep as a super straight-arrow simp. Maybe that done it."

"Think so?" Winger was after an angle all the time. "So you wised up. Hard to believe. Usually it takes—"

"I ain't as dumb as you think, Garrett." She refused to provide proof, though. "What Cleaver was up to, he called in this bunch of street brunos. Not his regular butt buddies, just some muscle. He told them he had this big problem name of you and asked could they solve it for him? How about they sent you off to the Bledsoe? The brunos said sure and laughed and joked about how they done it before with some guys Cleaver didn't like. He's got people on the inside on the pad. He's connected to the hospital somehow. Probably through that blond baggage you was drooling on when I was trying to get you out of there."

"Yeah. Probably." But I didn't believe that and neither did she.

"Anyways, it took me a while to get away without nobody noticing. I came straight to the hospital."

I could imagine why it had taken her so long to slip away. Once she decided to quit Cleaver, she would want to collect everything valuable she could carry. Then she'd have to take that wherever she kept her stuff. Then she might have tested the waters to see if she couldn't carry off another load before she finally got around to me.

She knew I wasn't going anywhere.

The big rat.

"So you came whooping to the rescue only to find out that, through my own cunning, I had proceeded to effect my own release."

"You was doing all right," she conceded, "but you wouldn't never of gotten out of there if I hadn't whipped up on all them guys what would've gotten in your way downstairs."

Whatever else, Winger was a woman. I granted her the last word.

"You can let go the hand now," she said. "There ain't nothing left to squeeze out'n me."

"That a fact?" Then how come the country was coming on stronger all the time? She was putting on her camouflage. "And just when I was thinking it might be useful to learn how Maggie Jenn knows you. Just when I was getting curious about your pal Grange Cleaver. Since I've never heard of the guy, it'd probably save me a lot of time if you were to clue me where he lives, is he human or whatever, is he connected with the Outfit or anybody, stuff like that. Details. I'm a detail kind of guy, Winger."

Winger is your basic jump on the wagon and head out without checking to see if the mules are hitched up kind of woman, never long on scoping out plans or worrying about consequences. Neither past nor future mean much to her. That isn't because she's stupid or foolish, it's because that's the way she's made.

"You're a royal pain in the ass kind of guy, Garrett."

"That too. Hear it all the time. Especially from you. You're going to give me a complex."

"Not you. You got to be sensitive to get a complex. You're sensitive like a stinky old boot. Grange Cleaver, now he's a sensitive kind of guy." She grinned.

"You ever going to tell me something? Or you just going to sit there smirking like a toad on a cowpie?"

She snickered. "I told you, Garrett, Grange Cleaver is the kind of guy wears earrings."

"Plenty of guys are the kind of guys who wear earrings. That don't make them poofs. They might be fierce pirates."

"Yeah? He's also the kind of guy wears wigs and makeup and likes to dress up in girl clothes. I heard him brag about how he used to work the Tenderloin without the johns ever knowing how unique an experience they'd had."

"It happens." In the Tenderloin, in TunFaire, everything happens. I didn't consider this big news, though Cleaver did seem careless with his secrets. You get too public you can end up with more trouble than you can handle. Asking for trouble is plain dumb.

"He human?" I asked.

"Yeah."

"And don't hide his quirks?"

"Not around home. I never saw him go out in the street and run after little boys. Why?"

"He don't sound careful enough. You got any idea what a poof goes through in the army? Hell like you wouldn't believe. Bottom line is, any of them that don't hide it damned good don't last. The Cantard is no place to belong to an unpopular minority."

"I don't think Grange was in the service, Garrett."

"You're on a first-name basis?"

"He has everybody call him Grange."

"Real democratic kind of guy, eh?"

"Yeah."

"Right. So. He's human and male, he had to be in some service, Winger. They don't allow exceptions."

"Maybe he was a dodger."

"They never give up hunting those guys." They don't. Not ever. There is no privilege when it comes to conscription. Say that for our masters. No favoritism is shown there. In fact, in that regard *they* pay more than their share of the price. They do lead from the front.

Notice how Winger got me off on a tangent? I did. She had dropped out on this Cleaver princess but did not want to give up any information about him. That meant she still saw an angle.

Winger always sees an angle.

"Let's get back to the high road. What's between Cleaver and

Maggie Jenn? If he's a shrieking faggot, why is he interested at all?"

"I think she's his sister."

"Say what?"

"Or maybe his cousin. Anyway, they're related somehow. And she's got something he wants. Something he figures is his."

"So she's going to kill him?" This was getting weirder by the minute.

I hate family wars. They're the worst kind. They put you out in no-man's land all alone without a map. Whatever you do turns out wrong. "What's he after, Winger?"

"I don't know." Now she was getting long suffering, the way people do when small children ask too many questions. "I just worked for the guy. I didn't sleep with him. I wasn't his social secretary. I wasn't his partner. I didn't keep his diary for him. I just took his money and did what he said. Then I came out to save your butt on account of I kind of felt responsible for getting you into a jam."

"You *were* responsible. You were running a game on me. I don't know what it was because you've kept it to yourself. Chances are you're still running a game on me, you being you."

I was a little tired of Winger, which was another of her talents. She could exasperate you till you ran her off, leaving you thinking it was your idea that she was gone; leaving you feeling guilty for doing her that way.

"So what're you gonna do?" she asked. I had let go of her hand.

"I figure I'll suck up a few beers, then I'll get me some sleep. After I get me out of this clown costume and delouse myself."

"Want some company?"

That's my friend Winger.

"Not tonight. I just want to sleep."

"All right. You want to be that way." She got gone before I could react to the smug smile she left floating behind her. Before I fully realized that she was going without having told me anything useful, like where the hell I could find friendly Grange Cleaver.

# 21

"I just want to get some sleep." Usually famous last words for me when I'm working. I'd get three hours of shuteye the rest of the month.

The gods were toying with me—nobody messed with me at all. So naturally I kept waking up to listen for pounding at the door. Somewhere up there, or down there, or out there, an otherwise useless godlet was earning his reputation by tormenting me in ingenious ways. If he keeps on, he may get promoted to director of heavenly sewers.

So I failed to rest well despite the opportunity. I wakened cranky and stomped around cussing Dean for being out of town. There was no one else I could make miserable.

The true breadth and depth of my genius didn't occur to me till I was well along toward whipping up a truly awful breakfast of griddle cakes. I had forgotten to ask Winger about the guy who had followed me to Maggie Jenn's place.

Someone tapped on the front door. What the hell? It was a civilized hour, almost.

The knock was so discreet I almost missed it. I grumbled some, flipped a flapjack, and headed up front.

I was astounded when I peeped through the peephole. I threw the door open to let the radiance of that blond beauty shine on me. "Didn't expect to see you again, Doc." I examined the street behind the lovely, in case she headed up a platoon of Bledsoe guys who couldn't take a joke. I didn't see anybody, but that meant squat. Macunado Street was so crowded you could have hidden the entire hospital staff out there.

"You invited me." She looked like she had come directly from work, like maybe she'd pulled a double shift cleaning up. "You were panting over the idea." She had a sarcastic tone to counterweight a blistering smile. "Your big friend dunk you in icewater?"

"I just didn't expect to see you again. Look, I'm sorry about that mess. I just get wild when somebody pulls a dirty trick like dumping me in the cackle factory."

Her lips pruned up. "Can't you use a less contemptuous term?"

"Sorry. I'll try." I encouraged myself by recalling a thing or three people have said about my profession, most of it unflattering.

She relaxed. "The dirty trick is why I'm here. What is that smell?"

I whirled. Tendrils of smoke slithered from the kitchen. I shrieked and bounded down the hall. Our lady of the marvelous legs followed at a dignified pace.

I scooped blackened griddle cakes into the sink. They sent up smoke signals denouncing my skills as a chef. Hell, I was so bad I might be able to get on in Morley's kitchen. They had an opening. "I can use these to patch the roof," I grumbled.

"Too brittle."

"Everybody's a comedian. You had breakfast?"

"No. But . . ."

"Grab an apron, kid. Give me a hand. A little food will do us both good. What you want to know, anyway?"

She grabbed an apron. Amazing gal. "I didn't like the way you were talking last night. I decided to check it out. There was no record of your commitment, though when I joined the orderlies carrying you they assured me that you had been brought in by the Guard and the records were in order."

I made rude noises, started flapping a new generation of flapjacks.

"That was easy to check. A ranking Guard officer is an old friend of my family. Colonel Westman Block."

I squeaked three or four times before I managed to ask, "*Colonel* Block? They made a *colonel* out of him?"

"Wes speaks highly of you, too, Mr. Garrett."

"I'll bet."

"He told me you were *not* sent to the Bledsoe by his people—though he wished he'd thought of it."

"That's Block. Playful as a hogshead of cobras."

"He did speak well of you professionally. But he warned me to remain wary in other respects." She could get a laugh into her voice, too.

"You going to want bacon?"

"You just starting it now? You're supposed to start the bacon first. It takes longer."

"I cook one thing at a time. That way I only burn one thing at a time."

"A daring approach."

"Holds down expenses."

We cooked together and ate together and I spent a lot of time appreciating the scenery. The lady didn't seem to mind.

We were cleaning up when she said, "I won't tolerate this sort of thing. I won't tolerate the corruption that allows it to happen."

I stepped back, checked her out with different eyes. "You just start working there? You'd have to look hard to find a place more corrupt than the Bledsoe."

"Yes. I'm new. And I'm finding out how rotten the place is. Every day it's something. This is the worst yet. You might've spent your whole life wrongfully imprisoned."

"Yeah. And I wasn't the only one in there. You an idealist and reformer?" TunFaire is infested with those lately.

"You don't need to make me sound like a halfwit."

"Sorry. Most wannabe utopians are, reality-wise. They come from well-to-do families and haven't the vaguest notion what life is like for people who *have* to depend on a Bledsoe. They can't imagine what life is like for the kind of people who work in a Bledsoe. For them taking bribes and selling donated supplies are perks of the job. They wouldn't understand you if you bitched about it—unless they figured you were trying to increase the override you take off the top."

She gave me a disgusted look. "Somebody suggested that yesterday."

"There you go. I bet you blew up. And didn't get through. And now everybody in the place thinks you're crazy. Maybe the better-placed guys in the bigger money are wondering if you're dangerous crazy. They worry about these new Guards kicking ass and taking names. It takes a while to corrupt reformers."

She settled with a fresh cup of tea, honey and mint in it. She eyed me, then mused, "West says you can be trusted."

"Nice of him to say. Wish I could say the same."

She frowned. "Point is, I'm dangerous already. A few days ago, several thousand marks worth of medical supplies vanished.

Right away I filled two orderly slots with men I knew personally. Men I can trust."

"I see." In view of her Guard connection, I guessed they were Block's men. He had a character named Relway working for him, running his secret police force. Relway was *nasty*.

If Relway became interested in the Bledsoe, heads would roll and asses get kicked. Relway doesn't let bureaucratic roadblocks and legal technicalities get in his way. He gets in there and rights those wrongs.

I suggested, "You be careful. They think you brought in spies, they could forget their manners."

She sipped tea, studied me, which made me uncomfortable. Not that I object to having a beautiful woman check me out. I was born to be a sex object. But this beautiful woman had something less thrilling in mind. "I'm not as naive as you think, Garrett."

"Good. That'll save you a lot of pain."

"You have any idea who signed you in?"

"No. I was asleep. But I hear the prince who paid for it goes by the name Grange Cleaver."

"Cleaver? Grange Cleaver?"

"You know him?"

"He's a hospital trustee. Appointed through the imperial household." She studied me some more. "I told you I'm not as naive as you might think. That does include understanding that I might be in danger."

Could be was not how I would put it. "So?"

"So maybe I should get somebody to stick close by till the dust settles."

"Sounds like a good idea."

"You game?"

I was game, but not for that. "You want a bodyguard?"

"Wes says you won't sell out."

"Maybe not. But there's a problem."

"What?" She sounded irked.

"I don't do bodyguard work. Sorry. And I have a client already. Wouldn't do to let that obligation slide, much as part of me wants to. Also, your staff is going to harbor grudges. I wouldn't dare hang out around there."

She looked like she was getting mad. "Then what would you suggest?" She didn't try to change my mind. My feelings were hurt. Maybe she could have talked herself into something.

She was too damned businesslike.

Maggie Jenn would have tried to talk me into something.

"Friend of mine, Saucerhead Tharpe, could do the job. Or several other guys I know. Trouble is the best guys all look like what they are." Then my muse inspired me. "My friend from last night will be looking for work."

My guest brightened, her mind darting past all the obvious caveats that would have obtained had Winger been male. "Can she do the job?"

"Better than I could. She doesn't have a conscience."

"She trustworthy?"

"Don't put her in temptation's way. The family silver might accidentally fall into her pockets. But she can get a job done."

"She tough?"

"She eats hedgehogs for breakfast. Without peeling them first. Don't get into a tough contest with her. She don't know when to quit."

She smiled. "I understand the impulse. When you step outside tradition, there's a temptation to show the boys you can do everything they can do better. All right. Sounds good. I'll talk to her. How do I get in touch?"

Finding Winger isn't easy. She wants it that way. There are people she'd rather not have sneaking up.

I explained what worked for me. She thanked me for breakfast, advice, and help, and headed for the front door. I was overwhelmed still. She was ready to let herself out before I got myself together. "Hey! Wait up. You didn't introduce yourself."

She smirked. "Chastity, Garrett. Chastity Blaine." She laughed at my goofy look, slipped out, and closed the door behind her.

# 22

By daylight, the Joy House is dull. Lately Morley has been open continuously, driven by some bizarre civic impulse that wants weeds and grass clippings made available to all. I was concerned. The place might start attracting horses.

I invited myself up to the bar. "Cook me up a rare steak, Sarge. And let Morley know I'm here."

Sarge grunted, scratched his crotch, hitched his pants, thought about it before he did anything—which was mainly to wonder aloud why I thought Morley Dotes gave one rat's ass whether I was infesting the Joy House or stinking up the place in Hell, where I belonged.

"You ought to open a charm school for young ladies of superior breeding, Sarge."

"Fugginay. Ain't dat da troot?"

I settled at a table. My steak arrived before Morley did. It was a thick, rare, prime center cut. Of eggplant. I forced part of it down by holding my breath and closing my eyes. If I didn't have to smell it or see it, it wasn't too bad.

Sarge's buddy Puddle trundled out of the kitchen, half a foot of hairy bare belly hanging out from under his shirt. He paused to blow his nose on his apron. He had him some kind of key on a rope around his neck. I asked, "What the hell are you supposed to be? One that got away? They didn't tie the noose tight enough?"

"I'm da wine stewart aroun' here, Garrett." My worst fears were confirmed—not only by ear but by nose. Puddle's breath told me he diligently tested his vintages. "Morley says we got to attrack a better class a' custom."

Time was you could have done that by dragging in a dozen derelicts. "You're just the guy who can do it, Puddle."

"Fugginay. Ain't dat da troot?"

These guys had the same rhetoric teacher.

"You want some wine, Garrett? To go wit' what you're havin' dere we got us a perky little fortunata petite what's maybe not as subtle as a Nambo Arsenal but—"

"Puddle!"

"Yeah?"

"It's spoiled grape juice. If they call it wine, it's spoiled grape juice. I don't care if you call it coy or brujo or whatever. Talk that wine snob talk till doomsday, that don't change the main fact. Hell, go look at the stuff while it's changing into brassy brunette or whatever. It's got mold and shit growing on it. What it is, really, is how you get alcohol that winos and ratmen can afford."

Puddle winked and whispered, "I'm wit' you. The gods meant real men to drink dat stuff dey wouldn't of invented beer."

"What you do, you get Morley to serve beer by telling him it's cream of barley soup?"

Morley arrived during this exchange. He observed, "Wine is how the smart restauranteur fleeces the kind of man who walks around with his nose in the air."

I asked, "How come you want that kind of guy cluttering up your dance floor?"

"Cash flow." Morley planted himself in the chair opposite me. "Plain, simple, raw money. If you want it, you have to find ways to pry it loose from those who have it. Our current clientele doesn't have it. Often. But I've noted that we've begun to attract adventurers. So I've started positioning us to become *the* in place."

"Why?"

He looked at me funny.

"Don't let me throw you with the trick questions, Morley. If they get too tough for you, holler."

"Look around. There's your answer."

I looked. I saw Puddle and Sarge and a few local "characters" using the place to get out of the weather. "Not real appetizing." I meant Puddle and Sarge.

"It's that old devil Time, Garrett. We're all a pound heavier and a step slower. It's time to think about facing realities."

"Puddle and Sarge, maybe." Morley didn't have an ounce of fat on him. I did my famous eyebrow trick, one of my more endearing skills.

He read that right. "A guy can get a step slow between the ears, too. He can lose that lean and hungry way of thinking." He eyed me as though I, of all people, should know that.

"Or he can start thinking like a cow because he doesn't eat anything but cattle fodder." I laid a pointed stare on the corpse of my eggplant filet. It had failed to live up to even my low expectations.

Morley grinned. "We're breaking in a new cook."

"On me?"

"Who better? Right, Puddle? No way we can disappoint Garrett. He was disappointed when he walked in the door. He'll bitch and gripe whatever we serve him."

I grumped, "You could poison me."

"If it would improve your disposition."

"There's an idea!" Puddle enthused. "Hows come I never thought a' that one?"

"Because you've never had a thought. If one got loose in that abandoned tenement of a head, it'd never find its way out," I muttered, but Puddle caught on anyhow.

"Yo! Sarge! We got any of dat rat poison left? Tell Wiggins to bring dis guy Garrett a special chef's surprise dessert."

I made noises to let them know what I thought of this level of humor and told Morley, "I need the benefit of your wisdom."

"You going to cry on my shoulder about one of your bimbos?"

"There's a thought. I never tried that. Maybe by way of a little sympathetic magic . . ."

"Don't expect sympathy from me."

"What I want to do is listen to you, not have you listen to me."

"This has to do with your Maggie Jenn thing?"

"Yes. The name Grange Cleaver mean anything?"

Morley glanced at Puddle. A shadow crossed his features. Puddle exchanged glances with Sarge. Then everybody faked indifference. Morley asked, "You saying the Rainmaker is back?"

"Rainmaker?"

"The only Grange Cleaver I know was called the Rainmaker. He was a fence. Big time. Where did you come onto the name?"

"Winger. She said she was working for him."

"That woman isn't your most reliable witness."

"You're telling me. But she did have an interesting story about how this guy was using her to keep tabs on Maggie Jenn. She said she thought Cleaver was Maggie's brother. Or some sort of close relation."

Again Morley tossed a glance at Puddle, then looked thoughtful. "I've never heard that one." He chuckled. There was no humor in the sound. "It can't be true, but it would explain a lot if it was. Maybe even including why *she* is back in town."

"You changing your position?"

"Huh?"

"You said she was in exile. What're you going on about, anyway?"

"All right. Grange Cleaver, alias the Rainmaker, was a very famous fence years ago."

"How can you be a famous fence? Seems to me you could be one or the other but not both."

"Famous among those who use the services of fences, wholesale or retail, supplier or end user. The Rainmaker operated on the swank. There were rumors he choreographed several big jobs himself, that he had a connection who got him the inside information he needed. He hit several Hill places. There weren't many guards back then. His raids were one reason the Hill folk set up their goon squads."

"This all connects with Maggie Jenn?"

"Maybe. It just occurred to me that the Rainmaker's heyday coincided with Maggie Jenn's famous affair. Specifically, with those months when Theodoric was dragging her around in public, not giving one good goddamn what anyone said."

"You have to admit nobody would've figured her for a spotter."

"Exactly. Her social crimes were reason enough to hate her."

"All of which is interesting but, as far as I can see, doesn't have anything to do with the job I'm getting paid to do." Though I might be wrong. Cleaver hadn't drafted me into the crackdome brigade because my colors clashed when I dressed. I was a threat somehow. "You still say Maggie Jenn doesn't have a daughter?"

"I said I didn't know about one. I still don't. But now I have a notion there's a lot I don't know about Maggie Jenn."

"Heard anything off the street?"

"Too soon, Garrett. It's a big town. And if the Rainmaker is in it, people who remember him might not talk."

"Yeah." A big town. And somewhere in it, a missing girl.

Somewhere in TunFaire there are scores of missing girls. More vanish every day. This just happened to be a girl who had someone willing to look for her.

I started toward the street.

"Garrett."

I stopped. I knew that tone. The real Morley was about to speak from behind all the masks. "What?"

"You be careful about the Rainmaker. He's as crazy as they come. Dangerous crazy."

I leaned against the door frame and did some ruminating. "I've got some real funny people in this one, Morley."

"How so?"

"They all have two faces. The Maggie Jenn I know and the one Winger told me about aren't much like the woman you describe. The Grange Cleaver Winger worked for and the one you describe aren't anything like the Grange Cleaver I heard about from another source. That Cleaver is one of the directors of the Bledsoe. He's connected with the imperial family."

"That's another new one on me. But so what?"

Yeah. So what? It occurred to me that Chastity's troubles with theft and corruption might stem from the very top.

For some reason, I just can't get used to the thinking it takes to encompass that kind of villainy. It doesn't seem reasonable to steal from the poor and the helpless, though I'm sure Morley could paste on his puzzled frown and make it all clear: you steal from the poor and helpless because they can't fight back. Because nobody gives a damn. But you do have to do one hell of a lot of stealing in order to make much money.

That's why most thieves prefer wealthier victims.

# 23

I decided my best course was to go home and settle in with a beer or five while I figured out how to do my job. Grange Cleaver was a side issue. Maybe I'd put time in on him after I found the missing daughter. I owed the clown. But Emerald came first.

Speaking of debts, by now his people inside the Bledsoe should have reported my brilliant, dashing escape. It might behoove me to keep a close watch on my behind.

You work yourself into the right frame of mind, it's sure something will happen. I was all primed to turn paranoid. Naturally, fate just had to set me off.

"How are you doing? I'm Ivy."

I squeaked and jumped up there where the pigeons fly. I could have clicked my heels and turned a somersault on the way down but was too busy making funny noises. I landed. And there, by the gods, was my old prison pal Ivy.

And not just Ivy. Behind Ivy, grinning merrily, was that big bozo who'd helped me with my breakout.

"You guys made it, eh? That's great." I tried easing around them. That didn't work. "How many others managed? Any idea?" I was just being sociable. You do that with unpredictable and potentially dangerous people. Hell, you should do that with anybody you don't know. You should be rude only to friends you're sure won't slice you into cold cuts. That's what manners are for.

The grinning fool grinned even wider. "Most everybody scooted, Garrett. The whole ward, I think."

"How did that happen?" I'd thought the staff were gaining control when I ran out.

"Some of us guys that had uniforms on decided to go get some paybacks after we got the smoke out of our lungs. And then a bunch of the guys still inside went berserk."

"Lucky for us they weren't crazy before." But they were crazy now and on the loose. I tried easing away again. The big guy had a knack for staying in my way.

I hadn't overlooked the fact that he knew my name even though I hadn't introduced myself. "How did you guys come to be here?" Here being Macunado Street less than two blocks from my house. A coincidence that monstrous could occur only every third leap year. It wasn't leap year.

The big guy got red. He confessed, "We was sneaking around trying to find a way out and we heard you talking to Doc Chaz. So we're on the street all this time, we don't know where to go or what to do. I ast Ivy and he don't got no suggestions."

Ivy's face brightened at the mention. He introduced himself, in case he'd forgotten his manners, then went back to studying the street. He seemed more perplexed than frightened, but I didn't think it would be long till he was ready to go back inside. I suspected that would be true for a lot of men.

"So you came looking for me."

The big guy nodded like a shy kid. "Seemed like you was a guy would know what to do."

I cussed myself silently for being the kind of fool I am. "All right. I got you into this, I'm kind of responsible. Come on. I'll get you fed, put you up tonight, maybe help you make arrangements."

Yeah. I know. Chances were good they would smell like long-dead fish before I got them out. But I did have a card up my sleeve. The Dead Man isn't handicapped by manners or an overdeveloped sense of social obligation. Guests don't overstay his welcome.

I wondered if it wasn't maybe time to start nudging him. I could use a little advice.

I let my guests into my house. The big guy was as nervous as a kid in unfamiliar territory. Ivy was as curious as a cat. Naturally, the Goddamn Parrot started raising hell in the small front room. Ivy invited himself in there while I tried to solve a problem by asking the big guy, "Do you have a name? I don't know what to call you."

Mr. Big cussed Ivy for not bringing him food.

I was beginning to miss Dean for yet another reason. He had dealt with that foul feathered fiend before he left. I still wasn't used to it.

It went into its act. "Help! Rape! Save me! Oh, please, mister, don't make me do that again." It managed to sound like a preadolescent girl. The only parrot in captivity smart enough to remember more than four words, and some wit had taught it that. I just knew if the neighbors ever heard the beast I'd never convince the lynch mob that a parrot had done the squawking. The bird would not say boo till I was swinging high.

Meantime, the big fellow stood around wearing a thoughtful look, trying to remember his name. His wits seemed to turn through seasons. Must have been summertime when he helped me at the Bledsoe. Now it was late autumn or early winter. I was glad I didn't have to deal with him all the time. I could go crazy myself.

Powziffle.

Ivy closed the door to the small front room. The Goddamn Parrot went right on screeching. Ivy grinned from ear to ear. I had a feeling I knew what was going to become of that bird. He could become the companion of a tortured fellow who needed a friend desperately.

The tortured fellow roamed on down the hall while his sidekick continued to ruminate the big question.

"Hey! Yeah!" His face brightened. "Slither." Brighter still. "Yeah! That's it. Slither." His grin dwarfed Ivy's.

"Slither?" What the hell kind of name was that? A nickname for sure, though he didn't look like a Slither to me.

Ivy had his face shoved into my office. He froze. Eventually he let out a little squeak of dismay, the first break in his six-word pattern. From the direction he was facing, I guessed he'd gotten a look at Eleanor. That painting had plenty to say to anyone with the open eyes of madness.

Slither preened, proud that he had recalled his name.

I said, "You guys come back to the kitchen. We'll have us a beer and a snack." I suspected that they hadn't eaten since their flight from the hospital. Freedom does have its disadvantages.

Slither nodded and flashed his grin. Ivy ignored me. He crossed the hall to the Dead Man's room, went inside, and got himself a shock even more horrible than the terror in the shadows behind Eleanor. The Dead Man isn't furry, little, or cuddly. He can't win instant love through cute.

I pried Ivy out of there and got him into the kitchen. We settled down to a snack of cold roast beef, pickles, cheese, mustard with verve enough to water your eyes, and adequate quantities of beer. I did more sipping than eating. Once Slither and Ivy slowed enough so they took time to breathe as well as eat, I asked, "You guys able to do anything?"

"Huh?" That was Slither. Ivy was sucking up another mug of beer, his fifth. He'd begun to look brighter, more human. I'd begun to suspect the nature of his madness. He was a wino.

"What did you do before they put you in that place?"

Slither started another five-fall match with his memory.

I wondered how well he'd done before his venture inside.

Ivy drained his mug and headed for the cold well. I caught his wrist. It didn't take much to set him down. "Don't let's overdo, Ivy."

He stared at his plate a minute, then lifted a sliver of meat to his lips. He chewed slowly for a long time. After he swallowed he startled me by saying, "You can't forget to eat, Garrett. That's the thing you've got to hang onto. You can't forget to eat."

I stared at him. Slither stared at him. Slither howled, "I'll be damned! I'll be double dog damned, Garrett! He talked. What did we do? I never heard him talk before."

The event seemed to give Slither's intellect a kick in the slats, too. He started chattering at Ivy, trying to draw him out. Ivy didn't want to be drawn. He stared at his plate and picked at his food. He looked up only once, to toss a longing glance toward the cold well. The object of his affection, my keg, lay there all alone.

"Well?"

Slither looked at me. "Huh?"

"I asked what you did on the outside, before you went in."

"How come you want to know?" The fires of genius never burned real hot here.

I had to move before he faded again. "I want to know because if I know what you can do maybe I can find somebody who'll pay you to do it." There is no shortage of work in TunFaire, honest or otherwise, what with all our young men spending five years in the Cantard and a lot of them never coming home.

"Mostly I done bodyguarding. I was pretty good when I started, but I figure I picked up something when I was down south. I started kind of fading out sometimes. I started making mistakes sometimes. I screwed up on a real good job I got on account of my size mostly, so I took another one that wasn't quite as good and I screwed up on that one, too, so I took another job and all the time the fading got worse and worse. I started not remembering anything sometimes. Nothing. Except I kept getting the feeling that I was doing things that weren't right. Maybe really wicked things,

only whatever I was doing I wasn't getting caught by nobody because I always woke up at home. Sometimes I had bruises and
stuff, though. And then I was right in the right place at the right
time and landed me a real sweet job. I don't know what happened
or how. One day I wake up, I'm there where you found me and I
don't know how long I been there or what I done to get myself put
inside."

I'd seen him during one blackout. Powziffle. Maybe that one
had been mild and harmless. Maybe he went berserk sometimes.

But then he'd have been in the violent ward. Wouldn't he?

"What did you do in the army?" I asked.

"Nothing, man. I wasn't no friggin' ground-pounder."

I knew that tone and that look and that fire in the eye. "You
were a Marine?"

"Absofugginlutely. First Battalion. Fleet Marines."

I was impressed. That meant something to a Marine. Slither
had been one of the elite of the elite. So how come ten years later
he set up housekeeping in the charity bughouse? The man had to
be tougher than rawhide.

On the other hand, how many tough guys fall apart with a
nudge in the right way at the right time?

Slither asked, "What about you?"

"Force recon."

"Hey! All right!" He reached out to slap my hand, a silly habit
left over from the Corps.

They told us when we went in we'd never stop being Marines.

"If you can keep your head together, I could maybe use you on
the job I'm doing."

He frowned. "What kind of work you do? Besides bust places
up like you was trying to turn the whole world into a barroom
brawl?"

I explained. I explained again. He didn't get it till I told him,
"It's kind of like being a mercenary—only I just find things or
figure things out for people who can't handle their problems
themselves."

He still frowned but got the basic idea. His trouble was that he
couldn't grasp *why* I'd galavant around like I was some kind of
white knight.

So I put that into terms he could understand. "Most of my
clients are loaded. When things go my way, I can soak them for a
bundle."

Even Ivy brightened at that. But he kept looking at my cold well like it was the gate to heaven.

I got up, dug out a bottle of wine that had been around since the dawn of time, plopped it down in front of Ivy. I drew more beer for Slither and me. I settled. Ivy went to work on his bottle. After he finished a long pull, I asked, "How about you, Ivy? What did you do in the war?"

He tried. He really did. But his tongue got tangled. Gibberish came out. I suggested he take another long drink and relax. He did. That worked. Sort of.

"So?" I urged, gently, in the back of my mind beginning to hear guilt nag because I was getting soaked with a pair of fruit-cakes when I ought to be hunting a missing daughter. "What did you do down there?"

"La-la-long ra-range re-re-recon. Ra-ranger stuff."

"Excellent!" Slither murmured. Civilians wouldn't understand.

I nodded encouragement and tried to cover my surprise. Ivy didn't look the type. But a lot of guys don't. And it's often guys who make the elite outfits who're good enough to survive. They know how to take care of themselves.

"Pretty grim?" I asked.

Ivy nodded. Any other answer would have been a lie. The fighting had been tough, vicious, endless, and unavoidable. Mercy had been an unknown. The war seems won now, years after our hours in the ranks, but fighting continues on a reduced scale as Karenta's soldiers pursue diehard Venageti and try to stifle the guttering republic created by Glory Mooncalled.

"Dumb question," Slither observed.

"I know. But once in a while, I run into somebody who insists he liked it down there."

"He was rear echelon, then. Or a liar. Or crazy. The ones that can't live no other way just stay in."

"You're mostly right."

In a thin voice, Ivy said, "Th-there's sp-space for them na-now we ga-got out."

I agreed with him, too.

"Tell us more about what you do," Slither said. "What you working on now that got somebody so pissed they shoved you into the Bledsoe?"

"I'm not sure anymore." I saw no reason not to so I shared most of the details. Till I mentioned Grange Cleaver.

"Wait a minute. Whoa. Hang on. Cleaver? Like in the Rain-maker, Cleaver?"

"He's called that sometimes. Why?"

"That last job I had. The plush one. I was running errands for that faggot asshole."

"And?" I suffered a little twinge.

"And I don't remember what the hell I was doing before I woke up in the bughouse, but I'm damned well sure it was the Rainmaker what put me there. Maybe on account of I bucked him."

"This is interesting. How come you're so sure?" It wasn't that long since he couldn't remember his name.

"Account of now we're talking about it, I remember two times I helped carry guys in there myself. Guys what the Rainmaker didn't figure was worth killing but what he had a hard-on for any-way, one reason or another. He'd say anybody crazy enough to give him grief belonged in the bughouse."

I held up a hand. "Whoa!" Once he got rolling he was a rattle-mouth. "I have a feeling I need to talk to Mr. Cleaver."

Slither got pale. I guess the idea didn't have a universal appeal.

# 24

My conscience insisted I do something to fulfill my compact with Maggie Jenn. What? Well, her daughter's backtrail had been strewn with mystical whatnots, supposed surprises to mom, indicators that Emerald was into that old black magic.

The juju stuff had been so plentiful and obvious that you had to wonder about a plant. Then you had to wonder who and why (guess I should have been digging into that), and then you had to wonder if the obviousness of the evidence argued against its having been planted. Could anybody be dumb enough to think someone would buy it?

Well, sure. A lot of TunFaire's villains aren't long on brains.

I decided I'd follow the road signs, genuine or false. If they were false, whoever planted them could tell me something.

I couldn't discount the witchcraft angle. My fellow subjects will buy anything if the guy doing the selling is a good enough showman. We have a thousand cults here. Plenty lean toward the dark side. Plenty go in for witchcraft and demon worship. Sometimes bored little rich girls amuse themselves by dabbling.

Maybe I should have inquired after the state of Emerald's virtue. That had not seemed important at the time. From her mother's account, she was in good health and otherwise normal. There was no apparent reason for her to suffer virginity at her age. Most adolescents cure that before they get rid of their acne.

If you want information about something, it always helps if you corner an expert. Sure, the street is a great source of news, but out there sometimes you have to separate raindrops from the downpour. That's maybe a lot of needless sorting if you know somebody who stays on a first-name basis with all the interesting raindrops.

People had called her Handsome for as long as I can remember, for no reason I know. Though mostly human, she had enough dwarf blood to give her a very long life. She'd been a cranky old woman when I was a kid. I was sure time had not improved her temper.

Her shop was a hole in the wall in my old neighborhood. It lay down an alley so dark and noisome even homeless ratmen would have avoided it had it not led past Handsome's place.

The alley was worse than I remembered. The trash was deeper, the slime was slipperier, the smell was stronger. The reason was simple. Every day things do get worse than they've ever been before. TunFaire is falling apart. It's sinking into its own offal. And nobody cares.

Well, some do. But not enough. Scores of factions front as many corrective prescriptions, but each group prefers to concentrate on purging heretics and infidels from the ranks, which is easier than improving the state of the city.

I should complain? Chaos is good for business. If only I could recognize lawlessness as a boon.

No wonder my friends don't understand me. *I* don't understand me.

There *were* ratmen sheltering in that alley, which was so insignificant it didn't merit a name. I stepped over one and his wine bottle bedmate to get to Handsome's door.

A bell jangled as I entered. The alleyway had been dark. Handsome's hole was darker. I closed the door gently, waited for my eyes to adapt. I didn't move fast, didn't breathe deeply for fear I would knock something down.

I remembered it as that kind of place.

"Gods be damned! It's that Garrett brat. I thought we got shut of you years ago. Sent you off to the war."

"Nice to see you again, too, Handsome." Whoops! Big mistake there. She hated that name. But she was in a forgiving mood, apparently. She didn't react. "You're looking good. Thank you for caring. I did my five. I came home."

"Sure you didn't dodge? Garrett men don't never come home."

Gave me a twinge there. Neither my brother nor my father, nor my father's father, had come home. Seemed like a natural law: your name was Garrett, you got the glorious privilege of dying for crown and kingdom. "I beat the odds, Tilly." Handsome's real name was Tilly Nooks. "Guess that old law of averages finally caught up with the Venageti."

"Or maybe you're smarter than the run of Garrett men."

I'd heard similar sentiments expressed before. Tilly spoke more forcefully than most. She carried a grudge. My Grandfather Garrett, who went long before my time, jilted her for a younger woman.

That bitterness never kept her from treating us kids like we were her own grandchildren. Even now I can feel her switch striping my tail.

Handsome entered the shop through a doorway blocked by hanging strings of beads. She carried a lamp that had shed no light on the other side. The lamp was for me. Her dwarvish eyes had no trouble with the gloom.

"You haven't changed a bit, Tilly." And that was true. She was just as I remembered.

"Don't feed me that bullshit. I look like I been rode hard and put away wet about a thousand times."

That was true, too.

She looked like a woman who'd survived seventy very hard years. Her hair was white and thin. Her scalp shone through even in that light. Her skin hung loose, as though she'd halved her weight in a week. It was pale though mottled by liver spots large and small. She moved slowly but with determination. It hurt her to walk, but she wouldn't surrender to her frailties. I recalled those making up the bulk of her conversation. She complained continuously but wouldn't slow down. She was wide in the hips and her flesh drooped badly everywhere. Had I been asked to guess, I would've said she'd borne a dozen kids from the shape she was in, only I'd never seen or heard of any offspring.

She peered at me intently, trying to smile. She had only a few teeth left. But her eyes glittered. The mind behind them was as sharp as ever. Her smile turned cynical and weary. "So, to what do we owe the honor, after all these years?" Maybe she wasn't going to catch me up on her lumbago.

The rest of "we" was the scroungiest calico cat that ever lived. Like Handsome, she was ancient. She, too, had been old and scroungy and worn out all those long years ago. She looked at me like she remembered me, too.

You can't lie to Handsome. She always knows if you do. I learned that before I was six. "Business."

"I heard the kind of business you're in."

"You sound like you disapprove."

"The way you go at it, it's a fool's game. You're not going to get you no happiness out of it."

"You could be right."

"Sit a spell." Groaning, she dropped into a lotus position. That she could had amazed me as a kid. It amazed me now. "What's your business here?" The cat set up camp in her lap. I tried to remember the beast's name, couldn't, and hoped the question wouldn't come up.

"Witch business, maybe. I'm looking for a missing girl. The only clue I have is that I found witchcraft type stuff in her rooms."

Handsome grunted. She didn't ask why that brought me to her. She was a major supplier of witchy stuff; chicken lips and toad hair and frog teeth. "She left it behind?"

"Apparently." Handsome provided the very best raw materials, but I've never understood how. She never left home to acquire stock and I never heard of anybody who wholesaled that stuff. Rumor says Handsome is rich despite the way she lives. Makes sense to me. She's supplied the witch trade for generations. She's got to have chests full of money somewhere.

"Don't strike me as the kind of thing a witch would do."

"Didn't me, either." Occasionally a bunch of baddies will ignore the lessons of history and try to rob Handsome. None succeed. Failure tends to be painful. Handsome must be a pretty potent witch herself.

She's never said she's a witch. She's never claimed special powers. The fakes do that. The fact that she's grown old swimming with sharks says all that needs saying.

I told her my story. I left nothing out because I didn't see any point. She was a good listener.

"The Rainmaker is in it?" Her whole face pruned into a frown. "I don't like that."

"Oh?" I waited.

"We haven't seen him for a while. He was bad news back when."

"Oh?" Handsome liked to talk. Given silences to fill, she might cough up something especially useful. Or she might take the opportunity to catch me up on her illnesses and infirmities. "People keep telling me he's bad, but it's like they're embarrassed to say how. It's hard to get scared once you've spent five years nose to nose with Venageta's best and more than that butting heads with people like Chodo Contague." Chodo used to be the kingpin of crime in TunFaire.

"A Chodo uses torture and murder and the threat of violence like tools. The Rainmaker hurts people on account of he enjoys it. My guess is he's anxious not to get noticed. Otherwise he wouldn't stuff people into the Bledsoe. We'd find pieces of them all over town." She went on to paint the portrait of a sadist, yet another view of Cleaver.

I was starting to have misgivings about meeting the guy. But I had to do it, if only to explain that not liking a guy isn't any reason to shove him into the cackle factory.

Handsome rattled on, passing along fact, fancy, rumor, and speculation. She knew an awful lot about Cleaver—in the old days. She could tell me nothing about him now.

"All right," I finally put in, stopping that flood. "What about witchcraft cults today? The kind of black magic stuff that would appeal to bored kids? Any of that going around?"

Handsome didn't say anything for a long time. I wondered if I'd overstepped somehow. Then she said, "There could be."

"Could be?" I couldn't picture her not knowing everything about such things. "I don't get it."

"I don't got a monopoly on witchcraft supplies. They's other sellers around. None to match me for quality or inventory, but they's others. Been new people coming into the trade lately. Mostly they go after the nonhuman market. The folks you want to talk to is Wixon and White. They don't ask questions the way I would and their slant is toward your rich crowd."

"I love it when you talk dirty."

"What? Don't you jump to no conclusions about folks on account of where you find them, boy. They's geniuses in the Bustee and fools on the Hill."

"I don't see what you're saying."

"You always was dense."

"I'd rather people said things straight out. That way there's no confusion."

"All right. I don't know anything about anything like what you're hunting, but I got me a strong suspicion that they's a whole passel of rich folks getting used by some real nasty demon worshippers. Wixon and White is where you start. They'll sell anything to anybody what's got the money."

"That's all I wanted. A place to start. You remember Maggie Jenn?"

"I recollect the scandal."

"What kind of woman was she? Could she have been connected to the Rainmaker?"

"What kind of woman? You think we was friends?"

"I think you have an opinion." If she didn't, it would be a first.

"They was a thousand stories. I think maybe they was some truth in all of them. Yes, she was connected. Bothered that Teodoric considerable. One time he threatened to have the Rainmaker killed. Worried the Rainmaker enough that he got out of town. I heard Teodoric was plotting to hunt him down when he got killed hisself."

"Any connection?"

"Coincidence. Every king makes him a crop of enemies. The Rainmaker staying away after Teodoric died says he had other reasons to go. There was talk he got the wise guys mad. I wonder what brought him back?"

She mentioned wise guys. It could have to do with Chodo's semi-retirement. Already several ambitious men had tried to take advantage, but Chodo's daughter played the game as hard as her father. She would cast a cold eye on the Rainmaker if he made a wrong move.

And on the law side we had us the new Guard, who would love to lay hands on a famous villain—if one could be found who didn't have connections. The Rainmaker might do.

I inched toward the exit. "Wixon and White?" I was afraid she'd do the old give us a kiss.

"That's what I said. You come around more than once every twelve years, you hear?"

"I will," I promised, with all the good intentions I always have when I make that promise.

She didn't believe me. It was getting so I was beginning to doubt myself.

# 25

I've done some dumb things in my time—for example, forgetting to ask Handsome where Wixon and White hung their shingle. I remembered after I was three blocks away. I hustled back—and got what I deserved.

Her shop wasn't there anymore. The alley wasn't there. I was boggled. You hear about that stuff, but you don't expect it.

After that disappointment, I just strolled to the nearest place where I knew somebody and asked if they'd ever heard of Wixon and White. It's a fact. Somebody you know will at least know somebody who knows the person or place you want.

That's the way I got to it. A bartender I knew, name of Shrimp, had heard of Wixon and White from a client. So Shrimp and I shared a few beers on me, then I started hiking. The Wixon and White establishment lay way out in the West End.

They were closed. Nobody answered my knock. The place was a rental. Wixon and White were so highly priced and cocksure they didn't live on the premises.

That part of the West End is pure upscale. The shops all serve those who have money they don't know what to do with. Not my kind of people. Not any kind of people I can understand, buyers or sellers.

I kept an eye out for armed patrols. Those had to be around, else the shops would all be boardups. I wondered if the Outfit wasn't involved. Some of the shops had glass windows. That meant real heavyweight protection.

Wixon and White looked like a place that would serve upper-crust dabblers in black magic, at embarrassing prices. Wixon or

White, whoever did the buying, probably acquired inventory from Handsome, tripled her retail, then tripled it again. Then they'd probably jack up the price on particularly thick-witted customers. The people who shopped the area would be the kind who got off on telling friends how much they paid for things.

Feeling my prejudices coalesce into an urge to break glass, I got me out of there.

I had nothing to do and no inclination to go home to a house where all I'd have for company would be a psychotic parrot and a couple of bark-at-the-moon boys. I hoped that foul-mouthed squab was starving to death.

I asked myself why I didn't stop in and see how Playmate was doing. He might have regained consciousness by now.

# 26

Damn! Playmate looked none the worse for wear. I snapped, "What the hell are you? Twins?"

"Garrett!" He swept out of the shadows of his stable, arms spread wide. He'd been using a pitchfork to do what you do a lot of if you operate a stable. He didn't seem stiff or sore. He swept me up in a hug. He's never stopped being demonstrative when I come around, though it's been a long time since I saved his business.

"Easy, man. I'm breakable. Unlike some I could name." The tenderness wasn't gone from my ambush bruises.

"You heard about my mishap?"

"Heard? I was there. I'm surprised you can walk, what they had to do to bring you down."

"I am a little sore. But somebody's got to care for the beasties."

"So send for the boys from the tannery." Me and horses don't get along. Nobody takes me seriously, but I know for a fact that the whole species is out to get me. The moment nobody is looking, the moment I have my back turned, those damned oatburners start moving in.

"Garrett! What a cruel thing to say."

"You think the best of everybody." They've got Playmate fooled. They stood right there in their stalls sneering and measuring me for a shroud while he defended them. He actually loves the monsters. He thinks I'm just ribbing him, making jokes in bad taste.

Somebody he'll learn. When it's too late.

I asked, "Got a lot of work to do?"

He indicated the manure pile. "You have to haul the hay in and the fertilizer out. They don't take days off."

"Make that pressing work. You have time for a few beers? On your old buddy? That pile won't go anywhere."

"Not if I don't move it." He frowned. "On you? Must be an awful big favor."

"What?"

"Must be some giant favor you want. You never offered to buy me a beer before."

I sighed. "Wrong." This was a battle I'd been fighting for years. All my friends insist I never come around unless I want something. Wasn't all that long since I'd bought Playmate dinner and all the beer he could drink, so he'd introduce me to a man who made coaches. "But I'm not going to fight." I'd show him. "You coming?"

The trouble with a guy Playmate's size is, he can't just drink *a* beer. One beer is a drop in the necessary stream. The man decides to get seriously ripped you have to send for the beer wagons.

He picked the place. It was a small, dark, shabby one roomer furnished in Early Thrownaway. Everyone there knew Playmate. They just had to come say hello. It was a long time before we could talk—and that got interrupted every time another body arrived.

Meantime, we ate. And drank. On me. Ouch, said my purse.

Hole in the wall though that place was, it served a fine dark ale supposedly brewed on the premises. And someone in the kitchen had a more than nodding acquaintance with the art of cookery. I devoured slice after slice of a roast that would have embarrassed Dean's best effort.

The prices were reasonable, too—for those not trying to support a one-man regiment in the habit of eating only when someone else was buying. I asked, "How come this place isn't swamped with customers?"

Playmate awarded me one of his righteous, thoughtful looks. "Prejudice, Garrett."

"Uh-hum?" It was testing time again. Playmate, who wanted to be a priest once, has to keep checking to make sure I stay more good guy than bad.

Forewarned, sure he was going to zing me by telling me the place was run by ratmen—whom I dislike more than I dislike horses, with, admittedly, weaker cause—I was pleasantly surprised when he told me, "It's run by centaurs. A refugee family from the Cantard."

"Where else?" Through a heroic effort I kept a straight face. "I can see how they might have trouble building a clientele." Centaurs aren't beloved. They'd long served Karenta's forces as auxiliaries in the Cantard. But when the mercenary Glory Mooncalled defected and proclaimed the Cantard an independent republic, every centaur tribe joined him. Chances were this family had fought Karenta till recently. When things fell apart down there, where did they run? Straight to the cities of Karenta, whose soldiers they'd been killing.

I don't understand why they're welcomed. Sure, there's room in the economy, what with all the young men gone for soldiers. But all those young men are going to be coming home. Venageta has been driven from the Cantard. Glory Mooncalled has been crushed. Sort of.

Centaurs. Bloody hell.

I kept my thoughts to myself, shifted subjects, told Playmate what I was doing for Maggie Jenn. I didn't overlook such embarrassing adventures as my unexpected visit to the Bledsoe. Playmate wasn't Winger. He wouldn't spread it all over town. He smiled gently and forebore the opportunity to score a remark on the state of my mental health. That's why I love the guy. None of my other friends could have resisted.

He asked, "What do you need from me?"

"Need? Nothing."

"You come, brought me out here, fed me, and filled me up with beer, Garrett. You got to want something."

"That stuff used to be funny, Playmate. About a thousand years ago. Ragging me for the fun, I can go along with that. For a while. But it's gotten real old. I wish you guys would find a new song to sing."

"You mean that?"

Butter wouldn't have melted in my mouth. "Damned straight." I was getting what I needed already, an uncritical ear and a break from loneliness.

"You just don't realize," he muttered. Louder, "In that case, maybe I can help."

"Huh?"

"I know a little something about the witchcraft scene. I have clients who belong to that world."

I was surprised. His religion, a self-defined offshoot of Orthodoxy, doesn't hold much truck with witches. Which doesn't make a lot of sense when you think about how big sorcery and demonism are in this burg. But I have a suspicion that religion isn't supposed to make sense. If it did, there'd be no buyers.

This was Playmate showing off his tolerance again.

"All right. I'll take you up on it. There any new covens around?"

"Of course. In a city this size, there are always covens forming and falling apart. Human nature, being what it is, there are always egos getting bruised and—"

"I understand. You heard of any in particular? Any that have been recruiting young women?"

"No."

"Damn! So, that's that. Well, then, tell me about Maggie Jenn. Morley tells me you've got the skinny on the royals."

"Tell me what you already know."

I highlighted.

He told me, "There isn't much I can add. She did have a daughter. I thought the girl died but evidently not. Nobody's proved it, but Maggie probably was a pricy pro before Teodoric took her up. Under a different name, of course. Morley was wrong about her being in exile. She does spend most of her time on the Isle of Paise, but that's preference. She spends a month each year in the Hill place. If she doesn't use it, she loses it. She does keep her head down when she's in town. She doesn't want her enemies to get too unhappy."

I nodded, understanding. I signaled for more of that excellent house brew. I had enough inside me already that sounds had buzzes around their edges, but that superman Playmate hadn't yet stumbled over his tongue.

"Grange Cleaver," I said. "The Rainmaker. What about him?"

"Been a while since I've heard of him. Curious that he's back in town."

"Maybe. I think it has something to do with Maggie Jenn."

"You be careful of him, Garrett. He's crazy. Blood crazy. They called him the Rainmaker because he left so many weeping widows around. He was big into torture."

"Just your average, everyday psycho next door. What was between him and Maggie Jenn?"

"I can't swear. From the little I've heard, he could've been her pimp."

"Her pimp?" I tried it out. "Her pimp." That had a feel to it, all right.

I dropped some money in front of Playmate, for the house. "Enjoy. I'm going to go put my thinking cap on."

Playmate divested himself of various remarks of the sort that have become fashionable among my acquaintances. I ignored him.

That last piece of news put a whole different weight on everything. Unless I was guessing way wrong.

It could happen.

# 27

Once bitten, twice shy? How often have I gotten nipped because I don't have the sense to get out of this racket? Often enough that I no longer wander around without tools to defend myself. Often enough that I stay alert once somebody starts getting physical.

Despite a few ales too many, I spied the ambush on Macunado—mainly because the night traffic was missing. The denizens of my fair city can smell trouble at a thousand yards, like small game when a troll is prowling the woods.

So it was as rowdy as a desert ruin around my place. It was so quiet I had trouble picking out the ambushers.

I finally caught the stir of a shadow in a breezeway across Macunado. There was no way to sneak up from where I was, so I retreated, took a long way.

All of a sudden I felt cheerful, the prospect of cracking heads making me high. That wasn't my way. The case was getting to me—if it *was* a case. I wasn't convinced.

I came at the guy from behind, singing a ratman working song. Far as I know it's the only working song they have, so few of them actually hold jobs. . . . Between the fake accent and fake drunken singing, my man was way off guard. He cussed me instead of getting set for trouble.

I staggered up and popped him between the eyes with my headthumper. He said "Gleep!" and stumbled backward, his knees watery. I grabbed his shirt, pushed him down onto his knees, slipped behind him, and laid the length of my stick under his chin. "All right, bruno, I lean back sudden and you find out what it'll be like the day you hang." I gave a little jerk to make my point. Also to keep him from getting too much air. He wouldn't be interested in much else if I kept him on short rations. "Get the point?"

He got the point. He grunted cooperatively—after I'd cut him off for a while.

"Excellent. Now here's the part where you tell me who sent you and how many buddies you have and where they're hanging out."

Give the guy credit. He was loyal to his pals. You don't see a lot of that in street thugs. He made me take him to the brink of the big sleep before he gave in. That was right after I whispered, "I've always found that the best way to run a bluff is don't be bluffing. You don't help me out here I'll just hunt me down another guy."

I was bluffing.

He made noises indicating that I'd smooth-talked him into co-operating. I eased off on the stick. "Maybe you better talk on the exhale. Or I might get edgy. You guys messing with me last night got my dander up."

*Wham!* I quick thumped him for thinking about what he was thinking of trying. "So who sent you?" I went back to choking him.

"Cleafer," he gasped. "Guy named Cleafer."

"Surprise, surprise," I muttered. "He happen to say why?"

Grunt and choke. Meant no, and who gave a damn why anyway? This Cleafer was paying real money.

"How many pals you got with you?"

Seven. Seven? "I'm flattered. This Cleafer must have a high opinion of me." I have a high opinion of me, but my enemies don't usually agree.

My man made sounds indicating he couldn't have agreed less. I took that to mean that he was recovering too fast. I popped him again.

I get less nice as I get older.

We chewed the fat till I knew where his buddies were hiding and I understood their grand strategy, which was to round me up and drag me off to their boss's hideout. Friendly Grange Cleaver, pre-owned property salesman, wanted to have a chat.

"Yeah. I like that idea. We'll do that. Only maybe we won't stick too close to the original scheme."

I popped the guy again, hard enough to put him to sleep. He was going to have a headache worse than the one his gang had given me.

Funny. I didn't feel bad about that.

So I went around pounding the stuffings out of guys till

thumping heads no longer made me feel better. I wondered what folks on the shadow side would say when word got around. After the usual exaggerations, it might start worrying the kind of people who get in my way.

Nobody would believe it, probably. Everybody thinks I use Morley Dotes for all my heavy work.

I rounded up the smallest thug, a bit of a guy so tiny he had to be a breed. I slung him over my shoulder and headed for the Joy House.

Sometimes you can use a helping hand.

# 28

Morley tousled the little fellow's hair. "He's mad, Garrett. This is one you'd better not leave behind." We were in Morley's office upstairs at the Joy House. The veggie killers were rioting downstairs.

"And after I decided to give him a break. Any of those guys related to you, Stubby? Your lover or something?"

The little breed glared.

"I like this guy." Morley frowned at Spud, who was sizing the prisoner up for some painful burns.

"What?" the kid demanded.

"He's still officially a guest."

"Sure. And if I was here with a guy who'd just offed my whole gang but me I think I'd be a little more disturbed. Look at that fool. He's already sizing us up for some pain when it's him that's in the shit."

"Narcisio! Language!"

"He's got a point, Morley," I said. "The clown ought to be more scared."

"He's going to be, Garrett. It's just that he's from out of town."

I agreed. "How can you tell?" I wanted to see if his thinking paralleled mine.

"Because he isn't scared. Look, now he's got an idea who has him. He's starting to tense up. They didn't tell him anything when they gave him the job. They just put money in his pocket and told him to help with a snatch."

"I do believe you're right." I tried out a ferocious smile, like the guys from the violent ward would wear if they were sent out to play.

Morley was right. The little guy had heard of Morley Dotes even if he hadn't heard of me. He squeaked. Maybe Winger was right about reputation's tool value.

"I do believe he has a notion to deal," Morley observed.

"So," I said. "You want to be lucky number seven, the one who got away, or just another stiff?"

"Lucky seven sounds great to me."

"Look at that. He kept his sense of humor, Morley. I think that's great. All right, Lucky, what was the plan?" I told Morley, "Be a shame to let it go to waste."

Morley flashed a humorless grin. "Best thinking you've done in years." He was ready to go. I'd been surprised by how quickly he'd agreed to help. I recalled the glances between him and Sarge and Puddle. Was there old business between them and the Rainmaker?

I worry when Morley gets agreeable. I always end up getting jobbed.

"How much are you ready to spend, Garrett?"

I considered my agreement with Maggie Jenn, then the size of my advance. "Not much. You have something in mind?"

"Recall the Rainmaker's reputation. We could use some specialists to calm him down if he gets excited."

"Specialists?" Here comes a sales pitch. "Like who?"

"The Roze triplets." Naturally. Perennially underemployed relatives.

Specialists I wouldn't call them, but those guys *could* calm people down. Doris and Marsha were about sixteen feet tall and could lay out a mammoth with one punch. Part giant, part troll, the only way to beat them was to booby-trap their resolve with barrels of beer. They'd drop anything to get drunk.

The third triplet was an obnoxious little geek barely Morley's size good for nothing but translating for his brothers.

"No, Morley. This is a freak show already. I just want to talk to the guy, find out why he's messing with me."

Morley stared at Lucky. "Garrett, Garrett, just when I thought you were developing sense. You don't talk to the Rainmaker. All he understands is raw power. Either you can kick his ass or he can kick yours. Unless he's changed his spots in a big way."

I grimaced.

"What?"

"My budget is pretty tight."

"Big news, big news."

"Hey!"

"There you go getting cheap again, Garrett. You want to save money? Don't bug the Rainmaker. Just lock your door and snuggle up to your moneybags and hope he can't think of a way to get to you. After tonight, he'll be trying for real."

I knew that. Cleaver sounded like he was all ego and no restraint. All the reason he needed I'd already provided.

What a dummy, Garrett. Your troubles are all your own fault. You should try a little harder to get along.

I mused, "How did he know I was out of the Bledsoe?"

Morley and Spud perked up, smelling a tale not yet told. I had to yield enough sordid details to get them off my back. Which was way more than I wanted anyone to know, really. "I get any razzing back off the street I'm going to know where to lay the blame."

"Yes." Morley gave me his nasty smile. "Winger." That smile turned diabolical. He saw he'd guessed right. I hadn't thought about who knew the story already.

What Winger knew could spread from river to wall in a night. She liked to hang out with the guys, get drunk and swap tall tales. The story would grow into a monster before she was done with it.

I said, "You *really* feel like we need the Rozes, get the Rozes."

"You gave me a better idea."

"Well?"

"Use those clowns you have stashed at your place. Make them earn their keep. You said the big one owes Cleaver anyway."

"That's an idea. Lucky, what direction are we going to head?"

Morley added, "Keeping in mind that I'll be a lot deadlier a lot quicker than Cleaver if Garrett is disappointed."

"West." The little fellow's croak contained undertones of frightened whine. I didn't blame him. He was in the proverbial between of the rock and the hard place.

"West is good," I said. "West means we can drop by my place on the way."

I assumed Lucky's buddies would have cleared off.

Morley and his bunch looked unexcited by this opportunity. They're villains, though, and no villain in his right mind got within mind reading range of the Dead Man. However strong my assurances that he was asleep.

"His bark is worse than his bite," I said.

"Right," Sarge sneered. Puddle and Morley backed him up. Spud took that as his cue to ape his elders. I gave up.

# 29

I found Ivy in the small front room arguing with the Goddamn Parrot. The Goddamn Parrot was making more sense. Beer and brandy odors were potent. Which had drunk more? Who knows? The Goddamn Parrot would suck it up as long as you let him.

Ivy seemed determined to clean me out before he got kicked out. I told him, "You'd better ease up or there won't be anything left for breakfast."

Ivy looked distressed. You could see him struggling to light a fire under the pot of his thoughts. I doubted he'd get them simmering. He did seem to grasp the notion that my alcohol reserves were finite.

"Where's Slither?" The big guy was nowhere in sight. There was a racket from upstairs, but nothing human could be making that.

I could see through the open kitchen doorway. The view set me to talking to myself. Friend Slither was trying to do to my larder what Ivy was doing to my drinking supply.

So much for good deeds.

They start preaching at you when you're barely old enough to walk. But what the hell happens when you *do* try to help your fellow man? You get it up the poop chute every time. Without grease.

Where do the preachers get their crazy ideas? How many cheeks do *they* have to turn? How come they aren't hobbling around with bandages on their butts?

"Where's Slither?" I demanded again.

Ivy answered with a slow shrug. I don't think he understood anything but my tone. He started trying to explain Orthodox transcircumstantiation to the Goddamn Parrot. The Goddamn Parrot made remarks with which I agreed.

I commenced a quest for Slither. Snores from above seemed worth investigation.

Slither was sprawled across Dean's bed, on his back, his snores like the bellows of mating thunder-lizards. Awe held me immobile. The man couldn't be human. He had to be a demigod. He was producing an orchestra of snores, humming and roaring and snorting and sputtering. He seemed capable of combining every known species of snore. All in the same breath.

When I could move again I went to my own room. I hate to disturb an artist at work. I shut my door, went to the window, checked Morley and his crew and the ever astonishing traffic on Macunado. Where could all those creatures be going? What drove them to be out at this hour? Was just my neighborhood in a ferment? I couldn't recall seeing as much traffic anywhere else—though the whole city seemed crowded these days.

I could hear Slither's every snore. I'd hear every snore plainly for however long he remained in my house.

So much for doing good deeds.

Morely gave the boys a glance and said nothing. He did shake his head. Even I now wondered if they hadn't made it all up about their service. Especially Ivy. He had the Goddamned Parrot on his shoulder. It mixed its finest gutter observations with declarations of, "Awrrgh, matey! We be ferocious pirates." That naturally drew a lot of attention. Just the thing you want when you're out to sneak up on a guy calls himself the Rainmaker.

My prisoner indicated a brick and stone monstrosity he insisted was the Rainmaker's headquarters. Dotes opined, "You get what you pay for, Garrett." His glance speared Ivy and Slither. "You didn't pay for the Roze brothers."

"Don't remind me." Slither was awake but might as well have been snoring. It was winter at his house. Ivy was still trying to argue with the Goddamn Parrot. The feathered devil figured he'd sorted Ivy out already and had turned to reminiscing about his sailing days.

Morley tossed a glance sideways, checking to see how near Spud was. He flexed his fingers like he suffered the same temptations I did. "Go ahead," I said.

He scowled. "Can't. But I'll figure a way."

I said, "The course of our relationship has shown me a few things about dear Mr. Big." More cunning than usual, having foreseen the possibility that the Goddamn Parrot might become a liability, I'd brought a little flask of brandy I'd dug out of a cache Ivy hadn't found.

Morley snickered. So, he knew. I said, "We need to keep Ivy away long enough to get the bird snockered."

"He was a scout, send him scouting. Along with Spud."

"You sneak." I looked at Cleaver's place. "What did they do to the guy who designed that place?" The building had been a small factory once. Undoubtedly manned by the blind. It was *ugly*. I was amazed that so much ugliness could be committed with simple construction materials.

"Probably burned him at the stake because they couldn't think of a punishment nasty enough to fit the crime." Dotes chuckled. He was going to have some fun with me playing high-nose elf.

His tastes in art and architecture naturally weren't human. For all I knew, the lunatic who designed that factory was one of his forebears.

I expressed that opinion and added, "It may be on the elvish list of historic structures."

Morley scowled. He wasn't pleased. He grabbed Spud and Ivy and told them to go check the place out. "And leave the bird here. It doesn't have sense enough to keep its beak shut."

Off they went. The rest of us got out of sight and listened to Cleaver's man bitch because I hadn't cut him loose yet. "I'm busy, man," I told him. "I'm feeding my parrot." The Goddamn Parrot was sucking up the brandy. "I'll cut you loose as soon as I know you didn't job us." I didn't think he had. Nobody sane would pick such an ugly hideout. Cleaver did sound like he had the kind of ego that would appreciate the place.

Ivy and Spud scurried back. The kid said, "The place is occupied. I didn't ask names, though. The guys I did see looked antisocial enough to be the sort Mr. Garrett wants to find."

I didn't *want* to find anybody. "You been giving him lessons?"

"It's in the blood. Needs to work on his diction and grammar, though."

"Definitely. Smartass ought to know how to talk good."

"Can I go now?" the prisoner asked.

Spud demanded, "What happened to Mr. Big? Hey! He's drunk. Uncle Morley, did you? . . ."

"No, Lucky," I said. "I still don't know you didn't job us. Suppose you just led us to a place where some hard boys hang out?"

Morley opined, "That monstrosity is the kind a fence would use. Plenty of storage. Probably an owner who hasn't been seen in years. No traceable connection to anyone if you looked for one. You going to do it?"

I considered my help. Neither Ivy nor Slither incited confidence. "Looks like we're as ready as we're gonna get. Any tactical suggestions?"

"Straight through the front door might work."

"Wise ass. Slither, Ivy, come on." I trotted toward that monument to ugliness. My strange assistants toddled after, bewildered but loyal. Morley told Sarge to stick with us, just in case. He came himself. So Spud and Puddle volunteered, too. Spud was protesting, "Mr. Garrett, you shouldn't give Mr. Big alcohol."

What I always wanted to do: storm a fortress at the head of a pack of killer elves, fugitives from an insane asylum, and a drunken parrot.

The Goddamn Parrot was muttering something about its imperiled virtue but in Drunkenese so fluent even a tipsy ratman would have had trouble following him.

Spud said, "Uncle Morley, did you? . . ."

"Be quiet."

I looked at that jungle chicken and grinned like a dwarf just awarded an army weapons contract.

# 30

The place was ugly, but it was no fortress. We found an unguarded side door. I cracked the crude stopper and invited us in. Dean should've been there to see how much good locks do.

"Dark in here," Ivy said. What did he expect?

He sounded troubled, like somebody wasn't playing fair.

"Crackbrain's got one sharp eye on him," Sarge sneered. "Goddamn Rainmaker can't fool him for a secont."

"That's enough," Morley snapped. He peered around. Elves really can see in the dark, almost as good as dwarves.

"What you see?" I whispered. We all whispered. Seemed the sensible thing to do.

"What you would expect."

What kind of answer was that? What I'd expect was filth and squatters and a lot of upset on account of the style of our entrance. But only the rats seemed disturbed—and they were so confident they just went through the motions.

According to Spud, the natives resided on the other side of the building. And so they did. Mostly.

We were sneaking along a hallway illuminated by one half-hearted candle, me thinking what a cheapskate the Rainmaker had to be, when some sleepy-eyed goof ruined everything.

He stepped out of a room just ahead, both hands harrowing hair already well-harvested by time. He woke up fast, generated one man-sized squeal before I bopped him with my second-best headthumper. He squealed even louder. I had to pop him four times before he laid down.

"That tears it," Slither muttered. It was hard to hear him be-

cause of the racket being raised by people I couldn't see wanting
to know what the hell was going on.

"Never mind the opinion survey. You know this place?"

"Never seen it before."

"Thought you said . . ."

"Never was here. That I remember."

The hall hung a right. I stayed with it. I met a native coming
the other way. He had a stick, too. His eyes got big. So did mine. I
swung first. He ducked, showed me some heel, whooped and
hollered.

"You could have moved a little faster there, Garrett," Morley
suggested. The racket ahead grew louder. Morley was concerned.

The fugitive blew through a doorway. I was only two steps behind, but when I got there the door was closed and locked. I flung
one granite shoulder against it. It gave about a thousandth of an inch.

"You do it." Morley indicated Slither. "Stop whimpering,
Garrett."

"I dislocated everything but my ankle bones."

Slither knocked on the door with his very large feet, smashing
away numerous times before he risked his own tender shoulder.

The door exploded like stage furniture. Guess you have to
have the knack.

We'd reached the warehouse area. Only a few lamps burned
there. Definitely a cheapskate, the Rainmaker. Looked like the
place was being used as a barracks. People flew around like startled mice, headed for other exits. Only the guys from the hall
looked like fighters.

Curious.

Amidst the howl and chaos I glimpsed a familiar gargoyle, my
old pal Ichabod. Excuse me. My old pal Zeke. Zeke did a fast
fade. I went after him. We needed to have a talk. My pretty Maggie Jenn had troubles enough without her butler being hooked up
with the Rainmaker.

I didn't find a trace. He vanished like the spook he resembled.

We searched the dump. We found no sign of Grange Cleaver.
We caught only three people—the guy from the hall who I'd
bopped, plus an old couple who hadn't reached their walkers in
time to grab a head start.

The old woman was about a week younger than Handsome.
Her husband and the thug showed little inclination to talk, but she
chattered like she was so full of words they ripped out of her like
gas after an unfriendly meal.

"Whoa, granny, whoa!" She'd lost me in some kind of twin track complaint that blamed her lumbago on the incredible ingratitude of her willfully neglectful children. "That's unfortunate. It really is. But what I need to know is where is Grange Cleaver?"

"You might try to be more diplomatic," Morley suggested. Like he had the patience of a saint when he was after something.

"I was diplomatic the first three times. I did my part. Now I'm not in the mood for diplomacy, I'm in the mood for busting heads."

I didn't do it good enough. Nobody was impressed until Spud let his young mouth run too long and the bad folks figured out that they were in the hands of the infamous Morley Dotes. Then, even the hard boy developed a mild case of cooperation fever.

Yep, maybe Winger was right.

Fat lot of good that all did. Granny Yak-Yak had the definitive answer and the definitive answer was: "He just went out, him and his boys. He never said where, but I figure he was gonna check on some guys he sent out a long time. He paid them and they never reported back." She laid a hard look on pal Lucky.

Lucky looked a tad frayed. The old folks understood whose information had brought us to uglyville. He was growing concerned about his boss's temper.

Morley spun him around. "Cleaver brought you from out of town. He do that with a lot of men, Lucky?"

Lucky gave us the daggers glare. We were leaving him no exit. "Yeah." Sullenly. He thought we were cheating on our end of the deal. Maybe we were. Tough.

"Why?"

"I guess on account of he couldn't find anybody here what was willing to work for him. 'Specially after they found out who he was when he was here before. Way I hear it, he made him some enemies back then what nobody wants to piss off."

I gave Morley a look. Some people might consider him major bad news, but he wasn't big enough bad news that his displeasure would intimidate thugs working for somebody he didn't like. I didn't think. "Chodo," I said. Call it intuition.

Morley nodded. "There was a little brother who died badly. Chodo was way down the ladder then. He couldn't get the go-ahead. But he didn't forget."

Not once in his life had Chodo Contague let a debt go unpaid. "But . . ."

"You and I know. No one else does."

He and I knew that Chodo had become a vegetable after suffering a stroke. These days, his daughter was the power in the outfit. She only pretended to take instructions from her father.

"Crask and Sadler." Those two knew, too.

Morley inclined his head slightly. "They might explain a few things."

Crask and Sadler had been Chodo's chief bone-breakers before they turned on him, caused his stroke, tried to take over. They disappeared after Chodo's daughter outmaneuvered them.

Coincidentally, there'd always been some doubt about their commitment to masculinity, despite the fact that they were two human mountains on the hoof.

I described them. Lucky's discomfort made it obvious he had met the boys. I shot Morley a look. "I don't need any more complications."

Morley prodded Lucky. Lucky admitted, "You won't see them guys around here. Grange, he's got a straight look to him back home. Didn't want them guys turning up in his public life. Figured they'd be lightning rods for trouble around here. So he gave them jobs in Suddleton."

Where, I had no doubt, they spent their spare time scheming revenge on me. "Morley, you get the feeling pal Lucky is holding out? He knows an awful lot about the Rainmaker's business."

"I noticed that."

Lucky protested. "I just heard his regular guys gossiping. You know how it is, guys sitting around, killing time drinking."

"Sure. Tell me, Lucky, where you going to run when we cut you loose?"

Lucky checked the old folks, shrugged. He was scared. They weren't, though the old woman had chattered. I wondered if they were something special to the Rainmaker.

I was about to ask about Zeke when Morley remarked, "We've spent enough time here, Garrett. Help could be on its way."

Yes, indeed. It could be.

# 31

"You just walk along with us, answer a couple more questions," I told Lucky and the old folks, "and we'll be done." I gestured, a comealong. "There was a guy named Zeke . . ."

The Goddamn Parrot did the only worthwhile thing I ever saw him do. He flailed out of the darkness shrieking, "Save me! Oh, save me, mister." His tone suggested he wasn't just being obnoxious.

He wasn't.

There were eight of them. Wasn't hardly fair to them, even considering they were all big, experienced villains. Sarge and Puddle pounded our captives, then vaulted the leftovers and began twisting limbs. There was something evilly fascinating about them at work. It was kind of like watching a snake swallow a toad.

I didn't have time to be fascinated. I was up to my crotch in crocodiles. I held them off till help arrived.

Morley and Spud flew around like they were part of some absurd combat ballet. Mr. Big flapped and squawked. He made more racket than a herd of peafowl. His vocabulary achieved new lows. Puddle, Sarge, Slither, Ivy, and Cleaver's thugs tried to help him expand that but had nothing to teach him.

Four brunos took quick dives.

I've heard people that've never been there claim it's impossible to lay somebody out with your fists. That's true for your average drunken amateur who gets into it with his brother-in-law at the corner tavern but not so for the unrestrained violence of professionals.

Puddle developed a bloody nose. Spud managed to get kicked in the funny bone. He leaned against a wall clutching his elbow, face pale, language vile. Such a look Morley gave him.

"Kill them, damnit! Kill them all!" The girlish voice slashed through the mayhem. "Stop playing with them and kill them!"

I spotted a short guy screaming from what he thought was a safe distance. Cleaver? The Rainmaker himself?

Morley spotted him. Cleaver's brunos were coming to the conclusion that it was not a bright idea to piss off guys who could handle them so easily. They didn't follow orders. Morley grinned and headed for the Rainmaker.

I was on my way already.

The Rainmaker, however, did not care to join the party.

That little bastard could run!

Naturally, our whole crowd dropped everything and lumbered after us, with predictable results. The Rainmaker vanished down the same rabbithole that had swallowed Zeke. His people grabbed up each others' parts and headed for the exits. Suddenly, we had us nothing but one big empty building and one hysterical parrot. And, according to Morley, "The Guard's on its way."

"You could be right." These days, people actually called for official help. These days, the police forces sometimes actually responded.

Morley snapped, "Narcisio, catch that faggot pigeon and shut it up." Mr. Big was no joke right then.

I checked to see if all our people could leave under their own power. No major injuries. Workable legs were available. It was brains that were in short supply.

Slither and Ivy helped round up the GDP. Mr. Big made it easy. He flew into a wall full speed, coldcocked himself.

Pity he didn't break his neck.

I considered wringing it and blaming it on the bird's own erratic piloting, but Spud kept too close an eye on the beast.

As we hustled into the street, I asked Slither, "That short guy was Cleaver, wasn't it? The shrimp with the girl voice?"

Morley seemed intensely interested in Slither's reply. Could it be he'd never seen Cleaver before?

"Yeah. That was him. That hunk a shit. I'da caught the little turd I'da turned him into a capon. Put me in the bughouse. I'da used my bare hands. Twisted 'em off. I'da fixed him." But he was shaking. He was pale. He was sweating. Rock-throwing range was as close to Grange Cleaver as he wanted to get.

Cleaver must be some swell guy.

I checked Ivy. Ivy didn't have an opinion. Ivy was all wrapped up in his feathery buddy.

Morley opined, "Cleaver is going to turn scarce now."

"Think so?"

"His being in town is no secret now, Garrett. A lot of people who don't like him will hear. And he'll have a good idea how many enemies he has once he gets together with Lucky."

"Think he'll leave town?"

"No. But he would if he had the sense the gods gave a goose. You going to have another chat with Winger?"

Guess who was hiding in the shadows outside when we came thundering out. "You saw her, eh?"

"I saw her."

We cleared the area before the Guard arrived. Safely away, I checked our surroundings more carefully. No more sign of my oversize blond friend. Maybe she wasn't interested anymore.

"You need to get her to talk, Garrett."

"I know. I know. But I want to let her come in when she's ready." I wondered why Winger wasn't off looking out for Chastity Blaine.

Morley made no mention so I supposed he'd missed the other watcher, the character who'd followed me to Maggie Jenn's place.

I was confused. Nothing made sense.

It wasn't going to get any better.

"Don't wait too long," Morley told me. "Two tries in two nights means the Rainmaker is serious."

"Seriously disturbed." Cleaver's enmity made the least sense of all. "Yeah. With that thought in mind, I'm going home and get some shut-eye."

Spud had the Goddamn Parrot. He kept whispering to the fancy pants little drunk. I tried to ease away before anyone noticed. Morley grinned and shook his head. "No, you don't. Narcisio."

My luck stays stuck in the same old rut.

# 32

Slither surprised me. He was a decent cook, which I learned when I stumbled down for breakfast, after having been rousted out by Ivy, who must have caught something Dean had left behind.

"You have to loosen up, Ivy," I grumbled as I toddled into the kitchen. "This isn't the service. We don't have to haul out before the goddamn crack of noon."

"My daddy always told me a man's got no call lying in bed after the birds start singing."

Inertia more than self-restraint kept me from expressing my opinion of that perverted delusion.

One songbird was wide awake up front, rendering chorus after chorus of such old standards as, "There was a young lady from . . ." I wondered if Dean still had some of that rat poison that looked like seed cakes. The rats were too smart to eat it, but that bird . . .

"You're working on a job, aren't you?" Slither was *still* vague about what I do.

"The mission," Ivy mumbled. "Old first rule, Garrett. Even a jarhead ought to know. Got to follow through on the mission."

"Watch that jarhead stuff, Army. All right. All right." Good old attitudes from the bad old days. But was the mission more likely to be advanced at sunrise than at high noon? Excuse me for entertaining doubts.

I wondered if they had noticed the changes in TunFaire. Probably not. Neither was in close touch with the world outside his skull.

I surrendered. "I guess we can hit Wixon and White."

At the moment, the occult shop was my only angle. Mugwump had not yet materialized with the promised list of contacts.

Slither's cooking would have appalled Dean and sent Morley into convulsions. He fried half a slab of bacon while baking drop biscuits. He split the biscuits and soaked them in bacon grease, then sprinkled them with sugar. Poor people food. Soldier food. Food that was darned tasty when it was hot.

# 33

It had rained during the night. The morning air was cool. The breeze was fresh. The streets were clean. The sky was clear. The sun was bright. It was one of those days when it was too easy to relax, too easy to forget that a brighter sun means darker shadows.

Fortunately, even the shadows were relaxing. Not a one belched a villain bent on mischief. The whole town was in a rare humor. Hell, I heard singing from the Bustee.

It wouldn't last. Before sundown, the wicked would be slashing throats again.

We did develop a following, including the inept creature who had followed me to Maggie Jenn's place and a guy with an earring who was maybe a ferocious pirate, but I doubted that.

Even Ivy noticed the clumsy guy.

"Let them tag along," I said. "They'll go cross-eyed. What I do is excruciating to watch. Not to mention tough on the feet."

"Be like being back in the Corps," Slither observed.

Ivy had the Goddamned Parrot with him. That obscene buzzard had a great time. "Holy hookers, check them melons. Oh. Look it there. Come here, honey. I'll show you . . ." We were lucky his diction was sloppy.

The streets were crowded. Everybody wanted a lungful of rain-scrubbed air before TunFaire returned to normal. The old and weak would be falling over left and right. All that fresh air would be poisonous.

Before we reached the West End, I spotted another tail. This guy was a first-string pro. I made him by accident, my good luck and his bad. I didn't know him. That troubled me. I thought I knew the top players.

It was quite a parade.

# 34

Wixon and White were open. I told Ivy, "You stay out here. You're the lookout." I went inside. Slither followed me. I wished I was as bad as I tried to look.

Both Wixon and White were on board, but no other crew or passengers were. "Bless me," I murmured, pleased to have something go my way. And, "Bless me again. More fierce pirates."

The guys eyeballed us and took just an instant to decide we weren't the sort of customers they hoped to attract. Neither mislaid his manners, though. Neither failed to notice that between us Slither and I outnumbered them by two hundred pounds.

"How might we help you?" one asked. He made me think of a begging chipmunk. He had a slight overbite and the obligatory lisp. He held his soft little hands folded before his chest.

"Robin! . . ."

"Penny, you just hush. Sir?"

I said, "I'm looking for somebody."

"Aren't we all?" Big smile. A corsair comedian.

Penny thought it was funny. Penny tittered.

Slither scowled. Garrett scowled. The boys got real quiet. Robin looked past us, toward the street, as though he hoped the answer to his dilemma might show up out there.

"I'm looking for a girl. A specific girl. Eighteen. Red hair. So tall. Freckles, probably. Put together so nice even fierce pirates might take a second look and maybe shed a tear about choices made. Probably going by either Justina or Emerald Jenn."

The guys stared. My magic touch had turned them into halfwits.

Outside, Ivy told a dowager type that the shop was closed, only for a little while. She tried to disagree. The Goddamn Parrot took exception and began screeching crude propositions.

I moved around the shop, fingering whatever looked expensive. The boys had a lot of square feet and plenty of bizarre furnishings. "That description ring any bells?" I couldn't read their reaction. Its schooled neutrality gave nothing away.

Penny sneered, "Should it?" I could tell him from Robin only by the size of his mustache. Otherwise, they could have passed as twins. A strong strain of narcissism united these wild and woolly buccaneers.

"I think it's likely." I described the black magic stuff I'd found in Emerald's rooms. My descriptions were faultless. The Dead Man taught me well. Those studied neutral faces betrayed teensy cracks.

Penny for sure knew what I was talking about. Robin probably did. Robin was a better faker.

"Excellent. You guys know the items. Presumably, you provided them. So tell me to who." I picked up a gorgeous dagger of ruby glass. Some true artist had spent months shaping and carving and polishing it. It was one beautiful, diabolic ceremonial masterpiece.

"I wouldn't tell you even if . . . Stop that!"

The dagger almost slipped from my fingers.

"What? You were going to say even if you knew what I was talking about? But you would tell me, Penny. You'd tell me anything. I'm not nice. My friend isn't as nice as I am." I flipped the dagger, barely caught it. The boys shuddered. They couldn't take their eyes off that blade. It had to be worth a fortune. "Boys, I'm that guy in your nightmares. I'm the guy behind the mask. The guy who'd use a priceless glass ceremonial dagger to play mumbletypeg on a tempered oak floor. The guy who'll vandalize you into bankruptcy. Unless you talk to me."

I put the dagger down, collected a book. At first glance it seemed old and ordinary, shy any occult symbols. No big thing, I thought, till the boys started squeaking answers to questions I hadn't asked.

They babbled about the man who'd bought the stuff I'd described. Puzzled, I examined the book. And still saw nothing special.

Why had it loosened their tongues so?

Its title was *The Raging Blades*. That made it the central volume of the semi-fictional saga trilogy *No Ravens Went Hungry*. *The Raging Blades* was preceded by *The Steel-Game* and followed by *The Battle-Storm*. The whole related the glamorized story of an historical character named Eagle, who plundered and murdered his way across two continents and three seas nearly a millennium ago. By today's standards, the man was a total villain. Friend or foe, everyone eventually regretted knowing him. By the standards of his own time, he'd been a great hero simply because he'd lived a long time and prospered. Even today, they say, kids in Busivad province want to grow up to be another Eagle.

I asked, "Might this be an early copy?" Early copies are scarce.

The boys redoubled their babble. What was this? They were ready to confess to murder.

"Let me check this. You say a man with red hair, some gray, green eyes, freckles, short. Definitely male?" Nods left me with one theory deader than an earthworm in the noonday sun. Not even these rowdy reever types would mistake Maggie Jenn for a man. "Around forty, not eighteen?" That fit no one I'd encountered so far, unless maybe that nasty runt in the warehouse. "And you don't have any idea who he was?" I hadn't caught the colors of Cleaver's hair and eyes. "You know anything about him?"

"No."

"We don't know anything."

Eyes stayed stuck to that book while their owners tried to pretend everything was cool.

"He paid cash? He came in, looked around, picked out what he wanted, paid without quibbling about inflated prices? And when he left, he carried his purchases himself?"

"Yes."

"A peasant, indeed." Smiling, I put the book down. "You see? You can be a help when you want. You just need to take an interest." Both men sighed when I stepped away from their treasure. I asked, "You don't recall anything that would connect all that junk together?" It had seemed of a sort to me when I'd seen it, but what did I know about demon stuff? Mostly, I don't want to know.

I got headshakes.

"Everything had its silver star with a goat's head inside."

Penny insisted, "That's generic demon worship stuff. Our stock is mass-produced by dwarves. We buy it in bulk. It's junk with almost no intrinsic or occult value. It isn't fake, but it doesn't have any power, either." He waved a hand. I stepped to a display box filled with medallions like the one I'd found in Justina's suite.

"You know the girl I described?"

Headshakes again. Amazing.

"And you're sure you don't know the man who bought the stuff?"

More of that old shaka-shaka.

"You have no idea where I might find this guy?"

They were going to make themselves dizzy.

"I might as well go, then." I beckoned to Slither.

Wixon and White ran for their lives for their back room. I don't know what they thought I meant to do next. Nothing pleasant. They slammed the door. It was a stout one. We heard a heavy bar slam into place. Slither grinned as he followed me outside.

# 35

Slither glanced back. "How come you didn't push them harder? You seen how they sweated, 'specially when you was messing with that book."

"Sometimes I take the indirect approach. Ivy, wait right here. Whistle if anybody comes snooping." Right here was the end of a breezeway that led to the skinny alley behind Wixon and White.

The shop had no back window. Surprise, surprise. Even in the best parts of town there are few windows at ground level. You tempt fate as seldom as possible.

The place did have a rear door, though. And that wasn't much more secure than a window. I wondered what the boys did that they needed a sneak-out door. Was that how they handled customer complaints?

That back door led to the room whither the boys had fled. It did little to muffle their argument.

". . . could you have been thinking of, leaving it lay out like that?"

"I forgot it. All right?"

"You forgot it. You forgot it. I don't believe this."

"He didn't think anything about it. You saw that. All he cared about is where the Jenn chit is."

"Then why couldn't you tell him and get him out? He has to be suspicious, the way you were . . ."

"I didn't tell him because I don't know, love. She hasn't been seen since her mother came to town."

Well, well, well.

"Stop worrying about the damned book. A thug like that can't read his own stupid name."

Slither said, "Garrett . . ."

I waved him off, listened as hard as I could. I had to fill in here and there, from context, to get everything.

Me and the occult corsairs were going to have another talk.

"Garrett!"

"Wait a minute!"

An unfamiliar voice observed, "You guys better be ratmen trash hogs in disguise because if you ain't . . ."

"Which one you want I should eat first, Garrett?"

". . . if you ain't, you're gonna be going outa here *on* a trash wagon." This sweet-talker was the spokesman for five thugs in slapdash butternut costume. I assumed that was the uniform of the neighborhood watch. I did mention how peaceful and confident the area seemed? Getting old and slow. I'd forgotten that, then I'd failed to stay alert.

They'd come from the direction Ivy wasn't covering.

I heard no more conversation behind the alley door. Naturally.

"Which one first?" Slither asked again. He was hot to go and sure he could handle them all. They weren't big guys and they all had bellies that hung over their belts. They had mean little pig eyes. Slither's growling got the boss pig thinking. He got a look like he thought maybe Slither could follow through.

Didn't seem like the best time to get into a fight. I still had a bottle of Miracle Milt's Doc Dread magic getaway juice. Last one. I whistled so Ivy would know something was up, then slammed the bottle into the bricks at the toes of the guardians of order.

I was lucky. The bottle broke.

A nasty dark stain spread like something alive. And nothing else happened. The brunos didn't twitch. They understood that something was *supposed* to happen. They didn't want to get it started.

I grabbed Slither's arm. "Time to take a hike."

A thin feather of mist curled up off the bricks. Well, better late than never. Only it leaned toward me, the one guy moving.

Slither said, "Aw, Garrett. Do I have to? Can't I just bust up one or two?"

"Go right ahead. But you're on your own. I'm leaving." The streamer of mist reached farther toward me.

I exercised my philosophy of discretion swiftly and with great enthusiasm. I grabbed Ivy as I flew out of the breezeway. That startled the Goddamn Parrot into one of his more memorable sermons.

Slither must have had an epiphany because he was stomping on my heels.

# 36

The Wixon and White street door was locked. The CLOSED sign stood in the window, supported by drawn shades. I had a feeling the boys wouldn't answer if I knocked.

I said, "We'll check back after those characters start thinking we've forgotten them. Right now, we'll find the weather friendlier in another part of town." I could see several butternut outfits. They weren't easily overlooked since all normal traffic had deserted the street. Way it goes in TunFaire.

We moved out as fast as Ivy would travel with that idiot bird. The butternut brunos were content to let us take our trouble elsewhere.

After a while, I asked, "Slither, you know why I like working alone?"

"Huh? No. How come?"

"On account of when I'm working alone, there's nobody around to call me by name in front of people I don't want to know. Not even one time, let alone four."

He thought about that and eventually concluded that I was peeved. "Say! That was pretty dumb, wasn't it?"

"Yes." Why shield the man's feelings? That kind of mistake can be fatal.

On the other hand, the butternuts had no reason to keep after me. They had run me off before my pockets filled with doodads they doubtless felt only they had the right to pilfer. They could beat their chests and tell the merchants association they were mighty hunters and protectors.

I couldn't see the swashbucklers pursuing the matter. All they cared about was that book. I growled, "Shut up, you mutant pigeon."

I wondered about the book. I'd read all three volumes of *No Ravens Went Hungry,* waiting around at the library. What set the story in motion was a dynastic squabble among mobs of people who were all related somehow. The prize was an almost nominal kingship over a loose association of barbarian clans. Not one person in the whole saga was the sort you'd ask into your home. This hero, this thug Eagle, murdered more than forty people during his life.

*No Ravens Went Hungry* was based on actual events that marinated in the oral tradition a few centuries before being recorded.

I hadn't enjoyed it, partly because no likable people were involved, but more because the author had felt a duty to name every player's antecedants and cousins and offspring and, likewise, those of everyone they ever murdered or married. After a while, it got hard to keep track of all the Thoras, Thoralfs, Thorolfs, Thorolds, Thords, Thordiscs, Thorids, Thorirs, Thorins, Thorarins, Thorgirs, Thorgyers, Thorgils, Thorbalds, Thorvalds, Thorfinns, and Thorsteins, not to mention the numerous Odds and Eiriks and Haralds—any one of whom could change his name any time the notion hit him.

"What now?" Slither asked, prodding me out of my thoughts.

Ivy looked over his shoulder, expectant. He seemed more disappointed than Slither about having missed a brawl. But he did stifle the Goddamn Parrot whenever that stupid harlequin hen started propositioning passersby.

"I'm going to go home, get me something to eat. That's what now."

"What good will that do?"

"It'll keep me from getting hungry." And it would set me up to get shut of him and Ivy and the parade that stretched out behind us.

I had plans.

# 37

I let Slither and Ivy make lunch. I retreated to my office to commune with Eleanor. Eleanor didn't help me relax. My restlessness wouldn't go away. Curious, I crossed the hall. The Dead Man appeared to be soundly asleep, but I wondered. I'd suffered similar restlessnesses before.

I didn't feel up to dealing with him, so I gobbled some food, fed the boys a quick, plausible lie about ducking out for just a minute, hit the cobblestones. I lost the people watching me by using the density of the crowds. The streets were busier than usual. There were refugees everywhere. In consequence, every street corner boasted its howling mad bigot who wanted to run them all out. Or worse.

I sensed another crisis in the wind.

Sure I was running free, I headed for the Hill.

I strode up to Maggie's door as bold as if I'd been summoned. I used that discrete knocker, over and over. Nobody responded.

Was I surprised? Not really.

I studied that grim, featureless facade. It remained grim and featureless. And uninviting.

I wandered the neighborhood for a while and wasn't challenged. I didn't stick with it long enough to press my luck.

I was halfway to Morley's place when I realized that I was no longer without a tail. The inept guy was on me again. Say what? Maybe he had something going after all.

\* \* \*

I walked into the Joy House. There sat my two best pals, Morley Dotes and Saucerhead Tharpe, making goo-goo eyes at my favorite fantasy. "Chastity! What's a nice girl like you doing in a place like this?"

Morley gave me a look at his darkest scowl, the one he reserves not for victims but for guys who venture to hint that they might possibly think the Joy House is less than the epitome of epicurean paradises.

Saucerhead grinned. He is one great huge goof. I love him in a brotherly way. I noticed he was missing another tooth.

Chastity said, "I was checking up on you."

"Don't believe anything these guys tell you. Especially Morley. Can't tell the truth when a lie will do. Just ask his wife or any of his seventeen demented children."

Morley showed me a bunch of pointy teeth. He looked pleased. Saucerhead's grin got bigger. He had teeth like yellow and green spades.

I figured it was time to check my shoes, see what I'd stepped in because my feet were whizzing past pretty close to my mouth.

Unlikely as it seemed, folks had been saying nice things. I sat down. "Puddle! I need some apple juice. Shoeleather leaves a bad taste in your mouth."

Dotes and Tharpe kept smirking. Spud brought me my drink, like to dumped it all over me. The kid couldn't keep his eyes off the lady doctor. I couldn't fault his taste. She sure looked good.

I told her, "You didn't answer my question."

"Why I'm here? Mr. Tharpe suggested we eat here before we go to the hospital."

"We? The Bledsoe?" Mr. Tharpe hated the Bledsoe with a blind passion. Mr. Tharpe was poor. Mr. Tharpe had been born in the Bledsoe and had been forced to rely upon its medical care all his life, excepting during his years in military service, when he had discovered what real doctoring could be. I could not imagine Saucerhead going near the place voluntarily.

A lot of people will suffer almost anything before letting themselves be committed to the Bledsoe. Many see it as the last gate to death.

"I'm bodyguarding her," Saucerhead told me.

"What? I thought . . ."

"I saw your friend." Chastity smiled. My best pals snickered.

"My friend? I'm beginning to wonder. She didn't want the job?"

"Sent her on to me," Tharpe told me.

That deserved some thought.

Morley asked, "Where are your buddies, Garrett?"

"Home minding the Goddamn Parrot. Slow roasting it, I hope. Why?"

"There's a story going around about the three of you trying to rob some nancys out in the West End."

I frowned. Strange that should be out already. "I was trying to get a line on Emerald. I never pushed that hard." I told the story.

Morley soon developed a deep frown. He let me talk, but when I finished he asked, "You're sure it was an old copy of one of the volumes of *No Ravens Went Hungry?*"

"It was *The Raging Blades*. You know something I don't?"

"Do you know the story?"

"I read the book."

"That doesn't surprise me." He grinned. He recalled my troubles with Linda Lee. "Since you've read it, you know what happens at the end. Eagle is in his eighties, still hale except that he's going blind. The women start pushing him around, probably getting even for the way he always treated them. He gets pissed off, grabs a couple of slaves, takes the treasure he's stolen over the past seventy years, and heads for the boondocks. A few days later, he comes home alone and empty-handed and never says a word about what happened to the slaves or the treasure."

"So?"

"So Eagle's treasure is one of the big prizes treasure hunters yak up when they get together. One of their myths says the earliest version of *No Ravens Went Hungry* contains all the clues you need to find it. The copyists supposedly actually found the treasure, after they produced maybe five copies of each volume, but they murdered each other before they dug it up." Morley touched the highlights of a tale of greed and double-dealing worthy of Eagle himself.

Tell the truth, Morley's story sounded like one of those worth the paper it was written on. If he hadn't had a certain familiar gleam in his eye, I would have ignored everything he said. But that gleam was there. I knew his gold sniffer had been excited. He believed. He was thinking of paying Wixon and White a visit that had nothing to do with mine.

"The second volume?" I asked, hoping to cool him down. "Why that one? It wasn't until the end of the third that Eagle buried the treasure."

Morley shrugged, smiled. Poor dumb Garrett couldn't see the obvious. Chastity gave us a funny look. She knew something was going on but wasn't sure what it was. Morley said, "You could be right," which I assume he said to confuse everybody.

He knew something he didn't want to tell. Like everyone lately. I shrugged and said, "I'm going to visit Maggie's house. Want to come along?" His gold sniffer would respond to that, too.

He said, "Why not?"

Saucerhead got it, too. He gave me a dubious look but asked no questions. No need letting Chastity in on everything. Especially since she had friends in the Guard.

She knew we were closing her out. She didn't like it, but she had a strong notion she wouldn't want to know anyway.

I asked her, "You familiar with Grange Cleaver? He ever hang out at the Bledsoe?"

"I've seen him. More lately than in the past. He seems to be living in the city, now. He's Board. Board are in and out all the time. The rest of us only pay attention if they start throwing their weight around."

"I see. What's he do there?"

"I don't know. I'm a ward physician. I don't fly that high."

Morley was ready to go. He asked, "What's he look like these days? He used to play around with disguises. Only his closest friends knew what he looked like."

Perplexed, Chastity said, "How would a disguise do him any good? There aren't many men that short."

"He wasn't always a man," Morley told her. "He could be a dwarf if he wanted."

"Or an elf?" I suggested.

"Never was an elf that ugly, Garrett!" Morley snapped. "Not that lived long enough to get out of diapers."

I thought about the prince at the warehouse. Effeminate but not ugly. Just an unlucky gal fate stuck with the wrong plumbing. "Could you describe him, Chastity? I mean, besides as short."

She did her best.

"Good enough for me. That's the guy, Morley."

Morley grunted irritably. Chastity looked perplexed again. "I'll explain later," I promised. I wondered what it was between Dotes and the Rainmaker.

Morley did have his share of feuds. I stayed out of them. And I figured it was just as well I didn't know their details. I hoped he would explain if I needed to know.

I would keep my eyes open, though. He'd been known to wait a bit too long in the past.

"You going or not?" he grumped.

"I'll catch up with you later," I told Chastity.

"Promises, promises."

Saucerhead gave me a look that told me, yes, he would look out for her. I wouldn't suggest it because it was a big sore spot with him. Once upon a time, I asked him to guard a woman and he didn't come through. She died. He slaughtered a whole herd of villains and came within an inch of death himself, but all he saw was that he'd failed. There was no talking him out of thinking that.

Chastity was as safe as it was possible for her to be.

# 38

"Hey, Garrett! How about you do away with the goofy grin and the glassy eyes long enough to let me in on the plan?"

"Jealous." I wrestled with the grin, got the best of it. "We're going to take what I call the Dotes Approach." We were nearing the Hill. Soon we would be on patrolled streets. I had to get my grin under control, stop daydreaming about remarkable blondes. The thugs up there had no patience with happy outsiders.

"The Dotes Approach? Dare I ask?"

"You ought to know. You invented it. Straight ahead and damn the witnesses—we'll just bust in."

"One time. During a thunderstorm in the middle of the night. Talk about exaggeration."

I didn't grace his protest with a reply. I told him, "There's an alleyway runs behind those places. Used for deliveries and by the ratmen who haul the trash away."

"Haul the trash away?"

"A novel concept, I admit. But it's true. This alley is cleaner than the street out front. I never saw anything like it."

"Almost unpatriotic, what?"

"Un-Karentine, certainly. High weirdness."

"A conspiracy."

He was needling me, probably because I was running the inside track with Chastity.

"That thing about a wife and kids wasn't playing fair." He glanced back casually.

"Sure it was. You're just sore because you didn't try the gag first. They still back there?"

"Stipulated. Maybe. She *is* worth a trick or two. They're still there. A whole parade of potential witnesses. This one is a first-class lady, Garrett. Don't mess up the way you did with Tinnie and Maya." Before I could object, he added, "You do attract it, don't you?"

"What?"

"You said it. High weirdness."

"I can't argue with that. Though this one is only weird because it doesn't make sense, not because I've got guys walking through the sky or refusing to stop committing murder just because we've killed and cremated them. I haven't seen any shapechangers and nobody is going around biting anybody's neck."

"There is an occult angle of some kind."

"I think it was planted by Cleaver. I think Cleaver has the girl. The occult crap is to throw Maggie off the trail."

"You going ahead anyway?"

I'd been considering. "For now. For them back there. Might be interesting to see who does what once they figure out what we're doing." We were on the Hill now, strutting like we were honest. Act like you belong, who notices you? Even on the Hill there's plenty of legitimate traffic. The local guardians didn't dare roust everybody. I remarked, "Someday these clowns will recall their training and set up checkpoints and start issuing passes."

Morley snorted. "Never happen." He didn't think much of the Hill brunos. "People who live here won't tolerate the inconvenience."

"Probably right." That's the problem with public safety. It is so damned inconvenient.

"You counting on those people back there being as crooked as you are? That would be as bad a bet as counting on everyone to be honest."

"Crooked?" I protested, but I knew what he meant.

"You know what I mean. One might be secret police." The secret police were a new problem for TunFaire's underworld. Always flexible, though, Morley seemed to be having no trouble adapting.

"Might be." But I didn't believe that and doubted that he did. The Guard were less shy than these people. Even Relway's spies.

Morley did have to say, "Winger could have that kind of connection."

Damn! "Yeah. If there's a profit in it." I wondered. Could

Winger turn up the closest thing she had to a friend, just for money? Scary. I couldn't answer that one.

I said, "You gave me some advice one time: never get involved with a woman crazier than I am."

"And I was right. Wasn't I?"

"Yeah. Oh, yeah."

We turned into the alley that passed behind Maggie Jenn's place. Luck had given us clear sailing so far. Not one patrol even came into sight. We were as good as ghosts in the official eye.

"Be careful with Winger, Garrett. She is crazier than you." He stared down that improbably clean alleyway. "Though not by much. It isn't closed off. Anyone could walk in here." He sneered, unable to believe the arrogant confidence that showed. *Nobody* lives so high on the Hill that they're immune. Even the great witches and wizards, the stormwardens and firelords, who set counts and dukes to shaking in their boots, get ripped off.

"I'll worry about Winger later. Right now we need to do a B and E before our fans show. Up there." I indicated a wrought iron balcony that existed as a drop point for garbage. The ratmen ran their waste wagons in underneath and household staff dumped away. Similar balconies ornamented the rough stonework all along the alley.

"Except for the clean, they didn't do much to put on the dog back here, did they?" Morley asked.

"You want they should've done fancy masonry for the likes of us?"

Sneering, Morley darted forward, found handholds in the rough stonework, scrambled up, did a job on the flimsy door, then hung over the rail to help me up. The balcony creaked ominously. I flailed my way aboard. An instant later, Morley and I were inside. We peeked out an archer's slit of a window, looking for witnesses. It was a minute before any of our tails entered the alley.

Morley chuckled.

I sighed. "Only Winger."

"Where does she get those clothes?"

"If I knew, I'd strangle the seamstresses. That stuff has got to be against divine law if nothing else."

"We're inside. What do we look for?"

"Hell, I don't know. Anything. Things keep happening that don't make sense, since I'm only supposed to be looking for a missing girl. I shouldn't be up to my mammaries in maneating pi-

rates. I'm pretty sure that finding Emerald isn't the main reason
Maggie hired me."

"Huh?"

"You recall I got into this because Winger wanted me to keep
tabs on Maggie. She thought Maggie wanted me to waste somebody."

"And now you're thinking maybe Winger was right, that the
whole point might have been to get you butting heads with the
Rainmaker."

"Could be. I thought I might find a clue here."

"So let's dig. Before Winger figures out what happened and
walks through the wall."

"Absolutely. But first let's see who else takes a chance on the
alley."

The whole parade passed by before it was over. Morley got a
good look at them.

"That one," I said. "That's the pro."

"I see it. I *smell* it. He's a major player."

"Who is he?"

"That's the rub." Morley looked worried. "I don't know him."

I worried, too. I could figure Winger was working for Winger
and anybody else she could get to pay her. The fierce pirate had to
be on Cleaver's payroll. But what about this slick pro?

They did seem to be aware of one another.

Their sneakery caught some squinty eyes. Guard thugs began
to appear. Even Winger cleared out rather than tempt those clowns
too much.

"Quit your snickering and get to work," Morley advised. "The
guys with the squashed noses won't hang around forever."

We started right there in that very room.

# 39

We had been whispering. Soon I wondered why. We found no trace of Maggie or her marvelous staff.

I thought it but Morley voiced it first. "People don't live here, Garrett. They haven't for years." Not one room that I hadn't visited earlier wasn't in mothballs and choked with dust. I kept hacking and honking.

"Yeah. It's a stage set they used to play out a drama for me."

"Make a guess. Why?"

"That's what I'm here to find out, if Winger wasn't right the first time."

Over and over, all we found was more of the same old dusty rooms filled with covered furniture.

"Some nice antiques here," Morley noted. He pretended indifference, but I sensed his disappointment. He could find no wealth that was easily portable. He *was* trying to think of ways to get the furniture out.

In time, because we had time to look, we did find an upperstory bedroom that had seen use but which I hadn't visited before. Morley opined, "This was occupied by a woman with no compulsion to clean up after herself."

And nobody to clean up for her, apparently. Remnants of old meals provided spawning grounds for blue fur.

Morley said, "My guess is this stuff dates from before your visit. Let's check this room carefully."

I grunted. What genius.

A minute later: "Garrett."

"Uhm?"

"Check this out."

"This" was a shocker. "This" was a woman's wig. "This" was a wild shock of tangly red hair so much like Maggie Jenn's that, in an instant, I was mug to ugly mug with a horrible suspicion.

"What's that?" Morley asked.

"What?"

"That noise. Like somebody goosed you with a hot poker."

"I tried to picture Maggie without hair." I lifted that wig like it was an enemy's severed head.

"Out with it. Out with it."

"Know what's the matter? Here's a hint. You take a wig like this wig and grab the Rainmaker and stuff his head into said wig, you'd have a dead ringer for the little sweetheart who hired me to find her kid—assuming you dressed her girlie style. A dead ringer for a sweetheart who all but point-blank invited me up here for . . ."

Morley grinned. Then he snickered. Then he burst out laughing. "Oh! Oh! That would have made the Garrett story to top all Garrett stories. People would have forgotten the old lady and the cat like *this*." He snapped his fingers. He started grinning again. "I'll bet you Winger knew. I'll just bet she did. At least she suspected. Maybe that's what she wanted to find out. Send in Garrett. He has a way with redheads. He'll go for it if you drop one in his lap." He was breaking up now, the little shit. "Oh, Garrett, she just rose way up in my estimation. That's a slicking *I* wouldn't have thought of."

"You have a tendency to think too complicated," I protested. "Winger don't think that way." I went on, arguing, I don't know with whom. My voice rose and rose as I imagined the myriad piratical horrors that might have befallen me simply because of my connoissieur's appreciation of the opposite sex. Just because Maggie Jenn, who had heated me to a rolling boil, might have been wearing a wig.

I glared at that wig. The fury of my gaze changed nothing. It remained a perfect match for Maggie's hair.

"You get it?" Morley asked, like it hadn't been my idea in the first place. "Grange Cleaver put on a wig and fooled you one thousand percent." His leer set my cheeks ablaze.

"Maybe he did. Maybe he didn't. Let's say he did. Just for now, let's say he's the Maggie Jenn who hired me. Let's ignore the fact that that makes things make even less sense than before. Cleaver wouldn't aim a dagger at himself. So let's look for the bottom line. Let's figure out what my employer really wanted, whoever he, she, or it was."

"Don't be so touchy, Garrett." He kept fighting the giggles.

"The question, Morley. The question. I got paid a nice advance. Why?"

"You could always assume you were supposed to do what you were hired to do. Find the girl. When you think about this mess, Maggie Jenn not really being Maggie Jenn makes sense."

"Huh?"

"Look. If she was Cleaver in disguise, then there'd be no conflicts in what us old experts told you about the woman."

"I saw that when you waved that damned wig in my face. The real Maggie Jenn is probably on her island with her feet up and not a suspicion that her old pal Grange Cleaver is blackening her reputation by pretending . . ."

"You have to wonder how much he did that in the old days. When she was involved with the crown prince."

"Not around the prince, he wouldn't have. The prince definitely preferred girls and wasn't patient with girls who played hard to get. He knew the real Maggie Jenn."

"But a fake Maggie could have gone around looking at places that interested the Rainmaker."

"Somebody told me Cleaver might be her brother. Maybe they were twins."

"He was his sister's pimp?"

"Like that'd be the first time a guy ever sold his sister?"

"You're right. I lost it for a second. Wishful thinking. Thought I'd outgrown that. Shouldn't ever forget what slime humans can be."

"We've still got rooms to search." I didn't want to get into the subject of necessity—though Morley would have to slither down there under a snake's belly to hold an opinion of my species lower than I do.

Necessity I understand. Necessity I won't condemn. The despicable are those who sell their sisters and daughters and wives because that saves them having to work. "Bear with me, Morley."

"I do, Garrett. And with all your kind. Like it or not, you're the present and future of the world. The rest of us are going to have to find what niches we can. Otherwise, time will pass us by."

"Bravo!" I clapped. "You've got the vision. Get yourself appointed to the city board of aldermen."

"I'm not human enough. And I wouldn't have time."

I boggled for an instant. My facetious remark had been heard seriously. Interesting. Morley Dotes, bonebreaker and lifetaker, your alderman and mine?

Actually, that could be an idea whose time had arrived. The Goddamned Parrot could do as well as the crooks and incompetents and senile halfwits running things now.

TunFaire is a human city in the human kingdom of Karenta. This is established by numerous treaties. It means human rule prevails except in such ways as may be modified by treaty in particular regards or areas. TunFaire is also an "open city," meaning any race with a treaty can come and go freely, essentially with the same rights and privileges as Karentine subjects. And, in theory, the same obligations.

In practice, all races come and go, treaty or no, and a lot of nonhumans evade their civil obligations. Centaurs are the outstanding example. All treaties with centaurs perished when the tribes went over to Glory Mooncalled. Legally, they're enemy aliens. But they've been flooding into city and kingdom as Mooncalled's republic fades and nobody except extremists seems to object.

Guest workers and resident nonhumans make up half of Tun-Faire's population. With the war winding down and ever more folks realizing that society is headed for dramatic changes a lot of resentment is building.

Shouldn't be long before the nonhuman question becomes a central fact of politics. It is now for splinters like the Call. You won't find any euphemism or circumlocution in the message of the Call. Their strategy is kill nonhumans till the survivors flee.

Gods, I didn't want this mess of mine to lead me into the snakepit of racial politics. Lords Above or Below, render me outside politics of any stink.

Morley and I pressed on. We searched high and low, right and left, north, south, east, and west. We placed special emphasis on the suite supposedly belonging to Justina Jenn. Morley opined, "Nobody lived here, Garrett. It was stage-dressed."

I agreed.

"Think there's anything else to find?" he asked.

"I doubt it. Want to try the basement?"

"Do you?"

"I remember the last time we did a basement. I'm more inclined to go shopping."

"Wixon and White. The hens' teeth salesmen. They actually knew the girl?"

"A girl," I grumped, identities being so shifty lately.

"Good point. But it's a start. Mind if I tag along? I haven't been out that way for a while."

"Gee. I'm psychic." I'd just known he would want to go. "Wasn't for those buccaneers, I'd have serious doubts that the girl exists."

"A girl. Like you said. What say let's don't just hit the street?"

"Good thinking." We checked for observers. Winger and a ferocious pirate type were holding down the alley, pretending they couldn't see each other. "Nice to see folks get along."

"Makes the world run smoother. Crack that view slit up front and check the genius out there."

The front face of the house wasn't as featureless as it had looked from the street. I peeked.

The pro had decided we would walk out the front door like we lived there. Which he'd have done himself. He had done an admirable job of fading into the background. Nobody looking for him was going to miss him, though.

There was no sign of the inept guy. Curious.

Chuckling, Morley asked, "How long will they wait if they don't know we're not in here anymore?"

"How?"

"The rooftops."

I chuckled right back. "Sounds like an experiment worth making. Let's do it."

"We could even sic the brunos on them after we're clear."

"No, no. That's too much. I don't want to spend the rest of my life watching over my shoulder for some of Winger's paybacks."

"Good point. Let's go."

We went. It was easy. The roofs were all flat. The only hitch we encountered was getting down.

# 40

We tried three downspouts. None would support me. "Need some home repairs in these parts," I grumbled. "People ought to show some pride. Ought to keep up their property."

"Or we could start a weight loss program at the Garrett dump." Morley, the little weasel, could have gone down any of the spouts.

Worse, last try we had caught the eyes of some prematurely cynical kids who'd jumped to the conclusion we were up to no good. Just because we were running around on the roofs. We could have been roofers shopping for work.

No more fun. The patrol would be along soon.

Morley bent over the edge, tried another downspout. A herd of preadolescents watched from the street. I made faces, but they didn't scare. Morley said, "This will have to do."

I shook it myself. Not that I didn't trust him. He was right. It would have to do. It *was* more solid.

Still . . .

"We have to get down now, Garrett."

"I'm not worried about getting down. What concerns me is how many pieces of me there're going to be after I get there."

Morley went over the side, abandoning me to my fate. I gave him a head start, then followed, my weight taken by different supports. I had descended about eight feet when furious elvish cursing broke out below me. For a second, I thought I had stepped on his fingers.

"What?" I demanded.

"I'm hung up."

I leaned out so I could see. Sure enough. His shirt was out and tangled in one of the supports that anchored the downspout to the building. He tried to climb a little to get loose. For reasons known only to the gods who engineer these things that only made things worse. I heard cloth tear. Morley started cursing all over again. He let go with one hand and tried to work his shirt loose.

It would not yield. But he was being awfully damned delicate about it.

Down below, some kid came up with the notion that it would be fun to throw rocks at us. First shot he got Morley on the knuckles of the hand he was using to hang on.

Only thing that saved him was that his shirt was hung up.

The gods give and the gods take away.

Morley's shirt tore a little more.

Morley's temper ripped. He invented new curses.

"Cut it loose!" I yelled.

"It's a new shirt. First time I ever wore it." He continued fighting with it.

Stones peppered the wall. A racket from up the street gave warning of the patrol. "You'd better do something. In a couple of minutes, you're going to have people throwing more than rocks at you."

"*I* am?"

"You am. I'm going to climb down over you and leave you hanging."

He started to say something testy, but a small stone hit him in the back of the head.

Blur of steel. Pretty cloth flying. Morley down that spout like a squirrel as kids shrieked and scattered. I caught up while he was trying to decide which kid to run down. "Let's go." The patrol were damn near in spear-chucking range.

Morley looked like he'd rather stay and fight. He wanted to hurt somebody. He rubbed the back of his head and got set.

"Come *on!*" I commenced the old high-speed heel and toe work.

Morley opted not to take on the world alone.

# 41

Even Morley was puffing before we shook the pursuit. Staggering, I gasped, "It was torn already. And you've got another shirt. I've seen it."

He didn't respond. He was holding a wake for his apparel, though you could hardly tell there was a problem if he stayed tucked in.

I croaked, "Those guys've been working out." My legs were rubber.

"Good thing you started before they did." He wasn't puffing nearly enough to suit me. I don't know how he stays in shape. I've seldom seen him do anything more strenuous than chase women.

Maybe he just lucked out when he picked his ancestors.

"How about we take five?" We could afford it. I needed it. Before I puked up my toenails.

We had ended up dodging into one of those small sin sinks that cling to the skirts of the Hill and cater to and prey upon the idle rich. Nobody would help trace us there. Patrol folks weren't welcome.

Morley and I planted our posteriors on a stoop where traffic seemed limited. Once I had sucked in enough air to rekindle my sense of humor, we began fantasizing scenarios wherein Winger did Winger sorts of things to find out what we were up to inside Maggie's house—only with her suffering my kind of luck instead of her own.

You would have thought we were eleven again. We ended up with the giggles.

"Oh, damn!" I couldn't stop laughing, despite the bad news. "Look who just showed up."

The clumsy guy almost tripped over us before he realized that he had found us. His eyes got big. His face went pale. He gulped air. I gasped, "This clown has got to be psychic."

"Want to grab him?"

The suspicion that we might try occurred to him first. He went high-stepping around a corner before we finished swatting the dust off the backs of our laps.

"Damn! Where did he go?"

"What I expected," Morley said, suddenly morose as he stared down that empty cross street.

"Expected?"

"He's a spook. Or a figment of your imagination."

"No. He's no ghost. He's just lucky."

"I've heard luck called a psychic talent."

"Give me a break, Morley. How can random results have anything to do with talent?"

"Luck was really random it would even out, wouldn't it?"

"I suppose."

"So you ought to have some good luck once in a while, right? Unless you're directing it somehow."

"Wait a minute. . . ." Our squabble wandered far afield. It kept us entertained all the way to the West End. For the heck of it, we set a couple of ambushes along the way. Our tail evaded both through sheer dumb luck. Morley did a lot of smirking.

I told him, "I'm about to come around to your way of thinking."

"You say this Wixon and White place has a flimsy back door?"

"A bad joke. Unless it's a trap." There are spiders that specialize in catching other spiders.

"Show me. We'll treat your friends to chills and thrills."

Right. Morley was along just for the fun.

Wixon and White were open for trade. We lurked, watched a few customers come and go. "We'd better get on with it," I said. "Their local watch is a little too serious for my taste."

Morley grunted. I introduced him to the alley door. He scoped it out, suggested, "Give me ten minutes."

"Ten? You going to take it out frame and all?"

"No, I was considering doing it quietly. You wanted fast you should have brought Saucerhead Tharpe. Finesse, Garrett. Surprise. I don't do Thon-Gore the Learning Disabled."

"Right." I left the artist to his easel.

My old pal was hustling a personal agenda again. I had a good suspicion, too. And I didn't care. I just wanted to get on with my job—the way I had defined it.

I wondered if I had an employer anymore. I hadn't heard.

I waited in the breezeway while Morley did whatever. He did keep the racket down. I never heard a thing. No butternut thugs showed up to inconvenience us, either. I tried to psych myself into a role.

Time. I walked to the shop door and invited myself inside.

# 42

"Howdy." I grinned. Wasn't nobody there but them and me. I locked the door. I put the CLOSED sign in the window.

One bold corsair demanded, "What *are* you doing?" He wanted to sound tough, but his voice scrambled right up into a high squeak.

The other one didn't say anything. After ten seconds frozen like those mythical birds that stare down snakes, he bolted for the back room. A moment later, he squealed like Morley was whipping him with a naked woman.

I trotted out my cheerful charlie voice. If you do that right, it's really sinister. "Howdy, Robin." It had taken me a moment to sort them out. "We just dropped in to get the real skinny on Emerald Jenn." I pasted on my salesman's smile. Robin squeaked again and decided to catch up with Penny.

Both those fierce buccaneers were taller than Morley. They looked pretty silly being held by their collars from behind, facing me, when I entered their lumber room. They were shaking.

I closed the door. I barred it. I leaned back against it. I asked, "Well? Want to pick a spokesman?" The room was an extreme mess. I'm sure it was a wreck to start but now had the air of a place hastily tossed, perhaps by a dedicated bibliophile in quest of a rare first edition. "Come on, fellows."

Heads shook.

"Let's don't be silly."

Morley forced them to kneel. He hauled out a knife way too long to be legal. He made its blade sing on his whetstone.

"Guys, I want Emerald Jenn. Also known as Justina Jenn.

You're going to tell me what you know about her. You'll feel better for it. Start by telling me how you met her."

Wixon and White whimpered and whined and tried to exchange impassioned farewells. Boy, I was good. Oh, the drama. Morley did his bit by testing his edge on Penny's mustache. A big hunk of lip hair tumbled to the floor. Morley went back to work with his whetstone.

"Don't nobody *need* to get killed," I said. "I thought I'd just skin one of you." I toed that glob of hair.

"Immigrants," Morley observed.

"Probably." Karentines don't rattle easily, having survived the Cantard. They would have made us work. "Talk to me, outlanders."

Robin cracked. "It was almost a year ago."

Penny glared.

"What was almost a year ago?"

"The first time the girl came to the shop. Looking lost. Looking for any handle."

"Just wandered in? Wanting to borrow a cup of frog fur?"

"No. She was just looking. In more ways than one."

"Uhm?"

"She was a lost soul, drowning in despair, looking for straws to grasp. There was a young man with her. Kewfer, I believe she called him. He was blond and beautiful and young and that was the only time he came around."

"Sorry he broke your heart. Don't go misty on me."

Penny didn't like Robin's wistful tone, either, but he just kept the glare cooking.

"Kewfer?" I stressed it just as he had.

Thoughtfully, Morley suggested, "Quince Quefour?"

"Quince." Left me thoughtful, too. Quincy Quentin Q. Quintillas was pretty enough to launch a thousand ships filled with fierce pirates. He was a small-time conman of the smallest time, too damned dumb to amount to anything. He was part elvish. Made him look younger than his real years and got him out of army time. A faked spook thing would be right up Quefour's alley.

I barely knew him, didn't want to know him better. I described him.

Robin nodded vigorously, eager to please. I wondered if he was just telling me what he thought I wanted to hear.

"Thank you, Robin. You see? We can get along fine. What was Quefour up to?"

Baffled look. "He wasn't up to anything. He was just with the girl. Wasn't much special about her, either."

Of course not. You were lusting in your heart. "Please explain."

"She wanted an easy answer. She was looking for easy answers."

"I thought she was desperate."

"Desperate after the fashion of her age. Kids want results without work. They believe they *deserve* magical answers. They don't want to hear that real magic is hard work. Your stormwardens and firelords spend twenty years studying and practicing. These kids think you just wiggle your fingers . . ."

Morley's magic fingers darted, slapped Robin's hand. Robin had started wiggling fingers as if by way of demonstration. He might have suckered us had we not been in the back of a shop that supplied witches and warlocks.

"Stick to Emerald Jenn. I develop a taste for social commentary, I'll head for the front steps of the Chancery." The most marvelous lunatics hold forth there. "Emerald, Robin. Qucfour didn't come back but she did. Talk to me."

"You don't need to be brutal. Emmy was a runaway. Came from upcountry. We knew that but not much more till a few weeks ago."

"A runaway," I repeated, trying to put an evil twist on everything I said. Morley rolled his eyes. "On her own here for a year." Scary idea. A girl can live a lifetime in a year on the streets of TunFaire. "What did she run from?"

"Her mother."

Who had been worried because her baby had been missing six days. "Go on."

"She didn't go into detail, but it was obvious the woman was a horror."

"Emerald spend a lot of time here?"

"She helped out. Sometimes she stayed back here." Gesture toward a ratty pallet. I didn't apologize for what I had thought about that. "She was a wounded bird. We gave her a place to feel safe." Hint of defiance.

I could see a girl feeling safer with Penny and Robin than on the street. Trouble was, I had trouble accepting them as philanthropists. Too cynical am I.

Robin was a real chatterbox when he loosened up. I spent a lot of energy guiding him back to the main path.

"Seen her lately?"

"No. She heard her mother had come to town."

"That would make her stay away?"

"She thought her mother would look for her. And she is look-ing, right? You're here. She doesn't want to be found. People who don't know where she is can't give her away."

Morley and I exchanged glances. "What's she scared of?"

Robin and Penny got into the look-trading business. A growth industry. Only they were puzzled.

"You don't know." My intuition was at work. "She told a tale but you didn't buy it. Think you know her? She the kind to fill you up and leave you to feed the wolves?"

"What?"

"She knows her mother. She'd know what kind of people would be sent."

More looks flashing. The ferocious pirates of this world are paranoid. Given our record, they are justified in expecting evil of the rest of us.

Penny had spent the interview glowering at Robin. He seemed to suffer a sudden pessimistic epiphany. He barked, "Marengo North English."

"What?" Tell me I heard wrong.

"Marengo North English."

I heard right. But why did he have to say that? Things had been crazy enough. I feigned ignorance. "What's that?"

Robin tittered. "That's a who. One of our biggest customers. A very powerful underground adept."

That was disheartening news, but useful if ever I found myself dealing with the lunatic fringe.

Penny said, "He met Emmy here. Invited her into his coven. She went a few times but didn't like the people or what they wanted to do."

Robin said, "We thought she might have run to him."

I stipulated, "He could protect her." Morley looked at me askance. I said, "I've met the man. I didn't know he dabbled in black magic, though." North English mostly concentrated on viru-lent racism.

Penny and Robin seemed surprised, as though they had not heard of Marengo North English in any but an occult context. Silly boys. The man had a special place in his heart for their sort, too.

Morley moved sudden as heat lightning, startling us all. He

ripped the alley door open, stepped out, stared for a moment, shook his head, and closed up. "Guess who?"

"Some guy who tripped over his own feet getting away."

"You win first prize. Near time to go."

"I have a few more questions."

"That guy is a lightning rod for the law."

Right. And I didn't accomplish much more, though I had hoped to get at their angle for helping Emerald. I did get the names of three people who were on speaking terms with the girl. Not real friends. Not people likely to be useful. Emerald evidently didn't have any friends.

We departed as suddenly as we had arrived. We were gone before those bold buccaneers knew we were going. We were out of the West End moments later. We were long gone before the boys in butternut closed in.

# 43

Miles from the West End, we ducked into a smoky dive fre-
quented by the lowest classes. The bar was wide planks on saw-
horses. The fare consisted of bad red sausages and worse green
beer. Nobody paid me any mind, but Morley drew some vaguely
hostile looks. Nobody would recognize him if he stayed a year,
though. You don't look for Morley Dotes in that kind of place.

Morley settled opposite me at a scarred trestle table and
steepled his fingers. "We have some names."

"Five. And none worth the paper it's written on."

"You reacted to one."

"Marengo North English. I don't know why the black magic
connection surprised me. The man has the brain of a snake."

"You met him? Tell me about him."

"He's a loony. A racist loony. The Call. Sword of Righteousness. He wouldn't be involved in this. He would have cut
Emerald off the second he heard about Maggie and the Rainmaker. Not our kind, you know, old bean."

"Wasn't what I meant. I think."

"He's the Call."

Not many patrons found themselves in circumstances sufficiently insufficient to have to take their custom into that dump, but
those that did were curious. Ears pricked up and twitched first
time I mentioned the Call. Second time, various faces turned toward us.

This was the sort of place where the Call would find recruits
for the Sword of Righteousness, the sort of place infested by folks
who'd never once in life had a bad break that was their own fault.

Morley caught the significance of my glare. "I see."

In a softer voice, I said, "He was a founding father of the Call. I met him at Weider's estate. I was doing security. Weider mentioned my military background. He tried to recruit me into the Sword of Righteousness. Sicking him on me was Weider's idea of a joke."

Party police isn't my usual, but Old Man Weider had asked nice and he's had me on retainer so long we're practically business partners. I said, "Be afraid of Marengo North English. He's crazy as hell, but he's the real thing. Had me ready to puke in his pocket two minutes after he started his spiel."

"But you didn't."

"Of course not. That was Weider's place. He was Weider's guest." The brewery retainer keeps me going through the hard times. "Like me, Weider can't help it if he has to do business with crazies."

"You didn't sign on with the Sword?"

"Give me a break. I grunted and nodded and got away from the man. The way you do when you don't want to make a scene. Why're you so interested?"

"Because I know Marengo North English, too. That man is going to be trouble. Why don't you sign up? Give sanity an agent inside."

I hemmed and hawed and cast meaningful looks at the big-eared clientele. I waved for another pint.

Morley got it. "Something to think over. We can talk about it later. Meantime, I think you're right. He might have seen a chance at some sweet young stuff, but he wouldn't keep her around ten seconds after he found out she had a scandal in her background."

I must have had a funny look on. He added, "I get to meet all kinds." I presume he had done some work for North English. I didn't ask.

"Where are you going from here, Garrett?"

"I was thinking Quefour. Not that he'll know anything."

"I need to get back to the store."

"Got to read that book?"

"Book?" He started out with a hard look, decided on a different tack. "Wasn't a book. It was gone already." He grinned. Beat me to death with honesty.

"I'm heartbroken for you." I tossed coins onto the table. The tavernkeeper made them vanish before they stopped rattling. "Thanks for your help."

"Hey, it was fun. Anytime. I have some advice for you, though."

"I can't wait."

"There's a chance black magic is involved. You should take precautions."

"I'm a certified genius. I was thinking that very thought." Really. Because I was getting uncomfortable about how easy it was for one inept gorilla to keep getting back on my tail.

I knew I would see him as soon as we stepped into the street. And he didn't disappoint me.

# 44

Handsome's alley was back where it belonged. I examined it as I ambled past, not wanting to lead trouble to the house of a friend. Neither did I want to make a fool of myself by stepping into something unpleasant.

Second time past I turned in, leaving the inept guy trying to blend into a mob of dwarves. What worried me was that my other fans might realize they could stay on me by keeping track of him.

The trash had deepened. It was deeper everywhere. Such was the nature of things.

The shop felt unnaturally quiet—though how that was possible I couldn't say. It never got rowdy. Maybe it was like the breathing of the mice and roaches was absent.

Handsome's ragged cat padded in, sat, fixed me with a rheumy stare. I wondered how bad its eyes were. I didn't move around. I killed time watching from inside while my eyes adjusted. No point finding out how Handsome protected herself.

Then she was there. For one moment, I lapsed into a daydream and suddenly I wasn't alone.

Spooky.

She looked me in the eye. "You grew up with some sense after all."

"Only a fool goes around touching stuff in a place like this."

"Not what I meant, boy. You learned better than that when you was a pup. I'm talking about you having sense enough to know you're in over your head."

I did? I was? I nodded. I never shatter illusions.

"Garrett men just bull ahead, confident they can handle any-thing."

That was me, sort of. Except the part about the confidence.

"Explains how you managed to come home when they didn't."

Mystified, I let her talk. Patience is a sound strategy when you don't know what is going on. When she did slacken, I wedged in, "Wixon and White did know the girl. But it looks like Grange Cleaver faked up the black magic connection." I related the details of my adventures as I would have done for the Dead Man.

Handsome let me run dry. She let me stand empty a while, too. Then, "Why would the Rainmaker want to find the girl?"

"I don't have a clue. Maybe her mother is dead and he needs Emerald to control the estate."

"She is valuable or dangerous. One or the other."

"Or both."

"You'll have to find her to know which. Can you?"

"Given time."

"You've made enemies. And you let someone mark you with a finding spell."

"I was afraid of that. The stumblebum?"

"He's tracking you. He didn't mark you."

"Winger or Maggie, then."

"And the Jenn woman seems to be the Rainmaker in drag."

"Who wants me sleeping with the fishes."

"And who wouldn't be above using a dollop of sorcery to get his way."

"No way can this klutz be Cleaver's. Whenever I sit still long enough to draw a crowd, I accumulate one of Cleaver's own kind. So who could the guy work for?"

"Am I a mind reader? You want that, go home."

"Why did Cleaver get after me in the first place? I just can't figure that."

"At this point, why don't matter. He is. Deal with that."

I moved slightly. Just a twitch of impatience, really. But the old cat hissed.

"Patience, boy. And caution. These days a hundred evils could jump you before you got a hundred paces from this shop."

"I know." That was why I was there.

She told me, "I'm not going to let you go back out there till you're better prepared."

Who, me argue? "Thank you. That was in the back of my mind."

"I know."

"I'd be eternally grateful for any help."

"Don't heap it on with a manure fork, boy. It's all part of putting the Rainmaker in his place."

She knew the rules. Never let on how much you care. If you care, you're vulnerable.

The cat hissed again.

"What? I didn't do anything."

"Never mind Malkyn. She can smell the trouble on you. She worries about me."

Malkyn. Of course. What the hell else? "I smell the trouble on me, too. It's a curse."

"Or a calling." Her right eyebrow rose. Excellent! There was one talent I hadn't known she commanded.

"No. I just wish I could wash it off. I don't *want* to get into all these crazy things. I'd rather sit around the house drinking beer and—"

"You're bullshitting an old bullshitter, boy. I know more about you than you think."

My cue to hoist a brow.

"That don't slice no ice." She started moving around, fiddling, muttering. I realized she was naming names. "Hey! Wait a minute! What do they have to do with anything?"

"You wouldn't have met one of those ladies if you'd stayed holed up. And you ain't going to meet no more—"

"All right!" Truth is pain. Female remains my great weakness. A flashy smile and saucy wink can lure me away from safety.

Grinning evilly, Handsome cleared nonhuman skulls off a fern stand, started assembling her candidates for weirdest items in the shop. I started to say something but didn't get past opening my mouth.

"Give me that stick, boy."

I surrendered my headknocker, then opened my flycatcher again.

She didn't give me a chance to speak. "We don't got no idea what you're gonna run into, so what I'm gonna do is give you a range of generic defenses."

Oh, that sounded good. If it meant anything. "What are you doing to my stick?"

"Toughening it up, boy. When I get done with it, you're going to be able to whack right through all the common protective spells. You see that red thing there?"

"Looks like a dried-out sow's ear somebody dyed red?"

"The very thing. It looks like a sow's ear on account of once upon a time somebody hacked it off the side of a pig's head. I want you should take it and put it in your right front pocket. And keep it there until you settle up with the Rainmaker."

"Why?" She was getting ahead of me.

"On account of the Rainmaker is the kind who would get a laugh out of fixing you so's you wouldn't have no more reason to leave your house looking for women."

Ouch! I needed only about a quarter-second to mull things over. I accepted the sow's ear, placed it as directed. "You're the expert." Some fates are too horrible to contemplate.

"Remember it." She aligned four more objects, then regrouped them. One was a small wooden box given to fits of angry buzzing. Whatever was in there sounded huge for a bug.

Handsome noted my interest. "It's more wicked than it sounds."

"I wanted to hear that."

"It's not gonna bother you, son. Once I tell it you're its friend."

"Oh, hey, by all means. I'm a bug-lover from way back. I probably met most of its family when I was in the islands. I got intimate with lots of bugs when I was down there."

"You always did have a tongue of nonsense, boy."

What the hell did that mean?

She continued, "You don't want to use the little devil, don't bother. What they call a last resort. When you and your tongue have gotten you into something where there ain't no weaseling out, just pop that lid open."

"Yeah?" Call me dubious. I stopped being a bug booster during my Marine days. "Then what? It bites a hunk out of me and I scare the bad guys away with my screams?"

"Maybe. Or maybe it just comes home and tells me you need help."

Somehow having a bug in a box didn't sound that useful if I was in it deep, but Mom Garrett never raised her boys to backtalk the likes of Handsome. She always said we should keep our yaps shut when we were around somebody who could turn us into table scraps. There were times when Mom was pretty astute. "Uhm," I grunted.

Handsome gave me the fish-eye, then resumed her explanations. I did listen. And found my imagination captivated immediately.

Handsome offered me a doodad that looked like a wood chip stained red on one side and green on the other. She told me, "When you want you should turn invisible to that guy following you, you should rub your thumb three times across the red side here. He shouldn't ought to turn suspicious because the spell he's using isn't all that reliable. You think it would be handy having him tag along, you rub your thumb three times on the green side."

"What? Why would I want him following me?"

"How would I know?" She shrugged. "Reckon that's all I can do for you right now. Time you were getting along, anyway, boy. I've got paying customers backing up."

Where? But I only thought it.

The old cat looked at me like she was thinking about taking a bite out of my ankle before I got away. Or like she thought she would take a bite, if only she had some teeth.

Handsome patted me down, making sure I was carrying everything exactly where she wanted me carrying it.

I kept at it. "What can you tell me about—"

"Go on, boy. Out of here. Shoo. Scoot. How do you kids expect me to get any work done if you pester me all day long?"

Had she gone senile all of a sudden? Or was she trying to make me nostalgic?

I treasured my childhood memories but didn't consider those times the good old days. The good old days never were. These are the good old days, right here, right now.

Won't never get no better than this.

# 45

I'd told Morley I would see Quefour while doubting there was any point. But brave soldier I, dedicated to my mission, I spent a half hour trying to trace that most useless of beings and learned that when last seen he had been floundering around with an inept homosexual murphy in the Tenderloin, which was a stupid game to play. The wise guys could help him take a swim with a hundred-pound rock strapped to his back.

The beauty of being your own supervisor is you set your own hours. If the spirit moves you, you can procrastinate till hunger boots you into action.

I headed for home thinking life couldn't get any better.

Of course, it could have a Chastity Blaine perched on your front stoop when you came home, so damned radiant all your male neighbors had found some reason to come out and gawk.

She was alone. I broke into a trot, wove through the crowd, felt the deep disapproval radiating from such bastions as Mrs. Cardonlos's rooming house. Chastity was the only woman in the neighborhood smiling when I puffed up. "Where's Saucerhead?" I demanded.

"Saucerhead?" She really seemed puzzled.

"You know. Saucerhead Tharpe. Big goof with snaggle teeth. Your bodyguard. Able to outsmart small rocks if you give him an hour."

She smiled grimly, not in the mood. "I let him go."

"Why'd you do a fool thing like that?" What a sweet tongue.

"I don't have to worry anymore. It seems the episode of the

escaping patient who couldn't have been in the first place because there's no record of any admission tore it for me. The Knopfler Bledsoe Imperial Memorial Charity Hospital no longer welcomes my services."

"They canned you. I'm sorry."

"Don't be. It was a learning experience."

"Uhm?" Philosophy straight from the Dead Man.

"I discovered that bitter old cynics like my father are right. No good deed goes unpunished."

"I like his thinking. So how come you're here? Not that I'm complaining. I couldn't have daydreamed a nicer surprise." I was hungry. I couldn't correct that hanging around on the stoop. I went to work with my key.

"I guess because you're the only one who knows what's going on."

"Boy, don't I wish." The door was bolted on the inside. I let out a shriek that got everybody within two blocks looking my way. I pounded away. Nobody responded.

"Is anyone in there? I couldn't get an answer."

"They'd better be dead. If they're not, I'm going to kill them. They're drinking up my beer and eating up my food and now they won't let me into my own house. I'm going to skin them and make myself a suit out of their hides."

"What are you going on about?"

"How many escaped patients have they recovered?"

"Only a few. It's not like they're trying real hard."

"A couple of them turned up here and I let them stay." The Goddamn Parrot was in there hollering so loud I could hear him through the door. I put on eternity's most forced smile. "You said it. No good deed goes unpunished."

"They're here now?"

"Somebody barred the door. If I have to break in, I'm going to carve somebody into rat snacks."

"Aren't you overreacting a little?"

Yes. "No!"

I received a completely unexpected hug. "Guess I'm not the only one who's had a bad day."

"Once we get in, let's butcher one of the clowns and discuss our bad days while we eat him."

"Don't be so gruesome. Who are they?"

"Ivy and Slither."

"Are you sure?"

"That's the names they use. What they want to be called." I pounded on the door and howled some more. "Soon to be past tense." Across the street, Mrs. Cardonlos came to her window and gave me that look. I was going to get another protest from the citizen's committee. How dare I raise hell on my own front stoop?

I sent Mrs. Cardonlos a smile. "Wait till I get my next psychopathic killer, lady. I'll tell him you're desperate to meet a real man."

"You don't have some secret way to get in?"

"You didn't grow up in this neighborhood, did you? If I had a secret entrance, the villains would have used it to clean me out a long time ago."

"You don't expect me to apologize for where I grew up?"

Careful, Garrett. "You didn't pick your parents. Just ignore me. I get testy when I can't get into my own house." I went to work on the door again.

The lady had begun to doubt the wisdom of being with me. I made a special effort to remain calm and reasonable when Ivy finally cracked the door an inch, keeping it on the chain while he checked me out.

"Ivy, it's me. I'm home and I'd really like to visit my kitchen. Think you could speed it up?" I scanned the street quickly. Looked like everybody who'd shown any interest lately was out there watching. Even a guy with an eyepatch and an earring. I couldn't see if he had a pegleg, but I knew where he could pick up a parrot cheap.

The door opened. There to greet me was Slither. "Doc Chaz. Garrett. Sorry. I was in the kitchen whipping something up. I thought Ivy was taking care here." Ivy was at the door to the small front room, looking inside with eyes that had glazed over. "Looks like he's having one of his spells."

"I'm about to have one of mine."

"Bad day?"

"That catches the spirit of it." Slither wasn't listening. He was headed for the kitchen.

Chastity asked, "These men escaped with you?"

"Not with me. But they were both in my ward."

"I know Rick Gram." She indicated Ivy. "The other one is a stranger."

"Slither claims he got in there the same way I did. And the same guy put him there."

"Grange Cleaver?"

"The very one."

"Maybe. I don't recognize him. But there were four hundred men in your ward. And I was expected to concentrate on the female population."

We hit the kitchen. Slither announced, "Not a lot of supplies left here, Garrett. You need to do some shopping."

Scowling, I put an arm around Chastity's shoulder and headed for the back door. I didn't want to be home after all. With the thumb of my free hand I stroked the red side of a wood chip. "I'm ducking out the back way, Slither. The front door ever gets barred again I'm going to cut somebody's heart out. You make sure Ivy understands." Intuition told me that was all Ivy. He'd been Long Range Recon once upon a time, but he was afraid of his own shadow now. "*My* house, Slither. My rules and my ways."

"Stay cool, Garrett. I got it under control. You and Doc Chaz go somewhere, have a good time."

# 46

"I hope every villain in town is camped out in front of my place."
Chastity and I were enjoying a perfect evening. Nearly perfect. I
had one bad moment at a place where I caught a glimpse of Maya
Stuub. Once upon a time Maya had thought more of me than I'd
thought of myself.

Maya didn't see me. I put her out of mind and had a nice time.

Chastity was all right. I could relax with her. I told her tales of
the Garrett that was, suitably edited for modern audiences, and
she did the same with Chaz Blaine—though she didn't say much
about her family. We lost track of time. Time lost track of us. An
apologetic fellow with a grungy towel on his arm advised us that it
was time to close. We nodded and apologized back and left too
much money and went out to wander streets we didn't see. For
both of us the world had come into narrow focus. We were our
universe—that teenage feeling. . . .

"My gods you're beautiful," I told her in a place that wasn't
mine. And she was. More than I had imagined.

Her insecurities burned through. She protested, "My nose is
crooked and one eye is higher than the other and my mouth is
tilted and one boob is bigger and higher than the other."

"You got weird toes, too, but I don't give a damn. You hear me
howling about what a prize I am? Lucky you, not even having to
find the end of the rainbow."

"We're all overstressed these days, aren't we?"

"Absolutely." Nobody anywhere was comfortable. Conflicts
were feeding upon one another. "A moment that loosens us from
the cycle of despair is a treasure."

"Was that a compliment? I'm going to take it in that spirit."

Actually, it was a quote from the Dead Man, but why disappoint the lady?

Got to be getting old. I woke up feeling guilty about not having done anything useful about Emerald Jenn. I watched Chaz sleep. I recalled Morley's comment about her quality. I remembered seeing Maya. I felt a twinge of pain.

Chaz opened an eye, saw me looking, smiled, stretched. The sheet slipped off her. I gulped air, astounded all over again.

Next time I knew it was an hour later and I hadn't heard a word from my might-have-beens the whole time.

"So what do you intend to do?" Chaz asked, having heard the details of the case.

"That's my problem. Common sense says walk away. Tell myself some people tried to use me, I made some money, we're even."

"But part of you wants to know what's going on. And part is worried about the girl."

I admitted nothing.

"Waldo told me about the case he helped you with."

Naturally. He wouldn't have missed a chance to play his big It Was All My Fault scene. "Waldo?" They were on a first-name basis?

"Waldo Tharpe."

"Saucerhead. Sometimes I forget he has a real name."

"And your friend Morley told me about a case involving a girl named Maya and something called the Sisters of Doom."

"He did?" That startled me.

"It's pretty obvious, Garrett. You're an idealist and a romantic. With big clay feet, maybe, but one of the last good guys."

"Hey! Wait a minute. I'm turning red here. Anyway, there's never been anybody more pragmatic than Mrs. Garrett's little boy."

"You can't even convince yourself, hard boy. Go. Find Emmy Jenn. Help her if she needs it. I'm getting out of the way. You don't need distractions."

"That's where we disagree."

"Down, boy. When you've wrapped it up, send me a message at my father's house. I'll be knocking on your door before you can say Chastity is a naughty girl."

"Uh-oh." Not again.

"What?"

"Don't get mad. I don't know who your father is."

"You didn't investigate me?"

"I didn't see a need."

"My father is the Firelord Fox Direheart."

Oh, boy. I made a squeaking noise.

"Can you remember?"

Squeak. I don't dally with the daughters of sorcerer nobility. I don't relish the honor of having my hide bind somebody's grimoire.

"Don't let the title intimidate you. He's just old Fred Blaine at home."

Right. What I've been looking for all my life, a girlfriend whose pop is a frontliner but wants me to slap his back and call him Fred.

"You'll get in touch?"

"You know I will, devil woman." I wouldn't be able to resist.

"Then get back to your quest. I can find my way home." Cute little frown. "And then Daddy will get in his 'I told you so' about the hospital job. I hate it when he's right, because he's always right about people being cruel and selfish and wicked."

I collected a farewell kiss and headed for home wondering why one of Karenta's leading sorcerers was here in TunFaire instead of working the cleanup detail down in the Cantard.

# 47

I slipped in the back door. Slither and Ivy were in the kitchen, one drunk and the other cooking. Slither said, "Yo, Garrett. The cupboard is bare."

"Need a new keg, too," Ivy slurred.

"Sing, Johnny One-Note," I grumbled. If they didn't like it, they ought to do something about it.

Up front, the Goddamn Parrot was squawking about neglect. I wondered if Slither had started eating parrot chow, too.

I wondered what the Dead Man would think if he woke to find himself in this zoo.

I said, "I guess that means it's time you moved on to greener pastures."

"Huh?"

"You done anything to find work? To find your own place? I think I've done my share."

"Uh . . ."

"He's right," Ivy said. His tongue tangled, but otherwise he was more articulate drunk than his sidekick was when he was sober. "We haven't contributed here. It's possible we're not capable. And this is his home."

Damn. The man made me feel guilty when all he was doing was telling the truth.

"I washed the goddamn dishes, Ivy. I did the laundry. I scrubbed woodwork. I even sprayed bugweed juice on the thing in the lib'ary to keep the crawlies off'n it. So don't go saying I didn't do nothing, Ivy. What the hell you keeping a mummy around for,

Garrett? And if you got to, how come you got to keep such an ugly bugger?"

"He makes a great conversation piece. The girls all tell me how cute he is."

That didn't wake him up, either.

Slither wasn't listening. "And how about you, Ivy? What've you done? Besides suck down that horse piss till you make me wonder where the hell you put it all? You hungry, Garrett?"

"Yes."

"Sink your fangs into these here biscuits. Gravy coming up." He wheeled on Ivy, but Ivy had gotten going, headed up front. I shut them out, ate hastily, wondered if they'd gotten married. Slither started hollering the length of the house.

"Enough!" I snapped. "Has anyone been around?"

"Shit, Garrett, you got to be the most popular guy in town. Always somebody pounding on your door."

"And?"

"And what? You ignore them, they go away."

"That's always been my philosophy."

Ivy stuck his head in. "There was that cute little girl."

I raised an eyebrow, which was talent wasted on those two.

"Yeah," Slither said. "Ivy answered that one. He's a sucker for a skirt."

Ivy shrugged, looked embarrassed.

"Well, guys?"

"I don't know," Ivy said. "I didn't understand." Hardly the first time, I thought. "She didn't make much sense. Something about could you help her find her book yet."

Find her book? "Linda Lee?"

"Huh?"

"She tell you her name? Was it Linda Lee?"

Ivy shrugged.

No good deed unpunished, Garrett. I downed a last bite, knocked back a mug of weak tea, headed for the front of the house. T.G. Parrot seemed less intolerable by the hour.

Everything is relative.

I used the peephole.

That was Macunado Street all right. Infested with quasi-intelligent life. Not much use studying it through a hole, though. I opened up and stepped onto the stoop.

I spotted nobody but sensed the watching eyes. I settled onto my top step, watched the sweep of commerce. As always, I wondered where everybody was going in such a hurry. I nodded at people I knew, mostly neighbors. Some responded. Some hoisted their noses and wished I would vanish in a puff of smoke. Old Mr. Stuckle, who roomed at the Cardonlos place, was one of the friendly ones. "How you doing, son?"

"Some good days, Pop. Some bad days. But every new day is a blessing."

"I heard that. You got Gert stirred, you know."

"Again? Or still?"

He grinned a grin with only two teeth left to support it. "There you go." Gert Cardonlos always took the other side when my neighbors got upset. I wondered whether she had changed her name to Brittany or Misty, she would have grown old without growing sour.

Probably not.

As I watched Stuckle breast the stream of flesh a neighborhood urchin sidled up. "There's people been watching your place."

"No kidding?" Becky Frierka had illusions about getting involved in my adventures. I don't mind having girls around, but they need to be a little older than eight. "Tell me about it." You never know where you'll learn something useful. And me listening would make Becky feel good.

I don't remember my father much. Mom always said one of his philosophies was each day you should do at least one thing to make somebody feel good. She probably made it up. People like Handsome let me know Mom did a lot of creative revision. But this was a good idea.

"Thank you, Becky. That's quite useful." I offered her a couple of coppers. "Better scoot."

"You took that lady to dinner."

"What?"

"Last night."

"So?"

"I don't want money. I want you to take me out."

Oh. Right. And would I ever hear the end of that? "How come you know what I did last night?"

"I saw you go out the back. I followed you." She put on her devil smile. "I know what you done."

"You a dwarf in disguise? You trying to blackmail me?"

"No. But I could tell you who else followed you."

Whoa! I hadn't noticed any tail. Not even her. "You have my attention, Becky."

"You going to buy me dinner? Same place as the blond lady?"

"You got it." No problem. Her mother would get me out of it. "Soon as I get this job wrapped. Deal?"

She was suspicious. I gave up too fast. But, "Deal. And don't think you're gonna weasel out."

"Talk to me about the somebody who followed me, brat."

"It was a man. A weird man. Not very tall but really huge-mongous anyway." She spread her arms. "He walked funny." She showed me how.

"Mugwump," I guessed aloud. I hadn't seen Mugwump's walk, but that had to be it.

"Mugwump?"

"Man's name. Probably who that was. He have really big hands?"

"I don't know."

Great. "What did he do?"

"Just followed you where you went. After a while he left. He's really weird, Garrett. He talked to himself all the time."

"Probably from living in a neighborhood like mine." I spied Saucerhead Tharpe headed my way. I could think of no reason for him approaching with such a purposeful stride. "Thanks, Becky. Time for you to scoot now."

"Don't forget. You promised."

"Who? Me? Get on with you." I hoped *she* would forget, but I never have that kind of luck. "So who died?" I asked Tharpe. The big goof wasn't even breathing heavy.

"Huh?"

"You were charging this way like a guy loaded with the worst bad news he could imagine."

"Really? I was thinking about Lettitia."

"Lettitia? That off the menu at Morley's?"

"My lady. You haven't met her yet." Saucerhead always has a new girlfriend. I didn't see any bruises so maybe this one was nicer than usual.

"You came for advice to the lovelorn?"

"From you?" His tone wasn't generous.

"From His Nibs in there. The world's foremost authority." On everything. According to him.

"Speaking of him, you give him the latest from down south?"

"Something happen?" The street didn't have the edgy feel it gets when there's big news from the Cantard.

"Ain't out general yet on account of it's supposed to be a big military secret, but I heard from my sister's husband who's got a cousin works for the Stormwarden Burner Skullspite, First Cav Spec Ops raided Glory Mooncalled's headquarters."

"Our guys have found his hideout about five times already, you silly groundpounder." A good-hearted fellow, Saucerhead didn't quite grasp reality. He'd been a plain old foot-slogging infantryman during his service. He suffered from the common army delusion that cavalry were some sort of elite. I mean, come on! They're not even Marines. You add in the fact that they're dimwit enough to voluntarily ride horses . . .

"This was the real headquarters. An old vampire nest."

Something about his tone . . . "Don't tell me."

"The very one."

"Life is weird."

An earlier case had taken me back to the war zone. In the course of events, Morley and I and some others invaded a subterranean vampire nest, a stronghold of horror. We were fortunate. We escaped. We passed word to the Army. The soldiers took time off from the war.

The war with vampires takes precedence.

That was before Glory Mooncalled rebelled. Just.

One of my gang had been a centaur. "There's more?" I asked. Tharpe was antsy. There was something.

"Yeah. The attack was a big ass surprise. They barely figured out what hit them before it was over. They hardly destroyed any documents."

So Mooncalled's deep well of luck was running dry.

"What's the bottom line?"

"Them documents showed he wasn't in the Cantard no more. Our big boys been chasing shadows."

I have my moments. "And the only documents the republicans did destroy were ones that might say where the boss was?"

"How'd you know?"

"I'm a good guesser." This would interest the Dead Man. His hobby was tracking and anticipating Glory Mooncalled.

"They get anything out of the prisoners?"

"Didn't take no prisoners, Garrett."

"You always take prisoners."

"Not this time. Them guys never had no chance, but they wouldn't give up."

I couldn't believe that. However fanatic a group is there's always a member who doesn't want to die.

"But that ain't why I come here, Garrett."

"Oh?"

"Winger wanted me to—"

"Winger! Where is that oversized . . . ?"

"If you put a clamp on it, I might tell you something."

The best advice I ever got. It repeated suggestions from my mother and the Dead Man. You have a hard time hearing with your mouth open. I shut mine.

"Winger said tell you that you and her ain't pulling the same oar no more but you ought to know them West End pansies was coached to tell you what they told you. You was supposed to head off in a new direction."

He looked at me like he hoped I would explain.

I considered. I thought Robin and Penny had talked straight. They maybe forgot a fact or three but steered a tack close to the truth. Why point me at Marengo North English? Why would Winger turn me away?

Smelled like somebody was dragging a squashed skunk across the trail. Somebody big and blond with too much faith in my naivete. "How would she know?"

"I figure she got it from her boyfriend."

"Her what? Boyfriend? Since when?"

Saucerhead shrugged. "Been around a while, off and on. She never made no announcement. I don't figure she wants us to know. You'd come out of your hole and hang out, you would know, though."

He had a point. Information was the blood of my trade and connections the bone. I wasn't taking proper care of either. I did before I moved in with the Dead Man. "Go on."

"She just wanted to warn you. Didn't want you should step in anything unexpected."

"That's my pal. Always thinking of me. She couldn't drop by herself, eh?"

Saucerhead grinned. "You ask me, she don't want to get close enough you can get your hands on her."

"Surprise, surprise." I glanced over my shoulder. The boys and bird weren't watching. "Think I'll wander over to Morley's. I'll buy, if you want to come along."

# 48

Morley didn't seem thrilled to see Saucerhead. He gave me a dark scowl. I couldn't understand why. Tharpe was a good customer.

Dotes joined us anyway. It was obvious immediately that he was distracted. He listened with half an ear, kept one eye on the door all the time.

I told him, "I've got most of it figured."

"Uhm?" How did he get so much incredulity into one grunt?

"When Maggie Jenn left town, she was so bitter she never wanted to come back. Her lover had been murdered, his people hated her, but she still had to go through the motions to keep what he gave her, for the kid's sake as well as her own. Her old pal and maybe brother Grange Cleaver played her to get the skinny on the Hill places he robbed, so she got him to play her whenever it was time to make her annual shows. Cleaver was happy to help. It gave him a way to get into and out of TunFaire without getting gobbled up by Chodo Contague. Along the way, he hooked up with the imperials, sold them some con, and got involved with the Bledsoe. Bet you he's been stealing from the hospital and the Hill place both.

"Now get this. One day along come Crask and Sadler with a tale about Chodo and his little girl. Cleaver eats it up. This is what he's been waiting for. This is his big chance to get back into the big time in the big town. But there's a loose end: Emerald Jenn. She's in the city. A runaway. She knows the truth about Maggie Jenn and Grange Cleaver. And she'll tell it."

Morley and Saucerhead looked like they were having trouble grasping it. Why? It wasn't hard.

"So Cleaver tries to set up an operation here, and nobody signs on because they know about Chodo's old grievance. Except Winger. And she starts wondering what's what. But she smells a chance to score. When Cleaver mentions he wants to look for the girl without it being obvious it's him looking, Winger drops some hints about me, figuring to use me somehow. Cleaver puts on his Maggie Jenn face and hires me, only I mess up by letting it drop that I was warned Maggie was coming. He smells a rat inside his outfit. Who it is doesn't click right away. Being a good actor, he doesn't have any trouble staying in character long enough for me to finish up at the Hill place. Soon as I'm gone, though, he takes off for his headquarters and sets it up to get rid of me. He'll get somebody else to look for the girl.

"Winger hears him sending his men out. She realizes it won't be long before he figures out who told me he was coming. She grabs anything she can carry and takes off. She helps me get away from the Bledsoe.

"She gives me a double ration of bullshit when I ask her what's really going on. She still thinks she can make a big score, so now she's staying away from me."

Sarge brought tea while I theorized. Morley poured, sipped, grimaced. Evidently the tea hadn't been brewed from anything off a tea bush. Big surprise. They serve nothing normal there.

Dotes was distracted. He was listening, but every time the door opened he lost his concentration. Still, he'd remained attentive enough to observe, "Your hypothesis doesn't contradict any of the known facts."

"Hell, I know that. I made it up. But? I can tell—you have a but."

"Couple of them. You don't contradict any known facts, but you don't account for everything that's been happening around you. And you've done a feeble job of examining Cleaver's motives."

"What? Wait. Whoa. You just lost me."

"Chodo's kid shirked any of the duties of a kingpin?"

"Hardly. Ice and iron." I had the gashes and frostbite to prove it.

"Exactly. So whatever Crask and Sadler might claim, being here is a major risk for Cleaver. I've identified the pro who's dogging you. His name is Cleland Justin Carlyle. He's a specialist assigned to watch you. You get three guesses why. Only the first counts."

I nodded. "And, wonder of wonders, C.J. was never seen in these parts before I mentioned the name Grange Cleaver to my pal

Morley Dotes, once said pal failed to meet up with Cleaver his own self."

Morley shrugged, which was as good as a confession.

He had no regrets. He never looked back and seldom apologized. He saw no need to apologize now. He asked, "What's Winger's angle?"

"I don't know. I doubt that it matters. She probably doesn't know what she's doing herself, she just wants to keep the pot boiling till she finds a way to score."

Morley slew a pity smile a-borning.

"You know something I don't?"

"No. You're ahead of me. Though you do seem to be late catching on to an essential point."

"Really? What?"

"That Winger lied about everything. Right from the beginning. That not one word she said can be counted on to be true. That anything that comes from her should be thrown out altogether."

"Oh. Yeah. I knew that."

I knew it now. Now that I looked at it. Forget everything Winger said. Sure.

# 49

"I conned Puddle into doing you a favor, Garrett," Morley told me. I didn't ask; I just waited for the inevitable wisecrack.

He fooled me again. The crack didn't come. "Uhm?"

"I had a feeling you wouldn't get around to Quefours."

"Puddle scare him up?"

Morley nodded.

"Waste of time, right?"

"Puddle's still sulking."

"What's the story?"

"Quefours hasn't seen the girl for eight months. His choice. He broke it off because she wouldn't play his way. Made her sound prudish."

"And Quefours doesn't have the ghost of a notion where to find her now. Right?"

"Wrong."

"Huh?" I've always had a knack for witty repartee.

"He said dig around among the witchcraft community. The girl is looking for something. His notion was you should start with the blackest black magicians. That was where she was headed when they split." Dotes appended a big nasty smile.

"You saying Cleaver framed her with the truth?"

"Maybe just to get you headed in the right direction." More teeth. He had to have about two hundred. Looked like he'd been filing them again, too. "Thought you'd get a kick out of that."

"A kick in the butt." It just got more confusing. I started to get up.

"Hey!" Saucerhead growled. "You told me . . ."

"Feed this beast, Morley. Something cheap. Like alfalfa."

"Where are you going?"

I opened my mouth to tell him and realized that I didn't know. "Like that? Then why not just go home? Lock your doors. Get comfortable. Read. Wait for Dean. Forget Grange Cleaver and Emerald Jenn."

I responded with my most suspicious look.

"You got your advance, didn't you? This Jenn chit sounds like she can take care of herself."

"Answer me one answer, Morley. Why did she run away from home?" Might be important if the whole thing had to do with a missing kid after all.

"There are as many reasons for going as there are children running."

"But they mostly boil down to a perceived need to escape parental control. I don't know enough about Emerald. I don't know enough about her mother. Their relationship is a mystery."

"What did I just recommend? Don't keep gnawing on it, Garrett. You don't have any reason. You don't need any more grief. Turn loose. Spend some money. Spend some time with Chastity."

"What?"

"Gods preserve us," Saucerhead muttered. He stopped attacking his dinner long enough to sneer, "He's got that look, ain't he?"

"Got what look?"

Morley told me, "The dumb stubborn look you get when you're about to jump into something without a reason even you understand."

"About to? I've been in it four days."

"And now you're out because you know it was a game that didn't take. You did your usual stumbling around and knocked over everybody's apple carts. Now it's over. You're out. You're safe as long as you don't go around irritating people. Consider it a phenomenon. You don't go charging around like a lunatic trying to find out why if it happens to rain live frogs for three minutes in the Landing. Do you?"

"But . . ." But that was different.

"There's no need to find the girl now. Not for her sake, which is the thing that would bug you."

"Garrett!" I jumped. I hadn't expected Saucerhead to horn in. Everybody in the place stared at him. He told me, "He's making sense. So listen up. Nothing I heared about this makes me think these folks're really worried about the kid."

"He's making sense," I admitted. "Morley always makes sense."

Dotes gave me a hard look. "But?"

"I'm butting no buts. I mean it. You're dead on the mark. There's no percentage messing with this anymore."

Morley eyeballed me like he believed me so surely he wanted to wrap me in another wet blanket. I complained, "I really do mean it. I'm going to go home, get ripped with Eleanor, grab me a night's sleep. Tomorrow I get to work on running my guests off. All of them. Only one thing I'm wondering."

"What's that?" Morley remained unconvinced. I couldn't believe that they really thought I had the white knight infection that bad.

"Could Emerald be another Cleaver disguise? You think he could manage makeup good enough to pass for eighteen?"

Morley and Saucerhead opened their mouths to ask why Cleaver would want to, but neither actually spoke. Neither wanted to feed me any reason to go chasing something potentially lethal.

"I'm just curious. He has a rep as a master of disguises. And Playmate told me he'd always thought that the daughter was dead. I wonder if maybe the plot wasn't more complex than we suspected. Maybe Cleaver didn't just plant clues up on the Hill. Maybe he created a whole character."

Morley snarled, "You're psycho, Garrett."

Saucerhead agreed. "Yeah." He was so serious he put his fork down. "I know I ain't no genius like neither one of you guys, but I do know you got to go with the simplest explanation for something on account of about a thousand times out of nine hundred ninety-nine that's the way the real story goes."

What was the world coming to when Saucerhead got a smart tongue on him? "Am I arguing? I agree. Sometimes I think this brain of mine is a curse. Thank you, Morley. For everything. Even when you didn't mean it." I left enough money to cover Saucerhead's meal, though I could have made it to the street before anyone realized that the tab hadn't been satisfied. I figured Saucerhead deserved it. His luck rolled down a steeper incline than mine. He seldom lived better than hand to mouth.

Me, I, Garrett, was out of the game. Whatever it might be. I was going to go home, get organized, drink some beer, have a bath, scope me out a master plan that included seeing a lot of Chastity Blaine.

But I left Morley's place with my hackles up, like some atavistic part of me expected the same old gang to be out there set to reintroduce me to the pleasures of the Bledsoe. I was on edge all the way home.

The Bledsoe was a sight, thcy said. Supposedly it was disappearing behind fast-rising scaffolding.

My tension went to waste. Nobody paid me any mind. I didn't even get followed. Made me feel neglected.

I'd never had a case as exciting as this just sputter and fade away, but some jobs have. Those kind usually see me ending up snacking on my fee. I recalled with pride that this time I'd been clever enough to snag a percentage up front.

I wouldn't win any kudos from the Dead Man, but he would have to admit that I was capable of being businesslike on occasion, even in the face of a lusty redhead.

# 50

Despite sleeping well I wakened restless. I chalked it up to rising before noon even though Ivy hadn't pestered me. Once again I wondered if the Dead Man wasn't stirring. I looked in but saw no sign that he was. But what could you expect? Awake or asleep, the Dead Man's physical appearance changes only as time gnaws.

Slither and Ivy were unusually subdued. They sensed that I planned to move them out. I had a notion where to send them, too. But old lady Cordonlos wouldn't believe a word I said to make them sound like worthy potential tenants. Darn her.

So after lunch I consulted someone who might actually give a rat's whisker about their welfare.

Wonder of wonders, Playmate had some ideas. Before long, my old campaigning pals had probationary jobs and probationary housing and I found me, O miracle of miracles, with my own place all to my ownself again. Except for the Dead Man and the Goddamn Parrot. That cursed bird had gone into hiding before Ivy could hunt him down and take him along. My generous self-sacrifice wasted.

It would be a while yet before I saw Dean again. I hoped. What with Chaz and all. . . .

I talked it over with Eleanor. She had no objections, so I wrote a letter and hired a neighborhood kid to deliver it to Chastity. He insisted on a bonus for approaching a wizard's house.

I checked and rechecked the street while I gave the little mercenary his instructions. I saw no one even vaguely interested in the Garrett homestead. Even my neighbors were ignoring me. Still, I was uneasy.

I squabbled with the Goddamn Parrot till that got old, then communed with Eleanor. I was lonely. Your social circle isn't much when it consists of a talking bird, a painting, and a character who hasn't only been asleep for weeks and dead for centuries, he hasn't been out of the house since you met him.

My friends were right. This was no way to live.

There was a knock. I would've ignored it had I not been expecting to hear from Chaz.

Even so, I used the peephole.

It was the kid. He held a letter up. I opened the door, tipped him extra, checked the lay of things again, still saw nothing unusual. I like it that way.

I settled behind my desk, read, then shared the news with Eleanor. "Chaz says she's gonna pick *me* up. How about that? One bold wench, eh?"

After a pause, I continued, "All right. Call her a role-breaker, not a bold wench. And she's gonna stay nontraditional. Taking me someplace she likes. And she's bringing her father."

Only a painting, I reminded myself. This chatter was only an affection. No way could Eleanor taunt me with a spectral snicker.

I didn't much want to meet Chaz's pop, him being one of the top twenty double-nasty wizards infesting this end of the world. I hoped he wasn't a real old-fashioned kind of dad. I don't deal well with foamy-mouthed avengers of soiled virtue.

Another ghostly guffaw? "She says he just wants to ask about Maggie Jenn and Grange Cleaver."

Right. That worried me more than if she'd tipped me to expect a daddy smoking with outrage.

No good kicking and screaming now.

Eleanor insisted this was a great opportunity to make contacts among the high and mighty. "Right, babe. You know how I value my contacts among the rich and infamous. Exactly what I've always never wanted."

I went to make myself lunch.

My guests had left me my shoes and half a pitcher of water.

# 51

I went into that evening with my philosophy of life firmly fixed in mind: expect the worst and you can't possibly be disappointed. Chastity's old man was a boomer. If he took a notion, he could flatten me like a cow patty and skip me across the river.

He surprised me. He was no centenarian gargoyle. He looked like an ordinary guy barely on the lying side of fifty. His black hair had gone half silver. He had a small paunch and stood four inches shorter than me. He was groomed till he gleamed. He glowed with good health. Those were obvious badges of power. But he dressed no better than me. And he had the tanned and roughened skin of a guy who spent a lot of time outdoors. He didn't seem taken with himself, either.

He turned out to be one of those guys who is such a good listener you tell things you didn't know you knew. That skill would have served him well in the war zone. The best leaders are those with ears.

He interrupted only twice, with penetrating questions. Before I finished, I adopted the attitude I take when reporting to the Dead Man or chatting with Eleanor. I talked to me, thinking out loud.

I finished. Chaz looked at her father. He stayed clammed. I asked, "So how come you're interested? Because of Chaz and the hospital?" He called her Chaz, too.

"Our home was looted during the crime spree that paralleled Teodoric's affair with Maggie Jenn."

I gave Chaz a mild fish-eye. She hadn't mentioned that.

"A few items were recovered. They traced back to a Grange Cleaver—who couldn't be found."

"You didn't connect him with the hospital Cleaver?"

"I wasn't here when Chaz decided to work charity. Nor would I have looked for a thief in such a high place."

"No? I think I'd look there. . . ." I got control of my mouth when Chaz kicked me under the table.

The firelord's expression told me I was fooling no one. He was right, really. We look for shady characters in the shade. Unless we're cynics.

"I always thought Jenn was involved, Garrett. That raid took military timing. No outsider knew the family schedule. But you can't accuse the royal mistress of theft."

"I see." Sort of. Chaz offered a smile meant to give me heart. Didn't work. I had a notion where her dad was headed.

I wasn't wrong.

Blaine said, "I'm as vindictive as the next guy. Even now I can't go after Jenn, however much the royals hate her. They take care of their black sheep, too. But Cleaver has no friends that count and no guardian angels. Chaz says she told you we know Colonel Block. I'm pulling strings with the Guard and elsewhere, but I'd really like you to find Cleaver. If Block does it, it ends up on a court docket. I want to deal with Cleaver personally."

*Ker-pungk!* The daddy of all fat leather wallets hit the table. "Nice workmanship," I noted.

Faint smile. "Chaz gives you glowing reviews, Garrett. West man Block, though, suspects that you *can't* dance on water." I gave Chaz a look. She reddened. "But I know Block, so I solicited other opinions."

Was I supposed to be impressed? Blaine had begun to sound pompous.

Maybe there was a problem with my hearing.

I gave the Firelord an opportunity to appreciate my raised eyebrow trick. It worked. He told me, "They say you're the best but you're no self-starter." He caressed that wallet like it was a special lady. "Devil snatch you, man! Don't you have a bone to pick with Cleaver? You could've spent your life in a lunatic ward." He edged that wallet half a foot closer.

Chaz smiled, nodded encouragement. Maybe her daddy danced on water, too.

"I did talk to Block, Garrett. There's more than money here." Caress, caress. "There's a letter of introduction over my chop. Use it any way you want. It says you're my agent and anyone who won't help you just might find life unrewarding. There's also a warrant from the good colonel that you can use to commandeer help from city employees. There are letters of credit that should be sufficient to cover your expenses and fees."

Oh? And the damned wallet jingled like it was stuffed with more gold than a troll could hoist.

Chastity's old man had come prepared to do business. He didn't expect to go home disappointed. And I couldn't argue with him.

He wouldn't let me.

He was like all his class—though he did seem inclined to play fair.

Chaz kept right on saying nothing and grinned like she was watching me being inducted into paradise. I stalled. "I'm not sure what you want."

"Find Grange Cleaver for me. Bring him to me or lead me to him. Once we're face-to-face, you're out of it."

Reluctantly, like that wallet was a real troll-buster, I dragged his bribe toward me. I peeked. I saw pretty calligraphy, nifty official seals, a sweet double handful of shiny gold. And . . . a wishbone? "A killing bone?" I asked.

"What? Oh. That's right. You served in the islands." Where the natives owned their own special nasty magic. To which Karenta and Venageta reacted by exterminating its practitioners wherever they were found.

"Yes." Growl and scowl.

"This isn't that. This is just a gimmick. Should you get into terrible trouble, spit on the bone. You'll go out of focus to anyone concentrating on you. Any disinterested observer will see you fine, but somebody trying to kill you won't be able to fix on you. Clever, eh?"

Maybe. I didn't say so. I didn't say his kind were so clever they fooled themselves most of the time.

"All right. It isn't much. My talents run more toward smashing cities."

And Chaz kept on smiling like she meant to melt me down.

The firelord excused himself. "Got to run. You'd think I could back off and take it easy now we've won the war. You two don't need me getting in the way, anyhow."

This guy couldn't be real. I waved bye-bye. My new boss. Like it or not.

The thrill doesn't last like it used to.

"Isn't it great?" Chaz asked. She was so excited. I wondered if somebody had hit her with a stupid spell.

"What?"

Her smile turned puzzled. "What's the matter?"

"Your daddy." I kept a firm grasp on that wallet.

"I don't understand." She thought I should be pleased.

"I'm concerned about his agenda."

"Was he indirect? Did he blow a lot of smoke?"

"No." I couldn't deny that. "What do you recall about this big ripoff?"

"Nothing. I wasn't here."

"Uhm?" I reached deep into my trick bag and came up with my best eyebrow lift. That drives them wild.

"I was away at school. Being finished. Boys go to the Cantard as subalterns." Her class, she meant. "Debs go to finishing school."

"Let's don't fight." Especially since I'd survived a face-to-face with a father who wasn't overburdened with ordinary paternal prejudices.

"Daddy's people are rustics, hon. He doesn't fake it. Forget his fire talent. *He* calls it a curse." She kept scooting her gorgeous little tail ever closer. I didn't think she wanted to talk about Daddy anymore.

But I had to ask, "Is this like him?"

"What?"

"Would he hire somebody to hunt somebody so he could settle an old grudge?"

"Maybe. We only got robbed one time. I know he's never stopped being mad about it. He'd go burn something down whenever he got thinking about it."

Interesting. Even curious. Not for an instant had he come across as hagridden.

"Come on, Garrett. Forget all that," Chaz cajoled.

"Yeah? Think I should?"

"I think you should think about what the doctor wants to prescribe."

I did my eyebrow thing. "Not another thought in my head." She did an old female trick back that set me to drooling on myself.

In a perfectly cool, rational, businesslike voice she said, "Daddy's paying. Make a pig of yourself."

"Oink, oink. But not here."

"Oooh! Promises, promises. Better be careful. I don't have to work tonight."

That was the best idea I'd heard in a while, but because she was one gorgeous woman, I let her have the last word.

# 52

A couple of regulars actually lifted welcoming paws when I drifted into Morley's place. The attitude didn't infect management, though. Puddle scowled like he was trying to remember where he put that damned rat poison.

Morley was in a good mood, though. He bounced downstairs as my tea arrived.

I said, "I know that look. You just won big on the water spider races. Or somebody's wife tripped and you ravished her before she could get up."

He showed me a mouth like a shark's. "I gather you're doing some ravishing yourself."

"What?"

"You were seen with a stunning blonde in a place way out of your class."

"Guilty. How'd you know?"

"You won't like the answer."

"Yeah? Hit me with the bad news. I'm overdue."

"A couple came in late last night. Slumming. He was mister Flashy. She was Rose Tate. She'd seen you earlier."

"Bet she had her nasty smile on." Rose Tate was the cousin of my lapsed girlfriend, Tinnie Tate. And Rose had a grudge.

"She did. You're going to star in some interesting girl talk."

"No doubt. But Tinnie knows Rose. Rose mention who else I was with?"

"You running a string?"

"Chaz brought her dad." I told the tale, then asked, "You ever seen Blaine?"

"No. Why?"

"Wondering about ringers again."

"You think Chastity is jobbing you, too?"

"It's paranoia time, Morley. My world has stopped making sense."

"When you're well paid, sense needn't enter the equation. Right?"

"But it helps."

"You're concerned about coincidence."

"What are the chances Chaz would work the same place as a thief that robbed her father?"

"What are the odds you'd get thrown in there where you could meet her? A lot longer, I'd say."

"How come?"

"Where would a female doctor have the best chance of getting started? Where would the imperials set Cleaver up if they wanted to put him into TunFaire?"

"You figure he's into something with them?"

"My guess is they think they are, but he's only using them so he can slide in and out of town without being noticed by people he used to know. You'll recall he meant nothing to Chastity at first."

"And her father?"

"You'll have to do your homework there."

"I've started. His place was cleaned out. It was one of the big jobs of the time. He only got back to town day before yesterday."

"After this started."

"And he's been away for years. Only came home for a few days each winter." Winter is the slack season in the war zone.

Morley looked at me hard, shook his head. "Your real problem is common sense is nagging you."

"What?"

"You can't let this thing alone. You have to keep picking at it. You set yourself up so you'd find an excuse. Now that you've done that common sense wants to make a comeback. Forget the Rainmaker, Garrett."

I jacked one eyebrow way, way up. "Oh?" Did he have a private line on Cleaver?

"He's on a traveling bullseye now, Garrett. Not mine. You get too close you could get hit by the volley that gets him." He gestured as though to push me away. "Go. I'll find out what I can about your lady's father."

# 53

Had to be magic. By the time I got home, after visiting a couple war buddies now in the extremist human rights movement, my place was surrounded. Ferocious pirates lounged on convenient corners. The guy from the outfit was back, with friends. The clumsy guy was there, and not alone, though I only glimpsed Winger before she vanished.

I'd even attracted some new folks. How many friends and enemies did the Rainmaker have?

I should have gathered the crowd and suggested we set up a pool, reduce duplication of effort, but I got distracted.

Slither and Ivy were camped on my front stoop.

Ivy had the good grace to blush. "We got thrown out," he told me. "I was trying to explain something to a guy and accidentally said the P word."

"What? What do you mean, the P word?" I checked Slither. The man looked awful.

"You know. Where he goes berserk."

Powziffle. Right. "Just out of curiosity, does he remember what he does after he hears that?"

The answer seemed a little much for Ivy's overtaxed intellect. He shrugged. I had a good idea, though. Might go a ways toward explaining Slither's problems.

Somewhere, sometime years ago, somebody twisted his mind trying to turn him into a human weapon, his trigger a nonsense phrase. Who and why didn't matter anymore, but they botched the job. Slither was out of control. He went into the Bledsoe improperly, but he belonged there. Out here he was going to get worse till somebody killed him.

Half the men roaming TunFaire belong inside somewhere. There aren't that many sane folks around, not that cross my path.

I went inside. The boys followed. Ivy headed for the small front room. The Goddamn Parrot started up. I paused to use the peephole. Morley must have run through the streets screeching about me being back on the job.

Interesting to note that the Rainmaker's pals were out as fast as his enemies. I wondered if some of those guys worked for Chastity's daddy.

With the boys so thick, it wasn't possible they were unaware of one another. That suggested possibilities.

If I was working for the outfit and thought somebody nearby worked for Cleaver, I'd snatch him and forget about Garrett. Were the lot so lazy they wanted me to do their work for them? Nah. They had to know about my lack of ambition.

Slither must have lost the landmarks blazing the trail to the kitchen. He just tagged along after Ivy. While the boys renewed acquaintances with TGD Parrot, I hit the kitchen fast and got my meager stores put out of sight.

Some forsaken jerk started pounding on the door. His knock was so diffident I almost let it go.

The Goddamn Parrot was heaping the Garrett lineage with fulsome praise. "Strangle that jungle chicken. I'm going to sell the feathers." I returned to the peephole.

Where did they find these guys? Slight financial types, they were the kind of guys who fought their war shuffling papers. The kind of ninety-three-pound brain cases anybody who ever did any real soldiering swore he was going to drown in urine if he ever got the chance. . . . Curious. Their kind seldom ventured into my part of town.

Macunado Street isn't the Bustee but is in a neighborhood silver spoons are scared to visit.

Maybe they had something to do with the Blaines.

I opened up.

Error.

Maybe I did sense something. I did have one hand on the grip of my headknocker. Useful. Because two men as big as Saucerhead Tharpe materialized from the blind spots beside my door and tried to run me over.

I stumbled back, astonished. I produced my stick. The guy nearest me tried to tackle me. I drifted aside and laid my stick across the back of his skull. These clowns had to be from another dimension. Nobody tries to take me at home.

The Dead Man doesn't suffer disturbances.

Well, not usually. If I hadn't been busy, I would've gone to see what was keeping him. He didn't stir a mental muscle.

That first guy curled up for a nap. His behemoth buddy scoped it out and opted for a less precipitous approach. He remained confident. He had valiant commodities brokers to harry my flanks.

Slither stuck his head out of the small front room. He didn't look like he could be much help, but he *was* behind the crowd. "Hey, Slither. Powziffle pheez."

My pronunciation was good enough.

The screams for help had died away. I didn't hear much groaning or furniture breaking anymore, either. Careful to make no noise, I moved the table away from the kitchen door, took a peek down the hall.

Ivy had Slither up against the wall, shaking a finger under his chin. The Goddamn Parrot was on the little guy's shoulder, singing. Near as I could tell, most of the invaders were breathing.

I stepped into the hallway.

"Why did you have to go and do that?" Ivy whined.

"Because these guys wanted to operate on me without getting patient permission." Even the guy I put down myself had bruises on his bruises. Slither must have been practicing his fancy dance steps. "He all right?"

"He will be. No thanks to you."

"Let's don't squabble. Prisoners of war here. Get it? Interrogation." I opened the Dead Man's door—like I'd be able to see what the hell he thought he was doing, sleeping through all this. I saw what I deserved to see, which was the corpse of a fat Loghyr slouched in a dusty chair.

My pals just needed guidance. When I finished checking on my one-time partner, the invaders were trussed like pigs set for live roasting. The action brought Slither back.

"You guys ever work interrogation?" I asked.

Ivy nodded. Reluctantly, it seemed. Slither looked dumb. He was real good at that. A natural talent.

"My style is to scare them without hurting them—if that can

be helped. We have four guys here. One ought to be a weak sister. Right?"

Blank looks.

"We try to figure out which one will tell us what we want to know without we bust them up."

"Can you do that?"

Why do I try to be a nice guy? Even people on the side of the angels, my side, don't understand.

I took my pals into the kitchen. We slapped together a really rough meal while we waited for those guys to wake up.

One by one they came around. They didn't seem thrilled with their circumstances.

# 54

Cup of tea in hand, accomplices at my sides, the Goddamn Parrot cussing like he'd invented the genre, I returned to the hallway. "All right, boys. Let's play a game. Winners get to go home with all their fingers and toes." If they didn't know enough to be wary of the Dead Man, they didn't know I seldom toast off villainous digits.

Slither had his own ideas. He broke a guy's arm. Casual, no big deal, just part of the job, all empathy absent. When his victim stopped squealing, I said, "Mainly, I want to know who you are. And why you busted in, of course."

The clerk type with two good arms volunteered, "We were supposed to discourage you. Warn you off."

"We're gaining ground. Now clue me in. Warn me off what? Why? And who says?"

He looked at me like I was retarded.

Maybe he was right. "I don't have a clue, friend."

"You've got to drop what you're doing. . . ."

"Let's try getting more specific."

That didn't elicit a response. "Lords of Shadow," I muttered, gesturing at Slither. Slither took a step.

"Hold on! Hold on! Mr. Davenport asked us to convince you that you shouldn't waste any more time looking for Miss Jenn."

"Good. Except I don't know any Davenport. I've never heard of any Davenports. Who the hell is he?"

My man got a big "Duh?" look on him. Which meant he did have brain enough to want to find a connection if he was supposed to pound on a guy who never heard of the guy who wanted him

pounded. We were confused, us two. But I had Slither to help clar-
ify. Slither glowered. Slither loomed. I remarked, "He likes hurting folks. You don't want to go home in a litter, you'd better
whisper in my ear. And tell me no sweet little lies. What'd I do
that got this Davenport clown upset?"

"You're trying to find Miss Jenn."

Miss Jenn, eh? "Give me some details. I'm a detail kind of
guy."

The staff type went to talking like he'd contracted diarrhea of
the mouth. I squatted beside the flood and panned for nuggets.

He claimed a character named Davenport, good buddy of
Marengo North English, didn't much like the idea of me maybe
finding Emerald Jenn, so he'd asked some pals to discourage me.
His pals had no idea why Davenport gave a damn who did or
didn't find Emerald.

I poked in a question whenever he paused for breath. He answered everything. He couldn't shut up now. In time I did understand that I hadn't gotten on the wrong side of Marengo North
English himself. This was Davenport's alone. Good. I have no desire to get noticed by the lunatic fringe.

I said, "I know this is going to break your hearts, guys, but I
don't give a rat's ass about that kid. I'm not on that case anymore.
These days I'm hunting a creep named Grange Cleaver. You help
me out there, I'll forget you messed up my hallway. I won't even
go break Mr. Davenport's arms."

I harvested a crop of blank looks. None of those guys ever
heard of Grange Cleaver.

"All right. Out of personal curiosity, because of all this, I
would like to talk to Emerald. Pass that on to her. I want to ask
about her mother and Cleaver." I gestured. Ivy and Slither both got
my drift without elaborate instructions. Ivy opened the door.
Slither herded the gang that way. The Goddamn Parrot got into the
game, encouraging their departure.

"Hey! You guys want a talking chicken?"

Sometimes people are just too fast. Those guys got out without
answering or even looking back.

You'd think a talking bird would be a real prize—wouldn't
you?—if you hadn't been around him long enough to know better.

I watched the watchers watch the flight of the four dismayed human rights activists. Their going didn't generate much excitement.

Could I lay hands on one of those fierce pirates? If he talked, I

could get the Firelord what he wanted fast. Maybe. Cleaver had
spent a life being light on his feet. He wasn't about to convenience
anybody now.

I went back to the kitchen, built another sandwich. I checked
on the Dead Man. Out of it still. I went back to the peephole. Evening had started lowering its skirts. Which made no difference.
The street was as crowded as ever. My fans hadn't called it a day.

My gaze swept a pair of earringed angels—and I suffered a
mighty intuition.

I knew where to find Grange Cleaver. He hadn't hauled his
buccaneer behind out of TunFaire. He was still around, laughing
at everybody trying to track him down. It was a game for him. A
vicious game. If he feared he risked losing, he'd cut and run.

I summoned Ivy and Slither. "I admit I wanted you guys out of
my hair. Didn't work, but my misfortune looks lucky now." The
Goddamn Parrot didn't like being left alone. He started spouting
off in a big way. I stepped over where he could see me, gave him
the evil eye. He shut up while he considered the situation. "I need
you to hold the fort."

Ivy stared. Slither said, "Huh?"

Great. "I'm going out the back way." I spoke slowly and
clearly. "I'm leaving you in charge. Anybody knocks, either ignore them or don't tell them anything." I donned my best scowl,
faced the Dead Man's door. Old Bones was way overdue.

Hell, maybe I'd grown too dependent on him. I reminded me
that in real life you can't count on anybody but you, yourself, and
you.

"All right, Garrett." Ivy's voice was half-strength. Was he
fading?

It could be worse. The Dead Man says it can always get worse.
Don't ask me how.

I slid out the back way.

# 55

"What's dis shit?" Sarge bellowed. "I got ta put up wit' you tree times a day now?"

"Bask in the reflection, my man. Morley is my number one boy now. He up there showing some married lady the ins and out of cross stitch? I could maybe tell him something he wants to hear."

"Yeah? Like what?" I wasn't selling Sarge no swamp.

"Like where to find some buried treasure."

Sarge moved out.

We've all endured one another so long we all know when the yak means something and when it's just macho yammer. Sarge figured I had something, so he got intimate with the speaking tube. I didn't hear what he said, but hardly three minutes passed before Morley descended the stairs. A woman of astonishing beauty peeked down for a moment, as though she just *had* to see what improbability could distract Morley Dotes from her. From what I saw of her, I had to consider that an excellent question.

"I'm sorry." The woman retreated, but my imagination went with her. I hated Morley for having found her first. How did he do it? "Who was that?"

He sneered. "Wipe the drool off your chin. Someone might mistake you for a mad dog werewolf."

"Who is she?"

"No, you don't. I was a gentleman about Chaz. I suffered in silence while you wasted Tinnie Tate. I didn't birddog when that went bad because it might get good again. So forget my little Julie, eh?"

"I'll give you half a minute."

"Generous, Garrett. Generous. How come you're down here making my life miserable again?" Oddly, he seemed anxious. He covered by glancing upstairs like he was thinking about maybe spanking somebody for revealing herself to the rabble. Then he eyed me like he really did expect to hear about buried treasure.

"While back I got the impression you wanted to get face-to-face with the Rainmaker."

He glanced at the stairway. Glorious, lovely Julie was very much with us even though she remained unseen. He said, "Tell me about it."

I wondered. I knew Morley's priorities. Seldom did he find a Julie less interesting than revenge. "I think I know where to find him."

Morley cast one more longing glance upstairs. "How did you manage that? You turn psychic? Or psycho? Or did the Dead Man wake up?"

"Through the exercise of reason, my man. Pure reason."

Morley offered me one of his special looks, just to let me know I couldn't fool a stone with a learning disability. "I'll bite, Garrett. Where?"

"On the Hill. Maggie Jenn's place."

He made a show of thinking about it before he smiled nastily. "Damn if I don't think you stumbled into it and came up smelling sweet. I should have thought of that. Let's go."

"What? Me? No way. I did my part. Take your help. Sarge and Puddle need the exercise. I'll stay here and hold the fort."

"Ha. That's ha, like in half a ha-ha, Garrett."

"Some guys got no sense of humor."

"You talking about me? I gave you a parrot, didn't I?"

"My point exactly."

"What can you do? People just won't show any gratitude anymore. All right. Let's go see the man."

I smirked. Behind Morley's back. No sense having him figure out who was manipulating whom. Not just yet.

# 56

I began to wonder if there wasn't an alert out with my name on it. Three times we tried to go up the Hill and three times patrols got in our way. Unbelievably bad luck.

Morley snapped, "Don't be so cheerful!"

I started to open my mouth.

"And don't give me that dog barf about never being disappointed if you only look for the worst."

"You are in a fine mood, aren't you?" I reflected a moment. "We've known each other too long, you realize?"

"You can say that again."

"All right. We've known each other . . ."

"And you turn into a bigger wiseass every day I know you. The Garrett I used to know . . ." Off he hared on an expedition into reality revision. We live in different worlds. He remembers nothing the way I do. Maybe that's cultural.

The old work ethic paid off. Fourth try we got through. As we gained the high ground, I muttered, "I was beginning to think my magic gizmo was working backwards."

"Your what?"

"Uh . . . I have this amulet thing. Somebody uses a tracing spell on me, I can steer them off."

"Oh?" Morley eyed me suspiciously.

I don't tell him everything. And he keeps things from me. You just don't share everything, friends or not.

As we neared that grim gray canyon of a Hilltop street we grew cautious. I found myself feeling nervous in a premonitory way. And Morley said, "I have a strange feeling about this."

"It *is* quiet. But it's always quiet up here. These people want it that way."

"You feel it, too."

"I feel something."

But we saw no one, sniffed out no slightest scent of a patrol ambush.

We approached the Jenn place through the alley. And strolled right on past, pretending we were scouts for the ratmen who would come for the trash.

Someone had employed the balcony route to get inside. Someone not very circumspect. We judged the break-in to be recent because there was no evidence of the patrol having taken corrective action.

I told Morley, "I need to go in there."

Dotes didn't argue, but he wasn't enthralled by the notion. He observed, "The roof hatch is unlatched—if nobody cared how we got out before."

We'd left it unlatched because the catch couldn't be worked from outside. "Just what I wanted to do today. Clamber around rooftops."

"You're the one can't leave well enough alone."

"The firelord is paying me very well not to."

"All right. Let's don't bicker." Morley looked around. I looked around. We could've been surrounded by a ghost city. Other than the buildings, there was no evidence of human presence.

"Spooky," I muttered, while Morley scampered up a downspout like some pointy-eared ape. I dragged my bulk after, groaned as he helped me roll onto a flat roof. "I thought I was getting back in shape." Puff puff.

"Tipping a beer stein doesn't stress your leg muscles nearly enough. Come on."

Beer stein? *I* was getting to be a wiseass? Uh-oh.

Starting after Morley, I glanced back into the alley and spotted a housemaid on a balcony down the way, gaping at us. She had come out while we were climbing. "Trouble," I told Morley. "A witness."

"Keep low, then. If she doesn't see where we go, we'll have enough time."

But time for what? I had real strong doubts about the wisdom of my approach, now.

As we neared the roof hatch, I noted that Morley seemed to lack confidence, too. But he was a dark elf, partly. He wouldn't back down without more reason than a growing premonition.

# 57

We listened intently, heard nothing on the other side of the hatch. Grimly, I prized it open an inch. Morley listened with his better ears, peered into the inner darkness with his better eyes. He sniffed, frowned slightly.

"What?" I whispered.

"I don't know."

"Someone there?"

"Not that. Open it up. We need to hurry."

I lifted. There was no racket in the street yet, but I doubted that that would last. Light poured into the stairwell. Neither villain nor monster rose to greet us.

Morley descended quickly. I followed less swiftly, it having gotten inky dark in there once I shut the hatch again. We entered the top story without incident. Morley kept sniffing the air. So did I. I sucked in enough dust to have to fight sneezing. But there was something . . .

A sound echoed up from below, a moaning wail like the last cry of a lost soul. "Spooks," I said again.

"No."

No. He was right. Somebody was being hurt badly. I'd just have preferred spooks.

We grew more cautious.

Confident that that floor was untenanted, we stole down a level. I murmured, "We're going too slow."

Morley agreed. "But what can we do?" Twice more we heard that cry of agonized despair.

What we could do was get out before the goon squad showed.

The next floor down showed evidence of human habitation. Morley and I held silent debate over the numbers, which had to have been more than a half dozen and possibly the whole crowd from that ugly warehouse.

Another cry. From the top of the stair that led down to the second floor we could hear remote voices engaged in argument. Morley held up three fingers, then four. I nodded agreement. Four. Plus whoever was getting hurt.

The Rainmaker had his reputation for torture, I recalled.

That smell in the air was stronger but not yet strong enough to identify.

Morley kept hesitating about going on down. I no longer wanted to risk even a whisper so had to trust his instincts. As he did start down, something made a clunking racket on the floor below. We froze. Surprise, surprise.

Three very large male individuals dripping sharp steel galumphed across our field of view and headed down the stair to the ground floor. Patrol thugs. Come on the scene via the balcony door, I guessed. Moving fast because somebody tripped over his bootlace and gave them all away.

Morley whispered urgently, "Hide!" He jerked a thumb heavenward. I nodded. It did seem likely that younger and more agile guards would take the path we'd used.

Our timing was superb. No sooner had we ducked under the dustcovers shielding adjacent antiques than we heard lots of boots hustling down from above. I worried about sneezes betraying me. Then I worried about footprints in the dust. I couldn't recall if there had been enough prior traffic to disguise our movements.

An uproar broke out downstairs. Sounded like a major battle: lots of metal banging metal, people yelling and screaming, furniture crashing. I guessed patrol types had entered at ground level, too.

A pseudopod of combat scaled the stairs. The expected gang from the roof arrived and jumped in. The hollering and cussing grew ferocious, but I kept squeezing my nose anyway. With my luck, those guys would notice even a little sputter of a sneeze.

It got brisk. For a while, despite their edge in the odds, I thought the patrol guys would lose out. They lacked motivation. They hadn't hired on to get killed protecting property.

I never doubted that people were dying.

The guys on the stairs launched an angry counterattack.

After that the battle lasted only minutes. Soon it left the house for the street. The patrol bunch hollered in angry pursuit of those they had routed.

Came a scratch on the sheet concealing me. I gripped my headknocker, ready for a mighty two-handed swing. Morley whispered, "Let's go. Before they come back to look around."

He was right, of course. They would be back. But at the moment we were invisible—assuming the patrol thought the people downstairs were the guys that maid had seen.

The silence didn't last. I picked out a groan followed by something I hadn't heard for years—the rasp of a man with a punctured lung trying desperately to breath.

Morley and I descended in spurts, always ready to flee. We encountered casualties, all of whom had rolled to the bottom of the stair ending on the second floor. None of the four would brawl again.

I knew that smell—now it was fresh and strong.

Blood.

Three of the fallen wore crude patrol uniforms. The fourth had fought them.

"Know this guy?" I asked Morley, sure he knew pro thugs better than I did. And I had recognized Hammerhand Nicks, middleweight enforcer type for the Outfit.

"Yes." Dotes seemed to grow still more alert.

I told him, "I'm going down." Not that I wanted to.

I made my feet move. I did want to know.

The smell of death grew dense.

Three more patrol types lay dead in the ground floor hall where the stair ended. Blooded steel lay everywhere. I found another syndicate character there, just less than dead. I beckoned Morley. "Gericht Lungsmark?"

He nodded. "Over there. Wenden Tobar."

More Outfit hitters. Lungsmark groaned. I moved away. Didn't want him seeing me if he opened his eyes. "She figured it out before I did."

"Maybe." Dotes eased toward the next room, whence came the sounds of the man with respiratory difficulties. "Or maybe she had help."

"Oh?"

"Lot of ears in my place." He started to say my name, recalled that this was not the best place. "If somebody told somebody and that somebody moved fast. . . ."

Maybe, but I shook my head. Likely the Outfit did have the pull to get the patrols to do a favor, but . . . "They—"

Morley made a silencing gesture.

No. The patrols wouldn't get into it with the Outfit without they didn't know they were up against syndicate guys.

Come to think of it, the hoods probably did the logical thing and snatched themselves a pirate off the street outside my place.

Morley gestured again, slipped through the doorway. I went to the other side, crouching.

We found the fellow with the breathing problem, one Barclay Blue, journeyman bonebreaker. "Going to be some advancement opportunities, looks like," I said.

Morley scowled. His situation was way less comfortable than mine. Further, there was the question of why Contague associates had gotten into a deadly battle high on the Hill. Not politic, that.

Next room boasted the remains of the main encounter. The Outfit guys had come from farther back and met the invaders there. At least one patrol bruno had carried a crossbow. I counted eight corpses. Four were Outfit. Some fine antiques had been rendered kindling. Blood covered everything.

I didn't like the implications. Things had gotten way out of hand.

We entered the dining room I'd shared with Maggie Jenn. I understood why the Outfit guys hadn't been willing to surrender.

The stench of death was heavy. Most of the chairs at the table had dead or probably soon to be dead people tied into them. I recognized the old guys from the warehouse, Zeke, the woman who had served Maggie and me, and others I'd seen on the street. Nobody's breathing was real robust.

I said, "They *were* hiding here."

"There were two battles. Belinda Contague won the first one."

Fourteen people were tied into the chairs. Zeke and Mugwump were among the breathing. Excepting several guys who obviously got themselves killed when the thugs moved in, everyone had been tortured. None of the survivors were conscious.

Morley asked. "You see any Rainmaker? I don't. No Maggie Jenn, either."

"He's famous for not being there when the shit comes down." I double-checked Mugwump. He was the healthiest of the survivors.

"Yes. He is. What are you doing?"

"Cutting the guy loose. Sometimes I do stuff just because it feels right."

"Think you'll find anything useful here?"

"Probably not." I noted that we were no longer a we. "Probably be a good idea to go." We'd have the victorious patrolmen back soon and the Guard right behind them.

A bloody knife lay on the floor, probably a torture instrument. I placed it in front of Mugwump. "So let's scat."

# 58

"Freeze, slimeblog!"

Huh?

I was always a rebel. I didn't freeze. I didn't even check to see if I was outnumbered.

Neither did Morley. And he was where the speaker couldn't see him.

I dove, rolled, came to my feet out of view, charged. Morley attacked from the other side of the doorway, low, shrieking.

One lone heavyweight had thought he could bluff me. He didn't pull it off.

Morley smacked and kicked him about nineteen times. I whacked away with a headknocker rendered magically unbreakable. Down the man went, his expression saying it just wasn't fair. Poor baby. I knew what he meant. Just when you think you've got it knocked, along comes some clown with a bigger stick.

Morley and I got no time to congratulate ourselves. More patrol types materialized. After the intellectual form of their subspecies, one demanded, "What's going on here?"

Bippetty-bappetty-bopp!

I was not unaware that real heroes flail around with singing swords while I rated only an enchanted hunk of oak.

Morley whooped and hollered and popped guys all over the place. He was having a great time. He could hustle when he was motivated.

We broke through. We headed upstairs, disdaining the front way because every thug on the Hill had gathered to attend the business of counting bodies, cussing villains, and abusing captives.

My normally abysmal luck failed to assert itself completely, mostly because the patrol guys were making so much racket. They couldn't hear me and Morley getting away.

"Let's try the balcony first," Morley suggested. "And quickly."

I didn't expect an easy getaway. Anybody with half a brain would have posted guards at every potential exit.

You never know, though, when you're dealing with Tun-Faire's bonebreakers. Most can't think past the next arm they mean to twist. They're efficient and technically polished within their specialty but feeble when it comes to planning and making decisions.

There had been a major engagement on the second floor, back toward the balcony door. There was a lot of blood but no bodies. Blood trails indicated that several bodies had been dragged out of what had been a lumber room last time I looked. My impression was that here was where the Outfit's invasion first met serious resistance. I wondered why. That room was no place to make a stand.

I took time out to look it over.

What the hell?

Seconds later, Morley called from the balcony exit, "What're you doing? Come on! There's nobody out there right now."

I finished scanning the vellum sheet, one of several pages come loose from a book evidently damaged during the fighting. The rest of the book was gone. The loose pages might have gotten lost during a hasty getaway.

"I'm going to leave you here," Morley threatened.

I folded the vellum, slipped it into my shirt. Best to get going and not pique Morley's suspicion. I'd read the story before, anyway. The whole book, not just one page.

I reached the balcony, saw that Morley had given up on me and dropped into the alleyway. I glanced right and left, spied no trouble moving in. I landed beside Dotes. "We probably ought to split up now."

He eyed me closely. He's sure that any time I know what I want, I'm up to something that won't be to his advantage. I can't fathom why he would think that way. I said, "Do me a big one. Couple hours from now I'm going to lead that clumsy guy down to your neighborhood. Help me grab him."

"Why?"

"I want to talk to Winger. He'll know where to find her."

He gave me another glimpse of his suspicious side, then told me, "Be careful. Right now, they're touchy around here. They'll jump anything that moves."

I nodded, less concerned about me than about him.

# 59

I wasn't in a real good mood. I didn't turn cartwheels when Colonel Block waved his clowns off and told me, "Cheer up, Garrett. It's all straightened out."

"How can you put these clowns on the street if they can't recognize a pass put out by their own beloved captain?" What, me worry about getting off the Hill? I had passes and paper from a troop of heavyweights.

"The fellow who reads and writes doesn't normally opt for a career in law enforcement. And you'll have to admit that you refused to provide any good reason for being where you were found."

"Where I was found? I was—"

"Detained, then."

"And with way too much enthusiasm. I did try to cooperate. They wouldn't let me talk."

"I will."

"Huh?"

"I'll let you explain. To your heart's content."

A wise guy. I admonished myself to be careful. Quietly. "I was just trying to do what the Firelord hired me to do. I'd heard a rumor the Rainmaker was hiding out on the Hill."

Block offered me a *try again* look. I wasn't snowing him. His agents would have relayed any such rumors. "What happened in that house, Garrett?"

"You have me at a disadvantage, Captain."

"It's Colonel, Garrett. As you know. And that's true. I do have you. If I wanted, I could send you over to the Al-Khar to be held for questioning. It's entirely possible for somebody to fall between the cracks there, same as in the Bledsoe."

The Al-Khar is TunFaire's city jail. "Why you want to be like that?"

"Mainly because I don't like to be jerked around. I have an eyewitness who saw two men climb a drain-spout. One of them was dressed exactly like you."

"Without so many rips and tears, I'll bet. Doubtless a daring youth out pretending to swash a few buckles. An amazing coincidence."

"Witness summoned the local patrol. Patrol went looking around and found a house showing multiple signs of forced entries. Inside they found lots of corpses and plenty of people willing to fight. I wouldn't accuse you of stretching any rules, Garrett. Not you. You're not that kind of guy. But I'd bet that if I wanted to spring for a cut-rate diviner, I could place you inside that house. Hm?"

I admitted nothing.

"Give me a hint, Garrett. Who were those people?"

I could discern no obvious profit in keeping my yap shut and sliding farther out of official favor. "Some were the Rainmaker's people."

"Was that so hard?"

Of course it was. Guys like me aren't supposed to cooperate with guys like him, especially if doing so would save some headaches. In my racket, you're supposed to be troll-stubborn. Apparently, dumb is supposed to help, too. "The others answered to the Combine. I've heard that a long time ago Cleaver had some part in the death of Chodo's brother." I doubted Block was hearing much that was news.

"I see. And Chodo pays his debts."

"Always."

Block had stayed seated, fortified behind his desk. Now he picked up a folded document bearing a fancy seal, tapped it against his desk top. "How bad will it get, Garrett? We in for a gang war?" That wouldn't look good on his record.

"I doubt it. You know Chodo's rep. Cleaver had to hire his muscle out of town. After this fiasco, he'll have no friends left. His dearest boyfriend is gonna ask 'Grange Who?' "

Block kept tapping that document. It looked more legal by the minute. He mused, "So many people interested in Grange Cleaver." He waved that paper. "Including mine, now." As if only then realizing what he held, he said, "This just came in. One Grange Cleaver is to be found and brought before the Court of Honor of the Magistry of Manpower Procurement. There's no record of him having performed his obligated service to the realm." You had to be there to get the full effect of Block's seditious sneer and sarcastic tone.

I grunted. Hadn't I thought maybe Cleaver was a dodger?

"I'm not going to strain myself trying to round up dodgers. Get out of here, Garrett."

I patted myself. Yep, I'd gotten back everything that was mine. Block's crew were almost honest. I started to take his advice.

"Wait!"

Damn! I knew he'd change his mind. "What?"

"You still seeing Belinda Contague?"

He knew too much about me. "No."

"Too bad. I thought you might suggest to her that her dad recall that it's to be kept off the Hill."

"Oh." A slightly more than gentle hint that he wanted all that passed along. "I don't think there'll be a problem again." Since all of Belinda's thugs dumb enough to get involved up there were no longer with us.

I got out.

# 60

It had been a long, hard day. And it was just getting started. Aching all over, looking way too much like a guy who got into one-sided brawls with zealous minions of public safety, I sneaked through the postern door of the Royal Library. Which was a whole lot less of a big deal than you might think.

Old Jake was supposed to keep that door secure, but when he did that his wartime cronies couldn't get in with supplies of liquid refreshments. Old Jake was all the security the library had. He didn't get around so well on his wooden leg, but his heart was in the right place. Linda Lee had a bad habit of saying he was me at twice the age.

Jake was asleep. What the hell. There wasn't a lot in the library your average thief would consider worth stealing.

I slipped past the grizzled old goat. He was snoring. I'd seldom seen him do anything else. Hard to believe he'd been given a job for life because he'd lost his leg becoming one of the all-time heroes of the Royal Marines. Sometimes it's better to have your legends dead.

I went looking for Linda Lee. I hoped I wouldn't scare many of her coworkers before I found her. They were easily spooked.

She found me.

I was peeking around the end of a stand of shelves—stacks, in the approved jargon—when she spoke behind me. "What the hell are you doing in here?"

I caught my breath, got it back where it belonged, made sure my feet were back on the floor, then turned around. "I'm thrilled to see you, too. You're as lovely as ever."

She looked me up and down. Her cute upper lip wrinkled. "You just stay where you are. And answer the question."

I opened my mouth, but she didn't stop. "You really ought to take more trouble with your personal appearance. Good grooming is important. Come on. What are you doing here?"

I opened my mouth.

"You're going to get me into bad trouble—"

I pounced. I clapped a hand over her mouth. She wiggled a little—a not unpleasant experience. "I wanted to talk about the book somebody stole from you. Was it a first edition of *The Raging Blades?*"

She managed to stop wiggling and started listening. She shook her head.

Startled, I growled, "Damn it! I really thought I had it locked." I turned her loose.

"It was a first of *The Steel-Game*. The library has had it since early imperial times." She went on about some ancient emperor having wanted to assemble a set so he could seek Eagle's fabulous horde, about how no outsider could have known the book existed.

I expelled some remarks of my own. "Ha! I *was* right! Wrong book but right idea." I produced the fragment of vellum I'd lifted from Maggie Jenn's place, a solitary page from *The Battle-Storm,* edition uncertain, but people had died trying to protect it from other people who hadn't cared about it at all. The intensity of that encounter had set the tone for the atrocities that followed.

Linda Lee asked, "What about *The Raging Blades?* We've never had a first of that one."

"Because I saw a copy the other day. Somewhere where it shouldn't have been. But I didn't realize that until today. Then I thought I could solve your troubles."

I'd begun developing troubles of my own. Linda Lee wouldn't stay still. I couldn't stay focused. She was too close and too warm and had begun purring like she really appreciated my thinking of her.

"You just come on down here, Jake! I'll show you. You wouldn't believe me, but I'll show you."

A voice muttered, "I wouldn't believe you if you told me the sky was up, old woman."

"You fell asleep. You go ahead and lie, but we all know you fell asleep at your post and let an outsider get in. You're too old."

I hated that woman's voice almost as much as I hated the voice of the Goddamn Parrot despite having heard it only a few times.

Those few were a few too many. It was nails on slate, whined through the nose, always complaining.

"Talking about old, you been dead three years but too damned stupid to realize it. Still got people to make miserable, too." Old Jake didn't care if he hurt her feelings, but it wasn't likely he would. She was two-thirds deaf.

"You were sound asleep when I came to get you."

"I was resting my eyes, you impossible hag." Clump! Old Jake collapsed. His fingers weren't too nimble anymore. When he got in a hurry, he sometimes failed to get his wooden leg strapped on right.

I gave Linda Lee a peck on the forehead. "I'd better run."

"Later." She winked fetchingly. I've always had a soft spot for women who wink. "Promise," she breathed, then went to help Old Jake. She ignored the old woman, who didn't miss the attention. She was doing just fine carrying two sides of an argument herself.

I ducked out of sight. The old man hadn't seen me, so he started spouting off about frustrated old maids who imagine men lurking behind every stack.

# 61

A long, hard day, and not yet done. I had aches where plenty of people don't have places. I'd walked too many miles and had been thumped too many times. Hell, this was like the bad old days when the Dead Man made sure I got no rest at all.

I told myself I would make one last stop, then I would hang it up for the day. Then I groaned. I recalled my arrangement with Morley.

Not Winger on top of everything else. Why had I done that?

Good soldier, I soldiered on.

I wondered what bean-brained civilian had come up with that one. Every soldier I ever knew never moved a muscle unless that was the final option.

I sensed trouble long before I hove in sight of Wixon and White. That end of town was silent with the silence that bubbles around immediate, terrible violence.

The moment passed. The ghouls were gathering when I reached the storefront, panting over the bloody wreckage.

One look and I knew smart money would choose putting one set of toes in front of the other and repeating the process briskly. In my case, while facing in a southeasterly direction. But I just had to take a fast look around the shop.

Colonel Block banished his henchmen with a wave. "Cheer up, Garrett. It's all straightened out now."

"Must be an echo in here." Not to mention way too much sunlight. The stuff flooded in through an open, eastern window casement at gale force. It was way too early for any reasonable man to be upright. Block obviously wasn't reasonable. Tell the truth, I wasn't feeling real reasonable myself. "We've got to stop meeting like this."

"Wasn't my idea, Garrett. You enjoy your accommodations?"

I'd spent a too-short night on a straw pallet in a stinking cell in the Al-Khar, charged with being a possible witness. "The fleas and lice and bedbugs enjoyed my visit." They should feel right at home. Block was a dirty dog.

"This is where you tell me why my men found you right in the middle of another massacre."

"Somebody yelled for help and your gang actually showed up. I was amazed." The old Watch would have headed the other direction, just to make sure nobody got hurt that didn't need hurting.

"Thought you said it was all straightened out."

"I meant I know you didn't slice anybody into cold cuts. Witness says you showed after the screaming stopped. I want to know why what happened happened. And how come you were there."

"Grange Cleaver."

"That's it?" He waited for me to say more. I didn't. "I see no connection. Maybe you'll enlighten me. Meantime, you should know it looks like some really nasty black magic did the killing."

I nodded, but I didn't believe it. "That's what doesn't make sense." Someone made it look like magical murder. I was willing to bet Robin and Penny had kept their appointment with doom through the agency of a devil named Cleaver, once again trying to point a false finger at Marengo North English. Made me think Emerald Jenn was holed up with North English and Cleaver wanted to bust her loose.

"Why do I got a feeling you're being too cooperative, Garrett?"

"What? Now what the hell do you want? I answer your questions, you get aggravated. I don't answer them, you get aggravated. If I wanted aggravation, I'd stay home and argue with the Dead Man."

"You're answering questions, but I got a hunch you aren't telling me what I want to know."

I took a deep breath. We were about set for one of those ferocious head-butting sessions so gratifying to men of our respective professions. I exhaled. . . .

An ugly little breed stormed in. He scowled at me like I had no right to be cluttering up Block's office. I nodded. "Relway." He didn't respond.

"It's started," he told Block.

"Damn them." Block lost all interest in bugs as small as me. Must be fatter victims available somewhere else. He glared at me, though. "The Call." He stalked after his secret police chief, who was gone already. "Get out of here. And try not to stumble over any more bodies."

Good advice all. Maybe he wasn't a complete dunce.

What was that about The Call?

Didn't take long to find out. I hit the street. Off east, looking like it might not be rooted far from my place, was a growing tree of smoke. I caught snatches of news from people rushing through the streets.

A bar brawl had turned into major racial trouble. Humans were going after centaurs. Apparently, it hadn't gotten out of hand till somebody in The Call had served up an inflammatory diatribe and people had responded by firing the homes of centaur immigrants. Other species were becoming involved. There had been some kind of deadly guerrilla battle in the scaffolding festooning the Bledsoe. They were losing ground getting the hospital repaired.

The insanity had begun. I hoped Block and Relway could contain it. At least this time.

There would be other times. And they would get worse before they got better.

People were going to get polarized real soon now.

I walked carefully. And went about it visible to anyone who might have a tracking spell laid on me.

# 62

Slither and Ivy got on me the minute they let me in the house. "Guys. Guys! I want this kind of crap I can get married. I need food. I need sleep. I need a bath. I need that foul-mouth flamingo strangled so I can do the rest without getting so aggravated I have to kill somebody." The bird must have saved up for my homecoming.

I got some money from the Dead Man's room, studied him suspiciously before I left. Was that a restrained amusement I sensed there for just a second?

I sent Slither out for supplies. I told Ivy to let me have three hours of sleep. When he woke me up, I wanted food and bath water ready. Then I dragged me upstairs and splashed me into my bed. The Dead Man could get the bugs out later. I lay there tossing and turning and listening to the Goddamn Parrot cackle for half a sentence, then it was time to get up.

Ivy did his part like that was all he had to live for. I rose on time. I scrubbed up in my ten-gallon copper tub. Downstairs, I found a classic breakfast waiting. Ivy was as drunk as a skunk, the Goddamn Parrot on his shoulder. The bird wasn't talking. It needed its whole attention just to hang on. Its breath was worse than Ivy's. Maybe Slither got him his own bottle. Good old Slither, looking out for everybody.

I stuffed myself, then told the boys, "I was going to run you guys off again today, but I don't think I'm going to have time. Either of you has a good afternoon, I want you to get out and look for a place, find a job. I'm not going to take care of you forever."

Slither nodded. Ivy said, "There's some letters for you."

"Letters?"

"We didn't let nobody see you," Slither explained. "Mainly on account of you wasn't here. So some people wrote you letters. We put them on your desk."

There were three letters. Two showed no indication whence they sprang. The other bore Morley's chop. It was a nag about where the hell was I last night? He couldn't waste all his valuable time playing my games if I wasn't going to show up.

By now he would know why I hadn't. Him and his thugs probably thought it was funny.

I opened a letter that purported to be from Maggie Jenn. She wanted to meet. Oh? Right. "Slither! You remember who brought these?"

The big man leaned through the doorway. "That one was brung by a lady. Cute little bug of a thing with red hair."

Surprise, surprise. Bold little witch. . . . Oh, horrible thought! What if this was the real Maggie Jenn, come in from her island hideout?

No. Because I didn't want that.

"That one you done opened come from your friend with the funny ears."

"Morley Dotes. I know." I picked up the last one. "How about this?"

"One of them fellas that was here when I had my seizure brung that one."

"One of those lunatics from the Call?"

"Them fellas what tried to push you around."

That didn't make sense. I supposed I'd have to open the letter to straighten it out.

It was from Emerald Jenn. She would talk to me if I would meet her at a certain estate south of TunFaire. I didn't know the estate, but I did know the area. I'd met Eleanor out there. Folks down there were a lot like folks from the Hill—only way more reactionary. Their wealth consisted of land rather than treasure or power. A more smugly self-righteous, bigoted bunch would be hard to imagine.

Emerald Jenn's suggested meeting place wasn't far from the main estate of Marengo North English.

Interesting.

"How is your memory, Slither?"

"I'm pretty good today, Garrett."

He didn't sound good, but I had to take his word. "Need you to run over to Morley's. Tell him I'm coming, he wants to get on with what we talked about last night. You manage that?"

He thought about it. "I can do it. You got it. Now?"

"Always a great time to start."

"Pretty rough out there, Garrett. They're killing each other in the streets."

"Take Ivy, makes you feel better."

"I was thinking about you."

"I'll take my chances." Wise ass. Do I carry a sign only I can't see? Garrett's ego. Kick here.

I occupied the stoop in order to field marshal Slither's departure. I checked the street, too. "I know how a horse apple feels," I told Ivy, who was inside the doorway and had to have the allusion explained. "Flies?"

All my fans were back. Except for the fierce pirates. Grange Cleaver friends seemed scarce.

I predicted that, didn't I?

I shrugged, went inside, and scribbled a note to Maggie Jenn. Ivy could give it to whomever came around to get my reply.

# 63

"Getting predictable in your old age," I told Dotes, settling beside him on the exact set of steps where I'd guessed he would be waiting.

"Me? I'm here because I knew this is where you would come looking. I didn't want you wasting time stumbling around looking for me."

Invisible sign. Absolutely. "Can we take him?"

"He's caught. Nobody is so lucky he gets out of what I have set." He glanced left, at smoke rising in the distance. "Quiet out." The street should have been busier.

All streets should have been busier. Slither was right. They were killing each other out here—though it wasn't as bad as it could have been. Block's heavies were fast on their feet. And they had the army garrison to help discourage disorder.

Trouble never got a chance to grow up.

Too, word was out that Marengo North English didn't approve. He said this wasn't the time. The captains of many sister nut groups agreed. They asked for restraint now, promising license later.

"Interesting times," I told Morley.

"It's always something." Like he hadn't the least concern. "Well, here's our guest."

The clumsy guy smelled a rat. He was moving carefully. Trouble was, his sniffer wasn't sensitive enough. It was too late by the time he got a good whiff.

Morley waved. "Come on over."

The guy looked around. Just the way he moved you could tell he thought his luck was with him still. He was in it up to his chin but knew he always got out. So maybe this time he would fall up and blow away on the breeze. A regular dandelion seed.

Morley's friends and relatives and employees closed a ring. Luck failed its compact with our man. Gravity didn't reverse itself.

I thumbed a wood chip while Morley watched the man get a grip on his disappointment.

"Pull up a step, Ace," I told him.

He did, but he had the fidgets. He kept looking for his lucky exit.

I told him, "I didn't really want you. But I can't get ahold of Winger." Not that I'd tried.

"What? Who?"

"Your girlfriend. Big blond goof with no common sense, always has an angle, never tells the truth if a lie will do. Her."

"Part of that fits everybody in this thing," Morley said. "Even up on the Hill, they turned the truth to quicksilver."

"Untruths, too."

"Quicksilver lies. I like that."

"Deadly quicksilver lies." I spotted friend C. J. Carlyle. "Look who missed the slaughter at Maggie Jenn's place."

Our guest eyed us as though he was sure we were loony. Winger must have mentioned my stint in the Bledsoe. He never noticed C. J. I said, "No telling what story you got from Winger. She comes up with some tall ones. I've known her since she came to town. I don't remember her ever telling the truth if there wasn't a profit in it."

Our man didn't reply, but his skill at hiding his thoughts did not exceed his skill at tailing.

He was inept but loyal. He stayed clammed. I told him, "I want to get ahold of her mainly as a friend." That hadn't been the case the night before. A few hours had altered my perspective. "I no longer think she could tell me anything I don't know. I am sure I know a few things she doesn't. Things that could get her killed. Maybe right after they get *you* killed."

Not only did I get him thinking, I got his attention.

He didn't plan to die for love. Guys just aren't romantic anymore. He had something going with Winger—and he had a real good idea just what that was worth.

He didn't speak up, though.

"She isn't going to get those books," I told him. "Not a chance. All the guts and luck you can muster won't get that done."

The man stayed clammed. So did Morley, though he looked

like he wanted to hear more. I told him, "When you get past all the blown smoke, Winger and Cleaver are after a set of first editions of *When No Ravens Went Hungry.* Winger has the notion she can get them away from the Rainmaker." She had an even sillier notion that she could decipher the clues in them once she had them.

"The woman doesn't suffer from any lack of self-confidence."

"Trouble is, she's digging through the wrong haystack. The Rainmaker doesn't have the firsts. He could have grabbed them all, but he didn't pay attention so the one he did come up with got away."

Morley gave me a big evil dark-elf grin. "Why do I get the feeling you're going to explain everything again? How come I have the notion I ought to bet the deed to the Joy House against you?"

I snarled at our captive, "Tell Winger she's wasting her dreams. Cleaver can't lay hands on more than two books. Go on. Get out of here."

Baffled, the man went, maybe thinking he had found another angle to his luck.

Morley asked, "What was that? I set up a major operation, then you mutter some cryptic stuff at the guy and let him go."

"You fooling somebody? You know this mess has got to do with Eagle's treasure."

"Maybe. Sort of. I had a passing interest when I thought you'd stumbled onto something there in the West End."

"What you told me then was the key to the whole thing," I exaggerated. That wasn't a lie. Not really. Not exactly.

The truth was I was guessing again, playing with the known information. I had it figured out, but as Dotes hinted, I'd been wrong before. I yelled after Winger's friend, "Tell Winger what I said." To Morley, "She'll ignore me and do something dumb, but this way my conscience will be satisfied."

# 64

I expected more grief about letting Winger's guy go. But after the one snip, Morley leaned back and, apparently, never gave it a second thought.

I started to nag him. . . .

"Can it, Garrett. Once upon a time I had a notion. But I changed my mind."

I awarded him the grandfather of all raised eyebrows.

"Last night Julie wasn't there to distract me. I got to thinking about Eagle's saga. And guess what I realized? Nowhere does it say that the jerk was really rich—by our standards."

I indulged in a self-satisfied smirk. My good buddy was telling me I'd figured the angles right. "You ever wonder how Eagle murdered those slaves? If he was so blind and feeble he needed them to haul and bury his treasure, how could he get the angle on them slick enough to off them all?"

Obviously, Morley hadn't wondered. "Sometimes I do like the way your mind works, Garrett."

"Let me tell you something you maybe don't know." I hadn't known till I got it from Linda Lee, back when I was reading sagas. "Most of the sagas were composed at the instigation of the guys they're about. The *No Ravens* thing was done by Eagle's sister's grandson, partly in collaboration with the old man himself. And they started long before the business of the mocking women, the treasure, and the murdered slaves."

"I'm sure you'll get to the point eventually."

"You see it. Unless you're slower than you pretend. Say a guy is paying to have puff stories written about him. Not only will he decide what he wants put in and built up, he'll decide what gets played down or left out."

"You mean like maybe Eagle wasn't a big success just because he was treacherous and quick with a blade? Maybe he had a small natural talent as a wizard?"

"Bingo! He was accused by others, but obviously it wasn't anything major, nothing backed by formal training. He wouldn't have stayed quiet about it if he'd had a sheepskin declaring him a heavyweight ass-kicker. But he had something that helped him slide through the tight places."

"There'll be curses on the treasure, then."

"That's the way these things are done."

"There'll be ill-tempered ghosts in the neighborhood."

"What are murders for?"

The Eagle sort isn't uncommon. Usually he tries to parlay his lucky genetic draw into a big, fast score. Manipulating the fall of dice is a favorite pastime. Hobbling around on crutches after getting found out is another.

"Also, if you ask me, it couldn't be much of a treasure, even if it hasn't been found. They figured wealth different back then."

"Indeed. And here's a thought." Which he didn't bother to relate.

"Well?" I snapped.

"Just checking to see if you've taken up your partner's evil habit of reading minds. Or have started reasoning from the available evidence."

"Not me."

"Silver, Garrett. Silver. You said it. They figured wealth differently in primitive times. Silver wasn't worth much."

It was now, though. Even with the war seemingly settled and the mines solidly in Karentine hands, the silver shortage was severe. The disappearance of silver coinage threatened to strangle business.

Silver fuels most heavyweight sorcery. Lately its value has been on a par with gold. The Royal Mint has been valiant in its efforts to produce alternate means of exchange, some of which are pretty unwieldy.

Silver. An apparent opportunity to unearth an old cache would excite all sorts of greed.

"By the Devil Harry," I swore, rolling out one of my granny's favorites. "Maybe you just tripped over the real core of the thing." That might even explain why a nose-hoister like Marengo North

English would take an interest in the daughter of the notorious Maggie Jenn. It might explain why all this insanity had come to a head at this point in time.

The silver shortage wasn't likely to ease soon. Maybe never if the wrong people grabbed control of mine production.

"But what do I do about it?" I muttered.

Morley frowned my way. "Excuse me?"

"I think you're right. We have all sorts interested in Eagle's treasure because of the distorted metals market. People who wouldn't have given it a thought in normal times. Probably including my honey's daddy."

"Here comes that explanation." He stunned me by hoisting an eyebrow.

I got my breath back. "You been practicing."

"Almost forever. What about Chaz's father?"

"Call it intuition, but I'd bet your deed to the Joy House that what he really hated losing to the Rainmaker and Maggie back when was a first edition of the middle volume of *When No Ravens Went Hungry*. Which Emerald took when she ran away from home. Which she gave to Wixon and White for safekeeping, or they got it away somehow. That book is why I was hired. It's why Emerald was framed up with the black magic stuff. Cleaver knew where she was. He couldn't get to her. He thought he'd toss me in there to butt heads with the human rights guys and maybe break her loose."

I rolled right along till I took note of Morley's smug smile. He stared into infinity, listening with half an ear. "What?"

"I was right. It's another explanation. You realize your theories clash?"

"We're not talking mutually exclusive, though. We have a lot of secret motives driving people. You aren't helping me for the same reason I'm helping Chaz's pop."

"I won't argue that, though I wish I was. You made up your mind yet?"

"Huh?"

"About what to do now."

"I'm going to stroll out to this estate. See what Emerald says."

"Flashing more nerve than brains, Garrett. You're jumping into deep doodoo."

I laughed. The professional lifetaker couldn't say one word that flowed easily from naughty six-year-olds. "With my eyes open."

"You're doing a Winger on me, aren't you?"

"What?"

"You've got an angle."

"I'm just not as paranoid as you. And I know how to talk to those people. You stroke their egos and let them think you love the cracks in their pots and they'll act like you're visiting royalty."

Dotes didn't agree but didn't argue. He suggested, "Maybe you'll take Saucerhead along?"

# 65

I didn't take Saucerhead. I didn't need any help. I was just going to chat with a teenage girl.

I didn't take anybody but me because I sold myself the notion that Marengo North English was committed to an old-fashioned, rigidly fair way of doing things.

So I fooled myself. Eagerness to meet Emerald Jenn didn't take me anywhere near Marengo North English. The estate belonged to the character who had sent his pals to roust me, a fact I could have determined had I bothered to do a little homework before hitting the trail. One Elias Davenport owned The Tops. Elias Davenport thought Marengo North English was a candyass who was just pussyfooting around the human rights thing. Elias was ready to *act*.

I didn't *listen* when Slither told me who brought Emerald's invitation.

Getting onto the grounds of The Tops wasn't a problem. Managing a sit-down with Emerald was a little more trouble.

Silly me. I thought they'd let me see her, get me out of their hair, forget the whole thing. I had no idea they were out of control.

I figured it out, though.

The guys who smiled me through the manor gate shed their senses of humor when the gate chunked shut. Their eyes got mean. They kept on grinning, but the only part of the joke they wanted to share was the punchline. Kidney high.

The guys who'd visited my place ambled out of the shrubbery. Didn't look like their manners had improved.

They made me so nervous I hit them back first, shielded by the spell that put me out of focus to anybody trying to concentrate on me. Damn, that was a neat one! They hopped and flailed and swung and cussed and missed me like a bunch of drunks. Meanwhile, I was hard at work with my mystical headknocker, scattering unconscious bodies. Davenport's gardeners were going to be busy picking up fertilizer for a while.

I amazed myself. But we're all capable of amazing behavior once we're adequately motivated.

The Davenport mansion couldn't be seen from the gate. I undertook an odyssey across vast expanses of manicured lawn, maneuvering between sculpted shrubs and trees. Almost got lost in a maze created from hedges. Gawked my way through an incredible formal flower garden, thinking half the people of the Bustee slum (every one a human) could've supported themselves farming that ground.

The Davenport place was enough to kindle revolutionary fervor in a stone. Something about it shrieked contempt for every race.

I didn't march up to the door and hazard the mercies of another Ichabod. Once I spied the main house I resorted to my old recon training. I sneaked and hustled and lurked and tiptoed till I got to the rear of the house. There were plenty of people around and plenty saw me, but they were cringing characters wearing tattered Venageti military apparel. They were employed at such socially useful tasks as trimming grass with scissors. They pretended blindness. I returned the favor, didn't see their humiliation.

Never had I thought prisoners of war might be reduced to this. Not that I had any love for the Venageti. You got people chasing you through the swamps, trying to kill you, making you eat snakes and bugs to stay alive, you won't develop much sympathy if they stumble later. Still, there was an essential wrongness about their situation. And the core of it, I suspected, was that Elias Davenport wouldn't distinguish between vanquished foes and the "lower orders" of Karentines.

Elias must have had him a cushy desk mission far from the fighting back when he was serving his kingdom. Most ruling-class types get out to the killing grounds and discover that when they're cut they bleed the same as any farmboy or kid from the Bustee. "Sharp steel don't got no respect," one of my sergeants used to say, wearing a big-ass grin.

I found a back door that wasn't locked or guarded. Why

bother? Who was going to do a break-in in this loony nest? Who would dare discomfit Elias Davenport?

(The name was a cipher to me at that point.)

I don't mind folks being stinking rich. I'd like to get there someday myself, have me a little hundred-room shack on a thousand acres well stocked with hot and cold running redheads and maybe a pipeline direct from Weider's brewery. But I expect everybody to get there the same way I would: by busting their butts, not by burying some ancestor, then raising their noses.

I know. It's a simpleminded outlook. I'm a simple guy. Work as hard as I need to, look out for my friends, do a little good here and there. Try not to hurt anybody needlessly.

That house was a house of pain. You couldn't help feeling that as soon as you stepped inside. Sorrow and hurt were in its bones. The house now shaped its inhabitants as much as they shaped it.

You find houses like that, old places possessed of their own souls, good or evil, happy or sad.

This was a house possessed by disturbing silence.

It should have had its own heartbeat, like a living thing, echoing comings and goings, creaking and rattling and thumping with the slamming of distant doors. But there were no sounds. The house seemed as empty as a discarded shoe—or Maggie Jenn's place up on the Hill.

Spooky!

I started thinking trap. I mean, those guys had been ready at the gate. A minute stalling around while somebody ran to the house, supposedly for permission, then they were all over me.

Was I expected to get past them? Was I supposed to walk into . . . what?

I grinned.

Saucerhead says I think too much. Saucerhead is right. Once you commit, you'd better give up the what-ifs and soul-searchings, do your deed and scoot.

I moved into the silence carefully, wearing a renewed grin. If I ever name my jobs, this one would have to be the Case of the Burglar Who Was the Good Guy. I was sneaking into every place I came to.

Not that I wanted it that way. People made me.

# 66

I didn't have the strength to lift my eyes in search of the source of the voice that said, "You're a resourceful fellow, Mr. Garrett. And remarkably adept with a truncheon." The speaker had the nasal drawl of an old-line aristocrat, scion of a lineage dangling down from the age of empire.

I barely retained the presence to wonder what had happened. One moment I'm trying to conjure a good rationale for my breaking and entering habit, the next I'm in a cold red place of echoes, tied into a hard chair, limp as a wet towel. No mental effort, however mighty, supplied details of intervening events.

"Pay attention, Mr. Garrett. Otto."

Fingers ungently buried themselves in my hair. The helpful presumptive Otto yanked my head back so I could do my blurry-eyed mouth-breather act in full view of a guy on some kind of elevated seat. He was just a terrible silhouette against a scarlet background.

I was too dizzy to be scared. But I was hard at work trying to get control of my head so I could be. I recognized my surroundings from whispers about it by some less than sane acquaintances connected with the Call. I was in the star chamber of the Holy Vehm, the court of honor of the Call. Not being an active member, I had to assume I stood accused of being a traitor to my race. Only . . .

The way I'd heard, there were supposed to be three judges. The spook in the high seat should've been the meat in a lunatic sandwich.

I focused my whole being on my tongue. "What the hell is going on?" I don't know why I bothered after the first few words. They all came out in a language even I didn't understand. But I'm an optimist. I kept trying. "I just came here to interview Emerald Jenn." Had I been given the tongue of a dwarf while I was out?

"It takes the spell a while to wear off, lord," a voice announced from behind me.

Can a silhouette glower? This one did. "I am aware of that fact, Otah." Otah? Like in Otto pronounced backward?

I sagged again. A hearty yank on my hair helped me stay focused on the silhouette. A guy started slapping my cheeks. That helped, too.

Oh, heavens. Another guy stepped in to help the first. He was an exact copy of the other. Identical twin thugs? This concept was too bizarre. Time to wake up.

I woke up but only to find identical cretins waling on my face. My tongue had lost its skill at dwarvish. I began to render opinions in only mildly accented Karentine. And my mind raced far ahead of my laggard tongue. "Do you realize to whom you are speaking?" the silhouette demanded. The guy sounded put out.

"I did, I could've said something more specific about angles of approach and velocities of insertion."

The silhouette snapped, "Control your vulgarity, Mr. Garrett. You broke into my home."

"I was invited. To see Emerald Jenn."

"I'm afraid that won't be possible."

"She not around? Then I'd better be going."

Davenport chuckled. He must have done well at crackpot villain school because he brought it up from the pit, full of evil promise. "Nonsense, Mr. Garrett. Really." He gave me another chuckle just as good as the first. "Where are the books?"

"Huh?"

"Where are the books?"

Uh-oh. "What the hell you talking about?" I never thought anybody would ask *me*.

"Do you think me naive, Mr. Garrett?"

"I think you're a raving lunatic." Pow! Right in the chops. Chaz was going to have to do without a kiss next time we ran into each other. I guess Otto or Otah didn't agree with me.

I also thought Davenport was a damned fool. He'd made the same mistake the Rainmaker's thugs had back in the dawn of time, when they hadn't emptied my pockets. His boys were fools, too, because they hadn't bothered to check. Davenport wouldn't have risked breaking a nail touching me himself.

I had my stuff.

I just needed to get to it. Nothing to that. Once I shed the twelve nautical miles of rope cocooning me.

"Where are the books?"

"Give me a clue, Bonzo. What the hell you talking about?"

"Otto."

Pow!

As the constellations faded I suffered an idea. It wasn't the best I'd ever had. It was going to hurt.

Typical Garrett plan.

"The books, Mr. Garrett. Unaltered first editions of *When No Ravens Went Hungry*. Where are they?"

"Ah. Those books. I don't have the faintest." Could he have been behind the wrecking of Penny and Robin?

"I don't believe you."

"You want to sell me the idea a jerk as stinking rich as you needs to bust people up and kill them and steal old books over a treasure as puny as Eagle's?"

"The record says that treasure consisted entirely of silver, Mr. Garrett. To accomplish its purpose, the Call needs that silver."

I lost my focus as I intuited the nature of his interest. He meant to become the boss crackdome.

Silver was the fuel of sorcery. Black magic lurked behind the Call. Maybe the silver shortage was holding the Call back more than was any excess of reason, humanity, or common decency. Maybe the guy who brought the silver in would own the Call. And maybe whoever ran the Call would own the kingdom if the lunatics got their racist revolution rolling.

"Marengo North English tell you to find it?"

Elias Davenport said nothing for a moment, which confirmed what I'd guessed. Then, still not speaking, he came after me. He didn't exactly bound my way, though, and when he stepped into a better light I saw why. He was probably around when Eagle sneaked off with his slaves.

He had a bulging, throbbing vein in his left temple. I suggested, "Don't have a stroke, old-timer."

Shucks. He didn't. He just got *really* mad. He made a gesture that must have meant punch Garrett in the face till you turn him inside out because the twins really went to work.

Felt great when they took a break. Gave me a chance to spit the blood out and suck some air.

"Where are the missing pages, Mr. Garrett?" Davenport was shrieking now.

# 67

Yep, it sure wasn't the cleverest idea I ever had and it sure did hurt. I decided I'd strung them along long enough. "Shirt. Pocket," I gurgled. "Box. Key. To house."

Davenport was right in my face, gagging me with foul breath caused by rotten teeth. He was so eager he didn't wait to hear the story I'd rehearsed. He pawed my shirtfront, found the box I wanted him to find, snatched it, and stumbled toward his high chair. Or whatever he called it.

My ears rang like church gongs, but I still heard the buzz when the whatever in the box woke up. The twins heard it, too. "Please be careful, lord!" one squealed. "There's something wrong. . . ."

Davenport fumbled the box open. I knew when because he screamed to let me know.

If I hadn't hurt so bad I might have felt sorry for him, such was the agony and despair in his shrieking.

One of the twins squeezed my throat. "You better make it stop. . . ." He went to work on his own screams before he made his point. That aggravated his backward named brother, who stepped up to maul me, only just as he reached for me he got a big look of surprise and started howling himself.

I never did see what got them. They'd tied me up real good. I do know the uproar attracted people from elsewhere because I heard new voices rushing around asking what the hell was going on. Then some of those started screaming, too. Their shrieks left the star chamber and dwindled.

Circumstances being what they were, I couldn't do much but

sit around plotting my next move. Despite my discomfort I even fell asleep (I'm too tough to pass out) for a while. Probably a long while, though in such situations the whiles tend to stretch longer than they really are. I doubt more than a couple months passed in the outside world.

My big worry was the killer bug coming back, but when sounds disturbed my nap I learned that I had more immediate troubles.

"Got yourself in it real deep this time, Garrett." Winger strolled around me while her boyfriend watched from a distance. This was my fault. I'd made it possible for him to track me again. But I'd had my reasons. They just didn't make much sense now.

Winger wasn't suffering from any overwhelming passion to set me free, so I didn't act like I was as aware as I was. I was confident that Otto and Otah had left me looking well done. I turned loose a moan that didn't take much acting.

"Think he told them anything?" the boyfriend asked.

"What? How? He don't know anything."

The boyfriend grunted but sounded unconvinced. But he'd been on my tail closer than Winger had.

Winger grabbed my hair, lifted my head. "You in there, Garrett? Where did everybody go? Where did you send them?"

"Hon? Wrong question," the boyfriend said. He was over by the judge seats now. "Ask him what he did to them."

Winger went to check what was left of Elias Davenport. "What would do that?" She glanced back at me nervously.

"I don't think I want to find out," the boyfriend said. "There are more over there. Four, maybe five. All torn up the same way."

"What did you do, Garrett?" Winger actually seemed concerned. Like maybe she was worried I might do it again. Maybe she was getting old.

I noticed that nobody was straining to get me loose yet. Winger asked, "They have all three books, Garrett? Or just the one the girl took from her mother?"

I wondered if I could lure her close enough to bite her.

"Hon!"

I couldn't turn, but I heard them come into the chamber, at least four men. Maybe more. Things froze. Winger was at a loss for what to do. I wondered why.

"Holy hooters! Looka them gazoombies!"

The Goddamned Parrot! What the hell?

Slither moved across my field of vision. For reasons known

only to him he was lugging a military entrenching tool. He brandished it at Winger but didn't say anything.

Next thing I knew Morley was lifting my head, looking into what little could be seen of my eyes behind the swelling. "He's alive. Get him untied." A second later, Ivy and Spud went to work on the ropes holding me. They didn't seem to be in any hurry, though. "Saucerhead. Cover that door. Sarge, get that one over there. Looks like they went that way when they ran." He lifted my head again. "What happened?"

"Mimble sif cubby bunka snot!" Oh, damn! I was speaking fluent dwarvish again. Courtesy of my swollen face and tongue. But this time *I* knew what I was trying to say.

The Goddamned Parrot definitely possessed a working man's taste in femininity. And he wasn't going to let Winger get away without hearing about it.

She and her boyfriend were making sure they didn't do anything to get anybody upset.

Ivy and Spud kept fumbling and I kept trying to tell them not to be so thoughtful of the ropes, just haul out a knife and hack away. They didn't understand me, though. They kept doing it the hard way till Morley snapped, "We don't have any call to be careful of property, Narcisio. The owner is over here full of holes. A prosecuter won't worry about a damaged rope."

Saucerhead scolded Winger. Spud and Ivy tried to get me to stand. Morley faked looking like my well-being was the only thing of any interest to him. Slither wandered around muttering and waving his shovel. Sarge studied the expanse of his belly, maybe contemplating drawing a map.

Somebody somewhere shrieked in pain, somebody not there in the chamber but not real far away. Then another somebody screamed. Then we heard a furious buzzing, getting louder. My pet was coming back.

That fool Slither chuckled like this was what he'd been waiting for all his life, like he'd finally found his chance to use that killer comeback he'd thought of fourteen years ago. He told Sarge, "Better get outa the way, Ace, 'less you want it coming right through you."

Sarge took a peek at the bodies. He opted for discretion and cleared the doorway fast.

An instant later, something came through that doorway so fast it was barely a blur on a course that curved right toward me.

Slither swung his shovel. He stepped into it, got his arms extended and all his arm and shoulder strength into his swing.

*Splang!*

He dropped the blade of his tool to the floor and began cleaning it with the edge of his sole. His grin was huge. "There's how you handle them little boogers. They're fast and they're mean, but you can handle them easy if you just don't take your eye off them. I guess nobody around here must've seen them before."

Morley asked me, "Will you be able to walk?" He left Slither's strokes to the others.

I tried to ask the big guy where he'd run into those devil bugs before. Only dwarvish came out. Morley thought I was talking to him. "Good," he said. "You're tougher than you let on. Let's get out of here."

A good idea. After making sure nothing got left that would implicate any of us. Though I couldn't see how it would be possible for some of us not to be connected somehow. There were live people in the house still, and the POWs outside could be forced to reveal whatever they had seen.

Winger and her pal tried to turn sideways and thereby become invisible, but as TG Parrot reminds us occasionally, Winger in profile is hard to miss.

"We can leave you here," Morley told her. "There is ample rope now." He indicated the chrysallis I'd left behind.

"No. No. That's all right." Winger didn't want to stay. It was likely the weather would turn real nasty soon. The Call wouldn't know that Davenport had gone rogue. They would want a blood price paid.

It was all my fault. I admit it. If I'd been able to shuffle my feet faster, we might not have had to play in the rest of the game.

# 68

We never cleared the star chamber. I mean, I was heeling and toe-
ing as fast as my heels and toes would cooperate, but we just
didn't get far.

Morley howled suddenly. That startled the rest of us into
freezing. Another bug? I thought. How? . . . Dotes leapt into the
air. As he peaked out, a guy stepped into the chamber and presented his chin for kicking. He dropped like his legs had been cut
off, but a whole herd of brunos stormed in over him. He was going
to have bruises on his bruises and powdered bones if he ever came
around.

Everybody but me got into the mix-up. Ivy and Spud propped
me against a wall and jumped into it. I stood there so focused on
trying not to fall that I had little attention left for rooting for my
pals. I did try fishing something useful out of my pockets, but the
effort was too much for what meager energy I had left.

I didn't even realize who this bunch were till Mugwump appeared admid the second wave. By then things had grown too serious to be settled amicably. We had dead and bad hurt people
everywhere, mostly on the Rainmaker's side, but poor addlepate
Ivy made a wrong move and accidentally got himself stabbed in
the back about forty-five times. The Goddamned Parrot ripped the
scalp off the character responsible, a ratman so weeded up he
couldn't stop stabbing long enough to brush the bird off his head.

Slither picked Mugwump up and tossed him about forty yards,
then headed for the Rainmaker, who had just made his appearance, had spotted Saucerhead already headed his way, and was
concentrating on evading that behemoth. Then Cleaver saw Slither

coming, squealed and ducked between the two big men. I wondered where he had managed to find so many brunos stupid enough to work for him, what with everybody in TunFaire out to buy his head. Maybe he put on his girl disguise and let them think they were working for a woman.

His thugs sure were disconcerted when they recognized my friends.

Slither was altogether too determined to pay Cleaver back for Ivy and his own old grievances. He threw pieces of people right and left as he stormed after the Rainmaker, but he never quite caught up and he didn't keep an eye out behind him. I tried to yell, but my yeller was out of action. Just as he grabbed the raving runt somebody stuck a dagger in his spine. I would have cried for him if I could. Instead, I spent my last reserve to bawl, "Pwziffle pheez!"

Slither was a dead man, but he didn't let that slow him down. Nobody he could reach enjoyed the experience. He broke Morley's arm. All Morley was trying to do was get out of his way.

I tried to get my feet moving toward a doorway, but they just wouldn't cooperate. Davenport's headbusters must have given me something more than a beating. I had a bad feeling I wasn't going to make a getaway the way I had at the Bledsoe, even with Slither demolishing the unenthusiastic crowd Cleaver had brought.

I did reflect that everyone who'd ever trailed me seemed to have come to the Tops. I guess everybody thought I was about to glom the mystic trilogy.

About the time Slither wound down, one of the Rainmaker's thugs got a knife into Winger's boyfriend. She had a blood fit, jumped some guys trying to get away. They didn't make it.

I glanced around. It looked like Winger and Grange Cleaver were the only players not hurt. Saucerhead was leaning against a wall, looking pale. Sarge was down, but I couldn't tell how badly he was injured. Spud, with T. G. Parrot on his back, cussing, was on hands and knees not having much luck getting back up. Morley, despite his injury, was making sure none of Cleaver's thugs ever inconvenienced him again.

Looked to me like the whole thing had been a blood sacrifice in aid of nothing. Nobody profited and a lot of people lost big.

I was proud of myself. With a little help from my pal the wall I was making headway toward a door.

Movement took all my concentration. I had to stop to catch up on the struggle.

Things had not gone well. The floor was littered with bad guys, but the good guys had vanished. Unless you counted the Goddamned Parrot, who swooped around exercising the slime end of his vocabulary. I wanted to yell for Morley or Winger or somebody, but my yeller was out of commission.

Cleaver was still upright. So was Mugwump, mainly because he was so wide he rolled back upright whenever somebody knocked him over. Slither had had the right idea: just hurl him through the wall.

Where were my pals?

Ducking somebody else's pals?

I was moving again when Cleaver and Mugwump got to me, just as yet another gang of players plunged into this pool of insanity.

I recognized one, Belinda's specialist, Cleland Justin Carlyle. I assumed his companions were Outfit heavyweights, too.

Now I knew why my friends had disappeared.

Carlyle and his buddies had blood in their eyes. Events at the Jenn house had to be avenged. Somebody messes with syndicate guys, somebody has to pay. Didn't matter than much who.

Mugwump grabbed me by the shirtfront. He snagged Cleaver with his other hand. He hauled us both to a door. I don't know what he was thinking. I guess he was a little distressed. He chucked Cleaver through, held me a second, rasped, "Even, fella," and chucked me, too.

Into some damned hidey-hole behind the ever-loving thrones of the lunatic judges of the Call. Not through an exit.

Mugwump made a whole lot of noise negotiating with the boys from the Outfit. Then the debate ended. Utter silence filled the universe . . . unless you counted the sonofabitching Goddamned Parrot, who wouldn't shut up if you drowned him.

Everybody else had left him behind. Maybe I could work it that way, too.

Not bloody likely. Not with my luck. The gods probably had me whipped up on like this just so I couldn't shed that talking feather duster.

It was real tight in that closet. It hadn't been intended to take two people. It hadn't been intended to take two people of the sorts we were.

Well, Mugwump *had* put me close enough to Cleaver to choke him, which is where I'd wanted to be for a while. But I didn't have the strength.

The squabble between the parrot and sanity continued as I

blurted, "Get your hands off me!" I suppose prowlers nearby, possessed of sharp ears, might have heard. Might have understood, too. My diction was improving. "I don't play your game."

Cleaver giggled.

And I blushed red enough to glow in the dark. Because Cleaver's movements had nothing to do with me. Sometimes the man did dumb stuff, but only a total damnfool would make a pass with slavering cut-throats stalking around looking to chop him into beagle chow.

"Garrett, you're a wonder." That was the voice of Maggie Jenn, sizzling like a red hot poker. "Maybe I will lay hands on. If we get out of here."

"Back off!" I barked.

He backed. But his Maggie voice chuckled wickedly. Evil, evil person. A moment later, he became all business. "You have your strength back?"

"They gave me something. I'm not going to be any good for anything for a long time."

"We have to step out of here sometime. And I don't have so much as a nail file."

I said "Fooey!" which is dwarvish for "Oh, shit!" Getting out was a significant goal. Out of the closet—out of *that* closet, damn it!—out of the Tops, maybe even out of the province for a while, all seemed attractive goals. The mess here was beyond any cover-up now.

The closet door whipped open.

Light poured in. It nearly blinded me. I could barely make out the silhouette of somebody short and impatient. The Goddamn Parrot swooped past, cussing.

# 69

"Get out of there!" a hard voice snapped. I shuddered—then recognized the voice.

"Relway?"

"Yes." The little halfbreed secret policeman was curt always, impatient forever. "Move it."

"I wondered if you or the Firelord's men would turn up."

"Direheart's guy was the first one here: you. And I find you in a closet with some bimbo in yet another place where we're gonna need wagons to haul the stiffs off."

Relway's men helped us out of the closet. They were particularly solicitous of the bimbo.

I covered my surprise. They said Cleaver was a master of disguise. Here was proof. That bit of wiggling in the dark had been him rearranging his clothing and donning a black wig. He looked like the devil woman lurking around many a man's fantasies.

Relway said, "I wouldn't be here if it wasn't for who owns this place. Block kowtows to the panjas, but I . . ." He stopped before he wasted half an hour on a favorite gripe.

"Panjas. I haven't heard them called that since I was a kid."

"Call me old-fashioned. What's your story, Garrett?"

"The girl I'm looking for was supposed to be here. I got a letter supposedly from her. Wanted me to come talk. I came. Some thugs grabbed me, I woke up here drugged to the gills, tied into a chair. They started asking questions that made no sense. Then a bunch of people busted in, there was a fight, somebody cut me loose maybe figuring I was one of their guys. I headed for cover since I wasn't in any shape to help myself."

He seemed somewhat less than convinced that I was telling the whole story. Can't figure why. He showed no interest in Cleaver and didn't ask questions about known associates of one Garrett who might have been seen lurking.

I asked, "Why is Elias Davenport of interest?"

"He's a lunatic panja who makes the rest of the Call look like a social club. He's behind most of the rioting. What kind of magic did they use?"

"Magic?"

"Something made a lot of corpses. Put holes right through them. No weapon will do that."

"Didn't play no favorites, neither, Lieutenant," one of Relway's men observed. Relway grunted.

I said, "I never got a good look, but I thought it was a giant bug. Some guy took it out by whacking it with a shovel." Said guy and his guilty tool weren't lying all that far away. Relway stepped over for a moment, scowled down.

He asked, "You get what you came for?"

"Hell, no! Never saw her. I came straight here. Wherever here is—I never saw the in-between."

Again Relway's look said he lacked conviction in his acceptance of my tale. People just don't take your word anymore. "That so? I'll be busy picking up the pieces here now. I'll want to talk later. Meantime, you might report to the firelord. I have a feeling he's uncomfortable with the bloodshed that follows you."

"I can go?"

"Just don't go so far I can't find you."

"Perish the thought." I tried to recall old war buddies who lived outcountry and might put me up.

"Garrett."

I stopped oozing toward the doorway. "Yeah?"

"Unusual mix of stiffs. You happen to notice who brought them in here?" His tone and expression suggested his thoughts were on a plane not even vaguely connected to my own.

"Not really. Not that I recognized."

"Any centaurs? Anyone with an unusual accent?"

"Huh?" He really was somewhere else.

"You see anybody might have been a refugee from the Cantard?"

"Not that I knew was. Why? What's up?"

"There's cause to think the refugees have organized for their own protection. Directed by fugitive Mooncalled officers."

"Oh." Now wouldn't that be the bloom on the rose? TunFaire hiding Glory Mooncalled's survivors. "Interesting notion." Relway would give it up as soon as he identified a few bodies.

I resumed traveling. I made sure I kept a deathgrip on my bimbo. And a close watch on her free hand, lest it dart into her bosom in search of some equalizer.

Cleaver always had a fallback.

# 70

Looked like Relway had brought the secret police cavalry brigade. Must have been ten thousand horses outside the manor house. Every damned one gave up tearing up property to glare malice my way. I limped and lumbered in between police equipment carts and made my getaway before they could get organized.

They aren't so bright. If you catch them by surprise, you can get the best of them.

A guy had passed me while I was creaking up the stair from Davenport's cellar. He must have given the word I was free to go. Hardly anyone even bothered to notice me, except a few vaguely familiar guys who nodded.

Cleaver kept his lip buttoned till we were far from anybody who might listen in. "That was nice, Garrett. You could've ratted me out."

"I didn't do you any favor."

"I didn't think so, but I wanted to check." He made a feeble attempt to get away. You could almost hear him sorting options.

I glanced back. Those horses had decided to let me go. This time. They seemed nervous, preoccupied. Weird, considering this was a chance to hoof me some major grief.

Cleaver sensed my unease. "What's up?"

"Something weird here."

"You just noticed?" That in a Maggie voice.

"Besides our weirdness. Walk faster." I smelled politics. Relway was around. Relway's world didn't encompass good guys and bad. Heads there didn't get busted for profit but for the power to make people do what they were told rather than what they wanted.

I let myself become distracted. Cleaver tried to yank my arm out by the roots. He got loose. I chugged after him, running weakly. The front gate came in sight. The little villain was gaining when he went through. I kept on plugging. I could outlast him. I was used to running.

Galoop, galoop, I turned into the lane. And, behold, there was my pal Grange Cleaver, passing the time of day, ducking around and betwixt Morley, Sarge, and Spud, who were trying to surround him. Sarge and Spud seemed to be in moods as dark as mine. Morley, though, was grinning like a croc about to pounce on a not very bright wild pig.

Cleaver chopped him on the bum wing. He yelped. Cleaver pranced past and darted away.

"Hi," I puffed.

Morley said a few things. Surprised me. Spoke quite fluent profanity when he wanted. Then he added, "Your luck with girls never improves, does it! Even that kind runs away."

"He bet he could beat me back to town. I was gaining on him." There was no hope of catching Cleaver now.

"Of course you were."

"Where's Mr. Big, Mr. Garrett?" Spud rasped. The kid was putting on a show of boldly standing up to his pain.

"Damn! It's silver lining time." I glanced back at the gate. "If we're lucky, by now Relway has taken all the beak he can stand and he's twisted its fowl head off."

The kid glared daggers.

I asked Morley, "You going to be all right?"

"I'm giving up cartwheels. Listen. Somebody coming."

Turned out to be a lot of somebodies.

We faded into the woods opposite the Tops before another troop of Guards arrived, their mounts acting spooky. "Those look like regular cavalry," Morley whispered.

Did to me, too. "Relway is putting on a big show." I wondered if maybe there wasn't something to his paranoia.

"We better scat," Sarge suggested. " 'Fore they get so thick we cain't move."

Good idea.

"Not yet," Morley said.

Baffled, Sarge asked, "How come you want to hang out?"

Good question. We couldn't do ourselves any good.

"I'm waiting for Tharpe."

"He all right?" I asked.

"Was."

"How long we gonna . . . ?"

"I'll let you know, Sarge. Garrett!"

I'd begun shaking, had lost focus. I had passed beyond the immediacy of the moment and had time to reflect on what I'd lived through. And on the fact that a couple of mentally handicapped guys hadn't made it. . . . "What?"

"You're the healthiest. Go watch for Saucerhead."

I sighed. I wanted to go home. I wanted to put myself to bed and sleep a week, till the pain and guilt were gone. Then I could get shut of this life. I could see Weider, tell him I was ready to take that full-time security job. They don't drug you and torture you and kill your friends at the brewery—and you're never far from a beer.

I found me a nice spot and settled to watch the manor gate.

I'd been there just seconds when buzzing flies and an odd odor grabbed my attention. Well. Fresh horse apples. And horsehair in the bark of a nearby tree. I looked around. Leaves on the ground had been turned. I found the impression of a shod hoof smaller than that of any riding horse. The shoe style would be recognized by anyone who had served in the Cantard.

It was a centaur's shoe.

The impression wasn't clear enough to tell me which tribe, but that didn't matter. What did matter was that a centaur had been watching the manor gate from this same spot until very recently.

The ugly angles grew heavier by the minute. I wanted away. None of this stuff out here had anything to do with me and my troubles.

# 71

That misbegotten Saucerhead. He didn't bother using the gate even though there was nobody there to contest it. He came over the wall, down the lane. I noticed when a major tree branch suddenly dipped its chin in the dust. It popped when Tharpe let loose.

He was carrying somebody.

How does the man do these things? He isn't human. I limped over. "What you got?" Like I hadn't figured it out at first glance.

Her mother had told me that she looked like her only with less wear. I promise you, Maggie Jenn turned them to stone in her day. The kid made it plain why Teddy went goofy back when.

"Spotted her when we was sneaking out. I figured it wasn't right we went to all that trouble, so many folks got hurt, you didn't get a crack at what started it all."

His shirt wiggled, heaved. Something made an ugly noise. I had a bad feeling.

Saucerhead worsened it immediately. "Oh. Yeah. I brung your bird. I stuffed him in my shirt on account of he wouldn't shut up."

I brandished a fist at the sky.

The breeze in the boughs sounded like divine snickers.

Saucerhead asked, "You want the bird or the girl?"

"Looks like I got the bird already."

"To carry." He did understand, though. "The chit, she don't really want to come."

"No. And you with your sweet tongue."

She hadn't said anything yet. She didn't now but did flash me a cold look that made me glad she couldn't do what she was thinking.

"Give me the talking feather duster. I can't manage anything bigger."

"Suit yourself." Saucerhead had kept the girl on his shoulder, sack of grain style. He asked her, "You want to walk? Or do I got to keep carrying you?"

She didn't answer. Saucerhead shrugged. He hardly noticed her weight.

The others joined us, drawn by our voices. Spud fussed over the bird. Morley had rigged himself some crude splints. I gestured at the parrot. "My pal had to do me a favor."

Morley tried to chuckle. Pain got in the way. I asked, "Can you manage?"

"Just won't play bowls this week."

"Poor Julie."

"We'll work something out." He offered a glimpse of his wicked grin. "Let's roll. Before Relway realizes he's played it wrong and wants us to explain."

"What happened to Winger? Anybody see?"

Nobody had but Morley opined, "She got away. She has her own guardian angels."

"She gets Relway after her she'll need them." We walked as fast as we could with wounds and burdens, the Goddamn Parrot denouncing the whole bleeding world for all the indignities he'd suffered. Even Spud's patience became strained.

Sarge sneered, "Least it ain't blamin' everythin' on you no more, Garrett."

Morley eyed that jungle chicken like he was considering abandoning the vegetarian life-style. I told him, "Thank Saucerhead. *I* left it for Relway. They're perfect for each other."

Nobody laughed. Sourpusses.

"Was that the Rainmaker you was chasing back there?" Saucerhead asked. He spat a wad of sourgrass he'd been chewing. He remained indifferent to Emerald's weight.

"Yeah."

"That runt? Hey!" The girl was wiggling. "Knock it off." He swatted her bottom. "I always thought the Rainmaker had to be nine feet tall."

"With hooves and horns. I know. I was disappointed, too."

Morley snickered. "He sure was." I gave him a dirty look. He never let up, pain or no pain.

# 72

I lost the election. My place got picked for the human reassembly party. Morley hinted that he didn't want word of his injury getting out right away. He didn't want the wolves smelling blood before he was ready.

I bought it. He has his enemies.

I had trouble getting comfortable. My home contained too many reminders of Slither and Ivy.

"It wasn't right," I told Eleanor. "They didn't deserve it." I listened momentarily. My kitchen had become an infirmary. Saucerhead had recruited a defrocked doctor who imagined himself a crusty town character. He reeked of alcohol and hadn't stumbled against soap or a razor for weeks so I guess he qualified.

"Yeah, I know," I told Eleanor. "Life don't make sense, it ain't fair and don't ever ask the gods for dramatic unity. But I don't have to like it. Got any idea what I should do with the girl?"

Emerald was confined in Dean's room. She hadn't delivered a word yet. She wouldn't believe me when I said I wasn't on her mom's payroll.

Could be she didn't care if I wasn't. You snatch some people, they never do warm up.

Eleanor had no suggestions. I said, "I'd cut her loose if there weren't people out there who'd jump all over her." Eleanor did not disapprove. "Speaking of whom, I wonder how long it'll be before Winger turns up with one of her outstanding stories?"

I was looking forward to that.

Morley howled. There was a crash. I headed for the kitchen.

Dotes began threatening bloodshed. "Not in my kitchen!" I yelled. I stopped to check on the Dead Man.

A bug darted across his cheek, hid behind his proboscis. If Dean didn't get home soon, I was going to have to clean him up myself. Maybe I'd bring him some flowers. He used to like bouquets.

The Goddamn Parrot started yelling louder than Morley. I told the Dead Man, "You're not earning your keep."

It wasn't pretty in the kitchen. All that whimpering and whining. The doc had finished, though. He was under an inverted wine bottle, using a half pint to clear his palate. I made a face. Even ratmen shunned the stuff he was swilling. "You all going to live?"

"No thanks to that butcher," Morley snarled.

Saucerhead asked, "You ever see him act like such a baby?"

"You oversized . . . If brains were fire you couldn't burn your own house down." He jumped up on a chair and started ranting like some Holy Roller soul-scavenger.

I asked Sarge, "The doc give him something?"

Sarge shrugged. "Come on, boss. Give Doc a break. He fixed your arm. And he ain't been getting much work since they cut him loose from the Bledsoe."

No wonder he was drinking bottom of the barrel. He *was* bottom stuff himself. . . . I glanced at Saucerhead. Doc must be some relative of his new lady.

Surly but silent, Morley paid his fees. Spud didn't look much happier. I decided to get the old boy out while Dotes was feeling generous. I got hold of Doc's arm and pulled.

"You really get the boot at the Bledsoe?" Hard to imagine that as possible, yet I'd met two such in just a few days.

"I drink a bit, son."

"No."

"Steadied my hands when I was young, chopping off arms and legs down in the Cantard, couple lifetimes ago. Don't work anymore, though. Barley kills the pain now."

He stepped outside, cloaked himself in what dignity he retained, started down to the street, stumbled, fell the last two steps. On her stoop, Mrs. Cardonlos paused to glare and nod to herself. I blew her a kiss. I studied the street.

It was hard to tell, but I thought I saw a few folks who didn't ring right.

Again? Or still? I eyed Mrs. Cardonlos again. Her being out

on point might mean she expected further proof that Garrett was a peril to the neighborhood.

I shut the door, thoughtful.

I had an idea.

I headed for the kitchen. "Saucerhead, want to run an errand?" I showed him some shiny copper.

"Talked me into it, you smoothie. What?"

"Give me a minute. I need to write a letter."

# 73

At last the house was quiet. The mob was away. The Goddamn Parrot had a full crop and was sleeping. I was in my office sharing the silence with Eleanor.

Naturally, somebody came to the door.

"My answer from Chaz." Or maybe Winger, if her creative side was hot.

I was hoping she had a block.

I used the peephole.

Got it right first guess. Mr. W. Tharpe with mail.

I leaned into the gloom of the Dead Man's room. Vermin scurried. I told him, "I'm off. And she's the most beautiful blonde you never saw. Don't wait up."

He didn't wish me luck.

I left the house without so much as a passing thought about the gorgeous redhead stashed upstairs.

It was the best table in the place but still only the Joy House. You do business with a world-class sorcerer, you can be a little more comfortable doing it on familiar ground.

Conscious of their bid to go upscale, Morley and his thugs were on their best behavior. Puddle even donned a clean shirt and tucked it in.

The Firelord had dressed down. Excellent. I didn't want casual acquaintances getting nervous because of my contact with him.

He looked like a big old dock walloper.

With him dressed down and Chaz dressed up, nobody paid him much attention. Even I had trouble concentrating. "Excuse me?"

"I said I'm serving my own interests."

I recalled now. I'd thanked him for not making a show. "Oh."

"Believe it or not, there are people who might do me an injury if they caught me off my usual range."

"Really?" My gaze swerved back to Chaz. The woman had dressed to kill and was armed with her best assassin's smile.

"Hard to believe, right? Big old cuddle bear like me?" He turned to Morley, who hovered at the head of a platoon of ready servers. "I'm not real hungry tonight. I'll take half pound of roast beef rare, sides of mutton, and pork. No fruits or vegetables."

Morley went paler than a blanching vampire. He nodded sharply, once, some postmortum spasm. He fish-eyed me and my grin. His eyes were the lamps of hell. I decided not to rub it in.

I ordered one of the more palatable house specialties. Chaz followed my lead.

Morley stamped toward the kitchen, dragging Puddle, muttering orders. I wondered which neighboring establishment would subcontract Direheart's order.

I fought the chuckles as I brought the Firelord up to date.

"You let him get away?"

"I didn't let. Let wasn't part of the equation. He got. You want, I'll take you to see him after supper."

Good Old Fred raised both eyebrows. But then he came after me about the centaur sign outside The Tops. His intensity confirmed my suspicions. He'd had definite reasons for coming home from the Cantard early.

In time, I led him back to the Rainmaker. He frowned, told me, "I'm generous to a fault, Garrett. Anyone will tell you that. Especially where my little girl is concerned. But I won't let you milk this forever."

"That's good to hear. 'Cause I'm sick of the whole damned thing. I've got one bruise too many, for nothing."

Morley returned to hover in time to overhear. He lifted an eyebrow.

I continued, "I'm closing this down soon as we eat."

Morley stifled his surprise, but Chaz and her pop both blurted, "What?"

"We eat, I take you to Cleaver, my part's done. You all settle up. I'm home having a beer before I hit the sack."

Direheart started to get up. He was ready.

Morley started slide-stepping toward the kitchen. Maybe he was headed for cover.

Chaz smiled like her brain had gone north. I'd begun to wonder about her. When her dad was around, she worked at cute and dumb.

"Sit down," I said. "Morley went to a lot of trouble with your order. And Cleaver will be there when we get there." Dinner hadn't yet arrived.

Morley could've been going to check its progress, but I wouldn't have bet two dead flies on that.

Nice of him to be so predictable.

After the Tops, I didn't have a trick left. What I hadn't used I'd lost or had taken. Might have been smart to see Handsome before dinner.

Too late now.

Dinner did come. I drooled over Direheart's while I choked down mine, a kind of souffle thingee I'd had before and hadn't found myself vomiting. . . . But this time somebody clever had chopped green peppers into the mix.

Morley looked so innocent I would've strangled him if I hadn't needed him.

I told Direheart, "There's no way you're going to get your book back. It's long gone."

The man was resilient. He displayed one scant instant of surprise. "Oh?"

"Near as I can tell, Maggie Jenn's daughter swiped it from Cleaver about a year ago, brought it to TunFaire, showed it to the wrong people, had it snatched by the human rights nuts." Which was true, to that point.

The Firelord smiled, in control. "I rather doubted I'd see it again, especially considering the bloodletting following it."

"Just wanted you to understand."

"Could you recover it if I hired you to?"

"I don't want the job. There're too many people ready to kill people over it."

Direheart didn't like what he heard. It wasn't Good Old Fred who laid that evil eye on me while he wondered what I was doing.

I saw him decide that I was too damned lazy to glom the book for myself.

The Firelord ate like a little dog trying to get his fill before the big dogs come. I ate at a leisurely pace, mostly staring at Chaz, who matched me bite for bite and stared right back, all but hollering her wicked intentions.

# 74

My stride faltered a few steps into the street. There should have been more people out. Some hint must have escaped the Joy House.

If the Firelord noticed he didn't let on. Maybe he didn't. He'd been in the Cantard forever. He'd be street naive.

Chaz was uncomfortable, though. She knew an off odor when she smelled one. The dumb blonde disappeared fast.

Considering my recent experiences, I didn't think it unreasonable to be alert to the point of frayed nerves. So, naturally, nothing happened. Except . . .

Wings beat the cool evening air. I braced for the advent of some batwinged demon belched from the hell of one of TunFaire's thousand and one cults.

The mythological is manageable.

Reality can be uglier.

The Goddamn Parrot plopped onto my shoulder.

I batted at it. "That goddamn Dean! Comes home in the middle of the night, lets that monster get loose." How did the damned thing find me?

The bird remained silent as it fluttered to Chaz's shoulder. It was unnatural.

"What the matter with you, bird? Chaz, he'll probably mess on you." This adventure wasn't going the way I'd hoped.

I didn't try to confuse anybody. I took the direct route. We weren't halfway there when Chaz chirped, "The Bledsoe?"

For Morley's sake—he had to be out in the darkness somewhere—I replied, "Where else? He's used up his other hideouts. And they don't know the real him there."

Maybe. I'd begun to doubt my intuition already.

And I'd begun to doubt my good sense. Head into danger with a sorcerer? I had no cause to trust Direheart. His sort were notoriously treacherous. And my only insurance was a dark-elf with a broken wing who might not remain devoted to my well-being once he sighted the Rainmaker.

People say I think too much. No doubt. . . . Why on earth did I think Cleaver would hang around TunFaire after his latest misadventure? Why, of all places, would he hide out at the Bledsoe?

I was one rattled guy when I pushed into the Bledsoe receiving lobby. But I got my confidence back fast.

Two steps in I spotted the female half of the elderly couple I'd held captive at that ugly warehouse. She spotted me, too, and headed out at her fastest shuffle. She made her break for the stairwell I'd used to make my getaway a couple of ages ago.

I won the race. "Hello again."

Direheart joined me. "Somebody you know?"

I offered a brief synopsis.

The Firelord surveyed the area. Our arrival hadn't gone unremarked. Staff were gathering. I saw familiar, unfriendly faces. "These guys can't take a joke, Fred." He'd heard a bare bones version of my incarceration. Those guys made the mistake of thinking it was payback time.

The Firelord did one of those things that make regular folks uncomfortable when his sort are around. It involved muttering and finger-wiggling and a sudden darkness as black as a lawyer's heart! An instant after that there were pillars of fire everywhere. Each contained a staffer who objected loudly. One unfortunate goose-stepped toward us. Direheart fixed it so we needn't hear his shrieks, but the guy kept on trying. He became a human torch to light our climb.

Chaz wasn't shocked. Her daddy hadn't disillusioned her.

The old woman broke away and tried to outclimb us. She failed. We passed the ward where I'd done my damage. The fixing up had hardly begun. I wasted a tear for Ivy and Slither.

The old woman suddenly wheeled like she had some mad idea about holding us off. She was a horrible vision, illuminated by the burning man. Her terror was absolute, but so was her determination. Death was in her eyes. She was a sow bear between hunter and cub. . . .

Bingo. I knew her now, nose to nose and her eyes on fire. Take away a few decades of pain and poverty and you'd have another Maggie Jenn.

Maggie hadn't said anything about her mother's fate.

# 75

The topmost floor of the Bledsoe was reserved for those who had no truck with poverty except by way of charity. It sustained an environment those folks would deem minimally adequate while they decided the fates of TunFaire's Waldo Tharpes.

We didn't need the burning man up there. Good Old Fred let him go. He collapsed, burnt meat and charred bone. Direheart ignored the old woman. We didn't need her. I tried to shoo her away. She wouldn't go.

Chaz wasn't frayed but didn't seem to be in close touch with reality anymore, either. During my own occasional brushes with sanity I'd begun wondering if she really was the girl for me. Her good points were obvious, but something was missing. When Good Old Fred was around she could turn into a zombie.

That green-and-yellow-and-red feather duster on her shoulder didn't betray any character, either.

Weird.

It got weirder.

First, Ichabod rematerialized. Pardon me. Make that Zeke. Maybe he came back from the grave. I'd thought he'd got plenty dead on the Hill. But here he was, all skin, bones, and white hair, trying to heft a big black sword that was beyond his strength. Good Old Fred did some evil things. That sword turned on Zeke. The old boy didn't even get out a good scream.

Mugwump emerged from the shadows. That human stump was not in a good mood. (He had to be immune to disaster.) I was glad Fred was in between us.

Direheart wasn't ready for a Mugwump. Mugwump like to

broke him into kindling before he conjured a bucket of eldritch fire. Mugwump ended up blind and burning. Direheart came away dragging a foot. He couldn't use his left arm.

Chaz showed no distress. She drifted along, gorgeous and empty and handy. Her dullness worried me more and more.

The Goddamn Parrot's silence didn't help.

Then we found a sleep-fuddled Grange Cleaver trying to pull himself together. Twenty feet separated us from him. Fred went out of control. He snarled, cursed, pulled a knife, and charged. Cleaver got loose from his cot and discarded his surprise. He pulled *two* knives. Lucky he wasn't one of those gods with a bunch of arms. He threw both blades. One knicked Direheart's right shoulder.

The blow wasn't crippling, but it did put the Firelord's good arm out of commission. Sorcerers don't do well when they can't talk with their hands.

I closed in on Cleaver. Cleaver had another blade. He assumed a knifefighter's crouch, edged sideways. His eyes were hard, narrow, and serious. He didn't seem frightened.

Chaz said something. I told her, "Take care of your father. After you lock the door." The Bledsoe was crawling with guys who begrudged me my fine escape.

Direheart shook Chaz off. Calmly, he explained to the Rainmaker how he was going to feed his scum-sucking corpse to the rats. Direheart had him an awful big anger about that old burglary.

Cleaver kept his knife weaving between him and me. He edged toward an outside wall. His caution seemed to be taking him back into a corner.

I got it way too late.

Direheart tried to let me become Cleaver's focus while he got ready to sneak in some deadly spell. . . .

Cleaver lunged at me. I stumbled back. Quick as a conjurer, the Rainmaker spun and flipped his blade. It sank into Direheart's throat.

I froze. Chaz screamed. Cleaver cackled, whirled, jumped out a window. Chaz grabbed me with one hand and her father with the other, pulled like I could do something.

A born gentleman, I grabbed blond hair and pried her loose. "You're a physician. Do what you trained for."

I threw one angry glance at the old woman, let her get on with her shuffling getaway. Oh, she was ready to go now. I went after Cleaver.

I'm not fond of heights—especially if Mrs. Garrett's boy might conceivably fall therefrom. I paused to eyeball the scaffolding below me.

Sneering laughter electrified me. I dropped the eight feet to the highest level the workmen had reached. I made a lucky grab and didn't plunge sixty feet to the cobblestones, where shadows darted. I was too far up to recognize anybody—not to mention I didn't consider trying.

The Goddamn Parrot swooped past, dove through the scaffolding. He zig-zagged like a bat, let out one serious squawk as he ripped past Cleaver. The Rainmaker cursed. Softly.

I concentrated on not achieving the unexpected experience of flight. All my hands grabbed anything convenient. All my feet assiduously maintained contact with whatever lay beneath them. I stormed slowly toward the Goddamn Parrot's noxious racket.

Cleaver cursed again. He'd looked down into a dark future. Big trouble was waiting.

I checked the street, too. Its shadows harbored folks who wanted to talk to the Rainmaker up close and personal. They must have picked up a clue or two via denizens of the Joy House.

Instead of heading down, Cleaver fled around the Bledsoe. Through one open window I spied Outfit hardcases on the prowl. Belinda must have had a crew on standby.

I don't quite get Morley's relationship with those people. He's no made man himself. He does them more favors than seems right.

The Goddamn Parrot kept beaking news of Cleaver's progress. I really wondered about that bird. This was out of character. His natural style would be to betray me, instead.

The thugs below couldn't see us. They tried to track the bird, too.

That hunk of spoiled hawk bait blew the big one. Cleaver set an ambush. He let me slink right into it.

I was twice Cleaver's weight and twice Cleaver's strength and that saved me a three-story decline in fortunes. He threw himself at me. I grabbed some scaffold and absorbed the impact. I tried to glom onto him while I was at it but didn't do real well.

He ricocheted off me, banged into an upright, bounced back toward the stone face of the Bledsoe, let loose one whimper of outrage, dropped into the gap between scaffolding and building. He scratched and grabbed and banged around as he fell but didn't verbalize at all.

I followed more cautiously. The Goddamn Parrot flapped around me but managed to keep his big damned beak shut. I caught up.

Cleaver had broken his fall and dragged himself onto planking maybe ten feet off the ground. His breathing was shallow and rapid. He wasn't in good shape. But he bit down on his pain.

The vinegar was out of him, but I moved carefully anyway. A guy has the Rainmaker's rep, you're careful with him even after he's dead.

# 76

I dropped to one knee. A hand seized mine. I jerked away for an instant, startled. That hand was warm and soft.

"We could have had . . . something. But you're . . . too damned dumb . . . Garrett. And stubborn."

I don't know about stubborn, but I was doing dumb pretty good. I didn't get it right away.

Cleaver was fading. Didn't seem right, considering his record. A long, agonizing cancer was more in order, not this just kind of drifting off into oblivion.

My hands were trapped. I didn't try hard to pull away. I had empathy enough to guess what was happening in Cleaver's mind. Though broken, he pulled himself toward me, closer, closer . . .

Realization came slowly, sort of sideways, without generating much shock. This creature desperately grasping at one final moment of human contact wasn't male at all.

I held her. I murmured, "Yes, love," when she returned to her notion that we might have had something remarkable.

I'd been wrong from the beginning. But so had all TunFaire. Past and present, high and low, we'd all seen only what society had conditioned us to see. And in her madness, she had exploited that blindness.

There never was any nasty little villain named Grange Cleaver. Not ever. Never.

I shed a tear myself.

You had to if you encompassed any humanity, recognizing the enduring hell necessary to create a Grange Cleaver.

You could weep for the pain of the child while knowing you had to destroy the monster it had become.

# 77

I lost Chaz at the Bledsoe. I don't know why. Maybe, emotionally, she chose to blame me for what had happened to her father.

Her medical skills hadn't been adequate.

Whatever the reason, the magic failed that night.

It was not one of my better nights. I blew the rest of it retailing explanations. Seemed anyone who'd ever heard of me or Grange Cleaver wanted all the dope. I was actually pleased when Relway materialized.

He was a magic man was Relway. People vanished in droves.

"It's all straightened out now, Garrett," Colonel Block told me. I was visiting him again. After having been allowed another ten hours of cell time to ripen. I'd had to do my time with the Goddamn Parrot, too. "Weren't nearly so many bodies this time." He looked at me expectantly.

I tried not to disappoint him but kept it short and got out. He wasn't much interested. Didn't even ask much about the Tops. He was preoccupied with the racial strife.

I headed for home. I didn't manage to leave the bird of doom behind. For no obvious reason, that breathing feather duster didn't have much to say. Even while we'd been locked up he'd held it down most of the time.

Maybe he was sick. Maybe he had some terminal bird disease. I couldn't be that lucky.

\* \* \*

Dean didn't respond when I pounded on my front door. Irked, I used my key, went in and stomped around hollering and cussing till I was convinced the old boy wasn't there after all. There was no sign he'd come back.

Huh? How'd the bird get loose?

Add another puzzle. Why hadn't Emerald taken advantage of my extended absence? The kitchen suggested that she had visited several times and was less than fanatical about order and cleanliness. But she hadn't tried to bust out.

Strange.

Stranger still, T. G. Parrot went to his perch without a squawk.

That was more than strange. It was suspicious.

"Justina? I need to tell you something." It wasn't going to be easy.

She was seated on Dean's bed. She looked at me without emotion but with what seemed too-knowing eyes.

Straight ahead seemed the best way. I told her.

She continued to look at me, apparently unsurprised.

But she did love her mother—despite knowing the truth about Maggie Jenn and Grange Cleaver. She broke.

I held her while the tears flowed. She accepted that but nothing more and never said a word, even while I led her to the front door and told her she was free to go.

"Chip off the old blockhead," I muttered, a little put out, as I watched her fade into the crowds. "Oh, but she was beautiful, though."

I was in no way pleased with the case. I don't like unhappy endings even though they're the most common kind. And I wasn't certain that much had been settled or wrapped up.

# 78

I locked myself in. I didn't answer the door. I just used the peep-hole whenever some sociopath compulsively exercised his knuck-les. I argued with the Goddamn Parrot. That squawking squab was slower than normal but nailed me with the occasional zinger.

Suspiciouser and suspiciouser.

Ever bold in the face of despair, I sent a letter up the Hill. Never got so much as a "Drop dead!" back.

And I'd just about decided Chaz was the lady for me. Oh, well. Live and learn.

I asked Eleanor, "Don't know what she's missing, does she?" That killed the ache, boy.

I swear Eleanor sneered. I could about hear her whisper, "Maybe she does."

I got the distinct feeling Eleanor thought it was time I stopped being stubborn about not apologizing to Tinnie Tate for whatever it was I didn't know I did, or maybe never did.

"Or I could look Maya up. She looked good the other night. And she's got her head on straight." Eleanor's smile threatened to become a grin.

I broke training once, allowed one special visitor inside. You couldn't refuse the kingpin of crime. Belinda Contague spent an enigmatic half hour at my kitchen table. I didn't disabuse her of her notion that, with the invaluable assistance of my acquaintance Morley Dotes, I'd engineered the fall of Grange Cleaver just for her. I guess for old time's sake.

She's one spooky black widow of a gal, bones of ice. Probably a real good idea she decided we should stay "just friends." Anything else could turn fatal.

Belinda expressed herself the one way she knew well, learned at daddy Chodo's knee. She gave me a little sack of gold. I passed it quickly into the Dead Man's care.

The Rainmaker business had been profitable, anyway.

Days slipped away. I sneaked out on several little errands, each time discovering that I still had one watcher on me. Becky Frierka was determined to collect her dinner. I saw no evidence her mother discouraged her from dating older men.

Mostly I kept it up with the bird and Eleanor, then went to reading with a frown that threatened permanent headache. I began to think Dean wasn't coming home and Winger might actually have the sense to stay away from me. Or maybe her luck had run out.

"It's gotten awful damned quiet," I told Eleanor. "Kind of like in those stories where some dope says, 'It's *too* quiet. . . .' "

Someone knocked.

Starved for real conversation, I scurried toward the door. Hell, a night out with Becky didn't sound that bad anymore.

I peeked. "Well!" Things were looking up. I yanked the door open. "Linda Lee Luther. You lovely thing. I was just thinking about you."

She smiled uncertainly.

I grinned. "I've got something for you."

"I'll bet you do."

"You're way too young and beautiful to be so cynical."

"Whose fault is that?"

"Can't possibly be mine. Come on in here. Got a story to tell you."

Linda Lee came in but made sure that I saw she still had her cynical face on. And that after she'd come all the way down to see me.

The Goddamn Parrot let out a whoop. "Hey, mama! Shake it up!"

"Stifle it, catfood." I closed the door to the small front room. "You interested in a new pet?" So happened I knew she had a cat.

"If I wanted one that talks, I'd pick up a sailor."

"Marines are way more interesting." I set us up in the kitchen, which was clean. Life had been that slow. I poured Linda Lee a brandy. She nursed that while I talked about the Rainmaker business.

One of Linda Lee's less blatant charms is her ability to listen. She doesn't interrupt and she does pay attention. She didn't comment until I paused to freshen my beer and pour her a dribble more brandy. Then she cut right to it. "What did you find when you went back?"

"Wreckage. The Guard tore the Tops up. Sending a message to the Call. Most of the Venageti were still there. They didn't know where to run. Guys like them could turn out to be another big headache. Come on to my office."

She gave me a kind of puzzled look, like my office was the last place she expected to be lured. She stretched like a cat as she left her chair. Woo!

I got my breathing under control. "Plop it into that chair." I squeezed around and into mine, dropped a hand down under my desk, dragged out one of those masterpieces that had been giving me wrinkles. "Look at this."

"Oh, Garrett!" She squealed. She bounced up and down. She squealed some more, jiggling deliciously all the while. "You found it!" She dashed around the desk and hopped into my lap. "You great big wonderful hero."

Who am I to complain? I had an idiot bird in the next room covering that. He went to carrying on like he was being murdered. I smirked and surrendered to Linda Lee's excitement.

When she paused to catch her breath, I leaned down and coaxed another book out of hiding. "Apparently nobody who knew those were there survived the excitement at the Tops. None of the interested parties thought to check, either." At least they hadn't before the notion came to me.

"This is a true first, too! I've never seen a *Raging Blades* before. Where did they find it?"

"It's the book Emerald stole from her mother. Her mother stole it from Firelord Direheart. No telling who he stole it from. The boys at Wixon and White got it away from Emerald somehow, but she complained to her pals in the Call. That wasn't real bright, but how many kids her age, spoiled the way she was, have a full ration of sense?"

Linda Lee snuggled down and opened the book.

"Wish you'd treat me that tenderly," I observed.

"Oh, no. I'm not going to be tender at all." She purred and turned a page.

I stretched down and retrieved the third book of the trilogy.

"*The Battle-Storm!* Garrett! Nobody's had a complete set for three hundred years." She let *Raging Blades* fall into her lap and grabbed *Battle-Storm*. I leaned back, relaxed, felt smug.

I got so relaxed I almost dozed off while Linda Lee sighed over her treasures.

A squeal of fury ripped me out of a reverie wherein I stood idly by while my old pal Winger enjoyed her just deserts. "What?" Silly me, for a second I thought she'd stumbled onto the secret of Eagle's treasure.

"This is a forgery! Garrett, look at this page. It shows a watermark that didn't appear till two centuries after Eagle's sagas were recorded." She seemed totally deflated.

"You were floating a yard off the floor when you only thought you had your *Steel-Game* back. Now you've got two originals and a copy. . . ."

"Grrr! Yeah, you're right. But it really makes me mad. It isn't really all a copy or forgery. Part is original. You see what they did? They took out some pages and replaced them with forgeries."

I showed more interest then. I leaned over. She was examining the book I'd seen at Wixon and White, not, as I'd expected, *The Battle-Storm*. "Emerald's book. Any idea how long ago it was altered?"

"The paper is old. It's just not as old as it ought to be. And if you look really close at the ink, you can see it isn't nearly as faded as it should be."

"Never mind the paper, love. I wanted old paper I'd steal an old book somewhere and scrape some pages down." Which is what master forgers do when a document has to look old.

"Oh. You're right." She studied the book some more. "I'd guess it was done quite recently. Somebody dismantled it, then put it back together with the new pages but couldn't match the original thread. This looks like a standard bindery thread like what we use at the library." She got after the other two books. "Damn! This *Battle-Storm* isn't even a first. It's early, though. Maybe a student's copy of the Weisdal Illumination. And look! Somebody's tampered with *Steel-Game,* too. This whole signature is a replacement. They're going to hang me out, Garrett. This book was all right before it was stolen."

Interesting. It occurred to me to wonder if Emerald Jenn wasn't just as clever and conniving as the woman who'd borne her. "You do have a copy, though. Don't you? Squirreled away, just in case?"

Linda Lee scowled. "Maybe."

"Of course you do. It might be interesting to compare texts."

Up front the Goddamn Parrot started having a fit. Sounded like he was laughing.

Linda Lee hugged a book to her chest with one hand, gulped the rest of her brandy. "I need you to walk me back to the library."

"Right now?" Boy, don't whimper.

"There's nobody there." She took a big key out of a pocket in her skirt. "They're gone for the weekend."

My white knight side took over. "Of course I'll go with you. People kill people because of these books."

I locked my door, pranced down to the street. I waved to Mrs. Cardonlos. She hoisted her nose so fast she threw her neck out of joint. Then I stuck my tongue out at my own house.

I was sure the gesture wasn't wasted.

# 79

Two days passed. I was distinctly distracted when I headed home. I entertained only one non-nostalgic thought during the walk home. Was I the only sucker who hadn't known about the tampering with the books? Was that why nobody raced to the Tops after the Guard cleared out?

My door opened as I dug for my key. An old guy about as impressive as Ivy glared out at me. "About time you made an appearance. You turned this place into a shambles. The cupboards are bare. You didn't leave me a groat to shop with."

Beyond him, the Goddamn Parrot went to work on me, too.

"I had a feeling my luck wouldn't last."

"What?"

"You didn't stay lost." He'd aged, it seemed. Must have been rough work, keeping reality from setting in on the young couple. "You know where the money is."

He didn't like getting close to the Dead Man so he'd moped around hoping to con me. He didn't say so, though. "And you let someone use my bed."

"Couple of someones. And a good thing you took your time getting back. Your heart couldn't have taken being around the last one. You going to let me get into my own house? It's too early to be out here." My master plan included half a dozen hours in my own bed. I'd had to vacate the library at that worm-catcher time of day when only abnormals like Dean are awake.

"Mr. Tharpe is here."

"Saucerhead? Now?" Tharpe's attitude is more flexible than

mine, but he isn't fond of getting out while there's still dew in the shade.

"He arrived moments ago. Inasmuch as you were expected shortly, I settled him in the kitchen with a cup of tea." Not to mention with most of the meager supplies I'd laid in recently, I discovered.

Saucerhead seldom lets a polite refusal get between him and a free meal.

I settled myself. Dean poured tea. I asked Tharpe, "What gives?"

"Message from Winger."

"Really?"

"She needs some help." He had trouble keeping a straight face.

"I can't argue with that. What's her problem? And why should I give a rat's whisker?"

Tharpe snickered. "Her problem is she needs somebody to bail her out of the Al-Khar. Seems she got caught digging around inside a certain country home and couldn't con the Guard into believing that she lived there. In fact, they were on the lookout for a big blonde who might be able to tell them something about what had happened there."

"I love it. But how did you find out? You sound like Colonel Block."

"Block came around to Morley's place on account of he couldn't find you here."

"Why'd he want me?" I could guess. Some little question about events at the Tops.

"He said on account of Winger claimed you as her next of kin when they asked who to notify she was inside so she could make bail or get bribe money for the turnkeys or whatever."

"I see." Boy did I believe that.

"And I went up and seen her. She already got into it with some screw thought he ought to collect special favors. Broke his arm."

"They charged her with anything?"

Tharpe shook his head. "Relway's just trying to squeeze her about what went down. But you know Winger. She's gonna be stubborn."

"I know Winger. She's lucky Relway's in a good mood these days. Things are going his way." Bad weather and ferocious behavior by the Guard and secret police had calmed the riots. For now.

There would be more. There had been no good news from the Cantard, like a resumption of the fighting.

"Yeah, I told her. Probably won't even beat her much."

"Then let her rot. No. Wait. Here. Run a message for me. Ask Block if he'll warn me before he turns her loose."

Saucerhead took my money. "How come?"

"So I can meet her coming out and tell her what a hard time I had getting her cut loose."

"You're wicked, Garrett."

"It's the company I keep. Been learning from a master." I jerked a thumb toward the Dead Man's room.

# 80

I shut the door behind Tharpe, locked up, strode to the Dead Man's door. I leaned inside. He looked the same: big and ugly. "I did all right for a guy whose help is so bone lazy. . . ."

*I kept close watch. You were less at risk than you imagine.* He puts thoughts directly into your head.

"After you started siccing the bird on me, maybe. By then I'd been through the hairiest part."

*You understand that the Winger creature knew the Jenn woman and Cleaver were one, right from the start?*

"Sure. And she knew you were snoring or she'd never have came in here to set her hook. She still has an angle. She thinks. Only Emerald was ahead of everybody, probably from before she ever left home."

*Indeed. The female of your species, if at all presentable, is capable of manipulating the brightest of you.*

"If that's her scheme. The Belindas and Maggies and Emeralds aren't that common, though. Luckily."

*Far be it from me to note your eagerness to be suborned by such females.*

"Yeah. But not far enough." In the other room the Goddamn Parrot started preaching what the Dead Man was thinking with one of his other minds. "Got to do something about that thing."

Somebody knocked. *Once more you have the opportunity to keep your word.*

Becky Frierka. And her mother, of course.

"Why should I be the unique truth-telling character in this part of town?"

As I went to the door the Dead Man sent, *The quest for Eagle's hoard is vain. The burial cairn lay on a slope overlooking Pjesemberdal fjord. That entire mountainside collapsed into the fjord during an earthquake three centuries before my mishap.*

"Really?" If anyone around today would know, he would. "Might have been handy to know that before. When you were watching so close."

*Any adventurer who deciphers the sagas discovers the truth eventually. But so much blood gets spilled that the guilty dare not give warning to the world.* He loaded that thought up with a cargo of amusement at human antics. But something unrelated leaked through, too. He was worried about the political climate. He had a stake in a tolerant TunFaire.

Details plucked from my mind didn't reassure him.

I pasted on my boyish grin and got to work. It took an effort to keep smiling. Becky's mother doesn't have a husband. She's actively screening candidates.

Couldn't have been a better time for my parrot to go berserk, for my houseman to show his mean streak, for my partner to be himself. Naturally, nobody cooperated.

I am nothing if not valiant in my efforts to do the right thing. Becky got her date, exactly according to terms.

# 81

Playmate was with me, trying to look fierce as a favor. So were Saucerhead and Winger, whom we'd collected from jail. Two weeks inside hadn't taught her a thing, which is why I had recruited my friends. I needed help getting Winger to go in the direction I wanted.

A couple weeks can make a big difference in the Safety Zone. Morley's place had a new name: the Palms. Scraggly palms in pots stood out front, already wilting in TunFaire's chunky city air. Street lamps had appeared. Elf-breed lads decked out like Venageti colonels stood by to handle horses and coaches, despite the time of day.

Playmate observed, "I don't think I'll feel comfortable around here anymore."

"That's the point," Tharpe said. "Dotes has got him some high-tone ambitions all of a sudden. No place here for the likes of us now."

I glanced at Winger. Still sulking, she didn't offer an opinion.

The interior of the Joy House had been redecorated to fake the inside of a lunatic's idea of some tropical shack. I've been to the islands. It didn't work. After Morley bustled us upstairs, so we wouldn't frighten the customers if any turned up, I told him, "There aren't enough bugs, old buddy."

"What? Bugs?"

"Tropical places got bugs. Bugs big enough you got to fight them for table scraps. Flies and mosquitos that'll hang you up in a tree for later. And lots of them."

"You can overdo atmosphere, Garrett."

"Bugs don't sell to the Hill," Saucerhead guessed.

Dotes scowled. Our presence made him uncomfortable. I hate it when people social climb. He asked, "What do you want?"

"Just a couple wraps on the Rainmaker thing. Winger's out, which you probably noticed. And all the trilogy books are accounted for, only somebody mutilated them. Which won't do them any good." And I briefed him on what the Dead Man had told me. Given their natures and acquaintances, these four would get the word spread. And people would stop following me around.

I'd begun to accumulate watchers again. I guessed the Venageti at the Tops had mentioned my visit to someone who cared.

Pained, Morley asked, "Seen the girl?"

"Vanished without a trace. Gone treasure hunting, I presume." I hadn't tried to find her.

"That's it?" He was puzzled. He didn't see my angle.

I didn't clue him in. "That's it."

"Then I have to rush you. I have a million things that need doing before our reopening tonight. One thing before you go, though. A favor I need desperately."

"You're starting to talk like those ferocious pirates. What?"

He faked hurt. "Friends are always welcome at the Palms. But we have to present a refined image. If you could dress a little more . . ."

I got no chance to respond because Winger unloaded first. "You guys ever stick a foot in a fatter load of camel shit? Can you believe this seeping sack of slime? You half-breed runt, I know who you are."

The lady is articulate in her own special way.

Winger and I came to a meeting of the minds, more or less. Playmate and Tharpe took off. I straggled homeward. Winger tagged along. She didn't seem eager to put distance between us anymore. "Garrett, it true, what you said about Eagle's treasure?"

"Absolutely. Came straight from the Dead Man."

She didn't want to believe me but decided she had no choice. I was too damned dumb straight-arrow. "That thing awake again?"

"*And* Dean came home. I'm back to being errand boy in my own house."

She snapped her fingers. "Shucks. Been a long dry spell, too."

I shook my head. This is where we started. "You never fail to surprise me, Winger."

"Huh?" She grabbed my arm, pulled me out of the way as a

flight of pixies, buzzing like angry hornets, harried several centaur kids they'd caught stealing. Idly, I noted what looked like one of Relway's spooks trailing the action.

"Last time you told me that, I found out you had a boyfriend you never mentioned to anybody and he can follow me around like he's got me on a leash."

She didn't lie straight up. "Hightower? Wouldn't exactly call him a boyfriend. . . ."

"No. More like a sucker who thought he was. And got dead for his trouble."

"Hey! Don't you go climbing on your high horse with me! I seen you with your pants down."

"I'm just reminding you that people you care about get hurt, too, Winger. Lies can kill. If you have to lie to your friends and lovers to get where you want to go, maybe you'd better stop and give a good hard think about whether this is the road you have to follow."

"Stick it in your do-good ear, Garrett. I got to live with me. You don't." Which was about as close to an admission of error or offer of apology as anyone was likely to get out of Winger.

"When you came down here fishing me in, you knew Maggie Jenn was the Rainmaker. You figured you could work an angle, you being the only one outside her crowd that knew. I won't forget you trying to do that to me."

Winger never apologizes in any of the customary ways. "I found out by accident. Pure dumb luck. And nobody but her kid really knew for sure. Her old lady and Mugwump and a few others maybe had all the facts right there in their faces, but they didn't want to believe it. . . . What the hell am I doing? It's over. Done. We got to move on. All the crap that's going on around town now, this racist bullshit, there's got to be lots of opportunities. But I'll check it out later. Why don't you come on over to my place?"

A temptation, if only to find out where she lived. But I shook my head. "Not this time, Winger." The Dead Man wanted me to bring him up to date on Glory Mooncalled, events in the Cantard, and recent events in general, real soon now. I knew because he had the Goddamn Parrot following me around, telling me all about whatever notions happened to be bubbling through his feeble minds.

My worst nightmare had come true. I couldn't get away from him even when I was away from him.

Also, I needed to consult Eleanor on potential career changes.

I had some ideas. At their root were the willies I got every time I thought about being caught inside the Bledsoe cuckoo ward.

If I had planned this thing out right, I would have been born rich and would have lived out a useless life as a wastrel playboy.

Doing that life somewhere besides TunFaire probably would have been a good idea, too.

Still, life won't be completely awful as long as I'm somewhere where they keep brewing beer.

# Petty Pewter Gods

This one is for Justin, aka Monkey Boy, Woozle, Boodle, and so forth. Without you this would have been completed months earlier. Love, Dad.

# 1

I greeted the morning the only way that makes sense. I groaned. I groaned some more as I pried me off the sheet. Several thousand maniacs were raising hell out in the street. I muttered dreadful threats, dropped my feet into the abyss beside my bed. My threats didn't scare up any peace.

Pain blazed from my right temple to my left, ricocheted, clattered around inside my skull. I must have had a great time. I told me, "You got to quit drinking that cheap beer."

The guy jacking his jaw was yakking way too loud. I clapped a hand over his mouth. He shut up. I used my other hand to open a curtain a peek. I had some morning-mad notion that by looking I could grab a clue about all that racket.

A club of sunshine whacked me right between the eyes. Like to laid me out. Gah! An ill omen for sure. These bright days are never kind. Everybody I ran into would be just like the weather: warm and sunny. Argh! I was in the mood for low overcast and light drizzle, maybe with a frigid south wind.

I peeled layers of fried skin off my eyeballs, took another look. Where there is life there is hope.

"Well." Across Macunado, standing out like she might be the source of the brightness, was a trim piece of work who would have no trouble making the short list for girl of my dreams. She looked right at me, like she knew I was watching. My toes curled. Wow!

I didn't notice the human rights guys and their ugly banners shoving dwarves and elves aside as they chased a gang of centaur refugees, flinging bricks and stones. I didn't chuckle when some fool bounced a rock off a fourteen-foot troll's beak and took up a brief career as a human club. Just another day of political dialogue in my hometown.

I was focused. Maybe I was in love. Again.

She had all the right stuff in all the right places in absolutely perfect proportion. She was a small thing, not a rat's whisker over five feet, and of the redheaded tribe. I would have bet the deed that she had green eyes. I drooled. I wondered what madness was loose upon the earth, that all those lunatics down there weren't dropping their sticks and stones and surrounding her, panting gales of garlicky breath.

"Whoa, Garrett," I muttered, after the curtain slipped from numb fingers and broke the crackling magic connecting my eyes with hers. "Where have we heard all this before?" Female is my weakness. Pretty redhead will do me in every time.

Oh, but what a delicious failing!

I wrestled with my clothes for a minute before daring another look. She was gone. Where she had stood, a drunken one-armed war veteran was trying to assault an even drunker centaur. The centaur was getting the best of it because he had more legs to keep him off the ground.

That troll must have been in a bad mood anyway. He bellowed his intention of clearing the street of anyone who didn't have green skin. He had a good work ethic, too.

Down the way Mrs. Cardonlos and her broom vigorously defended the stoop of her rooming house from fugitives. How would she blame this on me? I was confident that she could find a way. Too bad she couldn't saddle that broom and fly away.

Some dreams arrive stillborn. There wasn't a sign of that redhead anywhere.

But nightmares always come true.

Instead of young and gorgeous I spied old and homely and not even female.

Old Dean, my resident cook, housekeeper, and professional nag, was home from his journey north to make sure one of his numerous ugly duckling nieces didn't weasel out of her wedding plans. He was standing at the foot of the front steps. He stared up at the house with pinch-lip disapproval.

I shambled toward the stairs. Somebody had to let him in.

Dean's knock set the Goddamn Parrot to squawking obscenities.

*Garrett!* Oh, boy. That was my sidekick, the Dead Man, only recently awakened for the first time in months. He had a lot of vinegar stored up. *Kindly set aside your sensual maunderings and still that horrible thumping.*

It was, for sure, going to be one of those days.

# 2

T. G. Parrot—whose given name is Mr. Big—started whooping as I worked the latch. "Help! Oh, please, Mister, don't hurt me no more." He sounded like a terrified child. He thought it was great fun trying to get me lynched.

Mr. Big was a practical joke that had been played upon me by my alleged friend Morley Dotes, who must have spent years teaching that bird bad manners and worse language.

Dean wrinkled his nose as he pushed inside. "Is that *thing* still here? And what *is* that dreadful odor?"

By "thing" he meant the bird. I pretended to misunderstand. "He was too heavy for me to move by myself." The Dead Man goes somewhat over four hundred pounds. "Maybe he's getting ripe. You better work on his room first thing." Dean hates the Dead Man's room. He doesn't like being in the presence of a corpse, possibly because that rubs his nose in his own mortality.

*Your sense of humor has putrefied.*

Dean, of course, didn't receive the Dead Man's mind message. Wouldn't have been fun for His Nibs if he caused a reaction that the old man understood.

I didn't pay him any mind. That always irks him. I was preoccupied, anyway. Still looking outside, I noticed that the redhead was back, watching from across the street. Our gazes met. That energy crackled. Down the block my favorite neighbor, the widow Cardonlos, spotted my open doorway. She pointed, jabbered, probably telling one of her tenants that I was the linchpin of all the evils plaguing our street.

Her mind would not stretch any farther.

Other than making herself a boil on the bottom of my happiness, she did not much matter in my life.

Dean expelled one of his mighty, put-upon sighs. He dropped his duffel, stood there shaking his head. He wasn't three steps inside, but he had to assure me that his absence had been a domestic disaster. As had been inevitable.

I looked for the girl again. Redheads are trouble. Always. But that kind of trouble looked real appetizing.

Gone again, damn it. A mob of street rowdies had come between us, pursuing the ethnic debate with club and brickbat. Enterprising folk of several tribes tagged along, hawking sausages and sweetmeats and souvenirs to the participants. Never is there an event so wild, so dire or disgusting but what some entrepreneur can create collectible memorabilia.

Story of my life. Find my true love and lose her in a matter of minutes, while being tormented by a hangover and a carping housekeeper.

*What were you gawking at?*

"Huh?" You don't usually get much expression out of the Dead Man's mind messages. This time he seemed puzzled. "A girl." He ought to be able to figure that just because I was drooling.

More puzzled. *I see nothing but chaos.*

Neither did I, now. "That's the way it is these days. You didn't spend all your time napping, you'd know we're getting into the hell times." Damn! Me and my mouth. Now he would insist I spend another day bringing him up to date. A lot had been happening.

The Goddamn Parrot was squawking with a vengeance now. He had discovered that I had not put out birdseed before I'd hit the sack. Hell, I'd barely remembered to lock the door. I'd only just survived a near terminal case of redheaditis complicated by psychopathic killer transvestites and I had wanted to unwind.

Dean got to the kitchen before I could head him off. His howl stilled hearts for miles. Mr. Big squawked in fear. The Dead Man offered some mind racket meant as commiseration. Fetishist household order is not a priority with him, either.

Dean had started through the kitchen doorway. He froze there. He posed, the most put-upon old boy who ever lived. "*Mister* Garrett. Will you please come here and explain?"

"Well, I did kind of get behind on the dishes." I headed for the stairs. He wanted to give me a few choice pieces of advice, but the words all tried to come out at once. He began shaking in frustration when he could not get them untangled. I made my escape.

Sort of. I headed for his room upstairs, which I had not gotten straightened up after having stashed a fugitive girl there while he was away. He would get really excited if he saw the mess she had left.

I could feel the Dead Man's thoughts riding with me, amused, looking forward to the explosion. To him the world is one grand, enduring passion play, going on without end. He is settled comfortably in the wings enjoying it at little risk because he has been safely dead for four hundred years already.

Somebody clever and really fast stuck a knife into him way back then. That or some ordinary dumbbell caught him taking one of his naps. Did Loghyr take those long naps when they were alive? I'd never seen a living Loghyr. I knew nobody who had, save the Dead Man himself. He hadn't been born dead. Hell, I've only ever run into one other dead Loghyr.

A rare breed, they. And major pains in the social fundament, generally, which probably has something to do with why they are so rare.

*One is compelled to support your earlier remark concerning the quality of the beer you imbibe. Those cheap barley squeezings have poisoned your mind with premature bitterness and cynicism.*

"That's on account of my environment and evil companions. How come you're following me around the house?"

I hurled things around in Dean's room as fast as I could, but I knew I was fighting another losing battle.

Maybe the stress of the kitchen mess would burst his heart before he decided to put his stuff away.

It was unusual for the Dead Man to extend himself beyond the walls of his room, though he could reach a long way when he wanted. He claims he limits himself out of respect for others' privacy. I have never believed a thought of that. Laziness has got to be involved somewhere.

I am sure that even were he alive he would not move an ounce or an inch out of his room for years at a time. My guess is he died because it would have been too much trouble to get out of the way of the assassin.

*Not only bitter and cynical, but uncharitable.*

"You didn't answer the question."

*The deterioration has progressed faster than I anticipated. The city is at the brink. I have wakened to imminent chaos.*

"Yeah. We're beating up on each other instead of the Venageti."

*After so many of your mayfly generations.* Loghyr live for ages, apparently. And they do take their sweet time dying. *Peace. Can you stand the strain?*

Us humans are a hobby with him, by his estimation created exclusively for his amusement. He likes to study bugs, too.

I had gotten distracted from my mission. A sound like that of a strangling crow startled me. Dean stood in the doorway, duffel at his feet, mouth open. The noises came from behind his teeth but maybe started out in a dimension where people didn't let undisciplined young ladies invade your quarters in your absence.

"I had to hide . . ."

"Another of your bimbos. I understand completely." He articulated each word in isolation. "No doubt you had another already installed in your own bedroom."

"Hey! It wasn't *that* way at all."

"It never is, Mr. Garrett."

"What the hell does that mean?" Downstairs, the Goddamn Parrot went crazy. And the Dead Man insisted, *Come to my room, Garrett. You must tell me more. So much more. I sense so many wonderful possibilities. Glory Mooncalled is here in TunFaire? Oh, the marvel of it! The wonder! The insane potential!*

"Glory Mooncalled here? Where did you get that idea?" Mooncalled was a legend. He started as a mercenary general during the recent generations-long disturbance between Karenta and Venageta. He fought for the Venageti at first, but their arrogance offended him so he came over to our side. Where he was treated about the same despite his being the only skilled field commander in the theater. So somewhere along the way he got together with the sentient natives of the Cantard and the whole crazy bunch declared the war zone an independent republic. That led to some intriguing triangular headbutting.

In the end, though, Karenta triumphed, our generals and sorcerers having been marginally less incompetent than those of Venageta while outnumbering anything Mooncalled could muster.

The tribes were on the run. And every refugee seemed determined to immigrate to TunFaire—at the very time when returning soldiers were coming home to find most jobs already taken by nonhumans and most businesses now owned or operated by dwarves or elves. Thus the permanent floating riots in our streets.

*Is it not self-evident? He* must *be here.*

Actually, I had begun to suspect that weeks ago. So had the secret police.

The Goddamn Parrot grew louder and more vile of beak. Dean became more articulate with every word, nagging in double time. And the Dead Man grew increasingly insistent.

My hangover didn't bother me nearly as much as those three did.

It was time to go somewhere where I could be alone with my misery.

# 3

They didn't turn loose willingly. In fact, as I descended to the street, Dean wished me bon voyage in words I had not realized he knew. The Goddamn Parrot fluttered past him and chased me up the street. That flashy little garbage beak did tone it down because the Dead Man shut him up. I mean, if they hang me on the testimony of a bird, who's going to keep a roof over his head?

He would have no trouble finding somebody to take him in, but he wouldn't find anyone as undemanding. Most folks would expect him to stay awake and devote his multiple-brained genius to their enrichment.

Oh, yes, the Loghyr is a genius. His intellect dwarfs that of anyone else I have ever met. He just don't want to use it.

I was barely a block from the house, contemplating selling the Dead Man into slavery, when I glimpsed red hair. Since I was glancing over my shoulder at the time, it seemed possible the girl with the goodies was following me.

This did not excite me as much as you might think. Like the Dead Man, I am not big on work. Still . . . that was one tender morsel.

She wasn't much of a sneak. Her good looks weren't a handicap, though. You'd think every guy on the street would drop whatever throat he was throttling or would close the lid on his display tray so he could look without becoming vulnerable to shoplifters, or whatever, but hardly anyone noticed the girl. The few who did were nonhumans who shuddered as in a sudden draft an looked befuddled.

Of course you wouldn't expect a normal dwarf to get excited

about a sweet slip like that, but . . . It was weird. And I don't like weird. Weird comes at me like I am a lightning rod for the bizarre.

I left the house considering a visit to Morley Dotes' Joy House, to see how he was doing at turning that vegetarian thug's harbor into an upscale hangout called The Palms. But there was no way I was going to drag this redheaded sweetmeat across Morley's bow. He had dark elf good looks and charm to waste and was not a bit shy about taking unfair advantage of them.

I bustled down Macunado till I reached the mouth of Barley Close, a tight, dark alley no longer used to make back door deliveries because all the mom-and-pop businesses had been scared away. Buildings leaned together overhead. The alley was dark and dirty and stank of rotting vegetation despite recent heavy rains that should have sluiced it out. I stepped over the outstretched legs of a drunken ratman and tried to stay near the centerline of the Close, where the footing was least treacherous. I disturbed a family of rats making a holiday feast of a dead dog. They showed their teeth and dared me to try stealing their dinner. I gave the biggest rat a quick toe in the slats. My new honey might be scared of rats.

I drifted deep into the gloom, past sleepers of various tribes and sexes, careful to disturb no one. I'm a Golden Rule kind of guy. I don't like it when people bother me in my home.

I paused at a cross alley eighty feet in. The sunlight blazing in from the street dry-roasted my eyeballs.

I waited. I waited a little more. Then I waited some. Then, after I had done some waiting and was about to say oh well and give it up, a woman did come to the mouth of the Close. She was the right size, but her age was off by four generations. She was a slow, raggedy street granny propped up by a crooked cane. She peered out from under a yellow straw hat with devilish concentration, like she was sure some evil was afoot inside the Close. A woman her age could not have survived the streets without becoming constitutionally paranoid.

I like to think I'm a nice guy. I did nothing to frighten her. I just waited till she decided not to enter the alley.

To my utter astonishment the Goddamn Parrot never said a word. The Dead Man really had the muzzle on him.

Looked like my ploy had failed. A girl amateur had outwitted me.

I would keep that to myself. My friends ride me hard enough as it is. I did not need to pass out ammunition.

I eased back into the street. My luck turned no worse. No traveling brawl tried to suck me in. I went to a watering trough, used some green fluid to swab the muck off my shoes. I didn't mind making the liquid thicker. Provision of public horse troughs encourages the public to harbor horses. And horses are nature's favorite weapon when it comes time to tormenting guys named Garrett.

I had cleaned my left shoe and was trying to get the right off without getting anything on my hand when I spotted the redhead through a sudden parting in the crowd. Our eyes met. I gave her my biggest, most charming grin and a look at my raised right eyebrow. That combination gets them every time.

She took off.

I took off after her. Now I was in my element. This is what I live for. I would have called for foxhounds and a horn, but they would have brought horses along.

The Goddamn Parrot made some kind of interrogatory noise. I didn't catch it and he didn't repeat himself.

# 4

Again I noticed that curious phenomenon: guys didn't pay the girl any mind. Maybe my eyes were going. Maybe my run of bad luck was giving me a case of wishful thinking. Maybe those other guys were so happily married they never looked at pretty girls. Maybe the sun came up in the west this morning.

I ducked a swooping shoat and tried to catch up a little since I could not track the girl by the stir she was causing. The street was crowded like today was a holiday, but everybody was growling and snapping at everybody else. We needed some miserable weather to cool everybody down. A really hot spell might be like a torch to tinder.

I spied a familiar face headed my way, ugly as the dawn itself. Saucerhead Tharpe towered above the crowd. Nobody gave him any grief. He was a bone-breaker by trade, which meant prosperous times for him. He spotted me and hoisted a ham-sized hand. "Yo! Garrett, my man. How they hanging?" It is always good to have Saucerhead on your side, but he isn't overly blessed with brains or a flair for language.

"Low. You notice a cute little redhead about a hundred feet up? She's so short I can't keep track."

His grin broadened, exposing the remnants of truly ugly teeth. "You on a case?" Cunning fellow, he had an idea he could get me to hire him to help.

"I don't think so. She was watching my house, so I decided to follow her around."

"Just like that?"

"Yeah."

His grin turned into a horror show. "Dean come home? Or did the Dead Man wake up?" He winked at the Goddamn Parrot.

He was smarter than a rock, anyway. "Both."

Saucerhead chuckled. It was the kind of chuckle I get too often. My friends figure I was put here to amuse them with my travails.

"Look, Saucerhead, this gal is going to lose me if I don't . . ."

"Speaking of ones that got away, I seen Tinnie Tate yesterday."

Tinnie is one ex that my cronies won't let go away. "Great. Come by the house later. Tell me all about it."

"I seen Winger, too. She . . ."

"That's your problem."

Our mutual acquaintance Winger, though female, is as big as me and goofier than Saucerhead. And she has the moral sense of a rabid hyena. And, despite that, she is hard not to like.

"Hey, Garrett, come on, man."

I was drifting away.

"She had a good idea. Honest, Garrett."

Winger is chock-full of good ideas that get me up to my crotch in crocodiles. "Then you go in on it with her." There was a small thinning of the crowd uphill. I caught a glimpse of my quarry. She seemed to be looking back, puzzled, maybe even exasperated.

"I would, Garrett," Saucerhead shouted. "Only we need somebody with real brains to get into it with us."

"That leaves me out, don't it?" Didn't it? Would a guy with real brains keep following somebody when it was evident that that somebody had decided that she wanted to be followed and was getting impatient with my delays?

Seemed like a good idea at the time. We have all said that.

I considered waving so she would know I was coming, but decided to keep up pretenses.

Saucerhead followed for a way, babbling something about my manners. I showed him my worst. I didn't answer. I trotted after my new honey. The crowds were thinning. I kept her in sight. Her passage caused no more stir than if she were the crone I had seen looking into Barley Close.

We were just past where Macunado becomes the Way of the Harlequin when she glanced back, then turned into Heartlight Lane, where some of TunFaire's least competent astrologers and diviners keep shop.

# 5

"Hey, buddy," I called to a stout-looking old dwarf lugging an old-timey homemade club. That tool was as long as him, crafted from the trunk and roots of some black sapling that had wood harder than rock. "How much you want for that thing?"

The price went up instantly. You know dwarves. You show interest in a broken clothespin . . . "Not for sale, Tall One. This is the world-renowned club Toetickler, weapon of the chieftains of the Kuble Dwarves for ten generations. It was given to the first High Gromach by the demiurge Gootch . . ."

"Right. And it's still got dirt on its roots, Stubby."

The dwarf swung that club down hard enough to crack a cobblestone.

"Three marks," I barked before he gave me more details of the club's provenance or maybe demonstrated its efficiency by tickling my favorite toes.

"Not one groat under ten, Lofty." Even national treasures are for sale if you are a dwarf. Nothing is holy except wealth itself.

"Thanks for talking, Lowball. It was just an idea." I started moving.

"Whoa there, Highpockets. At least make me an offer."

"My memory must be playing tricks again. I thought I did make an offer, Shorty."

"I mean a serious offer. Not a bad joke."

"Three and ten, then."

He whined. I started moving.

"Wait, Tall One. Four. All right? Four is outright theft for such a storied weapon, but I *have* to get some cash together before you people run us out of town. I tell you, I'm not looking forward to rooting around in the old home mines again."

Sounded like there might be a tad of truth in that.

"Three ten and a parrot? Think what you could do with his feathers."

The dwarf considered Mr. Big. "Four." Nobody wanted the Goddamn Parrot.

"Done," I sighed. I turned out my pockets. We made the exchange. The dwarf walked away whistling. There would be tall tales told at the dwarf hold tonight, of another fool taken.

But I had me a tool. And with fate seldom able to gaze on me favorably for long, I would not have long to wait to field-test Toetickler's touch.

Heartlight Lane was not crowded, which surprised me. Given the political climate, more folks ought to be checking into their futures. I saw a lonely runecaster tossing the bones, trying to forecast her next meal, and an entrail reader much more interested in plucking his chicken carcass. Palm readers and phrenologists swapped fortunes. Aquamancers, geomancers, pyromancers, and necromancers all napped in their stalls.

Maybe customers were staying away in droves because they did not need experts to tell them that bad times were coming.

I got some interesting discount and rebate offers. The most attractive came from a dark-haired, fiery-eyed tarot reader. I promised, "I'll be right back. Save a dance for me."

"No, you won't. Not if you don't stop here. Now."

I thought she was telling me, "That's what you all say." I kept on keeping on. The Goddamn Parrot started muttering to himself. Maybe the Dead Man's compulsion was wearing off.

"I warned you, Handsome."

How did she manage to see her cards?

I had not seen the redhead since before my negotiations with the runt arms merchant. I didn't see her now, but something flashed around a turn of brick up ahead.

The guy who laid out Heartlight Lane was either a snake stalker or a butterfly hunter. It zigs and zags and comes close to looping for no reason more discernible than the fact that that is the way it has got to go to get between the buildings. A few quick turns and the lane became deserted except for a big brown coach, its door just closing.

Empty streets are not a good sign. That means folks have smelled trouble and want no part of it.

Maybe somebody just wanted to talk to me. But then why not just come to the house?

Because I don't always answer the door? Especially when somebody might want me to go to work? Maybe. Then there is the fact that the Dead Man can read minds.

I took a couple of cautious steps, glanced back. That tarot girl sure was a temptation. On the other hand, red hair is marvelous against a white pillowcase. On the third hand . . .

I got no chance to check my other fifteen fingers. From out of the woodwork, or cracks in the walls, or under the cobblestones, or a hole in the air came the three ugliest guys I have ever seen. They had it bad. I think they wanted to look human but their mothers had messed them up with their hankering after lovers who spelled ugly with more than one *G*. All three made me look runty, too, and I am a solid six feet two, two hundred ten pounds of potato-hard muscle and blue eyes to die for.

"Hi, guys. You think we're gonna get some rain?" I pointed upward.

None of them actually looked. Which left me with a nasty suspicion that they were smarter than me. I would have looked. And *they* hadn't followed some wench-o'-the-wisp up here where some humongous brunos could bushwhack them, either.

They said nothing and I didn't wait for introductions and didn't wait for a sales pitch. I feinted left, dodged right, swung my new club low and hard and took the pins right out from under one behemoth. Maybe the dwarf did me a favor after all. I went after another guy's head like I wanted to knock it all the way to the river on one hop. Big as he was, he went ass over appetite and I started to think, hey, things aren't going so bad after all.

The first guy got up. He started toward me. Meantime, the guy I hadn't hit planted himself resolutely in the way in case I decided to go back the way that I had come. My first victim came at me. He wasn't even limping. And his other buddy was back up, too, no worse for wear, either.

You could not hurt these guys? Oh my oh my.

"Argh!" said the Goddamn Parrot.

"You said a beakful, you piebald buzzard."

I wound up for a truly mighty swing, turned slowly, trying to pick a victim. I picked wrong. I could not have chosen right.

I took the guy I hadn't hit. The plan was to whack him good, then display my skill as a sprinter. The plan didn't survive first contact with the enemy. When I swung he grabbed my club in midair, took it away, and flipped it aside with such force that it cracked when it hit a nearby building.

"Oh my oh my."

"Argh!" the Goddamn Parrot observed again.

I went for the fast feet option, but a hairy hand attached to an arm that would have embarrassed a troll snagged my right forearm. I flailed and flopped and discovered ingenious ways to use the language. I got me some much needed exercise, but I did not go anywhere. And big ugly didn't work up a sweat keeping me from going.

Another one grabbed my other arm. His touch was almost gentle, but his fingers were stone. I knew he could powder my bones if he wanted. Which did not slow my effort to get away. I didn't give up till the third one grabbed my ankles and lifted.

The Goddamn Parrot walked down my back muttering to himself. Mumble and mutter was all he seemed capable of anymore.

The whole crew lockstepped to the coach. I lifted my head long enough to see a matched set of four huge horses, the same shade of brown. On the driver's seat was a coachman all in black, looking down at me but invisible within the depths of a vast black cowl. He needed a big sickle to make the look complete.

The coach was fancy enough, but no coat of arms proclaimed its owner's status. That didn't do wonders for my confidence. Here in TunFaire even the villains like to show off.

With nary a word, the ugly brothers chucked me inside. My skull tried to bust through the far door. That door didn't give an inch. My headbone didn't give much, either. Like a moth with his wings singed, I fluttered down into that old lake of darkness.

# 6

When you are in my racket—confidential investigations, lost stuff found, work that doesn't force me to take a real job—you expect to get knocked around sometimes. You don't get to like it, but you do catch on to the stages and etiquettes involved. Especially if you are the kind of dope who trails a girl you know wants to be followed, right into the perfect spot for an ambush. That kind of guy gets more than his share of lumps and deserves every one of them. I bet guys like Morley never get bopped on the noggin and tossed into mystery coaches.

Your first move after you start to stagger back toward the light—assuming you are clever enough not to do a lot of whimpering—is to pretend that you are not recovering. That way maybe you will learn something. Or maybe you can take them by surprise, whip up on them, and get away. Or maybe they will all be out to dinner and some genius will have forgotten to take the keys out of the door of your cell.

Or maybe you will just lie there puking your socks up because of a rocking concussion rolling your hangover.

"O what foul beasts these mortals be! Jorken! Fetch a mop!" The voice was stentorian, as though the speaker was some ham passion player who never ever stepped offstage.

A woman's voice added, "Bring an extra bucket. They leak at the other end as well."

Oh no. I already had a bath this week.

"Why me? How come, all of a sudden, I get stuck with scutwork?"

"Because you're the messenger," said a wind from the abyss,

cold as a winter's grave. That had to be my buddy the faceless coachman.

I was confused. My natural state, some would say. But this was bizarre.

Maybe it was time to get up and meet the situation head-on. I gathered my corded muscles and heaved. Two fingers and a toe twitched. So I exercised my skill with colorful dialogue. "Rowr-fabble! Gile stynbobly!" I was on a roll, but I didn't recognize the language I was speaking.

I cooled down fast when a load of icy water hit me.

"Freachious moumenpink!" Driven by a savage rage, I managed a full half pushup. "Snrubbing scuts!" Hey! Was that a real word?

Another bucket of water hit me hard enough to knock me off my hands and roll me over. A ragmop came out of the mist. It started swabbing. Somebody attached to the mop muttered while he worked. That was a dwarfish custom. But this beanpole was so tall he could only have been adopted.

There was something weird about the mopman. Beside the fact that he carried on several sides of a conversation all by himself. He had little pigeon wings growing out of his head where his ears ought to be. Also, you could sort of see through him whenever he moved in front of a bright light.

A really intense light blazed up. I managed to get into a sitting position but could not look up. That light was worse than sunshine on the brightest-ever morning after a two-kegger.

"Mr. Garrett."

I didn't lie about it. I didn't admit anything, either. I didn't react at all. I was busy trying not to make more work for that princely fellow with the mop. I succeeded. And I managed to get one hand clamped over my eyes. Somewhere way in the back of my head a little voice told me I should take this as a lesson in chemistry. Don't play with stuff that might blow up in your face. Like strange redheads.

I know. I know. All redheads are strange. But there is strange and strange.

A different woman said, "Ease up on the glow. You're blinding him." She had a voice of a type you never hear except from the women who haunt your fantasies. It was the voice of the lover you have been waiting for all these years.

Something was going on here.

The light faded till I could stand to open my eyes. It continued to wane till there was no more than you would find in your average torchlit dungeon, which was my first guess as to my whereabouts. But I didn't recognize any voices. I thought I pretty well knew everybody who had a dungeon in the family inventory.

Well, it's a big city.

Hell. No. Not a dungeon. This was some kind of big cellar with a high ceiling and only a couple of really dirty windows practically lost in rusty steel bars, way, way up at the back. The cellar was mostly empty except for pillars supporting the structure overhead. The floor was old stone, a dark slate-gray. Hard as a rock, hard on a sleeper's back.

I took inventory. I didn't have any bits missing or any open wounds. My headache had not abated, though. My main injury was a knot on my conk from my attempt to dive through that coach door.

And I still had a hangover.

Maybe they turned down the lights too far. Now I could see my captors. All eight of them. I would rather not have.

There was a long drink of water who maybe used to be a pigeon, your basic roof rat, leaning on his mop. There were the three characters I had met already, all looking bigger and uglier than ever. Those guys could get work as gargoyles at any of the major cathedrals. Then there were three females. None was my redhead. The closest to her was a brunette with a paler skin and eyes that were smouldering pits of promise and curves that had been drawn by a dreaming celestial geometrician. Her lips made me want to bounce up and run over there. Presumably she owned the sexy voice.

Next to her was a gal with the biggest hair I have ever seen. What looked like snakes seemed to peek out. Her skin was a sort of pale pus-green color. Her lips were gorgeously tasty but dark green. When she smiled she showed you sharp vampire teeth. Not to mention that she sported two extra arms, the better to whatever you with. I decided I would put off asking her out.

She stared at me with a heat—or a hunger—that set those old frozen-toed mice to rambling along my spine.

The third woman was a giant of a blonde, maybe ten feet tall and at least that many years past her prime. She had put on weight where women generally do not need much, and overall she projected a sort of middle-class goodwifely dowdiness—with a suggestion of all the hidden bitterness that so often goes with that.

A guy I took to be her old man sprawled on some sort of stone throne that was so chipped and crumbly it looked like it could collapse under his weight. He was a couple of feet taller than the blonde. He wasn't wearing much but a stripely leather loincloth that looked like it had been ripped off a saber-toothed tiger on the fly and nobody bothered to cure it. He was built like a muscle freak who had gone to seed. He could have lugged minotaurs on those shoulders in his prime.

His eyes were a blazing blue, almost as gorgeous as mine. His hair was white and there was a lot of it, flying out all around his head in tangles and spikes. His beard was white, too, and had not been trimmed in decades. Despite his lovely eyes he seemed to be bored or almost asleep.

Everybody stared at me like they expected me to do something clever. I did not have my cane nor my tap shoes, so I couldn't go into my dance routine. Those words that escaped my mouth still had no discernible meaning, so I could not sing. I reached deep into my trick bag for the last thing left.

I tried to stand up.

I made it! But to stay standing up I had to hang on to one of the ugly guys. This particular one lacked a forehead and had a mouth like a lamprey. I bet all the girls wanted to tongue-kiss him. His eyes were fish eyes, too, yellow and shadowy and covered by that milky membrane.

That popped up and down a couple of times, but otherwise he ignored me. I managed to croak, "Who *are* you people? *What* are you?"

Two of these characters could pass for giants and one for human, but the rest were not like anything I had ever seen on the streets of TunFaire. You spend any time at all out there, you will see members of virtually every sentient species, from pixies the size of your thumb to giants twenty feet tall. You will even see some horrors like the ratmen, who were created by sorcery run amok.

Maybe that was what we had here, fugitives from some cellar way up at the pinnacle of the Hill, where our magician masters live. Trouble was, for the last four generations most of them people had spent their lives in the Cantard, managing the war. None of them would have messed up this much.

Some things you could be sure of just by experience.

I sagged. My ugly buddy did not help. I hung on like a drowning man, gradually pulling myself back into our world. I had had practice climbing lampposts on nights when the weather had turned incredibly alcoholic. "I know you people can talk."

Speaking of talk, where was my curse, the feathered prince of gab, the Goddamn Parrot? He sure wasn't in this basement— unless he was dead. Even the Dead Man could not stop his beak from rattling here.

The big guy, who was pretty obviously the head weirdo, nod- ded to the guy who had feathers for ears. But Beanpole Man just looked at me and shrugged like he did not have a notion.

I muttered. "I have been kidnapped by morons."

Yeah. Right. And what did that say about the blinding intellect of the guy who got kidnapped?

Gravity would not leave me alone. I sagged yet again. Maybe I should let go, fall back down, go to sleep, and eventually wake up again somewhere else, where all the nightmares had not yet wormed their ways into every human mind.

*Et tu, Cthulhu?* The world is full of crackpots, and who can you trust?

# 7

The greenish woman moved toward me. "Please accept our apologies, Mr. Garrett. We needed to see you quickly. Daiged, Rhogiro, and Ringo," she said, aiming a wicked nail with each name by way of making introductions, "had to work fast. They aren't used to being gentle."

"No kidding."

I looked around for the Goddamn Parrot. Still no sign of him. Maybe he had had sense enough to get away. Maybe I was in real luck and he mouthed off and got his neck wrung.

Somehow some of the woman's arms had disappeared. Her hair had become more managable. Her color had improved, her teeth had lost their sharpness, and her neckline now plunged to navel level.

I had fallen in with shapeshifters.

Now that I noticed it, the giants were several feet shorter, the ugly boys were less repulsive, and the long pale guy had ears. The sexy gal had changed, too, though she had been fine the way she was. She had shortened up and gone blonde. She giggled. Her appeal had not faded a bit.

Why would she want to turn into a bimbo?

Soon they all looked normal, within the very extended range considered normal in TunFaire. They could have gotten by outside— except that they tended to be a little ethereal in a strong light.

Did somebody feed me magic mushrooms while I was asleep?

I said, "That's a better look for you." The woman was too close. I watched her hair. Fleas and lice are bad enough.

She flashed an inviting smile, licked her lips with a tongue that split at the end. She told me, "I appreciate your thoughts. They're flattering. But you don't want to get too close to me." She gestured at the blonde, who stared at me like she wanted me for dinner. In a less stressful moment I would have leaped onto her plate. I failed to correct the snake woman's misconception about her effect on me.

"You got any chairs around here?" I had a concussion for sure. I was keeping my balance about as good as a ratman on weed.

"I'm sorry. We jumped into this rather precipitously."

I lowered myself back down to the floor so I would not have so far to fall when the time came. "Tell me something useful. Who are you? What are you? What do you want? Give me some of the good stuff before I fade away again here." My head really hurt.

"We are the last of the Godoroth. Through no wish of ours, nor any fault, we have become entangled in a struggle with the Shayir."

"The sun of knowledge shines on me," I muttered. "I'm afraid not." I didn't have a clue.

"Only one group can survive. This place is the cellar of our last mortal follower. We will shelter here till the contest is decided. In his prayers our follower suggested we enlist your aid. By temperament you are well suited."

"Leave my tailor out of this."

She scowled. She didn't get it. "We were considering bringing in a nonbeliever already. The Shayir must have gotten wind of you and so set a trap for you."

"Must be the bump on the head. I'm not understanding any of this." I asked again. "Who are you? What are you?"

The blonde giggled. That rogue Garrett. He says the cleverest things. However, the boss guy didn't find me amusing. Lightning crackled on his brow. Literally. He had grown a tad again, too. Should have clued me right then. His type don't have any patience.

"You've never heard of the Godoroth?"

"'Fraid not. None of those other names, either."

"Ignorance was one point that recommended you." She didn't sound like she believed in ignorance, though.

Thunders pranced around the big guy's melon. The brunette flashed him a look that might have been disgust. Then she told me, "I'm Magodor. Collectively, we are the Godoroth. We were the patron gods of the Hahr, one of the first tribes to settle this region. They were primitive by your standards. They planted crops and herded cattle but were not very good at it. They lived as much by raiding as by agriculture. Almost all physical trace of them has vanished. Their blood still runs strong in the rulers of this city, but their culture is extinct. And their gods are on the verge of extinction."

That bad at agriculture—and the interest in institutionalized thievery sounded like a cultural aspect that had persisted amongst our rulers.

"The worship of the Shayir was brought into this region by the Ox-Riders of Gritn during the Gritny Conquest. The Gritny were much like the Hahr in the ways they lived. They did not last long. They were just the first wave in an age of great migrations. Every decade saw its raiders or conquerors. Each wave left its seed and a few settlers and their ideas. Of the Ox-Riders no physical trace remains. But their gods, the Shayir, are persistent and resilient. And now, brought low by time, we and the Shayir must fight for a place on the Street of the Gods."

Street of the Gods. That was the insiders' name for the avenue that runs the length of what cynical and undereducated types refer to as the Dream Quarter, that part of the South Side where Tun-Faire's thousand and one gods all have their main temples. Another legacy of the remote past, from an age when the temporal power reigned supreme and was totally paranoid about the worldly ambitions of priesthoods. Those old emperors had wanted every priest where he could be watched easily—and could be found easily at massacre time.

I looked around. Gods? Right.

"You know how it works on the Street? It's all marketing. If you win a good following, you migrate west to temples and cathedrals nearer the Hill. If you lose market share, you slide downhill eastward, toward the river. For three decades we have hung on by our nails, in the last temple to the east, while the Shayir holed up across the Street and one place west, with a monotheistic god named Scubs in the status niche between us. But Scubs won a family of converts last month. And immigrants from the Cantard have imported a god named Antitibet who has enough followers to seize a place a third of the way to the west. Which means a lot of shuffling around is due. And which also means that either we or the Shayir will have to leave the Street."

Yeah. I understood that. I knew how things worked in the Dream Quarter. I didn't have a clue why, or how, the priests worked it all out amongst themselves, but the results were evident.

Farthest west are the Chattaree cathedral of the Church and

the Orthodox compound. These are feuding cousin religions that, with their various schismatic offspring, claim the majority of Tun-Faire's believers. These are rich and powerful cults.

And at the east end are dozens of cults like this one represented here, gods and pantheons known only to a handful of faithful. At that end of the street the temples are really nothing but worn-out storefronts.

I thought I understood the situation. Which did not mean I believed these characters were actual gods and goddesses. Didn't mean I didn't believe, either. You ask me, the evidence in the god business is always thin and, in most cases, thoroughly cooked by priests who survive by charging admission to heavenly attention. But this is TunFaire, the wonderful city where any damned thing can happen.

"You are a skeptic," Magodor observed. She looked very pretty right then.

I confessed with a nod. I did not confide my own beliefs, or the lack thereof.

Wisps of smoke trailed from the big guy's nostrils. He was up to eighteen feet tall. If he got any more perturbed he would run out of headroom.

"We will explore your thinking another time. For the moment let's just say that we Godoroth are in a situation both simple and desperate. We or the Shayir are going to leave the Street. For us that would mean oblivion. The Street has a power all its own, a manna that helps sustain us. Off the Street we would be little more than wraiths, and that only transiently."

Maybe. The ugly boys looked as solid and eternal as basalt.

She reiterated, in case her point had gone over my head the past several times: "If we're forced off the Street we are done, Mr. Garrett. Lost. Forgotten."

I'm not often accused of thinking before I open my big yap. I could not be convicted this time, either. "What actually does happen to gods who run out their string? You have gods of your own to report to, stand on the scales, be judged and all?"

*Rumble-rumble.* A crown of little thunderheads rode the big guy's head now. He was over twenty feet tall. Too tall for the cellar, even sitting down. He was bent over, glaring at me ferociously. I got the impression that, despite being the boss, he was not too bright.

Isn't that a lovely notion? Even in the supernatural world it isn't necessarily the cream that rises to the top.

Lack of brilliance was a suspicion I had entertained concerning numerous gods. Mostly their myths consist of vicious behaviors toward one another and their worshippers, spiced up with lots of adultery, incest, bestiality, parricide, and whatnot.

"Some just fade till even the ghost is gone. Others become mortals, prey for time and the worm." I cannot say that she sounded entirely convincing.

The big guy closed his eyes, breathed lightning. His companion had better control. She had gotten herself down to six feet tall and was quite attractive in a mature, country sort of way. I had no trouble picturing her galloping across the sky on a stormy night, wearing an iron hat with horns, scattering ravens while harvesting the fallen heroes. Trouble was, she eyed me like she had no trouble picturing me dangling across the neck of her mount.

My head still hurt. My stomach kept rolling over. I wanted desperately to go back to sleep.

I said, "I'm not comfortable here." I was also, still, very confused, completely distrusting of my senses. "Is there somewhere we can sit down, just you and me, so I can get a handle on this without being distracted?" If I wasn't trying to keep from stepping on my tongue when I looked at the blonde I was worrying about the big guy's temper or about the ugly brothers taking a notion to bang me around again. I did know I was in one bad spot, whatever these things were.

The big guy spat from the side of his mouth, like those country boys who chew weed instead of smoking it. A ball of fire hit stone a few yards from my hand, melted right down into the slate. Charming.

# 8

There was another cellar above part of the one where I had awakened. It was more normal, used for wine storage and lumber rooms. Lots of dust and spiders. Plenty of rats. Refreshingly mundane. My companion illuminated our way with a light from within herself. She seemed fuzzy but appeared solid once we climbed into a kitchen where a dozen women were cooking and baking. They paused to stare, baffled. Who was this guy coming out of the cellar?

Apparently they didn't see Magodor. Nor did they seem inclined to challenge my presence. They went back to work. That was not reassuring. It meant they were used to strange doings and to minding their own business.

Their number meant I had to be way up the Hill. And that meant the house probably belonged to one of the great and most wicked of the sorcerers who are the true powers in Karenta.

I hate it when I get noticed by those people. That never is good for me.

Magodor led me into a small drawing room apparently set up just for us. She told me, "You will have to manage without refreshments. We're not allowing ourselves to be seen by mortals."

I dropped into a chair so overstuffed I sank almost out of sight. I caught an arm and saved myself. In moments I was so comfortable I was ready to sleep. I knew I had a concussion, so I fought the drowsiness. "How come?"

"Our enemies would find out where we are."

"That's a problem?"

She offered me a sour look. Must have been my tone. "You've

never seen a war of the gods. Pray you don't." The woman with all
the teeth and arms and the snake problem shone through momentarily. "Neither we nor the Shayir need worry about injuring mortals under our protection." But wasn't that sort of thing supposed
to be bad for business in general?

The nasty side faded. Lovely. Yum!

"That wouldn't be smart, Garrett."

"Huh?"

"Your thoughts are obvious. They were with Adeth. They were
with Star. They are with me. You should know that my lovers seldom survive. I offer the warning only because we need you
healthy. I am Magodor the Destroyer."

Into my head flooded images of famine and pestilence, of
acres of bones, of cities burning and ravens darkening the sky.
Boy, would she be a fun date. When the visions cleared, Magodor
looked her loveliest yet, a make-the-celibate-monks-howl-at-the-
unfair-moon sort of girl.

"Resist me."

"Will do." I was not sure that these Godoroth were not just
slick con artists with a little hedge wizardry, aiming to use me as a
stalking-horse. But why take chances?

"Until we triumph over the Shayir." If anything, she grew
more desirable.

"Uh," I said, wondering if I ought not to hold a hand over my
eyes. "Let's have some details. Like who was who down there and
what you expect me to do."

"Meaning, if we really are gods, why not handle our problems
ourselves?"

"Something like that." She talked too much for any god I ever
heard of.

"Even gods are constrained."

"How?"

"We cannot, for example, invade the temple of the Shayir.
More will become evident in time. You haven't agreed to help."

I didn't intend to, either. I didn't tell her that. I don't have
much use for gods of any sort. I figured what I needed to do was
be polite, stall, ride it out, and soon enough I would be out of
there. All the gods I had heard of had notoriously short attention
spans. They all wanted to go boff their father's girlfriend or their
brother or their pet three-headed dragon. Two hours after I was
gone, these characters wouldn't remember me.

"Are you going to help?"

"You haven't told me anything. I don't even know who I would be representing. I know the name of one lovely who dotes on devastation. I know the name of a long drink of water who has feathered ears. That's not much."

"Jorken the Messenger. He is of no consequence."

"Then there are the big guys. Daiged, Rhogiro, and Ringo? What are they?"

"Avars. We inherited them. They were servants of the Old Ones. They have no attributes but strength."

"Don't forget ugly. They're really big on ugly."

"You have no idea. And of course, being you, you're really interested in Star."

"Star?"

"She has an older name, but it means Morning Star. She is the whore avatar of Woman, the Temptress, the temple prostitute who always comes across."

"How romantic."

"I could see the romance in your eyes whenever you looked at her."

"Some things we can't control."

"Or you wouldn't have followed Adeth."

"Adeth?"

"The one trying to lead you into a trap. You are lucky we were watching. You would not have enjoyed her company as much as Star's."

"The redhead? Some things we can't control."

"If you must lose it, concentrate on Star. She might get interested. She hasn't turned it on for you yet, Garrett."

Wow. She ought to bottle and sell that indifference, then. Be a comedown from the god racket, but she would get rich and famous and maybe famous would put her feet on the ladder back to the top. I could get rich myself, managing her. Cut myself a percentage of the take and . . .

*Sssss!*

Snakes out of green hair. Magodor was irritated. I don't think she could read my mind, but she was bright enough to realize I wasn't paying attention. I came alert fast. They might not be gods, but they might believe they were and had every right to be vicious and capricious. I put on my killer grin, hoisted an eyebrow charmingly, said, "I'm awake! I'm awake!" same as I used to tell the sergeant of the guard when he caught me with my attention wandering back in those good old Marine Corps days, dancing with the Venageti in the islands.

"You don't seem especially interested."

"Consider the mortal's viewpoint. He's been kidnapped. He has a knife across his throat. Somebody supposedly wants to hire him, but he can't find out what for. You haven't said a word about payment. The one thing that does come across is that these would-be employers don't look any more trustworthy or stable than any other gods."

With every word sweet Maggie grew less attractive. I quit before she decided to drop me down a hole and interview elsewhere. "Why not finish telling me about the others?"

I basked in the pale green light of her disapproval. She wasn't used to backtalk. But she took control. Maybe she *was* desperate.

Doubtless, in the shadows of her heart, she put a tick beside "Garrett" in her book of destruction.

"How about the boss couple? Who are they?"

"Imar and Imara." I didn't have to be told. Both brother and sister and man and wife. "Lord and Mistress of All, Skystrider and Earth Mother. Sun and Moon, Scatterer of Stars and She Who Calls Forth the Spring."

"And so forth," I muttered. When you have the habit of back-mouthing crime bosses and Guard chieftains, it ain't easy to break the circle.

"And so forth. We tend to accumulate titles, of both supplication and accusation."

That fit with what I knew about other gods. The Church, where I was raised, didn't have a full crew of gods like most religions. We had one God, No God But God—and about ten thousand saints who covered the same ground as lesser gods and goddesses. The Church had a whole heavenly bureaucracy, with saints who didn't do anything more strenuous than find lost buttons or keep an eye on the wine grape harvest. The Church's supernatural establishment was so big the whole thing would continue on inertia for ages after its last believer perished.

"All right. Now that I know who you are, I have a vague notion what your problem is. One temple. Two bunches of gods. Whoever loses out loses big time."

"Exactly." She was all business now. As if a beautiful woman can ever be all business, however much she wants to think that.

Nature does not care about the clutter in the mind. Decorum is just another obstacle to be surmounted by instinct.

I tried being all business, too.

Instinct could get me dead.

I reminded me that lady spiders eat their mates.

# 9

"Listen," Magodor snapped. "You get to hear this once."

Generous. "I'm all ears, Maggie." I tried to wiggle them encouragingly, but I just don't have that talent. What an unfair world. A big goof like Saucerhead Tharpe can wiggle one of his ears, but I am stuck with . . .

"Garrett."

Whoops. "I'm awake! I'm awake!"

"You may not accept it, but we gods have dealings amongst ourselves. Few of your priests are aware of this."

"Yeah. Mostly they're big on declaring their own gods to be the only gods."

"Partly. Some younger religions are intolerant that way. About rules. There is a set that governs the situation that exists now. Additionally, there are custom and past practice. It's not explicitly forbidden, but past practice is that pantheons don't fight over places on the Street."

"Bad for business, eh?"

"You have no idea. Customarily, a committee of more successful gods oversee a competition. Winner takes all."

"Ah." That was my polished professional ah, my ah of illumination.

"The competitions are unique each time so the contestants cannot rig the results beforehand."

"I'll bet they never even try."

Maggie smiled me a genuine smile. "Indeed."

"So what's the contest? Where do I fit in?"

"The prize temple has been sealed. Neither the Shayir nor we can get in. Somewhere there is a key. Whoever finds it, and recognizes it, can open and take over the temple."

I used my eyebrow trick. "Oh?" She wasn't impressed.

"It's supposed to be ordinary but rendered invisible to immortal eyes. The lock it fits cannot be broken. It will open only to the key. The Board probably expects us to rely on our faithful to do the legwork, but there is no specific prohibition against employing a professional. So we turned to you. And it seems that the Shayir, apparently having gotten wind of our interest, tried to lure you away."

"I see," I said, not sure that I saw anything. "I'm supposed to find this key, scoot to this temple, and let you in before the Shayir find it."

"That's the meat of it."

"Interesting." If I was not caught up inside some bizarre con. That would fit my luck. Time and again I get dragged in where nobody plays me even close to straight.

All part of the business.

I had questions. Were the contesting gods, though discouraged from bushwhacking each other, allowed to make life hard for the opposition's mortals? I have enough troubles.

Maggie looked at me like she meant to glare a hole through.

"It's worth thinking about. My weirdest case yet. Great for my references later." I had to get out without making commitments. I knew I could not get away with a flat no.

"There's a time limit, Garrett. The sands are running already. We have maybe another hundred hours."

Gah. "What happens if nobody finds the key?"

"These southern immigrants could bring more gods than Antitibet."

"Everybody loses?"

"It has happened before."

"Let's talk money, then."

Her face tightened. Prospective clients never want to talk about money.

I told her, "I have a household to support. The usual story stuff—like maybe a night with Star, like a night in Elf Hill, wonderful as that might be—won't put food on the table."

# 10

"I have hovered above a thousand battlefields, Garrett. I can tell you where the treasure of a hundred vanquished armies are hidden."

Handy trick. "Excellent. Then clue me about one small one that's close by."

Her green began to rise. But she nodded abruptly. "Very well. The workman is worthy of his hire. And it is necessary that we trust one another. There is no time for anything else." She stalked across the room, bad Magodor becoming luscious Maggie as she walked. My instinctual side was adequately impressed. "Come see, Garrett."

She indicated a hand mirror on the room's small mantelpiece. There was nothing mystical about it. The dwarves produce them by the thousands. Maggie passed a hand over the metal in a circular motion, as though polishing it. A mist formed between her hand and the metal. That faded. The mirror no longer reflected here and now.

Woodland scene with men who rode desperately, low upon the necks of lathered horses. Arrows fell around them. A rider fell. The rest swept on into forest so dense their horses could make little headway. The riders dismounted and fled on foot. One led them to a trail hidden in the growth.

"Amis the Third. In flight from the uprising masterminded by his brother Alis. He failed to make proper sacrifices. We turned our eyes away. We were strong in those times. Here. This is the treasure they were able to carry away. They buried it in a badger's den. It is still there." Her hand made that wiping motion again.

The view backed off enough to give me a good idea where to look. Then the view changed.

Now the fugitives were cornered. Their guide had led them into a trap. Their pursuers showed no mercy.

"That's inside the wall now, isn't it?"

"Yes."

"Wonderful. That will do for a retainer if it's still there."

"I wouldn't have chosen something that wasn't. One thing more." She took a cord from around her waist, a cord that had not been visible till she unwound it. It was four feet long. She wrapped one end around her left hand once, let the cord dangle from between thumb and forefinger, drew the thumb and forefinger of her right hand along the length of the cord.

The cord became as stiff as an arrow. "Neat trick."

She jabbed it, swordlike, right into my breadbasket.

"Oof!" said I.

"Had I pinched the end down into a point, so, it would have gone through you."

"Uhn."

She swung the cord, hit me on the left elbow. Right on the funnybone. I said something like, "Yeow! Oh shining wondrous mudsuckers fingushing wowzgoggle! That hurts!"

"Pain is the best teacher. Watch." She reversed her fingerwork. The cord fell limp. She was a lefty. I was not surprised. Most artists and sorcerers I run into seem to be. So are most of the more successful villains. The really stupid bad guys, the kind who try to get in somewhere by sliding down the chimney without checking first to see if there is a fire burning, are always righties. But I am not a lefty myself, so not all righties are dumb.

Magodor grabbed the middle of the cord and pulled. It kept getting longer. "Just like this, Garrett. Hands extended, level, palms up, heels of your hands together. Pull outward from the middle. It will stretch as long as you need it to."

"That's one handy piece of rope."

"Yes. It is." She stopped when she had twenty-five feet of cord. "It can be used as a garrote, too."

"I saw that right off." It looked very much like the ritual garrotes the Kef sidhe use to carry out their holy murders.

"Pay attention. To shorten it you rumple it all up in a ball, so." The cord crushed up small. She rolled the wad around on her palms, grabbed the ends that were sticking out, pulled. The cord was four feet long again.

She stretched it to ten feet. "If you need more than one piece of line, tie a slip knot in the middle, so. Pull out a loop as long as you need. Cut the loop right at the knot." She held cord and knot with two hands. Another hand clipped the cord with a thin knife. Yet another hand dealt with the second piece of cord, which she handed to me. She dropped one end of what was left, grabbed the knot and slid it right to the end.

I had seen this trick's cousin before. It was in the arsenal of most street conjurers. Only it didn't seem to be a trick this time.

She took the cord back from me, wadded, rolled, had one four-foot piece again. "I will want this back."

"Darn! I was afraid of that."

She eyed me sharply. "I'll show you one more thing. For you this is likely to be its most useful facility."

She stretched the cord to six feet, tied a small bowline at one end, ran the other end through the resulting loop, forming a large noose. She set the circle of cord on the carpet, stepped inside, lifted the cord. Everything of her below the rising cord vanished. In a moment there were just hands floating in the air. Those disappeared as she pulled the loop shut. "Pull the cord inside but leave it hanging." I could hear her fine.

"That's astounding."

"There is still one little hole up high where someone can see inside. You must be careful about making sounds. You can be heard. If you take reasonable precautions neither people nor animals should be able to scent you." A knot appeared in the air. Fingers poked through, expanded the loop outward. It dropped. Magodor stepped out. She untied the bowline, handed me the cord. Her fingers were soft and hot, but I jerked away from the prick of a talon as sharp as a razor. She raised a finger to her lips.

I pulled that cord around my waist the way she had worn it. It stayed in place without any special tucking or tying. I couldn't see it but could feel it. I observed, "The sands are running. How do I get out of here?" See? No commitment at all. Any she heard she made up herself out of wishful thinking.

"Abyss."

The guy who had driven the coach floated out of a shadow. I had not suspected his presence. Magodor was pleased by my surprise. "Show Mr. Garrett to the street."

Abyss looked at me from eyes that were leagues away inside his hood. The air grew cold. I got the feeling he resented being forced to bother with me. I thought of a couple of cracks but doubted he had the brain or sense of humor to understand. And I still had to get out of there.

As I left that room, Magodor said, "Be careful. The Shayir are desperate and dangerous."

"Right." The Godoroth, of course, were just playful puppies.

I encountered several servants before leaving the house, startling every one. None paid Abyss any mind, though one who passed close by suffered one of those unexpected chills that sometimes fall upon you for no obvious reason.

Abyss never said a word. I felt his eyes upon me for a long time after I got my feet onto cobblestones.

# 11

Just playful puppies, the Godoroth.

I moved fast for a few blocks, just to get some distance. Then I stopped to get my bearings.

I had been right. The place was right up there. I didn't recognize the particular house, but it wouldn't take much effort to find out who owned it. I wondered if I should bother. Knowing might be too scary.

Before I moved on, I charted a course unlikely to lead me into trouble. I had to get to the Dead Man. I needed some serious advice. I had fallen into deep shit if I was dealing with real gods. I might be into it deep anyway.

I moved fast and tried to watch every which way at once, sure that the effort was a waste because I was dealing with shapeshifters who could walk behind me and just be something else every time I looked around.

My head still hurt, though my hangover had faded. I was past the sleepiness, but I was starved and all I really wanted was a sample of Dean's cooking.

The streets were not crowded. Up there they never are. But times have changed. I saw several enterprising pushcart operators trying to sell trinkets or services. They would not have dared in times past. Used to be privately hired security thugs would send their kind scurrying with numerous bruises.

They still did, I discovered. I came on several brunos bouncing an old scissor sharpener all over an acre of street. They eyeballed me but saw I was headed downhill. Why risk any pain encouraging me to hurry? I guess those other cartmen were

around because the thugs did not have time to get them all. Or
they had purchased a private license from the guards.

Not long after I crossed the boundary into the work-aday real
world, I realized that I had acquired a tail. She didn't give me a
good look, so I could not be sure, but I suspected she might have
had red hair when I was on the back end of the chase.

Sometimes you just got more balls than brains. You do stuff
that don't make sense later. Especially if you blow it.

I was lucky this time but still can't figure out why I headed for
Brookside Park instead of going home. If that was the redhead
back there she knew where I lived.

The park was a mile out of my way, too. It is a big tract of trees
and brush and reservoirs fed by springs that fill a creek running
off the flank of the Hill. There are Royal fishponds and a Royal
aviary and a stand of four-story granaries and silos supposedly
kept full in case of siege or disaster. I wouldn't bet much on there
being a stash if ever we are forced to tap those resources. Corruption in TunFaire is such that the officials in charge probably don't
even go through bureaucratic motions before selling whatever the
farmers bring in.

But, hell. Maybe I am too cynical.

The park police force, never numerous nor energetic nor effective at their best, had worse problems than the thugs up the
Hill. Whole tribes of squatters had set up camp. Again I wondered
why they found TunFaire so attractive. The Cantard is hell by anybody's reckoning, but a lot less so if you were born there. Why
leave the hell you know, walk hundreds of miles, plunk yourself
down in a town where not only do you have no prospects but the
natives all hate you and don't need much excuse to do you grief?

On the other hand—and I don't understand why—TunFaire is
a dream for this whole end of the world, the golden city. Maybe
you can't see why if you are looking at it from the inside.

The woman gave me more room out there, off the street, so
she would be less obvious. I didn't get a better look.

I strode briskly, hup two three four. Up and down hump and
swale, round bush and copse. I darted into a small, shady stand of
evergreens in a low place, careful not to disturb the old needles on
the ground. Hey, I used to be Force Recon. I was the bear in the
woods.

I selected a friendly shadow, did the trick with the cord that
was supposed to make me invisible. I waited.

She was careful. You have to be when you are tracking somebody and they drop out of sight. They could be setting an ambush.

I didn't plan to jump her. I just wanted to try my new toy and get a look at someone who seemed interested in me.

She was about six feet tall, dishwater blonde, sturdy, maybe twenty-five, better groomed than most gals you see on the street. She had an adequate supply of curves but wasn't dressed to brag. She wore a homespun kind of thing that would have looked better cut up and sewed up and used to dress large batches of potatos. From what I could see she lacked legs and feet. Her skirts were that long. She made me think of a younger version of Imar's wife, Imara.

She moved cautiously, as though she knew I had turned. She eased past not ten feet away. I held my breath. It was obvious she could not see me. It was just as obvious that she felt I was real close. She had the heebie-jeebies. I restrained my boyish side and didn't yell "Boo!" I studied her but didn't come up with a clue. She might be some nightmare in disguise. Whatever, she was no smouldering redhead.

She seemed human. Do devils get the heebie-jeebies?

She decided to get the hell out of there before bad things happened. Which suggested that bad things could. But that might only be because she was Shayir and knew something unpleasant about the Godoroth.

Some surprise that would be.

I do a good tail. I decided to put off seeing the Dead Man, and suffering his wisdom, long enough to see where this mouse ran. I spotted her a lead.

I discovered that becoming invisible imposes limitations. Like I was enclosed inside some kind of sack I could see through. There was plenty of air in there with me. The walls of the sack didn't collapse. It was like being inside a big, floppy bubble that wobbled and tangled and toppled when you moved. You could get around, but you had to be careful. If you got in a hurry, you stumbled and rolled downhill into a soggy low spot. The bag didn't keep water from soaking your knees and elbows.

Rorjfrazzle! Mirking sludglup! Everything just has to have a down side.

Or three. It took me ten minutes to get back out of the sack. The loop in the cord has to line up with the closed hole just right. If you have been moving around, you probably didn't keep track of where that hole went. Rotten racklefratz!

As I stumbled out and crawled away and started undoing my bowline, I realized that the tittering above wasn't the gossip of sparrows. A tiny voice only inches overhead piped, "We seen what you done. We seen what you done."

A pixie colony inhabited the grove. Now that they were bouncing around and giggling they were obvious. I hadn't noticed a thing when they were silent.

I didn't commence my rebuttal till I was safely away from any branch likely to serve as an aerial outhouse.

# 12

I headed for my house. The girl was long gone.

Used to be whenever I was out I had to knock so Dean would let me in. Before he left town he looted my savings to have a key lock installed so I could let myself in. Being a bright boy, I had my key with me. I used it.

The door opened an inch and stopped. Dean had the chain on.

I closed the door gently, took a moment to collect myself, knocked briskly. The Goddamn Parrot started up inside. O Wonder of Horrors, the little vulture had made it home on his own. I tried to avoid worrying about what kind of omen that might be.

I stepped back while I waited, studied the face of my house. It was a very dark brown, built of rough brick. I saw several places where the mortar needed tuck-pointing. The upstairs window trim needed fresh paint. Might be a job for Saucerhead some time when he wasn't tied up cracking skulls.

"Damn it, Dean! Come on! If you've had a heart attack and I've got to bust the door down I'm gonna break your legs."

There was a horrendous squawl behind me. I whirled. A huge, ugly ogre had gotten too near a donkey cart. A wheel had crushed his toes. He was bounding around on one foot offering to whip all comers.

"Ah, shuddup!" an old granny lady advised. She hooked the heel of his good foot with the crook of her umbrella. He went down hard. Ogres are solid-bottomed fellows, as a rule. This one was no exception. His breath deserted him in a mighty whoof. The cobblestones buckled. I might have a traffic hazard out front for months now. Maybe years. Who knew when a city crew would come and actually do something?

The crowd howled and mocked the ogre. Ogres are not popular because they are just not nice people, generally, but this was an especially tough crowd. They would have laughed had he been a sweet little old nun. Times had the mob in a vicious humor.

I spied my new friend Adeth. She wore a darker, longer wig and had changed apparel, but I was sure it was her. She moved like a cat now, without wasted motion, absolutely graceful. Maybe while Dean made up his mind to answer the door I could stroll over there and invite her to dinner.

I hammered the door some more. Then I got my key out again. I would unlock the damned thing again, then kick the chain loose. I was in one bad mood.

My head still throbbed like a couple of pixies were in there waltzing in combat boots.

Dean opened up as I reached with the key. "We have to talk," I told him. "Let's rehash the argument over that damned lock that cost me more than most guys make working twelve hours a day for two months."

"What happened?"

"I couldn't get into my own house, that's what happened! Some damned fool put the chain on!" The Goddamn Parrot was in fine voice. "When did that damned thing come home? How did it get inside?"

"Hours ago, Mr. Garrett. I thought you sent it." He nodded his head toward the Dead Man's room, scowled. "He told me to let it in." Dean shuddered.

On cue, I heard from Old Bones. *Garrett. Come here. I want to review events of the past few months.*

Him and his hobbies. "What you're going to hear about is events of the past few hours."

Dean shivered again. The Dead Man gives him the creeps. He has as little to do with His Nibs as he can.

"That dressed-up buzzard over there should of let you know I was having some trouble."

"I'll make some tea," Dean said, by way of offering a white flag.

"Sounds good. Thanks." When he gets those big hurt eyes it is hard to stay mad at him. "But you, you traitor, you deserter," I snapped through the doorway of the small front room, "you're going to star in an experiment to see if parrots make good ha-

senpfeffer." The shape my head was in, I was real short on tolerance.

I went into the Dead Man's room.

*Pickled parrot?*

"He must be good for something."

*Do I detect a measure of crabbiness?*

"Things are closing in on me. I was getting used to not having
to deal with Dean's nagging. I was getting used to not having to
deal with your outrageous demands. Then you woke up. He came
home. I went out for a walk and a bunch of ugly wazoos bopped
me on the head."

*The picture the bird brought in had you lunging through a
coach without the forethought to open the nether exit.*

He has moments when he looks beyond the end of his nose.
And an ugly nose it is, too.

The Dead Man has a human look to him. You glance into his
room—the biggest in the house and poorly lighted at his insistence even though he cannot see—and your gaze is drawn to a
wooden chair at the room's center. Maybe you could call it the
Dead Man's throne. It is massive—but it has to be to support four
hundred and some pounds. He has not moved in all the years I
have known him. He *has* grown seedier. Though he can protect
himself if he concentrates, mice and bugs do nibble when his attention wanders.

His outstanding feature, other than size, is his schnoz. It's like
an elephant's trunk a little over a foot long.

*Bad day?*

"It was a bad day when I got woke up at a totally ridiculous
hour, thank you very much. It has gone downhill ever since. Why
don't you just dig into my head?"

*I would prefer that you told it. I get more subtext examining the
subjective side.*

This from a guy who insisted I had to maintain my emotional
distance when I reported to him. We might as well be married. You
can't win with him.

*This is not good.*

"Hey, I hardly got started."

*I read you. These are not friendly gods. These are old-style
gods, all wrath and thou shalt not.*

"You know them?"

Dean brought in a tray with teapot, honey, cup, spoon. What?
Usually he just handed me a mug ready to go. Was he kissing up?

*Only by reputation. They have been marginal pantheons since the beginning, deities of ancient nomadic immigrants. Both religions were too cold and hard to win many converts. They are much alike.*

"Oh, your head!" Dean said. He was looking straight down at the top of my conk. "No wonder you're in a black mood. Don't move. I'll clean that up." He bustled out.

*Apparently your skull is as thick as I have claimed.*

"Huh?"

*Your head wound is worse than you realized.*

"What did I say? The good news just piles up." I reflected on what he had sent. "I got a question."

*Yes?* I felt a mental smirk.

"Back when we dealt with that crazy Loghyr you told me Loghyr never found proof of the existence of any gods and claimed logic suggests they can't exist. I believe you said 'They are not necessary to explain anything. Nature does not provide that which is not needed.' "

*That is correct. There is no concrete proof that any of the deities worshipped in this city exist as independent entities, outside the imaginations of those with the will to believe.*

"Who tried to toss me through that coach door, then? You telling me they were scamming?"

*That is a possibility deserving of examination. But to your question. For the sake of argument, your interlocuters were indeed Daiged, Rhogiro, and Ringo. Magodor gave you your answer in her remarks.*

Oh boy. Here came my favorite part of our relationship, the part where he tries to expand my horizons by forcing me to expand my intellect.

Dean came back with our first aid stuff. I keep a good home medicine cabinet. For a while I had a girlfriend who was a doctor. She fixed me up because I seem to get dinged up every time I turn around.

"I'm a little woozy here, Chuckles. How's about you just hand it to me this time?"

*All the sport is gone out of you, Garrett. The very nature of their situation should shriek the answer. If they fall off the Street of the Gods, if they are forced to leave the Dream Quarter, if they lose their last True Believer, they cease to exist.*

"Ouch!" Dean was dabbing at my head with a hot, wet rag.

"You mean I wouldn't have this dent in my head if somebody didn't believe in the ugly boys?"

*Essentially.*

Dean asked, "Who sewed this up for you, Mr. Garrett?"

"Sewed what?" And to His Nibs, "But they exist on their own. Nobody dreamed what was happening to me."

Dean told me, "You have three . . . six . . . nine stitches here. You must have bled pretty bad."

"No wonder I'm so weak. I thought it was a concussion."

"Might be that, too."

*They need only be imagined and believed in fervently enough, on the right level. They assume an existence of their own, within the attributes assigned them.*

"Careful!" I snapped at Dean. "That's tender. They must have given me something to make it not hurt. Ouch! Damnit! . . ."

"Don't be such a pansy."

"You aren't digging for gold. Old Bones, your theory is absurd."

*Gods are absurd, Garrett. And it is a hypothesis, not a theory. A theory is supported by experimental proof.*

"I'm just looking to see if there's any infection," Dean grumbled, doing his hurt thing.

I ignored him, told the Dead Man, "There you go splitting hairs."

*"Theory" is a much-abused word, particularly by those in the divinity trades. Be careful, Dean. If those stitches break, his brain may leak out. Have you formed any plans, Garrett? To deal with your situation?*

*My* situation. "I take it I need to worry in a big way." When the Dead Man sets aside his own self-centered interests, I know he is troubled deeply. It was obvious that he had no problem believing that I could have fallen afoul of real gods and not just sleight-of-hand con folk somehow setting me up.

I answered his question. "I don't have a clue. That's why I came home. Are you going to pay your rent?" Though *he* insists he is a full partner, the most work he does is aimed at getting out of doing anything constructive.

"Right now I don't see any choice but to play along."

*Indeed. Wriggling out of this will require intense self-discipline and long hours of work by all concerned.*

"Don't whine. I hate it when you whine. You were way overdue to kick in around here anyway. You could've saved me a ton of grief with Maggie Jenn if you would've just woke up." He had unraveled the mystery at the heart of my most recent case before I had finished telling the first half of the tale. It was a case he had slept through stubbornly.

# 13

It was great to be in the righteous right so solid I could bury my spurs in the Dead Man.

"Will you hold still?" Dean snapped. "Looks like a little pus here. Let me clean it out so we won't have to cauterize later."

I had a vision of my handsome face set off by a strip of scar tissue skewed across my scalp. I held still, but it hurt.

Dean said, "Miss Tate was here while you were away, Mr. Garrett. She . . ."

"She must have been watching the place." To know he was home so soon after he arrived. Tinnie probably shouldn't be the ex-girlfriend. She was waiting for me to make the first move toward reconciliation. I liked to think.

"News travels fast, Mr. Garrett."

"Did it have some help?"

"It's possible." Dean is as stubborn as I am. He is determined to get me hooked up with Tinnie Tate or Maya Stubbs, both of them beautiful, squared-away sweethearts who deserve Prince Charmings who are the real thing.

The Dead Man sent, *Miss Tate was as charming, witty, and beautiful as ever and her companion, Miss Weider, cannot be encompassed by normal superlatives. Nevertheless, their petition will have to wait.*

"Alyx Weider?" Those two must have buttered him up big. He has no use whatsoever for the female of my species—or any other species, as far as I have seen. I'm sure that is why he tries to sabotage most of my romances. He doesn't think most women deserve me.

Them pigs were flying formation today.

Dean tends toward the opposing opinion.

He said, "I believe Miss Tate did introduce her as Alyx." He did something to my head that sent a ribbon of pain streaking from my scalp to my toenails.

"You're on my list, Dean. Someday I'll get my chance to patch you up."

I am on retainer as chief of security at Weider's brewery. My role is to drop in unexpectedly and check employee honesty. I saved Weider from being robbed blind a long time back. The job was my reward. Old man Weider has been trying to get me on full time ever since. There are times when a regular job looks real good, even if I would have to call somebody else boss.

Alyx was the old man's baby, much younger than the rest of his sprats. I had not seen her for some time. She had been a lovely but shy girl at sixteen. I was surprised to hear that she had come to the house. Her dad wasn't the sort to let his baby girl out, especially in today's TunFaire.

*Miss Tate brought her. There is something happening within the Weider family, possibly having to do with The Call and other radical fringe human rights groups. We owe them an interest but this mess must take precedence. Gods! Garrett! Garrett! At best you are an agnostic. But still you become entangled with a clutch of redundant deities.*

"Like I went looking for them? I'm not agnostic, though. I'm indifferent. My philosophy is, you leave the gods alone and usually they'll leave you alone."

"Another one bites the dust," Dean said.

"Huh?" He find a nit?

"Another of your adolescent fantasies."

Dean is a religious man. I never pressed him, but I do not understand his blind devotion to his peculiar monotheistic mythology when we are plagued by a thousand other deities and, obviously, those gods occasionally really do mess around with mortals. The human capacity for selective blindness appears to be infinite.

For me the religion business becomes problematic when the gods outnumber their worshippers.

Well, in some cases. One of which I seem to have stumbled into. I told the Dead Man, "You sound like you're actually interested. Maybe I ought to be suspicious. But I don't think there's time."

*Exactly. Long hours and rigorous self-discipline lie ahead.
Your first chore will be to visit the Royal library and sweet-talk
your friend into loaning us whatever books they have devoted to
these religions.*

"Uh . . . that might not be so easy."

*Make peace.*

"It's not that. Linda Lee and I get along fine. I found some rare
books she let get away."

*Find me some books. Dean! Put aside your prejudice for a mo-
ment. Go to Mr. Dotes' establishment . . .*

"That may not be any good either. Morley has gone upscale.
He might be trying to put his whole past behind him."

*Must you interrupt?* He rooted around inside my head. He
never does that unless he is seriously provoked or concerned. He
reviewed my experiences during his nap. Usually he is overly
careful to respect my privacy.

His behavior was troubling. I had to suspect that he knew
something that had not occurred to me.

*Who do we know who has the ability to read? Other than
yourself?*

"Playmate," I replied, puzzled. "But not real good. Winger, a
little. Morley. Barking Dog . . ."

*Winger?* Astonishment.

"She's been learning. The better to con you with, my dear. Always a surprise, Winger is."

*Not good enough. Try to get your librarian friend to come in.*

"Why?" Talk about astonishment. The Dead Man asking for a
woman to be brought into the house?

*Any books you do obtain will have to be read to me. It is too
difficult for me to do it by myself.*

Turning the pages is a bitch when you're dead. Though he
could manage it if he had to.

"I got you."

*An even bigger problem is that he has a hard time seeing if he
can't use somebody's else's eyes.*

*Once you have dealt with Linda Lee I want you to go to the
Dream Quarter. Examine the temples involved in this business.
Move carefully. Waste no time but take all the time you need to
study the places right while maintaining your personal safety.*

"What? Shouldn't I look for this key?"

*That is of no concern now. Information is. If you collect the available information I will sift the clues. I am not as powerful as these gods, but I am far smarter.*

"No self-image problem over there," I told Dean, who had made no effort to leave.

*Much the same can be said of you, Garrett. I do not recall the Godoroth well, but do believe Magodor may be the only one smarter than a four-year-old.*

Wonderful.

*Time is wasting, Garrett. To the library. Then to the Dream Quarter.*

"What about the Shayir?"

*What about them?*

"Apparently they were on to me even before the Godoroth. What do I do if they close in on me?"

*Use your wits, guided by experience. You have your weapons and your physical skills. In any event, you will achieve nothing standing there. Dean. After you have spoken to Mr. Dotes, locate Mr. Tharpe. If Mr. Tharpe is unavailable, find Mr. Playmate. As a last resort, call upon Miss Winger. Then return here quickly. I will have more for you to do. Garrett.*

I paused at the door. I will say this about the Dead Man. It is blue-haired hell getting him started, but once he is into something he is a take-charge kind of guy. "What?"

*Take the parrot.*

"What? Are you crazy? I got lucky a while ago, but you know my luck ran out. He'll get me killed before I walk a block. He'll tell some giant his mother does trolls, and they'll find parts of me all over town."

*Take the parrot. Put a lanyard on his leg if you feel the need. I believe he will be more cooperative than usual.*

"Dead would be more cooperative than usual."

*Garrett.*

He was impatient. He had no time to play. When he is in a mood like that it is best to humor him.

The Goddamn Parrot offered me a black look but only nibbled my fingers once when I moved him from his perch to my shoulder. Hell if I would tie him down. Anytime he wanted to escape I would stand there grinning and waving bye-bye. But I knew how my luck would run already. Just like before, he would beat me home.

"I need an eye patch and an earring," I muttered. "Yo ho ho."

# 14

I stood on the stoop wishing for a beard to go with the earring and eye patch. I growled, "Argh! Prepare to repel boarders."

T. G. Parrot squawked, "Awk! Shiver me timbers!"

I tried to give him my best jaundiced look, but he couldn't get the full benefit perched as he was on my shoulder.

Neighborhood kids materialized out of the crowd. "Can we feed your parrot, Mr. Garrett?"

"Yeah. To one of those flying thunder lizards." A pair were circling high above, shopping for plump pigeons.

The kids didn't get it. Short attention spans, I guess. It had been a while since their elders had worried about trouble with thunder lizards. Now we had centaur infestations and whatnot.

As my old Aunt Boo used to say, "It's always something."

I looked up the street. Mrs. Cardonlos was out watching. I waved. Always a neighborly smile, that Mr. Garrett. It drove her crazy. Made her *sure* I was up to no good.

I'd barely entered the crowd when Dean left the house. He was pale. He didn't look at me. He headed downhill, toward Morley's Joy House, which now masquerades as The Palms.

I went the other way, amidst the fastest traffic. I didn't make much effort to see if I was followed. If I had gods on my case they would have resources better than mine. I headed where I had to go, wondering why the Dead Man was taking this so seriously.

I think I was followed by the same woman, only now she seemed taller and had a fall of white on the right side of otherwise raven hair that hung quite long. I didn't get a good look at her clothing, but it had a foreign air.

The Royal Library has a side entrance that isn't well known to those without friends inside. You do have to slip past an ancient guard who uses his job to catch up on naps he lost while he was off to war. Once he is behind you, all you have to do is avoid notice by the senior librarian. That isn't hard, either. She is ancient and slow and stumbles into things when she is moving around. Once you are inside, you have to decide whether to see your friend or load up with rare books to sell.

Turned out that was the way it used to be. Changes had been made. All my fault for returning the stolen books I had happened upon the other day.

The old man had been replaced. A hard young veteran manned his desk. He was snoring. A liquor bottle dangled from his hand. Sneaky was wasted on him. I was tempted to leave the parrot on his shoulder. Let him wake up and find himself infested. He wouldn't take another drink for hours.

I resisted. We must not dishonor our public servants.

I found Linda Lee in the stacks, peering intently at worn and flaky leather spines. She had a stylus in her mouth, bitten crosswise. She carried a wax note tablet and a small lantern. Her sleek brown hair was pulled back in an old maid's bun and, damn me, a few gray hairs showed on her temple. She might have a few years she hadn't mentioned.

Even so, she was the cutest bookworm I'd ever seen.

I asked, "What do you do when you have to make a note?"

She jumped. She whirled. Sparks danced in her eyes. I never knew how she was going to greet me. "What the hell are you doing here?" She had no trouble talking around the stylus.

"Looking for you."

"Can't get a date?"

"It's professional this time . . ." There you go shoving one of those big old dirty hooves of yours right down your throat, Garrett. You slick talker. "My mouth just won't say what my head tells it to today."

"Surprise, surprise. What the hell is that on your shoulder? You trying a new look?"

"You remember Mr. Big."

"Unfortunately. That's why I asked. Why haven't you drowned it? What's wrong with it?"

"Huh?" She wasn't herself. I wondered who she was. That might clue me in about who she wanted me to be so all four of us could get along.

"It hasn't said anything. Usually it's criminally obnoxious."

"The Dead Man did something to him."

Linda Lee shuddered. The Dead Man gave her the creeps. That might be a problem.

"So ignore the fact that I haven't seen you since I was a girl."

"Three days?"

"What do you want?" For all she apparently wanted to fight, she kept her voice down. Her superiors and coworkers didn't like me wandering in and out. It shook their confidence in their safety and the security of the Royal collection. If I kept it up, someday they would have to do something. Maybe even put out money for a real guard.

"Three days isn't long enough for you to turn into your own grandmother . . . Damn! Now I'm doing it."

"It hasn't been a good day. Time is flying, Garrett."

No need to cause more difficulties. I told the story, quick and straight, giving the most detail in the least time. I left out a few details she didn't really need, like how exciting some of those goddess types were.

She grew thoughtful before I finished. "Really? Gods? I never . . . You don't think about them actually getting in your way, do you?"

"No. They're like another remove beyond the firelords and stormwardens. They may shape your life, but you don't figure on banging into one going around a corner. Given my druthers, I'd never run into either one."

"Too much potential for disaster."

"Absodamnlutely. You know anything about these gods?"

"Only their names. There are a lot of old mythologies. They aren't my area. I could get Mad."

"I thought you were. I just couldn't figure out why."

"Mad is Madelaine. She handles our scriptures."

I recalled a harridan of satanic disposition old enough to have written the first drafts of most of her charges. "That's not necessary. I just need whatever I can get on the Godoroth and Shayir over to the house so somebody can read them to the Dead Man."

"You can't take books out of here."

"I thought I explained. I've only got a few days and I don't have a clue where to start." I touched the high points again.

She understood, all right. She was negotiating. If she was going to take risks she wanted something more than a kiss and a thank you. Maybe some yellow roses.

"All right. All right," she whispered, throwing a troubled glance over her left shoulder. She placed a finger against her lips. I nodded. Her ears were better than mine. First thing they check when you apply at the library is your ears.

She gestured "Go away!" with finger still to lips. I went. She would do me the favor. She might even read for the Dead Man. He could charm them when he wanted. But she was going to make me pay.

I eased into shadow at the nether end of the stacks as the mother of all librarians materialized at Linda Lee's end. The way she moved, she could have run the hundred-yard dash in slightly under a decade. She leaned on a gnarly, ugly cane notched once for every time she had caught someone talking. Her hair was white and thin and wild, and she was bent way over. She wore cheaters, which suggested she had wealthy relatives. Spectacles cost a fortune. But she still could not see her hand more than a foot from her face. I could have danced naked where I was and she would not have had a clue.

She croaked, "What's all the racket down here, child?"

On the other hand . . .

"Mistress Krine?"

"The noise, child. The noise. I heard it all the way upstairs. Do you have one of your men down here again?"

One of? Well. You devil.

"Mistress! I was only whispering to myself. I can't read the lettering on these spines. The gold flake is almost gone."

"And that's the project, isn't it? Find the volumes that need restoration? In future, restrain your expression of frustration . . . What was that? Is someone there?"

Not anymore. I was gone, down the back way to the back door, with less sound than a mouse on the run. I floated past the guard. His sleep remained untroubled.

What the *hell* was wrong with the Goddamn Parrot today? He just blew the opportunity of a lifetime. He hadn't made a whimper.

# 15

It was still daytime outside. I know because they took a couple of bars of sunlight and tried to drive my eyeballs out the back of my head. It wasn't morning anymore, but it looked like one of those days when the rest of the world would insist that it stay morning all day long.

Once the pain faded, I surveyed the immediate area. The library stands amid an infestation of official buildings, both municipal and royal. Traffic is different there, being made up mostly of functionaries. I saw nothing unusual—which meant only that I couldn't see any watchers.

I headed out.

The afternoon remained so relentlessly pleasant that I began to give in despite the state of my head. Infected by a lighter mood, I paused at the Chancellery steps to listen to the crackpots rave. Any wacko with a goofball grievance or a fanciful cause can use those steps as a forum. Never kindly, the rest of us use them as free entertainment. I know some of the less bizarre, habitual speakers. In my line, knowing people is a major asset. I didn't nurture my contacts enough anymore. Today I didn't have time. I gave Barking Dog Amato a thumbs up and dropped a groat into his cup, waved to a couple other howlers. I moved on. My head throbbed. My parrot never cracked his beak. The Dead Man must have destroyed his brain.

Around and down and off for the south side. I wasn't going to like this thing because of all the walking. There are less strenuous ways to get around, but none faster. Even the great wizards with their big coaches and running footmen and outriders and trumpeters can't get around as fast as a man on foot. Walking, you can cut through alleys and climb over fences.

I didn't shortcut much. I don't climb unless I have to, and alleys often harbor people or prospects best left unchallenged. Still, when the choice is a hundred yards straight or half a mile around . . .

I had used Slight Alley often. A lot of people do. It stays relatively clean. Heavy traffic discourages both squatters and the forces of free-lance socialism. It is difficult to manage what is essentially a privacy-oriented one-on-one transaction when at any time somebody troublesome may wander between you and your . . . er . . . client.

I risked Slight Alley.

The ramshackle frame half-timber structures popular in the neighborhood leaned in overhead, reaching out to one another like drunks in need of mutual support. Most of the afternoon's intense sunshine failed to penetrate, but there was more light than normal. The paving bricks were cleaner than usual, too. You could see their dark red. On the other hand, there were squatters in residence. Not only the ratmen you expected, but families of refugees.

The times they change.

I wondered how we would feed all the immigrants. If racist groups like The Call had their way, the refugees would eat the dwarves and ogres and elves already here.

I stopped. "What?" I had caught a strange smell. There was no describing it. It was neither awful nor particularly pleasant. Mostly it was startling.

It was gone in an instant. I couldn't catch it again. Happens all the time. I resumed walking, ignored the sleepy-eyed stare of a drunken ratman trying to decide if I was behaving strangely.

I was. At the first hint of the unusual my hand had darted to Magodor's cord. My habit is to face sudden threats with an eighteen-inch oaken nightstick into which has been introduced, by way of providing additional encouragement to the customer, a pound of lead at the business end.

Slight Alley has a couple of jags and an offset where it crosses another alley stretching east and west. I noticed that the light had a golden, autumnal cast. Though diffuse, it sent shadows crawling over the walls. Some of those seemed to assume almost recognizable shapes.

Then there were the whispers behind me, like the whispers of mocking children, perhaps speaking a foreign tongue. I felt a lot better when I reached a real street filled with real people.

As I hurried the last mile, I tried to think of somebody I knew in the religion racket who wouldn't run me off on sight. Most religious leaders are paranoid about their privacy. They feel especially threatened if they suspect an investigation of their finances. They have me run off just on the chance somebody might want me to check them out.

Playmate was the only religious character I knew. And he was just a wannabe preacher.

Then how about somebody who would answer my questions in order to get rid of me? Somebody who had no use for me at all. I tried to recall who all had been involved that time that Maya and I had straightened out the feud between the Church and the Orthodox over their missing Terrell Relics.

Hell. I didn't even have useful *enemies* down in the Dream Quarter.

I hit the Street of the Gods farther to the west than I had planned, but Slight Alley had given me a case of the willies. There was no reason not to feel safe now. The Dream Quarter is the safest neighborhood in town.

I hustled past Chattaree and other huge places belonging to successful cults, recalled from past cases. Back then, though, I was dealing with flawed holy men, not the gods themselves. What was Maya doing now? I could ask Dean in a few days. He would know. They stayed in touch.

The weather must have melted the stone hearts of the older priests because the acolytes and postulants and what-have-you were all out fluttering like mayflies. The scenery was positively brilliant around the female-oriented temples.

The first four or five people I approached had not heard of either the Godoroth or the Shayir. Farther east I got a couple of bewildered "I ought to know what you're talking about but don't" responses, like the guy seven and a half feet tall, pale as death, wearing a black robe and lugging an ivory staff topped by an angry cobra's head. This character had no more meat on him than a skeleton. He mused, "Shayir? Those the people with the squid gods?"

"I don't know." Squids? I'm not even fond of mortal cephalopods, let alone many-armed critters with delusions of being masters of the universe.

"No, wait. Those are the Church of the Nameless Unspeakable Elder Outer Darkness From Beyond the Stars folks. I'm sorry. I should know, but I don't. But you're headed in the right direction. They must be right on the bottom end, ready to fall into the river."

How you going to learn anything when nobody knows anything?

I thanked him, accepted a small card good for one admission into one of his snake-worshipping services, said I sure would stop by, I just plain loved snakes. The bigger the better. I had a few for breakfast in the islands.

He guaranteed me they had a serpent that was a genuine kickass god snake big enough to snack on horses.

"Excellent idea. Round them all up and let him get fat." Then feed him to the ratmen.

A block later I met a guy who knew about both cults. He was a free-lance guide and street sweeper. He did little odd jobs, and the temples fed him scraps and let him sleep in warm spots out of the way, as long as he didn't spook the marks. He was raggedy around the edges, so probably didn't get a lot of work at the high end of the street.

"Name's No-Neck," he told me, proud of the fact that once upon a time folks thought enough of him to hang a nickname. "Had a little muscle on me when I was young."

"I figured. Marine?"

"Hey! Fugginay! How'd you know?"

It might have been the tattoos. "You can always tell a Marine. Got that special attitude."

"Yeah. Ain't dat da troot? You too, eh?"

"First Force." I added the years, so he would know there was no chance we had acquaintances in common. I hate it when people play that game. They find out you are from a particular neighborhood, whatever, they spend an hour asking do you know this one or that like all you ever did with your life was keep track in case somebody asked.

"Good. Dat's good. You come wit' me. I show you where dey hang. What you say you want to know for?"

"I didn't, No-Neck. But I'm supposed to check up on some changes going on down here." I told him about the Antitibet cult coming in.

"Yeah, yeah," he said. "I'm gonna help wit' da moving. Dese here Dellbo priests from da Cantard, you ask me, dey got no business taking over from honest TunFairen gods, but rules is rules and the gods made dem demselfs. You can only have so many temples and stuff or pretty soon you lose control and have dem loony churches wit' only tree members where nutsos worship killer radishes and stuff."

I am no heartbreaker, so I didn't let him know there were some off-Street storefront temples where minuscule congregations really did worship holy rutabagas and snails and whatnot. If the mind of man can come up with a screwball god, however bizarre, a god will arise to answer that lunatic appeal. At least in the imagination of man.

Many of the nonhuman species have their religions, too, but they do not go for diversity and cuckoo. Only us humans need gods crazier than we are.

And we are the future of the world. The other races are the fading past.

Makes you wonder if there isn't a god of gods with a really nasty sense of humor.

# 16

For a couple of sceats No-Neck showed me both the former Shayir temple and the Godoroth.

"Couple of real dumps," I said. "Tell me what you know about these gods." Thought I would catch him while he had a grateful glow on. I glanced around. Once you have experienced Chattaree it is hard to imagine such squalor.

"Cain't tell you jack, pal. Wisht I could. But it ain't smart even ta name names, like Strayer, or Chanter, or Nog the Inescapable. Dey is nasty as hell, all a dem."

"That's no surprise."

The Shayir and Godoroth were competing for the last hovel on the Street. It was beyond the levee, leaned out over the river on rotting piles fifteen feet tall. One good flood surge and it would be gone. But it was home to the Godoroth, I guess, and nobody wants to get kicked out of their own house.

No-Neck told me, "Bot' places is closed down. Dey'll open back up in a couple days."

"Under new management?"

No-Neck frowned. He didn't have a lot of brain left over to untangle jokes and decipher sarcasms.

I asked, "Any reason I can't go in and look around?" There were no physical locks on the doors.

"You'd be trespassing."

Right on top of it, my man No-Neck.

"I wasn't planning to touch anything. I just want to see the set-ups. For my client's information."

"Uhm." He focused his intellect, frowning, investing heavily for a small return. The No-Necks of the world are great for getting work done as long as they have somebody to tell them what to do.

"I don't tink I unnerstand what you do."

I explained, not for the first time since we teamed up. I said, "It's like being a private soldier. A client hires me, I'm his one-man army, except I don't bust heads or break arms, I just find out things. The client I have now wants to find out as much as he can about these two cults."

No-Neck made a connection. "Like dat might be somebody what has to help decide who gets dat last temple."

"There you go." Far be it from me to disabuse a man of an erroneous intuition. Not that he was entirely off the mark.

"I guess it cain't hurt. You ain't involved wit' dem. If you was involved wit' dem I'd hafta raise a holler on account of some of dese gods would do any damned ting to stay on da Street."

"Ain't dat da troot." If you are big time, going off with the holy rutabagas won't get you no respect at all. Better gone than playing out of the Dream Quarter.

"Well, den let's look in dat dere place where da Shayir got bounced. But I guarantee you ain't gonna see nuttin' exciting."

We went into the Shayir place. Always quick on the uptake, I muttered, "Not going to find anything exciting here."

"Cleaned it out." No-Neck had a trained eye, too.

The dump was as bare as a thousand-year-old thunder lizard thigh bone, emptier than No-Neck's head. He said, "We done took all da stuff down to da place at da end. Goin' ta paint and fix up here."

I glanced right. I glanced left. I didn't stand all the way up because the ceiling was too low. The place was barely fifteen by twelve, last stronghold of an ancient religion, first bridgehead of a new one. It seemed touched by the same sad desperation you see in middle-aged men and women who can't let go of a youth that has long since stolen away.

"So let's stroll over there and count the silver."

"Silver? Dese is small gods, Garrett. Dey probably didn't even have no copper. Down here dey're da kind we call pewter gods. Petty pewter gods. Da pot metal boys." He leaned close, ready with a garlicky confidence. "You never say dat where dey might hear you, dough. Da fard'er dey slip da more dey demand respect, got it coming or not. You go on up dere to da high end of da Street, dem gods you don't never see no proof dey even exist. Dey ain't got time to be bodered. Down here, dough, dey might be running deir own bingos. And you better not cut dem where dey can hear it."

That sounded like a notion worth keeping in mind.

"I been front wit' you, Garrett. Tell me something straight."

"I'll try."

"How come you got dat stupid stuffed bird on your shoulder?"

The Goddamn Parrot. T. G. was being so good I'd forgotten him. "He isn't stuffed. He's just pretending." What the hell. I plucked the bird and studied him as we climbed crumbling steps on the face of the levee. They were the conclusion of the Street. No repairs had been offered them in recent lifetimes. The smell of river mud hung like an all-pervading mist. The air was thick with the flies that breed in the mud. They were nasty, hungry little flies.

The Goddamn Parrot was breathing, but his eyes were milky. "Hey, bird. Show some life. Got a man here wants to hear one of your jokes."

That flashy jungle chicken didn't make a sound.

"Just like a kid, eh?"

"How's that?"

"Clever as he can be when dere's nobody dere but you. Clams if you want him to show off." Maybe No-Neck was not as dense as he let on.

"You got it. Most of the time you got to hold him under water to shut him up. Got a mouth like a dock walloper. Gad! This place is a dump." The Godoroth temple hadn't been cleared, the movers had just piled the Shayir stuff inside where it could be unpacked or chunked in the river if things turned out that way. All the rats and roaches and filth were still on the job. No broom had gotten past the threshold any year recently. Definitely a place with character.

No-Neck chuckled. "Way I hear, da Godoroth got only one worshipper left, some old goof on the Hill wit' so much juice he's kept dem on way past dere time already. Say he was around when dey built dis burg. Been in a wheelchair more dan tirty years."

"And the gods won't sully their fingers cleaning up around here."

"You got it. Won't even run a message to dis dink when I want to offer to take care of da place for a reasonable retainer."

"Sounds like they're their own worst enemies." I put the God-damn Parrot back on my shoulder. All that vulture was going to do was breathe.

"You just said a mout'ful. I been working da Dream Quarter

tweny-eight years. You tink people fool demselves, you hang out down here, see what da gods do."

"You actually see them?"

He gave me a funny look. "You don't know much about how tings work here, do you?"

"No. I'm perfectly happy to let the gods ignore me, same as I ignore them."

"You cain't see dem. Not unless'n dey done gone to a lot of trouble to touch you, or you been working here a long time, like me. Den you maybe see shadows and glimmers or hear whispers or get chills and the willies. We could have a whole gang of dem standing around here right now. . . . Well, way I hear, dey wouldn't actually be standing. Shapes like dem little idol tings, dat's what dey might do if dey decided to come out and be visible a while."

I picked up a statue that had to be Magodor. Maggie was not a pretty girl. Her idol had more snakes, more fangs, more arms and claws than she had shown me. "How would you like this for a girlfriend?"

"Way da myts go, I wouldn't get dat close. Dat one's like a spider. Any mortals what do survive her, dey say she ruins for any mortal woman."

I examined one statuette after another. The ugly guys were even uglier, too. "Fun-looking bunch."

"Dem idols don't do dem justice, what da myts say."

"Bad?"

"Very. But dis one, she's da one I dream about. Call her Star."

"I've heard about her. I know what you mean. What about the boss couple? Imar and Imara? Big and dumb is my impression."

"Imar is your old-time always-pissed-off kind of god, real pain in da ass, loves da smell of burnt flesh, which is maybe why da Godorot' don't got dat many worshippers anymore."

"How about the Shayir? I know nothing about them. Who are they? How many of them are there? They have any really special attributes? Are they different from other gods? These Godoroth, overall, aren't anything special. There are gods or saints like them in most religions."

"Da Shayir ain't dat unusual neither. Well, Torbit the Strayer and Quilraq the Shadow, dey're weird. And Black Mona. But da All-Father god is Lang. He probably hatched out of da same egg as Imar. Dey even look alike."

No-Neck was not shy about digging in the boxes filled with Shayir relics. I wondered if he had rummaged through them before, supplementing his income. "Here. Here's all da idols." He held up one that did look just like the Imar idol up where the altar was.

"Let me see that." I upended Lang, probably an act of deadly disrespect. Sure enough, there was a dwarfish hallmark on the base, along with a date. That was dwarfish, too, but no mystery. Most scholars use the dwarfish dating system because human dating is so confusing, especially back a few centuries when every petty prince and tyrant insisted on setting dates based on his own birth or ascension.

I handed Lang back, went to the altar. The dust was thick. I sneezed, grabbed Imar, treated him with the same lack of respect that I had shown Lang. "Well. What do you know." Imar had the same hallmark and some of the same mold markings, though an earlier date. I could see the dwarves snickering. Stupid humans. Maybe there were thirty gods in the Dream Quarter who all looked exactly alike.

I wished I knew a good theologian. He could tell me how much a god's idol influenced his shape and attributes. Be funny if the gods headed downhill were on the skids because some mass-market idols of dwarfish manufacture didn't distinguish the little quirks that made an Imar an entirely different menace from a Lang.

"Can you read?" I gave a thousand to one in my mind.

"Never had da time to learn." I win. "Even when I was down to da Cantard and dey was trying to teach guys, just to keep dem out of trouble in da waiting time, I never got da time. How come you ask?"

"These idols came out of the same workshop. Out of the same mold. If you could read I'd ask you to look through the records, maybe find me something there."

No-Neck snickered. "You gonna tip me a reasonable tip for helping you out, Garrett?"

"Yeah. After I finish looking through this Shayir stuff." The Shayir were rich compared to the Godoroth. And even homelier, if their idols were accurate.

"You give me a good tip, you come on over to Stuggie Martin's, we can toss back a couple. I'll tell you how silly dis all gets around here sometimes."

"Sounds like a winner. If Stuggie Martin can draw a decent pint of dark."

"Top o' da line. Weider's."

Wouldn't you know?

# 17

After a few mugs, No-Neck and I had become friends for life. I told stories about my more outrageous cases. He told tales about his war days. I told stories about mine. Now that their hell is far enough away, I find that there are some memories worth saving. No-Neck told stories from his years in the Dream Quarter, and we giggled and laughed till the proprietor asked us to keep it down or do a stand-up so the whole place could enjoy our good humor. Sourpuss. Surprise! His name wasn't Stuggie Martin. The real Stuggie Martin did own the place once upon a time, but nobody living remembered him. It was easier and cheaper to stay Stuggie Martin's than it was to get a new sign.

All that fun and the Goddamn Parrot never horned in once. It was unnatural. I was beginning to wonder. Everybody in Stuggie Martin's thought he was some kind of half-alive affectation till I got him his own mug.

I was a little dizzy and it was getting shadowy outside when I told No-Neck, "Man, I got to get going. My partner will be having fits. Da way dis ting scopes out, I can't afford time to have a good time." It *was* time to get away. I was starting to talk like him.

The Goddamn Parrot was on the table, working on his beer, showing more signs of life than he had for hours. The bird was partial to the Weider Dark, too, which is all I can say positive about that animate feather duster.

What had the Dead Man done? That devil bird talked in his sleep.

Something was going on, I didn't have any idea what, and so what else was news?

An attraction that made Stuggie Martin's a popular and up-scale neighborhood hangout was an actual real glass window that let its patrons see the street outside. The window had lattices of ironwork protecting it inside and out, of course, and those didn't enhance the view, but you could watch the world go by. The name of the street out there was regional, after a province, typical of that part of town. I wouldn't remember it or be able to find it again, but that didn't matter. What did matter was that when I glanced out the window into the provincial street, amidst evening's shadows and oddly golden light, I spied that damned redhead whose twitching tail had lured me into this mess in the first place. She had taken station in a shadow across the way. The light didn't play fair. She stood out like a troll at a fairy dance contest.

I beckoned Stuggie's current successor, who had proven a fair keeper of the holy elixir, if short on good humor. "You got a back way out of here?"

He glanced at No-Neck, who put his seal of approval on me with a nod. "Sure. The back door."

Will wonders never cease?

I sucked down my beer, planted the Goddamn Parrot on my shoulder, said good-bye to No-Neck, scarfed the rest of the bird's beer and headed out. My navigation was unstable but under control. I looked forward to getting home and taking a nine-hour nap. I was a little less than fully alert. For some reason I had become preoccupied with significant persons not of the male persuasion. That can be the downside of a few good mugs. You start thinking about serious stuff and don't pay enough attention to what is happening around you.

I slid along the alley feeling totally cunning. If anybody was after me they would be watching the front door. Autumnal light illuminated the walls of the alley. Shadows played. I didn't pay much mind. It was late in the day.

I slipped around a corner, said "Awk!" at the same time as the Goddamn Parrot, pranced to one side and started running.

A guy had been waiting for me. He looked more human than troll or giant, but he was twelve feet tall and carried an axe with a handle as long as me. It had a bizarre double head, *big* curved blades, some kind of runes worked into the metal, a spike on the end of the handle. The handle itself looked like ebony or ironwood also deeply worked with runes. Some were inlaid with paint or metal. The guy had a wild long red beard and, probably, equally wild hair, but his head and the top half of his face were hidden inside an iron helmet that Dean could have used for an oven. He must have ridden in on a dragon or a big blue cow.

Maybe he didn't want me annoying his sister, following her around.

His clothes were not the height of fashion. Oh, maybe a thousand years ago, when people lived in caves and the badly-cured-hides look and smell was in. But not today, brother.

I had a hunch he was what I had smelled on my way down to the Dream Quarter.

The Goddamn Parrot came to life now. He flapped away. He squawked something outrageous at the big thing, distracting him for the moment I needed to get my rubber legs pumping. I banged into somebody. "What's the matter with you, buddy?" I was lucky. He was just some guy headed home from work, who hadn't had a bad day and was not in a belligerent mood.

"Sorry." I glanced back. The big character was slapping at the Goddamn Parrot like the bird was some annoying insect and his axe was a flyswatter. I probably couldn't have lifted the damned thing. He got a fix on me and started getting all that beef organized to head in my direction.

"Maybe keep an eye out where you're going." The working stiff headed right for the monster man, obviously not seeing a thing.

"Oh my," I told me. "I guess I just met one of the Shayir." I kept on moving as fast as wobble legs would allow.

Shadows and golden light ran with me. I suspected that meant something that might not be good.

A woman stepped into my path, possibly another version of the redhead I had tracked when the world was simple and gods were just bad practical jokes on the credulous. I faked left, got her off balance, and cut right. The Goddamn Parrot ripped past, flapping all out and cussing his fool head off. I would've cussed myself but needed to conserve my wind. I juked around a startled dwarf peddler and his cart full of knives, hurdled a water trough, zigged around an extremely short, fat character who might have been the world's only bald and morbidly obese dwarf, banged into an alley, and did quick and wonderful things with my piece of rope. I vanished.

I tried to hold down the racket I made huffing and puffing as I worked my sack of invisibility back into the street and kept on moving.

The Goddamn Parrot screamed past again, not seeing me.

Right behind him was the world's biggest owl. A shadow flickered past. I looked up. Another owlish overachiever cruised at a higher altitude, watching. Neither owl was real maneuverable. The Goddamn Parrot cut a tight turn. The owl behind him didn't make it. It banged into the side of a building, fell, looked foggy for a moment, like it was having trouble deciding what it wanted to be. The owl overhead took up the chase. It kept up easily on the straightaways.

Screeching like a sailor just awakening to find that last night's sweet luck not only had vanished with his whole fortune but had left him a nasty rash as a memento, T. G. headed for home, abandoning me to my fate again.

A gang gathered. The big character with the axe rumbled like a pissed-off volcano. The redhead stood by herself in some shadows and looked pretty. The fat bald dwarf guy looked puzzled. The owl that had hit the wall wobbled through the air, alighted, fuzzily changed into a perky lovely who looked about seventeen and wore nothing but thin lavender gauze. Golden light and shadow coalesced to become a guy about seven feet tall who was naked to the waist and from the waist down was mostly shaggy brown fur and goatlike legs that ended in hooves. He and the re-formed owl must have been in love. They couldn't keep their hands off one another.

Nobody else could see them, but nobody walked through them either. Not that there was much traffic anyway. It seemed some message had gone out at an unconscious level and most humans were staying away.

The guy with the weird legs pointed to where I had been when I slipped into my invisibility sack. I couldn't hear what he said, but his gestures gave me the gist.

He had seen me disappear. They all understood my limitations, obviously. They spread out and started feeling around for me. All but the young number. She turned into an owl and flew away, not in the direction the Goddamn Parrot had gone. My impression was that she was going after reinforcements.

I couldn't outrun them without becoming visible again, where I couldn't outrun them anyway. So I slid into the damp under a watering trough and got uncomfortable. I would try to wait them out.

They were stubborn. I guess you become patient when you are immortal. They knew I wasn't moving fast or going far. Soon enough, too, I began to suspect they were only interested in keeping me contained while they waited.

That didn't boost my confidence.

An owl arrived. She misted down and became another tasty delicacy wearing not much of anything. This was not the same sweetmeat as before. This one wore a different shade of purple.

The blind guys on the street were missing one hell of a show.

The faun guy—who actually bore only a passing resemblance to the faun tribesmen of the Arabrab Forests—seemed to bear no prejudice against this owl girl, nor she toward him. They engaged in a little heavy petting the others apparently failed to notice.

I began to study the lay of the land.

I wondered if the Goddamn Parrot had gotten away.

# 18

Soon I began to suspect that I had outwitted myself. I should have covered what ground I could. The Shayir lacked no confidence in the help that was coming.

I eased out of hiding, checked myself. Good. Mud had not clung to whatever surrounded me. I studied the Shayir. They had stopped poking and chattering, were looking out of the corners of their eyes or squinting like that might help them see me better. I guess they could sense that I was moving.

The first owl dropped out of the sky, changed, immediately started slapping the other girl away from the faun guy, who didn't apologize at all. The huge guy rumbled like a volcano getting ready to belch, waved his axe. The air shrieked. Passersby heard and looked around nervously. The owl girl relented long enough to deliver whatever message she carried. The others looked smug.

Big trouble, Garrett.

What could I do to fool them?

I didn't have a clue. Motion seemed the best course at the moment. I got over against a wall and drifted northward. Unlike the gods, I discovered, people who could not see me did not avoid me. Luckily, the guy I bumped was far gone. He mumbled an apology and stumbled on for another dozen steps before his jaw dropped and he looked around. I hoped the Shayir were not alert.

Just then some fool opened his front door but paused to yell back inside, reminding his missus of what a melonhead she was. The lady made a few pithy remarks by way of rebuttal. I took the opportunity to slide past the guy and invite myself into a tiny two-room flat that had to be the place where they made all the garlic sausage in the world. I felt a moment of sorrow on behalf of the couple who lived there. They hadn't had time to pick up after the Great Earthquake yet. You know how it is. The centuries just slip away. There was stuff in there that had mold growing on its mold.

The woman sprawled on a mat on the floor. That mat had been chucked out by more than one previous owner. She didn't care. She had one arm wrapped around a gallon of cheap wine while she soul-kissed its twin brother. She seemed accustomed to having invisible men move through the gloom around her. I positioned myself where I could watch the street through the peephole in the door, which was the only window that place had.

Right away I discovered that the skinny geek with wings on his head was peeking out of an alley half a block to the north. The Shayir spotted him about the same time, became agitated. The whole bunch surged toward that alley.

Winghead moved out.

The term "greased lightning" does not do him justice. He was a shadowy flicker moving between points. The weird herd rumbled after him, hollering and flailing bizarre weapons.

He had their full attention. I took my cue. I got out of my bag, so startling my roommate that she actually spilled a precious cup of wine. "Take it easy, lady. That stuff costs money." I waved good-bye, stepped into the street like her man before me, walked off like I was just another local going about his business. I made believe I had a stone in one shoe. That altered my way of walking.

It worked.

Three blocks later I could not see an immortal anywhere. I settled into a trot, headed for home.

With a whoosh Winghead settled in to jog beside me. "Thanks," I told him. He offered an enigmatic look and flickered into the distance ahead. He was not hard to track when you were behind him. He just dwindled fast.

I slowed to a pace that didn't mark me out from the crowd. I started feeling smug.

# 19

Owls have always been birds of ill omen, particularly when they fly by day. Owls were my first clue that I was, perhaps, premature in my self-congratulation. But the owls themselves were preceded by the uproar of a crowd of crows.

Crows are common, and they get rowdy when they get together, like teenage boys. They get triply rowdy when they find a feathered predator to pick on. Or two. Two familiar owls in this instance. And the crows were so numerous they attracted the attention of everyone in the street.

I listened to people talk. Nobody but me and the crows could see the owls. There was a lot of chatter about omens. It was a trying time. People would look anywhere for guidance. That ought to make religion and divination growth industries.

Maybe crows have better eyes than people, or maybe they just can't be fooled. Of course, they could be semidivine themselves. They and their cousins turn up in a lot of myths and religious stories.

They kept the owls on the move, which was dandy by me. They wouldn't have time for aerial spotting.

I continued my jog, wondering if I might not have done better running back to the Dream Quarter. I could have taken refuge in one of the big temples where these small-timers couldn't come after me.

I cut across Gravis Convent Market, where they had torn down an abandoned convent and used the brick to pave a square that became a flea market, thieves' market, farmers' market, haymarket, so people in the neighborhood would not have to walk miles to do their marketing. There must have been scandal and corruption involved, a construction scheme that fell apart, else the square would have been gone long since. Corruption and scandal are always involved in any public works scheme, sometimes so much so that they poison the well.

The square sinks a little toward its middle, probably settling where the convent's vast basements had been filled with rubble. It is two hundred yards across. I was about twenty yards in when old Jorken Winghead zipped up. I was puffing heartily. He wasn't breathing at all.

He suggested, "You should move faster."

A genius. I glanced back.

He was right.

"Good idea."

But not entirely practical. The square was packed ear to elbow with buyers and sellers and pickpockets and sightseers and people who just plain couldn't think of anything else to do or anywhere else to go.

I glanced back again. Jorken was for sure right. New players had come onto the pitch for the Shayir. A woman on unicorn back, not wearing much but showing muscle tone on muscle tone, probably six and a half feet talk, dark as eggplant, iron helmet with a crescent moon up top, herself festooned with weapons and stuff. Ropes. Nets. A falcon. Dogs cavorting around her steed's legs, critters that looked like half wolf and half whippet and were maybe big enough for dwarves to ride.

Well. Your basic huntress goddess. Probably with a list of nasty quirks, like most of the older deities. Ate her firstborn, or whatever.

Amidst the barking and yelping and galloping another form stood out, something like a haystack of black cloth with tails fluttering, dripping an occasional wisp of dark smoke, more floating than running. I saw no limbs, nor any face, but when I looked directly at it I staggered. A voice thundered inside my head. *Nog is inescapable.* The voice was like the Dead Man's, only with mental bad breath.

Jorken showed up again. He seemed exasperated by my lack of progress. "Follow me." He started to pull away but did keep it down to a mortal pace. The crowd parted for him without seeing him. I zipped along in his wake, making much better time.

The effort only delayed the inevitable.

# 20

The huntress wasn't thirty yards behind me when I fled the north side of the square. The voice in my head told me, *Nog is inescapable.* The black thing fluttered and flapped amidst the hounds. It seemed bemused by my attempt to get away.

I ducked around a corner and into a narrow breezeway, readying my magic cord as I went. Jorken didn't like that. He shook his head violently, snapped, "Don't!"

I popped into my sack of invisibility anyway and kept moving through the breezeway. There wasn't much light back there, but enough for me to see the huntress and her pets race past the breezeway. I chuckled. "There, Winghead." But Jorken had taken a fast hike, last laugh choking him.

The bundle of black appeared, hesitated, drifted into the breezeway behind me. The horsewoman returned. Her four-legged pals climbed over one another, trying to sniff out a trail that wasn't there. But everybody trusted Nog's nose. Or ears. Or whatever.

I kept humping that sack but never got out the other end of the breezeway. I was trying to slide into the cavity at someone's back door, without making a racket, when Nog caught up. I heard a slithering snakes sort of sound, like reptilian scales running over scales. Something like black worms, nightcrawler size, began oozing into the sack through the little hole left by the knot when I had closed up. The voice in my head reminded me, *Nog is inescapable.*

Old Nog knew his limitations.

Old Nog smelled pretty damned bad. I didn't get a chance to offer him any man-to-man advice on personal hygiene. Paralysis overtook me. I felt like a stroke victim. I was fully aware, but I couldn't do anything. Nog slipped back out the hole, content to leave me in the sack. I saw nothing that looked like hands or arms, but he took hold anyhow and dragged me back into the street, to the huntress. She leaned down, felt around, grabbed hold of my arm, hoisted me like I was a doll. She flipped me down across the shoulders of her mount. She let out an earsplitting shriek of triumph, hauled back on her reins. Her unicorn reared, pounded the air with huge hooves, then we were off at a gallop, hounds larking around the great white beast's pounding hooves, Nog the Inescapable floating alongside. Owls passed overhead, still fleeing the crows but finding a moment to send down hoots of congratulations. The huntress laid a silver-tipped arrow across her dark bow—weapon and shaft both just materialized in her hands. She sped the arrow. A monster crow became an explosion of black feathers. The missile flew on through, took a big turn, came back home. Mama snatched it out of the air, on the fly.

The crows got the idea. But they didn't back off entirely. Whither the owls flew they followed, waiting to flash in and rip a few more feathers off heavy wings. The owls were looking pretty ragged.

Not that I got a real good look, sprawled in that undignified position. But it was a long ride, out of the city completely, into the region of wealthy estates south of town. I don't like it out there. Every time I go I get into big trouble. This time didn't look like it would be any exception. I was in trouble before I got there.

I wondered why nobody remarked on me floating through the streets.

Along the way we accumulated the rest of the Shayir crew, some of whom had real trouble keeping up—especially that wide, stubby guy. None of his pals seemed inclined to make any allowances. Sweethearts, the gods.

# 21

The place was huge and well hidden by trees and a stone wall ten feet tall, a quarter mile before you got to the house itself. There were guards at the gate, in keeping with the spirit of the times, but the gate stood open and they didn't notice our entrance. I realized that nobody saw me floating around because I was still inside that damned invisibility sack. All I had done was make their job easier for them.

It was dark when we reached the manor house. I couldn't see much of it from my position. I wondered if I would recognize it in the daylight. I wondered if I wanted to. I wondered if the Dead Man had any idea where I was or what was happening to me. I wondered why I was doing so much wondering lately.

The huntress dismounted, tossed her reins to a lesser deity of some sort who looked like a pudgy kid with the world's foremost collection of golden curls. She dragged me down and tossed me onto her shoulder. Into the house we went. The pudgy kid flew away on impossibly small wings, leading the unicorn.

I hit the floor on a bearskin rug in front of a merrily crackling fireplace at one end of a room they could have cleared of furniture to use as a ball field on rainy days. I lay there looking up at my captor, who was as beautiful as any woman I'd ever seen. But there wasn't an ounce of warmth in her. Cold as ebony. No sensuality whatsoever. I was willing to bet a mark she fell into the virgin huntress subcategory.

Nog crackled. The owl girls passed near the fire, as lovely as ever but sadly tattered. Hardly a thread remained of their wispy apparel. In better times I would have applauded the view.

The dogs, the stubby guy, the giant, all stood around staring at the bearskin. I didn't think they were trying to bring Bruno back to life.

I spied other faces great and small, humanoid and otherwise, all with a definite mythological caste. Shadows played over the walls. The faun guy began consoling the owl girls. A pleasant, avuncular sort of voice said, "Might I suggest, Mr. Garrett, that as an initial gesture you come forth from that pocket clipped out of reality?"

I wiggled and rolled and looked at a guy who was sitting in a big chair, facing the fire. He had his hands extended to the flames as though he had a circulation problem. He did look enough like Imar to be his brother. Maybe Imar's smarter twin brother, since he could articulate a civilized sentence.

Straining and groaning—I do not recommend horses in any form as transportation—I wobbled to my feet and fumbled with my cord till I was able to step out into the room with my hosts. None of them seemed interested in the cord. I made it disappear, hoping nobody would have second thoughts.

But why should they care? They had Nog, god of litter piles.

"I apologize for the less than genteel means by which you were brought here, Mr. Garrett. You have made it difficult to contact you."

I stared for maybe fifteen seconds. Then I said, "I guess you're not one of them."

"One of what?" Puzzled.

I waved an inclusive hand. "The Shayir pantheon."

He frowned.

"I've never heard of a god who has manners, let alone one who treats mortals with respect."

Shadow touched his face. It wasn't one of the shadows that infested the place, it was a shadow from within, a shadow of anger. "Would you prefer to be treated the way you expect?"

I am, I thought. "Actually, I'd rather not be treated at all. I ignore you, you ignore me, we're no problem to one another."

"But you are a problem. Of the worst sort. You threaten our existence. You cannot possibly expect us to overlook that."

I swallowed about three times. The guy in the chair projected a furious temper, restrained only with great effort. I must have some power in the situation, though I couldn't catch a whiff. "How am I a threat?"

"You have been enlisted by the Godoroth to find the Temple

Key. That simple name doesn't tell you that the group who fails to take possession of it will perish."

"I think you got the wrong guy. I don't know anything about any Temple Key."

A whispering filled the air. Ice formed on my tailbone and crawled northward.

"Curious, Mr. Garrett. Torbit says you are only partially lying. But." He rambled through an eyewitness review of my visit with the Godoroth. Maybe he was Imar in a good mood.

I searched the crowd, trying to get a good picture of faces. The Dead Man would want every detail—if ever we met again.

I said, "You got all the details, then you know I didn't agree to do anything. I just slid on out of there."

"There was an implication. You did not refuse."

"Won't stand up in court. Duress and coercion." Which got me a blank look. Duress and coercion? Wasn't that what being a god was all about? You could make people do what you wanted? Weren't mortals toys?

He took it his own way. "Granted, you did not swear allegiance to the Godoroth. That is good. But why, then, were you on the Street of the Gods asking questions? Why were you visiting temples?"

"I was pretty sure it was a con of some kind. Those Godoroth characters didn't convince me that they were real gods. They just told me that they were. They hadn't shown me anything a clever conjurer couldn't manage." If you overlooked my magic rope. "I figured somebody wanted to set me up."

My audience stirred. Most probably didn't understand me. The guy in the chair had to mull it over before he got it. Give him that. He could step out of his own viewpoint. Not that he credited the mortal viewpoint with much value.

That chill whisper filled the air momentarily.

"It appears that, once again, you are telling most of the truth. Very well. I believe you understand the situation. Foreign gods have come to TunFaire. They have been awarded a place on the Street of the Gods. This means great inconvenience and dislocation for many gods, but for us and the Godoroth it means one group or the other has to go. For my part, I do not care to fall into oblivion."

"Me neither."

"You still believe you are being hoodwinked?"

"It's starting to look like the real thing."

"I want that key, Mr. Garrett."

"I'll say a prayer for you."

Teensy thunderbolts crackled at his temples. Maybe it was something I said. He regained control. "You fled from my friends. If you are not in the service of the Godoroth, why run?"

"Give them an eye, chief. Most of them look like nightmares come true."

More teensy thunderbolts flickered. I wasn't doing too good here. I looked around. Things moving in and out of the light *might* have lurked under my bed when I was a kid. This was a much bigger crowd than the Godoroth. And not real friendly. Bad cess to the infidel, I guess.

"Where will you look for the key?"

"I'm not interested in any key. I just don't want to be between gangs of divine sociopaths who have no interest whatsoever in my welfare."

Crackly whisper in the air. Stir in the crowd, which seemed larger every time I checked. They were not all nightmares, either. This pantheon was well supplied with attractive goddesses, not one of whom had trouble with her hair and all of whom had normal teeth and the usual complement of limbs.

I didn't need the whispers translated. Torbit the Strayer—whatever he, she, or it was—had reported the truth of my lack of interest. No grail quest for me. Forget that Temple Key. Garrett has no desire to save any holy bacon. I said, "I have friends in the beer business who do care and who do need my help. I'd rather be solving their problems."

"There is little time, Mr. Garrett. We need a mortal to rescue us. Our remaining worshippers are few and of little value because of their age. Belief is not a requirement. Free will is. I see no more likely candidate than yourself. You work for hire. We have resources beyond your imagining."

Yeah. Everything but loving followers eager to bail your asses out.

# 22

I'm sure I didn't say that out loud. Must have been my body language. Dumb, to be twitching and aggravating the gods like that.

The head guy growled, "Put him into the lockup room. Some time with his thoughts should help him develop a new perspective."

I liked my old one fine, but several unpleasant fellows disagreed. I had seen them on their day jobs as gargoyles. And not only did they have heads like rocks, they had muscles of stone as well. We took a vote. The majority elected to go along with Lang's plan for an attitude adjustment. They lugged me through the house, up various flights of stairs, past a scattering of antique humans who had no trouble seeing us and who kowtowed to anything that moved. My companions chucked me into a large closet containing one ragged stolen army blanket (I knew it was stolen; otherwise it would still be in the army), one feeble fat candle, and two quart jars, one full and one empty. I presumed I was to be the middleman between jars.

The door closed. I gathered I was supposed to ruminate and quickly conclude that signing on with the Shayir was preferable to the alternatives. At the moment it looked like that could be true. I might have gone with that option had I not become distracted.

The dust hadn't settled when the door popped open and the owl girls invited themselves in. They hadn't bothered finding fresh clothing. They had mischief in their golden eyes, and "Uhoh!" was all I got to say before they piled onto me.

They weren't great conversationalists. In fact, I didn't get anything out of them but giggles. I did my best to remain stern and fatherly and aloof, but they just took that as a challenge. I am nothing if not determined in my pursuit of information, so I continued to ask questions while I endured the inevitable.

After a while I began to fear the interrogation would never end. Those two only looked like girls.

Then they were gone and I was collapsing into exhausted sleep while trying to figure out what that had been all about. They hadn't tried to worm anything out of me or to get me to promise a thing. They were very direct, very focused, and very demanding.

The door opened. The woman who had gotten me into this mess stepped inside. She was in her redhead phase, and a very desirable redhead she was. She sniffed. "I see Lila and Dimna have been here." Her observation was as neutral as a remark about the weather.

"I don't know what they wanted . . ."

"What they wanted is what they got. They are direct and simple."

"Direct, anyway."

"Simple." She tapped her temple. "You find this form attractive?"

"I'll howl at the moon." Though she made no effort, she exuded sensuality. "But that won't get you anything."

"You're sated."

"Got nothing to do with it. I'm being pushed and bullied. I don't take to that much. I get stubborn."

"You have to understand something. If the Shayir don't get what they want, neither do you."

"And the Godoroth will think the same, so I can't win. But I can stay stubborn and take everybody with me." Damn. I didn't like the sound of the slop gushing out of my yap. I don't know if I believed it. I hoped that Torbit thing wasn't listening.

"What do you want?" she asked.

"To be left alone."

"That isn't going to happen. And you know it. A sensible man would cut himself a deal."

"I've already referred to the fatal flaw that renders that idea specious. Based on the record, it's only reasonable to assume that you all will fail to keep your half of any deal. Promise the fool mortal all the gold and girls he can handle, tell him he gets to be ruler of the world and several provinces in hell as soon as he delivers this nifty key that will save some divine butts." Speaking of divinity of the foundation, she knew the nature of perfection. "When we're done we'll turn his mortal ass into a catfish or something."

"You're certainly a cynic."

"I didn't create myself."

She appeared thoughtful. "You may have touched on a real problem. I'll think about it." She looked straight at me, radiating that heat but not extending any invite.

"What?"

"You're a true curiosity. I've met believers, unbelievers, fanatics, skeptics, and heretics, but I don't think I've ever met a man who plain just didn't care." She did not, however, seem displeased by my indifference.

"I do care. I care a whole bunch about being left alone."

"Only the dead are left alone, Garrett."

"And even that depends on which gods they chose while they were alive."

"Perhaps, stubborn man." She left me with an enigmatic smile and a philosophical conundrum. She seemed content with my attitude.

TunFaire has innumerable clots of gods. Each bunch anchors a different belief system. Some of those are as crazy as pickled cats. If competing groups of gods, like the Godoroth and the Shayir, actually revealed themselves to mortals and confirmed not only their own existence but also that of their enemies, by implication, the existence of all the rest of the gods would be validated. In my skewed view it further implied that any given value or belief system must be just as true as any other.

Maybe I should start my own Church of the Divine Chaos. Everything is true and nothing is true.

I had no trouble with the idea that all the gods might be real. I'd always liked the notion that gods will exist as long as there is someone who believes they exist. The solidity of my intuition was now at the root of my difficulties. What troubled me was the possibility that the dogmas surrounding various really wacko religions might bear equal validity while there were true believers. If the general population reached that conclusion, there would be a big winnowing fast. Some belief packages just look a whole lot better than others. I would much rather kick off and fall into a paradise stocked with wild women and free beer than just become part of a ball of light or shadow, or become some dark spirit that necromancers would summon, or be gone to eternal torment, or, as had always been my personal suspicion, be just plain dead.

Deserved some thought.

# 23

I didn't get time. I had too much on my mind. And I kept getting interrupted by one god person after another, each with the same mission: convince Brother Garrett to scare up that precious key. I had several truly intriguing offers from a couple of goddesses who looked like I had made them up. Maybe I did, come to think. One side of me wished I had a really remote deadline so I could take advantage of all these wonderful offers.

I dozed off at last, started sighing my way through a marvelous dream wherein all these randy goddesses decided I should go in with them on starting a new paradise. We would forget all those stuffy, weird shadow lurkers and hammer pounders and generally unfun, gloomy-gus guy gods. Then the bane of my existence raised its ugly head once again.

Somebody tapped on my cell door.

Something buzzed like the world's biggest bumblebee. Voices clashed in whispers. The buzzard-size bee went away.

Somebody tapped on the door again.

I did not respond, probably because I was so amazed that anyone here would have the courtesy not to walk right in. I decided to play possum. I cracked an eyelid and waited.

The door opened.

This one was a girl. Surprise, surprise.

At first watery glimpse she seemed chunky and plain, and at second glimpse she seemed vaguely familiar. She had the glow of a peasant girl lucky enough to have enjoyed good health, with a body designed for serious work and frequent childbearing. As lesser gods went, she might be some sort of spring lamb or crop planting specialist.

She poked my shoulder. She was between me and the candle. Nothing insubstantial about her. My earlier visitors, however determined or enthusiastic, had not been entirely impervious to the passage of light.

I opened my eyes completely, startling the girl. I frowned. I did know her . . . Ah. She looked like a young version of Imara, Imar's wife. But the head god here looked like Imar, too. Maybe Lang had a kid. No! Hell. She was the girl from Brookside Park.

"What?" I asked.

She didn't seem to have in mind using woman's oldest tool of persuasion.

"Hush. I'm here to help."

"Funny. You don't look like any royal functionary I ever met." I touched her. She flinched. Earlier visitors had felt just as solid but had seemed awfully warm. This one was a normal temperature and lacked the absolute self-confidence the others had shown.

"You're mortal." Clever me. Now I was sure she was the girl I had seen in the park. The pixies had seen her, too.

"Half mortal. Come on! Hurry!" An angry buzz waxed and waned in the corridor outside. "Before they realize there's something happening outside their set pattern."

I debated it for a long time, six or seven seconds. "Lead on." I couldn't see her getting me into the hot sauce any deeper, whatever her scheme.

Sometimes you just got to roll the bones.

"Who are you? How come you've been following me? Why are you doing this?"

"Hush. We can talk after we get out of here."

"There's an idea I can get behind." And right in front of me was a behind I could get behind. She wore the peasant skirt again, whitish linen under a pale blue apron. I liked what I could see.

This mess had its aesthetic up side. I could not recall ever having run into so many gorgeous females in such a short time.

So some were a little strange. We all have our moments of weird, and life is a series of trade-offs anyway.

Blonde braids trailed down the girl's back. "Wholesome" was the word that came to mind. Generally, wholesome is the last thing most guys find interesting. But . . .

She beckoned. I rose to follow. She opened the door a crack, beckoned again. I caught a bit of that buzzing racket again. It had an angry edge. Or perhaps it was impatience.

I don't think the Shayir ever posted a guard. I guess when you have a Nog on staff you don't much worry about prisoner escapes. Or maybe it was just divine hubris.

I wondered how my new pal planned to cope with the owl girls and Nog and his girlfriend with the dogs and weapons and no sense of humor.

"Come on!" She was intense but would not raise her voice above a whisper. Which was a good plan, probably.

She was flesh for sure. The floorboards creaked under her, ever so softly. They groaned under me. My earlier visitors had not made the house speak.

"This way, Mr. Garrett."

Her chosen route was not the one the Shayir had used when escorting me to my spacious new apartment. It was not the route I would have chosen to make my getaway. It led down a narrow hallway only to a small, open window. A chill breeze stirred the thin, dirty white cotton curtains there. Outside, an almost full moon slopped light all over and made the whole manor look like a haunted graveyard. Maybe it was. How were we going to deal with that?

There was a whole lot of buzzing going on out there, suddenly. Somebody said, "Come on, babe, getcher buns moving." Outside. Stories and stories up.

The girl went right out the window, indifferent to the fact that she was not dressed to play monkey on the wall. I stuck my head outside—and discovered that the big darling was not going downward. Gulp! What the? . . . Where was the rope? There wasn't any rope. I had expected a rope from the moment I'd realized her plan included us climbing out that silly little window.

Buzz overhead. I looked up in time to glimpse just a hint of movement vanishing behind the edge of the roof.

Meantime, the girl had gotten herself onto a ledge that was not much wider than my palm. She was sidestepping industriously, headed I couldn't tell where.

I then noted that the ledge was not a ledge as such. It was the top side of some kind of decorative gingerbread I could not make out because I wasn't out there in the moonlight. I drew a deep breath, meaning to tell the young lady that I preferred my adventures at low altitudes with solid footing. Somebody behind me spoke up first. "Here, now! You! Who are you? What are you doing there?"

The speaker was a real live human old man, possibly of the butler calling. He wore only nightclothes but was armed with one truly wicked-looking meat cleaver. A door stood ajar behind him. Feeble light leaked into the hallway. If he had pests in his room the way I'd had them in mine that might explain why he slept with kitchen utensils.

The old man didn't look like he was interested in conversation. He began slicing the air. I considered using my magical cord to climb down. But there was no time to stretch it. Nor did I see any handy place to tie it off.

Why not just jump? Falling would be less unpleasant than an encounter with a slab of sharp steel. The ground wasn't more than a mile down.

That bumblebee buzz whirred off the roof and dropped down behind me. "Why you want to waste your time on this candyass pug, sweetheart?" I caught a strong whiff of weed smoke.

I looked back. Floating behind me was a pudgy baby with a thousand-year-old midget's head. The critter wore what looked like a diaper but was actually a loincloth. "What you gawking at, Jake?" it snapped. And, "Get your lard ass moving." He yelled upward, "Hey, babe, this one's a fourteen-karat dud."

The critter carried a teeny little bow and a quiver of little arrows and had the world's biggest weed banger drooping from the corner of his mouth, smouldering. Here was the source of the buzz. And of the weed stink.

I managed to stand myself up on that ledge. A dud, huh? Look here. Sometimes a military education *is* useful in civilian life. Watch me now.

The old man leaned out the window and took a swipe at me. Rusty iron dealt the air a deep, bitter wound entirely too close to my nose. For a moment it looked like pappy was going to come outside after me.

The buzz changed pitch. I glanced back but kept my feet moving. The little guy doing the floating and cussing slapped a little arrow across his little bow and plinked the old man in the back of his meat-chopping hand. "Get moving, ya drooling moron!" he growled at me. "If you'd hauled your ass from the start they'd never have seen me."

"I wouldn't have missed you."

Sometimes it's wonderful to be young and dumb. A stunt like this would not have bothered me ten years ago.

About twenty feet from the window a bit of rope hung over the edge of the roof, which at that point descended to within eight feet of our footing. However, the roof did overhang us by several feet. Young and dumb, my new friend just leaped, grabbed the rope, clambered right up, skirt flying. Although he was busy cursing his wound, the old man caught that action. His eyes bugged more than mine did.

As the girl's feet vanished, the flying critter soared up after her with the same sort of ponderous grace you see in large flying insects, the sort of stately defiance of gravity of a thing that don't look like it ought to get off the ground at all. He filed various verbal complaints as he went. What a team the girl and I would make, her with her chattering whatisit and me with the Goddamn Parrot.

I shut my eyes, took a deep breath, considered the racket the old man was raising now, opened my eyes, offered the old boy a salute, took the plunge.

That sort of thing was all very well when I was nineteen and only one of a bunch of lunatics who tried to outdo one another in the face of an implacable enemy and almost certain premature death, but I was thirty now. I had a reasonably ordered and comfortable life. Well, sort of. Why the hell couldn't I remember the moments like this when Old Man Weider made one of his pitches aimed at getting me to work the brewery full time?

I grabbed the rope, found arm strength I had feared was not there anymore, scrambled toward the roof. No longer did I possess the liquid grace of youth, but I did manage to get the job done.

"Can ya believe it, toots? The wuss actually dragged his lead ass up here."

"Hurry!" The girl beckoned from the top of a slope of slate. "The alarm is spreading."

Wouldn't you know. I hurried. After bellying up twenty feet of steep and treacherously dew-slick slate, I dragged myself onto the flat part of the roof, which was large enough for a battalion's drill ground. You could farm there if you wanted to haul the soil up first. I got to my feet. The girl beckoned anxiously. Beckoning had to be her top skill. I got the notion this was going slower than she'd planned.

The flying baby with the hallucinogenic stogie watched sourly from the back of a horse big enough to haul ogre knights around. The little guy had wings sprouting out of his shoulder blades.

They looked just about big enough to lug a pigeon around. I guess he had to work hard when he flew.

There were two horses. "Oh no," I said. "No. I've done all the riding I want for today." Me and horses never get along. My ribs informed me that Black Mona's mount had made every effort to ensure that my immediate future was one filled with misery. And that thing was only related to horses. Did I really want to escape badly enough to put myself at the mercy of these monsters?

"Look at this clown, babe. He don't . . ."

"Please stop horsing around, Mr. Garrett." The girl was exasperated.

"You don't understand. They have you fooled."

The house shuddered underfoot. Somebody big had begun to stir downstairs.

"See ya later, Sweet Buns." The little thing's wings turned into a blur. He buzzed off into the night.

I started climbing the one horse that didn't already have a blonde on top. It was a monster the color of old ivory, maybe even big enough to haul a troll into battle. For a while there I thought I would need ropes and pitons to make it to the top.

I completed the long climb. I swung my right leg over, was pleased to discover that the horse and I both had our heads facing the same direction. The extra altitude gave me a fine view of the roof.

The roof?

It occurred to me that I was about make my getaway on horseback from a rooftop. How far could I get? Was I the victim of an all-time practical joke? I do have friends who would consider this kind of situation a real howler.

I didn't see anybody standing around snickering behind his dirty elven hand.

I didn't have any friends who would, or for that matter could, spring for the cash a setup like this would cost.

The girl howled like a merry banshee. The child was happy. She kicked her horse in the ribs. It took off down the roof, chasing the baby whatisit. My horse was exactly as treacherous as I expect every equine to be. He took off, chasing his pal, without ever consulting me.

# 24

Those goddamned horses were stupider than I thought. They decided to race. The girl's mount had shorter legs but a head start. When mine got up to speed it started to gain. All I could do was howl and hang on as my brave but terminally stupid steed pulled even. The girl grinned at me and waved.

We ran out of roof.

Neither horse blinked. Neither horse slowed down either, though they did angle away from one another at the last second.

The shapeshifting started well before the leap into space, but it was only as we ran out of roof that I noticed it. In scant seconds huge wings burst from my mount's shoulders. Those broad shoulders narrowed dramatically. The beast's whole back slimmed down until it was barely wider than a trim woman's waist. All that bulk turned into wings. Those great wings hammered the air.

I hoped my whimpering wasn't loud enough to hear.

We climbed toward the moon. The girl's laughter tumbled back toward the manor like the tinkle of celestial windchimes. Possessed by the confidence of youth, she thought we were safely away. I was too busy not falling off to worry about owls and fluttering shadows and whatnot.

We went up and up till all TunFaire lay sprawled below us, more vast than ever I had imagined. To my right the great bend of the river shone like a silver scimitar in the moonlight. Lights blazed everywhere, for the city never sleeps. It boasts almost as many nocturnal inhabitants as daytime ones. It is several cities coexisting in the same place at the same time. It changes faces with the hours. Only in the hour before dawn is TunFaire ever more than coincidentally quiet.

I buried my hands in horse mane and hung on for dear life. I didn't pray, though, if that was what they were trying to get me to do. Soon I became engrossed in that remarkable view of the city I call home. When I saw it from up there I didn't wonder that half the world wanted to come here. From up there you could see only the magnificence. You had to get down on the ground to capture the stench and filth, to see the pain and poverty and cruelty, the irrational hatreds and the equally mad occasional senseless acts of charity. TunFaire was a beautiful woman. Only when you held her close and buried your face in her hair could you see the lice and scabs and fleas.

Not even in my most bizarre dreams had I ever drifted above everything like some great roc of darkness. I boggled while moonshine turned reservoirs into glimmering platters and drainage ditches into runes of silver. The earth seemed to wheel as the animals turned in flight. Amazing! My hands were cramped from holding on so tight, but I knew only the awe.

The girl shrilled, "Isn't this wild, Mr. Garrett?"

"Absolutely." I would tell her that Mr. Garrett was my grandfather after I got my feet back onto solid ground.

I looked back the way we had come. Trouble, if it was after us, was not yet close enough to pick out of the night. Trouble was sure to follow, though. That could be the title of my autobiography. *Trouble Follows Me*. Though usually it ambushes me. I wondered if Nog was capable of tracing me through the air.

The girl let rip a wild yodel, swung one hand violently overhead. Lilac and violet sparks flew off her fingers. Her mount pointed his nose down. He plunged toward the earth.

Mine followed. "Oh, shit!" The bottom fell out. Mine wanted to race again. TunFaire hurtled toward me, getting less enchanting by the second.

My stomach stayed back up there among the stars. Good thing I'd had no supper. We would be racing it to the ground, too.

The winged horses actually descended in a great circle, tilting slightly, moving their wings no more than buzzards on patrol. The streets and lights turned below. Soon I could make out individual structures, then individual people, none of whom looked up. People seldom do, and I take advantage of that fact occasionally, but seeing my world from the back of a horse cruising above the rooftops gave that concept new dimension.

My fright had ebbed. I was thinking again. I was proud of me. I wouldn't have to change my underwear. I must be getting used to these bizarre adventures.

What were these winged horse things? What was the little flying thug in the diaper? He was around somewhere. I couldn't see him, but his voice carried altogether too well. The only place I had seen their like was in old paintings of mythical events.

Unicorns, vampires, mammoths, fifty kinds of thunder lizards, werewolves, and countless other creatures often deemed mythical I had seen with my own eyes. Too often they had hammered bruises into my own flesh. But these flying horses and the bitty bowman constituted my first encounter with a class of critters I thought of as artists' conventions. Symbols. These guys, griffins, ostriches, cameleopards, cyclops. All of them supposedly as uncommon as lawyers driven only by a need to see justice done.

We dropped lower. The horses glided wingtip to wingtip. The little guy buzzed, but I could not spot him. We seemed to be headed back into the heart of TunFaire, down toward Brookside Park.

I still had not gotten a name out of my demigoddess benefactor, nor did I have a ghost of a notion of her true motive for helping me. She offered up another amazing yodel. I began to fiddle with my amazing cord. We could amaze one another. "Hey, girl! Who are you? You got a name or not?" There was a lot of wind noise in my ears, not to mention the powerful hum of the little guy's wings. I couldn't spot him no matter how hard I looked.

Crystal laughter rang out off to my right. It looked like the horses were thinking about landing. The girl was pulling ahead to go down first. "Call me Cat, Mr. Garrett. Bad Girl Cat."

"I like bad girls." I would have said more, but my throat tightened up. We were down so low the peaks of buildings with pointy roofs were at eye level. My mount started using his wings to slow down, but still structures whipped past at a speed beyond my imagining. I could not believe anyone could travel so fast and still be able to breathe.

My mount reared back and presented the entire undersurface of its wings to the onrushing air. We slowed violently, shuddering, air roaring. The beast's wings shrank. Its shoulders began to bulk up. Its speed dropped. Then it hit the ground galloping. And there was nothing upon its back. Or so I hoped the casual observer would conclude. The horse had to sense my weight.

I had strained my courage to its limits to get myself inside my sack of invisibility.

Actually, initially I pulled the noose up only to my armpits. I needed my arms free. Once the horse touched down and began slowing its run, it trotted in amongst some trees. It promptly lost two hundred pounds as I grabbed a sturdy branch. Oof! Rip the old arms out by the roots, why not?

I dropped to the ground, pulled the sack of invisibility over my head, moved along before my self-proclaimed rescuers had time to realize that I had disappeared.

Pixies laughed and yelled, "We saw what you did. We saw what you did." But if you were not listening for them they just sounded like sparrows complaining about having been wakened in the middle of the night.

# 25

"Mr. Garrett? Where are you? Are you all right? Answer me if you can."

I could but I didn't. She could not be sure I hadn't fallen during our landing. Damn! If I had kept my mouth shut, if I hadn't asked her her name, she couldn't have been sure I hadn't fallen earlier, when she was having too much fun to concentrate.

The bumblebee whir of the runt's wings came toward me, wordlessly putting death to my maunderings. He knew I hadn't fallen. He was on patrol now, running a slow search pattern. The little rat couldn't shut up. And everything he said was less than complimentary toward my favorite working stiff. Me.

To know me is to love me.

I headed for home full speed, encouraged by a racket behind me that suggested a welcoming party might have been waiting. Sounded like lots of folks were in a sudden bad mood, including a nation of pixies untimely rousted from their sleep. Over what sounded like a hen-house disturbed I heard Cat shout at one of her horses. She wanted to get airborne again.

The little winged guy buzzed up to within a few feet of me. He settled his plump rump onto the outstretched bronze palm of one of the few nonmilitary statues in the park. He had an arrow across his bow. His moonlighted expression said he meant to use it. "Know you're around here somewhere, Slick. Know you're close enough to hear. That was a nifty stunt, turning sideways to reality to give the kid the slip." Weed smoke had begun to cloud up around his head. He ought to be too stoned to breathe. "But fun is fun, and I don't think you're gonna have much more if you don't come in now. You don't got no other friends."

I figured the Godoroth crew had tried to reel me in, irked because I had been trafficking with the enemy, and now they were triple irked because I had done a fade. I considered taking advantage of my invisibility to get a closer look at them. But I was worn out. I just wanted to go home. Reason told me home was no safer than out here, but the animal within me wanted to believe otherwise, wanted to slide into its den and lick its wounds. I kept the sack of invisibility around me till I was sure the flying runt had gotten lost.

I caught his buzz again as I was about to leave the park. I stepped into deep shadow and froze. Thus I was out of sight and motionless when two huge owls flapped over moments later. Though they were talking owl talk, the girls were bickering virulently.

I chuckled. To myself, of course.

Let them go butt heads with the Godoroth.

Knowing the Shayir were around put some extra hustle into my step. Good thing, too. Wasn't long before I began to feel a chill. It grew. I found another deep shadow and shrank down into it. I was crouched there when Abyss the Coachman floated across my backtrail like a black, wind-tossed specter. Looked like he had been sent to patrol the routes from the park to my home.

Had that been set up ahead? Had they expected an escape attempt?

You get paranoid.

I'd always thought gods were big on omniscience and such. Maybe as your followers become fewer you have less ability to draw on the power leaking over from the old country. Certainly if either bunch had any way of knowing things for themselves they would have no need for me. And I wouldn't be running around loose.

Paranoia. I had a bad feeling that when the smoke cleared and the earth stopped rocking and the dust settled, neither bunch would have much use for a mortal pug who had gotten his nose into too many divine secrets.

Something to keep in mind.

I heard a rustling. It came from the south. It grew louder quickly. Nog? No. Not Nog the Malodorous. Marvellous. I crouched in another shadow. Something passed overhead like a flight of bats but was not bats. More like fluttering paper shadows in a big hurry, moving with great purpose, hunting. Might that be the thing called Quilraq the Shadow? I wasn't inclined to hang around and find out.

I stuck to alleys and breezeways that would not have been graced by my presence at any other time. I even crossed the Bustee, the deadliest slum in town, where nine of any ten inhabitants would have cut my throat for the shoes I was wearing and the gods themselves would walk in peril. Twice I turned to Maggie's wonderful cord to fend off overeager shoppers. That was one handy tool, but I was getting reluctant to use it. It could be no coincidence that every time I did one of the Godoroth turned up soon afterward.

No exception in the Bustee, either. Each time it was one of the ugly guys that came, too, like the Godoroth knew those mean streets well enough to send only their meanest and most expendable. The streets emptied quickly after that, even though the locals could not see what was scaring the bean sprouts out of them.

I tried to see the bright side. The Shayir were not turning up at the same time. They were, apparently, only running random patrols in areas that interested their opponents.

The ugly guys were not Nog. Nor were they especially powerful other than in the scary department. I ducked and dodged them with little difficulty. On the other hand, I suspected everyone now had a solid idea of where I was headed. Whole platoons of divine beasties might be setting up camp near my house.

Owls and paper shadows, flying horses and flying babies who smoked weed crisscrossed the night, possibly taking their bearings from Godoroth on the ground. It was a wonder they didn't collide.

I changed course the minute I cleared the Bustee, skirting its eastern edge as I headed north. I mean, what would Mrs. Cardonlos say if I brought this all home and the gods themselves started duking it out in Macunado Street?

It seemed a better strategy would be to go where the gods wouldn't look, then stay put till their deadline passed. Put them all out of business.

Faces and figures flickered through my memory. Such a pity I couldn't pick and choose. There were some divine ladies amongst those gods, and the world might become a lesser place for their absence.

# 26

I drifted more than a mile north and east of my original course. I attracted no attention but never made up my mind where to go, either. Then I changed my mind.

This was like being back in the Corps. The people in charge didn't know what they were doing. I cussed the guy giving me orders. I told me to shut up and do what I was told.

I'd decided that I did have to go home. I needed to see the Dead Man. He needed to know what had become of me. Maybe he could find a thread of sense in this madness. There was more going on than I had been told, and I still had only a glimmering of the rules of the game I was being forced to play.

Surely both god gangs had my place staked out. I needed to draw them away. So give them a sniff of the false trail, Garrett.

Out came that cord. I turned it into a poking stick and swished it around, relaxed it and trotted a third of a mile northeast, toward TunFaire's northernmost gate, then I played with the rope in an alley infested with snoring drunks. I hurried on, used the cord one last time on the street that leads directly to the gate.

TunFaire's gates all stand open all the time. Only once had they closed, when some thunder lizards from the north had been ravaging the countryside. A guy with the need could make a high-speed exit anytime of the day or night. I suspected the gates would be of particular interest to the new secret police.

The street to and from the northeastern gate is always busy. I tied my rope around my waist and plunged into traffic headed south. I didn't think the Godoroth and Shayir, busy tripping over one another, would become sure of where I wasn't for a good while yet.

My plan worked like they write them up in a book. For a few minutes.

I was preoccupied. The texture of the night changed, and I failed to notice because there were no mad little gods weirding around me. The street grew quiet and tense and the crowds thinned out, but I caught on only after a howl arose ahead and I discovered the street blocked by a bunch of guys carrying angry red-and-black banners. They were armed with clubs and staves and were whipped along by drums and trumpets. They sang some really vicious racist song.

Startled, I stopped to take stock.

More human rights guys came from cross streets. They appeared to have a specific objective, attainment of which required the physical battery of everyone in their way, human or otherwise. It seemed that, for the purposes of the moment, anybody not actively marching with them was deemed to be against them.

People on the street fought back. The nonhumans went at it with great verve. The rightsists didn't care if those folks were apolitical and there by accident. They were not human. That was guilt enough.

I saw banners from several organizations. The demonstration would be something unusual, then. These groups fought one another over subtle points of dogma more than they battled their declared enemies.

Up ahead, where the rightsists were thickest, the northbound side of the street dissolved into ferocious turmoil. The center of violence appeared to be a caravan intent on slipping out of town under cover of darkness.

Stones flew. Clubs flashed. People hollered. I ricocheted back and forth, banged around, finally came to rest in a pile of mixed casualties. The cobblestones exercised no favoritism toward anyone. I got back onto one knee, muttering curses on all their houses. My headache was back. How could I douse all the streetlamps? But they would keep fighting anyway.

A knot of nasty-looking rightsists drifted my way. Ever flexible, I dived down and liberated an armband from an unconscious guy who didn't really need his right now. I put it on fast. Then I did what I have been doing so well lately, which was act like I'd just had my brains scrambled and couldn't quite get myself put back together. "Garrett? Hey, Wrecker, is that you?"

"I think so." I knew that voice but couldn't place it. It was a voice from long ago and far away. I faked an effort to get up that failed and left me down on my face.

Somebody else asked, "You know this guy?"

"Yeah. He was in my outfit. In the islands. He was our wreck."

I got it. "Pappy?" That was the voice. Pappy Toomey, also known as Tooms. The old man of the outfit at twenty-seven, a lifer, like a father to the rest of us, like a sergeant without official authority. Pappy never got out but never wanted to advance either.

"Yeah, Garrett. Help me get him up, Whisker." Hands hoisted me. "Who you with, Garrett?"

I didn't know who he was with, so I wobbled a hand vaguely, muttered vaguely, "Them."

A piece of brick whizzed by. They ducked, nearly dropping me. "What's wrong?" Pappy asked me.

"Somebody whacked me with a log. Everything keeps turning around. My knees won't work."

"Lookit here, Whisker. Already got his head sewed up once today. Right in the thick of the Struggle, eh, Wrecker?"

I tried for a grin. "Hey, Pappy. Butter and bullshit to you, too. How's it going? I thought you was dead."

"I heard that rumor, too, Garrett. It's almost all horse puckey. You gonna make the big rally?"

"I'm still walking," I said, knowing that was the answer Pappy wanted. "I got to roll, Tooms, catch up with my crew. Nice meeting you, Whisker." I took a couple of steps and glommed onto a lamp post that already supported two addled lovers against the seductions of gravity. Why does my luck run this way? On the lam from my personal armageddon and I stumble right into a guy I haven't seen in a decade and he recognizes me and throws my name out where anybody with an ear can catch it.

What next?

Aunt Boo was right. It's always something.

Nothing dropped out of the night or poured out of an alleyway. I saw no sign that anybody but Pappy and his pals had any interest in me. I held a conference. My feet agreed to stay under the rest of me. We all got going. My head hurt bad. I cursed softly and steadily, a vision of my own bed the carrot that kept me moving.

And still nothing plopped out of the night or boiled forth from the sewers while I was still in a part of town where they have those.

# 27

I was bone-tired. I wasn't smart, but I was lucky. It was a quiet night. Everybody with a taste for trouble had gone to the riots. My own brush with those, I learned later, was little more than a glance off the fringes of a minor skirmish far from the center of conflict, where matters grew serious. The push and shove and shouting escalated into massacres when real weapons came out. Nonhuman shops got plundered by the hundred. Refugees and squatters got tormented and beaten too often to number.

The scary thing was, the men responsible were out of control now but were all trained soldiers and combat veterans. If they reclaimed military discipline and organization, TunFaire could witness some real bloodshed.

I wondered what Relway and the secret police were doing to stem the tide. Maybe nothing. Serious bloodshed might serve Relway's personal agenda.

Bad as I wanted to get home to my bed, I entered my neighborhood with care. The temptation to make myself invisible was almost overpowering. Instead, I took my mind back in time, again became the company wreck. "Wreck" was what the regular grunts called us recon types when we were stuck with an infantry outfit. Wrecks got lots of training in sneakery and the mental skills important to the recon mission. I retained the physical skills, but getting to that place in my mind where there was no uncertainty, no nervousness, no worry, no lack of self-discipline, eluded me. That was something you had to work on every day. I had been slacking for years. I felt all the things your master wreck is supposed to set aside.

But I was quiet. I was one with night and shadow, never mind that big moon up there. I was fluidity itself, illusion flowing over the faces of walls in silence of stone. I passed sober but sleeping ratmen and they stirred not a whisker as I ghosted through the alleyways they called home.

I jumped about nine feet high when a sudden weight plopped onto my shoulder, grabbed hold like the cold, clawed hand of something risen from the grave. Every damned time I start telling me how great I am doing.

I returned to earth without screaming, having realized that the clawed hand was two bird feet. Attached to those feet was the ugliest duckling that ever lived. This one couldn't even swim or honk like a swan.

It said, "Do not approach the house yet. There are watchers. They must be diverted. Do not move at all until I give you the word." The voice did belong to the Goddamn Parrot, but there was only one horrible possible source for its dialogue.

I froze, the sheer horror, the terrible implications, leaving me completely blind to the fact that my venture northward, which had cost me such pain coming back south, had not broken the stakeout around my place. "No!" I whined, envisioning a future wherein there was no escape, no safe place. "Tell me it isn't so." He would be able to nag me anywhere.

"Awk! Garrett?"

"I understand and obey, O babbling feather duster." He was doomed. He had to go. If he could be used to follow me around carping, his fate was sealed.

It was him or me or the nightmare. Him or me. Heh heh. Accidents happen, Morley. Terrible accidents. Every day.

"Garrett! Please respond."

I was so involved in scoping out Mr. Big's short future that I had forgotten to keep my eyes and ears open. But luck looked the other way. No evil happened. "I'm right here. Right under this stinking vulture."

"Do not talk that way. The creature could have feelings, too. Hurry home. This diversion will not last long."

"On my way, Old Bones." I could sell him into slavery. Plenty of big-time wizards wouldn't mind having a dead Loghyr on staff. Well, a tame one anyway. Maybe I could give him away. Anybody wanted him, they could just come by and haul him off. I was not going to endure having him looking over my shoulder and criticizing me all over town.

# 28

I sensed the Dead Man's presence long before the house came in sight. He was wide awake and totally involved, which was a little disconcerting.

"Hurry!" the bird muttered. "Hurry!" *Hurry!* echoed inside my head.

I ran, still horrified by the possibility that there might be no escape from the Dead Man ever again.

My block of Macunado was filled with smoke. A few neighbors were out asking the night what the hell had happened. Seemed a waste if this was the Dead Man's doing. Gods, even of No-Neck's petty pewter stripe, were without doubt capable of seeing through smoke screens both physical and metaphorical. But I soon discovered that this smoke was full of specters flittering hither and yon, like the ghosts of childhood nightmares conjured for but an hour.

I scrambled up my front steps. My front door popped open just as a bumblebee hum grew in the darkness. I dived through. It popped shut behind me, hopefully before that banger-smoking runt caught a glimpse. For once Dean was on the job.

He was pale, frightened. I said, "Maybe you should have stayed another couple of days. You would've missed all this fun."

He gulped and nodded, but said, "I will have your supper ready in a few minutes. Meantime, Himself insists on seeing you."

Now didn't that dovetail sweetly with my own master plan?

I let myself into Himself's room, rehearsing some choice remarks. "We're into some really deep shit, Old Bones, and it isn't going to be good enough to just tread water."

"I am aware of the peril . . ."

"Can it with the talking bird, will you? Let's do it the way we always have. No! Wait. Stay awake . . ."

*Sarcasm is inappropriate, Garrett. We will proceed as you wish.*

"I figure you can see how my day went with one glance at the inside of my head. I hope yours was better."

*Indeed. I had a very instructional evening with your friend Linda Lee, once she gained the upper hand on her prejudices. That child has potential, Garrett. I approve.*

Uh-oh. He never approves of any woman. "Don't let her image fool you, either. She knows exactly what to do with all that potential."

*I fail to see any humor in your insinuation, Garrett. Linda Lee is that rarest of all mythical beings, a woman of reason and . . .*

I burst out laughing. "I don't believe it. She got to you." I chuckled some more, telling me I would have to look out for my librarian. If she could turn the Dead Man's head she was dangerous. "Of course you don't see any humor. You don't have a sense of humor. Come on. What's the word on these gods? They the real thing? How do I get out from under?"

*The Word is Trouble. In your vernacular, trouble in a big way. From the sheer scope of events around you we have to conclude that this is not an elaborate confidence game.*

"No shit."

He failed to catch my sarcasm this time. Or he ignored it, which he will do.

*Not even a government would go to the expense and trouble of staging something this difficult to manage.*

"You're kidding. Imagine that. No government willing to fool me?"

*Not in this pinpoint fashion. The expense anti-militates.*

"Not to mention that I'm completely unimportant in the mortal scheme. A little nil."

*Not to mention that no one on this earth has to work that hard to fool you. Some long legs, a bit of jiggle, some flouncing long hair, perhaps red for extra effect . . .*

Sigh. "Great, Chuckles. We're really getting somewhere here, aren't we? We are really getting diddled by gods?"

*They believe they are gods. And almost certainly they are within the liberal definitions employed by your primitive ancestors.*

"All right. Whatever, they're bad. I'm a fly and I see the flyswatter coming. Do I get philosophical and suffer it? Or can I do something?"

*There are several somethings available as options. Perhaps the most attractive is to lie low and do nothing at all while the situation runs its course. I would not be repelled by this option were it possible to sustain it. Your world and the Dream Quarter would be no poorer for the loss of these pantheons.*

"The trouble is, they don't plan to go quietly into that gentle night."

*Not at all. And since you have been given the opportunity to save them, any disaster is sure to come to roost here swiftly, whether or not they are able to discern your presence.*

"They want a key, Chuckles. And I don't have a clue where to look for one. Or what it would look like if I tripped over it. Did Linda Lee help us out there?"

*With her invaluable aid—and I cannot overemphasize just how much the child impressed me—I reviewed the available literature both on these pantheons and on those mechanisms used to determine presence, place, and status in the Dream Quarter.*

"Wonderful. Does all that wind mean you figured something out?"

*Restrain yourself. You are not safe here, nor is time ours to squander.*

I rolled my eyes and beat back the urge to head upstairs right now. I was more than ready to get intimate with my bed. "I'm not the one blowing like the wind."

*Based upon available information, supplemented by reason, I have concluded—albeit with a reluctance approaching despair—that you yourself are the anointed key. Additionally, it seems improbable that the interested parties have yet entertained that possibility.*

"Say what?" I squeaked.

*You are it, Garrett. They do not know yet. That has been your grand piece of luck to this point.*

"No shit." If he was right. He couldn't be right. I didn't want him to be right.

They would break my legs so I couldn't run, then clap me in irons and toss me into a cage and rivet it shut, then surround that with magical spells.

*I have no doubts whatsoever.*

"Shit," I said again. I was going through one of those vocabulary droughts that set in after a really bad shock. "Shit. It's me? I'm the key? How the hell does anybody fit me into a lock?"

*You have to begin from the fact that where religion is con- cerned, as is the case with magic, much of what you deal with is metaphor and symbol. In this instance metaphor and symbol have taken life.*

That kind of babble usually sets me off. This time I was too tired and achy to squabble.

Dean brought a tray. I stared at a gigantic lamb chop, vegeta- bles, cherry cobbler fit for the king and a mug of beer big enough to suit one of the divine thugs making my life miserable.

"Is there some metaphorical way to kick symbols in the ass so they leave you alone?"

*Doubtful. They are gods—albeit as petty as they get. You are not. In all the histories of all the races of this world there have been only two methods proven efficacious in dealing with the gods. You must appease them or you must befuddle them.*

"There you go stating the obvious again. Let's back it up some. What makes me the key? How and when did I get hung with it?"

*I cannot offer an informed answer. I have a theory, but it is too tenuous and unsettling at this point.*

"Bullshit." My buddy, my pal, who don't like getting caught being wrong so won't say anything till he is certain he is going to be right. "I'm not buying any of this premature . . ."

*Though time is indeed precious, your best option now is to rest. It should be possible to maintain the illusion of your absence for a time. Sleep. And, henceforth, please do not resort to any of the op- tions offered by the cord given you by that Magodor creature.*

"I done figured that one out for myself, Smiley."

*I suppose you have, at that. Sleep, Garrett.*

My bed felt like a little slice of heaven, with whipped cream on top.

# 29

It was a night too short. Some thief of time ripped off the four best hours. Cruel wakeup arrived with a crueler sunup. Somehow, my curtains stood open. Sunbeams flailed around like whips in the hands of morons. I faced away, tried to den up like a groundhog under the covers, but there was no escape. There is no enemy so relentless as the sun.

I know I shut my door before I collapsed into bed. It stood open now, perhaps betraying the first feather-stroke of Dean's vengeance campaign. My struggle against a return to the realm of the waking suffered savage reverses at the beak of the Goddamn Parrot, who was perched atop the open door and deft enough of wing to evade a flying shoe traveling at high speed.

This was the last straw. He was gone.

I was not likely to fail to remember who was operating him, either. The very bone-lazy bonehead who had helped so little with my recent cases, the deadbeat who would not wake up if you set a fire under his chair.

To hell with him. I packed my blanket tight around my ears.

Stubbornness gained me nothing. I stayed in bed, all right, but didn't get any more sleep. I just lay there wishing. While the Goddamn Parrot preached sermons.

"Bird, your life expectancy is minutes. You don't shut up you're going to be creamed chipped squab on toast." Dean would put together a championship gourmet experiment.

The bird got the message. His inclination toward self-preservation overrode the Dead Man's low, practical joke kind of humor. For the moment. That was one stupid bird.

All right. I could tuck that triumph in my pocket. So how come I couldn't get back to sleep? How come some sadistically self-abusive part of me kept insisting it was time to get up and get at it?

"Get at what?" I muttered. I dropped my feet into the same abyss as yesterday. "There ain't nothing, but nothing, out there that can't get through the day without me."

*Good morning, Garrett. Please exercise emotional caution today. The house is being observed. I believe I have your presence adequately masked. To maintain the illusion I must have you remain placid. Please refrain from these unproductive outbursts.*

"Then don't provoke me," I grumbled. I staggered around and fell into some clothes I found lying around, mostly what I had shucked in the middle of the night. They were not completely ripe. They would do.

I took my life in my hands, peeked out my window. "Damn!"

*Garrett! Calmly, please.*

"It's *bright* out there." Whatever happened to all those gloomy, overcast days we'd been having? The world seemed to be getting warmer.

*Stay away from the window. Someone might see the curtain move and reason that you are here after all—particularly since the movement came at your window.*

It was going to be one of those days, was it? Nags punctuated by nagging? I reconsidered my bed. It had been so nice in there, so toasty warm. My dreams had been of a paradise where the motives of all the beautiful women were blatant and straightforward and the "me key, you lock" symbolism was direct and obvious. There were beer taps everywhere, and you would gain five pounds a day on the food if you ate it in the waking world.

By jingo june, as Granny used to say—I *did* hear her say that once—I ought to get my buddies together so we could cook us up our own religion. Most of them believed in booze and bimbos, and some enlightened religions already considered that sort of stuff important enough to rate its own underling gods and goddesses. Star was one example. Maybe we could get Star to jump the Godoroth ship by offering her a better contract.

A diffuse wave of disgust emanated from downstairs. "You don't like the way I think, quit poking around inside my head."

*I was not seeking adolescent fantasization. I was trying to re-examine your experiences of yesterday.*

"You were playing voyeur because you can't think that stuff

up for yourself. The best you can come up with is bug parades and goofball political theories."

*I cannot deny what is self-evident. I am a creature of intelligence and intellect, disinclined toward obsession with pleasures of the flesh.*

"You can't deny what is self-evident, which is that you couldn't do anything about it if you wanted, so you just sit there making sour remarks about those of us who still have a little fire in our blood."

While we amused ourselves, I negotiated the stairway, an epic adventure any morning early. I trudged into the kitchen and drew a mug of tea from the pot. Dean was at the stove. He offered me a look of exasperation, like I had ruined his whole day by not staying in bed so he could experience the enjoyment of rousting me out. I tapped every reservoir of contrariness within me, put on my brightest Charlie Sunshine face, chirped, "Good morning, Dean. Did you sleep well?"

He glowered a deep black glower, sure I was putting him on. "Breakfast will be a while yet."

I poured myself a refill. "Take your time. Me and the big guy got schemes to scheme and cons to crack." I was sure that, immortal players or not, there were charades going on in this temple squabble. Overall, the Shayir probably were more straight with me, and one sex of them sure was friendly, but I was sure we didn't have the full map in front of us yet.

"Dean?"

"Sir?"

"Did the wedding go well? Was the trip worth it?" I could not recall having asked before.

"It all went quite well. Your gift was received with considerable pleasure. Rebecca expressed amazement that you even remembered her, let alone thought so well of her."

"There was a time when neither one of you let me forget for a minute. That gift was a sigh of relief." Back then Dean's whole mission in life, it seemed, was to get me married to one of his numerous nieces.

A hint of a smirk pranced around the corners of the old boy's mouth. He said, "It was an interesting journey. We even fell afoul of highwaymen on the return leg, gentlemen so inept they didn't know what to do when they found out that everyone aboard the coach was stone-broke. I enjoyed myself a great deal, but it's good to be back home."

"Yeah. No place like." Especially for me. "Sounds like somebody pounding on the door."

*Garrett. Please step into your office and close the door.*

"Huh?"

*Our visitors are Mr. Tharpe, Miss Winger, and an associate of Mr. Dotes' known as Agonistes. They will leave shortly. I should like them to depart convinced that you are not on these premises.*

That sounded like a reasonable idea, but who would want to admit it to Himself?

Who was this Agonistes? I didn't know anybody by that name in Morley's crew.

*"Agonistes" is what you people call a street name.*

"Oh. Silly me. I really thought somebody's mother would hang a tag like that on him."

Dean passed me, headed for the front door, wiping floury hands on a dishrag. I ducked into my office, which is a large, messy closet across the hall from the Dead Man's spacious suite. I swung the door most of the way shut. I left it cracked both so I could hear what was said in the hall and so I could peek at the Dead Man's visitors. "Dean, remember to keep an eye on Winger. She'll try to kype something."

"I always do, sir. All of your friends."

He started fumbling with locks and latches and chains, taking away any chance I would have had to speak on behalf of my friends.

*The man's birth name was Claude-Ned Blodgett.*

I didn't know that name, either, but I could see why he would take up just about anything else. Who was going to be scared of a gangster named Claude-Ned Blodgett? Was he going to pop you with a farm implement?

Agonistes, though, had a kind of self-selected sound to it. Names picked up on the street don't usually come that dramatic. Pretty often, they really sound plain stupid. Our great wizard lords on the Hill pick their own business names, and they always choose something like Raver Styx.

Winger started barking before Dean got the door all the way open. I hoped the Dead Man just had her doing legwork. She could complicate things real bad if she got in far enough to get ideas for some scheme.

# 30

"Garrett here?" Winger demanded.

"I fear not, Miss."

"I'd swear I heard his voice."

"Holy hooters!" the Goddamn Parrot squawked. "Look at them gazoombies!" He managed a creditable wolf whistle. Winger is blessed. Nobody will ever doubt that she is female, despite her six-foot stature.

"If Garrett wasn't my best friend I'd throttle that critter," Winger said.

I wanted to jump out and tell her not to hold back on my account, go for it, turn the little vulture into mock chicken soup.

Though he knew I would do no such thing, the Dead Man did brush me with a cautionary touch. Up front, the Goddamn Parrot continued to flatter Winger. Saucerhead's rumbling laugh filled the hallway. "I think he's in love, Winger. I bet you Garrett would let you take him home." He knew.

"Shee-it."

"Think of the advertising. That bird around wherever you went."

"Double shee-it."

I leaned in an effort to look through the narrow crack by the door hinges. I wanted to see this Agonistes character. I didn't get much of a look, though he waited for Winger and Saucerhead to go into the Dead Man's room first. He didn't look like a thug. He looked like a lawyer, which is a whole different species of villain. But, then, Morley is trying to polish his image these days.

I listened carefully. I couldn't catch a sound from the Dead

Man's room. Dean went back to the kitchen, prepared a tray with tea and muffins. My mouth watered. I was hungry. I resisted temptation. Those three did have to leave the house convinced I was still on the run.

Dean wouldn't be able to go out at all now. We would have to survive on whatever we had on hand. Unless Dean had managed some marketing, that would not be much. I had eaten out while the old boy was gone.

On his way back to the Dead Man's room, Dean stepped in and quietly handed me tea and several hot muffins. He winked, crossed the hall. Before the Dead Man's door shut I heard Winger carping about me being so cheap I wouldn't serve a decent breakfast.

Winger is one of those people you love because they have style. Anyone else who did the things she does would have no friends. Winger does it and you just sort of sigh and chuckle and shake your head and say, "That's Winger."

That kind of person always irritates me—along with guys who never get dirty or rumpled—but I fall under their spell as easily as anybody.

I munched a muffin with one hand and felt the stitches in my scalp with the other. They were tender. Surprise, surprise. But when I didn't touch them they itched. At least my hangover was long gone. I wished I could sneak into the kitchen for a brew. But there wasn't a drop in the house.

Oh my. No beer. And I couldn't go out. And Dean couldn't go out. Even having Dean have Saucerhead bring in a keg wouldn't work. Nobody out there would believe the keg was for Dean or the Dead Man.

That led to the really uncomfortable question. Were those god gangs likely to come play rough? Would they bust in here just to poke around?

"They're gods, Garrett," I reminded myself. "Maybe they aren't as powerful and all-knowing as they want people to think and most people usually think gods are, but they're still a long way up on us mortals." I could not see them having much trouble figuring out where I was.

And that being the case, why shouldn't I just cross the hall and hand Saucerhead a few marks and a nice fee for fetching me a keg?

*Continue to assume you are the focus of a mighty confidence scheme, Garrett. It will help if you believe we are not powerless in this.*

I jumped. For a moment after the touch opened, I expected it to be *Nog is inescapable.* I'm not sure why.

What was that all about? He did not expand upon his remark, which only indicated he was monitoring my thoughts, something he wasn't supposed to do except in extreme circumstances.

Dean stepped in. "More tea?"

"If you can manage. What's going on over there?"

"He has them collecting rumors so he can compare and collate them and test some theory about the true intentions of Glory Mooncalled."

My expression scared Dean. He grabbed my mug and platter and scooted. I squeezed the edge of my desk so hard I ought to have crushed fingerprints into the wood.

I wanted to blow up in a shrieking rage. I wanted to stomp around the house breaking things. I wanted to use words my mother would have disowned me for even thinking. I wanted to grab a certain humongous sack of petrified camel snot and drag him into the street, where he could become snacks for homeless and otherwise disadvantaged vermin. I couldn't do any of that without giving myself away, so I sat there rocking back and forth and making weird, soft noises that could get me committed to the mental ward at the Bledsoe Imperial Charity Hospital.

I had a feeling Dean had just let slip the real con going on around here. My esteemed sidekick was using my concern about my own dire situation to gull me into thinking I was getting something for my money when it was really him getting something else.

*Child and Loghyr, living and dead, I have been in this world more than a dozen centuries, Garrett. Never have I encountered a creature as cynical and selfish and penurious as you. There are great changes stirring. True marvels and wonders are transforming today into history out there. And you insist we all focus completely on a squabble that may work itself out just fine without you or me.*

I didn't shriek. I didn't foam at the mouth. I didn't go over there and choke him. For what good would that do me? It would not have any effect on him. And until his guests departed, I could do nothing but fume and paint mental pictures of vast, complex, and exquisite torments to try out on the Dead Man.

*Were you to distract me so, I might not be able to maintain the webs of deception I have woven to keep your presence here concealed.*

He could deal with me and his guests both because he has more than one mind. Which mainly means he can be a pain in the butt several places at the same time. Not what I count as a big plus talent.

The fact that I could fight back only in the darkness of my heart only made my situation more unbearable.

*Perhaps you should spend less bile upon me and invest more thought in the situation you fancy has engulfed you.*

Standard fare from the self-declared brains of the outfit. Tell me to figure it out for myself.

Not easy. The situation was unlike any I had faced before. With me identified as the divine key, there was no mystery involved— unless it was why I had gotten trapped in the first place.

I did not like being the key, but I believed the Dead Man was right. Though No-Neck had made nothing of it, I was able to stroll right into a temple that was supposed to be sealed so tight that gods couldn't get inside.

How had I become the key? When had I? How come I hadn't been consulted? The virgins who give birth to the children of gods, the men compelled to beat into those sprats the principles of offering accounting and believer manipulation later, those folks always got an advisory visit from a messenger angel before the fact. Just to smooth the road, you know. Me, I'd gotten diddly. Squat. Zilch plus zip. Hell, I was out of pocket on this thing. And I could be helping people I actually liked to handle problems I actually cared about.

Not that I wanted to dive into the Weider family troubles. That just looked less treacherous than where I was at now.

The Dead Man may have been amused by my quandary, but he was preoccupied with his visitors. He spared me no more attention while he extracted whatever it was he wanted from the crew, then filled them up with new instructions and sent them on their way.

Winger was the last to leave. Of course. Dean shepherded her carefully, stopped her from entering my office, then stayed between her and anything valuable that she might find too tempting.

# 31

*You do overestimate Miss Winger's cupidity and amorality.*

The front door had not yet closed behind the overestimated lady, who had started swapping compliments with the Goddamn Parrot. I had to wait till the door slapped her behind before I could respond.

"I really doubt that."

*She has a code of right and wrong. She sticks to it firmly.*

"Yeah. Her code is, If it ain't nailed down it's hers to carry away. And if it can be pried loose it ain't nailed down."

*You do the woman an injustice. But, then, you feel you have been through trying times and are justified in demonstrating a foul temper.*

"It's no feeling, Smiley, it's fact. And my temper is going to turn even more foul if you keep indulging your hobbies while I'm getting batted around by characters who actually make you look attractive."

I stormed across the hall, burst into the Dead Man's room. Dean entered behind me, stood around nervously waiting to find out what was going on. He was scared. However casual or indifferent the Dead Man seemed, Dean's intuition told him we had big trouble. Usually he copes with big trouble by going wild in the kitchen.

*Though you want to believe otherwise, I have given your god problem some attention. Your friend Linda Lee brought a cartload of books here last evening. She and your friend Tinnie and her friend Alyx and their friend Nicks spent hours reading for me. I learned very little that you do not already know. Neither the Godoroth nor the Shayir pantheons represent golden examples of the brilliantly absurd natural imaginings of humanity. If some unimaginably great beings were to be connoisseurs of absurdities, these would form the centerpieces of their collections. These pantheons slithered from the bottom depths of lowest-common-denominator minds. Thud and blunder, sex and scandal, and afflict your mortal followers with pestilences and famines, disasters and humiliations, for fun, is what they are all about. And in that, of course, they mirror the souls in their care. All gods are shaped by the hearts of their believers.*

What a sight that must have been, the Dead Man surrounded by beautiful women reading aloud, him absorbing the information they provided while smugly ignoring the fact that I was flailing around on the bottom in the deep smelly stuff somewhere else. And he had been aware of my plight—the Goddamn Parrot, having abandoned me to my fate, had flown home to him.

*There is one aspect in need of deeper consideration. The girl who brought you out of Shayir captivity does not appear in any recorded account of either pantheon. Nor does your air-mobile infant. Which, by the by, is usually called a cherub.*

"Hell, I remember cherubs now." They were part of the mythological hardware of my mother's religion. Mostly they just appeared in religious art.

*They are part of the background populations of divine beings common to most religions springing from the same roots as the Church.*

So he still had a spying eye inside my head.

*For efficiency's sake only, Garrett. About the girl. It is your feeling that she is the by-blow of either Lang or Imar, her mother having been a mortal woman?*

"She didn't tell me a whole lot about herself."

*No. She did not. And you were too taken by the imaginary possibilities of your circumstances to try to elicit any useful information.*

"Hey! . . ."

*I reiterate. She does not figure in either mythology. The cherub springs from another family of religions entirely.*

"I heard you. Give me a break. Imar and Lang are both the kinds of guys who grab whatever and whoever wherever and whenever they think they can get away with it. And probably don't much care if they get caught."

*Stipulated. That is not in dispute. It is beyond dispute. But it may not be relevant. What troubles me is this anomaly, these players who do not fit the game. This girl, the cherub, even the winged horses. Anomalies always worry me. Your better course may have been to stay with the girl until you learned who she was and what she wanted.*

"Maybe." Hindsight makes geniuses of us all. "And maybe if I had done that, right now I would be the meat in somebody's stew."

*We really are contrary this morning, are we not?*

"Damned straight. The whole crew. Me, myself, and I. Happens every time I find my partner blowing my hard-earned in order to collect political rumors. Wasting it on people like Winger, that we know too well, and on that Agonistes, that we don't know at all."

*Both are entirely trustworthy within the limits of the tasks they were asked to perform.*

"Yeah? What happens when somebody out there starts wondering why you're asking questions? Political people are born paranoid. If they interrogate Winger, she'll tell them anything she thinks they want to hear to get herself out of it. We could end up with Relway's thugs all over us, or The Call, or somebody out of the Cantard, or the for gods' sake Pan-Tantactuan Fairy Liberation Army . . ."

*You are becoming excited. Please restrain yourself.*

Grumble grumble.

*You fail to appreciate the real magnitude of the crisis gripping TunFaire. And you fail to accept my ability to protect myself.*

"It ain't you looking out for your butt that I'm worried about, Old Bones. You've always done a truly outstanding job of covering number one. It's my ass ending up in a sling that worries me."

*Always the self-centered, demanding . . .*

"Don't play that game with me, Chuckles. It's time you paid your rent. I'm calling. Tell me how to deal with this gods mess."

*What do you know about the rash of strange fires in the Baden neighborhood?*

"Huh?" Talk about your blindsider. But he does that. One of his minds will be mulling over something not remotely related to anything under discussion and it will pop right out. "I've been busy. You would have noticed if you weren't worrying about things like fires and Glory Mooncalled. What about these fires?"

*I do not know. Several of my visitors have mentioned a series of unexplained, fatal fires. Not arson. Nothing burns but the victim himself, apparently, unless he sets fire to something himself.*

"Sounds grisly."

*Perhaps. It is only a curiosity, of course, but I gather there was no connection between the victims, none of whom were the kind of people who get themselves assassinated.*

"Great. Sounds like the perfect puzzle to keep you out of my hair on a long winter's day. So put it on the shelf till the snows come back. Give me a hint here. What about these gods? Are we even dealing with gods?"

*Again, the amount of energy being expended and the number of players involved militates against it being a confidence action. Indeed, it would be possible for a cabal of wizards to produce the effects you have encountered. But to what purpose such effort? There is no hint of any stake other than that proclaimed by the principals. This appears to be a straightforward struggle for divine status.*

"Status?" Got me again. Another blindsider.

*Of course. Do you accept as absolute and literal their expectation of total oblivion if they are driven from the Dream Quarter?*

"Pretty much. They were real intense about it. You're right, though. They could set up in a storefront somewhere. Plenty of crackpot outfits do."

*And there you have it. If you are not established in the Dream Quarter, yours is not a serious religion. You are a focus for lunacy. A bad joke. Even if you have a hundred times the followers of a respectable cult.*

"But that would win you a place in the Dream Quarter."

*True. Although you would carry a stigma for generations. Like new money amidst old. You see my point?*

"Theirs, too. You got only a couple, three followers left and you get the old eviction notice, then you try to set up shop in an abandoned sausage cookery, your followers maybe won't show up for services anymore. Too embarrassing. They might sign on with some other crew who knew the right people and worshiped in the right place. So maybe you are dead if you're out. It's just not sudden."

*They might see it that way.*

"So suggest me a plan. Sit tight?"

*I am applying some thought to the matter. I feel it is unlikely that the pantheons remain ignorant of your whereabouts, despite our*

*precautions. It remains to be seen if they will accept inactivity—*
*especially once someone realizes that you are the key.*

"You think they will?"

*I reasoned it out easily enough. They are less able, constitu-*
*tionally, to consider a mortal closely, but eventually it will occur*
*to someone that you entered that temple as though there was no*
*seal upon it.*

"Could have been No-Neck. He was with me."

*No doubt he will pay for that.*

"He deserves a warning."

*He does. I will see to it.* He seemed to mull something over. I
let him ferment. *Events could become exciting, I fear, once that*
*conclusion is reached. Particularly if one of the Godoroth reaches*
*it first.*

"Huh? You want to explain?"

He *was* in a mood. His usual response would be to tell me to
work it out for myself. *You suggested that Lang had eyewitness*
*knowledge of your visit with the Godoroth. I suggest we seri-*
*ously entertain the possibility that, in fact, he did hear from an*
*eyewitness.*

"You think one of the Godoroth is a traitor?" There was a bog-
gler. Not that treachery isn't a favorite divine sport *inside* any
given pantheon.

*And perhaps the other way as well. During your encounter*
*with Magodor there were hints. In fact, you were, apparently, inter-*
*cepted on your way to a rendezvous with the Shayir, though there*
*is no mention of any Adeth amongst them, according to Linda Lee.*

"The more you complicate this the worse it smells. It could get
real nasty."

*Indeed it could. That is why I have devoted such a great store*
*of energy to ferreting out potential twists before we find ourselves*
*caught in the claws of an unexpected turnaround.*

Although he was probably blowing smoke and wasn't really
doing anything, it was refreshing to hear him claim that he was.

"Sit tight?" I asked again.

*Sit tight. And keep your hands off that rope.*

"I'd say something about grandmas and egg-sucking, but it
would fly right over your head."

*Like a child who cannot focus its attention long, you require*
*frequent reminders. It is inevitable that some will be superfluous*
*or redundant.*

Was that a put-down?

Yes. It was. He was in full command of his powers, which meant there would be no getting any last word.

I jerked my hand away from my waist. That rope was damned seductive. It was hard not to fiddle with its ends.

*A pity that we cannot interview the Cat person. She might be a sizable gap in these gods' wall of secrecy. It is possible she is knowledgeable but unable to protect her knowledge.*

"Guess I should have turned on the Garrett charm and sweet-talked her right on home here. Eh?" His opinion of my ability to cope with women has no connection with reality.

He responded with an unfocused mental sneer.

I countered with another grumble about him spending my hard-earned, then retreated to my office.

# 32

When the going gets tough the tough guy takes his problems to Eleanor. "What do you think, Darling?" Hell, Eleanor might be more use than the Dead Man.

She was all the way Over There.

Eleanor is the central feature of a painting of a frightened woman fleeing a dark mansion. Shadows of evil tower behind her, suggestions of wickedness hunting. The painter had a great talent and incredible power. Once his painting had been possessed by a dread, drear magic, but most of that had leaked away.

Eleanor had been a key player in an old case. I had fallen for her, only to learn that she had gotten herself murdered while I was still wearing diapers.

It isn't often the victim helps solve her murder, then breaks a guy's heart when she's done.

It had been a strange case.

It had been a strange relationship, doomed from the start, only I hadn't known until the end. The painting, which I seized from her killer, and some memories are all I have left.

When I have a problem that cuts deep or just tangles my brain I talk it over with Eleanor. That seems to help.

The Dead Man doesn't have any soul. Not the way Eleanor does.

For an instant she seemed thoughtful, seemed to have a remark poised right behind her parted lips.

Take charge. Start acting instead of reacting.

"Right, Honey. Absodamnlutely. But clue me. How do I grab Imar—or good old Lang—by the gilhoolies while I kick his butt till he starts talking? Tell me. I'll strut out that front door with my ass-kicking boots on."

Which was the crux, the heart, the soul of my problem. And ain't it always, when mortals deal with the gods? Almost by definition, Joe Human has no leverage.

Dean appeared. He carried a big platter of stew. He set that in front of me while he frowned at Eleanor. Me talking to her makes him uncomfortable. There is enough residual sorcery in the painting to set his skin crawling. "I saw Miss Maya while I was doing our marketing last evening."

That explained why there was food in the house. He had wasted no time. I don't like stew much, and his latest effort didn't look even a little appetizing but it smelled tempting. I dug in and discovered the stew tasted way better than it looked. It was lamb. We hadn't had lamb for a long time.

Dean has his weaknesses, but bad cooking isn't among them.

"That's amazing, Dean."

"Mr. Garrett?"

"I can wander all over town for months and never once run into Maya or Tinnie. I live here, but I never see either one of them come to the door. But let me take a walk around the block, when I get back I hear all about how Miss Tinnie or Miss Maya was around and I get all the latest news from their lives. How does that work, Dean? Do you hang out some kind of sign to let them know the ogre isn't in his cave?"

Dean was both taken aback and baffled. I had lost him several sarcastic snaps earlier. "I'm sure I don't know, sir." He looked like he thought his feelings ought to be hurt, but he wasn't quite sure why.

"Don't mind me, Dean. I'm not in one of my better moods."

"Really? I hadn't noticed."

"All right. All right. The stew is better than ever. You didn't think to order a fresh keg, did you?"

"I thought of it."

We were going to play that game, eh? "And did you follow through?"

"Actually, I did. It appears Miss Winger will be spending some time here, off and on, and Mr. Tharpe enjoys a mug when he comes by, so that seemed the hospitable thing to do."

"Better have the empties taken away. I forgot to take care of that while you were gone."

"I did notice that." Since he had to work around the stack in the kitchen. "I cautioned the delivery outfit to bring a wagon or an extra cart."

Smart aleck. He disapproves of my hobby. He doesn't have a hobby himself. He needs one bad. Never completely trust a guy who doesn't have a hobby. He takes everything too damned seriously.

Maybe he and the Goddamn Parrot could go for long walks together.

"I just had an idea, Dean."

He backed off a step, beyond the sink. Beyond the kegs.

I gave him a look at my raised eyebrow. "What?"

"You are at your most dangerous when you start having ideas."

"Like a newly sharpened sword."

"In the hands of a drunk."

"You would make somebody a really great wife. Here it is. We let it out that Mr. Big knows where there is buried treasure. We say he used to belong to a Lambar pirate, Captain Scab, who taught him the major chart keys. Somebody will hold us up for him next time we take him outside."

Dean chuckled. He doesn't like the Goddamn Parrot either. That parti-colored crow is as hard on Dean as he is on me. I owed Morley a big one. I ought to lug the Dead Man and his bug collection over and dump them in The Palms.

"It would be far easier and much less complicated just to wring its neck."

It would indeed, but we humans seldom pursue the pragmatic course. We let ancillary factors influence us. For example, Morley would be offended if I murdered his gift.

Dean pulled a baking sheet out of the oven. I grabbed a biscuit while it was still smouldering, drenched it in butter, splashed on a little honey. Heaven.

Paradise has a way of running off faster than I can sprint trying to catch it.

*Garrett. Presences have begun gathering in the neighborhood.*

"My friends?"

Dean gave me a look, then realized I wasn't talking to him.

*I cannot sense them clearly. It may be that most are not entirely present in this level of reality. I do sense a great deal of unfocused power out there, and barely restrained fears and angers. That is not a combination that bodes well.*

"No shit. The master is back, folks. Do you get any sense of immediate intent? Can you make out any identities?"

*No. In my youth I went to sea. You have been there, on a day when the storms stalk the horizons, balanced on slanted towers of dark rain, and the winds rise and die in moments. Sitting here sensing those creatures is like standing on the deck of a galleon watching those storms walk about.*

"Very picturesque, Old Bones." I knew exactly what he meant. I *had* been there. "I didn't know you were a sailor."

*I was not.*

"You said . . ."

*I went to sea.*

"Probably one step ahead of the loan sharks. You mean they're just out there, hanging around, pissed off, but without any special villainy in mind?"

*Yes.*

I headed upstairs so I could peek out the windows. Excepting one barred one in the kitchen that allows Dean to get some air while cooking on a summer's day, we have none on the ground floor. That is characteristic of TunFaire architecture. We like to make our thieves work. "Are we under siege?"

*Not as such. We are under observation.*

"Don't go showing off."

*In your own vernacular, Garrett, go teach your mother to suck eggs.*

Grandmother, Old Bones. It's go teach your grandmother to suck eggs. You're going to talk like the rabble, at least try to get it right.

# 33

Bizarre. The street was almost empty. A brisk but confused wind flipped leaves and rubbish this way and that. It looked colder than it ought to be. There was an unseasonal overcast. Mrs. Cardonlos was out in front of her rooming house taking advantage of the light traffic to clean the street. For reasons that would make sense only inside her strange head, she was staring at my place like the weird weather had to be my fault.

She can lay anything off onto me.

While I watched, she put her broom down, went inside, came out wearing another sweater. She glared at the sky, daring it to darken any more.

"You using my eyes?"

*Yes.*

"Looks like late autumn, except the trees still have their leaves." Not that there is a lot of greenery around. My neighborhood isn't big on tree-lined streets, lawns, gardens, and such. Brick and stone, that is us. Brick and stone.

"Can you tell anything useful?"

*No. Have Dean put the bird out the front door. Back him up but stay out of sight.*

"Right." What the hell? Oh, well. Let *him* explain to Morley.

Mrs. Cardonlos stopped working. She stared malevolently, but not my way. Remarkable. I leaned so I could see the object of her wrath.

"See that woman, Chuckles? That's the redhead who led me into all this. Adeth." Curious, the old woman being able to see her.

*She looks forlorn. A sad waif.*

"What's gotten into you? You have bad dreams last nap?"

*Sir?*

"You usually take a more mechanistic, colorless view of the world."

*Surely not. Please dispatch the bird.*

"I'd love to if I could find a way to make somebody else take the rap." I went and told Dean what His Nibs wanted. Dean just shook his head, dried his hands on a dishtowel. He left the sink to its own devices, headed for the small front room. Mr. Big had no premonition that he was about to enjoy a new adventure. Dean collected him unprotesting while I checked the stoop and street through the peephole. "All clear, Dean."

He fiddled with locks and latches and chains. I take back what I said about him not having a hobby.

The Goddamn Parrot looked like he was about half alive. He was behaving himself. It was scary.

I hoped I didn't start missing his obnoxious beak.

Dean pulled the door halfway open, leaned out far enough to chuck the flashy little squab into the wind. A puff of that got inside and, yes, it was chilly.

Dean jerked back inside, started to push the door shut.

"Wait! No. Go ahead. I can look through the peephole."

Dean stepped aside. I peeped. "I was right. The beer wagon is coming. Get an extra keg if he has one. We may be locked up a long time."

Dean glowed with dark disapproval. Then, "Are we actually involved in something serious?"

All the activity had not clued him.

"We are. And it might be the most dangerous thing yet." I hit the highlights while we waited for Charanagua Slim to bring his cart to the foot of our steps. Slim was part elf, part troll, an improbable mix that had to be seen to be believed. He was short and hard as a rock, and both his parents had to have been the ugliest of their kind ever to reach breeding age. He was a sweetheart when you got to know him, but he made nails look soft when money was involved. He was important in my life only because he was my main source of fresh kegs of the holy elixir.

Dean slipped out to help Slim. Slim was going to be irked. Not all of my empties carried his chop.

I denned up in my office. Slim didn't need to see me. He might tell somebody later. Or he might insist we review my fickle relationships with beer haulers.

I heard the door close barely after I sat down. I never caught a snarl of complaint from Slim. Something was wrong. I headed for the hallway.

Dean had just passed my door. He had a pony keg on his shoulder. That's hardly enough beer to wet your whistle. "What's that?"

"All he could deliver right now. All he had left on his cart. I took what I could get."

I followed him into the kitchen. The empties had not stirred. "What about those?"

"He didn't have room on his cart. He'll be back, he said. He said business is good, what with the soldiers coming home. Said he's working fourteen-hour days."

Wouldn't you know? "I smell a beer shortage coming on. Another of the unexpected horrors of peace." I went scurrying toward the front door. Better have Slim bring me a cartload all my own. I would become a beer hoarder.

*Garrett, please.*

I gave it up, just took a peek through the hole. Slim sure enough did have kegs and barrels practically dripping off his cart. "I guess those human rights guys need a lot to keep them going." Beer drinking is an essential part of the preliminary rituals of political demonstrations.

"Hang on, Smiley."

*Yes?*

"Use my eyes. Take a gander up the street, past Old Lady Cardonlos' place."

*I see nothing but a somewhat substantial peasant girl.*

"That's Cat. The one who gave me the ride on the flying horse."

*I have her.* Half a minute passed. *She is not quite mortal, Garrett. Ah. She is an interesting child. And this house is her destination. She is not aware that it is the center of a great deal of attention. She lacks some very basic divine senses despite being the child of a god.*

"She never struck me as any genius. Hey, Dean! We're going to have company. Take her in to His Nibs. We don't want her to know I'm here."

Dean offered me a look at his hardest glare. "I hope there is money in this somewhere. I have no interest in putting on a show for one of your prospects."

"It's all business. Just let her in. Offer her tea and a muffin and hand her off to the Dead Man."

"Yes, sir."

*Thank you.*

Both sounded as though no greater imposition had settled upon their lives before.

"You wanted to interview Cat, Smiley. Now's your big chance."

# 34

*Those things out there do not appear to be aware of her as anything but another mortal. I sense no interest at all.*

"Intriguing."

*Extremely.*

Nobody knew who Cat was, but Cat was in the game. "Old Bones, this may be more complicated than I thought."

*Probably. And she may be more of a challenge than I had anticipated. Her mind has a remarkably stout shell surrounding it. It conceals her memories and all but her surfacemost thoughts. There is enough on the surface, though, to confirm the notion that she serves neither the Shayir nor the Godoroth.*

"That's hot news. Shucks. Recomplication wasn't what I wanted right now."

Dean continued to grumble his way up the hall. He had a pie in the oven and didn't think it was reasonable that he be expected to watch the door as well. We were turning into a bunch of cranky old men.

Had to be the Dead Man's wicked influence.

*Pshaw! Allow her to knock a second time before you open the door, Dean. I need time to get the bird back here.*

Dean responded with select commentary worthy of Mr. Big himself. I have to admit I felt a certain sympathy for his position.

*Go into your office, Garrett.*

He was surly. Still had that one eye inside my head.

I went, but watched as long as I dared.

Dean stiffened, presumably getting instructions. He really

hates having the Dead Man get into his head. I managed to get out of sight before he yanked the door open, not waiting for any damned second knock while his pie was baking.

The Goddamn Parrot blasted inside, staggering the old man, arriving with his beak going full speed. "Lay your glims on this bimbo! Hooters deluxe!"

"What is *that*?" Cat squeaked. My erstwhile traveling companion seemed a touch irritable.

Welcome to the house of aggravation, dear.

"A pet. Ignore it. Product of a wastrel youth. It doesn't understand that it is offensive," Dean replied. "It escaped some time ago, going out to search for Mr. Garrett, my employer. Mr. Garrett has vanished. Wenching again, no doubt. They were inseparable."

I considered what choke holds might best serve in a debate with a man Dean's age.

*Garrett. The creature No-Neck has been warned. He recognized the bird but failed to take its message seriously. He seemed to think you were trying to pull some clever practical joke.*

Great. "He didn't get the name No-Neck for no reason," I whispered. But would I have listened to a talking bird I had met only once, when both of us were drinking?

Probably not.

*Unless it was a redhead. Dean. Please close the door.*

"Cheap shot!"

The Goddamn Parrot kept yapping like he thought Cat was Winger. Maybe he couldn't tell the difference.

Near as I could tell from the racket, she kept getting in Dean's way, possibly because she didn't know how to deal with the Goddamn Parrot. No matter how obnoxious the critter gets it's never good manners to stomp somebody's pet in their own house.

Then the awful truth plopped like a great stinking lump falling behind the tallest herbivorous thunder lizards.

"Hey, Honeybuns, dig the weasel out of this dump and let's get going." Yes. Him. And his humming wings.

The Goddamn Parrot shrieked and headed down the hall. Dean clumped after him, exercising his own vocabulary. The bumblebee buzz drifted. I heard rattling at the door to the small front room.

"Nothin' in there. Stinks, though. That bird. Let's look at this next one."

I went over behind my desk and picked up the spare headknocker. It was time to find out how much power a cherub had.

*Calmly. Calmly.*

The runt's mouth never stopped. Neither did his banger. The smoke began coming in under my office door.

The Goddamn Parrot's beak never stopped.

Dean kept swearing.

Cat kept after everybody. She sounded like she was about to break down crying.

*Be patient,* the Dead Man sent. *The girl is rattled. This is to our advantage. I see weaknesses in the armor around her mind.*

"Oh, excellent," I muttered. "And what about that stinking, banger-smoking cherub?"

*Cherub?*

"The one in the hallway with the rest of that baby riot? The half-bug little guy trying to get into everything?"

Cat shrieked, "Fourteen, stop that!"

*Oh. That cherub.* And, somehow, I knew he could not sense the little monster at all except through the senses of others. Presumably he was seeing through Cat's eyes, since I was not out there. Unchosen mortal Dean ought to be blind to the critter.

Would ordinary mortals smell the smoke even if they could not see the smoker?

"That very cherub," I said. "Since you've found these chinks, chip away." And good luck with the runt. You marvel, you.

*Your attitude needs adjustment desperately.*

"And you need to get back outside of my head, Chuckles." Gotcha.

I felt his withdrawal. He didn't do it as a favor to me.

He was going to need all his minds to deal with Cat and her pet.

I tried to commune with Eleanor. Eleanor wasn't interested. And who could blame her?

# 35

*Garrett. I have attained control. You may join us if you so desire.*

"Oh, I will. I've got to see this."

The Dead Man was smugly self-satisfied. Which was not an unusual state of affairs. When things go wrong for him that is always someone else's fault, but his triumphs are all his own, brilliantly unshared. Just ask him.

"A prime candidate for Amazon school," I cracked. Cat did look like a leading contender for future queenship of the women warriors. "Another Winger."

*Not quite. This one is completely healthy and totally honest and wholesome. The girl you will want your daughter to be.*

"There anything inside that handsome head?" Cat was that kind of girl when you got her out into the light.

I was paying her no mind, really. I was studying the cherub. It was perched on the arm of the Dead Man's chair, frozen solid as some stone gewgaw on a temple wall.

Handsome, by the way, is a physically pretty woman who has no attractive pizzazz whatsoever. Something like being your good-looking sister. A perfect match for your feebleminded cousin Rudolf from Khuromal. Give her a pat on the hand and a weak smile, then go find the girls who want to be bad.

"You accomplish anything with the runt there?"

*I succeeded in extinguishing his smoke.* The room stank. The hallway outside stank. *I managed to petrify him. Otherwise he has proven intractable.*

"Shut up and put out is good enough for me. How about Cat?"
*There is a great deal in there, but I cannot reach it without her cooperation. She is quite strong.*

"Must be the blood."

*Sneer.* A mental sneer is a remarkable thing.

"Hey! This is a woman who rides flying horses and thinks it's fun."

The Dead Man relaxed his grasp ever so slightly. The light of awareness grew in Cat's eyes. She shuddered, shifted her gaze to stare at the Dead Man. Her expression became one of horror. "We didn't know that," she murmured. She looked at me. "So you are here."

"I are. I live here. What's your excuse?"

She remained cool under pressure. She reached out to the cherub, touched him gently. "Poor Fourteen. He'll be unfit to live with after this."

"He's fit now? Ratmen would run him off."

"I came looking for you."

I settled into the chair that we keep there for me. It doesn't see much use. I put my feet up on a stool and examined my left thumbnail. Yep. Still there. "Why? Do I know you? Do we have a relationship? I don't think so."

"You deserted me before I could . . ."

"Definitely. Before you could anything. Especially anything unpleasant."

"But I got you out . . ."

"I haven't forgotten. Last night wasn't that long ago. But I can remember rescuing a light colonel from the Venageti so the Karentine army could hang him. I walked before you finished haggling with whoever you were delivering me to."

"I was taking you to my mother. We argue all the time. That's just the way we are."

Maybe. It happens. I waited.

*It may be true.*

Cat said, "She was the one who wanted you freed from the Shayir."

"I appreciate that. She didn't have time to spring me herself?"

*Gently, but continue. She is beginning to leak. This is very interesting.*

"Mother doesn't dare stay away long. It might be noticed. They're all so paranoid these days. Because of the temple business. And she can't manage Chiron and Otsalom."

Was I supposed to have a clue here? "Hell. I have trouble with five-card pitch."

*Chiron and Otsalom, it appears, are winged horses common to the myths of the peoples of the city states of the Lambar Coast a few dozens of your generations ago.*

"Back around the time you went to sea?"

Cat looked baffled. The Dead Man ignored the remark. *Coincidentally, cherubs appear in those myths, none of them named. And that whole family of religions is a branch from the trunk that produced the Church and its local relatives.*

"Chiron and Otsalom are my horse friends, Mr. Garrett. Mother never learned to manage them. She never had time. It's very difficult for her to get away. And I have a knack. She asked me to get you out and bring you to her. I tried."

"I'm grateful. I wasn't enjoying captivity at all."

*Then I suggest you get rid of that goofy grin.*

Darn. He can see through others' eyes.

"Savage." I continued, "I just wish I knew who she was and why she bothered." I recalled that the Lambar Coast has been a Karentine tributary since imperial times. For so long that there is no separatist sentiment there anymore.

*The ships and boats and barges that dock in TunFaire often carry Lambar sailors, Garrett. Working ships is what the Lambar peoples do.*

"They do. And that's interesting. What's going on, Cat?"

She put on a stubborn face.

*We live in a time of amazements, Garrett. Would you suspect the existence of a temple serving the needs of Lambar sailors, down in the Dream Quarter?*

"Some of us are surrounded by amazements. Some of us are just too lazy to die. Of course there's a temple for Lambar sailors. I'd almost bet your life there's more than one. You're a soldier or a sailor, even a merchant sailor, you have to do something after you've spent your wages in the Tenderloin and they've thrown you out of your rooming house for not paying your rent. Come on. You've had time to dig. What's her story?"

Cat gaped at me. She moved nearer the cherub, though reluctantly because that put her nearer the Dead Man. Being able to touch the little guy seemed to boost her confidence.

*You told me she looked like Lang and Imar. Not so? But the fact is, she looks even more like Imara.*

"You're pulling my leg."

*I am not. Her divine half comes from her philandering mother. She is unaware of her father's identity. She knows only that he is not Imar, for which she is grateful. She does not think this consciously, but she suspects that her mother may not know who her father is. Imar, by the way, is unaware of her existence and, it would seem, Imara is eager to maintain his ignorance. I suspect that, should he learn the truth, he would indulge in one of those infamous celestial rages that tear down mountains and sink continents. Or he would at least cause the creeks to back up and mice to get into the corncrib.*

"Huh?" Whoa. Who was getting wound up now?

I didn't figure Imar and the horse he rode in on had much heavenly oomph left between them, but why thumb our noses? You ask for trouble and you're damned well going to get it. "That's ringing the changes on the old holy bed shuffle, isn't it? Where do I fit?"

I intended the last question for Cat. She didn't answer me. Neither did the Dead Man, really. *I am unable to reach that information, Garrett. She may not have it. She seems to be motivated mainly by a desire to be a dutiful daughter.*

"Don't look to me like she's all here right now." Maybe she was mentally allergic to the Dead Man. She seemed to be aging before my eyes, taking on that lost look you sometimes see in stroke victims. She had a firm grip on the cherub. I doubt I could have beaten it out of her hand.

*Easy, Garrett. Calm yourself.*

Sometimes you stumble without seeing it coming. My mother suffered a series of strokes. A stroke finally killed her. In between the first and last, my cousins took the brunt because my brother and I were in the Cantard. She outlived my brother, but I got home often enough to see it at its worst.

It will tear your heart out when your mom all of a sudden can't remember your name.

*Easy, I say.*

" 'The pain still remains,' " I told him, quoting a popular soldiers' poem. He would be hearing that a lot if he kept up his interest in current politics. The Call had set it to music. When the fighting is done and the long night is gone, the pain still remains.

*Manage it, Garrett.*

"Getting short-tempered, are we?"

*We have an opportunity here. This child is the stone at the center.*

"The fruit outside looks pretty tasty, too."

Mental sneer. *She cannot be reached. Not at her heart. And now I see that it is not of her own choosing.*

I'm a normal, red-blooded TunFairen boy, so I wasn't much concerned about her heart when I looked her over. I grumped, "You manage your own pain."

Cat was drifting, but she was not catatonic. She knew we were talking about her and probably did follow my half of the conversation. She did not appear to resent it. Assuming the Dead Man was right about her birth, she undoubtedly had had plenty of experience being an outsider.

*Ah. A plan presents itself. Inasmuch as you find Cat such a delectable morsel, you might try doing what you do so well. Charm her. See where that goes. She may lead you to valuable information.*

"Like we have that kind of time?" He dwells entirely in the realm of fantasy when he pictures my abilities to understand and communicate with the opposite sex. Old Bones, they are way too opposite for me.

And it was not like him to give up on himself so easily. Let Garrett do it? Not when he thought so much of his own ability to get inside another mind. Either he overestimated Cat or he was sneaking around to get an angle on me. This news could break his heart, but it seemed to me that, as is the case with so many young ladies her age, there just wasn't a whole lot in Cat's head to find.

Faintly, faintly, like the remotest, most tenuous whiff of weed smoke drifting from an alley, gone in a blink: *Nog is ines . . .*

I shuddered.

*That was not pleasant.*

"You ought to smell him."

*Not a problem for me anymore.*

"Nice to know there are advantages to being dead."

*The watchers have begun to move in slowly as members of each pantheon try to stay a few feet ahead of their competitors. I need Dean to send the bird out again.*

From the kitchen came an uncommon construction blurted in response to the Dead Man's touch. I heard Dean stomp toward the front door. I heard him say something very unpleasant to Mr. Big. The Goddamn Parrot did not respond. Maybe he had discovered manners.

Maybe there were blizzards in the hot place and all the young devils were sharpening their skates.

Dean stuck his head into the Dead Man's room. "Mr. Dotes is headed this way."

"Morley?" It had been a while since I had seen Morley Dotes, my sometime best pal. He was trying to go high class, which apparently meant scraping old buddies off the soles of his shoes.

"Do we know another Dotes?" Dean does not approve of Morley. Of course, he doesn't approve of much of anything but marriagable nieces and his friends Tinnie and Maya. But not many other people approve of Morley, either. Morley is what discreet, gentle folk would call a thug.

In the real world Morley is known as one badass bonebreaker. Who has developed delusions and illusions.

*Please await Mr. Dotes at the front door, Dean. Bring him straight here. I am certain we will find his news enlightening.*

# 36

Morley Dotes is part human, part dark elf. His eleven side dominates. His choice. He seems embarrassed by his human side. Can't say I blame him.

He is short and lean and so damned good-looking they ought to jail him and lose the key. So the rest of us get a break. I have known him a long time. Sometimes we are best pals. Sometimes he does stuff like give me a talking buzzard that is possessed by an insane demon that causes diarrhea of the beak.

"Mr. Dotes," Dean said, showing Morley into the Dead Man's room.

"Egad," I said. I've always wanted to say that. The opportunity never presented itself before. "Your boys knock over a tailor shop?"

He was dressed to the nines. Maybe even to the tens or elevens. He had on a silver-trimmed black tricorner hat, a heavy, bright red-, black-, and silver-trimmed cut-away over a white shirt wild with lace and ruffles at throat and wrists, a skinny sword cane, natty cream hose, and incredibly shiny shoes with huge silver buckles. He even had a little twitch of a black mustache coming in.

"Some high-class Hill couches must have died to make that coat."

Morley removed a white silk glove, took out a scented little hanky, held it beneath his nose. He sniffed and eyed Cat speculatively, wondering if there was something between her and me. That is the one line he never crosses.

"Really putting on the airs now, isn't he?" I asked the Dead Man.

*A man has got to do what a man has got to do.* The Dead Man's sarcasm would have rattled the windows if the room had had any windows to rattle.

Morley took it in stride. We peasants could not be expected to appreciate his improved, refined station. "As you requested," he told the Dead Man, flouncing that damned hanky like he belonged in the West End, "I inspected the site you specified. In fact, I soiled a perfectly beautiful . . ."

*Nog is inescapable.*

This one was a lot stronger. Nog was close. And his thought did not touch just the Dead Man and me. Morley lost his color.

I told him, "That's not just another Loghyr. That's a for sure howling petty pewter god whose specialty is hunting people down. Right now he's looking for me."

Cat had caught it, too. She started moving around nervously. "I need to get out of here, Garrett. If Nog finds me here . . ."

*Show the young lady to the small front room, please, Dean. Miss Cat, I wish to speak to you for a moment privately before you depart. In the interim, I need to consult with these gentlemen.*

"Where will I be able to get ahold of you?" I asked Cat, as though I believed the Dead Man really did plan to cut her loose.

"I'll find you."

"Sure you will. Good-bye, then. Behave yourself."

She gave me a funny look, then went with Dean. She failed to take Fourteen with her. That had to mean something to somebody.

In the background Nog faded away, but he left no doubt that he was not far off and in a foul mood besides. His pals were bound to be around, too, and I couldn't see their tempers being any more pleasant.

*I fear it will not be long before they come visiting.*

Morley asked, "Are you into something weird again, Garrett?" He stared at the cherub like he half expected it to come to life and snipe an arrow right into his black heart.

"Me? Into something weird? The gods forfend." I told him all about it. And concluded, "It wasn't my idea."

"But then, it never is. Is it? I take it that was some other clown named Garrett who went chasing the skirt up Macunado."

"Here's the pot calling the kettle. You never saw a skirt you wouldn't chase."

"Technically incorrect, although true in spirit. If you will recall I was able to resist several of the old man's nieces."

"They're a pretty resistable bunch."

I remembered the owl girls. I chuckled. They would make a fine payback for the Goddamn Parrot. I could give him back birds with interest. If I could fix it so he couldn't get away from them for a month or two.

"Great story, Garrett. Real interesting. I'm sorry I can't help you with this one." Dotes shrugged. "And I didn't come over to trade insults." He pumped a thumb. "That one asked me to look into something. I came to tell him what I found."

*That you have appeared in person leads me to believe that the treasure is, indeed, hidden exactly as Magodor suggested.*

"There's one to wake up to in the morning, Morley."

When money was involved Morley trusted nobody. I have become so cynical I even wondered why he hadn't just grabbed the treasure and reported it nonexistent. I wondered why the Dead Man had chosen to send Morley. I would have used Playmate. Morley's ethics are not as flexible as Winger's, but they still have plenty of elastic in them.

Actually, he wouldn't do me that way. He might use me in a scheme without consulting me first, as he had done a few times already, and he might dump a Goddamn Parrot on me as a practical joke, but he would not steal from me.

*Excellent. Then there is a possibility Garrett's latest misadventure will not turn up a complete loss. Will you contract to recover the treasure for a percentage?*

"Hey! . . ."

*You will be busy running, Garrett.*

I caught just the faintest parting echo of Nog. How long before he passed this way again?

"Mr. Garrett?" Dean was in the doorway. "Slim is here for his delivery and pickup."

"Good." I hadn't gotten a chance to steal a sip off the emergency pony keg. Life is a bitch. "That gives me an idea. Go let him in."

# 37

Slim doesn't find my line of work believable, but the notion I tossed out captured his imagination. "All right, Garrett. I'll do it. Might be fun."

Might turn painful if some Godoroth thug got pissed off, but I forbore mentioning that. We need not trouble him unnecessarily. It might disturb his concentration.

"All right, Dean. Let's get the barrel up here."

I had a huge old wine cask in the cellar. It had been down there for ages. One day real soon now I planned to clean it up and fill it with water so we could withstand a protracted siege. I have all sorts of great ideas for that sort of stuff, like running an escape tunnel or two, but I never get around to working on them.

Slim removed a couple of beer kegs while Dean and I wrestled the barrel up from the cellar. Dean mostly kept his opinions to himself because he didn't have anything positive to say. He did bark at Cat when she dared peek out the door of the small sitting room.

The barrel was thoroughly dried out, which meant its ends and staves were not as tight as they would be when soaked and swollen. That left me worried that the damned thing might fall apart while they were carrying it out to Slim's cart. I wouldn't look real dignified falling out of an exploding barrel.

As soon as Dean shut me in, I knew I had made a mistake. I should have just walked out the door. The results would have been less unpleasant. This was like being trapped in a wino's coffin. And I am not comfortable with tight places. Smelly tight places are worse. Getting rolled down steps inside a smelly tight place is worse still. And no effort to make me unhappier was spared when the bunch of them tossed my conveyance onto Slim's cart. Vaguely, I heard Morley mixing complaints about what could have happened to his clothing with chuckles about my probable discomfort.

I should fix him up with Magodor. Maggie was just the girl for him. Snakes in her hair. Fangs. Claws at the ends of all those arms.

Matters did not improve anytime soon. The cart started moving. Slim did not ride it, he led his team. He had no need to ease the bump and bang of solid wooden wheels rolling over cobblestones.

It seemed I was in there for several infant eternities. Slim was supposed to head straight for his Weider distributor to get shut of me and my empties and reload with full kegs, but soon I became convinced that he was going the long way, looking for the princes of potholes. Every bump we hit made the barrel creak and move around the cart a bit.

Bang! We hit a big one. I thought I was going over. Slim growled at his donkeys. I swear one of them laughed—that honking bray they have.

Donkeys are relatives of horses.

Bang! again. This time we got the mother of all potholes. My barrel bounced off the back of Slim's cart. It fell apart when it hit the pavement. I staggered up dripping staves and hoops, looking around fast to see if I needed to run. I didn't see a cherub, let alone a full-fledged third-rate god.

"Sorry," Slim told me. "These damned donkeys seem to be taking aim at every damned pothole."

The animal nearest me sneered.

"Throw them to the wolves. Use them for thunder lizard bait. Don't suffer them a minute longer. If you do, someday they'll get you."

Slim gave me a really strange look.

"Thanks for the help," I told him. "You want what's left of this thing?" A barrel is a valuable commodity even if it requires some assembly.

"Yeah. Sure."

No danger greater than the bile of donkeys presented itself. I helped Slim get the barrel pieces into his cart. People who had watched me get hatched from a wooden egg just stood around and stared. They worried me only because they would brag about what they had seen and somebody somewhere sometime would realize that the clown in the barrel had been me.

Could not help that. Could get my feet to stepping.

The Goddamn Parrot swooped past, vanished without any comment.

I had my feet moving now but did not know where to let them take me. South seemed good. If I made the Dream Quarter, the Godoroth and Shayir would not be able to bully me without irritating all the other gods.

# 38

I got so close I began to think I was going to make it. But I hadn't put enough thought into planning. I took almost the same route I had followed before. All too soon I began seeing strange shadows in golden light. I heard whispers just beyond the edge of hearing, though some of those emanated from the Goddamn Parrot, who was trailing me.

The bird swooped in, plopped onto my shoulder while squawking something about changing course right now. I told it, "I've picked up something that I think is called Tobrit the Strayer. Shayir. It's more like a fear than anything. If it's the same one, the one time I saw it materialize it turned into an oversize and over-ugly imitation faun that was hornier than a three-headed horned toad."

I spoke in a normal voice. The Goddamn Parrot screeched. Naturally, people stared. I made the turn the bird demanded. I tried not to dwell on the nightmare that life could become if the Dead Man kept the bird on me all the time.

The Goddamn Parrot guided me to Stuggie Martin's. That swillery, for all its lack of glory, had seen a dramatic improvement in business. Overflow guys were standing around outside, drinking and muttering. Some of their buddies preferred to mutter and drink.

Having failed to get so much as a taste off the keg delivered to my house, I decided to stop in, maybe revel in the ambience for one beer. My spirits were flying too high anyway.

It did not occur to me that the Dead Man actually wanted me to visit the place.

Yesterday Stuggie Martin's had been depressing. Today it was like the dead of winter inside. I called for a dark Weider's, then asked Stuggie's successor, "What's with these guys? They look like they just found out rich Uncle Ferd croaked and left everything to the home for wayward cats."

"You ain't heard? Got to be that you ain't heard. It was your pal No-Neck, man. Most everybody 'round here liked that old goof."

"Did something happen to No-Neck?"

"They found him a little while ago. He was alive, but that wasn't 'cause somebody never tried to make it go some other way. They tortured him really bad."

I smacked a fist down hard on what passed for a bar in there. "We tried to warn him. He didn't want to listen."

"Huh?"

"He did a favor for somebody that was sure to piss somebody else off. We tried to tell him they wouldn't let it slide."

The barkeep poured me another and nodded. He had been sampling his wares, no doubt making sure he was serving only the best. He was having trouble keeping up.

Hell, I was having trouble and my first few sips hadn't hit bottom yet.

"You guys friends?" the barkeep asked, topping my mug for me.

"Not really. Just had things in common. Like the Corps." This guy had the right tattoos. He could be diverted.

When I arose a while later I was in a bitter, black mood. No-Neck had been tortured to death only because his precognitive sense had failed him and he had gone walking around with me.

Thus we rail, in vain, against the whims of gods and fates.

Unless his killers were really stupid, one god-gang would have it figured out and would be out of control.

Getting into the Dream Quarter, fast, sounded like a really good plan now.

The barkeep asked, "No-Neck have any people?"

"I didn't know him. Just met him yesterday. He never mentioned any."

"Too bad. He was a good guy. Be nice to let somebody know. So somebody could do right by him."

Had I not been at the bottom of a deep barrel with herds of gods out to get me I might have volunteered to find No-Neck's family. But I was so far down there the open top looked no bigger than a bunghole.

So No-Neck would be seen into the great beyond by the city's ratmen, who would cart his remains to the nearest public crematorium.

# 39

The Goddamn Parrot plopped onto my shoulder as I hit the street. "Shiver me timbers," I muttered. "Do I live a blessed life, or what?"

"Awk. Something is following you."

"Am I surprised."

"Many of the presences are coming this way."

People stared. It was not often you saw a man chatting with a parrot. "And I'm headed thataway." I began trotting toward the Dream Quarter. Shouldn't be that hard to make the safety of the Street of the Gods. Getting back off again might turn out to be a grand adventure, though.

Apparently the Dead Man had little trouble detecting gods once he took an interest. In fact, there was an amazing array of things he could do if you could just get him started. *That* was a secret I really wanted to crack. I might trade my keyness . . . Nah.

I wondered if the Dead Man being able to spot them meant that my divine acquaintances had chosen to manifest themselves especially strongly during their struggle or if, perhaps, TunFaire was always infested with petty gods and we were detecting this bunch only because we were watching for them. My guess was that these two gangs were obvious mainly because they were fighting for their lives.

The Goddamn Parrot fluttered up and away, off to I-don't-know-where, once again leaving me to dread a future in which the Dead Man could tag along wherever I went through that bird-brained feather duster.

I walked around a corner and there was Rhogiro, bigger than

life and twice as ugly, holding up a wall like your everyday garden-variety street thug. Obviously he wasn't really waiting for me but was there just in case something turned up. I never slowed a step. I whipped across into a narrow breezeway. It dead-ended on me. I put my back against one wall, my hands and feet against the other. Up I went. Meantime, Rhogiro realized who he had seen, came to the end of the breezeway and did some holy thundering. He was too big to get into the crack and too stupid to recall that he had divine powers. At least in the moments it took me to get up top.

My luck, as always, was mixed. The climb was just two stories. Good. The roofs up there were flat and identical and stretched on and on. Excellent. They could be run upon almost like the street. None of the buildings were more than three feet from their neighbors. Fine.

But in this part of town the slumlords wasted no resources on maintenance. My foot went through a roof almost immediately. I didn't get hurt, but I realized that I had to slow down or get down.

Slowing down gave me time to think about what I was doing, which, mainly, was heading *away* from the Dream Quarter. I needed to get down and head the other way.

I got down rough, after jumping to a roof so fragile I punched right through. I caught myself before I plunged into whatever disaster lurked below. I stared downward. My eyes were not used to the gloom there, but the area immediately below me looked empty. I lowered myself as far as I could, let go. The floor was not that far. And it held.

The place had been abandoned. Only the masonry was more substantial than the roof. Now that I was into the gloom I could see light leaking through the overhead in fifty places.

The walls consisted of plaster crumbled till it was almost gone, the lathing behind it mostly fallen too. The floor groaned and creaked. The stairway looked so precarious I backed down on all fours. I was interested only in getting out but did note that there was nothing left worth stealing except the brick itself and some wooden bits that would end up as firewood.

I was surrounded by things on their last legs. My partner was dead already. My housekeeper had one foot in the grave. The city where I lived seemed ready to commit suicide.

The street out front was almost empty. That was an ugly omen. These tenement blocks swarm with kids playing, mothers gossiping, grannies whining about their rheumatiz, old men playing checkers and complaining about how the world is going to hell in a handbasket. Where was the Goddamn Parrot? I could use a good scouting report.

Didn't look like I had time for anything fancy. I ran toward the Dream Quarter. On the other side of the tenement row Rhogiro continued to bellow and blunder around. Maybe his displeasure was leaking over enough to have startled the locals.

I could not see that some gods would be much missed.

# 40

I almost made it. The story of my life. A lot of almosts. I was almost king, except right at the last minute I got born to the wrong mother.

I turned into Gnorleybone Street a few blocks short of the Street of the Gods. Gnorleybone isn't much used because it don't go anywhere, but it did offer a nice look at the distance I still had to travel. I saw only normal traffic for the place and the time of day. No funny shadows or lights, no big ugly guys, no pretty and deadly girls, no huntress or hounds, nothing but clear sailing. I slowed to a brisk walk, tried to catch what of my breath hadn't gotten so lost it was out of the kingdom.

*They* say it's always darkest before the dawn. *They* ought to live my life. With me it's always brightest just before the hammer of darkness comes smashing down.

I don't know what hit me. One minute I was just a-huffing and a-puffing and a-grinning, and the next I was crawling through a molasses blackness. Time passed there, inside my head, but beyond me seemed a timeless sort of state. Maybe I was in limbo, or nirvana, depending on your attitude.

I sensed a light. I struggled toward it. It expanded to become a face. "Cat?" Fingers touched my cheek, caressed. Then pinched cruelly. The pain helped clear my head and vision.

"No. Not Cat."

Cat's mom. Imara. The Godoroth had gotten to me first. But when I looked around I saw no one but Imara. We were in a place like the inside of a big egg furnished only with a low divan draped with purple silk. The light came from no obvious source. "What's going on? . . ."

"We will talk later." She laid a fingernail on my forehead, over that spot sometimes called the third eye. Then she trailed it down between my eyes, over my nose, across my lips. That nail felt as sharp as a razor. I shivered nervously but found her touch weirdly exciting, too.

"You have a reputation." Her hand kept traveling. "Is it justified?"

"I don't know." My voice was an octave high. I couldn't move. "Whoa!" That was a squeak.

"I hope so. I seldom get an opportunity like this."

"What?" I wasn't putting up much of a fight. This matronly goddess was about to have her way with me and, incidentally, establish her husband as my mortal enemy. There was no arrangement between them, only the arrangement Imar had with himself. Gods are always jealous critters, turning their spouses' lovers into toads and spiders and whatnot.

Which seemed of no particular concern to her. She had one thing on her mind and pursued it with a single-minded devotion more often associated with less than socially ept adolescent males. I began struggling too late. By then the inevitable was upon me. I had no heart for a fight. I hoped she wouldn't turn into something with two hundred tentacles and breath like a dead catfish.

I am one agnostic who got made a believer. I should have brought help.

If they were all that way no wonder they were always getting into trouble.

Panting, I asked, "You make a habit of just grabbing guys and getting on with it?"

"Whenever I get away long enough. It's one of the little rewards I permit myself for enduring that bastard Imar."

The Dead Man hadn't said anything about Imar's legitimacy. No doubt being a bastard was part of his divine charm.

"Please stop for a while. I'm only human." Imara seemed human enough herself, except for the scale of her appetites.

"For the moment, then. We have to talk, anyway."

"Right."

"Have you found the key?"

"Uh . . ." I was at a serious disadvantage here. I was getting sat upon at the moment. "No."

"Good. Have you bothered looking?"

Good? I ground my teeth. She was a goddess of some substance. "Not really. I haven't been given a chance."

"Good. Don't bother."

"Don't?"

"Ignore it. Hide out. Let it go. Let the deadline pass."

"You *want* to get kicked out of the Dream Quarter?"

"I want Imar and his band of morons to get kicked out. I've made arrangements. I've wanted to get shut of that belching idiot for a thousand years, and this is my chance."

She began numbering Imar's faults and sins, which reminded me of the main reason I avoid married women. I didn't hear one complaint that I haven't heard from mortal wives a thousand times. Apparently, being a god is domestic and deadly dull most of the time. Pile it on for millennia and maybe some divine excesses start to make sense.

Those recitals are boring at best. When you have no particular desire to be with the reciter they can become excruciating. Despite my improbable situation, my mind wandered.

I came back fast when she decided I had recovered. "Ulp! So you're gonna dump the Godoroth and sign on with the Shayir?"

How could she manage that? Any honest historical theologian will admit that deities do move shop occasionally, but the mechanism by which they do so eludes me.

"The Shayir? That's absurd! Lang could be Imar's reflection. Why would I want more of that? And his household has nothing to recommend its survival. Let them sink like stones into the dark cold deeps of time." She said all that in a sort of distracted, catechistic manner. Her mind was on something else.

Maybe the wrong gal got the temple whore job.

"You haven't communicated with the Shayir?"

"No! Shut up." She pressed her fingernails into my forehead again. I shut up. She took charge. She had her way with me for about a thousand years.

That molasses darkness reclaimed me eventually. The last I knew, Imara was whispering a promise that I would never be sorry if neither Lang nor Imar ever got hold of the key.

Why do these things happen to me?

# 41

I ached everywhere. I felt like I had done a thousand sit-ups, run ten miles, then finished with a couple hundred push-ups to cool down. I had bruises and scratches all over me. I was thinking about finding a new hobby. My favorite was getting dangerous.

Then once again there was a face in my face. This one was uglier than original sin. It was the face of a ratman that not even a female of his own kind could love. I grabbed him by the throat. Ratmen are not real strong. I held on while I climbed to my feet.

I had been lying on a bed of trash in an alley I did not recognize. The ratman had been going through my pockets. I relieved him of his ill-gotten gains. He wanted to whimper and beg, but I didn't give him enough air. I was in such a bad mood I considered putting him out of my misery.

My headache was back.

Though the world would be better off for his absence, I just slapped him silly. Then an idea occurred. An experiment to try. I didn't have much to lose. The gods all had a fair idea where I could be found.

I did a quick stretch job on a bit of my mystic cord, cut that piece off, tied it around the ratman's tail. He was too groggy to notice.

I got my behind moving. My feet worked hard to keep up.

Maybe the Godoroth would jump on a false trail.

I found myself on Fleetwood Place, one of the many short and lightly trafficked streets that enter the Dream Quarter. Fleetwood Place runs right through the Arsenal. Even now, with the war gone moribund, the place was going full blast. I don't know how the workers there put up with all the rattle and bang.

I darted from cover to cover, confident that a few hundred yards would get me into the safety of the Dream Quarter. During one pause two huge owls hurtled overhead, tracking a blur up the far side of the street. I grinned. Had to be Jorken, going for my fake.

A trickle of golden light leaked over the brick wall back up Fleetwood. That rustling-paper sound passed overhead. Hundreds of black leaves fluttered in a minor whirlwind. Wolves howled in the distance. I'd like to say dragons roared and thunder lizards stomped, but it did not get that dramatic.

I resumed putting one foot in front of the other as briskly as I could. A remote, foul bit of mind breath reminded me, *Nog is inescapable*. Nog didn't have much of a vocabulary.

As I ran I rehearsed what I had done to frame the ratman. Maybe I would work the stunt again, if I had to. I kept glancing back, expecting Jorken.

A huge boil of dirty brown smoke burst upward back whence I had come. Lightning ripped through its heart. An owl came flying out, folded up on its back, following a high ballistic arc. A thunderclap reached me moments later. And these were not phenomena that only I could see. People ran into the street to gape.

The Godoroth and Shayir were butting heads. I didn't wait to see if they got down to it seriously. I kept sucking wind and pounding leather. A wolf, or maybe a dog the size of a cow, hollered behind me. It was a cry whose tone said, "I got the trail, boss." I put my head down and went for new records.

I sensed something in front of me, a picket of shadow forming out of nothing, right in front of the line where I thought I would get safe.

That thing howled behind me. It was gaining fast. I didn't even try to zig, zag, or stop. I went for the hurdle.

# 42

There was a face in my face.

"This is getting old," I muttered. I tried to move. The darkness held me tightly, except for my eyes. I realized that that was all I controlled. My ability to see. No other sense was working.

The face in my face drifted back. It seemed to be a metal mask, its features stylized. Nothing but darkness appeared through the mouth, eye, and nose holes. It dwindled to a point of light.

Countless similar points materialized over what seemed like several minutes. A few began to drift, loop, swoop toward me, pursuing some pattern I did not recognize. These few became faces and even figures. Some resembled our better-known local gods. No two sprang from the same mythology.

Oh boy.

I grew up in Saint Strait's Parish of my mom's peculiar religion, so wouldn't you know the Strait Man himself would come shining up night center? "Are you with us, Mr. Garrett?"

"Wouldn't be smart to be against you."

Saint Strait was the patron of seekers after wisdom. And he looked out for fools, drunks, and little kids, which shows you that divine bureaucracies lump stuff together as rationally as do the mundane.

Saint Strait didn't get sanctified for his heavenly sense of humor or his divine tolerance for alternate viewpoints, but he was too preoccupied to indulge his famous temper. "If you will restrain yourself we can resolve several questions swiftly."

"Who is we?" I was in a mood so black I didn't much care if I was toe to toe with the gods themselves, including a leading saint of the religion that I had disdained and mostly disbelieved from eleven years old onward.

"We are The Commission, also sometimes called The Board, a permanent standing committee tasked with mediating and refereeing any arguments or contests between deities of different religions. Commission makeup changes continuously. Board service is a duty required of everyone. The Commission's mission is to ensure peace in your Dream Quarter. We arbitrate entries and exits of the mainstream religions there."

"I've always been content to ignore the gods. How come you can't return the courtesy?" These Commission types would be the clowns who had stuck me with being the key to divine nightmares—probably as a reward for past slights.

"There was no better candidate than you. However, we did not anticipate your being so much at risk. Apologies. Estimates were that you would become wealthy off the interested parties."

"Thank you very much. That sounds great. There'll never be another black day in my life. When does the bribing begin? I'd really like to get those bars of gold stashed away. And what sort of protection will I be getting?"

"Protection?" The concept was so alien he had trouble pronouncing the word. Him who looked out for our less-capable folk. How can you be labeled a hopeless cynic when your cynicisms prove valid all the time?

His response was an answer all by itself. But I soldiered on. "Protection from those lunatic Godoroth and Shayir who have started figuring out the fact that I'm the key they want. You guys set it up winner-take-all—including me. But the losers aren't going to just go away, are they? Maybe they'll want to lay their despair off on somebody. Maybe they'll want to hurt somebody by way of getting even with the universe. So who are they going to look for?"

While I rambled, the good saint had his eyes closed, either enduring my diatribe or communing with his associates.

He opened his eyes. "You will be protected. You have been troubled excessively already. They were supposed to win your support, not take it by intimidation. We will issue some addenda to the ground rules."

Divine figures moved toward and away from me in some rhythm known only to the gods themselves. I felt some poke around inside my head, picking my mental pockets as habit rather than policy. They were bored and wished those creatures from down where celestial glamour turned to celestial slum would take a powder and save their betters all this ugly, finger-dirtying *work*.

"Was there some point to my being dragged here?"

"The Shayir and the Godoroth collided not far off. They were out of control. It seemed possible the key might be at risk at an insalubrious juncture. You must remain alive for a while longer."

Had I been anything but disembodied vision I would have sniffed the air and checked my soles for accretions.

"Gracious of you. Can we work it so I can hang in here, the age I am now, for a couple thousand more years? Say until the last one of you Commission characters goes?"

"I could tell you what you want to hear, but you would realize its worthlessness as soon as the air blew past you." Saint Man had him a sense of humor after all. "If we made an exception for you, every man, woman, and child out there would petition us with unique circumstances."

Grumble grumble whine whine. Gods forfend anybody actually has to do their job.

"You were made the key because it was our hope that you, being mortal, could distinguish the superiority of one pantheon over another and thus resolve the question of which should remain on the Street of the Gods."

Boy, did they pick the wrong man. So much for omniscience. "I haven't fallen in love with any of the contenders. How about you hide me out till after the deadline and let them all suck the death pipe?"

"That is not an option. Persevere, Mr. Garrett. And work on your decision. Which temple should remain with us?"

He had rejected my suggestion already.

He began to shrink away from me. "Few mortals ever stand in judgment upon the gods."

Other Commission members fluttered about. Some swooped toward me, apparently curious. I got the distinct feeling that the gods from the uptown pantheons were way out of touch. They were like factory owners who never entered their factories for fear they would, somehow, sully themselves by associating with the people whose labor made it possible for them to live the high life. It was blatantly plain that for many, the notion that they had a responsibility to their followers was entirely alien. Many of these gods were what human teenagers would turn into, given unlimited resources and time. They watched me like I was a bug under glass.

"Good-bye for now, Mr. Garrett." His voice was a fading whisper.

Then I wasn't in a place where remote shimmers became curious gods and goddesses. I was where darkness was as thick as treacle. I swam hard. I was going to get out of town for real, let these crazies finish their incomprehensible game without me.

A genie in a bottle would have been a nice find. I could use her to straighten things out. But instead of something gorgeous and eager, I got another wave of darkness, of an altogether different kind. This invaded me, penetrated right down to the core of me. I began to feel better. Aches and pains vanished. My headache went away. Bruises and scratches healed. I felt the stitches in my scalp fall out. Suddenly I felt so good I almost turned positive. I almost wished I was bald so I could grow new hair. I felt younger, bouncier, eager to get into action—and more likely to do something stupid because I was regaining youth's impatience.

Then yet another darkness engulfed me. In a moment I felt nothing at all.

# 43

I awakened in an alley. Surprise. Surprise, I did it with a face nose to nose with mine. I was going in circles. At least it was a different face each time. "This is getting old." I tried to grab a throat again, but this scroat was no ratman. He was strong. He lifted me one-handed and shook me till my teeth wobbled. "Mom?" I asked. She used to shake me if I did something especially irritating. When I was still small enough to shake.

"Huh?"

Oh-oh. Another mental marvel.

He held me at arm's length so he could check me out. Turn-about is fair play. I checked him out right back.

He had long, wavy blonde hair. He had blue eyes to kill for. One blue eye, anyway. The other was covered by a black leather patch. He was nine feet tall. He was gorgeous. He had muscles on top of his muscles. Obviously, he didn't have much to do but work on his physique and study himself in a mirror.

I'd never seen his like running loose in TunFaire, so I assumed he was another pesky pewter god, though neither Godoroth nor Shayir.

"Now what?" I muttered. "Who the hell are you?"

My body still felt young and tough enough to whip its weight in wildcats.

Pretty boy shook me again.

Whip its weight in gerbils?

"You will speak when spoken to."

"Yeah. Right." Thought I was supposed to get protection?

Shake shake.

"Rhogiro! Trog!" I needed somebody big enough to get this guy's attention.

What I got was the Goddamn Parrot, who plummeted into the gloom from the afternoon sunlight above. "Where have you been?"

"Trying to deal with a whole parade of these characters." I got shaken again.

The bird said, "An apparent retard."

"You see him?"

The huge guy took a swipe at Mr. Big. He missed. The bird stayed over on his blind side, obviously seeing him.

"Be quiet, Garrett."

"Hard to do."

Pretty boy looked baffled. He wasn't used to having his orders ignored. He took a stab at Mr. Big. Maybe he was prejudiced against talking birds. The Goddamn Parrot evaded the blow.

"You try to talk to him?" the bird asked.

"Yeah. He told me to shut up. Then he started playing ragdoll with me. Got any idea who or what he is?"

The big guy pulled me right up close, eye to eye.

"There any divine dentists? He's got teeth all over his mouth, and most of them are rotten. He's got breath like a battlefield three days after . . ."

Bingo.

The Dead Man got it at the same time. "A war god."

Baffled, the war god set me on my feet and squatted. "You do not fear me?"

"I spent five years at your birthday party. You got nothing left to scare me with." I hoped he didn't have a big talent for bullshit detection. "Who are you? What do you want?"

"I am Shinrise the Destroyer." Roll of drums, please. Thunder of trumpets.

"I know your sister Maggie."

He frowned. He didn't get it. Maybe the world wreckers didn't get together and talk shop.

Where did I get the idea that gods were smarter than people?

"Garrett?" The Goddamn Parrot fluttered to my shoulder. "I don't know the name. Do you?"

"Actually, it seems I should. Maybe from somebody in the Corps."

Shinrise the Destroyer swung a fist in a mighty roundhouse. It tore a few hundred bricks out of the nearest wall. On the far side a couple in the throes of lovemaking took a moment to react. They gaped. The woman screamed. She had no trouble seeing Shinrise, either.

He stomped a foot. Bricks fell out of the wall. I said, "I'd better get out of here before he knocks everything down."

As suddenly as the rage took Shinrise it passed. He grabbed me again. "Have you found the key?"

"No."

"Don't even look."

Far, far off I sensed an echo of *Nog is inescapable*.

"Why not? What do you care? You're not Godoroth or Shayir."

"I have cause to wish misfortune upon both houses. You will refrain from . . ."

"Sure, big guy. Like your wishes are going to override theirs."

He started to shake me but frowned, tilted his head to one side. Maybe an idea was trying to get in.

The bird told me, "Others are coming." He fluttered upward.

"I know."

Shinrise completed his thought. He grinned. His teeth definitely were his weakness. "I will protect you." He sounded proud of himself.

"Of course you will. And here's where you start. Nog the Inescapable is coming here to snatch me. Discourage him while I find someplace to hide."

I jumped through the broken wall into the room just vacated by the lovers, then used the only door. I glanced back. Shinrise looked like he was beginning to wonder if he had been hornswoggled. Behind him, but close, came *Nog is inescapable!* strong and tinged with triumph. Nog had the scent.

What did Strait tell me? The Commission was going to caution the players about being so rough? Must not have gotten the word out yet. And Shinrise sure wasn't working for the Board. What he wanted was directly opposed to their desires.

Why didn't I find out what his interest was?

Oh, yeah. Nog.

Nog arrived.

Bricks flew. Thunder boomed. Lightning walked. I clamped my hands over my ears and kept moving. Shinrise the Destroyer lived up to his name by using Nog to finish off the damaged tenement and several of its neighbors.

People screamed.

These petty pewter gods were very much into our world now.

Maybe whole platoons of minor gods would come out as the deadline got closer. Maybe . . .

But gods had moved up and down the Street before without the
town getting torn up.

*Nog is inescapable.* Nog seemed amazed that he could be
thwarted.

I wished I knew where the hell I was so I could get to where
the hell I ought to be. Which, I had a notion, might be right in
front of the main altar at Chattaree.

I was about to step into the street when I saw a blur coming.
Jorken was earning his pay today. He streaked past, headed for the
divine ass-kicking contest.

The excitement began to draw a crowd. I saw Shayir and
Godoroth alike heading for the turmoil. I moved out, a man in
shadow, employing all the caution I had learned during the big
dance with the Venageti.

The racket got louder. Chimneys fell. Chunks of roof flew
around. Members of the Guard arrived. Residents lost interest and
fled the area. I went with them.

# 44

The Goddamn Parrot located me, dropped onto my shoulder, grabbed hold hard, then faded out on me. He would not answer questions. Apparently the Dead Man had no minds to spare for him. But he did not revert to his naturally obnoxious birdbrain style.

Unseasonal clouds were gathering. Lightning flickered within them. The wind suddenly seemed possessed of a hard, dark edge of desperate anger. The people in the street shivered, cursed, acted more bewildered than frightened. This was something new to everyone.

This was something that was getting out of hand. The Commission had to be napping. This couldn't do any religion any good. I wished I could stop it . . . I knew how, yes. But I had no viable excuse to pick one god gang over another.

I got my bearings and wished I had not. The Board had done me no favor. I was miles from the Dream Quarter, or any sanctuary. Unless I wanted to duck into Ogre Town. No self-respecting human god would go in there.

No human who wanted to survive the gathering night would go there, either.

I was tired and hungry and thirsty and pissed off about being used and abused. Time was the only weapon I could turn against the gods. I was, definitely, inclined to let as many as possible drift off into oblivion.

It grew dark fast. The breeze became a chill wind. No stars came out. In the distance, lights continued to flicker and flash and reflect off the churning bellies of low clouds. Fires burned and

smoke rose and emergency alarms beat at the cooling evening air.
Drops of moisture hit my cheek. The last one came in chunk form
and really stung.

The air was getting colder fast.

I trotted southward, making good time. Boy, was I getting my
exercise today. I reached a familiar neighborhood. It was dark
there, and unnaturally quiet. The strangeness was spreading
throughout the city. I ducked into a place where I knew I would
get served a decent pint and a sausage that wouldn't come with
worries about the inclusion of rat, bat, dog, or cat.

"Yo, Beetle."

The proprietor glanced up from his mug polishing. "Garrett!
You son of a bitch, where the hell you been? You ain't been in here
in three months."

"Been working too hard. Don't get time to get over here the
way I used to."

"I've heard some stories. I never believed them."

"The truth is worse than anything you've heard."

I took a pint, sucked down a long swallow, started telling him
what had happened the past day and a half.

"Hope you brought a pitchfork, Garrett."

"Huh?"

He pretended to examine the soles of his shoes. "If you don't
have a pitchfork, I'm going to make you clean that bullshit out of
here with your bare hands."

He didn't believe me.

"I have a hard time believing it myself, Beetle. I wish I could
introduce you to those owl sisters."

"My wife would never understand."

"Where the hell is everybody? I haven't seen the place this
dead since Tommy Mack's wake."

"Weather."

Something was bothering him. "That all?"

He leaned closer. "Big part of it is, The Call won't put me on
their approved list. Account of I let nonhumans drink here."

Only dwarves and ratmen do much drinking. And the dwarves
tend to keep it at home.

I don't like ratmen much. I had to work to find the charity to
say, "Their money is no different color than anyone else's."

"There's scary stuff getting ready to happen, Garrett."

I touched my cheek where the sleet had bitten me. "How right
you are, without knowing the half. What's ready to eat?"

He had drawn me another mug of the dark. I dropped a groat onto the counter. That would serve us both for a while.

"Specialty of the house. Sausage and kraut. Or sausage and black beans. Or, the missus made a kidney pie nobody's touched but old Skidrow yonder." He indicated the least respectable of his few customers.

"Where's Blowmetal?" Skidrow was half of the only pair of identical twin winos I'd ever seen.

Beetle shrugged. When his shoulders came up like that, you could see why the nickname. Back when he was a lot heavier it had fit much better. "Heard they had a fight. Over a woman."

"Shit. The guy is a hundred and twelve."

"That's in street years, Garrett. He's only a little older than you are."

I finished my mug, pushed it over for a refill. "Give me the sausage and kraut. And remind me not to get so far down on my luck that I've got to live like a ratman."

Beetle chuckled as he started digging around in a pot. He gave me an extra sausage. Both looked a little long in the tooth. They had been in the water a long time.

"Hey, Garrett. Don't get down on your luck. And try to turn the beer-drinking back into a hobby. Or you might get there."

"What's this about The Call? They trying to work the protection racket on you?"

"They don't call it that, but that's what it amounts to." He plopped a couple of boiled potatoes on the plate on top of the kraut.

"I know somebody who might get them off your back."

That was just the kind of thing Relway and his secret police liked to bust up, and I had no love for The Call.

"Appreciate it." Beetle turned to hand me my plate. His gaze went over my shoulder. His face turned pale.

# 45

I turned.

A cascade of black paper was fluttering through the doorway, buoyed by no obvious wind. Through that came a huge dog, tongue dangling a foot, eyes burning red. A second dog followed, then Black Mona herself, bearing up well under the weight of all those weapons.

"What did you do now?" Beetle croaked.

He could see them?

"Who, me?"

"They ain't after me, Garrett."

"Yeah. You're right."

The doorframe behind Quilraq began to glow golden.

Shadows crept in. Good old Torbit was here, too. Maybe it was a Shayir family reunion.

Had they whipped the Godoroth?

I started wolfing kraut and sausage. The Shayir glared at me.

Beetle filled my mug. "What are those things?"

"You really don't want to know." He was a religious man. He would not want to think ill of the gods.

Cold air blasted through the doorway.

Blur. Black Mona staggered. Her hounds yipped. Quilraq rustled. Jorken materialized in front of me. He was not in a good mood. What a day he must have been having. He grabbed me by the shirt and tossed me over his shoulder.

The side wall of Beetle's place exploded inward. Daiged, Rhogiro, and Ringo charged through. I thought that now Beetle would have to believe my story.

Imar himself followed the flying wedge of double uglies, baby lightnings prancing in his hair. His eyes were not pleasant when they touched me, but his immediate attention belonged to the Shayir.

"Run for it, Beetle." As Jorken turned, though, I discovered that Beetle was prescient. He had taken my advice before I offered it.

Jorken sprinted through the hole opened by the ugly boys. Egad, we could have used a few like them down in the islands. The war wouldn't have lasted nearly so long.

The air ripped past so fast I could hardly snatch bites out of it. Light sleet was falling steadily. That dark coach loomed out of the night. Abyss, that darkness in darkness, stared down as Jorken tossed me inside without bothering to open the door. I picked up fresh scrapes on the window edges. I got a pat on the cheek from Magodor before she dismounted from the far side. Her tenderness was false. She was in full Destroyer avatar. She hurried off to do whatever she did. Jorken went with her.

I was alone. With Star. Who had what it would take to make a statue stand up and listen.

The coach started moving. So did Star.

That gal knew her business.

This insanity certainly did have its moments. The bad part was putting up with what went on in between.

Star relented after I begged for mercy. She settled opposite me, gloriously disheveled. She giggled like the last thing you could expect to find in her head was a thought. Every boy's dream.

I was tying my shoes when the horses screamed and something ripped the top off the coach.

"Damn!" I said. "Now for more of that stuff in between."

I flung myself out a door, into the cold. I rolled in sleet half an inch deep. A stray thought: What had become of the Goddamn Parrot?

Not far away, Abyss was pulling himself back out of the hole in a wall through which he had been thrown. He was not pleased. The darkness within his hood was deeper than ever. Maybe the madder he got the more fathomless the nothingness there grew.

The right rear wheel of the coach collapsed. The nearest side door flopped open. In a sort of ghost glow I saw Star still sitting there jaybird, grinning, totally pleased with herself.

Time for Garrett to get in some more exercise.

Abyss moved to intercept me. Something whooshed through

the night, slammed him through the air. He smashed into another wall. Business would be great for the brickyards tomorrow.

Abyss slid down, did not bounce back up. So. Even a god can go down for the count.

I heard the approach of heavy wings. Lila and Dimna dropped out of the night, became their charming girl selves. "It worked!" one piped. She started toward me like she had that old wickedness in mind. The other one clambered into the coach and planted a distinctly unsisterly kiss upon Star's lips. Star snuggled right up.

Golden light rippled through the night. Shadows pranced. Faun guy Torbit coalesced. He seemed baffled. "Stop that! All of you. Trog. Grab him and get out of here." Torbit and Star looked at one another. I had a feeling they would not stick to business long. Make love, not war.

The humongous guy with the club and divinely potent body odor came close enough to be seen. Chunks of coach still stuck to his weapon. He grabbed me up like a little girl grabs a doll. It took me only a moment to discover that struggling was futile.

I was not real happy. It had been one damned thing after another. And now sleet was getting down the back of my neck.

# 46

It didn't do any good to get mad. I wasn't going to kick any divine butts. The one weapon I had in this scrap lay between my ears, and it hadn't been real deadly so far.

I don't like whiners and excuse-makers, but . . . it's hard to think when you're getting lugged around in one humongous hand, hardly gently. With hailstones hitting you in the face and sliding inside your clothing.

The bizarre weather had to be connected with the solid materializations of all these divinities. Maybe that required pulling the warmth right out of the mortal plane.

If only we could get the effect under control and harness it for use during high summer, I could make my fortune. How could I work a partnership deal with a god?

The big guy stopped walking. He began turning in place. *Zoom!* I saw why. Old Jorken was on the job, circling us. Poor Jorken. He'd had a rough day. If I was him I would demand a raise. *Boom!* Down came that tree of a club. It bashed a hole in the street. Jorken missed getting splattered by barely half a step.

I had an idea. I decided to put it to work before it got lonely. The Godoroth knew where I was, anyway.

I worked Magodor's cord loose from my waist. That was a real adventure, what with the big guy prancing around trying to get a solid whack at Jorken. I stretched an inch of rope out to four feet, tied a bowline, made the loop for getting invisible with the stretched section and got my feet worked through it all while being flailed around by the dancing giant. I saw scores of faces at windows, being entertained. I hoped nobody out there recognized me.

Trog's club flailed. A water trough exploded. A porch collapsed. Jorken stayed a step ahead. It was plain he was keeping the big guy in one place till slower Godoroth could catch up.

I wiggled until I got the invisibility loop over my top end, too, then continued to work the loop around so I could tighten it around the big guy's wrist. Then I stroked the cord the way Maggie had shown me, so it would shrink back to normal.

Old Trog froze, looked startled, then produced an all-time bellow of amazement and pain. And I splashed into the inch of melting sleet and hail masking some of TunFaire's more rugged cobblestones. The big guy's severed hand scrambled around inside the sack of invisibility with me.

That hand would not stop, I guess because it had been nipped off an immortal. I slithered to the side of the street, hoping my trail would not be too obvious. But nobody had much attention left over for me. Trog was in a real fury now. Jorken had a full-time job staying out of his way. Trog's club swished close enough to make him dizzy.

I wormed into a shadow and started sliding out of that sack. No need to tell anybody which way I was headed.

Jorken noticed me as I kicked Trog's hand away from me. He lost his concentration for an instant as he turned my way.

*Wham!* Trog gave new meaning to the expression "pound him into the ground." He was winding up for another swing when last I saw him.

I got the hell out of there fast.

Daiged and Rhogiro arrived just as I did my fade. Then the masonry really started to fly.

Something flapped past. I dodged, afraid I had an owl girl after me. "Awk!" The flyer smacked into a brick wall. "This thing cannot see in the dark." *Flap-flap.* "Garrett?"

"Where the hell have you been?" I felt around till I found the bird. It was really dark out now.

"You lost me when you stopped to eat. I had to tend to business elsewhere. I returned to a situation fraught with anticipation. As I flew up to reconnoiter it, the excitement began in earnest. I managed to trace you by staying close to the ugly one."

I muttered something about pots and kettles, got the critter installed on my shoulder, and resumed moving.

"Gotten real exciting, hasn't it?"

"They have begun to indulge in brutal destruction, like petulant children. Make for the park. And do move faster if you wish to get away."

"I can't go any faster." I was slipping and sliding all over, barely keeping my footing. The water under the sleet had frozen into a treacherous glaze.

And then it started to snow.

Snow leaves great tracks—unless it comes down real heavy. It began to look like this was just the night for that.

Another big blockbluster of a battle shaped up behind us. The gods shrieked and squawked like divine fishwives.

"I need warmer clothes," I said. "I'm going to freeze my butt off."

"You can afford to lose some of it. Head for the park. Miss Cat should meet us there. She will take us to safety." The bird was shaking too.

The snowfall lessened as we distanced ourselves from the battle, where thunder and lightning had begun to lark about. In fact, for a while that got so enthusiastic I figured Imar and Lang must be working it out god to god.

Them dancing gave us a chance to grab a new lead.

"I don't got much go-power left," I whimpered at the Goddamn Parrot as I stumbled into the park. The snow there was ankle deep and rising fast, but there was no ice or sleet underneath. It had to be real nasty back where it all started.

A breeze was rising, speeding toward the center of conflict. It slammed snowflakes into my face. They were big wet ones. I muttered and cursed. The Goddamn Parrot, just to be difficult, cursed and muttered. I trudged in what I guessed to be the general direction of the place where Cat had landed before. I couldn't tell anything for sure. It was darker than the inside of a shylock's heart.

# 47

"Garrett! Over here!"

Cat. I turned my head right and left to get a sense of her direction. I caught a toe on something, tumbled into a low place where snow had gathered eight inches deep. The Goddamn Parrot cussed me for being clumsy.

Cat appeared out of the milky shower. "Here." She offered me a blanket. I noticed that she was dressed for the weather. Which suggested she had an idea what was going on. But I didn't get a chance to ask. "Get up!" she barked. "We have to hurry. Come on! Some of them are on your trail again."

Her name was apt. She could see in the dark. She seemed to have trouble hearing in the dark, though. My "What the hell is going on?" fell into the snow without so much as a muted thump.

Cat led me about a hundred yards at right angles to my previous course. And there stood all her winged sidekicks, muttering seditiously amongst themselves. The weather didn't seem to bother Fourteen. The horses awarded me equine looks more laden than usual with the semi-intelligent malice of their tribe. But we did have something in common at last. They weren't happy about being out here, either.

"Shake your tail, Sugar Hips. Ya got bottom feeders headed your way."

I got a look at Cat's crew because way up in the snow clouds a pinpoint of light brighter than any noonday sun had popped and had taken a dozen seconds to fade away.

Cat helped me mount one of her beasts. It seemed to be the same one as before. And, behold! For the second time running I managed to get on top facing the same direction he was. It was an age of great wonders.

The Goddamn Parrot wanted to say something but couldn't squeeze it out. He couldn't control his shivering. Parrots are not meant for cold weather. I tucked him inside my blanket. He slithered around till he found a way inside my shirt. Then he settled down to shiver and mutter to himself.

"Cat, will you please tell me . . ."

Somewhere a wolf howled. Somewhere something named Nog polished its only thought. I didn't catch Cat's shout, but it was no answer.

The horses started to run. My blanket flapped in the wind. I held on with my legs while I tried to get myself wrapped again. I was shaking beyond all hope of control. It couldn't be long before the cold caused irreversible damage.

Fourteen zoomed past, bumblebee wings humming. "Grab your ass, Slick." He giggled. The bottom fell out.

My mount had run off the end of something again. Its huge wings extended, beat the flake-filled air. The cold breeze roared past, not quite as chilly now. I started to worry about frostbite but soon had trouble keeping a sharp edge on my thoughts.

Fourteen buzzed around running his mouth till even my ride got fed up and tried to take a bite out of him as he zipped past. A couple of cherub feathers whipped past me. Fourteen squealed and headed for Cat, plopping down into her lap.

Another one of those incredibly bright points of light popped over the north side of TunFaire. There was too much snow to tell anything else about it. I was trapped in a cold bubble in a sea of milk.

That flash made the flying horses whinny in dismay. They redoubled their efforts to gain altitude. Fourteen started cussing. Cat asked him what was going on. The horses turned directly away from the flash. Cat's mount drifted away from mine.

Curious. But I didn't have much hope of finding out what was going on. Everybody was giving me the mushroom treatment, keeping me in the dark and feeding me horse manure.

It all had to do with the feud going on back there, of course.

Something came down from the north and passed between my mount and Cat's. It went by too fast to see, arriving with a hiss, then leaving a baby thunderclap to mark its passing.

The horses yelped and tried desperately to get going faster.

Did my honey shout an explanation across, just in case it

would help me stay alive? Sure she did. Right after she told me the guaranteed-to-win numbers I ought to bet in the Imperial Games.

I discovered that our course was southward because we arose above thinning clouds. I made out what had to be the Haiden Light at Great Cape, downriver thirty miles, south of town. We were way up high now, moving fast—and finding warmer air quickly, thanks to no gods. A little thumbnail clipping of a moon lay upon the eastern horizon, smiling or smirking.

I looked over my shoulder. TunFaire lay under an inverted bowl of clouds that flickered and glowed. Serpents of mist writhed upon the surface of the bowl and gradually sank toward the epicenter beneath.

The Goddamn Parrot got active suddenly. He wriggled till he got his ugly little head out into the wind. "Garrett. A dram of information. Shinrise the Destroyer turns out to be . . ."

"A Lambar Coast war god? Hangs around with cherubs and winged horses?"

"How did you know?" Next thing to a whine there, Old Bones.

"I remembered." Under stress some guys just can't shut up. Back when I was in the Corps we had had us one of those for a while, a kid from the Lambar Coast. He had called on Shinrise whenever the going got tough.

One of those awful pinpoint flashes occurred on the far side of the city again. Ectoplasmic light expanded around it. For just an instant a point of darkness existed within that globe. Then cloud serpents began to spill down and twist into the lightning-laced mass below.

Lightning popped to our right front, *close* and overpoweringly intense. Cat and the horses screamed. Fourteen went on a cussing jag. Because I was still looking back to the north, I didn't suffer the blinding worst of it, but a brick wall of wind did smack me and almost bust me loose for one long and thrilling downward walk in the chill night air. I clutched mane hair and turned to see what had happened.

As I turned I thought I saw something cross the fragment of a moon. If I had not known that such things were mythical, the imaginings of men who hadn't ever seen an actual flying thunder lizard, I might have believed it was a dragon.

I faced front as that insane light's intensity dwindled to where it did not hurt the eye anymore. It was the same phenomenon again, only this time so close we got hit by the expanding ectoplasmic sphere. It smashed past me. My mount staggered. Blinded by the flash, he tried desperately to stay level while he recovered.

There was a hole in the night where the pop had taken place. It was a darkness deeper than that inside a coffin buried in an underground tomb on the dark side of a world without a sun. Then, just for an instant, something reached through that hole, something that was darker still, something so dark that it glistened in the light. Rainbows slithered over it like an oil film on water. It came my way, but I don't think it was after me.

The Goddamn Parrot went berserk inside my shirt. Either he wanted to get away bad or he had decided to snack on my guts.

Fourteen squealed like somebody had set his toes on fire.

Suddenly it was colder than any cold I had endured yet. The reaching something popped back through its window of darkness. For an instant, before the hole shrank to invisibility, a dark alien eye glared through, filled with a malice that was almost crushing in its weight.

All that didn't last more than a couple of seconds. My horse barely had time to beat his wings a full stroke.

The cold penetrated right down to the core of me. I knew, whether I wanted to believe it or not, that I had looked right into the realm of the gods. Maybe the eye belonged to something so unpleasant that the gods would willingly destroy my world rather than be forced to go back where that waited.

Hmm. That didn't feel quite right, though I had a suspicion that I had just seen something a lot nastier than any of the gods who were complicating my life now.

Damn! I couldn't see Cat anywhere. And my mount seemed to be having a seizure. Not to mention the fact that the ground looked like it was about eleven miles down.

I don't like heights very much. They give me the jim-jams in a big way.

# 48

"Worse things waiting." When I was a kid, that was the inevitable response of the old folks if you complained about anything. "You got it easy, young man. They's worse things waiting."

They knew what they were talking about, too.

I hung on. I kept my eyes closed tight while we fell. My mount banged the air feebly with spasming wings. It screamed a horsey scream, only about fifteen times as loud as a normal ground-bound beast might have.

Just the way I always wanted to go, at the age of four hundred and eight. Riding a waking nightmare.

"They finally got me," I muttered. I took even tighter hold of the creature's mane. This one damned horse was going with me.

Another horse shrieked from far above. Sounded like it was coming closer fast. I cracked one eye to see how far we had fallen. "Oh, shit!"

I should have known better.

My mount didn't like the prognosis either. He got serious about the flapping and flopping and got his hooves right side down and his wings floundering around in the right direction.

The cherub came whirring out of the night, hummed around and around, just hanging out like he enjoyed watching things fall. He chuckled a lot. Then he held up suddenly, staring, aghast. "Oh, no! That blows everything."

I looked around, spied a half-dozen tower-tall, transparent, and obviously pissed-off figures striding toward TunFaire. None of them were Shayir or Godoroth. Neither did I think they be-longed to the Board, whose controls had failed so abominably. It looked like some of the really big guys had decided to forgo normal business—making guys sacrifice their firstborn or sneaking up on virgins disguised as critters—while they attended to some emergency heavenly housekeeping.

Fourteen shot toward me, grabbed hold, scrambled up under my blanket. I grumbled, "It's getting a little crowded in here." That distracted me from the screaming I wanted to do.

The damned horse got it all together. It beat hell out of the air with its monster wings. To no avail. We had too much downward momentum. *Whamboney!* We hit. We shot on down through about half a mile of tree branches. Lucky us, they slowed us down. Lucky us, none of them were big enough to stop us cold. Lucky us, when we hit water I only went in up to my ears.

We surfaced. The horse whooped and hooted and gasped after its lost breath. The Goddamn Parrot wriggled its head out of my clothes again, began a wet and lonely soliloquy filled with every cussword the Dead Man could recall from about fifty languages.

Old Chuckles has been around a long time.

The cherub came out and hovered. He agreed with the bird.

It was all my fault.

Same as it ever was.

Personally, I was too busy being glad I was still in one piece to give either one of them a hard time. But good ideas for later did occur to me.

"Where the hell are we?"

Fourteen snapped, "In a freaking swamp, moron."

That wasn't exactly hard to miss. There were mosquitoes out there big enough to carry off small pets. Otherwise, though, it was your typically wimpy Karentine swamp. If you overlooked a few poisonous bugs and snakes, it would be completely safe. Nothing like the swamps we endured down in the islands, where we faced snakes as long as anchor chains *and* the alligators who survived by eating them.

I found myself not feeling at all awful—for a guy who had just missed falling to his death and had missed drowning only by inches.

That horse had one ounce of brains. He didn't try to fly out of there. As soon as he got his breath back, he let out a couple of forlorn neighs. He seemed surprised when they were answered from above. Fourteen buzzed upward, rattling and clattering and cussing his way through the branches. In minutes he was back, a fresh, competition-class banger in his mouth. "This way." My mount headed out. He was not inclined to hear suggestions or commentary from me.

The beast pulled in his wings completely. He proceeded as straight horse and regained his strength quickly. The cherub led us to solid ground fast. Minutes later, we left the trees. The horse broke into a trot that graduated to a canter and then a vigorous gallop. This continued for a while, the horse not growing winded but not getting off the ground either. We went over hill and dale and farm while Cat and her mount cruised overhead. Our course tended southwest. Time seemed to take the night off. Before long we left the farmlands.

I checked the moon. For sure, it hadn't traveled nearly as far as it should have. We were on elf hill time. And covering a *lot* of ground. Already we were in territory that remained unsettled because people were too superstitious to live there.

A sudden vague glow limned some hills up ahead. It made them look like they were standing in a circle, looking down at something they had surrounded. "Oh boy." It just got worse. I poked the Goddamn Parrot.

That gaudy chicken did not respond—except to bite my finger. Evidently we were beyond the Dead Man's range. At last. With the Goddamn Parrot, mercifully, left with little command of his vocal apparatus.

Great. Once again I was getting a lesson in watching out what I wished for because my wishes might come true.

Those hills had to be the Bohdan Zhibak. That name translates into modern Karentine as "The Haunted Circle." Over the ages a lot of really awful things are supposed to have happened there. And tonight, it seemed, the fabled Fires of Doom were ablaze inside the Circle.

Fourteen didn't want to get any closer. He was not shy about telling everyone about it.

# 49

Cat landed. We dismounted. She told Fourteen to shut up or go away. I hung on to a stirrup in order to maintain my defiance of the seductions of gravity. I felt like I had been living in that saddle for days. I glared at Cat. "You saved me from those lunatics back in town so you could sacrifice me out here?"

"Calm down. Fourteen, you shut up. You can be put back away with your brothers and sisters."

That worked on the cherub but not on me, though I protested, "I am calm. If I wasn't a veteran of all that screwiness in TunFaire I might not be calm. I might have a case of the rattlemouth like my buddy Fourteen. But, I mean, what's to get excited about, just because I find myself alongside the Haunted Hills? Just because there's all that doom light burning up out of the ground over there without, I bet, there being a real fire anywhere around? None of that ought to frighten a mouse."

I saw something move across the valley ahead of us, little more than a shadow hurrying, late for work. I didn't want to be on its list of chores.

"Plans change, Garrett. Originally Mom just wanted to get you out of there. But that was before the disaster."

"Which disaster? They come in strings lately." I dug the God-damn Parrot out of my shirt, looked around in there to see what damage he had done. I wasn't going to die, but I was sore enough that I would have strangled the ridiculous little feather duster if he had not been too dull-witted to appreciate what I was doing. I parked him on my shoulder. He had just enough wit to hang on.

Fourteen had a notion to take up residence opposite him. I did not feel guilty when I swatted him away.

"Which disaster? The breakdown of discipline. The squabbling. When they use their powers that way they weaken the walls of reality. What *is* that thing?" She meant the Goddamn Parrot.

"A really bad practical joke."

"Excuse me?"

"It's a parrot. Argh! Shiver me timbers! Like that."

"I'm so pleased that you can maintain your sense of humor." But she didn't sound pleased.

"It's all I've got that's all mine. What the hell are we doing out here?" Not even Winger would have the numskull nerve to go wandering around the Bohdan Zhibak.

"Because of the holes in the fabric. You saw what was happening. One blew out right in your face. If the walls really break down . . ."

I knew enough mythology to guess. Cold beyond imaginable cold. Eternal darkness beyond imaginable darkness. The end of the world. But just the unspeakable beginning for the unnamable eldritch horrors from beyond the beginning of time. Never mind it all sprang from the imagination in the first place. "Come on! This is some game between two gangs of petty half-wit gods who needed me to sort them out to see who gets to stay respectable. All of a sudden I've got to save the world?" I'm not big on world-saving. Way too much traveling and not nearly enough reward in the end. Not to mention you don't get much sleep.

"No! Of course not. Don't be absurd! You think too much of yourself. If you keep your mouth shut except when somebody asks you a question and you don't smart off when they do, you may survive long enough to see the world get saved."

Put me in my place, she did. "What's going on here?" We were sneaking between a couple of hills, crunching dry grass and bare stone, in weather that was appropriate for the season. Fourteen buzzed hither and yon, ahead, but very tentatively and very low to the ground. He wanted to be there less than I did. There was an astonishing shawl of stars flung across the shoulders of a cloudless sky. The moon was in no hurry yet, though it had climbed higher.

The light up ahead wavered, waxed, waned. Sounds came down the valley, inarticulate but angry. "I don't like this, Cat. Last time I came home from the Cantard I swore I'd never leave Tun-

Faire again. Till now I've stuck to that." More or less. But no lapse of mine had brought me this far afield.

Damn! This could turn *real* nasty. I might have to walk home.

"The gods have a secret, Garrett." She allowed the cherub to settle into her arms for a moment of rest. She held and patted him as if he were a baby. He seemed to like that.

"Just one? Then a lot of paper has gone to waste turning out holy books that claim to explain the ten million mysteries . . ."

"There you go again. Can't you ever just listen?"

Maybe when I run my yap I feel like I'm in control. I needed some control here. Desperately.

"Go ahead."

The cherub lit up a fresh banger that he pulled out of his diaper. He got fire by snapping his fingers.

Cat took the smoke. "Not now. Not here. Garrett, all gods, whatever their pantheon, whatever dogma has accreted around them, came from the same place and started out much the same. You looked into that place a while ago. The gods fled it because it's so terrible. But over here they can't stay functional, can't hang on, without belief to sustain them. Or without drawing power from the other side, which risks opening new gateways. If they have no sustenance at all, eventually they fall back to the other side. Naturally, they don't want to go home."

"You mean they're all related?"

"No. Is everyone in TunFair related? Of course not. They're not even all of the same race. Say this is like some of the humans going off somewhere together, in search of a better life. If they found it they might not want to come back."

"You telling me they're refugees?" The gods are refugees from somewhere else? Wouldn't that stir some excitement in the Dream Quarter? Wouldn't that be dangerous knowledge for some non-god to be lugging around?

This was no place for me. I had a notion I was one of the non-gods.

"Cat, you're a doll and I love you, but this isn't my idea of the perfect date. I've got a sneaking suspicion my prospects would be a lot better if I headed some other direction." Like any damned direction but this one.

Cat grabbed my hand. She was strong. My course remained steady, straight ahead. She told me, "You have a tool."

"Huh?"

"You can make yourself invisible."

"Yeah. But when I do, the Godoroth always know where I'm at."

"And you think they'd try something here?"

"Why the hell not? They've already proved they're bonkers. But you know them. I don't."

"We should remain unnoticed. For now."

"That's what I had in mind when I said let's go." I started to head for the horses. Just this once they looked like the lesser evil.

Cat still had my hand and she hadn't gotten any weaker. I got nowhere.

We were near the edge of the light and had attracted no attention yet. Shapes and shadows haunted the hillsides. Wouldn't you know a place called the Haunted Circle would be like that? I didn't recognize any of them. Few were in anthropomorphic form.

More arrived by the moment, flopping, flying, slithering, jogging in on two hundred legs. "Sooner or later something is going to trip over us." I tried beating feet again.

Have I mentioned Cat's unusual strength? I didn't go anywhere this time either.

I took out Magodor's cord, stretched it, knotted it, created a loop big enough for two. We hopped inside. "This may get real friendly," I warned.

Cat smiled a wicked smile that told me the deviltry was in her but she wasn't feeling flirtatious right now. She could stick to business where her mother could not.

It seemed my sack of invisibility could be made as big as whatever loop I started with, plus however high I could raise that loop before I closed it up. By holding hands and staying in step, Cat and I were able to move the sack with little trouble. She insisted on heading right out into the middle of the lighted ground. Once we were there we could see all the hillsides. Our presence didn't attract any attention.

Still I saw nothing I recognized.

The mob fell silent. The result was spooky. All that many humans in one place would have created a racket like hurricanes raising hell amongst the boughs of tropical forests. I turned slowly, examining every hill. I was scared, but I was not out of control. Not like Fourteen, who was down between our feet trying to vanish into our footprints, unable, apparently, to believe we were truly invisible.

I whispered, "I take it little ones like him don't get treated real well by the big guys."

"Cruelty is in their nature."

I didn't stop turning, studying. Few of these gods clung to any shape I had seen in the Dream Quarter. Maybe out here the belief of their worshippers was attenuated enough to let them relax. Scary to think things as ugly as Ringo and as attractive as Star might be identical blobs on one of those hillsides.

Pity, that.

I whispered, "You know any of those things?" I noticed a few taking imaginable shapes for flickering instants. Maybe their worshippers were thinking of them.

"No. My mother worked hard to keep me a secret from them. If Imar found out about me . . ."

Of course. It was just ducky being a half god if a god was your pop and your mom was human. A divine tradition. The great heroes of antiquity all had some heavenly blood. But goddesses aren't supposed to boff the suckers, apparently.

The old double standard was alive and well amongst the sons of heaven. Or whatever you called that over there. Always nice to know that some things are the same in heaven as they are on earth. Lets everybody know where they stand.

The shadows continued to gather like buzzards to a freshly fallen thunder lizard. The great towering ones began to arrive, their eyes like cities burning, their hair the ugliest thunderheads. I whispered, "What's happening here, anyway?" I was sure no such assembly had taken place before, ever.

"When they came here the gods left weak places in the fabric of the barriers between. When they want to show off or perform miracles, they use power they pull through those weak places. When they do they create a momentary opening. There are worse things still back there. They would like to come here, too. The fighting between the Godoroth and Shayir would have opened a lot of holes. Some of those things over there found them before they closed up again. They tried to break through. That's what caused those flashes. The stupid fighting went on so long and the fabric of the barrier grew so weak that those horrors might actually bust their own hole through. This assembly is going to decide how to handle that. It's also going to discuss the Shayir and Godoroth. They aren't so stupid they didn't know better. A universal terror of the evils left behind has underlain all divine law for ten thousand years."

"How the hell do you all of a sudden know all this?" I knew she couldn't have known much of it when we arrived.

"I can catch snatches of their debate." She tapped her temple. "It's really hot."

On that level where the Dead Man communicates with me, inside my head, I was aware of a continuous dull buzz, like I was catching just the remotest edge of mindspeech going on in a somewhat similar manner. That buzz was extremely stressful. Before long I was going to have one ferocious headache.

Then I spotted somebody I knew.

# 50

Magodor stalked along the foot of a hill about a hundred feet away. She was no shadow. She was set solidly in her nastiest avatar. She looked right at me. She knew I was there. Good old Driver of the Spoil. She didn't look pleased but seemed unlikely to try making my life less pleasant than it was already.

I recalled that people in TunFaire had been unable to see the divine clowns lurking around me. "Cat, you can see these things, can't you?"

"I see Magodor. She sees us, too."

"No. But she knows I'm here. She gave me the cord. She can tell where it is."

"Uhm!" She seemed to have lost interest. Aha! Her mother had arrived. Imara seemed quite regal and totally indifferent to the censure of fellow gods.

The rest of the Shayir and Godoroth arrived, all frozen into their city forms. The anger around us grew palpable. My headache began worsening fast. Among the stragglers I spotted interesting faces. "Cat. Do you know that character there?" I indicated a huge, handsome, one-eyed guy who was neither Godoroth nor Shayir.

"That's Bogge. He's Mom's lover."

"Bogge? You sure?" He looked a lot like Shinrise the Destroyer. "Gets around, don't she?" I wondered if a god would lie to a mortal about his identity. Or if a mother would lie to her daughter.

My thoughtless remark earned me a dirty look.

I asked, "How about the redhead there? The one who looks

like an ordinary mortal." Ordinary, hell. All women ought to look so ordinary. She looked like Star might if she decided to conform to my peculiar prejudices.

"Not in that form." There was a small catch in her voice.

"She got me into this. She was watching my house. I decided to follow her."

"She isn't Godoroth or Shayir."

Indeed. But you do have some ideas . . .

*Nog is inescapable.*

Well, of course he was. He kept coming back like an unemployed cousin, Nog did.

I recalled a little old lady at the mouth of an alley and reflected that goddesses were not required to keep one look. "The name Adeth mean anything? Magodor said an Adeth was trying to trap me. I thought she meant that woman."

Nervously, Cat said, "One of the Krone Gods is called Adeth . . ." and cut herself off.

"What? Give, darling. Look around. We don't need to play games."

"Adeth is one of a bunch of tribal deities from way down south. The people are fur traders and rock hunters. They've never had enough people here to win a place on the Street of the Gods."

Now that rolled off her tongue so smooth it must have been distilled twice.

She said, "I don't see why some primitives like that would get involved. Though her name does mean Treachery, I think."

"There's a lot of that going on these days." That redhead was just too polished to be the wishful thinking of fur trappers still using stone tools. Those guys go for malicious rocks and trees and such. And storm gods. They love gods who stomp around and bellow and smash things up a lot.

Be right at home around here.

*Nog is inescapable.*

"That boy needs a hobby," I muttered. The thing itself oozed out of a valley, stopped, turned in place slowly for half a minute, then began to shuffle our way.

"Oh, damn," Cat murmured.

A spear blade twelve feet tall slammed into the earth in front of Nog, nearly shaving his nose off. It was slightly transparent but did have a definite impact when it hit. Clods flew a hundred feet. Lightning slithered down the spear shaft. Sparks played tag along the edges of the blade.

One of the very tall, very big-time gods had admonished Nog.

Fourteen was whimpering out loud now. He was down flat on his pudgy belly with his chubby, too short arms trying to cover his head.

I said, "I'm beginning to wonder, Cat."

She grimaced but didn't answer.

Nog considered his situation, decided that since he was inescapable he could afford to wait. He resumed moving along a new course. He joined the rest of the Godoroth gang. Those swinging party guys had gathered at the foot of a slope opposite the Shayir. Both crews looked troubled. And angry, though no actual lightning bolts flew.

The last stragglers must have arrived because all of a sudden most all the gods tried to assume their worldly avatars. About a third were not successful. Maybe there wasn't enough power to go around.

I had an idea. This happens on occasion. "Are the walls between the worlds thinner in the Dream Quarter?"

"Will you stop blubbering?" Cat stuck a toe into the cherub's ribs. Then she looked at me almost suspiciously. She seemed reluctant to answer my questions now.

I said, "It seems reasonable to assume that they would cluster where it would be easiest to tap their sources of power." Which, of course, added meaning to the struggle of the Shayir and Godoroth to remain on the Street.

Cat grunted.

There was a change in the painful background racket gurgling down in the bottom of my mind. It faded. I caught the edge of what had to be one big guy really booming. There was no motion at all on the surrounding slopes.

The meeting had been called to order.

I thought about gods and points of power. Seemed likely that in addition to collecting where power was most accessible they would develop caste systems based on ability to grab and manipulate that power. Somebody like my little ankle-biting buddy Fourteen would be way down at the bottom of the pile.

If I have the innate ability to seize sixty percent of the power available and you can grab only thirty percent, guess who is in charge? Assuming we subscribe to the sociopathic attitudes generally ascribed to the gods.

Sudden anger surged along the thought stream I sensed so marginally. With the pure cold voice I had felt no pain, but this anger was a powerful blow, however glancing. It sent me to my knees. I ground the heels of my fists into my temples. I managed not to scream.

Imar came out from the Godoroth team. Lang moved forward, too. They raced to see who could grow big the fastest. Each surrounded himself with all the noisy, dramatic effects demanded by mortal worshippers.

Since I was down already, I settled against a not entirely uncomfortable rock. I patted Fourteen's bottom like he really was a baby and reflected, "I should have brought a lunch. This punchout is going to take a while."

I saw representatives of the Board called on the carpet while the mirror-image boss gods looked one another over. The mind stream had a blistery touch. The supreme busybodies seemed to want to give everybody a yellow card for unnecessary roughness.

Me, I thought they all deserved big penalties for unnecessary stupidity.

I kept one eye on Imara and another on her boyfriend, whatever name he was using. I kept one on the incipient ruckus out front and another on the redhead Cat was determined to keep mysterious. That didn't really leave a lot of eyes for anything else.

# 51

Boy. Talk about a big bunch of nothing! There I was, all bent over and scrunched up expecting the Midnight of the Gods, or at least the little ones getting their pants pulled down and their holy heinies spanked, and all I got was a headache that left me nostalgic for my hangover.

"Nobody is doing anything," I whined.

"There's plenty going on. You don't see it because you can't listen in. The Shayir and the Godoroth are really upset."

I did note a certain restlessness on the sidelines, reflected by the squared-off boss gods, who, I now suspected, were supposed to shake hands and make up. And I noted that Imara sort of drifted slowly throughout the midfield confrontation. She got smaller as she moved. And she assumed a whole new look.

Interesting. *Very* interesting.

"Cat. You keeping an eye on your mom?"

"Huh? Why?"

I pointed. "That's her there. Sliding over to her boyfriend. She's been changing her looks as she goes." I assumed she was disguising herself on levels seen only by gods, too.

"Oh. She looks a lot younger."

"She sure does. She's turning herself into a dead ringer for you." I kicked the cherub. I wanted him to stop whining long enough to get a good look at this transformation, too. "You got any thoughts about this, Cat?"

My suspicion was that Cat might not be as big a secret as she thought. I had a hunch she might be just another angle in a carefully managed escape maneuver.

Cat's eyes narrowed. She glared at her mother. She glared at me. She didn't have to be told that I suspected the worst. We both knew that gods and goddesses don't cling to any wordly code of conduct.

Cat said, "Maybe we ought to leave."

"That might have been a good idea a while ago. Before anybody knew we were here. But now? How far could we run? Could we run fast enough?"

"Nothing is settled here. The deadline still hasn't come." But she climbed to her feet and grabbed up her little buddy, plainly interested in quick relocation.

I got up myself. The whole situation had me thinking, which, according to some, doesn't happen all that often.

And according to the Dead Man, not often enough.

"Cat. The world was here before the coming of the gods. Right?"

"Yes. Of course it was. Why?"

Because, then, these were not really gods in the way I had been taught to think of gods. Even the gods I had been told were the one and only real and they're-gonna-send-all-them-infidels-to-burn-in-hell gods just belonged to the same bunch of transdimensional refugees. Or fugitives?

"Cat, did these gods come here by choice?"

"What?"

"It occurs to me they might be exiles. Thrown out of the old home for bad behavior or just excessive stupidity."

"No. None of them want to go back. That's what the fighting is all about."

"Maybe." I had some thoughts that included suspicions of setups. I surveyed the audience. More gods had settled into their earthly forms. I saw some really big names. Out here, though, they just looked luckier than bunches like the Godoroth and Shayir. Probably had better publicity wazoos.

What I didn't see anymore was a goddess named Imara. What I didn't see was a redhead maybe called Adeth hanging out with raggedy-ass jungle gods. I did see Shinrise the Destroyer—or maybe Bogge the Sucker—standing around stupidly now, looking like he had just lost something.

The ranks of the Godoroth and Shayir seemed short handed on females.

I checked some of the more successful gangs but couldn't tell if they had gone shorthanded, too. They just looked more prosperous. A supply of believers surely helped, but maybe also a knack for drawing power from beyond this reality.

Maybe gods are like sausages and politics and should not be examined closely.

I always expect the worst. That means I can be pleasantly surprised sometimes. This didn't seem to be one of those times. Circumstances appeared to support my most cynical suspicions.

There were thousands of gods there, though most were hangers-on, many even smaller than Fourteen.

The cherub seemed to have settled down. Maybe he realized that nobody was paying him any attention. I *knew* I was invisible but still felt naked to every divine eye.

There was some subtle movement out there, and tension rising. The hair on my arms tingled.

# 52

There was big anger in the air again, much worse than before. Fourteen whimpered. Something had happened. The crowd around Lang and Imar were all in a rage.

"We need to leave now," Cat said. Her voice squeaked. "A ruling was handed down. The Shayir and Godoroth refuse to accept it."

Holding hands, in step, each laboring under the weight of a garbage-mouthed curse, we headed for our horses. "Explain," I squeaked. My throat was tight, too. I noticed Magodor drifting through the mob. She seemed intent on tracking us. I wondered why.

"Because of their behavior in town, the senior gods have banished the Godoroth and the Shayir from the Street of the Gods *and* TunFaire."

"And our boys won't go quietly?"

"Imar and Lang pretty much said, 'Stick it in your ear!'"

"Can they do that?" Of course they could. Anybody can tell anybody anything, anytime. The tricky part is surviving the aftermath.

"There may be a confrontation."

Oh. "Uh-oh."

"And this is definitely the wrong place for that. This is where the gods originally arrived. It takes a lot longer than ten thousand years for wounds like that to heal. The walls here are tissue."

Which might explain why the little guys thought they could thumb their noses, except that I didn't credit them with sense enough to consider that subtle an angle.

"Keep hiking, girl. Runt, you stop sniveling or I'll kick you out of here."

Fourteen sneered. He wasn't afraid of any mortal. I was too busy staying in step with Cat to follow up.

I glanced back. I didn't see Magodor anymore. I did see a whirlwind of black paper chips and a mist of golden light around Lang, who raised his left fist and pumped his thumb in and out of his clenched fingers in a classic obscene gesture directed at the big boys. Then he struck suddenly right-handed, swinging a sword of lightning at Imar's throat. Just as suddenly, you had Jorken streaking around, the ugly guys looking for throats to crush, Imar flailing around with his own lightning. Trog went berserk with his hammer. Torbit, Quilraq, and others went wild. Black Mona galloped in with her hounds, her weapons flying everywhere.

"Hang on, Cat. Just a second." I watched as the fray disappeared inside a cloud of dust, then a light storm as those incredibly brilliant pops began ripping the fabric of reality. In seconds it began to snow. And Cat and I were moving again, faster than ever.

"Why did you stop?"

"Wanted to make sure I'd seen something right."

"What?"

"None of the females are in that mess, except Black Mona. And she's got more hair on her ass than anybody but Trog." Not even Magodor was involved. Maybe especially not even Magodor. What's an end of the world dustup without a Destroyer?

The temperature plummeted. My headache worsened till Cat had to help me stay on my feet. Numerous top god types tried to break up the fight. The Godoroth and Shayir went on like fools with nothing to lose and a complete willingness to take everybody with them. And they seemed to get support from some odds and ends of petty pewter types from other pantheons, mainly of the strike-from-behind, score-settling sort.

We made good time despite being inside the bag. We were behind the knee of a hill when the Bohdan Zhibak lit up with the grandaddy of all light pops.

I went down. "Bet they saw that back in town." My headache grew so intense I blacked out.

I recovered in seconds. "What are you doing?"

"Trying to get us out of this."

Trying to take a powder, actually. Hell. Give her the benefit. Say she was trying to scram because I was out and she couldn't move the sack with all that dead weight in it.

My head didn't hurt nearly so much now. I found the knot, got us out in seconds. Fourteen went catatonic with terror. I restored my cord to normal, wrapped it around my waist again.

There was a lot of noise from the other side of the hill. Cat told me, "We've got to keep going."

"In a minute." I wanted a peek. Just one little look. I was pretty sure my Midnight of the Gods was cooking now. Be a shame not to witness some of the action.

# 53

I kept a tight grip on Cat. Just in case. Much as I hate horses and heights, I hated the prospect of walking home more. Especially walking home while suffering a headache and a psychotic parrot.

She had the strength to break away. She just didn't try.

Ever seen a sea anemone? Thing like a little flower a couple inches across, pale tentacles that just drift around? Maybe not. I had the advantage of an all-but-the-pain expenses-paid trip to remote islands. Anyway, these little guys just sit there with their arms up and when something drifts by they snag it.

A black version thirty feet in diameter with two hundred tentacles fifty feet long was stuck in a hole in the air where Lang and Imar had been banging on each other. It was twenty feet off the ground, tilted forty degrees and wiggling like crazy. "No wonder the gods wanted to come over here."

The thing plugged the hole so tight no cold could come through. The snow had begun to melt.

The gods were active. Frantically. Some tried to deal with the interloper. Some tried to get loose from it. The really big guys were feeding it. I saw Ringo get flung into the middle of the tentacle forest. Many of the visible victims, in fact, seemed to be of Shayir or Godoroth extraction. Guess this will settle that question.

Other old scores were being recalculated as well. A general trimming of the divine population was under way.

There seemed to be enough gods actually taking care of business to push that thing back. While I watched, the hole shrank several feet.

*Nog is inescapable.* Oh my. Somebody fell through the cracks.

"Time to go."

Cat had gotten it, too. She outran me, though not by much. Wonder of wonders, her flying pals had not left us twisting in the wind. Considering Fourteen's timidity, I'd figured to find them long gone.

*Nog is inescapable.*

Maybe so. He was closing in fast.

He was so close, in fact, that he leaped and landed a raking blow on my mount's left flank as we went airborne. Which naturally irritated the horse. It gained some altitude, turned, dove, did a fine job of thunking all four hooves off Nog's noggin. Nog said, *Ow Stop! That hurts!*

The retard had double the vocabulary I had thought. But I didn't dwell on that. I was too busy screaming at the horse to get the hell out of there before I fell off or Nog showed us what other divine talents he possessed—or Magodor caught up or the other gods got bored with feeding each other to their new pet.

The winged horse took my advice.

As we gained altitude again my headache diminished. I was soaked with sweat from gutting it out.

The moon had climbed only slightly higher. At this rate, if we hustled, we could get back to town before we left. Or at least meet ourselves on the way. I could warn me not to go.

I looked down. The Haunted Circle crawled like the proverbial anthill. There had been a lot of breakthroughs. The one I had seen was just the biggest. In numerous places one or two tentacles reached through and tried to find something to grab. But the gods had covered themselves. There wasn't so much as a bush out there. When a tentacle grabbed a boulder somebody zapped that into pea gravel. The home gods were winning. Rah! The wannabes were being driven back. Rah! Rah! But at terrible cost. Boo! This insanity would decimate every pantheon in the Dream Quarter. Wait! Would that be so awful?

None of this was likely to touch the man on the street. I could not see, for example, the New Concord Managerial Recidivist gods informing their faithful that good old Gerona the Tallykeeper was no more, so they needn't trouble themselves with bringing in those tithes. More likely they would hear about several new diocesan appeals, maybe aimed at fixing up the mother temple in Tims-Noroë or financing another mission to the heathen Venageti. And one sceat out of every silver mark really would go toward carrying out the fund's dedicated purpose.

Not that the gods would themselves be much concerned about money or precious metals.

Well! Look at this. Not every god is woven of the stuff of heroes. I was too far up there to recognize individuals, but quite a few had run from the bad place. Was it all cowardice, though? One group of several dozen was headed north in a purposeful manner. I had a notion that if I dared swoop down there, I would find some very familiar folks.

In fact . . .

# 54

In fact, a pair of familiar shapes hurtled past, *zip! zap!* to my right front from my left rear, angling down from above, too swift to see but trailing giggles that gave them away. One looped back and took a seat right in front of me, where she changed into a half-naked girl. The other one circled and complained.

"I got here first, slowpoke. Hi, Garrett! Surprised? Can we talk? We're lots smarter than we always acted."

"I'm real uncomfortable up here. That first step down is a killer. No offense, but do you think you could maybe keep your hands to yourself till we get a little closer to the ground? I don't have your advantages over gravity. If I get distracted I just fall."

The circling owl girl giggled. The other answered peevishly, "He is not! He's just behaving like a mortal." She did not take her hands off me. "Wouldn't it be exciting way up here, Garrett? I've never played with mortals anywhere but down on the ground."

Does a bimbo become any less a bimbo because she is smarter than everybody thinks?

"For about as long as it takes for me to lose track and let go here." I tried to get a hint of the color of her rags. "Look, Dimna, darling, you're just about the greatest thing that ever happened to me." Wow! I got it right first try! "But now just isn't the time to show you just how much I mean that. I hate horses. I'm terrified of heights. I have a murderous headache from all the power in that mess back there, and I haven't eaten or slept since this insanity began."

So I exaggerated. We all do that to save somebody's feelings.

Or to avoid getting tossed off a two-thousand-foot drop for our thoughtlessness.

She sure did look good, though.

I am a pig, I know. I have been told. But I can't help it. Maybe if I didn't run into this kind of woman all the time? Maybe if I got into a more boring line of work?

Maybe I could just drop over the side right now, die happy making Dimna squeal all the way down.

She rubbed her firm little puffies up against me, let a hand drop familiarly, told me, "I don't think you're that incapacitated."

"Darling, I promise you, if I give in now I'll be incapacitated forever. Because I'll fall off here for sure. And I can't turn into anything else but a tired old ex-Marine."

The owl girl actually seemed flattered that I considered a dalliance with her potentially suicidal.

Who am I to argue?

"Awk?" said the Goddamn Parrot, making a sound for the first time since the latter stage of the journey outward.

"You aren't going to believe this, Old Bones." I didn't know if he was listening, but anticipating his nags about paying attention to business, I turned Dimna's temptations back upon her, a tickle here and a pinch there that she seemed happy to accept. She sneered at Lila, closed her eyes and relaxed. Her twin flapped off in a huff.

I kept talking, mostly just making noise with a little content in case the Dead Man could hear but occasionally asking a question and leaving a silence for Dimna to fill.

She might claim to be smarter than she let on, but she was no genius. Too bad that was recognized by others. She had been let in on very little of substance. But she definitely enjoyed being interrogated.

I felt so used.

Right.

"Talk to me," the Goddamn Parrot squawked.

You get distracted.

"You know I have company."

"Not, I suspect, another No-Neck."

Did he hear in monotones? Couldn't he see through Mr. Big's eyes? Interesting. "The sweetest company a growing boy could imagine, Chuckles. Every boy ought to meet Dimna on his sixteenth birthday." I gave Dimna a strained smile and a kiss. If she wanted anything more out of life she sure didn't tell me.

In pain still, sweaty, tired, and hungry, all I really wanted was to get home. I felt safe enough now.

I could not tell what Cat thought about the owl girls. She was too far away and staying slightly ahead, navigating.

# 55

Cat landed in Brookside Park. The snow there had not yet all melted. I told her, "Cat, I've had all the fun I can stand with you and your mom and your friends. Suppose you all carry on without me? The Shayir and Godoroth shouldn't be a problem anymore."

She dismissed the horses. They trotted into the darkness. Fourteen stayed with Cat. He was about as active as a twelve-pound brick. Cat stuck with me. So did Lila and Dimna. Maybe they just didn't know where else to go now that the Shayir pantheon was defunct. I can't say I was thrilled, though it would be fun to walk into Morley's joint with an owl girl on each arm.

At first Cat wouldn't talk in front of them, but finally she grumbled, "If you add everything up, you have to believe my mother and her cronies engineered what happened."

"That bothers you?"

"Because it looks like they didn't think about the consequences. They wanted rid of some deadwood, so they put Imar and Lang in a spot where they would betray themselves for the duds they were. I don't think Mom realized that could damage the barriers between the worlds."

I reserved my opinion, naturally, but that told me Mom was as much a dud as her husband. She just hadn't had as much chance to show it.

"Cat, you glance over history, you'll see that females, on average, aren't brighter or better than males. They can be stupid or wise, foolish or crafty, too. They can be petty or magnanimous, and blind to the blazingly obvious. One thing some religions push that I agree with is that people ought to be trying to improve themselves as a whole. But I'm a cynic. I see no evidence that it's ever going to happen."

"You may be a realist, not a cynic. I've been closer to more gods and goddesses than anyone who ever lived."

She did not seem inclined to expand upon her remarks.

I didn't get to bed. I didn't even get to eat right away. In fact, if it hadn't been for the Dead Man pushing Dean, I wouldn't have gotten in until morning. The old man had all the chains on and was sound asleep.

I gave it to him good.

An hour later I was in the Dead Man's room. Cat and Fourteen were with us. The owl girls were in the small front room with the Goddamn Parrot. I was barely awake. Dean was sulking in the kitchen, fixing something to eat. I think he was waiting for it to grow up so he could butcher it. I thought about siccing the twins on him. He needed an attitude boost. Unfortunately, only the Dead Man, Cat, and I could see them or Fourteen.

His Nibs issued an opinion. *Imara and several other goddesses engineered this thing. I imagine they just intended to rid themselves of stupid males who . . .*

"Cat already told me that."

*. . . gave no thought to consequences.*

"And didn't listen, no doubt."

He ignored me, began spinning out a storm of dreamlike images and speculations. My weary brain tried to translate them, but his thinking was alien because he experienced the world in so different a way. Once my mind processed his thoughts I drifted through a fairy-tale realm where all lies and surface posturings were illusions to be ignored because truths and real motives could not be hidden behind them.

"Can you get anything from the girls?"

*They are exactly what they appear to be. They do not have the depth to be anything else. They could if they so desire, but they are perfectly happy with themselves just as they are. This should thrill you. For you they are a dream come true, saddled by no more inhibitions than alley cats in heat.*

"That is wonderful, isn't it? But, to paraphrase the immoral philosopher Morley Dotes, what do I do with them the other twenty-three hours a day?"

*Not to fear. You will not remain amusing long. Some insects have longer attention spans.*

Not exactly an ego bash, that. I figured that out moments after meeting those dolls.

My own attention began to slip its moorings. Nothing would keep me awake much longer.

The Dead Man continued to spin confusions off all his minds at once.

"You tossing a mental salad, Old Bones?"

*My apologies, Garrett. I was not aware that I was drawing you in. I am trying to identify the missing ingredient. I am reviewing events as reported while sorting the clutter in your head. There must be something you know, although you are unaware that you know it. You would be unaware, in fact, that there is knowledge of which to be aware.*

"You're zigging before I even get the chance to zag, sidekick."

*There has to be something more to this.*

"You've been inside my head. You know I didn't want to hear that. You say nothing is ever what it seems?"

*It never is when I get involved.*

*Actually, I fear that, in this particular case it did indeed start out being what it seems. However, as is often the case with both human and divine endeavors, powerful outside forces and normal social dynamics will force what ought to be simple to become complex and devious.*

I leaned back and swilled me a long, long draft. Dean had bent that much. I had been so ragged when I turned up he hadn't considered arguing over a few beers. Possibly he received some encouragement from the Dead Man. The Dead Man has no interest in whether or not food or drink is good for you.

"At least the original problem is solved."

*Is it?*

"There's no need for anybody to choose between the Shayir and Godoroth. They don't exist anymore."

*Nog is inescapable.*

"Oh, shit!" I gulped air. I had forgotten Nog. Couldn't he wait until I'd gotten some sleep? Then I caught on. "You had me going for a second."

Amused. *I see. I do not indulge in practical jokes, do I?*

"Not too often."

*Consider it a dramatized warning.*

"It *was* you?"

*Reminding you that at least one survivor of the Haunted Circle massacre likely carries a grudge.*

"Wish I could figure out a way to make this all your fault. But all I can think of is I didn't have problems like this before I moved in with you."

Life was simpler in the old days. Not more pleasant, but definitely simpler. Life in the islands had been simpler still, if pure hell.

The Dead Man made a mental noise that sort of implied intense festering disgust. *If the anomaly is there, even I am blind to it. Maybe there is nothing after all. Possibly no one had any real, long-term plans. Self-proclaimed masters of the universe, yet they do everything by improvisation.*

"Tell you the truth, I've never seen any gods whose depth was more than a few pages."

*Clever boy.*

"Yeah. So clever I go out chasing redheads because they look interesting. I'm dead. I can't stay awake another twenty seconds."

*Wait.*

"Come on. It can keep for a few hours."

*The redhead. The shapechanger. Adeth? There is no place for her in the central events.*

"I told you that already. She led me into it but hasn't been around much since. She visited me once—I think it was her—when the Godoroth had me. She didn't make much sense. I saw her once in the Haunted Circle. Maybe one or two other glimpses round and about. Talk to Cat about Adeth. She knows something she won't tell me." I didn't bother to glance at Cat. "I'm gone upstairs. Tell Dean to do whatever he wants with these people."

The beer, while just about the most wonderful liquid I had ever swallowed, had sapped my ability to stay awake.

I met Dean in the hall, headed toward the Dead Man's room. I grabbed a greasy sausage off the platter he carried. I gave him a quick review of what I had told Himself.

I was asleep before my head hit the goosedown.

# 56

I plunged down the well of sleep faster than ever I had without the aid of somebody whapping me on the gourd. Only the well became a tunnel. At its far end an incredible woman waited, radiant in her dark beauty. She extended a taloned hand in welcome, offered green lips for my kiss. A snake winked at me from her hair.

"Not yet, Maggie."

She smiled. The tip of a fang sparkled, though there was no light. Still smiling, she touched my cheek with a forefinger—then raked me with its nail. I felt hot blood on cold skin. It was chilly there, though I had been unaware of that until that moment. Soon it was cold beyond any imagining.

Magodor tugged at my hand. She didn't speak. Words wouldn't carry there. She led me to the tunnel's end, high on the face of an immense black cliff, on a constructed balcony overlooking a vast black lake, facing a city on the far shore, that made TunFaire seem like a pig farmers' village. Some towers had fallen. No light showed. There were no lights anywhere. The sun in the sky shed no light either. Neither did three black moons.

Things swam in that lake and crawled across that landscape and flew in that sky so cold it held no air. They were things like nothing of our world, cold things that ate only the strange rays that wander between the stars, things for whom hope and despair and all other emotions were notions without meaning, utterly beyond comprehension. They were all ancient things, half as old as time, and for an eon they had been trying to escape that cold prison. They were not evil as we conceive of evil. There was no more malice in them than in a flood or earthquake or killing storm. No more than in the man who plows a field and turns up the nests of voles and rabbits and crushes the tunnels of moles.

Yet they were imprisoned. Something had felt obliged to isolate them from the rest of existence. Eternally.

Out in the lake something broke the surface of liquid as thick as warm tar. The light of remote and feeble stars was too weak to provide me a good look. Maybe that was just as well. I did not want a good look at something like that, ever.

I think somebody, possibly in drug dreams, must have seen that place before me. That would explain all those tales of eldritch horrors and unnameable names and unspeakable spooks—though I expect a lot is exaggeration for the sake of extra impact.

I wouldn't want to live in that place either, though.

A glimmering, pale, drowned man's sort of hand reached up from the darkness and grabbed the edge of the balcony. A corpse with pools of shadow for eyes pulled itself up until its empty mouth was level with the platform. It took me a moment to recognize the face, it was so filled with despair. Imar. The All-Father. The Harvester of Souls. Lord of the Hanged Men. Ass-Kicker Supreme.

He extended his other quaking hand toward Magodor, the Destroyer, the Driver of the Spoil, and all that stuff, his Executive Officer and First Assistant Supreme Kicker of Butts.

Magodor stomped his fingers. She put a foot in his face and shoved. So much for company loyalty. Without a sound, Imar twisted and fell into the gulf below.

I started walking back up the tunnel. Magodor stayed beside me a while, smiling up like we were headed home after a perfect date. She was excited. She could not stop shifting shape—although she never drifted far from human.

Maybe we had grown on them over the millennia, too.

Might be worth some speculation. Might have something to do with why they weren't as all-powerful as they wanted us to believe.

I faded out of the tunnel into normal sleep. Normal sleep did not last nearly as long as I would have liked.

Surprise, surprise.

# 57

When first I awakened I was confused. My head hurt. But I hadn't been drinking. There was noise outside in the street. But it was way too early for any reasonable being to be up and about.

Didn't I do this already? Had I been dreaming, and been dreaming dreams within dreams?

It was the same damned racket out there. The same damned bigoted morons trying to start the same damned brickbat party.

I groaned as I tried to get up. My imagination was so good I had bruises and sore muscles.

I just had to try to destroy my eyeballs. I pulled a corner of a curtain back . . . Whoops! They had thrown extra logs onto the fires of the sun this morning, then done away with any clouds that might temper its brilliance. I backed off until my eyes stopped watering and aching. Then I eased into it.

Yep! Same old bunches of fools with too much time on their hands. Same old mischief looking for a place to happen.

Across the street there . . . rooted in exactly the same spot. Exactly the same redhead. Looking right at me, just like before. But this time I knew what she was. Trouble. This time I knew better. This time I wouldn't chase her and let her make a fool of me. I can manage that fine all by myself, thank you.

I felt a slight tingle way back in my mind. The Dead Man was there. I realized he must have been there all night. Meaning maybe he had had a thread connected during my nocturnal adventure. Which suggested that he was very concerned indeed. I tried to give him a good look at the redhead.

As though she realized she was under special scrutiny she sort

of stepped sideways and backward and evaporated into a mob surrounding two women glaring at one another nose to nose. One
was a very short, fat, ugly human woman. The other was a tall,
skinny, beautiful dwarf. They looked like sisters.

Somebody had noticed and made mention of that fact. Somebody had been stirring with a big, big spoon.

A woman left the knot. There was a ghost of a hint of furtive-
ness about her. "That her?"

*Indeed. I am able to follow her by sensing her as a sort of ab-
sence of presence in motion.*

I didn't ask him to explain. I didn't care. I was watching the
wonder of the latter half of our century. Mrs. Cardonlos and her
broom were breaking up the all-female confrontation. She found
the assistance of a public-spirited giantess invaluable.

"Damn me, the old harridan ain't all bad after all. What'll I do
for somebody to hate?"

The Goddamn Parrot squawked on cue.

"Of course. Thanks, Morley."

Mr. Dotes himself was coming up Macunado, his sartorial el-
egance causing a stir all the way. Or maybe that stir was caused by
the grolls accompanying him, a pair of ugly green guys fifteen feet
tall. They had snaggly fangs in their mouths and knobbly clubs in
their hands and raggedy sacks on their shoulders. They were smiling, but a smiling groll looks twice as fierce as a frowning groll.

Grolls are the result of careless dalliances between giants and
trolls. These two came from a single lapse in judgment. They were
brothers. Doris and Marsha by name.

Nobody alive in TunFaire would rag those two about their
names. They are slow of wit and slower to anger, but once they get
started you really don't want to be in the same county.

They were related to Morley in some obscure fashion.

Why was he leading them to my house?

"You still tracking Adeth, Old Bones?" Looking at Doris and
Marsha left me wondering how The Call could take itself seriously. Boys like these could be more trouble than any fool wanted.

*I am. Her movements seem haphazard. Perhaps even aimless.*

"Think she knows you're onto her?"

*Improbable.*

I considered reminding him that *he* was highly improbable,
but now Morley was just fifty feet from my stoop. The grolls were
not his only companions. Several of his old crew, including Sarge,
Puddle, and Dojango Roze, pint-size brother of the grolls, were

with him. All were armed as heavily as the law allowed. All in all, that crowd had barely enough candlepower to light up the inside of a one-hole outhouse, but they had muscle enough to toss the toilet half a mile.

The Dead Man warned Dean. As Morley reached the foot of my steps the Goddamn Parrot went flapping into the morning, turning to follow Adeth. The shiny little buzzard was entirely under the Dead Man's control. He let fall a gift that would have spoiled Morley's splendor in a grand way, but Dotes was far too alert and quick. He eased out of the way.

Chuckling, I dropped the curtain, got myself dressed in something presentable, stumbled downstairs. I had aches and pains everywhere. And my head hurt, too. For nothing. Damn! You get up feeling awful, you ought to at least have had some drinks and fun.

# 58

At the foot of the stair I turned right into the kitchen. Dean wasn't back yet. I snagged a couple of fresh biscuits, broke them open and pasted them with butter, then smeared on great gobs of honey. Then I poured me a mug of tea and put some honey into that. Then I dug out an old teapot and put some water on to heat so I could follow the regular tea with an infusion of willow bark.

Dean returned to the kitchen shaking his head. "I hope he knows what he's doing."

"That pot is for willow bark tea."

"Don't talk with your mouth full. You didn't drink anything last night."

"Just one long one. This pain is from the job."

He frowned suspiciously. "What *is* this job? Nothing honest would pay so much."

He always worries about us getting paid at all. I've never heard him carp about us getting overpaid. "Huh?"

"Mr. Dotes just brought in what looks like a pirates' treasure."

"Argh! And she be a huge un, aye, matey?"

"Too huge."

"Great. I won't have to work for a while."

"Wrong. Mr. Weider requires your help as soon as you clean up this mess."

I sighed, buttered another biscuit. "It's a conspiracy. Everybody thinks I should work. You ever see a cat do anything more than he has to to get by? The world would be a better place if we all took a lesson from the cat."

"Cats don't leave anything for their children."

"Dean, take a quick head count here. How many kids? How many can even have kids? We don't need to give a damn about posterity because we don't have no posterity."

Dean sighed. "Perhaps not. You can't even learn not to talk with your mouth full."

He should have been somebody's mother. He was a worse nag than my mom ever was. He was more determined, too.

"I'll be in there with the rest." I left him.

I visited the front door first and used the peephole to check the stoop. Sure enough, the grolls and Dojango were seated out there, gossiping in grollish. Dojango Roze was Morley's size but claimed he and the grolls were triplets born of different mothers. Morley backed him up. I'd always considered that a bad joke, but after having wallowed in the mythological for a few days I had no trouble imagining one of our religions boasting some dire prophecy about the coming of triplets born of different mothers.

I took one cautious peek into the small front room. No owl girls. Maybe they left with the Goddamn Parrot. I wasn't surprised to see them gone.

I headed for the Dead Man's room. "You put out the Cat?"

*Upstairs asleep.*

The cherub, I noted, remained immobile. And visible. Sarge and Puddle were looking it over. Curious. "And the owls?"

*Gone. Bored. But they will return. I fear they may be so simple they will think of nowhere else to go.*

"That could make life interesting."

*Pshaw!*

"Thought you didn't like cats?" Morley said.

"You know me. Big soft spot for strays."

"Two-legged strays. Of the under twenty-five and female sort."

I turned. "How you hanging, Puddle? Sarge? The new business going all right?"

"Fugginay, Garrett. Only problem is da kind a people ya got ta put up wit'. All dem highfalutin, nose-in-da-air types, dey can be a real pain in da ass."

"Hell, people are the big problem in any line of work."

"Fugginay. 'Specially dem Call guys. Dey's gonna find some a dem cut up inta stew meat . . ."

Morley cleared his throat.

"Fugginay. Boss, you really need us here?" Puddle, doing all the talking, had been keeping one nervous eye on the Dead Man.

The Dead Man can be salt on the raw nerves of folks without clear conscience.

"Wait out front with the Rozes. Try to keep them from getting into another brawl." Dotes shrugged my way. "Every time I turn around some damned human rights fool is starting something with Doris or Marsha."

"Sounds like a problem that will cure itself, given time. Good for the human race, too. Eliminate the stupid blood from the breeding stock."

"There aren't enough grolls and trolls and giants in the world to accomplish that, working full time. I dug up your treasure." He indicated the sacks scattered around us.

It wasn't likely that he'd done any digging with his own hands. These days he was acutely conscious of the line between management and labor.

Just for grins I remarked, "I see you've gotten your share already."

He gave me exactly the look I expected. Little boy caught with hand in cookie jar. Only, "I took some to pay the guys to dig and carry and guard. They don't work for free, Garrett."

Not when they were exhuming a treasure. I was surprised that any of it had made it to my house.

I poked around like I knew what I was doing. Morley couldn't know that I had no real idea of the size of the treasure, or of its makeup.

He said, "Instead of playing games you could ask your partner."

I could. But where was the fun in that? "He's a tenant here, not a partner. Tell you what. Since you've been such a big help I'll see that you get something unique in all TunFaire. Maybe in the whole world."

"I'm not taking the parrot back."

Damn! Everybody is a mind reader anymore.

When he wants to bother, the Dead Man can move stuff with his thoughts. The treasure sacks tinkled and stirred. "Big mice around here." What was he doing?

Morley asked, "What's this all about, anyway? How did you find a treasure right here in town?"

"Eyewitness to the burial told me all about it. It was her way of paying me to do a job." Which, I had to remember, had not been completed to her satisfaction.

Morley didn't believe me. "Those coins are ancient, Garrett."

*There are artifacts here which we dare not market as they are.*

"Huh?"

*There are crowns and scepters and other royal insignia that today's Crown would demand if its agents became aware that they have been recovered.*

"What? Karenta didn't even exist then. Even the Empire was still up the road. It would take some really bizarre legal reasoning to . . ."

*Nevertheless.*

"Of course." Silly me. Logic, right, and justice had nothing to do with it. Royal claims are founded rock solid upon the inarguable fact that the Crown has more swords than anybody else. "You didn't give your guys anything unusual when you paid them?"

Morley shook his head. "I've handled treasures before, Garrett. You need somebody to break that stuff down and move it, I know somebody who'll make you a deal."

No doubt. And he would get a couple points back for steering the fence.

That's the way it works.

I said, "I know people who might be interested in the coinage for its collectible value. How about we just bid out the rest as a lot?"

*Not a good idea. That might put us at risk, as we would be identifiable as the source of the whole. Also, many of these items have value well beyond the intrinsic.*

"But this stuff has been out of sight for ages. Nobody ought to even remember it."

*Put the material under my chair and elsewhere out of sight. Give Mr. Dotes his fee.*

"No need to get testy. I was just ribbing him."

*I am aware of that, as is Mr. Dotes. The cleanup is necessary, as we are about to receive guests who may ask embarrassing questions should those bags be lying about, dribbling coins and bracelets.*

"Huh?" I started slinging sacks. Morley helped, paying himself off as he went. He was not unreasonable about how much he hurt me. "What kind of guests, Chuckles?" Off the top of my head I couldn't think of anybody with nerve enough to push through the group on my stoop just so they could aggravate me by pounding on my door.

But somebody started hammering away.

*Priests,* the Dead Man sent.

Help!

# 59

Not just priests. A whole gang of priests, some of them quite well armed. I looked them over as I let a few come inside, a courtesy they obtained only at the Dead Man's insistence. None of them looked like they were used to the streets. Maybe that explained the numbers and the weapons.

"Who's minding the store, guys? Thieves are going to be carrying off everything but the roof tiles."

A guy so old they must have carried him over squinted. He grunted. He dug inside his cassock till he located a pair of Ten-Hagen cheaters thicker than window glass. He readied them with shaking, liver-spotted hands. Once he got them on, he pushed them away out to the end of his pointy nose, then leaned his head back so he could examine me through them. He grunted again. "You must be Garrett."

His voice was a surprise. It was not an old man's voice. And it belonged to somebody used to telling others what to do. But I didn't recognize him. I had thought I knew the faces of the key people at Chattaree.

"I fear you have me at a disadvantage, Father."

The old man tilted his head farther. "They did say that you are lapsed. Perhaps even apostate."

No argument there. *They* were right. But who were *they*? I had had a brush with the powers at Chattaree, but I'd thought that was forgotten. Maybe not. Maybe all those saints have nothing better to do than to keep track of me and to report me to the priests.

"I am Melton Carnifan." Pause. Grown pregnant before, "Secretary to His Holiness."

"Gotcha, Mel." Yep. A real heavyweight in his own mind. Bishop Melton Carnifan was a power-behind-the-throne kind of guy capable of putting a bug in his boss's ear. They were scared of him inside the Church. Only the Grand Inquisitor and his merry henchmen frightened them more.

Any good religion has to have a really sound foundation of personal terror.

As Brother Melton suggested, I wasn't inside anymore. And today way less than ever before.

I said, "I suppose I should be honored. A whole platoon of you guys just to win me back? No?"

Carnifan smiled. The old man did have a sense of humor, though it was in the same class as silk flowers. No doubt it showed best when he and the Inquisitors were showing heretics the incredible extent of their errors.

"I am entirely indifferent to the welfare of your soul, Mr. Garrett. Your record suggests that the Church would get nothing but grief out of you even if you did reach out for salvation."

No doubt. "I didn't figure you were here to refund my dear mother's tithes." I swallowed any further comment. These guys might not be the big deals they pretended to be or wished they were, but they could still make life miserable. Religion is always a good excuse for unpleasant behavior.

"No, Mr. Garrett. Not at all. No. Actually, His Holiness had a dream. Or a vision, if you will, because he was awake at the time that it actually happened."

"Don't tell me. Saint Strait showed up, slung an arm around the old boy's shoulders, told him he ought to get together with me for a game of backgammon."

The old man's jaw dropped again. I had him going. He huffed and puffed for a couple of seconds. The two younger priests I had let in with him moved closer, maybe to catch him if he collapsed from apoplexy. Neither one actually dared to touch him.

*Bring them in here, Garrett.*

Good idea. "Come with me. We can get off our feet."

They came. Ha.

The Dead Man is impressive first time you see him, even if you know about him. Even if you think you're hot shit yourself. The old man paused a couple of steps inside the doorway, stared. Just to tweek him I said, "Yep. Every single thought. Especially everything you want to hide because you can't help thinking about it now."

*Garrett!*

I ignored the Dead Man, said, "Get to the point, Bishop. I've had a rough few days lately because of the gods. I'm not in a real hospitable mood."

*You have him, Garrett. He is quite rattled. He is very much the sort of creature your cynical side believes all priests to be. However, his disbelief in his own religion's dogma has been seriously rattled. It seems many of the Church's senior people shared the vision of Saint Strait.*

I won the intelligence award with my response. "Wha?"

*Although Bishop Carnifan was sent here, he came principally to satisfy himself that his own disbelief is justified.*

*Ah! He has decided to be straightforward and forthcoming, having realized that it is impossible for humans to lie to the Loghyr.*

Bullhooley. You can lie to a Loghyr any time you want. You just have to know how. And have to be willing to practice on a daily basis.

Bishop Carnifan hobbled to the chair I usually used, lowered himself gingerly. He folded his hands in his lap. He looked the absolute picture of the perfect holy man and he knew it. It was the sort of image cynical priests have cultivated for generations. He intoned, "Kamow. Bondurant. Would you step into the hallway for a moment, please?"

"Sir?"

"I want to consult Mr. Garrett privately."

*He is about to exercise his curiosity.*

I caught the edge of his message to Dean cautioning him that brothers Bondurant and Kamow would be leaving the room and ought not to be allowed to exercise their own curiosity about our domicile.

The door closed behind the last young priest. I told Carnifan, "They're all real. Every last one of them, from the least sprite to the biggest thunderbasher, no matter how ridiculous we've imagined them. But they sure aren't what you priests have been telling the rest of us."

The Bishop's jaw sagged again. He glared at the Dead Man. "Of course." He considered Morley, who leaned against a bookcase and said nothing, just looked like a stylish mannequin. I had, quite intentionally, not introduced him, nor had I explained his presence.

The Dead Man nudged me.

I said, "You want to know what happened last night, eh? You want to hedge some bets by getting the straight skinny from a guy who really has talked to gods? You want to know if there's an angle for you or the Church anywhere in this? I don't blame you. If I was a priest I'd be feeling *real* uncomfortable about now."

The Dead Man decided to have fun with the situation, too. Suddenly I was reliving the highs and lows of recent days as His Nibs sucked them out of me and pounded them right into the Bishop's brain.

He didn't leave out one damned thing. He rooted through my head for every glimpse and nuance, exactly as I had suffered it all, and he put good buddy Bishop Melton Carnifan through it exactly as though he was living it all himself. This time around it lasted only half an hour—and didn't hurt near so bad because I knew I would get through it—but that old boy came out exactly familiar with what it was like to deal direct with TunFaire's swarms of gods.

What a cruel thing to do, even to a man who had been an atheist on the inside.

Morley stood with fingers pinching chin, puzzled, as Carnifan displayed a catalog of changes. The Dead Man had given him nothing.

*Give the Bishop time to get his bearings, Garrett.*

I did so.

Carnifan recovered quickly. His eyes focused. He demanded, "That's really true?"

"Would I make up something that absurd? That's exactly the way it happened."

"I can't go back with that."

"Make something up." He didn't get it. He just looked at me strangely. I asked, "Who's going to believe you?"

Carnifan actually smiled. "Point taken. Nobody is going to want to."

"What did you really want here?"

"Not what you've given me. I didn't believe all that was anything but extremely weird weather. I thought we were just jumping on it to market our product. But now you've convinced me that the gods *do* exist. *All* of them, probably including a lot I've never heard of. But you've also convinced me that that is worse than having no gods at all."

I agreed, privately. "But the belief in what they could be . . . That's a comfort to a lot of people."

"And just the opposite to me. This has been a cruel day, Mr.

Garrett." His eyes glazed momentarily. He asked, "It's not over yet, is it? This shakeout. There are loose ends. There are traces of several conspiracies, some of which may not have run their course."

I rubbed my forehead. I had enjoyed life much more back when my worst worry was how unhappy I had made some crime kingpin. The Bohdan Zhibak returned to mind. Ten thousand shadows had infested those hills. Every single one of those absurdities had to know my name now. I never liked catching the eyes of the lords on the Hill. How much more dangerous would catching the interest of the gods be?

And I had, for certain. Else this sleazeball bishop would not have come visiting. Saint Strait, eh? Spokesman for the Board. Probably as straight as his servant Brother Carnifan. I wondered if every church and temple in the Dream Quarter was bulging with priests experiencing bizarre visions featuring me in some role.

Worse, were they all going to turn up here to hear words of wisdom, like I was some kind of prophet?

"Damn! What an opportunity," I mused aloud. "I could . . ."

Morley and Bishop Carnifan eyed me curiously. The Dead Man sent a mental chuckle. *A pity you do not have an appropriate mind-set. It might be amusing to play the prophet game— particularly if we could arrange continued contacts with these deities.*

I said, "Weider's difficulties are starting to look attractive." I turned to the bishop. "Brother. Father. Bishop. Whatever. I don't want to be rude, but I've had a real rough couple of days and you're not helping anything."

The Dead Man continued to speculate. *Perhaps Mr. Playmate could join us as front man. He has wanted to assume the religious mantle for some time.* My partner was as cynical as I about some things. It seemed that even concrete proof of the existence of gods didn't soften his religious skepticism.

I told Carnifan, "Unless there is something specific I can still do, I really wish you would go away." I softened that with a conspiratorial smile. "And please spread the word in the Dream Quarter. I can't do anything for anybody else, either. Far as I'm concerned, my part in this insanity is over."

*Nog is inescapable.*

I jumped a yard. But the Dead Man couldn't keep a mental straight face.

# 60

Carnifan departed. His gang looked like a small, dark army slithering up Macunado Street. Using the peephole, I watched the redhead watch them go.

"Hey, Old Bones. What was that really all about?"

*The Bishop—and, presumably, many other shakers in the Dream Quarter—erroneously assumed a greater and more favored role for you than was the case. If you examine their position and way of thinking, it should be no surprise that many priests will set new records for conclusion jumping.*

"What?"

*You have been driven into an untenable position. You are dealing with men who, in most institutions, have taken their gods entirely on faith for dozens of generations. Now they are learning that one man's genuine contacts have proven the whole process trivial. The gods, of all stripes, turned out to be small-minded, petty creatures with no more vision or aspiration than most mortals.*

"I never did worry much about being popular."

*Life could get difficult.*

"Hey, I'm a famous cynic. Remember? I can talk, but I can't produce concrete proof. Even if I got some great god like Hano to step up and confess, most true believers wouldn't buy it. You ask me, the great wonder that makes religion work is the fact that otherwise rational beings actually accept the irrational and implausible dogmas underlying them."

*Believers are not a problem. However, those who live off the believers could be—particularly if their continued existence and prosperity depend upon the good will of their believers.*

Morley asked, "What's going on, Garrett?"

We ignored him.

I entered one of my more intellectual remarks. "Huh?"

*The man in the street will be no problem. He has other troubles. Economics and riots are more threatening today. Priests, feeling their livelihoods imperiled, might represent short-term threats, till they understand that we are indifferent . . .*

"Speak for yourself, Chuckles." I'd as soon put them all out of business. The sanctimonious emotional gangsters. I reminded, "Adeth is back across the street."

*Indeed. And the one great tool we need has not yet been invented.*

"Huh?" That was fast becoming my favorite word.

*A godtrap!*

"Ha ha. What did Cat have hidden inside?"

He avoided a direct answer. *That child can be very opaque.*

Morley headed for the door. "I'm not big on being talked around and over. Obviously, I'm not needed here anymore."

*Not entirely true, Mr. Dotes. Exercise patience, if you will, while Garrett and I discuss threats more immediate than any you yourself can help us avert.*

That was sufficiently obscure. Morley donned an air of put-upon patience.

I told him, "You want to break away from The Palms and meet me someplace in keeping with my station, I'll tell you about the whole mess. After we figure out how to keep from getting gobbled up by the loose ends."

Dotes eyed me briefly, some secret smile stirring the corners of his mouth. "It's always the loose ends that get you, Garrett. You particularly because you refuse to take the pragmatic step when you can. You love this grand pretense of cynicism, but whenever you face what you consider a moral choice you inevitably opt for belief in the essential goodness of humanity—however often humanity grinds your nose in the fact that it is garbage on the hoof."

"We all need a moral polestar, Morley. That's how we convince ourselves that we're the good guys. Garbage on the hoof is garbage because somewhere somebody told it it's garbage on the hoof."

"Which, of course, absolves those guys of all responsibility for their own behavior. They don't have to stop and decide before they do something."

Wait a minute. How come the professional bad guy was dish-

ing up the law-and-order arguments? "What's this devil's advocate stuff?"

"Because you try to complicate everything with peripheral
issues."

"I can't help that. It's my mother's fault. She could bitch for
an hour about anybody, but she found the good in everybody, too.
No matter how bad somebody screwed up, she could find an excuse for them."

*This discussion, in one form or another, has been going on for
years. Neither of you has done more than entertain the other with
it. I suggest we not waste time on it. Mr. Dotes. Unless you would
like to assist Mr. Tharpe and Miss Winger . . .*

I lost him there, except for an echo that included Glory
Mooncalled's name. I wished he would forget Glory Mooncalled,
the Cantard war, and all his other hobbies. I wished he would
stick to business, just for a while. Maybe a couple of weeks.
Maybe till we got everything squared away and he could snooze
to his heart's desire while I loafed and experimented with new
strains of beer. Till Dean could spend his days just being inven-
tive in the kitchen, with no need to distress himself answering the
door.

Idly, I wondered how expensive it would be to have a spell cast
so people couldn't find any particular address when they came
looking.

*Nog is inescapable,* the Dead Man reminded me.

"I know. I know. Morley, take your ill-gotten gains and scoot.
Go con the rich johns so they'll pay big money to suck down carrot juice cocktails while gobbling turnip steaks."

Dotes took that opportunity to explain to me, at some length,
how my health and disposition would improve dramatically if I
would just let him set up a dietary plan customized to my peculiar
lifestyle.

"But I like being just plain old crabby Garrett who gorges on
bloody steaks and leaves the rabbit food for rabbits so they get
nice and plump before we roast them."

" 'Crabby' is the key word here, Garrett. You take most of your
vegetable input in liquid form. I'm sorry, beer just doesn't contain
enough essential fiber, which you have to have to . . ."

"Yeah. I know you get plenty of fiber because you're full of it
up to your ears."

He offered a mock two-finger salute and a thin smile. "Like I said. Crabby." He asked the Dead Man, "Did you have something for me? Or not?"

Old Chuckles did, in fact, have a lot to talk over with Morley, but it had no bearing on the problem at hand. I would not have stayed around at all if it hadn't had to do with my future, too.

# 61

Morley was gone. After five thoughtful minutes I asked, "You really think the troubles might get that bad?"

*They are barely into their infancy now and people are dying every day. Glory Mooncalled appears to be contributing by neglect, if not by plan.*

"You're determined to have him here in town, aren't you?"

*There is no doubt whatsoever that he is either in the city or somewhere close by. You came close to him last week.*

"Why?"

He could see my thoughts. He understood the question.

*Glory Mooncalled has betrayed no lack of confidence in his own abilities. About that all respondents always agree. Nor do they disagree that he has only disdain and contempt for the various persons who manage the Karentine state. He knows only those he encountered in the Cantard. And in the Cantard he did learn to respect the overwhelming force that lords and wizards could bring to bear—by direct experience. He believes it will be an entirely different game in TunFaire.*

"I got a feeling maybe friend Mooncalled is gonna run into a couple of surprises here." Here at home not all our functionaries are people who inherited their jobs, nor are all of them so enchanted with their own importance that they do nothing but polish their images.

*Exactly.* The Dead Man was still tapped into my mind. *And there is every possibility that someone like Relway may be the real best hope for averting complete chaos.*

"You think Glory Mooncalled might *want* to precipitate such a state?"

*Perhaps. As I observed, he suffers from no lack of confidence. And he is aware that he has been something of a folk hero here, in the past. He might believe that ordinary Karentines will proclaim him their savior if things turn bad enough.*

Which is really what happened in the Cantard during the war. The native tribes, tired of generations of being caught between two vicious, corrupt, inept empires, had fallen in behind Glory Mooncalled.

Hell, Glory had been a hero of mine because he had bucked the ruling classes and had shown no tolerance for corruption or incompetence. Without Mooncalled there would have been no victory in the Cantard. No one, from the King to the least trooper, would deny that—though different interpretations can be placed upon the exact nature of his role in the triumph. He has no friends on high. And guess who pays the salaries of the guys who are going to write the histories of the great war?

"I wouldn't like to think that he would be that cold-bloodedly, blatantly manipulative."

*He has little more love for the Karentine aristocracy than he did for the Venageti.*

Coldly and systematically, practically from the moment he had come over to our side, Glory Mooncalled had embarrassed, humiliated, and eliminated a parade of Venageti generals, wizards, and lords who had abused his dignity.

"Could it be that this man who never guesses wrong has, just marginally, misinterpreted the Karentine character?"

*He has, without a doubt. Karentines are inordinately fond of their Royals and aristocrats—although you murder them with alarming frequency.*

Actually, they murder one another. We have some outrageously bizarre revolutionaries on the streets these days, but I have never heard even the most deranged suggest that we dispense with the monarchy.

*I have heard the suggestion, though. Only from nonhumans. And guess who is the one big lump really sticking in the craw of the mob already?*

*Miss Winger and Mr. Tharpe are due here soon, should you be interested in an update on Glory Mooncalled's latest efforts.*

"Tell you the truth, I'm a whole lot more interested in the activities of certain gods and goddesses who may save us the trouble of having to survive your coming troubles."

Reluctantly, the Dead Man admitted that that might be a more immediate concern.

"Can you read Adeth at all?"

*Only her presence and general location.*

"If I get her in here, can you do anything with her?"

He didn't answer for a while. I was about to nudge him when he offered, *What good is nerve if you do not employ it?*

# 62

I peeked through the peephole. Adeth continued her vigil. My estimation of the gods continued its decline. This one did not seem omniscient enough to know when she was being observed by a mortal.

Maybe she didn't believe that that could be done. Conviction leaves us all with huge blind spots.

"What are you doing?"

I jumped. "Don't sneak up like that."

Dean glowered. Somehow, he was a lot less diffident than he had been before he had discovered that he could get a niece married without me—either as victim or as co-conspirator. And he was just a tad too confident of his employment here.

"I've been thinking, Dean. It might just be worth doing my own cooking to be able to get into my house whenever I want."

"Excuse me?"

"I've been thinking. And one worry that came up was, what do I do if the Dead Man decides to take a nap right before you have one of your paranoid seizures and go berserk with all your locks and chains? Here I come, dead on my feet, looking forward to ten hours in the sack. But he's snoring, you're off to bed, and there's enough iron holding the door to drag a groll to the bottom of the river. Wahoo! I get to spend the rest of the night on the stoop because I can't get into my own house. Seems to me it would be worth doing my own cooking to avoid that inconvenience."

I peeked again, while Dean struggled to invent a new line of excuses. The redhead hadn't moved. I didn't see the Goddamn

Parrot. I crossed my fingers. Two good omens. Maybe my luck was turning.

*Slip out the back. See if she can be approached unexpectedly. I will keep watch and inform you of any changes while you maneuver.*

"Right." I peeked once more, while Dean still sputtered. The Dead Man had allowed him to listen in because his help would be critical if I were to depart via the back. We undertake that means of egress in extreme circumstances only, it ordinarily being our intent to have the bad boys think there is just one way to get in or out. "Oh my. Here comes your company, Old Bones."

Saucerhead and Winger were coming up the street. Some strange half-breed, all white bony knees and elbows, skipped along between them. He grinned like somebody had promised him a hundred marks. He wore tan leather shorts and a vile green shirt. I'd never seen the look before.

I wondered what had become of their earlier accomplice, Morley's man Agonistes.

*There is no end to the demands of the living once you allow them the slightest opening.* Like them coming here wasn't his idea. *Dean, please get Garrett out of here. Garrett, sneak up on her, see if she can be surprised, then bring her to me.*

"Suppose she don't want to come?"

*Then you will have to resort to your usual charm. Let confidence and a boyish smile be your tools just this one more time.*

Well, I did come up with the idea originally, but . . . He was possessed of the misapprehension that anytime I want I can grin and hoist an eyebrow and great ladies and maybe even goddesses will melt. At least he pretends to believe it, maybe because he thinks that forces me to live up to his expectations.

I could sense him chuckling to himself as he nudged Dean to rush me off so he could be at the front door when Saucerhead and his companions arrived. But there is no hurrying when it comes to getting out the back. If it was easy, folks from the street would come in to do their shopping. Winger and Saucerhead would be thoroughly peeved before Dean got to them. And Winger isn't big on coddling people's feelings. I hit the alley smiling, even greeted a couple of self-employed ratmen with pleasant greetings. They responded suspiciously, not because they knew me but because of the current social climate.

I jogged down to Wizard's Reach, cut across to Macunado, looked uphill toward the house. I couldn't see the redhead. I crossed Macunado and found myself a slice of shade miraculously free of tenants. It was early still, but it was warm. It promised to be a blistering day.

Chatter on the street was all about the night's bizarre weather, the devastation, the strange things seen prowling and brawling. There was still plenty of snow in areas where the scrap had turned bitterest. There were witnesses who thought we faced the end of the world. Others were sure TunFaire was about to be punished for its wickedness. And, of course, a variety of entrepreneurs were taking advantage of the windfall.

Just goes to prove no wind is an ill wind for everyone.

I had my breath back. I rose on tiptoe, tried to spot Adeth. I had no luck, but that might have been just because the crowd was so thick.

The Goddamn Parrot dropped in out of nowhere, smacked down on my shoulder, staggered me. Several people nearby jumped. He startled them even more when he squawked, "Why are you just standing here?"

"I don't see her."

"She has not moved an inch. Get on with it. I need to free up another mind to deal with Miss Winger."

A long, lean, ratty character with the look of the born hustler eyed the bird. "How much ya want for dat crow?"

"Ha! Walk with me, my man. Let us negotiate." As I stared I glimpsed a wild spray of red hair tossing in the breeze. "Start by making me an offer." Try any number greater than zero. I'll lie to Morley. Poor Mr. Big. A hero! He flew into a burning building to waken sleeping babies.

I guess I was too eager. The mark grew suspicious. "I get it. You're one a dem ventrical twisters and dat's yer con. Sellin' talkin' birds."

"He has your number, Garrett. Whawk!" There is nothing quite like the sound of a parrot snickering.

"I'd drink a beer to show him it's really you who does all the talking for both of us, but then you wouldn't say a word just to spite me."

I caught another glimpse of red hair. She was exactly where I had seen her last, but obscured by windrows of taller people.

My new friend told me, "Be worth somethin' ta me ta learn dat trick. How you get it ta move its beak like dat?"

"You take a strand of spider silk and tie it around his little bird balls. You run it down your sleeve. You tie it to your pinky, which you wiggle whenever you want him to move his mouth."

"Hey! Slick." Then he realized that he was being put on. He suggested I engage in an act of self-admiration physically impossible for most of my species and then flung himself into the crowd. He was so irritated he lost his concentration and moments later became involved in a scuffle when he tugged a purse a tad too hard and numerous dwarves began to admonish him with cudgels.

"Please move faster, Garrett. That could be the seed of another riot."

He was right. Already some humans were wanting to know why dwarves were abusing their brother. If they were the sort who believed dwarves deserved to be robbed just for being dwarves, the fur would fly.

# 63

I scrambled up a stoop on the south side of Macunado, opposite my own, trying for a better look at Adeth. At that moment a very large fellow, who had some nonhuman in him from several generations back, broke up the developing melee. He asked what happened to start it. People shut up when he said he wanted to hear the dwarves' story first. Something about him suggested secret police. Nobody argued with Relway's men. By the time I'd gotten a look at Adeth and plotted my course, the big guy had allowed the dwarves to go back to pummeling the cutpurse. Everyone else just stood around watching justice take its course.

As I descended the steps a wiseass neighbor asked, "What you supposed to be now, Garrett? Some kind a pirate?"

"Argh! Shiver me timbers. Keelhaul the blighter."

I slipped into the press before further distraction could develop.

Being taller than most people and now closer, I found it easier to keep Adeth's position fixed. Of course, she didn't move. And there seemed to be an island of stillness around her. Nobody saw her, but nobody tried to walk through her. Everybody gave her a foot and a half of clearance.

I stayed as far to the side of the street as I could. Stoops and stairwells down to low-level apartments got in my way. Beggars and homeless people had mats and blankets spread in odd shady corners, as did small businessmen who dealt in trinkets of dubious provenance. How much worse would it be on the commercial streets? Macunado is just a meandering trafficway passing through an area that is mostly residential.

Something stirred in a shadow beside me, suddenly. Something stung my left cheek. A woman in front of me, headed my way, flung a hand to her mouth and shrieked. I touched my cheek.

It was bloody.

Magodor occupied the shadow. She smiled as she tasted a razor-sharp fingernail. "Tokens of love," I muttered. I shook out a grubby handkerchief. I might end up with a scar. I could claim it was a saber wound. I could make up a story about a duel in defense of a virgin princess's honor . . . Nobody would believe that. All the women I know are neither.

The Goddamn Parrot squawked, "I'm blind. Talk to me."

"Magodor just ambushed me," I said. "You read me?"

"Only the bird." The Goddamn Parrot took off, putting distance between himself and risk before Magodor understood that he was more than decoration. Seconds later Winger and Saucerhead burst out my front door, descended the steps part way, paused in a stance that meant they were harking back to the Dead Man. Dean stepped out behind them, holding the door open.

The cavalry was on the scene, but there wasn't much it could do.

Magodor laughed, though not cruelly. She was amused.

I slowed but kept moving. Only steps away now. Adeth looked like she was in a trance. Or on weed. Which reminded me. We still had a banger-loving cherub in the Dead Man's room, solid as an ugly hunk of rock, visible to anyone who looked.

I felt a vague brush. His Nibs was trying to reach me. His touch was being turned away.

Maggie laughed again.

I took Adeth's hand. She did not respond. I slipped an arm around her waist. Had I been snookered again? People passing tried not to stare at the goofball dancing with air.

"Is that some kind of mime, Momma?"

Adeth started. "Easy," I pleaded, before she did anything I would regret. "I just want you to come over to the house for a minute."

People gaped.

"Momma, mimes aren't 'sposed to talk."

Could you make a goddess visible by tossing paint on her? I wondered.

Adeth didn't speak. She flickered, though. People jerked their heads, having caught something from the corners of their eyes. A ripple spread, the old TunFairen sixth sense for the strange or dangerous. Open space expanded around me.

Maggie laughed yet again, softly, behind me. She was having fun. I told her, "Come on, darling. You're invited, too."

"Momma, who is the mime man talking to?"

Momma didn't want to know. Momma just wanted to get on down the street. Not that that was likely to position her more securely in regard to TunFaire's weirdnesses. Things were strange everywhere, and bound to get stranger.

"Wonderful. I've wanted to see your place," Maggie said, accepting my invitation. That both astonished and frightened me. What the hell? What was I in for now?

She came up and slipped under my free arm. She flickered, too. I got the impression some people caught glimpses from straight on. The open area expanded rapidly.

And, of course, Mrs. Cardonlos was out on her stoop to observe everything.

Winger and Saucerhead sort of oozed down to street level and out of the way. I think Dean really wanted to slam and bolt the door. As he was about to surrender to temptation, a pair of owls swooped down and changed over right there, without bothering not to be seen. He went catatonic in mid-motion.

Magodor went angry.

Saucerhead and Winger went away, as fast as their heels and toes would shuffle. I have no idea what became of their funny-looking friend.

# 64

"Maggie. Maggie! Darling! Nobody, not even the loveliest goddess, ever learned anything with her mouth open."

"You are insolent beyond all tolerance, Garrett."

"Yeah. Show me where I've got a lot to lose. I'm not on anybody's side. Never have been. But I can't make any of you gods accept that. I don't care any more about your survival than you do about mine. Since everything I do offends somebody, why should I worry about it? Come on and join the Garrett zoo."

Dean forced the door open wider as we mounted the steps, but he did not look at us. His whole attention was on the shadows in the hallway. I told him, "You want to drool, you ought to see Star."

Magodor spat, "She's a moron."

"It isn't her mind that precipitates salivation."

"I am aware of how males see these things."

On my other hand, Adeth seemed to regain the lost spark of life. Suddenly Dean could see her.

He did not lose interest in the owl girls, but he was distracted. A redhead will do that to the most stouthearted of men.

I said, "Sometimes daydreams come true." He would recognize Adeth as a close approximation of my perfect fantasy woman. "And some nightmares do, too." Because Magodor suddenly chose to materialize in one of her more unpleasant forms.

Dean said, "I'll make tea," and headed for the kitchen.

I returned to the door long enough to get the Goddamn Parrot inside. He was perched on the railing out there, reciting poetry. I have trouble enough with the neighbors.

Magodor eyed Adeth warily but behaved herself. I guided

them into the Dead Man's room, though I had no idea what good this would do.

Cat was there already, a recovered Fourteen in her lap, shaking. Magodor seemed surprised. "Who is she?" The cherub she recognized, at least by tribe.

The Dead Man touched me weakly. *Bring the Shayir girls, Garrett. Ladies, if you please, a little less intense.*

Like the Loghyr said, what good is nerve if you don't use it?

I went to the small front room. The owl girls cowered in a corner, too frightened to try a getaway. Maggie must be a real smouldering bitch.

Guess you don't pick up a nickname like The Destroyer because you fudge at marbles.

"Come with me, girls. Calmly. No need to be scared. We're just going to talk."

One—Dimna, I think—tried to run. I caught her, held on, patted her back. She settled right down. I opened an arm, and the other came for a hug. They really were simple.

The followers of the Shayir pantheon must have been pretty simple themselves.

Hell, I think No-Neck said they were lowest common denominator back when we were field-testing the Weider product. Or was that the Dead Man? Did it matter?

"It'll be all right," I promised the girls. I didn't mind seeing Imar and Lang plop back into the Black Lake of Whatsis, but to condemn similarly these two would be too cruel. The world could use more happy gods and goddesses.

I yelled, "Dean! Bring beer for me."

Dean came from the kitchen as I held the Dead Man's door for the girls. He had a big pot of tea, several mugs, and all the side stuff. The water must have been on. My beer was there. With backup. He told me, "I thought you *might* need fortification." He could not keep his eyes off the girls. His tray started to shake.

"That's an understatement."

Dean started to ask something but then saw Magodor trying to intimidate everyone with one of her nastier looks.

"Maggie, knock it off!" I snapped before I thought. "No wonder you guys worked your way down to the strong end of the Street. You had a stupid boss, yeah, but I haven't seen much to recommend the rest of you, either. Cat! Stop shaking. That cup belonged to my mother. It's about the last thing of hers I have left."

The Dead Man managed to slide in, *What are you doing?*

# 65

I was trying to break everybody's mental stride. If they were off balance they might think instead of just reacting.

It worked. Sort of.

Everybody stopped to gawk at me.

I said, "We came close to disaster last night. Because of stupidity and thoughtlessness. Imar and Lang nearly cost us the wall between this world and the darkness. The goddesses who set them up didn't show any forethought, either. It shouldn't have taken any genius to anticipate their behavior. Magodor, you never seemed stupid. When you maneuvered the ladies so they would manipulate the males . . ."

*Garrett.*

I was on a roll. I didn't want to hear from anybody yet.

"No," Magodor snapped.

*Garrett, I fear it may be less simple than you think, complex as that is.*

"Huh?"

Cat, Fourteen, and the owl girls contributed silence. I expected nothing more. Adeth, though, was turning out to be an unexpected zero.

*The Adeth creature is no goddess, Garrett. I can read nothing there. And this is for the very good reason that there is nothing there.*

"What?" It was me off balance now.

*This Adeth is a construct. A golem or dibbuk, if you will, here specifically to catch your eye. We should get it out of the house. Its ultimate purpose may be more sinister.*

I slipped my arm around the redhead's waist. I tried to lead her
away.

Nope. Nothing doing. All of a sudden that little bit had the inertia of a pyramid.

"Cat. You know something about Adeth. You'd better let us
know." I watched Magodor. Near as I could tell, she was unaware
of what the Dead Man had sent me.

*She cannot read me at all. I cannot get through to her. Pre-*
*sumably the dibbuk is blocking me.*

Cat did not respond immediately.

I relayed the Dead Man's observations. The owl girls developed cases of the sniffles. Magodor considered Adeth. "Interesting. You were trying to get rid of her?"

"Yeah."

Magodor seemed to vibrate. A baby thunderclap announced
Adeth's departure. "She is in the street again."

"Do you know anything about Adeth?"

"She was someone Imara knew. I never heard of her before
Imara organized the plot to rid us of Imara and Lang and the others. She had no trouble making herself visible to mortals and
could change her appearance quickly. Her only direct part was
supposed to be to bring you to us, making Abyss, Daiged, and
those think she might be one of the Shayir."

Cat said, "Mother got the whole plot idea from Adeth."

Did that make Maggie sit up? You betcha. Me, too.

"How long ago?" I asked. "Cat, I don't think you were any accident. You were created deliberately so your mother could assume . . ."

"Stop."

"I'm sorry. But . . ."

"Just stop."

"Plausible," Magodor observed. "Very plausible. Assuming
she feared someone very powerful, a mortal identity would be a
good place to hide."

"Please stop."

*Adeth.*

"Who or what is Adeth? It's very important."

"She was my mother's friend. I don't know. Maybe even her
lover. She had a lot. When Imar wasn't looking. Adeth was just always around, ever since I was little. She never even noticed me."

Magodor snapped, "Where is your mother now? Where is the
real Adeth?"

"I don't know. I've been here."

I heard Dean scoot along the hallway. The front door opened, then slammed. "What the hell?"

*The bird. I had him put out.*

"Good. Find him a cat to play with." I asked Magodor, "What do you know about Adeth?"

"Nothing. The name was new to me when Imara said we would use her to manage you. Her plot had many friends."

"How many of you are there? You really don't know everyone in your racket?"

"No, I don't. No one has any idea how many thousands or what kinds of us came across in the great migration. There's never been any reason to know. Do you know everyone in this great sump of a city?"

No. Of course not. I don't even know everybody on my block. People come and go. But that was different. Wasn't it? I wasn't in the Three-O racket. Nobody expected omniscience, omnipotence, or omnipresence from me.

Petty pewter, No-Neck. Petty pewter. All of them.

The more I had contact with them, the smaller the gods seemed. Maybe the poet was right about familiarity breeding contempt.

*Garrett. The dibbuk has decided to return. Or has been instructed to do so.*

Whichever, a tremendous crash came from the front of the house. A moment later Dean and the Goddamn Parrot both started exercising their voices in protest.

I told Magodor, "It came back."

# 66

Magodor tossed the goddess-golem back into the street. "I'm not strong enough to push it any farther." She was surprised.

The dibbuk headed for the house again.

People were aware that something weird was happening. The street was clearing fast.

I whimpered about the damage to my door until I saw smug Mrs. Cardonlos staring, grinning because she'd just found fresh ammunition to use in her campaign to condemn me.

"What do you think, Old Bones?"

*Wholly on an intuitional level, I suspect we would find no Adeth—not this Adeth—on any roll of gods.*

Intuition, for him, is filling gaps in already chancy information webs by applying his several minds. He is very good at filling gaps with plausible and possible gossamers. But he won't betray his thinking until he has everything nailed down, beyond dispute. He hates being wrong way more than he hates being dead.

"You're that sure? That you'll tell me now?"

*No. There is a matter of probabilities and risks and their comparative magnitude. If I am correct, time wasted filling the remaining gaps is time we can ill afford to waste. Particularly now that the villains must face the possibility that I suspect the truth.*

Only the Dead Man would think enough of himself to fancy himself a threat to the gods.

"Better come out with it, then."

*Relay this. I cannot reach the others all at once.*

"Listen up, folks. His Nibs has a big story coming out."

*The Adeth dibbuk was created specifically as an instrument by which you could be manipulated, Garrett. You were chosen because you were certain to become a focus for conflict. You were intended and expected to become a continuous provocation.*

"Little old me? Broke their hearts, didn't I?"

*Enough, Garrett. Listen. You can do your tongue exercises later.*

The reprimand seemed to get through to everyone else.

*Behind the contest for the last place on the Street of the Gods, behind the feminist schemes of Imara and her allies in several pantheons, beyond even Magodor's secret ambition to anoint herself the senior power of a grim new all-female religion, there has been a manipulator whose sole mission has been to provoke clashes like those at the Haunted Circle.*

*Wait!* he snapped as Magodor started to snarl something in reply.

*The ultimate cause behind the conflict is not that animating Imara and her sisters, Garrett. You told me that numerous gods not of Godoroth or Shayir provenance joined the fighting. But there is no reason they should have favored one cause above another. Revenge amidst confusion, of course, makes sense. But they would have needed to be primed and ready for sudden opportunity. Having followed the road this far, the questions I come up against are Who? and Why? And the why comes easier than the who.*

"I'll bite," I told him. Magodor and the owl girls, even Cat and Fourteen, were intrigued, too.

*Your dream, in which Magodor showed you the home of the gods, indicates that at some level it is possible to communicate between this world and that. I am going to strut out onto a limb now. I am going to postulate that the Great Old Ones over there have seduced someone here into opening the way. He or she has failed a few times. Another effort will be imminent. Even the dullest conspirator would have to be concerned that enough random evidence is loose to suggest the truth to anyone interested enough to put the pieces together. Add the fact that I am known to be involved, and desperate measures are sure to follow.*

The Dead Man lacks nothing in his confidence in his own significance.

I thought maybe he was reaching a little, but I couldn't think of any reason to reject his big picture. It did not contradict any known facts, nor did I notice any left over. That wasn't the case with any of my theories.

"Maggie?"

"Garrett, I weary of your familiarities. But I will restrain my ire. There may be substance to what you say. It illuminates many strangenesses of recent times." She became introspective. Her appearance deteriorated. She developed a bad case of too many arms and fangs. Body odor began to be a problem, too.

I started to say something. She raised a hand. "Wait." She thought some more. "I cannot guess who is at the center. But I am sure that someone knows or soon will know whatever the Adeth thing learned here. There will be an effort to silence us."

Oh boy. What a promotion. I always wanted to be the dot at the center of a really big target. "Ah . . ."

"Word must be spread, even if it isn't believed. Fast. Everywhere, like a tree spreading a million seeds. So that one takes root somewhere. You. You. You." She seized the owl girls and Fourteen. She glared into their eyes. They shuddered, whimpered, disappeared. For an instant I feared Magodor herself might be the mole of darkness.

"I scattered them, Garrett. Sent them to deities I know well, armed with tokens guaranteeing that I sent the message. I asked for help, too. I will stay here. Adeth will come here."

"I applaud your confidence."

"I am Magodor the Destroyer. I deal in violent confrontation."

"I know, but . . ."

"Reinforcements will be welcome."

"Witnesses, too."

I looked at the Dead Man. He sent, *I am trying to fathom the identity of the traitor. There is insufficient evidence.*

I relayed that to Magodor, said, "There isn't any evidence. But at this point I don't think it much matters. We just don't turn our backs on anybody who might be a holy shapeshifter."

In a tiny voice Cat suggested, "It must be my mother."

I hadn't seen a lot of Imara, but I felt comfortable saying, "No. She isn't smart enough."

The Dead Man offered his own opinion. *Not impossible, Garrett. If the genuine Imara has been displaced. You said it yourself. Adeth is a shapechanger.*

I saw something then. "The plan wouldn't have been for Imara to replace Cat. It would've been for Adeth to. Cat has a real history, even if it's been secret. And a mortal is easier to do away with and dispose of. Cat's demigoddess nature would cover a lot of questions about her replacement being odd. And the whole imposture would only have to last till the breakthrough came."

My guesses meant it had to be an old, old plot, reaching back for decades, always pointed toward the moment when pantheons like the Godoroth and Shayir could be brought into conflict. But the gods have time to unwind protracted schemes.

Cat was in a bad spot emotionally. I was willing to bet that she'd entertained similar suspicions for quite a while. Like everyone dealt a cruel hand, she had trouble facing the truth squarely.

The tears started. I held her. She shook violently with the hurt, with the grief.

# 67

*We do not know that Imara was lost.*

"Doesn't matter, though. If we've guessed right."

*No.*

"You feel Magodor?" Old sweet and deadly had vanished while I was getting Cat settled.

*She is all around us. I have a better sense of her inner being now that she is not incarnate.*

"For some reason that don't sound good."

He avoided the implicit question about the nature of the soul of a goddess. Such a goddess! *She is troubled. There has been no response to her messages. She fears they were intercepted.*

It could not have been more than ten minutes, but, "Shit!" I don't swear a lot, but I don't make last stands against hordes of male-bashing goddesses very often, either. And that is what I expected. All Imara's pals would turn up to put the last seal on their triumph. "It was nice knowing you, Old Bones. Once in a while. We'd better get Dean out of here." I didn't see any reason for them to be after him. He didn't know anything.

*Make haste.*

I went into the kitchen. Dean was boiling water for more tea. But it was just boiling. He was terrified, trying to cope by working to rote. "Go to one of your nieces' places, Dean. Now. Don't stop to pack. Don't stop to do anything. Just put the pot down and get out."

He looked at me, jaw frozen. He must have overheard and guessed enough.

Too bad. He'd been a religious man.

"Now, Dean. There's no time for anything else." I gripped his shoulder, shook him gently. His eyes unglazed. He moved, but without much speed. "Hurry!"

There were people in the street when I let him out, but only the most daring souls. There was a crackling sense of expectancy out there. I saw no sign of the Adeth golem.

Mrs. Cardonlos seemed positively orgiastic, so eager was she for the gathering shitfall to head my way. Someday I need to take time out to figure why she has so much bile for me.

I waved, tossed her a kiss.

*That will help.*

"Nothing will help. Might as well have fun with her." Considering what could be headed our way, Mrs. Cardonlos' displeasure wasn't particularly worrisome.

The light began to take on a strange quality. It went to a dark butter tone and on to butterscotch.

"What's happening, Old Bones?"

*Magodor is forming herself into a protective dome.*

Sweet, sweet Maggie. I never had a bad thought about you, darling.

She was just in time. As Mrs. Cardonlos began to glower nervously at whatever she saw from her vantage, and as the handful of folks in the street hastened to correct their error, a lightning bolt struck from the cloudless sky. It ricocheted, crisped down the street scant yards from my irksome neighbor, spent itself on the lightning rod of a small apartment building.

Its sparkle had not yet died when a humping lump of darkness appeared, coming down Macunado. *Nog is inescapable.* Just in case I had forgotten.

"Gods damn."

*Easy.*

"He's not alone." All the Shayir females except Black Mona accompanied him, as did that flutter of black leaves. Quilraq had not been lost at Bohdan Zhibak. I chuckled. Today Mrs. Cardonlos could see them, too.

*Lila and Dimna got through.*

I glanced down Macunado's slight grade. Dean was still visible, but he was wasting no time. I wished he would turn into a side street and get out of sight.

He staggered as something flashed past. An instant later,

Jorken materialized in the middle of Macunado. He trailed a mist that gathered itself to become Star. She certainly bugged Mrs. Cardonlos' eyes.

The Godoroth and Shayir ignored one another. The air crackled as Magodor communicated with everyone. My head began to hurt.

"Old Bones, how come Star and the Shayir girls are here? Weren't they part of Imara's plot?"

Another lightning bolt ricocheted and racketed around.

*In Star's case, Imara probably was not willing to trust so shallow a mind. With regard to the Shayir, the question deserves close scrutiny. Obviously, Lang was slated for disposal. Black Mona remained loyal and shared his fate. Therefore one or more of . . .*

Whatever he sent I repeated aloud. As I said "Therefore . . ." small hell broke loose. Paving geysered amidst the Shayir. A frosty brick fell at my feet. One female surrendered immediately. I got the feeling, on that level where pain was gnawing its way into my head, that she accepted Magodor's accusations and wanted to change sides. She was a spring-type goddess, into renewal and that sort of thing.

Another, darker sort ran for it. Nog whooped, *Nog is inescapable* and took off after her. I sensed an old animosity.

Minutes of quiet followed. There was nobody in the street but gods. Each time I glanced in a new direction, I saw that more had appeared. I didn't recognize many, but I was pleased. Somewhere, somehow, Lila, Dimna, Fourteen, and now Jorken were getting the message out. The owl girls must really have been concentrating.

A fusilade of lightning ripped the neighborhood. Not one bolt did any damage.

"Maggie, Maggie, I love you," I said. "Just keep going this way. Passive and controlled."

Apparently she did understand that this was no time to let herself be provoked into drawing energy from the other side. And I could sense that she was trying to get that message across to the gathering crowd.

Gargoyles settled onto neighboring rooftops. Things with no name floated on the wind. Shapes almost human gathered in the street. Shapes not human moved among them, some bigger than mammoths.

Mrs. Cardonlos saw them all. Nothing was going to intimidate her into going inside.

A massive bombardment began. The temperature dropped

swiftly. The wind rose. Clouds formed. Rain fell. Soon it became sleet.

And then it stopped, sharp and sudden as a knife slash.

The sun came out. Shadows scampered across the city.

Word had reached the big guys in the high end of the Dream Quarter. The air throbbed with their irritation. Their hands moved. Messages went out like puffy cloudlets, spinning off truths to Adeth's dupes. Wherever they fell, something happened. Each happening I sensed as a slight turning of the tide.

Those top guys were near Three-O.

A wobbling lump rolled into sight. Triumphantly, it announced, *Nog is inescapable.*

Good old Nog. I hoped he didn't think he still had a contract on me.

*The pain.*

Damned right, the pain. There was pain enough for seven hells.

Cat came outside. She stared in awe. Gods filled the street. They perched on rooftops and flew through the air and clung to balconies. They wore every size and shape ever conjured by the imagination of man. And they kept coming, most now females who seemed chagrined and eager to make amends.

There was one truly huge difference between here and the Haunted Circle, where they'd all been farther away. Here they smelled. Awful. Apparently not many ever bathed their physical avatars.

"All-smelling" isn't usually listed among the divine attributes, is it?

The pain began fading. The really big guys started going back to their cribbage games or whatever filled their time. The sense was that it was all over but the weeping. Only a handful of villains were unaccounted for. Hardly any of those would dare be so recidivist as to actually stick to a plot to bring the Great Old Ones across.

I even spotted Imara amidst the crowd, looking seriously sheepish as she came toward the house.

I nudged Cat, pointed. "All's well that ends well."

# 68

Cat started forward. I caught her arm. "There's still no reason to let those guys know about you." Many were the sort who didn't mind erasing mistakes.

In the back of my aching head I wondered if I had any chance to survive this thing.

Fourteen fluttered down to perch on a rail post. The Goddamn Parrot flapped around above the god mob. It looked like he was following Imara, but that made no sense till Cat, staring, said, "That's not my mother." She eased back behind me.

*Get inside fast, Garrett.*

I whirled and dove. Fourteen hit me in the back in his own sudden desire to be anywhere but out there. Cat and I rolled around in a tangle of limbs. Thunder barked, drowned out imaginative remarks by the Goddamn Parrot. Lightning struck the remains of hinges and locks in and around the remnants of my door. Splinters flew. Wood smoke filled the entryway. I separated myself from Cat, cursing. Good doors are expensive. As Cat rose, I swatted her behind to get her moving. I could make no tracks with her in my way.

The very air reddened with rage as Magodor realized she had been caught flat-footed. I yelled, "No!" for whatever good it might do. Even as I tried to keep from drizzling down my leg in terror, one screwball part of my mind wondered if I could sue some Dream Quarter temple for damages. Your mind goes weird places under stress.

A blow hit like an earthquake, banged me off the wall, spun me around, dropped me to my knees. I clung to the bones of my doorframe with one hand. It felt like all the air was being sucked out of the house.

Uh . . . Well. Maybe all the air was being sucked out of Tun-Faire.

There was a hole in the air out there, halfway between my place and the Cardonlos homestead. The hole was fifteen feet across. It gave you a tourist's-eye view of that huge black city on the other side, along with a gang of characters distinguished mainly by festoons of tentacles. They galumphed in mad circles while what had to be a raging hot wind blasted across their treacle lake, blowing harder than any hurricane. All sorts of trash and loose whatever was whipping through that hole.

The big boys got busy doing a little trash duty. A few unfortunates suddenly found themselves deported to the old country. Despite the howl of the wind, I heard Mrs. Cardonlos' bellow of rage when part of her roof pulled away and ran off to visit another world. She was far too damned solid to go there herself.

She would become impossible now.

Look on the bright side, Garrett. The Goddamn Parrot was outside when the big guys opened that interdimensional oublictte. That damned talking chicken had to be over there where they deserved him.

Gah! He might take over and do a better job breaking through next time.

"Gather up all the ratmen," I muttered to the wind. "Get all the human rights nutcases. Sweep this burg clean while you're at it."

A nice sentiment, perhaps, but all the gods were involved in this. That meant everybody's gods, including the gods of the ratmen and the nuts. Nobody's prayers were going to get answered today.

The hole to the other realm shrank. In moments it was a point, then it ceased to be.

The street was now almost the same as before my dive. Every god and goddess and weird supernatural critter was right where it was before, excepting Imara who was Adeth, nearly the most perfect redhead of all time.

I could shed a tear.

Almost.

All of a sudden one fine-looking woman was standing in my doorway, right shoulder leaning against the frame. She looked like she had done a lot of research on arc and proportion. Definitely legs that went all the way to the ground and ample amplitude in the curves and softnesses departments. Somebody must have been peeking over Star's shoulder when she was doing her design layouts.

"It over?" I gasped.

"Wrapped, Garrett. It's time."

"Uh . . ." I said. "Like . . ." She was for sure no Destroyer now. "I'm not feeling real suicidal right now, Maggie."

Her smile was deadly. My spine turned to gelatin. "No risk, Garrett. Except you might not want to come up for air." Her eyes were as hypnotic as those of the snake that supposedly entrances a rat.

*Help! Eleanor! Save me!* But I didn't want to be saved. Not really.

One divine arm went around my neck. Then another. Then a hand trailed down each of my sides, toward my belt buckle. Interesting, those extra . . .

# 69

"Excuse me."

The voice came from behind the new, improved, impossibly sensual Magodor. She glanced back, displeased. Can't honestly say I was thrilled, either.

I said, "Go away."

I could see parts of the street. There were no gods out there now. There was no strangeness at all. Just silence. My part of Tun-Faire was five minutes short of being back to the way things always had been.

"I cannot. I remain the Board agent assigned to you. And you remain the key to the untenanted temple on the Street of the Gods."

"You sonofabitch. Godsdamned bureaucrat. Where the hell were you when my ass was in a sling?"

I caught a whiff of weed. Fourteen drifted up in a cloud, an all-time smouldering banger in his mouth. His eyelids drooped. He was happy. "You tell 'im, Chief."

I guess my complaint was the last straw. Strait went off on all the grief I had caused him. I was amazed. You don't often hear that much whining outside Royal offices, where some functionary always resents being asked to do his job.

"Go away, Strait."

*Open the temple, Garrett. It is the last act necessary in this divine comedy.*

Maggie, snarling, leaned forward. Her lips touched my left ear. "Later, Garrett," she whispered. Sudden pain. Blood trickled down my neck. A needle tooth had pierced my earlobe.

Then Magodor was gone.

Maybe Eleanor was on the job after all.

Magodor never came back. Thank you very much. Because I had a bone to pick with Miss Nastiness, and not the one you think.

All those clever hands at the last minute had made a certain very useful piece of cord vanish. A piece of cord I'd had in mind trimming some in the middle of a loop before I gave it up . . . Damn my habit of vacillating.

Spilled milk, Garrett.

Maggie never came back. She left me with some powerful curiosities, but I never went over to the temple where she set up as boss yahoo of the combined and restructured and now intensely feminist Shayir/Godoroth cult. Whenever I was tempted, I had only to touch my scarred earlobe, my thumping carotid artery, and I had little trouble resisting. If I still felt the tug, somewhere in the back of my mind I heard *Nog is inescapable* and I recalled who all else might be there waiting for me.

No pack of earth mothers, that bunch.

I was too busy to commit suicide, anyway.

The very next time there was a shakeout in the Dream Quarter, Maggie's gang headed west ten places. They had managed to turn the near destruction of TunFaire into a public relations coup.

The really bad, horrible, awful part of the whole ordeal, more a cause for despair than any interdimensional hole with a starving tentacle factory stuck in it, came when a nasty little neighbor brat pounded on the drunken, leaning remains of my door and hollered, "Mr. Garrett?"

"What?" demanded the drunken, leaning remains of me.

"Mrs. Cardonlos told me bring this back to you." He handed me a bedraggled, frosty, half-drowned parrot. At the exact moment that Morley Dotes chose to arrive, having hustled over to see if I was all right.

I cursed some. I whined some. To no avail. Mrs. Cardonlos tossed me a cheerful wave motivated by 190-proof malice. And the Dead Man sent, *I had to prevent his being pulled through, Garrett. He is far too valuable to let go.*

"Valuable to who?"

Morley stood there smiling wickedly.

As I carried the bird to his perch I wondered if I burned the house could I get him and the Dead Man both?

# Faded Steel Heat

For all the wonderful people of the Baltimore SF Society but especially for Sue Who & her Little New Who

# 1

It ought to start with a girl. The best ones always do. She ought to be kick the lid off your coffin gorgeous. She ought to be in hot water right up to her cute little . . . ears. She shouldn't quite know why, or maybe she just won't say why the guys with the bent noses are after her. She ought to have eyes full of mischief and not be afraid to get mischievous with the right guy.

That's the way it ought to be. But this time it started with *three* darling gremlins, any one of whom could sprain a set of male eyeballs at thirty paces.

Oh. I'm Garrett, aka Mr. Right. Although a jealous acquaintance might lie about it, I'm six feet two inches of handsome ex-Marine. Yeah, sure my face has a few nicks and dings but those just add character. They let the frantic cutie in the deep gravy know she's found a stand-up guy. Or maybe, a guy too dim not to lead with his chops.

Dean, my cook and housekeeper and Door-Answerer General and (a legend in his own mind) majordomo, was out. I had to answer the tap-tap-tapping myself. It was noon. I'd been enjoying my first cup of tea. I was still a little tousled, wearing my charming rogue look. I had treated myself to a late nap in celebration of having survived an infestation of Great Old Ones, olden gods more like world-devouring termites than the woosie celestial accountants populating today's Dream Quarter.

What the heck. Real women like their fellows a little rough around the edges.

I put a bloodshot peeper to the peephole. The day looked better right away. "Eureka!" My stoop was overrun with lovelies cooked up from all the right ingredients. Youth. Beauty. Curve and flow and swoop to make drooling geometricians opt for a very specialized area of study. And right behind them hulked several ugly thugs who provided the element of menace.

I flung the door wide. "How lucky can one guy get?"

The blond was Alyx Weider. She gawked like she'd just seen something pop up out of its grave. She was five feet four and sleek as a mink but nature hadn't shorted her on the extras. "Garrett? Is that you?" Like I was wearing a disguise.

"You grew up." She definitely grew up.

The redhead said, "Stop drooling, Garrett." That was Tinnie Tate, professional redhead. And she took her calling seriously. My semi ex-girlfriend. "You'll get the floor all nasty. Dean will make you mop."

This was the first time Tinnie had spoken to me in months. Right away she had to start in on chores.

"You look lovely this morning, darling. Come in. Come in." I eyed the third woman, the brunette. She had done herself a cruel disservice by falling in with Tinnie and Alyx. She wore plain clothing and had taken no special care with her grooming. Tinnie and Alyx made her seem mousy. But only at first glimpse. The sharp eye could tell she was the most gorgeous of the three. I have an eye like a razor.

I didn't recognize her.

Tinnie said, "You're really working at the bachelor business, aren't you?"

"Huh?" Usually I'm armed with a rapier wit—well, actually, a gladius sort of wit—but when Tinnie comes around my brain curdles.

"You look like death on a stick, Garrett. Slightly warmed over." Tinnie has a way with words. Like the guy at the end of the chute at the slaughterhouse has a way with tools.

"That's my honey," I told the crowd. I backed into the house. "Ain't she precious?"

"You got a honey, Garrett, I don't think her name is Tinnie Tate. Unless there's more than one of us."

"Awk!" I said, stricken. "Impossible! You're unique."

"Did you break a leg? Or forget the way to my house? Or forget how to write?"

She had me. The slickest stoat that ever slank couldn't have weaseled out of this one. I'd done one of those things guys do, that they don't know they're doing when they do them and still don't know what they did after they're done, then I'd had the brass-bottomed gall not to rush right over with a public apology. Lately, I have begun to suspect that standing on principle is a strategic error of the first water.

"I think you didn't come here to bicker in front of your friends." I showed her a lot of shiny teeth.

She showed me a scowl that told me, once again, I had everything all wrong but she was going to let it slide for the moment.

This visit was no surprise except in its timing. The ladies had been around to see me before, while I was otherwise preoccupied saving the world. Alyx's daddy had problems. She thought I could unravel them.

Tinnie knows the hours I keep. Bless her sadistic little heart.

Old Man Weider owns the biggest brewery empire in Tun-Faire. That's because the clever rascal brews the best brew. The first time he hired me I saved him from an inside theft ring that was devouring his business like a raging cancer. He's had me on retainer ever since. He wants me to work for him full-time. I'm not interested in a real job. When you're your own boss you don't have to please anybody but yourself. Though that arrangement doesn't leave much room to pass the blame.

In exchange for my retainer I make frequent surprise visits to the brewery. Random appearances make it difficult for organized villainy to take root again.

In the old days Alyx was a scrawny kid barely threatening to become a heartbreaker. Her older sister, Kittyjo, was a lot more interesting.

Time trudges on. Sometimes it plays a pretty melody.

I tried again. "Let's not argue, Tinnie. I can't possibly win."

"If you know that how come . . ."

"I didn't say you were right." Damn! I knew I'd blown it before I finished saying it.

"Garrett! I . . ."

# 2

"Quiver me heart!" a voice squawked. "Feast yer glims, mates! It must be heaven! Where do we start?"

"Is that the infamous parrot?" the new girl asked. Alyx and Tinnie glowered into the small front room. They put enough kick into it to freeze water and crack glass. The room opens off the hall to the right just inside the front door. I hadn't remembered to close up before admitting the ladies.

"That's Mr. Big, yes. Trash beak champion of the universe. Ignore him. Otherwise, he'll get excited."

"Excited?"

"He's restraining himself right now."

Tinnie observed, "Garrett calls him the Goddamn Parrot."

How did she know that? The feathered mosquito didn't arrive till after her famous parting tizzy.

Of course. Her effort to twist my mind around till the last sense-juice leaked out didn't mean that she didn't see Dean. And Dean thinks Tinnie is the next best thing to immortality. He's her enthusiastic mole in the garden of my life.

I said, "I'd call him kitty food if I could wring his neck without offending the guy who gave him to me." Someday I'll get even with Morley. But it's going to be tough.

"He's kind of neat," Alyx decided, changing her mind on the fly. "But I wouldn't take him to visit my Aunt Claire."

"Come here, Sugar," the bird squawked. "Awk! Check them hooters! I am in love."

I muttered, "The only goddamn bird in the world with a vocabulary and he uses it up being obnoxious."

"Before you pop trying to find a safe way to ask," Tinnie told me, her finest taunting smile prancing across her lovely lips while she leaned against me and looked up with total green-eyed innocence, "this is Nicks. Giorgi Nicks for Nicholas."

"Hi, Gorgeous Nicks for Nicholas." Whoops! That slip earned me a pinch.

The Goddamn Parrot sang the praises of Alyx Weider in language that would embarrass stevedores. But it was hard to fault his eye.

Tinnie kept looking up and pinching, the devil in her eyes. "Guess what, lover? She's taken."

"Lucky guy. Mr. Big will be devastated." That foul-beaked jungle buzzard had spied Nicks now. Nicks winked at me. She had an incredible smile and eyes as blue as a cloudless sky.

She said, "I'm only engaged, Garrett. I'm not dead."

Alyx whistled. "Nicks!" Tinnie laughed but her eyes narrowed wickedly.

This looked like a good time to run down the street and see if Dean needed help with the groceries.

Nicks said, "Whoops! That didn't come out right. Are you the Garrett Tinnie brags about all the time?"

"Last time I checked that was still the name. I'm not sure about the brag part."

That earned me a fingernail in the ribs from the nearest beautiful redhead, who observed, "It's going to be mud if you're not careful."

"Just don't put me in the middle of anything, darling."

Alyx said, "Nicks is just being Nicks. She can't help it."

I said, "Huh?"

"Nicks flirts. She's been doing it since we were seven. She can't help it. She doesn't mean it. She doesn't realize she's sending come-on signals. Nicks, for heaven's sake. You can get in real trouble out here in the world."

Alyx was right. There's always trouble if a woman shows she's willing when she's not.

I asked, "Did I miss something? Did you spend your whole life in a harem, Nicks?" That isn't a Karentine thing but the rich do have strange ways. Alyx had been incredibly sheltered as a child.

"Practically." The Goddamn Parrot flapped over, settled on her wrist like a falcon in a clown suit. "My father has strong ideas about saving me from the world. The Weiders and a few other families are the only people I've ever met. Till recently."

Alyx said, "She's staying with us, now. Daddy isn't the big ogre he used to be."

He never was with his baby. Alyx always got anything she wanted with just a cute pout.

Nicks used a finger to stroke the top of the jungle chicken's head. The little monster went along enthusiastically. He tilted his head back so she could get a finger under his chin. I'd never seen him take to anyone so wholeheartedly.

I looked to Alyx. I didn't get anything. What was she doing out of the family fortress herself? Old Man Weider must be losing his grip.

Hell, I knew that already. Didn't I? Wasn't that why the toothsome threesome had come? If Max was on top of everything he wouldn't need help and his baby wouldn't be out looking for it.

I shrugged. "I'll find out what I need to know as we go. Let's visit His Nibs, get comfortable, and talk about it."

Tinnie stepped back. She glared at me. "Shouldn't you get dressed first?"

My gal Tinnie, always looking out for my best interest. "Not a bad idea, sweetheart," though I was perfectly happy dressed the way I was. So what if I was a little rumpled? That was part of my rough charm. "Be right back, my lovelies. If you want tea or anything, you'll have to help yourselves. Dean's out shopping. Tinnie, you know where everything is."

Sneaky Garrett. He will get fresh tea brewed by the very viragos who think they've got him in a clean pin.

I trotted upstairs before Tinnie caught on.

# 3

I descended the stairway wearing my clotheshorse best only to discover skinny old Dean newly returned. He wrinkled his bony nose, shook his bony head, proceeded into the kitchen. Alyx's blue eyes twinkled. "You don't waste much time picking out your clothes, do you?"

Tinnie was in the kitchen. Dean brightened right up. "Miss Tate! This is a pleasant surprise. May I observe that you are looking particularly lovely today?"

"Mr. Creech! You rogue. Of course you may. Somebody ought to notice. Let me help you with that."

I leaned into the kitchen. Damn! The old boy was being victimized by a hugging redhead.

Life ain't fair. Not even a little. Me she pokes and pinches.

A crackling sense of amused anticipation grew around me. Somehow the ladies had both wakened my partner and put him in a good mood. That filled me with foreboding. Eclipses and planetary conjunctions are less common than the Dead Man awakening in a good mood when the house is infested with females.

I took a deep breath.

Here we went again.

I led the ladies into the Dead Man's room, which takes up most of the lcft-side ground floor of my house, excepting the pantries off the kitchen.

The cuties made themselves right at home. Without asking they dragged chairs out of my office, which is an ambitious closet across the hall from the Dead Man's room. Tinnie perched on the guest's chair. Nicks claimed the comfortable one that belongs behind my desk. I would cherish the warmth forever. Meantime, Alyx decorated the chair I usually use when I'm in with the Dead Man. The Goddamn Parrot still perched on Nicks' hand, nibbling bits of something she offered him. He cooed like a goddamned turtledove.

*You might reserve that admiration for Miss Tate. If you were a gentleman.* That was my partner, shoving unwanted advice directly into my head.

"But I'm not. She's told me so lots of times." I glared. Alyx and Nicks smiled as though enjoying a private joke. Maybe Old Bones had shared his remarks with the three heartstoppers, not just me.

Perhaps I blushed, slightly. Tinnie sure grinned.

The Dead Man resides in a huge wooden chair at the heart of the biggest room in the house. Usually the room isn't lighted. In his present state he doesn't need light. But the ladies did and had brought lamps in from other rooms.

They shouldn't have bothered.

The Dead Man isn't pretty. That's partly because he isn't really a man. He hails from a rare species called Loghyr who resemble humans only vaguely. He goes four hundred plus pounds, though the vermin keep nibbling off bits so he's probably dropped a few. He's uglier than your sister's last husband and has a snoot like an elephant. It hangs about fourteen inches long. I've never seen a live Loghyr so don't know how they use that.

He was called the Dead Man when I met him, ages ago. One of those clever street names, picked up on account of he has been dead for four hundred years. Somebody stuck a knife in him way back when, probably while he was taking one of his six-month siestas. He's never bothered to explain.

But he is Loghyr and Loghyr do nothing hastily. They especially don't get into a rush about giving up the ghost. I hear four hundred years is far from a record stall.

Nobody knows much about the Loghyr. The Dead Man will babble on for weeks without dropping a hint himself.

I leaned against a set of shelves loaded with souvenirs from old cases and knickknacks the Dead Man likes to grab with a thought and send swooping around if he feels that will rattle a visitor already distressed by his less than appetizing appearance.

*Could you not have selected clothing less threadbare? In business it is important to present a businesslike appearance.*

Him too? Steel yourself, Garrett. It's teak on Tommy Tucker

time with you in the coveted role of Tommy in the brown-bottomed slit trench. "That's how we'll justify my fee."

*Fee?*

"Money? Gold and silver and copper. That stuff we use to buy beans for me and Dean and keep the leaky roof from leaking on your head? You recall your days in that ruin on Wizard's Reach? With the roof half-gone and the snow blowing in?"

The women looked at me weirdly. Which meant that they were getting only my half of the conversation. But their imaginations were perking.

*Of course. You must maintain a businesslike approach—if not a businesslike appearance. But, perhaps, you have overlooked the fact that we have a retainer arrangement with Mr. Weider and are, therefore, expected to provide our services against fees already paid.*

"You got a point." The Weider retainer had seen me through numerous dry spells. "Hey, Alyx. Before we worry about anything else, are you here for your dad or you?"

"I'm not sure. He didn't send me but he asked Manvil if they should think about calling you in. This thing will affect the brewery. He might've sent me if it ever occurred to him that a daughter could do something productive. I think he hasn't sent for you just because he's embarrassed to admit that he can't handle everything himself. He's still hoping he can get by without you but I think it's been too late for that for days."

I didn't have a clue what it was all about yet. I glanced at Nicks.

Alyx told me, "Nicks is in it because my brother is in it and they're engaged and she's worried."

What a cruel world it is where a beauty like Nicks wastes herself on a creature like Ty Weider. Though Nicks did not appear excited by her impending nuptials.

*She is not. But she does not have the heart to disappoint two sets of parents who have had this alliance planned for twenty years. She has found ways to delay it several times. Now her time has run out.*

"And Tinnie?"

"She's my friend, Garrett. She's just here to lend emotional support."

*A wise man would not now insist on subjecting all things to a rigorous scrutiny, Garrett.*

I have lived with His Nibs so long that even his obscurantisms and obfuscations have begun to make sense. This time he was hanging a codicil on the rule about not looking too closely at politics, sausage manufacture, or the teeth of gift horses. Tinnie was here. I should enjoy that, not go picking the scabs off sores.

"All right. I still don't have a clue. Start at the beginning and tell me everything, Alyx. Even if it doesn't seem important."

"Okay. It's The Call."

I sighed.

It would be.

Already I knew I wasn't going to like any of this.

# 4

I asked, "What are they doing? Strong-arm stuff? Extortion?"

"Tinnie says you call it protection."

I glanced at the professional redhead, so silent of late. At the moment she wasn't into her favorite role deeply. "They tried it with my uncle, too." She smiled nastily.

I worked for Willard Tate once. He was a tough old buzzard with a herd of relatives willing to do whatever he told them. He wouldn't be threatened. "He sent them packing?"

Tinnie grinned. "You know Uncle Willard. Of course he did. Dared them to come back, too."

"That might not have been too bright. Some human rights gangs are pretty wicked. Alyx. No. Both of you. Was it The Call specifically?"

The Call—as in "call to arms"—is Marengo North English's gang and is the biggest, loudest, best financed, and most vigorously political of the war veterans' groups. The Call includes a lot of wealthy, powerful men unhappy with the direction Karenta is drifting. As far as I knew The Call only raised funds by donation. But they might extend their reach if rowdier, more radical groups began to attract more recruits.

North English has a big ego and a personal agenda that's never been clear.

Alyx said, "Yeah. No. I don't know. They talked to Ty. He claimed he knew some of them. He said they told him Weider's has to contribute five percent of gross receipts to the cause. And we'll have to get rid of any employees who aren't human."

Ty is Alyx's brother. One of three, all older than she is. Two of those three didn't make it back from the Cantard in one piece. The other one didn't make it back at all. I don't like Ty Weider, though for no concrete reason. Maybe it's his relentless bitterness. Though he has a right to be bitter. He gave up a leg for Karenta. The kingdom hasn't given him much in return.

Ty is not unique. Far from it. Just look down any street. But he belongs to a family with wealth and influence. "Why would they take a run at Ty instead of your dad?"

"Daddy doesn't spend much time with the business anymore. Momma is lots sicker. He stays with her. He only goes to the brewery maybe every other day and then mostly he only stays for a little while, talking to people he's known a long time."

"So Ty is more likely to bump into the public." I glanced at the Dead Man. Was he mining the unspoken side of this? He didn't send me a clue. That suggested Alyx was being as forthright as she knew how.

"Yes. But Mr. Heldermach and Mr. Klees are still in charge."

"Of course." Because Ty Weider is no brewmaster and not much of an executive. Because nobody at the brewery likes Ty. Because Heldermach and Klees are more than Weider employees. They are more nearly junior partners. Their investment in the brewery is skill and knowledge. Both operated their own breweries before consolidating with Weider.

The Weider empire isn't just the big brewery downtown, it's a combine of smaller places scattered throughout the city. Most were struggling when Weider took over and rooted out the inefficiencies and bad brewing policies that kept them from prospering.

The best brewmasters and best recipes stayed on.

"Mr. Heldermach and Mr. Klees were there when The Call talked to Ty."

"They were?" I glanced at the Dead Man. He did not contradict Alyx.

Surprise, surprise. The moment she'd mentioned Ty as interlocuter I set a new conclusion-jumping distance record, figuring Ty for trying to scam his own dad.

I'm convinced Ty was at least marginally involved in the skimming operation whose breakup endeared me to Old Man Weider back when. That involved barrels of beer vanishing into thin air and becoming pure profit for those enterprising characters who used that method to reduce overhead in the tavern business. I spent months posing as a worker to unearth what I had. I never nailed Ty. What evidence I did find was all circumstantial and

could have been explained away as easily by stupidity and gulli-
bility as by evil intent. I never mentioned him to his father—
which, maybe, was one of the services Weider had expected.

Whatever Ty's role, I closed the brewery's bleeding belly
wound without any scandal. And I've kept the stitches from tearing loose again. For which the old man has been more than necessarily grateful. He's kept me on that retainer ever since and even
sends the occasional lonely keg of Reserve Dark over to spend the
holidays.

Though the Dead Man would have explored any thoughts in
the area already, I asked, "What do you think about Ty, Alex?"

"I try to make allowances. We all do. Because of his leg." She
wouldn't look me in the eye.

"But?"

"Hmmm?"

"I hear a but. A reservation?"

Alyx glanced at Nicks. She looked like she thought she had
said too much already. I glared at the Dead Man.

*Bingo! She is concerned about Miss Nicholas' feelings, Garrett.*

"Huh? Why?" I blurted.

The Dead Man seemed amused. He is whenever I stick my
foot into my mouth, though I hadn't gotten a good taste of dirty
old leather yet here.

*Miss Weider conceals a considerable affection for her brother
although she does understand why others find him unlikable. She
has an even stronger regard for Miss Nicholas. They have been
friends from childhood. Miss Weider will not knowingly cause her
pain.*

*For her part, Miss Nicholas does not care to hear evil of her fi-
ancé because she plans to accept this marriage despite having no
desire to do so. She will not disappoint the expectations of so
many. She consoles herself with the certain knowledge that Ty Weider, although no Prince Charming, stands to be one of the richest
men in TunFaire. And the wait may not be protracted if there is
substance to the cluster of fears infesting Miss Weider's head.*

I glanced at Nicks, remembered Ty. Money sure can get the
blood moving, too.

Tinnie seemed to be getting sour. I was too introspective to
suit her today. That was a problem most days as far as she was
concerned. "All right, Alyx," I said. "The Call made a threat. They
don't have a history of that but there is a first time for every extor-
tionist. What do you want me to do about it?"

"I want you to stop them but I don't think you could do that by yourself, so I don't really know."

"I can be pretty persuasive." Usually with Morley Dotes and Saucerhead Tharpe helping me drive my points home.

Alyx didn't hear me. She was too busy talking. "I guess if there's anything I really need it's for you to watch out for Dad. He was pretty blunt in public when he heard about the demands. Somebody might want to make him an example."

*Exactly*.

Tinnie said, "The men who came to our compound did claim to be from The Call." The Tate clan manufactures footwear. They got rich making combat boots during the war. "But I don't think they really were. They were too nervous."

The Dead Man sent, *I have compared the recollections of Miss Weider and Miss Tate and must submit the possibility that we have afoot several bold operators moving in where they believe they can score quickly by exploiting fear and hatred.*

There's nothing so holy some scroat won't try to turn a few marks on it. "Somebody's trying to scam the rich? They'll have to stay way ahead of Marengo North English, then."

And I kept right on having trouble getting my mind around the notion that a honey like Nicks would even talk to Ty Weider. Maybe I'd just always caught Ty at bad times. Maybe he wasn't as hopeless as I thought.

# 5

"Have you done anything?" I asked Alyx. "Besides coming back here till you caught up with me? Did you talk it over with your dad? Or Ty? Or Manvil? Have they done anything?"

"I didn't discuss it with them. Daddy would say it wasn't proper for a lady to take an interest. But if I went to anybody, he'd want me to go to you. Ty, though, will get mad when he finds out. He doesn't want outsiders around. He's argued with Dad about you."

Big surprise. But Ty's likes and dislikes never were high on my list of concerns. "Think he'd cut off my supply of dark?"

Nobody got it. Not even the Dead Man, apparently. So much for a new career in comedy.

*Ladies, you must excuse Garrett. The presence of so much loveliness in such tight quarters has disoriented him completely.*

Sarky bastard.

Nicks jumped at the Dead Man's first touch but settled down quickly. She had been forewarned.

Tinnie and Alyx showed the nonchalance of old hands.

His Nibs continued, *And I cannot say I blame him this once. I am overwhelmed myself. And I was dead ages before any of you were born.*

What a sweet-talker. "Thank you, Old Bones. Maybe if I shut my eyes and pretend I'm not a robust, hearty, virile young man whose special lady has shunned him mercilessly . . ."

*You might consider supplying shovels, high-top boots, and nose plugs, Garrett.*

"How sharper than a serpent's tooth. My eyes are sealed. My breathing is almost normal."

Nicks asked, "Is he always like this, Tinnie?"

"He's pretty tame right now. Wait till he wakes up."

"Not a tooth, teeth," I grumbled. "Alyx. Did your dad take this seriously?"

"He's worried. He's been asking our employees what they think about The Call. He's decided we won't hire anybody but veterans."

He never had. But that wouldn't satisfy The Call. Although most human males are veterans not all veterans are human. And Weider never made a distinction. He wouldn't now. He protects his employees like a she-wolf protects her young. Most give him complete loyalty in return. Me, I even drink his beer.

But there are always a rotten few who slip through any screen, or who are brought in by a big wormy apple already loafing in the barrel.

The ladies babbled on but I got nothing out of them. I turned to the Dead Man. He sent: *They are frightened. Time is passing. Nothing has been done to disarm or appease The Call. Apparently there is a deadline unknown even to Miss Alyx.*

Miss Alyx now, huh? I watched the Goddamn Parrot nibble out of Nicks' fingers. "You want that critter, Nicks? Take him. Call him my wedding present."

Alyx broke into laughter.

So maybe I'm not a complete bust as a comic. But it would help to know why they laugh.

"Sorry," Alyx said. "But I had this picture of Mr. Big kibbitzing Ty and Nicks on their wedding night."

That would be something. Unless they tied the bird into a gunnysack and hung the sack out a window. I glanced at Nicks.

She wasn't smiling.

She looked like a young lady who didn't believe in her future at all.

I couldn't disagree with her. But I had that deep prejudice against Ty Weider.

*She is an excellent actress, Garrett. Perhaps inside as well as out. Perhaps able to fool even herself. Even I see something different each time I look at her. I have to remind myself to recognize the surface.*

"Interesting."

*Save your interest for Miss Tate.*

"That was my plan."

*Stick to it. This matter will become complicated enough without adding the machinations of women scorned.* He does not have a high estimation of the fairer species.

Tinnie, I noted, seemed to be daydreaming. Which meant she was communing with the Dead Man. He can do that. He has several distinct minds and can go several directions at once.

I asked Alyx, "Could there be trouble on the shop floor?"

"There's always sympathy for The Call, anywhere you go."

"I doubt they cheer The Call much in Ogre Town or Dwarf Fort or the elven neighborhoods. I haven't seen many ratmen or pixies carrying banners in The Call's parades."

"Well, they wouldn't, would they?"

Maybe there was some rightsist sympathy right there.

From the sounds of it somebody nonhuman was being real unsympathetic to human rights out front right now. The neighborhood attracts more than its share of political debates.

"Alyx. The guys who brought you. They going to hang around?" Some situations can't be managed with cute and beautiful, a wiggle and a giggle.

"They went to lunch. They're supposed to wait out front afterward."

"Good. It's starting to sound excitable out there." The Dead Man evidently wasn't interested in what was going on. He didn't bother to report.

"We could stay till it quiets down." Alyx winked.

"I couldn't stand the heat. I'm about to melt down into a puddle of tallow now."

*Garrett.*

"Garrett!"

"Ah, Tinnie me love. My hottest of flames. You're awake after all."

Tinnie gave Alyx a look of exasperation. How was she going to get me trained if even her friends encouraged my delinquencies?

Nicks stayed out of it. She concentrated on the Goddamn Parrot.

Except that when I glanced at her she winked, too.

Help.

They do it just to watch you crackle and fry like bacon left too long in too hot a pan.

# 6

The ladies departed, headed not for the brewery but Tinnie's family compound. The Tates had to be hurting. The recent outbreak of peace had to be terrible for business.

That's the trouble when some darn war goes on too long. Life begins to revolve around it. We live and die by it at home as much as do the soldiers on the battlefields. Now that the fighting is over, except for mopping-up exercises against the last of Glory Mooncalled's raggedy-ass republican partisans, regiments are demobilizing as fast as the navy can haul them home.

These days many jobs belong to nonhumans because we humans went off to war and only a fraction returned. Today's soldiers come home to find there's nothing to come home to.

The door closed behind those three luscious behinds. I returned to the Dead Man's room and settled into my own chair. The seat was still warm. A clash of perfumes hung in the air. I asked, "What's your boy Glory Mooncalled up to?"

Years ago Mooncalled entered the war as a mercenary captain on the Venageti side. Though a successful campaigner, he failed to have been born into the ruling clique of sorcerers and nobles and so was treated badly. He resented that so much he changed sides. He spent the next decade embarrassing and picking off the men who had injured his pride.

His treatment by Karenta's overlords was not much better. He got paid on time but received few honors, however dramatic his victories. He defected again. This time he collected the tribes of the Cantard under the banner of a republic that rejected both Karentine and Venageti territorial claims. He provided spankings to armies from both kingdoms.

But fate wasn't kind. Karenta got some breaks. The Venageti collapsed. Karentine forces began exterminating the republicans.

The peoples of the Cantard immediately began migrating into Karenta, and especially to TunFaire, where their presence only adds to the social stress. Something I stumbled over during a recent case made me suspect that Mooncalled himself was now in TunFaire.

The Dead Man seemed disgruntled. *In all likelihood he is fomenting disorder under the illusion that his past popularity still assures him support amongst the lower classes.*

"You seem disappointed."

*Perhaps heroes are best kept at arm's length. Up close their flaws are too easily seen.*

The Goddamn Parrot had taken station on his shoulder. Nicks' fault. She'd put him there. I hadn't been able to talk her into taking the flashy little vulture with her.

The bird started to relieve himself.

He ended in a tangle amongst the mementos on the Dead Man's knickknack shelves. He was so startled he could hardly squawk in parrotese. He got his feet under him, shook his head, took a tentative step, fell off the shelf, and smacked into the floor.

*If that thing fails to survive please extend my deepest condolences to Mr. Dotes.*

"Wow! What a great idea! Why didn't I think of it before? I'm slow but I'm brilliant. I'll tear him apart in here and blame it all on you. I'll have Morley come over, see all the feathers and parrot shit, he'll just shake his head and forget it. He won't go getting into a feud with you."

*Very creative. Try it and I will hang you by your bootlaces from the rooftree. That bird is far too valuable even to joke about.*

"Valuable? You can't even eat those damned things unless you're so hungry you already ate up all the snakes and buzzards and crows."

*I mean valuable as a communications tool.*

"Not to me."

*Silence!*

"I was only going to—"

*We are about to have company. Strangers. Receive them in your office. They do not need to be made aware of my existence.*

Dean beat me to the front door but got a silent warning from the Dead Man. He peeped through the peephole, backed off frowning.

"What's wrong?"

"I don't like the looks of those two." He retreated to the Dead Man's room. The Goddamn Parrot flapped into the hall when he opened the door. It landed on my shoulder. "Argh!" I started to swat him. Dean came out of the Dead Man's room, lugging the chairs back to my office.

*Easy on the bird, Garrett. Dean, when you finish, shut the door to this room. Do not open it again while those people are in this house.*

"Put a kettle on, too. For hospitality's sake."

Dean gave me the look that asked what I thought he should do in his spare time.

The pounding resumed. It had started polite. Now it seemed impatient. I used the peephole myself. "Do I really need to talk to these guys?" The two men on the stoop looked just like the guy Dean wanted me to be when I grew up.

*It might be of value. Or instructive.*

"To who?"

*That would be* whom, *Garrett.*

"I'm beginning to get it already," I grumbled, starting in on Dean's battery of latches. He was done moving furniture.

The Dead Man would stir the sludge inside their pretty gourds, ever so discreetly, while I sat through some kind of sales pitch.

Those two were selling something. They were so squeaky-clean and well groomed that I feared their scam would be religion. I'd have trouble staying polite if they were godshouters. I've suffered an overdose of religion lately.

I changed my mind as soon as the door opened, before anybody cracked a word. The erect postures and humorless mouths said they were selling a true belief that had nothing to do with pie in the sky by and by.

Both were five feet six and unreasonably handsome. One had blond hair and blue eyes. I wish I could report that the other had blue hair and blond eyes but he didn't. He was a pretty hunk of brown hair and blue eyes. Neither had visible scars or tattoos.

Clerks, instinct told me.

"Mr. Garrett?" the blond asked. He had perfect teeth. How often do you see good teeth? Never. Even Tinnie has an incisor that laps its neighbor.

"Guilty. Maybe. Depends on what you want."

Nobody smiled. The brunette said, "A friend gave us your name. Said you would be a good man to see. Said as you were a bona fide war hero."

"I could throw bricks with my eyes closed and hit a bona fide war hero eight tries out of ten. Anybody who made it home is a hero. Which Free Company are you guys with?" They wore clothing as though they were headed for the parade ground. Like appearance wasn't just part of being a soldier, it was the whole thing.

Clerks.

*Do not antagonize them simply for the sake of deflating their pomposity, Garrett.*

I need a new partner. This one knows me too well.

They seemed surprised. "How did you? . . ."

"I'm a trained detective." Self-educated. From a very short syllabus.

"It's obvious?" The brunette almost whined. These would be guys whose self-image included no whinery but who would whine a lot and call it something else. In their own minds they were big hairy-assed he-men.

Clerks.

"When you're headed wherever you go when you leave, compare yourselves to everybody else. To human male people, anyway." That might have the unfortunate side effect of encouraging their feelings of superiority, but they *might* see what I meant. "You can't be a secret agent if you're wearing a sign."

They exchanged baffled looks. They were lost. Pretty but not bright. The blond asked, "May we come in?"

"By all means." I stepped aside. "We can talk in my office. Second door to your left."

*Be hospitable, Garrett.*

"Either one of you guys want a parrot?"

*Garrett!*

Both men had wrinkled their noses when first they saw me and my bird. Everybody was a clothes critic nowadays. Why? I was decent. I was even clean. These guys looked around like they expected the place to be a dump. They seemed pleasantly disappointed that it wasn't.

Dean does good work.

We trooped into the closet I call an office. I told them, "My man Dean will bring tea in a minute."

They eyed me uncertainly. How could I know?

My office is less ordered than the hallway. I don't let Dean loose in there. And behind my desk hangs a painting that Dean hates.

At first you just see a pretty woman running from a brooding darkness. But as you stare at the painting more and more of that darkness reaches out to you. The artist who created it had been possessed by a talent so fierce that it amounted to sorcery. It drove him mad. He put everything into this painting, including his insanity. It was personal. At one time it told a whole story and indicted a villain. It doesn't have a tenth its original charge now but still retains an immense impact. It exudes terror.

"That's Eleanor," I said. "She died before I was born but she helped me crack a case." She did a lot more.

The portrait once belonged to the man who murdered Eleanor. He's dead now, too. He doesn't need the painting anymore. I do. Eleanor makes a better sounding board than Dean, the Dead Man, or the Goddamn Parrot. She's seldom judgmental and she never gives me any lip.

Blondie said, "We understand you're often involved in unusual affairs."

"I'm a lightning rod for weird stuff. Thanks, Dean." The big tray carried the right number of cups, cookies and muffins, and a steaming pot of tea. The boys exchanged glances, nervous under Eleanor's piercing gaze and Dean's stern disapproval.

Dean left. I poured and asked, "What can I do for you guys? Really."

They exchanged glances again.

"Look, boys, I'm working hard here." The Goddamn Parrot squawked in my ear. "If you just need a place to get in out of the rain I recommend Mrs. Cardonlos' rooming house up the street. On the other . . ."

"Awk! Queen bitch! Queen bitch!"

"It's not raining." Literal-minded clerks.

"Stow it, bird," I growled at the Goddamn Parrot.

My visitors exchanged looks again.

This could go on all day.

# 7

The blond said, "I apologize, Mr. Garrett. We were cautioned that we might find you unconventional and should try to become comfortable with that before proceeding."

"Puny penis!" the parrot squawked.

I snarled, "You're going into the sack again, you animated feather duster."

The brunette smiled insincerely. "Is that ventriloquism? When I was little I had an uncle who could—"

"Why does everybody ask that? No. This devil-spawn of a seven-color jungle pigeon does it all on his own. He's got a vocabulary bigger than yours or mine and every word is foul. Fowl. Maybe there was sorcery done him sometime. I don't know. He was a gift. I can't seem to get rid of him."

"Pencil dick."

Now nobody was smiling. Again I thought about choking the Dead Man, only what good would that do? Strengthen my grip?

The blond said, "My name is Carter Stockwell."

So we were going to do business after all. "I'm not surprised. And you?"

"Trace Wendover."

"Of course. Hello, Carter and Trace. Sure you don't want a talking parrot? Cheap? Make a great holiday gift for the kids."

*Garrett, once again I must caution you against antagonizing these men.*

"No? All right. I made my sales pitch. Your loss. You guys make yours. Or go away."

"We were told you might be ill-mannered." That was the darker one. Trace.

Carter said, "Our mission is to interest you in contributing to our cause."

"Right now I've got about six copper sceats to clink together. The only cause I'm going to contribute to is the Garrett household supper fund."

"We don't want money. Please. Give us a chance to talk."

"You've been here ten minutes. You haven't said anything yet."

"You're right. We are Free Company men. Black Dragon Valsung." Carter watched for my reaction.

"What's that?" I asked.

Trace countered, "You don't know the Dragons?"

"Sorry." Heeding the Dead Man's advice I forebore remarks that might betray my feelings about those quasi-military gangs called Free Companies. There are so many of them that not having heard of a particular one was no big deal.

"Our leader is Colonel Valsung. Norton Valsung." I got intent looks from both pretty boys.

I shrugged. "Doesn't ring a bell, guys. He must have been army."

Carter began to puff up. He'd caught the slight. Trace, though, was made of sterner stuff. "Yes, Mr. Garrett. Colonel Valsung was army. He commanded the Black Dragon Brigade." Trace tossed him a warning look but he continued, "You would be impressed if you were to review his record."

No doubt. War does tend to expose men for what they really are. "Wouldn't be a relative, would he?"

"My uncle."

"The ventriloquist? I recall several colonels who were masters at putting words into other people's mouths."

"No, Mr. Garrett. Not that uncle."

"We're getting somewhere now. We have a colonel who isn't a ventriloquist. What does your uncle the nonventriloquist want with me?"

"Your peculiar combination of talents and expertise, both from your service and your career since."

I didn't get it. "You need a Force Recon guy with experience ducking vampires and sorcerers and tracking wayward wives to help you beat up old dwarves and crippled ratmen?"

*Garrett!*

Both of my visitors turned red. But Carter was out in front because he'd gotten a head start. Trace said, "Mr. Garrett, we do not roam the streets assaulting people. We are a veterans' mutual assistance brotherhood, not a street gang."

"The other day a veteran, who'd done five five-year hitches, three in the Cantard, was almost beaten to death right outside. He'd won eight decorations, including the Imperial Star with Swords and Oak Leaves. In one battle he lost half of his left arm and most of that side of his face in a blast from a witch ward. He's in the Bledsoe now. He probably won't get out alive. Those butchers won't pay any attention to him. He doesn't have any money. Go down there and mutually assist him. His name is Brate Trueblood."

"But the Bledsoe is a charity hospital, isn't it?"

"You didn't grow up in TunFaire, did you? In this town charity is available only to those who can pay for it."

"No. That's ugly." Trace seemed genuinely touched. Carter obviously didn't care but was cooling down. "That's exactly why we have to band together."

"But there's a problem, Trace. Brate was a real hero and as good a soldier as ever soldiered. Unfortunately, he made one really huge, stupid mistake."

My visitors looked at me expectantly.

*Garrett, please! Stop now.* The Dead Man seemed almost to despair.

"He was so stupid he picked an ogre for one of his grandparents."

It took them a while to catch on. I watched their eyes narrow and go shifty as they figured it out. Carter was slowest but he was the first to stand up. He told me, "You have the wrong idea." And, "Trace, we're wasting our time here."

"You're not wasting your time, Carter," I said. "I just want you to understand that nothing is black-and-white." I tried to hold Trace's eye. He seemed to be mulling my parable. "What did you guys do down there? You were clerks, right? Your uncle got you some safe assignment, right? Trace? Carter? You had an angel, too? So who do you suppose did more to defend and preserve the Karentine Crown? You guys or my ugly quadroon?"

Carter said, "You really don't know what's happening, do you?" And that actually seemed to please him.

I left my chair, moved to the office doorway. "You aren't wasting your time, guys. I'm right behind you. I just need to know how to reconcile the Brate Truebloods."

Trace started to say something. Carter squeezed his arm.

In moments those earnest young men were back in the street. Carter, I was convinced, would ignore my story, which was true only in a moral sense anyway. There really is a Brate Trueblood but he was just a small hero and the thugs who jumped him didn't put him in the hospital. Ogre blood made him hard to hurt. But these two creeps did want Brate in the Bledsoe. Or worse.

I might have done the devil's work with Trace, though. He looked like a young man who might, on occasion, actually have a thought.

I whistled as I bolted the door, blissful in my ignorance.

# 8

*That was not one of your more salubrious performances, Garrett. That flake of moral hubris may come back to haunt you.*

"Come on! They're jerks. Especially the blond one."

*Their minds did not reflect the prejudice you expect. But such jerks are quite common today. They are aggrieved. They need targets for their frustration. Those two seemed to be fundamentally good men. . . . Yet—*

"Yet? What?"

*They had no depth. Even a mind as dim as Saucerhead Tharpe's has its deeps.*

"No kidding? They're a couple of pretty boys who never worked a day—"

*Not shallow, Garrett. Not that way. Just all surface. Inside. Humans are filled with turmoil. Continuous dark currents collide and roil down deep where you do not see them and do not know them. Always. Even in Mr. Tharpe or Miss Winger. But those two had nothing beneath the fanatic surface. And that fanaticism was not as narrow and blind as is common. They grasped your Trueblood parable. They seemed unable to deal with it only because doing so would not have been in character.*

Well, he'd lost me. Except for the part about being all surface. "That don't surprise me. I know those guys. I've seen a lot of them. They just give up everything and let somebody else do their thinking. Life is easier that way."

*Perhaps. But I have a strong intuition that we would have been better served had you held them here whilst I milked them rather than driving them away.*

"Milked them? I didn't hear a moo from either one."

*Intentional obtuseness seldom finds a complimentary acute observation. You should have probed them for information. You should have held them while I wormed in under their surfaces.* He refused to let me exasperate him more than I had already. *Their particular Free Company may finance itself by extorting funds in the name of The Call. But we are in no position to winkle that out now. Are we?*

I hate it when he's right. And he was right. I let my emotions take over. I hadn't thought of those two in relation to the Weider problem. Yet they could have had that in mind. One of their cronies might have noticed the girls coming to my place.

*Your problem far too often, Garrett.*

"Huh?"

*You do not think. You emote. You act on that emotion in preference to reason. However, there was nothing in their minds to tie them in to the Weider matter. Which, of course, is no guarantee that those who sent them are equally innocent.*

"Aha! They knew about you."

*Those two did not. They knew nothing about you, either, except what they had been told. I believe you muffed this one, Garrett.*

I don't know about that. They probably wanted me to work. But I sighed. He really was right. And I definitely hate that. I hear about it forever. "I think I'll just go over to the brewery and—"

*Yes. You should do that. But not right away. Go later. After the night crew comes in. They will be the younger men who have the Cantard more freshly in mind. If there are human rights activists there, they are most likely to be found among the younger workers.*

What could I say? When he's right he's right. And he has been right a little too often lately. "All right. What're you going to suggest instead?" There would be something.

*See Captain Block. Ask him about The Call. Let fall some gentle intimation of the threat to Mr. Weider.*

Captain Westman Block runs the Guard, TunFaire's half-ass police force. The Guard is lame but more effective than the predecessor from which it evolved, the Watch, which existed primarily to absorb bribes to stay out of the way. The Watch still exists but only as a fire brigade.

The reason the Guard works is a little guy who is part dwarf, a touch of several other things, and maybe an eighth human. His name is Relway. He's the ugliest man I've ever met. He's obsessed with law and order. His conversations all revolve around his New Order, by which he means the absolute rule of law. When I met him, on a rainy night not that long ago, he was a volunteer "auxilliary" helping Block's tiny serious-crimes section of the Watch. I said something unpleasant to Relway that night. He assured me that I ought to be less unpleasant because he was going to be an important fellow before long.

His powers of prophecy were excellent.

Prince Rupert created the Guard and installed Westman Block as its chief. Then Block sanctioned Relway. And Relway immediately put together a powerful and nasty secret police force consisting of people who thought his way. Offenders have been known to just vanish once they attract the notice of Relway's section.

Probably no more than a thousand people know the section exists. He doesn't blow his own horn. And I'd bet there aren't more than a dozen people who can identify Relway by sight.

I'm one of them. Sometimes that makes me nervous.

That all rips through my mind whenever anyone mentions Block. I get the exact feeling Relway wants everybody to feel— that somebody is watching.

Old Man Weider is one of TunFaire's leading subjects. He's a commoner but is rich and powerful and influential. He has friends in high places who are real friends simply because he is the kind of man he is. Block would take an extra step to protect him.

Relway, being what he is, might take a few steps more if The Call was involved.

"Maybe that's all I really need to do. Get the Guard on the case. Block has more resources."

*There is more going on.*

"Why am I not surprised to hear that?"

*Because you are, at last, becoming somewhat adept at reading people—though not yet at a conscious level. At that same shadow level both Miss Weider and Miss Nicholas fear that Ty Weider was not the recipient of the threat but its source.*

"I don't like the guy but I could be wrong about him. Nicks thinks he's got something going."

*Miss Nicholas is torn in many directions. I feel for that child. She does indeed think some good things, though. She has known Ty Weider as long as she has known Miss Alyx. She makes allowances because she knew the Ty Weider who existed before the*

*Ty Weider who returned from the Cantard missing a leg. Have
lunch, then see Captain Block.*

"Yes, Mom."

Dumb move, Garrett.

The Dead Man took the mental muzzle off the Goddamn Parrot. That freaking jungle chicken just stores it up when he's under control. It gushed.

# 9

Block's headquarters were inside the Al-Khar, TunFaire's city prison. Handy, what with criminals being rounded up in gaggles lately. The place is huge, stark, cold, ugly, and badly in need of maintenance. It's a wonder prisoners don't escape by walking through the walls. Or by powdering the rusty bars in the infrequent windows. Ages ago some Hill family fattened up by cutting corners on construction, particularly in the choice of stone. Instead of a good Karentine limestone, available from quarries within a day's barge travel, somebody had supplied a soft snotty yellow-green stone that sucks up crud from the air, darkens, streaks, then flakes, leaving the exterior acned. The streets alongside the Al-Khar always boast a layer of detritus.

The mortar is in worse shape than the stone. Luckily, the walls are real thick.

I stopped, stunned, when I rounded a corner and saw the prison.

Scaffolding was up. Some tuckpointing was under way. Some chemical cleansing was restoring the youth of the stone.

Even clean that stone was butt-ugly.

How were they financing the face-lift? Till recently TunFaire jailed hardly anybody so no provision had been made to help maintain the seldom-used prison.

They'd had to evict squatters when Block moved in.

Captain Block not only was in, he was willing to see me. Immediately.

"You're a bureaucrat now, Block. Even if you haven't opened your eyes for fifteen years, you're supposed to be too busy to see somebody without an appointment. You'll set a precedent. You really live here? In jail?"

"I'm single. I don't need much room."

He seemed a little sad and a lot weary. He had shown fair political acumen getting the Guard created but, perhaps, didn't have the moral stamina to keep diverting frequent attempts to scuttle the rule of law.

"You look more relaxed these days." Block's quarters definitely didn't match his standing in the community. Neither did his dress. He should have been decked out like an admiral with two hundred years of service, but he just didn't care.

Block told me, "That business with the serial-killer spell that kept recasting itself made the prince love me. I'm almost untouchable. Almost. My cynical side says that's because nobody else wants the job. It certainly is thankless. But business is good. New villains jump up as fast as we harvest the old ones. They're like the dragon's teeth in that old myth. I'm endlessly amazed that so many of them survived the war."

I shrugged. I didn't know the one about the dragon's teeth.

Block is a compact, thin man with short brown hair quickly going gray. He needed a shave. He'd make a fair spy because there was nothing remarkable about him. You wouldn't notice him unless he yelled in your face. When I first met him, at a time when the law was honored more in the taking of bribes than actual enforcement, he'd had a mouth as filthy as the Goddamn Parrot's and all the manners of a starving snake.

I wasn't sure I liked the new, improved, mannered and unantagonistic, *dedicated* Block better than the angry old one.

I told him, "In the old days you never seemed like the dedicated type. You only did what you had to to get by."

A shadow brushed his features. "I got religion, Garrett."

"Huh?"

"I let Relway talk me into putting him on full-time. Big mistake. His conviction infects everybody around him."

"It does." Given his head Relway will exterminate the concept of crime by the end of the year. He's a man with a holy mission. He's scary.

"So what's up? Going to collect favors owed?"

"Not entirely. I want to ask about The Call. And I want to talk about Max Weider. Somebody's trying to squeeze him." I betrayed tradition and fed him all the details.

He was suspicious. "Why tell me?"

I would have been suspicious, too. In the past I'd kept him in the dark on principle.

"My partner insisted. And I owe Weider. It would be handy if somebody official was watching if something happened."

"What could happen?"

"With these rightsists? Anything."

"No shit. You heard about those people burning up on the north side?"

"I heard. I didn't pay attention. I've been busy."

"They're people with no connection to each other, drunks and no-accounts who couldn't make an enemy on a bet. But they've been burning up."

"You're pulling my leg."

"No. It's happened six times. It's got to be sorcery. Relway wants it to connect with the rights business but I don't see it. I can't see some teetotaling sorceress setting drunks on fire, either, though."

"You think it would be a woman?"

"If it was a teetotaller. You know any men dead set against spirits?"

"Only one." And I have to live with him. "So what about it? Is The Call moving into the rackets?"

"I haven't heard that. Jirek!"

The door opened. A creature limped in. He wasn't human. Not much, anyway. There was a little of everything in him but the three main ingredients appeared to be ogre, troll, and ugly. The whole was complicated by birth defects and wounds. Jirek moved sort of sideways, stiffly and bent, like his back hurt all the time.

"Jirek was injured in the ambush at Council Wells."

A veteran, then. Yet not human. Another one of those inconvenient complications I'd pointed out to Carter and Trace. Some of our biggest heroes aren't even human.

"Council Wells. One of our great victories," I observed.

"Do I detect the odor of sarcasm?"

Council Wells was supposed to have been a preliminary peace conference. The Karentine army concealed commando forces in the surrounding desert. Those patriots murdered the Venageti delegates in their sleep.

Another of those little triumphs that, when totalled, helped Karenta win the war.

"Me sarcastic? The gods forfend."

Jirek's great knobbly green mess of a face twisted and wriggled into a grotesque smile. Then he guffawed. His breath could gag a maggot. But he had a sense of humor.

Block told him, "Relway should be in his cell. Tell him I need him."

Jirek told me, "Good joke," then left.

"What was that?" I asked.

"Jirek. A unique." Which was slang for a breed who had extremely complicated antecedents. "He saved my ass a couple times in the Cantard. He was a perfect soldier. Too dumb to question authority. Just did what he was told. And was one bad boy in a fight."

"I just might change my mind about you."

"Don't brag about it. People might wonder why it took so long to rid yourself of the old, clogged one."

"And I thought I was developing a new relationship with the minions of the law."

Relway arrived. A little guy, he sort of oozed into Block's cell, no knock, like a shadow that didn't want to be noticed.

Relway is another unique, a completely improbable mixture. His interior landscape is a strange, strange land, too. He has a chip on his shoulder big enough to provide lumber for four houses. He's so far into law and order that he considers himself above any law that might restrain his efforts to crush crime. Now his auxiliaries and spies and midnight avengers are everywhere. It shouldn't be long till his name becomes one of the most feared in TunFaire.

Relway the man (using "man" generically, to indicate a sentient creature that walks on its hind legs) is almost unknown. I know him only because chance put me in the right place back when.

He nodded. "Garrett. You been keeping well?" His voice was hoarse, cracking, only half there.

"I'm fine. You pick up a cold?"

"The weather's been strange. I hear you might know something about that."

"Me? I was out there freezing my butt off with everybody else." Why relive my misadventures amongst mobs of low-grade, feuding gods?

He gave me that look all lawmen develop. It says not one word dripping from your filthy mouth is true now, nor ever has been. The power had gone to his head, though there was no denying the good being done. He had the bad guys rattled.

"What's that on your shoulder, Garrett?"

Block had done me the courtesy of ignoring that owl in a clown suit. "My lunch. I'll share. Stoke up the fire."

The Goddamn Parrot—or the Dead Man speaking through the buzzard's beak—had to have his word. "Awk! Jerk alert!"

"How do you do that without moving your lips?" Relway asked.

"It's a trick they teach Marines."

Relway asked, "We got something, Wes?"

They were getting cuddly now?

"Maybe. You've been working the rights gangs?"

"Where I can. They're hard to infiltrate. Mostly they form from groups who knew each other in the Cantard."

I still hang out with guys I knew down there. We don't spend good beer-drinking time trying to figure out how to hurt people, though.

Relway continued, "Big mobs like The Call are more vulnerable. Everybody doesn't know everybody. The Call proper is organized like the army. And Marengo North English is building a real private army. Freecorps Theverly, they're calling it."

"Is Colonel Theverly with them?" I was surprised, though I hadn't known Lieutenant Colonel Mochcs Theverly well enough to make sound assessments of his feelings toward nonhumans. He treated everybody the same in the zone. He was one of few officers who didn't go around with his head firmly inserted in a dark, stinky place.

"A man of conviction, the colonel." Shadows stirred behind Relway's eyes. "You know him?"

"I worked for him in the islands. Briefly. He got hurt and they pulled him out just before the Venageti overran us. The wound cost him a leg if I remember right. He was a good officer."

"That's not why you're here?"

"No. I didn't know about that."

Block asked, "Is The Call moving into the rackets, Deal? As a fund-raising activity?"

Relway frowned. "You have a run-in, Garrett?"

"I have a client. Max Weider. The brewery Weider."

Relway nodded. My relationship with Weider was no secret.

"His daughter Alyx says somebody claiming to be from The Call took a run at her brother Ty. They wanted a piece of the gross. That didn't sound like The Call. But if they need money to conjure up their own army, they might try more creative ways of getting it."

"They might," Relway agreed. "I haven't heard of it being discussed seriously. Yet. On the other hand, they have discussed
other areas traditionally associated with the Outfit—where those
exploit nonhumans."

"Two birds, one stone?"

"Exactly. The Call's Inner Council put it, 'We deem it fitting
that the disease provide the means of sustaining the cure.'"

Interesting. Sounded like he attended Call council meetings
himself. "They're pushing Chodo and they're still healthy?" I
wouldn't have thought even the most fanatic member of The Call
would dare jostle Chodo Contague. Chodo was the king of organized crime. Nobody poached in Chodo's territory. Nobody, that
is, who wasn't ready to fight a major war. It's impossible to imagine a deadlier enemy than Chodo Contague.

I knew the real head of the combine more intimately than Relway suspected. Chodo's daughter Belinda is young but so hard she
can cut steel.

Relway smiled his nastiest. "That'll be temporary. You know
the Contagues. And what they can do."

"O evil day," I said.

"Cute. The short answer is, The Call have shown no interest in
extortion. But this could be a test case. If Weider knuckles under
and they get the brewery in their pocket, Weider's peers will fall in
line."

"I know Max. He won't give in even if it costs ten times as much
to fight. Most of the commercial class would agree—even where
their political sympathies belong to The Call. They won't want the
precedent set. They didn't get rich by being easily intimidated."

Tinnie and Nicks running with Alyx might be as much business as friendship. The Tates were big in shoes. The family
Nicholas, in its several branches, were involved in winemaking,
coal mining, and inland shipping.

In each case, possibly even including that of the beer baron, I
would have been reluctant to listen to a standard appeal. But send
a beautiful girl and you can get Garrett's attention every time.

I'm too damned predictable. But they keep on making pretty
girls.

The shadows still swirled behind Relway's eyes. And those focused on me while the darkness pranced. "We have a basis for a
deal, Garrett," he mused.

"Uh. . . ."

"Apparently you don't approve of my methods. You don't

need to and I don't care if you do. You're a textbook case of inflexible goodguyitis." He chuckled at his own neologism. Scary, a Relway with a sense of humor. Maybe this one was a changeling. "But that don't mean we can't help each other."

That's why I came back to see Block. "I'm listening."

"Overwhelm me with enthusiasm."

"I'm a regular ball of fire. Everybody says so."

"You'd fit with the rightsists without any effort. You're the kind of guy they want."

Must be. Else yahoos like Stockwell and Wendover wouldn't come pounding on my door. "I'd only have to shuck about half my beliefs."

Relway's grin revealed teeth definitely not human. "You served with those people. You know how they think. You've heard all their knee-jerk crap. How hard could it be to parrot it?" His grin got bigger. He stared at Mr. Big. "Put some words in your own mouth."

I grunted, hoped Relway and Block didn't think too much about the bird. I didn't need them figuring out the fact that the Dead Man was riding my shoulder by proxy. "I could. But why should I?" This was starting to sound like work.

"I can't get my people inside. These crackpots are abidingly paranoid. If a man has even a tenth part nonhuman blood, he's a breed and part of the problem. Never mind he might have been a war hero. The spiders spinning the web of hatred are sure humankind can be redeemed only through the extinction of the rest of the races. Even to the extreme of hunting down and expunging every drop of nonhuman blood. Otherwise us uniques might breed back to original stock."

I guess my mouth was open. Luckily no flies were working the cell. "That's so damned ridiculous--"

"What does ridiculous have to do with belief? Those people are out there, Garrett."

I wanted to argue but my last case had involved several religions, each more unlikely than the last.

People will believe anything when they need to believe something. A lot *have* to believe in something bigger than themselves, whether that is a cause or a god. *What* doesn't necessarily matter as long as *something* is there.

"I understand."

"You don't have to sign a pact in blood. Just drift farther inside than you planned, then let me know what you find."

"And what'll you do for me?"

"Keep you posted on what I learn. And protect the Weiders—if it comes to that."

I owed Old Man Weider a lot. I owed the Tates some, too. "Could you keep an eye on the Tates while you're at it?"

Relway sighed. "I suppose I can do that." He smiled. Pity about those teeth. "You make peace with your friend?"

My life is an entertainment for all TunFaire. Everybody knows every time Tinnie winks at me. "They're special to me."

"You have a deal. Wes, I've got to wander, see what's new on the street." He can do that. Little scruff like him, nobody would believe he's Relway.

"Wait up," I said. "Couple things more. Ever hear of Black Dragon Valsung?"

Relway shrugged, showed me his palms. "Which is what?"

"Supposed to be a new freecorps. Colonel Norton Valsung commanding, lately of the Black Dragon Brigade."

Relway shook his head. Block said, "Never heard of either one."

"Me neither. That's what made me wonder."

"What?" Relway wanted to know.

"Two squeaky-clean clerk types named Carter Stockwell and Trace Wendover came to the house today. Wanted me to join their outfit."

Block and Relway glanced at each other. Block said, "Means nothing to me."

Relway said, "There're always new gangs. I'll keep an ear open."

Block waved. Relway headed for the door. I started to go myself. Block told me, "Hang on, Garrett."

"Uhm?"

"If you do get involved, you be real careful. These people are nasty."

"I've been playing with the bad boys a long time. I don't make mistakes anymore."

"Only takes one, Garrett. Smart guys get dead, too."

"Point taken. Thanks."

"One more thing. Relway gets too focused sometimes. Doesn't think about whatever don't bear on what interests him right now."

"You leading up to something?"

"Yes. His people saw Crask and Sadler yesterday. Remember

them? You should. They're back in town and too stupid not to be seen."

"Never heard either one accused of genius." I shivered. Not much scares me but Crask and Sadler are stone-cold professional killers of the worst sort. The sort who want to hurt Mrs. Garrett's only surviving son. They're that lucky kind of professional who get to do work they really enjoy.

Crask and Sadler have a sack full of bones to pick with Mama Garrett's favorite boy. I helped run them out of town. I helped fix them up with a Combine price on their heads.

"I'll watch out."

"Do. Hey! Teach that ugly sack of feathers to scout for you."

"You hear that, bird?"

The Goddamn Parrot kept his beak shut. A remarkable state of affairs.

# 10

Crask and Sadler. Damn! I thought those double-uglies were out of my life for good.

They tried to take over when Chodo had his stroke—which few people knew about. Most think he's still in charge. They wouldn't if Belinda hadn't outfoxed Crask and Sadler when they made their grab. Them knowing about Chodo, and their deadly enmity, explained Belinda's eagerness to elevate them to the next plane.

Nowadays Chodo is a lump of meat imprisoned in a wheelchair. Belinda has no use for him except to pretend her orders come from him.

Block again told me, "You take care."

"You too." I decided to say it. "I like this Westman Block better than the old one."

That got me a sour look and, "Might be smart not to turn up here again. You go out on the fringe, you'll never know who's watching or what their real loyalties are."

I paused outside the jail, studied the street. At the best of times watching your surroundings closely is wise. Our great city never lacks for characters willing to steal your gold tooth in broad daylight while you're watching.

Nobody was interested in me. I didn't appear threatening, nor weak enough to be an easy victim.

I felt good. I had an accommodation with the law—which would work for me because Max Weider is a municipal treasure.

It was a gorgeous day, a tad warm but with a nice breeze, a few scurrying clouds dancing on a sky so blue it defined the color for all time. It was the kind of day that makes us daytime people feel good. The kind of day when people laugh, visit friends not seen for a while, conceive children. The kind of day when bloodlettings are few and even the scroats take time off to appreciate what a wonderful world it can be. It was the kind of day when Relway's crew might get into mischief because they had too much time on their hands.

I headed east and north. It was time I visited an old friend of my own.

The streets were crowded but the activists were having trouble working up much indignation. If the weather held, the coffinmakers and crematoria would catch up and have to cut prices.

A centaur clip-clopped past. He wore an old army blanket. I couldn't make out the regimental mark. He couldn't be real bright. If that blanket was loot and not a Crown issue to an auxiliary formation, possession could get him killed.

Some days it could anyway.

He was drunk. He didn't care.

The air above swarmed with pixies and fairies and whatnot, the young ones tormenting the pigeons. That wouldn't earn them any enemies who weren't pigeons themselves.

Birds were out courting, too. I noted a few hawks and peregrines way up high. The little people better stay alert. . . . A dimwit peregrine dived at a pixie girl. It drew a flurry of poisoned darts. The wee folk were using the nice day to educate a new generation of predators.

It's a pity people are stupider than falcons. Otherwise, we could teach them not to prey on their own kind.

On days like this, when everyone comes out to soak up the warm, it seems impossible that so many beings live in this city. But TunFaire is really several cities occupying the same site. There are evening peoples and night peoples and morning peoples who never see one another. It is both an accommodation and a way of life. It used to work.

The tip of a wing whipped across the back of my hair. The Goddamn Parrot was showing off for his plain-feathered cousins. "I know a Yessiley place where they put pigeon in everything they cook. And they don't care if the pigeon is really a pigeon."

"Awk! I want to soar with eagles and am forced—"

"You want me to call one of those hawks down? They'll soar with you."

"Help!"

"Hey, Mister. Does your bird really talk?"

"Hush, Bertie. The man's a ventriloquist." Bertie's mom gave me a look that said I ought to be ashamed, trying to scam people with an innocent bird.

"You're probably right, ma'am. Why don't you take the poor creature and give him a decent home?"

The air crackled around woman and child so swift was their departure.

Nobody wanted poor old lovable Mr. Big.

# 11

The place has pretensions toward being a class eatery. It doesn't compete for the Yessiley trade. Its fashionable dishes never include anything harder to catch than squash or eggplant. Its name varies with the mood of its owner, Morley Dotes. The Palms is the moniker he's hung on it lately. His target clientele has gone from being blackhearted second-string underworlders foregathering to plot, negotiate, or arrange an expedient truce to upscale subjects foregathering to plot, negotiate, or arrange an expedient truce.

The staff, however, is a constant.

It was an off-peak hour when I invited myself into Morley's place. Diners of any station were conspicuous by their absence. Staff were making preparations for the hour when the crowd would show. Morley's new gimmick was a money cow. The place reeked prosperity.

"Shee-it! I done thunk we was shut of dis perambulatin' sack a horse apples."

"Better watch using words like perambulate, Sarge. You'll throw your tongue out of joint." How long did it take him to latch on to the word's meaning, so he could use it? It was several syllables longer than any in his normal vocabulary.

A voice from the shadowed back growled, "You let dat damned dog in here again, Sarge? I smell doggie do."

"Dat ain't dog shit, Puddle. Dat's Garrett."

"Tossup which is worst."

"Fugginay."

"You guys ought to take your routine on the road." I couldn't see Puddle but he had been struck from the same mold as Sarge.

Both are big and fat and sloppy, tattooed and almost as bad as they think they are.

"Fugginay, Garrett. We'd have 'em rollin' in da streets. Be up to our friggin' noses in hot little gels. . . . Nah. I don't tink. I'm gettin' too old for all dat."

"Watcha want, Garrett?" Puddle demanded. "I tink we done you 'bout enough favors for dis week."

"I don't need any favors," I fibbed. "I wanted to let Morley in on some bad news."

Back there in the shadows Puddle must have reported through the speaking tube to Morley's office upstairs. Dotes' voice came from the stair. "What bad news is that, Garrett?"

"Crask and Sadler are back."

Morley didn't say anything for a good ten seconds. Then he asked, "Where did you get that?"

"Can't tell you." Which told him.

"Shee-it!" Sarge observed. "What'd I say? It smells like poop it's proba'ly gonna be poop. He wants sometin' again."

"Fugginay," Puddle replied. "I'm gonna have me a case a da brown-leg trots he comes in here someday an' he don't want nuttin'."

I tried a ferocious scowl on Sarge as I passed him. He grinned amiably. He doesn't scare. "Nice shoulder ornament dere, Garrett. We knew you'd take to da bird eventually."

These people are my friends. Allegedly.

I told Morley, "You know eggplant used to be poisonous?"

"Yes. I keep a few of the undomesticated variety around in case I want to cook up special dishes for people who don't respect our dress code here." He led the way upstairs. "So who's going to hear you now? Block told you about Crask and Sadler?"

"He got it from Relway."

"Oh. In here." Morley ducked across the room he uses for an office, settled into a plush chair behind a big table. He slipped a toothpick into a forest of nasty sharp teeth, looked thoughtful. "Crask and Sadler. Interesting."

# 12

Morley Dotes is the kind of guy nightmares are made of if you have a daughter. He's so damned handsome it's painful, in an olive, slim, dark-elven fashion. Anything he throws on makes him look like he spent all last week at a tailor's. He can deck himself out in white and prance through a coalyard without getting a spot on himself. I've never seen him sweat. Females of numerous species stop thinking while he's around.

For all his faults he's a good friend. Albeit a friend of the sort who would give you a talking parrot as a gift—and do it in a way that would tie you in knots of obligation that keep you from disposing of said gift in any sensible fashion. Sort of the way an old hag witch might put a curse on you that you can shed only when some other fool volunteers to take it upon himself.

No doubt Morley chuckles himself to sleep every night thinking about me and the Goddamn Parrot.

I said, "Looks like the new scam has the marks rolling in."

"It was the right move at the right time, Garrett. Took a while to convince the neighbors that they would benefit, though."

I could imagine. The area had been known as the Safety Zone till recently. It was neutral ground where gentlemen of unsavory enterprise who were business rivals or outright enemies could sit down with some expectation of personal safety. The Joy House had been the heart of the Zone. Morley made the Zone work and therefore profitable for the whole area.

A shift in market focus certainly would disconcert the neighbors.

"Rich people have the same requirements and vices as poor

people," Morley observed. Lamplight sparkled off the points of his unnaturally white teeth. "But they have more money to pay for them. That convinced everyone."

That and, I didn't doubt, the marketing strategems of Sarge and Puddle and their compatriots.

"Uhm. Crask and Sadler."

"Block do any guessing about who brought them in?"

"Nope. I thought Belinda should know they'd been seen." Morley has better contacts in the Outfit.

"If she doesn't know, she'll be grateful for the warning."

I said, "I'd like to break the news personally."

Morley gave me a double dose of the fish-eye. "You sure that would be smart?"

"She used me up and left. No hard feelings from me."

"From you. Belinda Contague is a strange woman, Garrett. Might not be healthy to get within stabbing distance of her."

"We understand each other. But it'll be easier for both of us if I have you contact her."

"I'll pass it on this time, you bullshitter. But you need to find somebody else to run your love notes. I'm out of that life."

Who was bullshitting who? But I didn't ask. Let the man think he can kid a kidder. If he did. It could be a useful lever later.

"What have you been into lately?" Dotes asked. "We haven't had a chance to just sit and talk and find cures for the ills of the world." His notions for the latter involve either forcing everyone to turn vegetarian or necessitate wholesale slaughters. Or both.

I told him about my adventures among the gods. And goddesses. "I thought about getting you together with Magodor. She was your type."

"Uhm?" He looked speculative.

"She had four arms, snakes for hair, green lips, teeth like a cobra. But she was to kill for otherwise."

"Oh, yes. I've dreamed about her for years."

"Elves don't dream."

He shrugged. "What about now?"

"Now?"

"You didn't visit Block to tip a few beers and reminisce about old murders you solved together."

"Sure I did."

"I know you, Garrett. You have a case."

"It isn't really a case. I've got the deal with the brewery. Somebody threatened the old man. Maybe." I sketched the situation.

"You have yourself a situation fraught with peril, Garrett." He smirked.

"Potential violence. Weider won't stand for it. And if The Call tries moving into the rackets—"

"The Call probably wouldn't. But several fringe groups are trying. They don't attract people with money. We'll see some excitement there. I can hear Belinda sharpening her knives. You going inside?"

"Inside?"

"Into the movement. As a spy. You wouldn't have any trouble. You're ethnically pure. You're a war hero." Morley is a war hero himself, in his own mind. He stayed behind and did yeoman service comforting many a soldier's frightened wife. "You're healthy enough to stand on your hind legs. You're unemployed. Makes you the perfect recruit."

"Except for I don't buy the doctrine."

Morley smiled his sharp-toothed finest. "You better not be seen here if you're going inside. You shouldn't even be around the Dead Man."

"Oh." I didn't swear any oaths with Relway, did I? No thumb-cutting and blood-mixing. Obvious as it was I hadn't thought about the fact that infiltrating the rightsists meant my own lifestyle would have to reflect rightsist prejudice.

Adopting a false identity would be too iffy. Too many veterans knew me. One thing you do when you're single and don't work is hang out with people like yourself. I prefer the company of women but there are rare occasions on an almost daily basis when no woman prefers mine. Hard as that is to believe.

"It won't go that far." I hoped. "I'm going to the brewery to poke around. If Ty is trying to scam Pop's cash prematurely, I'll scare him off. If he's playing straight, I'll still get an idea of the real problem. I can't believe any of our racist lunatics have balls big enough to go after Weider."

"You have true believers involved, Garrett. You ought to know reality doesn't faze those people. They're right. That's their armor. That's all they need." Morley sat up straight. He wanted to move on to something else. "Be careful out there, Garrett."

"I'm always careful."

"No, you're not. You're lucky. And luck is a woman. Be careful. You learned from the best. Take my lessons to heart."

"Right." I chuckled. Morley doesn't lack for self-image.

"Tell Puddle to come up. I need him to run a message."

"I don't think he'll do much running." I did as Dotes asked, though.

Morley never said a word about the Goddamn Parrot. Never asked a question. Never even looked at the bird. Never smirked or rubbed it in.

Morley was playing with me again.

I ought to slice the little buzzard into thin strips and slip them to him buried in one of his strange, overly spiced vegetarian platters.

# 13

I watched Puddle strain his way upstairs. "That man needs to eat more of what he serves," I told Sarge, who isn't a single pound lighter.

"Fugginay. We're all puttin' on da pounds, Garrett," Sarge muttered, polishing a mug. Though they're all thugs, Morley's guys pretend to be waiters and cooks. "Ya tink about it hard when ya ain't eatin' but den ya wander inta a place where dey got da good beer and da great food, ya go bugfuck and don't tink what ya done till ya done et half a cow."

"I know what you mean." Dean was too good a cook.

Couldn't be the beer. Beer is good for you.

"Fugginay. Hey, I got work to do, Garrett."

"Yeah. Later."

"You be careful out dere, pal. Da world's goin' crazy."

That was the nicest thing Sarge ever said to me. I hit the street wondering why.

A bird's wing brushed the back of my head. Again.

My live-in clown was restless. He didn't speak, though. Luckily. Had the Dead Man not been controlling him, he would have screeched about me abusing infants. Or something. There was an unnatural rapport between the Loghyr and the bird. The Dead Man could touch his mind from miles away. Me he can barely reach in the street outside the house.

It's bad enough to have the Dead Man after me constantly at home. Having him use Mr. Big to keep tabs everywhere else had gotten old two minutes after he found out he could do it.

I reminded him, "I'm going to the brewery." Shift change was coming up.

People noticed me talking to the bird. They gave me a more than normal amount of room.

Because the streets are filled with men who talk to ghosts and shadows. For them the Cantard opened doors to realms the rest of us never see.

War may not be Hell itself but it definitely does weaken the barriers between us and the dark regions.

The Goddamn Parrot took wing. He followed me from above. The Dead Man's control slipped. The jungle vulture squawked insults at passersby. Some hurled sticks or bits of broken brick. The bird mocked them. He fears nothing that goes on two legs.

Hawks are something else.

A pigeon killer of uncertain species arrowed down out of the blue. Mr. Big sensed his peril at the last instant. He dodged. Even so, bright feathers flew but only the parrot's feelings suffered any real injury. He shrieked curses.

I chuckled. "That was close, you little pervert. Maybe next time I'll get lucky."

The little monster returned to my shoulder. He wouldn't leave again. The hawk circled but lost patience quickly. There is no shortage of pigeons in this burg.

"Argh!" I said. "Where's me eye patch, matey?" I took a few crabbed steps, dragging my left foot. Folks didn't appreciate the effort, thought. Almost everybody has a disabled veteran in the family.

# 14

Stragglers from the early shift still drifted into the street as I reached the brewery. The stench of fermentation drenched the neighborhood. The workers didn't notice. Neither did the residents. Their noses were dead.

Weider's main brewery is a great gothic redbrick monster that looks more like a hospice for werewolves and vampires than the anchor of a vast commercial empire. It has dozens of turrets and towers that have nothing to do with what goes on inside the building. Bats boil out of the towers at dusk.

The monstrosity sprang from Old Man Weider's imagination. A smaller duplicate stands directly across Delor Street, Weider's first effort. He'd meant that to be a brewery but it turned out to be too small. So he remodeled and moved his family in while he built a copy ten times bigger, to which all sorts of additions have attached themselves since.

We TunFairens love our beer.

The brewery don't have a real security team. Senior workers take turns patrolling and watching the entrances. Outside villains don't get in. The workforce protects the place like worker bees protect their hives.

A spry antique named Geral Diar had the duty at the front entrance. "Hey, Gerry," I said as I walked up. "Checking in."

"Garrett?" His eyes aren't the best. And he was surprised to see me. That was a good sign. If nobody expects me, any bad guys will have no time to cover up. "What're you doing here?"

"Snooping. Same as always. The big house says it's time. Been stealing any barrels?"

"You enjoy yourself, young fellow. Somebody should."

"Oh? You're not?"

Diar is one of those guys who can't not talk if anybody stops to listen. "Not much joy around here lately."

"How come?"

"State of the kingdom. Everybody's got a viewpoint and no-body's got a pinch of tolerance for the other guy's."

This might be germane. "Been some political friction here?"

"Oh, no, not around here. Mr. Weider wouldn't put up with that. But it's everywhere else and you got to get through it to get to work. You can't hardly go anywhere without you run into a brawl or demonstration or even an out an' out riot. It's all a them foreigners from the Cantard. They just act like they *want* to cause trouble."

"I know what you mean." I was in my chameleon mode, where I mirror whomever I'm with. That loosens people up. Diar's comment, though, complimented the Dead Man's suspicion that Glory Mooncalled was trying to destabilize Karentine society.

"Gets depressing, Garrett, knowing you have to go out there. Things was better back when all you had to worry about was thieves and strong-arm men."

"I'm sure the King will do something soon." Like the traditional turn-of-the-back till the mob sorted itself out. Not that the royals deign to spend time in TunFaire, where the upper crust bears them far less goodwill than does the factious, fractious rabble.

"Well, you just have yourself a wonderful day, Garrett."

"And you, too, Gerry. You, too."

When you think brewery mostly you picture the finished product: beer, ale, stout, whatever. You don't consider the process. First thing you notice about a brewery is the smell. That isn't the toothsome bouquet of a premium lager, either. It's the stench of vegetable matter rotting. Because that's the process. To get beer you let vats of grain and water and additives like hops rot under the loving guidance of skilled old brewmasters who time each phase to the minute.

There are no youngsters working in the brewhouse. In the Weider scheme even apprenticed sons of the brewmasters start out as rough labor. Weider himself was a teamster before he went to the Cantard and believes that physical labor made him a better man. But when he was young everybody over nine had to work. And jobs were easy to find.

Weider does know every job in the brewery and occasionally

works some of them just to keep in touch with a workingman's reality. He expects his senior associates to do the same.

Manvil Gilbey wrestling beer barrels is a hoot. Which might explain why Gilbey isn't entirely fond of me. I've witnessed his efforts and feel comfortable reporting that as a laborer he's pretty lame.

I said hello to the brewmasters on duty. Skibber Kessel returned a sullen greeting. Mr. Klees was too busy to notice a housefly like me. They were dedicated men, disinclined to gossip at the most relaxed times. I supposed they were happy with things the way they were. No brewmaster is shy about raising hell when he's bothered. The finest brewmasters are like great operatic performers.

When I go to the brewery I try to stay unpredictable. The bad boys don't need to catch me in a routine. Sometimes I hang around only half an hour. Other times I just won't go away. I become like some unemployed cousin loafing around the place, though I will help the guys on the docks, loading and unloading. I shoot the bull with the apprentices, shovel with the guys in the grain elevator, just watch the boys in the hops shed. I wander, double-check counts on the incoming barley, rice, and wheat, calculating inflow against recorded output. In all ways I try to be a pain in the ass to would-be crooks.

The brewery's biggest problem always was pilferage. That's been a lot smaller since I came around but, unfortunately, human nature is human nature.

# 15

I knew some of the teamsters and dock wallopers well enough to drink with so it seemed I ought to start with them. They wouldn't hesitate to talk about conflicts within the workforce.

There are two ways to reach the loading docks—besides going around to the freight gate. One leads through the caverns beneath the brewery, where the beer is stored. The caverns and the proximity of the river, on which raw materials arrive, are why Weider chose the site.

The caverns are the more difficult route. The other way runs through the stable. That's huge. Few other enterprises require so much hauling capacity.

I chose the caverns. It's almost a religious experience, wandering those cool aisles between tall racks of kegs and barrels.

They work round the clock down there and I always find Mr. Burkel there with his tally sheets. "Mr. Burkel, don't you ever sleep?"

"Garrett! Hello. Of course I do. You're just a lucky man. You get to enjoy my company every time you come around."

"How can I argue with that? How are your numbers running these days?"

"As good as they've ever been. As good as they've ever been."

Which still meant a slight floor loss in favor of the workforce, probably limited to what was consumed on the premises. Which was fine with Old Man Weider.

Mr. Burkel handed me a huge stein. As chance would have it, that stein was filled with beer. "This is a new wheat we've just started shipping." I sipped half a pint.

"And a fine brew it is, Mr. Burkel. It's heavier than the lager but lighter than the dark I usually prefer." I forebore tossing in some wine snob chat. He wouldn't get the joke. "This's why I like Old Man Weider. He's always trying something. Thanks. Maybe I'll come through again on my way out."

"Do. Now answer me something, Garrett. How come you got a stuffed bird on your shoulder? Looks goofy as hell."

"It's not stuffed. It's alive. It's kind of a signature thing. Other guys in my racket all got a gimmick."

"Oh." You'd have thought I was threatening to tell him about my new wall coverings. "Well, you be careful out there, Garrett."

"Likewise, Mr. Burkel."

# 16

The Weider freight docks are chaos incarnate, yet out of that confusion flows the lifeblood of the tavern industry. From its heart to its nethermost extremities beer is the blood and soul of the metropolis.

The teamsters and dockhands received me with mixed emotions, as always. Some were friendly, or pretended to be. Others scowled. Maybe some of those were involved in the theft ring I rooted out. They might figure I done them wrong because stealing from the boss is a worker's birthright.

Shadows were gathering in the dockyard. Hostlers had begun retiring the incoming teams. After dark only outside haulers would be loaded. This was a time of day the dockworkers liked. They could get lazy.

It was also the time of day when a keg or three could disappear most easily.

I planted the other side of my lap on a returned empty meant to go back to the cooperage yard for repairs. I stayed out of the way, let the noise and chatter wash over me. The Goddamn Parrot muttered but did not lapse into filth. What little I understood sounded like random thoughts from one of the Dead Man's secondary minds. He must be distracted.

I listened. I overheard almost nothing about the political situation and less about what everybody thought I might be after. I didn't mind. I didn't expect anybody to be dumb enough to plot right in front of me, though the criminal class does boast a rich vein of stupidity.

Mostly I watched how guys behaved when they knew I was watching.

Nobody acted guilty.

"Garrett?"

I opened my eyes. I'd been on the brink of falling asleep. The long nights were catching up.

"Gilbey?" Manvil Gilbey masquerades as Old Man Weider's batman but he's no servant. The bond between them goes back to their army days and is unshakable. Nobody can indict its rectitude, either. Gilbey had a wife who died. Weider still has one he worships. If Max is the brain of the brewing empire, Manvil Gilbey is its soul and conscience.

"Max requests the honor of your company whenever you can get over to the house."

Gilbey needed a few quaffs of the product. He's all right once he's had a few.

"I'll be over before it gets completely dark."

"Good enough." Gilbey turned and marched away.

A driver called Sparky observed, "That's one guy what never should of got outta the army."

"Always on the parade ground, isn't he?"

"He's all right, you get to know him."

"One of the good people," I agreed.

"He just never learned to take it easy."

"The streets are filled with people like that these days."

"Tell me about it," Sparky grumbled. "When I get off I've been driving and hossing them barrels for twelve, fourteen hours. All I want to do is get home and collapse. So what happens every goddamned night? I've got to walk a mile through morons trying to save the world from the guy next door. And every damned one of them wants me to join his mob. They get deaf as a cobblestone when you tell them to just leave you the fuck alone."

Another driver said, "I'm thinking about just camping out here till this shit blows over. I'm fed up having to duck a fight every time I go somewhere."

I suggested, "Maybe you could try a different route. Those rights guys only show up where they think they can start something. I didn't get any hassles coming down here. I don't get much trouble at all, really."

"You think walking around with that stick and stuff don't

make a difference? Them assholes ain't ready to work for it yet."

"Yeah, Garrett. Mosta dem fucks be scared shitless of a guy wit' a eagle on his shoulder."

"Thank you, Zardo. But don't give the buzzard a swelled head." I tote my headknocker everywhere these days. Times have grown so interesting that I no longer feel foolish being cautious. "You want to buy this bird, Zardo? Sparky? I'll cut you a deal. I'll throw in an eye patch."

"Dat'd just be askin' for trouble. I couldn't fight my way outta a weddin' reception."

Sparky said, "I spent my five doing the same thing I do here, Garrett. I never touched a weapon after Basic."

I didn't know Sparky well enough to preach to him so I just shrugged. "Life's never kind to the good-hearted. I had a friend once who recited a poem over and over about how good men die while the wicked prosper. One of the best men I ever knew. What the crocodile didn't eat we buried in a swamp on an island down south."

"I know that pome."

"I'd better head for the big house."

"Sure. Something I wanted to ask you, though."

"Yeah? What?"

"That bird. It's stuffed. Right?"

"You got a bet on? It's alive. It's just doped." On idiocy-suppressing thoughts from the Dead Man. "If I don't dope it, it cusses worse than old Matt Berry. Usually at somebody who could yank off both of my arms with one hand tied behind his back."

"Oh." Sparky seemed disappointed. He must have lost the bet.

# 17

I dropped off the dock, strolled toward the stables. Going through was the fastest way to the big house.

I was halfway through, stepping carefully, when I found myself at the heart of a sudden triangle of guys who didn't look very friendly.

Morley's oft-given advice was sinking in. Or maybe I was just in a bad mood. Or maybe I was just impatient. I didn't ask what anybody wanted.

I spun. My oak headknocker tapped the temple of the guy moving up behind me. The pound of lead inside the stick's business end added emphasis to my argument. His eyes glazed. He went down without a word.

I continued to turn, dropped, laid my next love tap on the side of the knee of a huge Weider teamster. He was just getting a fist wound up.

His legs folded. I rose past him, tapped him on his bald spot, stepped aside as he sprawled, turned to the last character. "Something on your feeble mind?"

He kept coming even though he had no tools. That didn't seem encouraging. Why the confidence? I feinted a tap at an elbow, buried the tip of my stick in his breadbasket. He whoosed a bushel of bad breath. I whapped the side of his head, then found out why he kept on coming.

A second wave of three materialized. These boys looked like they were accustomed to muscle work. I didn't recognize any of them. On the plus side, none of them were behind me.

While they decided what to do because Plan One had burned

up in their fingers I rethumped everybody already down. I didn't want any surprises.

One of the new bunch grabbed a pitchfork. Another collected a shovel. I didn't like the implications.

The Goddamn Parrot, who had elevated himself to a stringer overhead when the excitement started, said, "Awk! Garrett's in deep shit now."

The third man, who seemed to be in charge, hung back to direct traffic. He and his pals all looked up when the bird spoke.

I didn't.

I charged.

A pitchfork is nasty and a shovel unpleasant but neither was designed to hurt people. My stick, though, has no other reason for existing. A feint and a weave gave me a chance to reach in and crunch knuckles on a hand gripping the pitchfork. Shovel man froze momentarily when his too-slow buddy shrieked. I skipped aside and cracked his skull.

I swear, he shimmered. I thought he was going to fade away. I wanted to whimper because I was afraid some gods were after me again.

I whipped back to pitchfork man. He was too slow to be a threat by himself. A moment later he was sinking and I was ready to go after the last man.

The clown shut the stall gate between us, leaned on it, and smiled. "I'm impressed."

"You ought to be. You're about to be flat on your back in the horse fruit yourself. Who are you? Why the hell are you bothering me?"

"Awk," the Goddamn Parrot observed from above.

"I'm nobody special. Just a messenger."

I rolled me eyes. "Corn by the bucketful. Spare me. I don't mind crippling the messenger."

"Not scared?"

"Just quaking in my little shoesies." I banged a toe off the temple of the guy who had tried to fork me. For half a second he shimmered like his buddy had.

"No skin off my nose, you listen or not."

"Want to bet?" I popped my stick against my palm. "Let's see if you shimmer, too."

"Here's the word. We know where you live. Stay away from the Weider brewery."

"A joke, right?" I indicated my collection of unconscious bodies. "I know where I live, too. You guys want, come on over."

For just a second his confidence was shaky. "I'm telling you. Back off. Stay away."

"Says who? You've gotten something turned around inside your head. You and your company-clerk buddies here are going to keep your lardy asses off of Weider property. Next time you trespass you'll get hurt."

The guy smirked. I flicked the tip of my stick at the fingers of his right hand where he gripped the top of the gate. He bit, yanked back. I kicked the gate. He staggered backward. Unfortunately, my balance wasn't perfect either. My follow-through was a plop into not-so-sweet-smelling straw.

The Goddamn Parrot guffawed.

"Your day is coming."

The big guy bounced off a post, got his balance back. He grabbed a handy hay hook, whooshed it back and forth. He wasn't happy anymore. He snarled, "That was a big mistake. Now you got me pissed off. And I don't need you in one piece."

There are people so stupid they just can't imagine somebody hurting them. And some of those are so dim you can't even teach them with pain. This guy looked like one of the latter.

The Goddamn Parrot made a distressed noise.

I dived for my stick. It had gotten away from me when I fell. I slithered over an earlier victim. He groaned when I got him with an elbow.

"What are you men doing there?" That sounded like somebody used to being in charge. I glanced sideways as I got hold of my stick, saw Ty Weider and his wheelchair maybe fifteen feet away, beyond a couple of stalls. With him were his full-time helper Lancelyn Mac and two stable hands.

The big guy looked, too. He dithered a second longer than I did. Without getting up, I swung my stick and got him in the kneecap. He yowled and raised his leg. I rolled into the one still on the straw.

"Lance. Ike. See what's going on there," Ty ordered.

I got up. "It's me. I was crossing from the dock to the big house when these guys jumped me." I kicked the big man in the side of the head before he got organized. I wasn't fond of anybody right then. I planted a foot on his butt and pushed him into a manure pile.

Lancelyn and Ike joined me. I asked, "You guys recognize any of these thugs?"

Both looked toward Ty for advice. Weider maneuvered his chair through the mess. "Sit them up so I can see their faces."

I lifted guys. So did Ike. Lance didn't want to get anything under his fingernails. He elected himself director of field operations.

I'd always suspected him of being that kind of guy. He was a tall, golden-haired boy with an inflated notion of his own worth. Women of the shallow variety drooled when he walked past. We'd never gotten along but, then, we'd never had to. I didn't hang out with the younger Weiders anymore.

"You play rough, Garrett," Ty said.

"I took them by surprise."

"In more ways than one, I'd guess."

He was right. For sure these guys hadn't been clear on who I was. Otherwise, they would have been better prepared.

Ty said, "Lance, those faces look familiar." He pointed, indicating the men I'd seen before myself. "What're you doing, Garrett?"

"Going through their pockets." I tapped a guy's head to keep him down. "Might find something interesting."

"You saying this wasn't personal? None of these guys have a sister?"

"Some of them probably do. But I don't know them. It didn't get personal till they tried to thump on me. The one I was wrestling when you showed up told me they were supposed to tell me to stay away from the brewery. He was the only one who ever said anything."

"You don't know him?"

"No."

"Neither do I. Lance? No? Ike? Mays? No? Looks like we have a mystery, then."

"This is Votil Hanbe," Ike said, indicating one of the familiar men. "He cleans stables nights. That one works the dock nights. I don't remember his name."

"Kessel," Lancelyn said. "Milo Kessel. Skibber Kessel is his uncle. Mr. Klees hired him. As a favor to Skibber. I was there when they discussed it."

"We can talk to them, then. Don't beat on those two anymore, Garrett. And what should we do with the rest of them?"

"Whatever you do with trespassers."

"Keelhaul 'em," the Goddamn Parrot suggested.

I continued, "Beat them some more and toss them into the canal. Hello."

"What?"

"All of them have one of these armbands tucked away." I lifted one. It was the black and red and blue common to all the human rights groups. This one boasted a black two-headed dragon on a red field as its main device. "I don't recognize this."

Nobody else claimed any knowledge, either. Ty said, "Lance, get them up and get them out of here. Ike, Mays, lend a hand."

I asked, "Is there any reason one of the nut groups would want me to stay away from here? I'm part of the scenery."

"Who knew you were coming?" Right to the point, old Ty.

"Nobody," I fibbed. He should know, though, unless he didn't talk to his intended. Nicks wouldn't be hiding what she and Alyx were doing from her fiancé, even if Alyx wanted. Or would she? "But I've been here long enough for somebody to send out for help. Only, what would political guys be afraid that I'd find?"

"These people are mainly lower-class veterans, Garrett. You need money to become a political force. Did you check to see if someone's been skimming again?"

"I did. I didn't catch any bad smells."

"I'll reexamine the accounts myself. I'll let you know if I find anything. You say my father wanted to see you?"

"Gilbey caught me on the dock. Soon as I finished I headed for the big house."

"Dad's probably grumbling about you taking so long. I'll let you know what these two have to say. If they don't talk, they'll be looking for work."

The unknowns were headed for the street already, partly under their own power. Those boys would have a fine crop of aches and bruises in the morning.

Not me, though. I'd saved myself all that by moving fast and hitting hard, *first*. Just what Morley has been preaching for so long. Pretty soon I'd be leaving them with their throats cut.

Ty muttered, "I'm going to be late again." He worked his chair around until he was right in there with the brewery employees, both of whom were conscious now. "Lance. We'll question Hanbe first. No sense upsetting Skibber Kessel if we don't have to."

The Goddamn Parrot dropped out of the gloom, satisfied that it was safe to show his ugly beak around me again.

Ty started. Then he grinned. "Put one on the other shoulder, too, Garrett. Add a tricorner hat, a bad limp, some facial scars, and an eye patch. You could pass yourself off as Captain Scarlet." He smirked.

The Goddamn Parrot brings out the worst in everybody. Except me.

"I'll just go see your dad now."

"Yo ho ho."

# 18

Manvil Gilbey was waiting for me. I barely finished cranking the bell handle before he stuck his bleak face outside. I was surprised. A stiffneck named Gerris Genord usually answered the door.

His nose rolled up instantly. "What in the world? . . . Are you aware of the state of your apparel?"

"Plenty. I was headed over here. I got ambushed in the stable. I'll want to talk that over with the boss, too. But first, why don't I go around back, shuck out of all this horse flavoring, and wash down? If you've got somebody who can bring me a towel and something else to wear."

"Thoughtful of you, Garrett. Take care you don't fall afoul of any pigs or cattle on your journey."

"Careful is my new middle name."

The Goddamn Parrot decided that was his cue to laugh. He sounded like a donkey braying.

I strolled around to the tradesman's gate. I waited there for ten minutes. I started talking to myself, or maybe thinking out loud to the Goddamn Parrot. Gilbey himself finally showed up to open the gate and let me into a large paved courtyard that would have been the shipping point had the mansion actually become a brewery.

"You get lost backstairs? Or are you just the only one home who'll risk—"

"I ran into Alyx. I had to discourage her from supervising your ablutions personally."

That might have been interesting. "Must be this glamorous life I lead."

"I wouldn't get too interested in Alyx."

"Me neither. Max is my bread and butter." Oh, did it hurt to say that and actually try to mean it. The more I thought about how wonderfully Alyx had grown up the more—

"And I understand you're taken."

"Awk!" Chuckles in parrotese.

"This bird and me, we're a hot number. Nothing is going to come between us."

"I expect Miss Tate will be devastated."

Manvil is business all the time. He took himself and life and everything else much too seriously. "You should relax, Gilbey. Take a night off. Go out somewhere where nobody knows you, get fucked up and party your ass off."

Gilbey's eyes widened a skillionth of an inch. "Sound advice, no doubt. It's certainly done you well. I'll consider it."

"Go after it the way you did when you were young and in the service."

"I was in the Judge Advocate's office."

"Wouldn't you know." He probably prosecuted guys for smiling on the job.

"I don't recall ever having criticized the way you live your life, Mr. Garrett."

"Ouch!" Despite his obvious disapproval. "Point taken, Mr. Gilbey. And that makes you a treasure. *Everyone* else *is* critical, including my partner, my housekeeper, my girlfriend, my best friend, even this ludicrous buzzard."

The Goddamn Parrot cracked an eyelid and went to all the trouble of interjecting an "Awk" as bitterly cold as any corpse.

For a second I thought Gilbey might crack a smile.

He didn't but I knew how to get to him now. With the unanticipated. With the kind of humor that blindsides you with the unlikely.

"A troll, an ogre, and a barbarian walk into a tavern. The elephant behind the bar says, 'We don't serve—' "

"Mice are never amusing."

"You've heard it." I hadn't finished the setup.

"I hear them all. Kittyjo collects them. The more off-color the better. I have to listen to them. Here we are. I had several buckets of hot water brought around. Use them as you will."

"Can I ask you something, Gilbey?"

He waited, neither offering permission nor denying it.

"You're a right guy. You're Max's pal. His sidekick. But half the time you talk like some kind of butler or something."

"We are what we are, Garrett. You should find soap, towels,

and fresh clothing inside. Rinse down the floor when you're done. Courtesy to the next bather. When you're ready, meet us in Max's study."

"Thanks. For everything and whatever."

I stepped into the place he had made available. The floor was zinc. So were the walls. The staff were allowed to bathe there. Horses got scrubbed down there, too.

A selection of clothing, soap, a brush, and three steaming buckets all sat on a bench. A doorway without a door in it opened into a chamber about five feet by nine, also floored and walled with zinc. The floor sloped to a central drain. A bizarre apparatus consisting of a barrel and lead pipes hung overhead. You filled the tank by climbing a ladder in the outer room.

I figured it out because it resembled a contraption we'd built from a hardtack barrel in the islands, using bamboo for pipes.

I scrubbed up as good as I have in years.

The clothes were not the sort you'll usually find on one of Mama Garrett's boys—mainly because Mom and all her boys together couldn't afford them. Nor were they a choice I would've selected, given a choice. They were too dressy, formal, dull, too dark, more suited to the funeral racket. Also, there was a waistcoat. And ruffles. Not a plethora of ruffles. Not ruffles like you see when Morley dresses up. But ruffles.

Ruffles aren't me.

The Goddamn Parrot resumed station on my shoulder. He made no effort to control his snickers.

The clothing smelled like it had been stored. Maybe it had belonged to one of the Weider boys. In happier times. Not Ty, though. He was smaller than me. Probably the only one who hadn't come home. I couldn't remember his name.

The tools were there so I shaved. I don't know why I didn't seize the opportunity to cut the Goddamn Parrot's throat. It was one in a thousand. And nobody was looking.

# 19

Old Man Weider stands about two hairs over five and a half feet tall but he has a much bigger presence. He's a round-faced, ruddy-skinned guy with close-cropped white hair, most of which has migrated to the sides of his head, I suppose to escape the direct impact of sunshine and rain. His mustache is doing much better, thank you. Maybe it gets more fertilizer. It's a huge gray bush with flecks of yesterday's brown still hanging on stubbornly.

Weider smiles readily but his smiles seldom take up residence in his eyes. It's like he's really glad to see you but the moment you're actually there he starts calculating all the angles.

He grabbed my hand, pumped it. His fingers were plump little sausages. He grinned as he said, "I hear you had an adventure over in my stables." He has remarkably good teeth for his age. "Ty sent Ike Khame over. He told us what happened while you were cleaning up."

"Ah. An adventure. That don't capture it. I was lucky Ty and Lance turned up when they did."

"Why?"

"What?"

"Sorry. Sit down. You look good in those clothes. They were Tad's. I suppose you guessed. Keep them. In fact, Manvil, tell Genord to have Tad's whole wardrobe shipped over to Garrett's place. You don't have any objection, do you?" This was the boss. Chatter chatter, off in seven unpredictable directions.

"No."

"Sit down. Sit down. You want something to drink? We've got beer. Or beer. Or you can have beer." He worked some change on that joke every time I visited. Which wasn't often. Our relationship may be based on absence makes the heart grown fonder. "Why would anyone jump you?"

"Good question. I don't know. Two were your employees. Ty said he'd get an answer. They all carried armbands from some rights gang. Their emblem wasn't one I've ever seen before."

Gilbey brought a schooner of beer, a Weider Dark Reserve with a strong yeast flavor. The very beer the goats in heaven give instead of milk. He said, "It's spooky, seeing you in those clothes."

Weider agreed. "If we got a surgeon to cut that growth off your shoulder, you'd look a lot like Tad." The old pain rose into Weider's eyes. It was the pain we all know because we've all lost somebody to the war. I took a long drink and tried to forget my brother. My father doesn't hurt because I don't remember him.

Weider didn't have that solace. Nor that of beer. He drinks nothing. He stays away because he loves the stuff too much.

Gilbey drew a mug. He would nurse it all evening. "I don't get out much anymore, Garrett," he said as he settled into the chair he always used, not far from Max, where he could scoot over and get into a cutthroat game of dominoes when the mood hit. "I'm out of touch with popular culture. Are stuffed birds some new fad?"

"A present from a friend." I let it go at that.

With my luck the Dead Man was napping and catching nothing through that hideous jungle chicken.

Weider mused, "So Alyx went to you."

I nodded.

"I didn't send her."

"So she said. But she hinted that you wouldn't run me off if I turned up."

"It's good that you came. You've already generated evidence that something is going on. This cancer people call a human rights movement. It *has* penetrated the brewery."

"Alyx said somebody's trying to extort money on behalf of The Call."

Weider seemed surprised. He glanced at Gilbey. "Manvil?"

"News to me." Gilbey sat forward in his chair, alert.

"She said Ty told her. Tinnie and Nicks backed her up. A couple of brewmasters supposedly saw it happen."

"They did? The Call? Nicks?"

"Miss Nicholas. Ty's fiancé. It doesn't sound like The Call's style."

"Absolutely not. Marengo North English has more wealth than any three men deserve."

Interesting. Weider should be North English's equal in that. "I'd gladly relieve the man of some of the responsibility."

Weider chuckled. "No doubt. But his wealth is why The Call is the biggest rights group."

Gilbey amended, "His wealth and his connections. Most of his social peers share his prejudices."

Max said, "I don't. Even though I consider him my friend. He wouldn't try something that underhanded. He'd come ask for support."

I said, "He might have some renegade troops." I'd had an unpleasant encounter with a Call splinter group not that long ago.

"Plausible." Gilbey took my schooner, restored it to a happier estate, then added, "The men in the stable weren't from The Call."

Weider told me, "Ike seemed certain that Ty had made sure of that."

"Oh."

"Tomorrow night I'm hosting a gala where Ty and Giorgi will announce their engagement. Everybody who is anybody will be here. Including Marengo North English and Bondurant Altoona. And you, I hope. Won't you join us?"

"Uh . . . Me? Socializing with socialites?" I've done that, mostly in shady places, street corners, alleyways, taverns where their own kind won't notice them rubbing elbows with a disreputable character like me.

"You'll manage, Garrett. Just bring your manners. Pretend the guests are all beautiful women and you have charm to waste. Get him an invitation, Manvil. You'll come in like any other guest, Garrett. The security people won't know who you are. Not right away."

I must have let another expression get out and go scampering around my face. Maybe I need to hit the Landing and hang out in the gambling dens until I get my betting face back.

"I didn't have you do security because you're only one man, Garrett."

That was hopping on a crippled leg but I ignored it. I accepted a fancy folded paper from Gilbey, asked Weider, "So why did you send Manvil to get me?"

"An impulse. Possibly driven by an unconscious surge of common sense. I wanted to give you that invitation. Because I suddenly realized that by shutting you out I was putting myself entirely in the hands of amateurs and strangers at a time when I was going to have a house full of outsiders, many of whom I couldn't call friends even during a wedding celebration. And I wanted to find out why you suddenly decided to show an interest in the brewery. Just when things are showing signs of getting weird. Call it my old-age paranoia suddenly flaring up."

I looked at Gilbey. Manvil thinks much less of me than Max does. "You approve?"

"I do." But his gout was nipping him, or he was having a problem with gas pains.

"You have other troubles?"

Max said, "I expect to find out for sure tomorrow night. I mean to flush the snakes out of the grass."

There would be a few of those amongst the bourgeois robber moguls likely to be invited to a Weider soiree. Vipers the size of the crocodile killers we used to cut up and feed to the saber-toothed cats in the islands . . .

Gilbey volunteered, "Alyx wanted you invited, too."

The little darling. "Huh?"

"On behalf of Miss Tate. But also because she's wary of snakes herself."

Tinnie seemed to be wriggling her cute little tail right back into the center of my life. And I didn't mind at all. "I'll see if I can't find something to wear."

"Manvil will have Genord make sure Tad's things get to your house in time. Please avoid the stables until after the affair."

"I think I can resist the urge to visit them."

Grinning, Gilbey suggested, "If you arrive early, you can critique our arrangements and watch the villains—make that guests—arrive."

I pretended to be businesslike. "A reasonable plan, gentlemen."

"Awk! We'll be here."

"We? I'll sell your feathers first, you glorified duster."

Weider chuckled. He said, "At least one of you ought to show up."

"One of us will. Me. The one with half a brain." I got up. I must have moved too fast. The floor got awfully unsteady suddenly.

Couldn't have been that little dribble of beer.

# 20

"Will you quit stomping around?" The Goddamn Parrot kept getting more and more restless. I hoped that didn't mean he wanted to exploit me the way pigeons traditionally do statues of forgotten generals. I'd seen enough animal by-product for one day.

Weider's personal sitting room was in a corner of the front of his mansion, on what was called the second floor despite being only slightly above street level. The ground on which the mansion stood sloped. In back you could walk straight out but in front you climbed fifteen steps to reach the front door, then descended half a dozen back to street level. So the first floor lies below actual ground level almost everywhere. Only the rear of the house, including the kitchen, family dining room, and back stairs sees daily use. Most of it is reserved for entertainment.

Even the second floor mainly serves business and entertainment purposes. Weider rules his empire from there. The family lives higher still, on the third and fourth floors. Servants who live on the premises do so in nooks and crannies and under the eaves.

I didn't envy them.

I was about to head down the grand staircase to the first floor when a remote scream stopped me. I glanced back. Gilbey stood in the doorway of Weider's study, silhouetted. He shrugged, pointed upward.

I clomped downstairs muttering, "Tom is still with us." I took several deep breaths crossing the pink-marble floor so when I got to the steps I could bound up to the front door with the spring of a misspent youth. The Goddamn Parrot never stopped prancing on my shoulder.

Max had three sons: Tad, Tom, and Ty. Tom and Ty made it back from the Cantard but Tom left his mind and soul behind.

Rich or poor, we have that in common. We've been to the Cantard. And we've lost somebody. And none of us who survived came home unchanged.

But the war is over. Karenta has triumphed. The Cantard's fabulous mines now serve the sorcerers, who are our real masters. Karenta is the most powerful kingdom in the world. We should be proud.

This month, for the first time in three generations, the Crown conscripted no one.

We won. And because we did our world is falling apart.

Boy, am I glad we didn't lose.

It seemed like a mile to the door. My heels clacked hollowly. Their sound echoed off the walls. Preparations were under way for the party but so far only to the extent that the hall had been stripped of clutter like carpets, furniture, portraits of imaginary forbears, old armor, crossed swords and pikes, and most anything that could become a weapon after the weather turned drunken.

There was no one watching the front door. The old man's paranoia couldn't run too deep. I clomped up and let myself out while making a mental note to suggest a less relaxed security posture.

I surveyed the neighborhood from the porch. Daylight was a ghost of its former gaudy self. "You got to dump, you'd better go do it now, you runt turkey."

The bird squawked, said, "I wanted you outside so I could talk."

The Dead Man. Of course. I knew we were headed this direction as soon as he started insisting that I take the little vulture everywhere. Not only would he use that ugly feather duster to spy on me, he meant to nag me like he was my mother.

I muttered, "Bird, you are doomed! Doomed!"

"What?"

"You've got me talking to myself. What do you want?"

"You need to come home. We have company only you can handle."

"Damn." What did that mean? I didn't ask because he wouldn't tell me. His excuse would be that the bird could talk only so much before he injured his throat, a limitation I've never witnessed when that vulture—or the Dead Man—had something to say that I didn't want to hear. "Want to name names?"

"No. Don't waste time."

I'll strangle them both. It's got to take more effort to deny me than to say a name.

I took the direct route, which turned out to be a poor choice.

Grand Avenue from the Landing south to the Dream Quarter was choked with prohuman demonstrators. They were mostly younger than me. It didn't seem possible that there could be so many, that they could all belong right here instead of scattered amongst a hundred towns and cities and a hundred thousand farms. But, of course, resentment of nonhumans is an ancient exercise. We had great and vicious wars in ages past. And today plenty of men older than me, secure in their trade or employment, are as intolerant as any youngster with no prospects.

I hit Grand where six hundred guys from The Call were marching back and forth practicing their manuals at arms using quarter-staves and wooden swords instead of pikes and sharp steel. Their apparel was moderately uniform. Their shields matched. Most wore light leather helmets. They were true believers in the highest cause and they had faced deadly enemies on the plains of war. This night would turn nasty if some genius on the Hill decided the army should disperse the demonstrators.

Any troops sent in faced demobilization themselves. An interesting complication.

I relaxed, awaited a chance to cross when I wouldn't inconvenience any nut. You don't want to irritate somebody who has several thousand of his best friends handy. Not unless you're armed with the headbone of an ass.

A nice gap opened. Me and fifty other apolitical types decided to go for it.

"Hey! Garrett! Wait up!"

I knew that voice. Unfortunately. "Damn!" Maybe I could outrun her.

# 21

"Garrett!" That was my pal Winger doing the hollering. Winger is a big old country girl as tall as me, a good-looker, who abandoned her husband and kids to chase her fortune in the city. "Dammit! You stop right there, Garrett!"

"Wait," the Goddamn Parrot squawked in my ear. I stopped. I was well trained. Several people nearby stopped, too, all startled by the bird's having spoken.

A kid asked, "Does your bird really talk, Mister?" She was maybe five with blond hair in ringlets and the biggest innocent blue eyes ever invented. I wanted to make a date for about fifteen years but her dad looked like a guy who thought too much like a father. "Yes, he does. But it's hard to get him started."

"Awk! Pretty baby! Pretty girl!"

"Unless you're someone special."

The bird spotted Winger. "Awk! Holy hooters! Look at them gazoombies!" Nature had been generous to Winger.

I squeezed the bird's beak before he got me assassinated.

"I love you, too, Mr. Big," Winger said, hustling up. She ignored kid and dad completely. The father decided he wanted nothing to do with lowlifes like us. He took off across the street. Winger demanded, "Where do you think you're going, Garrett?"

"I was seriously contemplating crossing the street while the goofballs don't have it blocked, Hawkeye."

"He was trying to get away from you, genius," said a voice from behind me.

"Saucerhead!" I turned. Saucerhead Tharpe is a mountain of a man whose face has been rearranged several times too often. He grinned down at me. His teeth were stunted, black, and broken.

Between them Saucerhead and Winger have about enough sense to get out of the rain. After a lively debate obese with irrelevance. But you can count on their friendship. Well, all right, you can count on Saucerhead's friendship. Winger's tends to get slippery if money is involved.

"Hello, Winger my love. Hello, Saucerhead. How are you? I'm just fine myself, thank you. Nice to see you. I can't chat right now. I've got to run."

"We'll run with you," Winger told me.

"Why?"

"Because your sidekick isn't athletic enough to do it hisself so he hired us. He figures you might need your diaper changed."

"Yeah," Saucerhead said. "He's got a notion somebody might actually want to hurt you."

"I can't imagine why."

"I can't imagine why, neither, Garrett," Winger grumbled. "I mean, you only trample all over people's feelings—"

"Stuff it, Winger. Last time you had a feeling you beat it to a midwife to find out if it was gas or pregnancy."

Winger grinned.

The man with the cute little girl increased his pace. He ignored her demands to hear the pretty bird talk again.

The Call guys started a chant and cheer combination that was both moving and chilling. Then they started marching in place. Their feet shook the pavement. They had a band, too, we discovered to our dismay.

I never liked military bands. I don't get real excited about patriotic marches, either.

I paid attention and concentrated when I was in the Corps. I got real good at what I did. I became one of the best in a force made up of the elite of the elite. That helped me stay healthy. Never before then, then, or even now, has my soul suffered any compulsion to become an anonymous fraction of a brainless mass that has its thinking done for it by somebody who shouldn't ought to be trusted to water horses.

Another chance to cross presented itself. I stepped out. Winger and Saucerhead stepped with me, one on either side. What was going on in the Dead Man's minds?

Maybe he was finally drifting away for good, tarrying in a paranoid fantasy before letting go?

"This political crap is out of hand," I told Saucerhead.

Tharpe is no thinker. He takes a while to form an opinion so he must have applied some serious mind work to the matter. "I don't get it, Garrett. They're overreacting. It's like they're screaming because TunFaire is full of people who live here."

If Saucerhead has a prejudice, I've never noticed. Of course, he can develop one professionally if the pay is right. He's a bonebreaker by trade, though he needs odd jobs to keep body and soul together.

"The other day you told me these times would be good for you."

"Yeah. But times being good for me don't mean it's right, what's happening. People are going crazy. It's like some mad wizard cast a hate spell so everybody would act twice as stupid as usual."

Saucerhead and Winger searched the shadows as we walked. I kept an eye on the darkness myself. I was edgy. Times had not been easy lately. I thought about penning an autobiography called *Trouble Follows Me* or maybe *Danger Is My Business*.

Nothing happened except that we had to detour one small riot. Straggler rightsists had run into night folks who didn't share their viewpoint. Most of the night crowd aren't human and none have had sensitivity training so they respond to offensive behavior by breaking heads.

I don't know why when you put three drunks together they decide they can conquer the world. If they choose to start with a troll, they get hurt. No matter how much they drink that troll is still impervious to just about everything but lichen infections.

Beer may not be the root cause of social problems at all, despite what the teetotallers claim. Old Man Weider may be producing the cure for our social ills. Suppose we let the morons get tanked and go looking for big trouble? Big trouble can eliminate them. Bingo. No more problem.

You can't convince me that I'm obligated to save you from yourself. If you want to head for hell by way of smoking weed or opium, or by drinking, or by being dim enough to call a giant names to his face, go head. Enjoy the slide. I won't get in your way.

Nope. I won't hand you a bucket of grease, either. You've got to do it on your own.

# 22

"What's the drill?" I asked as we turned into Macunado east of my place. I spoke for the Goddamn Parrot, in case the Dead Man needed to let me know about any special plans. Saucerhead and Winger thought I was asking them. They were unaware of the special relationship between the character with no mind and the one with way too many.

Winger said, "We walk you to your door and make sure you're safely inside. You pay us."

"Pay you? That's going to come out of the Dead Man's side of the business. I didn't ask for baby-sitters."

His Nibs didn't rise to the bait. He didn't want anybody to know he used the parrot.

Saucerhead said, "Will you look at them kids, Garrett? That's disgusting."

He meant several youths of preconscription age gathered on a street corner. They were baiting a covey of adolescent elf girls who were way out of their own neighborhood, not to mention out after dark. Their fathers would have whipped their bottoms purple had they witnessed what was happening. The boys were uncomplimentary in the extreme, their vocabularies heavily racist— although the clothing they affected was borrowed directly from elven styles. The girls giggled at the boys and dared them to do something. Anything. Because then they would make the boys look as stupid as they were talking.

"You want me to go tell them to mind their manners?" I asked.

"Huh?" Tharpe responded, baffled. "Manners? What're you talking about, Garrett?"

"No. What're *you* talking about? If not their behavior?"

"Their hair, man!" Tharpe eyed me like he wondered if I was going blind. "Look at their hair."

"They've got a lot of it." Most of them had it up and artificially curled and it looked like hell, but so what? It was obvious already that they didn't mind being the butt of mockery.

Saucerhead never outgrew his military haircut. He grumbled, "What kind of parents would let their kids go around looking like that? You want to know why Karenta is going to hell . . ."

I did but I didn't think Saucerhead's theory would hold much water.

Hair had nothing to do with those boys' behavior—though behavior and hair might be two symptoms of the same disease. And the girls bore an equal responsibility. Hardly anybody, human or elven, would argue that there are any women more beautiful or sensual than the elven—and these girls were blessed additionally with the glow of youth. And they flaunted every weapon they had to get those boys to humiliate themselves.

The boys were too naive to realize they were going to lose no matter what they did. That's a hard lesson for even a man of my mature years. I'm past standing on street corners and howling at the unattainable but I suspect no woman ever gets entirely beyond belittling you, however subtly, for finding her attractive.

I was stretching Saucerhead's mind to its limit trying to explain what was going on across the street when Winger opined, "You're really full of shit, Garrett."

"Tell you what, Winger. You tell me about the women you hang out with."

"Huh? What's that got to do with anything?"

"You're going to tell me how women really think. But you hang out with me. You hang out with Saucerhead when he doesn't have a girlfriend tying him down. You hang out in lowlife taverns trying to get into fights with guys who remind you of your husband. You hang out with thieves and thugs and confidence men and none of them are women so I don't think the fact that you squat to pee qualifies you as an expert on female culture as practiced in our great metropolis."

"Shee-it. There you go cutting me down again 'cause I come from the country."

This could go on for hours. Winger always has a comeback, even if it doesn't make much sense. Lucky for me, we came to my house. It was night out and as quiet as it gets in my block but damned if Mrs. Cardonlos wasn't outside watching my place like she expected entertainment of the sort only I can provide.

I studied the area carefully. First I get an armed escort, then I find my neighborhood nemesis on point. "What's happening, Old Bones? How come the wicked witch of Macunado Street is on patrol?"

Saucerhead looked at me like I'd gone goofier than he'd ever expected. "Just thinking out loud," I said. "Priming him."

"Yeah?" Winger said. "Then tell him to read his account book. There's two marks each due here."

"Two marks? Don't be ridiculous."

*It is indeed ridiculous, Garrett. The woman has swung into her avaricious mode. And she is testing our ability to communicate, to establish, if she can, our limits. Two pennyweights silver was the agreed upon fee. And that was overly generous. On reflection I believe you ought to convince them to take an equivalent value in copper sceats. The price of silver is depressed. It will stabilize at a higher level once the euphoria of victory is swept away by reality's breeze.*

What was he going on about? "Euphoria? You've got to be kidding. You know what's happening in these streets?"

Winger and Saucerhead gaped.

*Yes. I do know. Would you say that what is happening involves the sort of people who deal in large quantities of noble metals?*

"All right. I understand." Dummy me. I understood, too, that I had given Winger a bucket of information for free.

*Please deal with those two quickly. We have company and I am impatient to correct that.*

Oh my.

# 23

Winger wouldn't take copper. She wasn't bright but she was possessed of a certain cunning. If we didn't want to let go of our silver, we must know something.

She respected the Dead Man's brains.

Saucerhead followed her lead though he wasn't sure why. He gave me a black look for trying to pay him in copper. I told him, "Don't spend it all in one place."

"It's already spent, Garrett. I owe Morley."

Imagine that. Tharpe runs a tab at Morley's place. Even now that it's The Palms. How come Morley lets him?

Winger told me, "You need to consult some kind of expert, Garrett."

"Expert?"

"About your habit of talking to birds."

"I could cure it in a minute. Faster, even. Take him home with you. He idolizes you. And he makes more sense than most people do."

Winger responded with a big raspberry. As they walked away Saucerhead tried to convince her that she'd just blown the best offer she'd had all year. Nobody human had shown as much interest.

"You want a knuckle sandwich for supper you just keep on jacking your jaw," Winger growled.

"Where we gonna eat, anyway?"

I shut the door, pleased that we'd gotten by without Winger trying to enlist me in some harebrained scheme for replacing the Crown Jewels with paste. They say you can't pick your relatives

but you can pick your friends. I must have some really strange secret urges.

*Garrett. Cease dallying.*

I entered the Dead Man's room, calling to the kitchen, "Dean,
I need you to come bear witness." I knew the signs. I was about to
be granted a nose-to-the grindstone lecture by the all-time grand-
master procrastinator and slough-off artist. Trouble was, the only
witness who could really indict him would be another Loghyr. "A
little chow wouldn't hurt, either." My own particular Loghyr, despite having been dead for ages, has the reputation of being one of
the most ambitious of his kind ever.

Some battles you can't win. Wisdom is attained when you
start to recognize those beforehand and slink onward in search of
ground you do have a chance to hold.

*Dean, please bring our guest when you come. And do put to-
gether a platter for Garrett, if you will be so kind. He is hungry
and becoming cranky.*

I was going to get crankier. His attitude earlier and that message told me our guest was female and under forty. Dean has a
way with women young enough to be his daughters. They like to
hang out in his kitchen. Partly that's because he's safe, partly because he indulges them like they were favorite daughters, partly
because he's a nice old guy.

"Is Tinnie here again?"

*No. Tell me what happened out there.*

"The Goddamn Parrot was on top of me the whole damned
time."

*The beast is more limited than you believe. The bird is keen of
ear but only in a narrow range. And his visual acuity and sense of
smell leave much to be desired.*

"You ought to find yourself a human tool." But not me.

*Perfect idea. Unfortunately, no human has a mind sensitive
enough for remote access. No intelligent creature, whatever the
species, fits my particulars exactly. There would appear to be a relationship. I must examine that someday.*

"Yeah," I muttered, completely confident that I was a failed
experiment.

The door swung open. Dean, platter in hand, held it for
someone.

Someone stepped inside.

"You?" I was surprised.

"Me," said Belinda Contague. "Your lack of enthusiasm is breaking my heart."

The woman doesn't have one. But I didn't remind her.

She likes black. She positively *loves* black. She wore a black evening cloak over a masculine-cut black suit of very supple leather. She wore black boots with raised heels. A pair of long black-silk gloves were folded over her black-leather belt. When she arrived, I was sure, Dean had taken her black hat and veil and put them in the small front room. She'd painted her nails black and had put something on her lips to darken and gloss them. Then she'd used a face powder to make her skin appear more pallid.

I have seen vampires with more color.

Despite all that, or perhaps because of it, she was incredibly beautiful. More, she exuded something that made it difficult to cling to common sense and the urge to self-preservation. That bizarre look was very erotic.

"You sent a message. I was in town. I had no other demands on my time. I came here. You were out but Dean was kind. As he ever is."

I glared at the Dead Man, thought hard: You should have warned me.

He didn't respond.

Damn, the woman was bold. She knew what the Dead Man was. Nobody with a conscience as black as hers ought to be anywhere near him.

Back in those remote times when the Outfit was in transition, passing into Belinda's regency, we had a brief fling. I might consider myself lucky because I got out alive. Belinda is very strange. And when it comes to hardness she makes her daddy look like a pet bunny.

I gobbled, "I'm sorry. You took me off guard. You're the last person I expected."

Belinda Contague stands five feet six inches. She looks twenty-five, says she's twenty. She lived a rough life before she took over. Lived like she was trying to kill herself. She was in good shape now, as her apparel proclaimed eloquently. Nature blessed her with a shape that would have them kicking the lids off their coffins if she strolled through a mortuary. Her dark eyes fell smack into the center of that semi-mythical "windows of the soul" class. You will discover more warmth and compassion in the stare of a cobra.

I can't imagine what she ever saw in me.

I always knew she would come back to haunt me, though.

"I'm not as bad as you think, Garrett."

Her daddy used to say the same thing. "Huh?"

"My father turned out to be a good friend, didn't he?" She sounded wistful.

I grunted. My relationship with Chodo Contague had been strange, too. I did him a big favor once, accidentally, and forever afterward he felt he owed me. He did me good turns even when I didn't ask. He covered my ass. He tried hard to entangle me in the Outfit's webs so I'd become one of his soldiers. I repaid him by helping take him down.

"Crask and Sadler are back in town." That would take the play out of Belinda.

"You saw them?" She actually became more pale.

"No. I heard it from Relway. Via Captain Block. He traded the information for a favor." She understood that kind of deal.

She didn't question my source. "What favor?"

"It doesn't involve you or yours."

"Relway isn't interested in us?"

"Of course he is. He's interested in everything. But he's a realist. He knows you offer services the public wants, nor are you breaking the law, mostly. Whatever the priests and reformers say. He's really interested in people who hurt people. Or people he thinks threaten society. But he's Relway. He's a slave to his obsessions. He wants to know everything about everything."

*Garrett, being able to read your mind and intentions helps but even so what you have just said makes only marginal sense.*

I had no trouble understanding me.

Belinda got it, too, though her coal-chip gaze never stopped boring holes through me.

I asked, "Darling, why couldn't you be somebody else?" Nobody grabs the unreasoning side of me like Belinda Contague.

"Sometimes I wish I was somebody else, too, Garrett. But it's too late."

"Do we have to be enemies?"

"Were we ever?"

Yes. Careful, Garrett. "No. But what we are can drive us places where we're out of choices."

"Sufficient to the day the evil thereof."

I gave her a look at my raised eyebrow. That always charms them.

"And don't try that on me, Garrett. You're in my heart. Suppose we just go on the way you did with my father?"

"Your dad thought he owed me." The final account left me way in his debt, though.

"I owe you. In a different way. You're the only guy I know who treats me like a human being. Even when I was completely weird you treated me right."

"That's just me." I glanced at the Dead Man. He was one witness too many.

"Shut up. I'm not proposing. I'm not going to steal you away from the Tate woman." She has more spies than Relway. "But I do have my small claim on you."

*Control your breathing, Garrett.*

When I was younger the old guys promised me I'd grow out of the heavy breathing. Maybe you have to be dead, though. There's always a Belinda or Tinnie or somebody scrambling my brain.

"If what Relway wants doesn't involve me, what's the secret?"

Good point. Perhaps. "He wants to infiltrate the rights movement. And I'm involved because some rightsist group is trying to extort money from the Weider family."

Belinda became the kingpin completely, a stone killer handicapped only marginally by her sex. "I have rightsist problems, too," she said. "Those people have no respect. They believe they have the right to do whatever they want because their cause is just."

I grunted agreement. That was their thinking exactly.

"I won't let them tread on my toes."

Oh-oh. Somebody else wanted to sign me up.

*I am going to take a short nap, Garrett. I expect it will last all night.*

What? Now I knew why I hadn't seen Belinda's coach outside. She'd had no plan to leave and His Nibs suddenly was inclined to humor her. Which he had not been only a short while ago. What intriguing thought had he plucked from her spider's nest of a mind?

# 24

I'm a devil pig, I'm told, because I like women. A lot. Go figure that kind of thinking.

The preference has gotten me into trouble occasionally. With Belinda trouble could get ugly. The spiders in her head spin strangely kinked thoughts. And she had to turn up just when Tinnie's stubbornness had begun to crack.

I heard about it over breakfast, basking in Dean's disapproval. I hated to let him waste all that bile.

"Thanks," I said, accepting the tea. "You'll need to do up the guest bedroom after Belinda gets up."

The old boy had an idea in his head. He wasn't going to let me confuse him.

"You're wasting an ulcer, Dean." Help! I appealed to the Dead Man. Tell him nothing happened.

*I was asleep, Garrett. However, if a small prevarication will oil the machinery . . .*

Dean made a sound of disgust. He didn't want to believe the Dead Man, either.

Belinda came downstairs. She was in a bitter mood. She didn't like not getting her own way. She glared at Dean. He responded with the indifference of a man so old he has nothing left to fear.

Belinda shrugged. She cared for no man's opinion, which wasn't always wise. Her world was unforgiving and the penalties for failing to observe its rules often lethal. She worried too little about making enemies inside her own circle. She could have worked something out with Crask and Sadler.

Belinda was Chodo Contague's child, both his creation and his doom.

It must have been hell to be his kid. Belinda wouldn't talk about it but there was no doubt that she was bitter.

There are suspicions that Belinda's mother went to her eternal reward early because Chodo disapproved of her infidelity.

That was common rumor before I ever met Belinda. It might have plenty to do with Chodo's condition now.

I feared Belinda's obsessions might compel the Outfit to take her down. But she was quite capable of taking it down with her.

Belinda asked, "Suppose I explain in person?"

"That might get exciting."

"Is the woman irrational, Garrett?"

"Is any woman reasonable after she makes up her mind? Tinnie's not. I can't figure her out. I hardly try anymore. What're you trying to do to me?"

"Nothing anymore, Garrett. It's just business now."

Did I need to concern myself with the hell hath no fury syndrome?

"Don't worry, lover. These crackpots are bad for business. They'll be dealt with. But—"

"Hey! Could that be why Crask and Sadler are back? Because somebody wants their knowledge about you?"

Belinda smiled like a cat contemplating a cornered mouse. "Possibly. I have an idea. Why don't I be your companion tonight? I can see people I'd never run into otherwise."

"I'm dead."

*She has put forth an outstanding idea, Garrett. Consider it.*

I had a good notion where she came up with it, too. "You consider it, Chuckles. You don't have to get along with Tinnie Tate."

*As Miss Contague has suggested, Miss Tate cannot be entirely irrational.*

"Then you know a different Miss Tate." He did see more of Tinnie than I did, though. Maybe he knew something. Maybe the leopardess had changed her spots. Maybe she'd traded them in for saber-tooth tiger stripes.

I told Belinda, "Me and the junior partner need to butt heads. He agrees with you."

"Tell him I take back all the wicked things I ever said about him."

"I won't. I'm going to invent new words so I can say more."

# 25

"What is this?" I demanded as I blew into the Dead Man's room. "Are you determined to get me lynched?"

*I reiterate. Miss Tate is not irrational. Enough of that. There are larger issues at hand.*

"Larger to who, Old Bones?"

*Thousands. Even tens of thousands. Name for me, if you will, just five nonhumans murdered today who considered Miss Tate's potential ill will an eventuality more dire than the catastrophe which actually afflicted them.*

"Unfair. Unfair." He was deft at carving holes in the thickest smoke when the mood took him. "None of them knew Tinnie like I—"

*Garrett.*

"All right. How is taking Belinda along going to be useful?"

*We want to situate you so that you become a recognized intermediary between as many interests as possible. So you can dip into the information flows. This will position you to take advantage of anyone wishing to communicate with the Syndicate. Particularly as regards those with little sympathy for The Call and its ilk.*

Ilk? What kind of word is ilk? "Relway?"

*An excellent example. With Max Weider and his moderate friends, perhaps, as another spoke to that wheel. With effective guidance I can even see you situating yourself on the axis between the radical parties and Glory Mooncalled's people.*

Guess who would do the guiding.

He was feeling smug about his genius. His true plan drifted too near the surface of his thoughts. "Hang on there, Old Bones.

There ain't no way I can sell me to all those folks as the hero of their prophecies."

*You do not have to sell yourself to Mr. Weider or Mr. Relway. You serve their interests already. No effort is needed to bring Miss Contague along, either. She wants to come aboard. That leaves only the rightsists and the rebels. The former are after you already.*

Aw, hell. Why not link up with the nonhumans and all those wannabe revolutionaries who have been lying low since the explosion of rightsist terrorism? The rightsists have no use for those guys, either. Rightsists don't like anybody very much.

"Nothing to it, Big Guy. A piece of cake."

*The rightsists should be fish in a barrel, to use your vernacular. You are exactly what they want. A certified war hero.*

"I'm a war hero who lives with a Loghyr and a psychotic talking bird and my best friend is part elf."

*All faults that are correctable. A man can come to the truth late. You can sell the rightsists because they want to be sold. Glory Mooncalled's is the organization I am concerned about cracking.*

"Why bother? I don't share your infatuation with Glory Mooncalled."

*Truth be told, Garrett, I no longer share that infatuation with my younger self. When Mooncalled was a distant gadfly yanking the beards of the lords and ladies we love to hate it was easy to cheer him on. But he is among us now and the glimmers of purpose I catch are depressingly sinister. Perhaps the Mooncalled I treasured perished along with his dream of an independent Cantard. Or he may have elected to become Karenta's great foe because we no longer have serious enemies but deserve them.*

"There's that damned word again, Smiley."

*Which word?*

'We.' I find nonhumans fond of reminding the rest of us that Karenta is a human construct. They make big shows of negotiating exemptions from human law and rule.

*Excellent. Maintain that capacity for dredging up irrelevant sophistries and The Call will clutch you to its bosom. You may be promoted directly into their Inner Council.*

"I don't want to do this."

*There is little choice, Garrett. These are pivotal times. Everyone must take a stand before it ends. Who refuses will be devoured because he will be out there alone. But we who recognize the signs and portents have the opportunity to deflect or defeat the gathering darkness.*

"I know where I stand, Windy. But I'd rather be noble and honorable and defend true justice and the divine right of Karenta's kings while I'm sitting in my office with a mug in my hand, chatting with Eleanor."

*And you insist that I am lazy.*

"Only because you have no more ambition than a bone that's been buried for twenty years. You don't have to go out there and try to run between the raindrops, partner."

*That is another matter which warrants future discussion.*

# 26

"Right on time," I said when somebody hammered on my door late in the afternoon.

Belinda said, "My people are expected to be punctual and to do their jobs well. And they deliver."

"You should take life easier, Belinda. You don't always have to be—"

"I try, Garrett. But some demon keeps pushing me. I can't beat it. And it'll get me killed eventually."

I nodded. That came with the territory. I looked out the peep-hole. An unfamiliar hulking creature of mixed ancestary shuffled impatiently on my front stoop. "I think I understand. Is this thing somebody you know?"

She leaned past me, so close I had trouble breathing normally. "That's Two Toes Harker. My driver."

"Driver? He looks like he wrestles ogres for a living."

"He looks badder than he is. He doesn't move very well any-more."

Two Toes knocked again. Despite plaster dust falling all over the house Dean didn't come out of the kitchen. He was exasper-ated with everybody. And for once he did put the blame where it always belongs: squarely on the shoulders of the Dead Man.

"I'll get my shoulder ornament and we'll be set."

"Why? That bird is disgusting."

Finally, somebody who agreed with me.

The Dead Man relaxed his control of the Goddamn Parrot. The little monster barked, "I'm in love! Look at this sweet fluff!"

"I already looked, you deadweight jungle buzzard. And you're right. She looks damned good. But she's a lady. Mind your stinking manners."

"That was really good, Garrett," Belinda told me. "Your lips never moved once."

Argh! But the bird was right. I was right. She *did* look good, if a little too vampiric for current fashion. She'd had people in and out all afternoon, some to elevate her to this supernal state. She didn't want to go unnoticed tonight. Hell, she was going to raise the dead. I thought about wrapping her in a blanket so we wouldn't have crowds chasing us through the streets.

This evening would be easy on my eyeballs. Alyx was sure to give Belinda a run. So would Nicks. And Tinnie would be absolutely killer if she bothered to try. Belinda would be a blood-dark rose in a garden of brilliant whites and yellows and carmines.

"If I was doing the talking this little shit would say things to score points for me, not to get everybody pissed off."

Belinda laughed. Then she demanded, "What?"

"You startled me. You don't laugh very often. You should."

"I can't. Though I do wish I was different."

A shuddering *déjà vu* overcame me. I recalled her father once suggesting that he didn't really want to be a bad guy but he was in a bind where his choices were to be the nastiest bad boy he could or end up grease under some climber's heel. The underworld is strictly survival of the fittest.

The Contagues survive.

I opened the door. Belinda pushed past, murmured something to Two Toes.

Dean bustled out of the kitchen. "Did you remember your key, Mr. Garrett?"

"Yeah. And this door better not be chained when I get back. Got that?"

He had talked me into installing an expensive key lock, supposedly so I wouldn't need help getting in late. But maybe he just wanted to aggravate me.

It used to be cats. He was always adopting strays, apparently because I didn't want them around. I attract enough stray people.

"Absolutely guaranteed, Mr. Garrett."

I looked at him askance. I didn't like his tone. "Thank you, Dean." I shut the door. "Living with him is like being married without any of the perquisites." I waved to Mrs. Cardonlos, who was outside watching again. I wondered if she knew what she was looking for. I wondered what had become of Mr. Cardonlos. I have a suspicion he's alive and well and happy somewhere far from here.

She got an eyeful of Belinda. That one and its sister both liked to pop. I thought her chin would hit her knee.

Now she had something juicy to chew up and pass around. *What do they see in that man?*

Two Toes had left the Contague coach around the corner on Wizard's Reach. As we strolled behind him I noted that he had earned his nickname the hard way. He had a weird, crooked limp.

I gave him a significant glance, then raised my eyebrow to Belinda. She'd relaxed. She understood. "Old family obligation." She made a noise I would have called a giggle had it come from another young lady. "Guess what? He has a twin brother. No-Nose Harker. The Harker boys didn't have much luck in the army."

I gave the automatic response of every guy who ever made it back from a war when most soldiers didn't. "Sure they did. They got out alive."

If you check the men in the street, particularly in the rightsist freecorps, almost every one bears some physical memento. And beyond the outside scars there are still suppurating wounds of mind and soul. And those affect our rulers as well as the least man among us.

You won't find a duke or stormwarden crouching in a filthy alleyway trying to exorcise his memories with wine or weed but up on the Hill, or out in the manors, the great families have locked doors behind which they conceal their own casualties. Like Tom Weider.

You don't hear about that in histories or sagas. They whoop up the glory and forget the horror and pain. The Dead Man assures me that all histories, whether official or oral, bear only coincidental resemblance to actual events—which few principals considered to be history in the making at the time.

# 27

Belinda said, "You used to be a lighthearted guy, Garrett. A little cynical, yeah, but it's hard not to be cynical nowadays. What happened to the wisecracks?"

"Darling, a wise man once told me each of us is allowed only so many wisecracks. Then life stops. That's how he explained there being so many sour old farts. I've only got one smart-ass crack left. I'm saving it. Which means that for the next four or five hundred years I'm going to be a sour old fart, too."

Her sense of humor was underdeveloped. She didn't get it. Or just didn't appreciate it. "You making fun of me?"

"No. Never. Just ringing changes on something an old-timer did tell me when I was a kid. This guy was so ancient he could remember when Karenta wasn't at war with Venageta."

"A human?"

"Yeah. I said he was old."

Dwarves and elves and some other species hang around as long as the Loghyr, given sufficient good luck. In fact, elves claim to be immortal. But even the Dead Man isn't sure about that. He hasn't been around long enough to see one never get killed.

Stories about elven immortality come from the same myth cycle that tells us that if you con a dwarf into coming out of his mine in the daytime or riddle a troll into staying up past sunrise they'll turn to stone. Word to the wise. Don't bet your life. Don't bet your favorite cockroach. You'll find out what that red stuff is between trolls' toes.

Sure, you don't see many trolls on the daytime streets of Tun-Faire but that's because trolls don't like cities. Things move too fast. But if you insist on looking for trolls, be sure you don't get trampled by all the dwarves trying to separate humans from their money, day or night.

I continued, "This old man was a real storyteller. Tall tales. I wish somebody had written them down. He claimed he was so old because there was one last joke that Death came and told you and he hadn't heard it yet."

"My father used to say that."

"Chodo?"

"Yeah. Really. Maybe he knew the same old man." She became the cold, hard Belinda I'd come to regret.

"Someday you have to tell me what it was like being Chodo's kid."

"What?"

"Most of the time I like you. But whenever you even remotely connect with your father you go all cold and spooky." The coach stopped. I shut my yap, peeked between curtains. "We're here. Without any trouble."

Two Toes dismounted and came to the coach door. "One minute," Belinda told him. "Garrett, sometimes I'm halfway in love with you. Most of the time I'm not. You treat me decent. I like that. But we can't ever go anywhere. I can't always control the part of me that you don't like. If you shoot your mouth off when I'm out of control . . ."

I hadn't thought she could see it herself. As always, Belinda insisted on being a surprise.

Two Toes helped her down. He worshipped the ground she stalked on. And she didn't notice.

One of those sad songs.

Two Toes gave me a look that said I'd better treat her right.

Manvil Gilbey was out with the hirelings making sure no great unwashed types penetrated the perimeter. "Glad you're here, Garrett. I'm getting nervous. They started arriving before we were halfway ready." He checked Belinda. He was impressed. "I am amazed, young woman. What could such a lovely creature possibly see in this battered rogue?"

"Gilbey?" I asked. "Is that really you?"

He winked as he took my invitation. I wondered if they were keeping count. He said, "We assumed you'd pair off with Miss Tate."

"Life is chock-full of surprises."

"I believe Miss Tate planned along those lines."

I didn't doubt it for a second. "I'm ready for her." Right. "Can we gossip later? I want to check all the arrangements for myself."

"Of course. I just wanted you to realize that the situation could become complex."

He was rubbing me the wrong way and I didn't know why. "Look, this isn't important now." Maybe it was having to face Tinnie. "My partner felt I should bring the lady along. Because of the other guests likely to appear." I didn't dare proclaim my date as being queen of the underworld.

Gilbey was disinclined to quibble. Neither did he satisfy me that he'd made any outstanding effort to protect the Weiders.

I had cause to be touchy. I was descending into a cone of trouble where the secret police, the rightsists, the Outfit, Glory Mooncalled, and maybe even the business community might want to roll rocks down on me.

"Have a wonderful evening, Garrett. Miss, I'm sure the Weider family will be honored that you choose to share their joy."

Manvil could lay it on with a trowel. And Belinda could make a determined holy celibate regret his vows. Gilbey certainly looked like he had suffered a stunning recollection of what women were all about. He had trouble looking at anyone but Belinda for the next several minutes.

# 28

Inside the doorway stood Gerris Genord. Genord had a voice like a thunderstorm. He refused to let me sneak in unnoticed. He announced, as though the end of the world was imminent and it was critical that everyone knew, "MR. GARRETT AND MISS CONTAGUE." Genord was the Weiders' majordomo. I did not like him. He sneered at me. I did not belong in this society.

I suppose my chances of getting inside unnoticed with Belinda along were as likely as those of the Crown cutting taxes because the war was over.

We were early, though, so only a small horde heard Genord's bellows.

The Goddamn Parrot made his entrance separately, sneakily. Wearing a parrot to a betrothal ball might be considered a lapse of etiquette.

We got down the steps all right but didn't make it twenty feet farther before I got pinned in the cold-eyed crossfire of Tinnie Tate and Alyx Weider. Tinnie was closer. I shifted course. Best get the worst over now.

I ignored Tinnie's expression. "I've got a letter for you from an old gentleman you know better than I do."

The Goddamn Parrot plopped onto my shoulder. So much for good form. He said, "Read it, Pretty Legs. Bust his head later."

Tinnie gaped. I wondered if I shouldn't have read the letter before I let her have it.

Dean transcribed it for the Dead Man—after I promised not to peek. Belinda glowered because I gave it to Tinnie. Tinnie—and Alyx and everyone else with eyes as good as a mole's—eyeballed

Belinda in her vampiric heat and wondered. Frumpy Garrett faded from their awareness, though wearing one of Tad's outfits I was as spiffy as I've ever gotten.

Well, I didn't want to be noticed, did I? Not in my line.

Tinnie read. Tinnie gave me the fish-eye. Tinnie cold-eyed Belinda. Tinnie glared at me some more. The Goddamn Parrot cleared his throat. I got his head in a one-hand squeeze before he made things worse. He flapped and squawked but didn't get any rocks dropped on my bean.

Tinnie decided she needed some fresh air. Her stride was efficient. Her feet pounded the floor, eating up ground. Her red hair tossed behind her.

Alyx caught her. They argued instantly.

Belinda stayed close as I moved toward the far end of the hall. The place wasn't crowded yet but was more so than I'd expected. Where I knew names I named them so Belinda would know. Her name began to circulate, too, after somebody realized which Contague she had to be.

"Yonder are the happy couple," I said. "We ought to pay our respects."

"They don't look happy."

I didn't think they did, either. Ty looked like he had a bad case of constipation. Nicks looked like she'd rather be anywhere else.

Ty perked up when he saw Belinda. And how could you blame him? He asked, "And who is your lovely companion, Garrett?" He never was nicer.

His own lovely companion bestowed a truly ugly look upon him. She didn't really want him. He didn't want her. But, boy, he better not even think about being interested in anybody else. And Garrett was a natural-born pig dog for daring to be seen with somebody as exciting as this wannabe vampire woman.

"Belinda Contague. Belinda, this is Ty Weider. Crown prince of the Weider brewing empire."

Ty failed to recognize Belinda as the crown princess of organized crime. But why should he? Her name was not a household word. Even her father was not universally known. "Charmed, Miss Contague. How long have you known this rogue?"

Did they take a vote on what to call me? Maybe I could be a rake next time around.

"Almost forever, Ty. He used to do favors for my father."

I winked at Nicks. She had made the connection. Maybe she

and Belinda had met in another context, though Belinda showed no sign of recognizing Nicks.

Nicks said, "I'll bet your father doesn't know you're out with this rake Garrett."

I didn't want to wait long, did I? I ought to get into the sybil racket. How cruel to label a man a garden tool.

I was sure the women had met before.

Belinda smiled wickedly. "Daddy would have a heart attack if he saw us holding hands." She grabbed my right mitt. "I'm still his little girl."

Daddy Contague might render me down for candle tallow if he knew the whole history of our friendship.

Whatever the game, Nicks was ready to play. Belinda pulled me away. She had to control her surroundings completely. I watched Nicks whisper to Ty, mischief in her eye.

She winked again.

These women might put me in more danger than The Call, the Outfit, and Relway put together, just for the long-legged, red-haired, howling wolf sexy fun of it.

The color left Ty's face.

Chodo really did have a bad reputation.

Genord bellowed, "Mr. Marengo North English and Miss Tama Montezuma."

"Whoa!" I barked. "This might be interesting."

"Why?"

"North English claims Montezuma is his niece. I've never seen her but she's supposed to be . . ." Wrong angle. Belinda's face darkened. When would I learn? "Rumor would lead one to suspect that North English regularly violates the rules about consanguinity. Not to mention he maybe cheats on his wife."

"Everybody loves a scandal."

"Don't they? Let's go over there. I've never seen North English up close."

"Why bother? He sounds like your typical sleazy male to me." But she watched the entrance intently. North English would be one connection she wanted to make, sleazy male or otherwise.

"You're too young and too beautiful to be so cynical."

"It's all your fault. You ruined me. You beast."

The newcomers paused to be seen before they descended to the great hall floor.

"Put your eyes back in, Garrett." Tinnie had materialized behind me. "And shut your mouth before swallows nest in it."

I did as I was told. I'm a good soldier, me. But, boy oh boy, that Tama Montezuma was something!

She was as tall as me, narrow of hip. She moved like a panther on the stalk, radiating an overpowering sexual urgency. Her face seemed animated by a secret knowledge, an abiding amusement at the follies of the world—which is, after all, only a dream. Her muscles were as hard as stone. Her walnut-stain skin was without flaw, showing no hint of a wrinkle, and a shocking amount of square footage was available for inspection. It glowed with a satin sheen of health so good it ought to be illegal. Her eyes sparkled with humor and intelligence. Her teeth were almost too perfect and white to be real. She reeked animal magnetism. Somebody— probably her Uncle Marengo—had invested a fortune in her scant but flattering elven fashions.

"Down, Rover," Alyx whispered over my other shoulder. I hadn't heard her sneak up, either. Maybe I *was* a tad distracted.

I grumped, "You guys are wearing that out, you know." Tinnie, especially, had a tendency to push the needling past the playful stage. "I thought you were just going to work it on each other."

"Tsk-tsk. His skin is thinner than I thought, Tinnie."

Lightly, Belinda observed, "I may be leaping to conclusions here, Garrett, but that woman doesn't look like she could be that man's niece—and not just because he's so pale." North English did look pallid next to Tama Montezuma. "In fact, she doesn't look much like anybody's niece. She looks a lot more like something a dirty old man dreamed up."

She did indeed. Or even some pure-hearted young man. Tama Montezuma had something that would make people suspicious of her even if she was out with her twin brother and wearing full nun's gear. But her being Marengo's niece was not impossible, technically. Dark-skinned adventurers visit TunFaire all the time. A few have stomachs strong enough to stay around.

North English didn't look at Montezuma like she was any relative, though. Guys who hit a number big and win buckets of cash get the look Marengo had. It says, "I do deserve this but I can't believe it's real."

Belinda asked, "Can you introduce me to these people, Garrett?"

"Me? You know I don't run in their circles. Alyx?" Her family did share those circles.

"Daddy invited him, Garrett. He'll remember me only as a lit-

tle kid. It's been a long time since he was here last. He and Dad argued. Politics."

Tinnie shook her lovely head. "I can't help. I never met the man."

Belinda demanded, "How would you suggest I meet him, then?"

"He's got a hungry eye. Walk up and tell him who you are and say you need to talk. He'll find time."

Tinnie grumbled something inaudible. I bet it had to do with it not being right, women taking advantage of their looks. That from a lady who grabs every possible advantage out of being a gorgeous redhead—at least when guys named Garrett are around.

"Maybe I'll do that."

"He doesn't look preoccupied right now." North English was posturing, peacock proud, basking in male envy, not noticing that no one hurried to get close to him. "And I've got to desert you anyway. It's time for me to look for bad guys."

Belinda touched my hand lightly, the gesture entirely for the benefit of Alyx and Tinnie.

The big cats really try to hook their claws in one another.

Belinda strode away.

Tinnie smoldered. Alyx demanded, "Who is that woman, Garrett? Why did you bring her?"

Tinnie answered for me. "Her name is Belinda Contague, Alyx. Her father is the number one crime boss in TunFaire. She's here because our friend the Dead Man asked Garrett to bring her."

So that was what was in that letter. But Tinnie still wanted it to be my fault.

"How long have you known her?" Alyx demanded. "How come she acts like she owns you?"

"A few months. But I've known her dad a long time. Same as I've known your dad for a long time. She acts like that because she knows it'll irritate Tinnie and because she likes to make me squirm. Just like you."

That was a good shot. But not good enough. They didn't want to believe it. I reiterated, "I need to wander around now."

"You're really working?" Tinnie asked.

"Yes. Gilbey's no professional and he knows it. That's why I got an invitation." I started walking.

Both women followed.

"Uh . . . Ladies . . ."

Alyx said, "I can show you around."

Tinnie's expression said she was going to make damned certain Alyx did nothing of the sort. I sighed. This was a fifteen-year-old's dream. At my age it was too rife with complications.

I sighed again. "Suppose we stroll around and see how easy it would be for somebody to get in uninvited."

# 29

Tinnie and Alyx stuck like my shadow. Once, when we were close and Alyx was a step ahead, I grabbed Tinnie's hand for a second. I asked Alyx, "How many people came in to handle the work on this?"

"What?"

"The extra staff. How many outsiders?"

"A bunch in the kitchen. A bunch to handle the service. Some musicians. I don't know. Ask Manvil or Gerris. Or Lance."

I guess she noticed me touching Tinnie.

If somebody really wanted to get into the Weider house, coming now as occasional help would be a good way.

Sometimes you just have intuitions.

Or maybe you see something and don't recognize it consciously but your mind works on it and you come up with an idea that, later, makes it look like you read the future.

I said, "Let's check the kitchen." The largest mass of outsiders ought to be there. The shindig would require tons of special food.

"Stay with me," Alyx said, eager to regain my attention. Maybe she hadn't gotten her full share growing up the youngest of five, with a father dedicated to empire building and a mother who was already dying slowly.

Following Alyx was no chore. The hardest work I did was to pretend I didn't find being a few steps behind a shapely behind all that interesting.

"You're not fooling anybody, Garrett," Tinnie whispered. I glanced back. She had her devil grin on. I like her best when she's

in that mood. Unfortunately, Alyx was right there to keep me in trouble.

We entered the kitchen.

Several religions boast hells that are less crowded, cooler, and quieter. The master of ceremonies was a devil woman so large that at first I thought she must be part troll or ogre. But no, she was just large and ferocious and determined that her domain should be an extension of her will. She never shut up. Her voice was a continuously constrained bellow. She was an immigrant with a strange accent. Platoons of cooks and bakers and their assistants, and boys who stoked the stoves and hauled firewood and charcoal and worked bellows and whatnot in a wild rush to achieve the impossible, were all lashed on by her scorn.

Our entry attracted attention instantly. She spun, prepared to repel boarders. She recognized Alyx only after she'd drawn in a bushel of air. "Miss Alyx," she boomed, "you shouldn't be back here now, you. Dey a party tonight, dey are. And you in your finest, you."

"Mr. Garrett needs help finding his way around."

The big woman dropped her chin to her chest. She glared at me from beneath eyebrows like hedges. "Garrett? Be you dat Garrett, you?"

"Which Garrett?" I had no idea who she was but it sounded like the reverse might not be true. She might even harbor some old grudge. "I don't recall our having met."

"You never did, you. I an' I want to know, I, be you de Garrett, he helps de mister sometimes, him? Dis Garrett, was a Marine, him. He saved my Shoeman from de swamp, him. From de debil crocodile."

"Yes. Yes. And I'm not sure. We all pulled each other out of the swamp a few times. I remember a guy named Harman and somebody called Bobby Ducks. Nobody knew why."

"Dat be him, yeah. Dat be my baby, him. He never like his god name, him. Always want it be Bobby, him do."

I vanished into a huge and powerful hug, me. As my last breath fled me I reflected that Bobby Ducks' daddy must have been a real man's man, him.

The big woman turned me loose. I gulped air like a fresh-caught fish. She told us, "But I have a big job to do now, I an' I. An' if'n I an' I turn my back one solitary minute on dese lazy debils—"

I interrupted. "How much outside help came in for tonight?

Some of them may be here to hurt the Weiders." I hoped my imagination wasn't running too wild.

She understood immediately. "In de kitchen us added fourteen pairs of hands, us. For de work on de other side of de door, Genord, he hired sixteen men, him."

Gerris Genord. We knew one another only well enough to dislike one another. He was a bigger snob than even Ty Weider could be. He spent his life scandalized because people like me were allowed inside the house. Unless he had orders from Gilbey, he wouldn't work with me at all.

Maybe I could get around him.

Maybe I'd be lucky and not have to do anything.

"Those the only outsiders here?" I asked. "Besides our guests?" I recalled a mention of musicians.

The big woman nodded and turned away, unable to restrain her bellows any longer.

"And who would she be?" I asked Alyx. Earlier contacts with the Weiders hadn't taken me into the kitchen.

"That's Neersa. Neersa Bintor." She pronounced it Nay-Earsah. "She's been in charge down here since before I was born. Even Daddy is afraid to argue with her."

The big woman stopped bellowing, turned back to me. "You, Garrett. Maybe you want to know dis, you. Some of dese hirelings, dey maybe not so trustworthy, dem. Some keep trying to sneak away into de house, dem. Maybe to steal someding, eh? Dey have not get away from Neersa yet but maybe I an' I, maybe not be so hawkeye sometime, maybe."

"Thank you." That was support for my hunch. Wasn't it? I glanced around. "I'll keep an eye open. None of these people could melt into a crowd." Most looked like the sort who worked only as occasional labor even in a robust job market. Not backbone of de kingdom, dem. "They all accounted for now?"

Neersa allowed as how she believed that was so by way of an imperious nod.

"I'll circulate here for a while, see if I recognize any villains."

Alyx asked, "What should we do?" like she suspected me of first-degree intent to ditch.

"Wait. I won't be long. I promise." The girl had a vulnerable air that made you want to make promises—even if they were promises you couldn't keep.

Maybe she did need Daddy watching out for her.

# 30

I wasn't long, either. The odors of cooking combined with the smells of too many unwashed bodies crushed into too tight and too hot a space quickly discouraged me. Also, few of these people appeared smart enough or stupid enough to get involved in a plot against the brewery. And if they did get out of the kitchen, my nose would warn me.

If I was a villain who wanted to make an impact, I'd get in with the serving crew. They would be more presentable and more socially adept. And they would be welcome in parts of the house denied the kitchen staff.

I rejoined Alyx and Tinnie. "Too hot in here." I herded them toward the exit. From the corners of my eyes I watched for anyone paying me any special attention. Once we were out I asked, "Either of you notice anybody watching me?"

"I did," Tinnie replied.

"Uhm? And?"

"I mean, I watched you. Close." She winked.

Which irritated Alyx for sure. "How about you, Alyx?"

"She stole my line." She stuck out her tongue, so maybe Tinnie had. "No. Nobody even looked at you. You blended right in. Looked like you belonged there. Even in that outfit."

Belinda had assured me the Tad Weider hand-me-down was perfect for the occasion. "What's wrong with this outfit?"

Tinnie smirked. "We're talking silk purses and sow's ears, Garrett."

"If I wanted verbal abuse, I'd get me a talking parrot." Speaking of whom, he'd disappeared. If there are any gods . . . What I

mean is, if there are any *responsible* gods, one or two might make
sure the Dead Man didn't fade while the bird was here. I shuddered to think what might happen if that gaudy cowbird became
himself.

"He's not here," Tinnie explained. "Somebody has to take up
the slack."

"Where're we going?" Alyx asked.

"Around the corner to where the serving folks should be getting ready to—Hello."

"What?"

"I see a familiar face. In fact, I see two." They belonged to
Trace Wendover and Carter Stockwell, erstwhile recruiters, all
spiffy in servants' livery. The outsiders were all dressed in the
same threadbare outfits. The contractor probably rented them, trying to expand his margin.

Trace noticed me an instant after I spotted him. He didn't acknowledge my interest but did drift toward Stockwell. Carter
came alert before Trace got close enough to whisper.

"I was right," I mumbled, smug. "There was something going
on."

"What?" Tinnie asked.

"I see two rightsists who have no business being here." Stockwell and Wendover weren't the sort to be reduced to daywork.
Those pretty boys had to come from families of substance.

Alyx asked, "Should I get Manvil?"

"No. You guys just watch out behind me. Oh, hell!"

"What?"

I'd taken my eyes off the boys for a few seconds. "They're
gone." But how? There was no exit they could have reached that
quickly, nor did the server gang seem diminished. But Stockwell
and Wendover weren't among them anymore. "You'd better get
Manvil after all." I didn't like the implications of what was happening.

# 31

Gilbey brought Ty's pal Lancelyn Mac and a brace of hulking, uncomfortably out-of-place dock wallopers. "You got something?" he asked. He was ready for war.

"I spotted two rightsists who definitely don't belong here. They called themselves Carter Stockwell and Trace Wendover when they tried to enlist me yesterday."

"Interesting coincidence."

"Ain't it, though? They came to my house claiming they wanted me to join a freecorps called Black Dragon Valsung."

"Doesn't ring any bells."

"Not for me either. Just now they spotted me the same time I made them. They did a grand disappearing act. I rounded up Mr. Gresser. That's him with the ladies. He says nobody named Stockwell or Wendover belongs to his crew." Gresser was boss of the contract servants.

"They wouldn't use their real names, would they?"

"Only if they're stupid." Entirely possible with TunFaire's bad boys. "Gresser did concede the possibility that he *might* have employed men who answer the descriptions of Trace Wendover and Carter Stockwell. He doesn't seem close to his help."

Gresser was a weasely little functionary type in a state of high agitation. He was a naturally nervous sort terrified that his plans for the evening would collapse and his reputation would follow. All because we insisted on making a fuss about a few of his people.

Gilbey skewered Gresser with a hard stare. "You know *anything* about your people, Gresser?"

I sighed. I hadn't been sure Gilbey would take me seriously. I still wasn't sure *I* ought to take me seriously. I was running on hunch power. Hunches are one of my more sporadic talents.

I listened with one ear while Gresser whined, "There just ain't no way to check them all out. You do the best you can in the time you got. You come up with a job, first you got to get word out that you need people. Then you take the ones you know. Then you look the rest over and pick the ones that seem the soberest and most presentable, that ain't gonna blow their noses on the table linen or grope the female guests. Then, if you got the extra minute, maybe you ask around does anybody know anything down." And so on.

I kept one eye on Tinnie. She was put out about the whole situation. I kept the other on Alyx. For her this had become a great adventure. She remained poised on the verge of bouncing around like an excited kid.

She did bounce nicely, thank you.

With my free ear I eavesdropped on Gresser's grumbling troops.

One voice stood out. I whirled. They all stopped talking, startled.

I didn't spot the man but I knew the voice from the brewery stable.

I jumped again as Lancelyn materialized beside me, tense as a hunting dog on the point. "You heard that?" Then he relaxed. "Must have been my imagination."

"You thought you heard the big mouth from the stables yesterday?"

"Yes."

"So did I."

"I don't see him."

"And I just saw two guys who aren't there now."

"What's going on?"

"I don't know. But it smells like sorcery." Wouldn't you know, just when I'd started to think it would be straightforward. "And that's an odor I hate. How's Ty holding up?"

"He's in heaven. He's the center of attention. Which is where he always wants to be. Nicks is the one hurting. You're spooky in those clothes. When I came up behind you you were standing exactly like Tad used to."

"Sorry."

"No need. You think we need to do something more to protect the old man?"

"I don't think he should come out at all. What about those guys in the stable?"

"They didn't know anything. They joined a rights group just last week. They were asked to discourage you if you started nosing around. They didn't like bullying one of their own kind but you were always a pain in the ass so they didn't have much of a conscience problem. Until Ty told them this could get them fired."

"Did they cooperate?"

"Of course. They weren't so fanatic they wanted to go jobhunting. But they didn't even know the names of the men they were helping. They never introduced themselves. They just used the right recognition phrases."

"Things are getting absurd," I grumbled.

"People are scared, Garrett. Times are changing. It don't look like they're going to get better. People want to blame somebody. You put thousands of men used to violence into conditions like that and it would be absurd to expect nothing to happen."

He was right.

I spotted a guy who seemed very interested in me. I didn't recognize him. I tried to keep track as he moved around.

Lance asked, "Have you seen Kittyjo?"

"Not for several years." Kittyjo was older than Alyx by a decade. Like Ty, she was always unhappy. Rumor said she'd tried suicide.

Maybe there's one envious devil god determined to punish Max Weider for his success. Great villains steal and murder and torture and pay only if they get gobbled up by even bigger villains. Weider never played it any way but square, his tools intelligence and hard work. So he loses one son, has another driven mad, has a third crippled forever, has a daughter twisted by severe emotional problems, has a beloved wife dying unpleasantly by degrees, seemingly never more than one breath away from the end. And now the man who deserved none of that had poisonous political snakes trying to slither into his life.

Much more and I was going to get mad.

"She came down before you got here. She couldn't wait, she was so excited. She was like a kid on her birthday. It's the first time she's broken through the melancholy in months."

I asked, "Do I sense a more than casual concern?"

Lance showed me a sick smile. "You found out, Garrett. I don't know how it happened. I figured it would be Alyx. I worked hard at being interested in Alyx. Common sense says Alyx should be your choice if you have to fall for one of the Weider girls. She's the only normal one here. Besides the old man."

Me, I'd assumed he had an unhealthy attachment to Ty. Goes to show you. Nobody is what they appear.

I stared at Lance too long. Naturally, when I checked the serving crew I couldn't find my interested man. "We need to pin numbers on these guys."

There was sorcery in the air for sure.

Gilbey bustled up. "I sent word upstairs, Garrett. Max says screw you. He don't care if you've got Venageti rangers on the roof and commandos in the kitchen, we go ahead with the show. He says it's time to earn your keep."

"I hope his arithmetic is better than mine. Because I flat don't like the way things are adding up."

# 32

An uproar arose in the ballroom. Feminine shrieks preceded bellows of masculine laughter. "Oh-oh." I had a bad feeling but headed that way anyhow.

My bleak premonition was dead on. My partner's control had slipped. The Goddamn Parrot had done something. Women were trying to catch him. Men stood back offering valuable parrot-stalking advice.

It occurred to me that I wouldn't enjoy myself much if that foul-beaked feather duster fled to me for help.

Mom Garrett didn't raise her boy to die for the sins of over-trained pigeons. And nobody out there looked smart enough to believe I wasn't fooling around with some kind of ventrical locationism.

One of these days, Morley Dotes. One of these days.

"Aren't you going to do something?" Alyx asked.

"And admit I know that babbling vulture?"

"But—"

"He wants to run his beak, let him suffer the consequences. Manvil, do we have enough friendlies to watch all of the serving staff?"

Gilbey made a noise like a infant's whimper. He sputtered in frustration. The Weiders wanted to throw the social event of the season. Its legs were wobbling already. Any more security headaches and the thing might collapse. "Can't you just stay in the middle of them?"

"It's a big ballroom and there're eighteen guys."

Gresser had hung on. He protested, "There's sixteen, sir. Sixteen. That was what was contracted." Righteous indignation bubbled off the man. "I won't provide more than my specific commitment."

"I counted eighteen heads, Gresser. Twice. You got many two-headed employees?" The difference might be why Gresser never heard of Trace or Carter, though. "Why don't we take care of this? There're at least two imposters in your crew. Collect them up."

"Oh, gods! This is terrible! I'm ruined! No one will hire me . . ."

"Gresser! Please! We'll lie for you on your wedding night. Just don't hold us up now."

"Yes, sir." Gresser hustled off to assemble his troops.

"Changeable sort," Gilbey observed.

"Where did you find him?"

Gilbey shrugged. "Genord picked him. He's supposed to be good."

"Mr. Gilbey! Mr. Gilbey!" Gresser was back. Lance Mac was right behind him. Lance looked grim. Alyx, who had begun prowling out of boredom, headed our way, too. "Mr. Gilbey!"

"Yes, Mr. Gresser?"

"Mr. Gilbey, it is my sorrowful and shamed duty to admit that this gentleman was correct. There *were* more men here than I hired. They all agree there were more than sixteen. Estimates vary from eighteen to twenty. I can't understand how that happened. I concern myself deeply with the sanctity of my clients' persons and properties. I'm sure there were only sixteen of them when we entered the service gate."

I'll bet. Gresser found himself in sudden deep sludge and wanted his butt covered when the brown stuff flew.

Lance confirmed my suspicions. "A couple of waiters just did a dash into the kitchen. I couldn't find them again when I looked."

Alyx said, "Garrett, I just saw a waiter take off."

"I know. Lance says two of them just headed into the kitchen."

"Not the kitchen. This one grabbed a food tray and went into the ballroom."

"Another one?" I asked. "Or one of the two?"

Gilbey frowned at Gresser. "How many bandits did you bring?" I added my most ferocious glower to Manvil's. Gresser glowered back, sullenly defiant. We weren't going to make this his fault. We enjoyed a veritable glowerfest. Lance added his glower to ours and slid into position behind Gresser.

"I only hire them!" the little man protested. "For big jobs like this sometimes I have to take on people at the last minute that I don't know. I explained that."

I asked, "Anybody think the man is too enthusiastic in his protests?"

"Yeah. Way too. Bet you he never saw any of those men before today." Gilbey acquired a remote look. "Lance, stick close to Ty. Garrett, I'm going to send some men to watch over Max. Check in when you can."

"Will do. Meantime, I'll prowl. Wherever these villains go, they'll stand out."

I was worried. Those guys had to have a definite plan. Stockwell and Wendover didn't look like commando types but didn't have to be. Had I not been here they wouldn't have been found out.

Which was cause for speculation: How much had I been calculated into their plans?

I had to be. First, they tried to enlist me. Then they tried to scare me. Black Dragon Valsung had some strong interest in Weider brewing. I would worry what later. Right now we had baddies in the house, probably not inclined to be good guests.

I glanced around. Lance and Gilbey had left. Alyx and Gresser awaited instructions. "Carry on, Mr. Gresser. Make this the best damn shindig you can. I'll try not to bother you again. And I'll stop thinking bad thoughts about you."

He bowed. Damn, was he eager to please.

"You do realize that nobody is happy with you right now?"

He bobbed his head, stared at the floor.

"Scoot."

Alyx said, "I don't trust that man, Garrett. He's tiny and he's slimy and every time he looks at me I feel like he wants to pull my clothes off."

"Wow! You're as smart as you are cute. Of course he wants to pluck you naked. I'd worry about a guy who didn't give it a thought."

That improved her mood. She began to look at me like she hoped I might indulge in some plucking myself.

I didn't need to open that hogshead of worms. Not tonight.

I quipped, "Maybe he wants to wear your stuff himself. How about you keep an eye on him for me? What happened to Tinnie?" The redhead had become as scarce as Carter and Trace.

"I don't know." She was irked that I would even ask when I

was with her and some banter about getting more comfortable was on her own agenda. "She was here a minute ago."

Ah, well. Might be better not to have her underfoot. I said, "I'm going to prowl." Before really big trouble caught up with me right here, right now.

# 33

I took the main stairs to the second floor. Bad guys headed up wouldn't use an open route, though, so I set course for the back stairs after pausing outside Weider's study door. Nothing loud was happening in there. And there was no one on the floor except the people in that room. I could hear nothing but the musicians tuning up downstairs.

I climbed the service stair cautiously. The way these spooks faded out indicated a fair knowledge of the layout. *That* suggested inside intelligence, which wasn't a thought I cherished.

I had no weapon sharper than my wits, which meant those guys might not have much trouble disarming me. And the ones I'd bested before would be laying for me.

Somebody fooled somebody. Or maybe I fooled myself. I was sure I would run into an ambush getting to the third floor. But nothing happened.

I didn't find anybody on that level, either, though I didn't check one suite. The Old Man's own was sacrosant. Hannah was in there, committed to the long, slow process of dying miserably. Everyone else was downstairs.

A spine-stiffening scream clawed its way downstairs. Tom would not join the festivities, either. But this shriek seemed different. Had the devils in his mind taken concrete form?

I didn't abandon caution. I did feel naked without my head-knocker. But that thing just didn't go with formal attire. I needed a fancy-dress something, maybe a cane, that could be applied to admonitory effect in genteel surroundings. Maybe a sword cane, good for thumping *and* stabbing. Morley carries one of those.

I saw nothing useful around me. The Weider house is sparsely furnished above the second floor. Not even an old mace or morning-star decorated the walls. All the stuff from downstairs was piled at one end of Weider's study now, out of temptation's way.

Another scream. This one spoke of true physical anguish. Were my missing servants torturing Tom? Why bother? Assume somebody had a grudge left over from the Cantard. How could he get any satisfaction out of hurting somebody who didn't know who he was? Tom lived in a world no one else could enter.

Nothing made sense.

That was only because I didn't have enough information. So the Dead Man would remind me. The bad boys wouldn't be confused about what they were trying to do.

I heard a light step on the stair below me, just out of sight around one of the tight turns. Somebody was being sneaky without being good at it. Easy meat—if I could get out of sight.

I sat down and waited.

Alyx appeared on the tight little half-floor landing. She was watching her feet as she moved with exaggerated care. She squealed when she noticed me.

"Got to watch where you're going, darling," I told her. "Which, by the way, would be where?"

"What?"

"Why are you up here?"

"I'm looking for you." She made big eyes. She could do cute and dumb really well. But she couldn't work that one on me, no sir, not even when she leaned forward so the view down her bodice was open all the way to her waist, not much. I was onto her tricks. "I saw you go into the back stairs."

"You're just as dangerous as you think you are, Alyx. Or maybe more so. You get me boiling like an unwatched pot. But we've both got to get along with Tinnie."

Alyx squeezed down beside me. Those stairs were tight. And warm. They were awfully warm.

"Alyx. . . ."

"Don't hurt me now, Garrett."

I clamped my mouth shut. There are times when I can do that. Alyx's tone suggested that this time would be a good one.

# 34

"Shh!" Alyx rested a warning hand on my knee.

I nodded. I'd heard it. Someone had entered the stairwell above us, carefully, barely making the door whisper. I signed Alyx to stay still. She nodded. I shifted my weight slightly.

They made enough racket up there to let me rise without giving myself away. I helped Alyx rise, too. I pointed downward. "Slow. Careful," I mouthed, not even whispering. Alyx was pale now. This was no game.

Carter didn't see me till it was too late to help himself. He was burdened with the downhill end of a body, backing downward.

"Hey, Carter."

He jumped. At the body's nether end, Trace froze. I popped Stockwell under the ear. He sagged. I thumped him a few more times while Wendover gaped. Somebody still out of sight barked, "What's happening?"

I climbed over Carter. Trace groaned. He was trying to hold all the weight at his end. "It's me again," I told the guy from the stable. "I need to see your invitation."

Wendover went right on trying to keep the body from falling—whether dead or alive I couldn't tell. The guy from the stable came down behind Trace. He was angry. I thought he might jump over Trace to get at me.

He settled for slamming his fist into a wall so hard he dented the plaster. He retreated, whimpering and blowing on his knuckles. Trace finally let go and took off himself. I was almost close enough to grab him. I leapt, got a pinch of his trouser leg. Not smart, Garrett. Even a clerk can hurt you when he's scared. Good old Trace kicked me in the chops. Oh, that hurt! And me with bruises on bruises already, still not recovered from my last adventure.

My eyes watered. Trace seized the day. He undertook the one-man version of the retrograde action the Corps would call an attack to the rear.

I was beginning to think that me and Trace weren't ever going to get to be good buddies.

Somebody grabbed my leg the way I'd grabbed Wendover's. I fell on the body. Lying there, face-to-face with it, I decided that it had to be Tom the Screamer. The face was that of an older, less vigorous Ty Weider.

Was he breathing?

Maybe . . . No time, Garrett. Somebody is trying to pound you.

Actually, the somebody was climbing me like a ladder. Carter wanted to get back up the stair. Bright boy. He only needed to get by Alyx on the downhill side. I sat up so I could pretend to defend myself.

Alyx, who had not listened and gone downstairs, yanked off a shoe and clouted Stockwell alongside the head with its heel. *Thwock!* Carter went down for his second nap.

"Thanks." I wriggled out from under. "Is this Tom? And why didn't you go when I told you?"

"Yeah." She didn't answer my other question. "Garrett, what the hell is happening? Why would anybody want to kidnap Tom?"

"It makes no sense all right. Let's tie this clown up. We'll ask him about it later." I wanted to chase the others.

I'm no math genius. Obviously. There were still two or three of them and one of me and there was sorcery in it. I shouldn't forget that factor.

"Tie him up with what?" Alyx asked. And she had a point. There wasn't one single coil of rope hanging on a convenient hook.

"All right. I'll find something upstairs. Whap him again if he gets frisky." I wasn't feeling charitable toward Mr. Carter Stockwell.

I hit the fourth floor reluctantly. I'd worked out the math part now. It wasn't impossible for a gang of clerks to beat up on a solitary Marine if he'd lost a step since his glory days.

The clerks, however, failed to discern their opportunity with equal clarity. They were in evidence no longer. The fourth floor was as still as a crypt.

This was my first visit in years. The Weider sprats and some

senior servants had quarters there, suites for the former and
ratholes for the latter. One door stood slightly ajar. I approached
carefully. Must be age making me cautious.

I miss the old Morley Dotes. Used to be, whenever I went into
something tight, Morley would be right behind me—or even out
front if the mood was on him. But he was changing. He might
even go legit—really—and slide away from the underworld. He
seemed concerned about growing too old to keep up.

Nobody jumped me when I did dash through that doorway.
The bad guys were elsewhere, handling their business, snickering
because they'd left me coughing in their dust.

This was Tom's room. The furnishings were spare. A selection
of restraints were available on pegs beside the doorway should
Tom get frisky.

The air was ripe enough to gag me.

Maybe they should try Tom in a different setting. Something
pastoral or sylvan. Wondering why I bothered, what with this
world being just one endless bleak season milemarked by pain and
death, I held my breath and dragged myself out where there was
air that was fit to inhale.

I stood gasping in the hallway while my head cleared, amazed
that a place could become so infected by its tenant's madness. Or
was it the other way around? Had the room created Tom? Could it
be that stifling air?

Someone started to step onto the floor from the main stairway,
spotted me, ducked back. I caught just a glimpse of red fabric vanishing. I tried to dash over there but a terrible lethargy slowed me.
I needed me a double shot of ambition just to keep on breathing.

There was nothing to see when I got there. Of course.

I checked the other rooms and suites, found no one and nothing interesting.

Where was Alyx? I'd expected her to be underfoot again by
now, despite my instructions.

# 35

As the mists of depression dispersed I grew more alarmed. I headed back to the stairwell.

You're seldom disappointed when you always expect the worst but sometimes you're pleasantly surprised.

This wasn't one of the latter occasions.

Alyx was out cold. Somebody had bopped her upside the head and was beating feet down the stairs. Mr. Carter Stockwell was no longer in evidence. Tom Weider was gone. Somebody had started undressing Alyx before I interrupted, not a project any red-blooded Karentine boy would disdain but I wouldn't consider a stairwell the most romantic site. Nor are unconscious lovers much to my liking.

"Wake up, sleepyhead," I said. "Alyx! Snap out of it!" I considered swatting her the way they do in stories. Not a bright idea here. I had plenty of people unhappy with me already.

Alyx tried to sit up. I helped, asked, "What happened?"

"Are you stupid? Somebody slugged me." I could understand her mood. "They came from downstairs. Didn't you hear me yell?"

"No." It was true. I hadn't heard a thing.

"Well, I did yell. Loud as I could. And when I tried to run away I tripped over Tom and got hit before I could get back up." She became aware of the state of her clothing. "What's this? You only need to say when."

"It wasn't me. I like my girls awake."

"I don't know if I should be glad or have my feelings hurt."

"I wouldn't presume to tell you." Women always take me the wrong way. I assume they do it on purpose.

"I'm wide-awake now."

"Sweet as that sounds, there isn't time. There're bad guys in the house. We don't have a clue why. Any idea what happened to Tom?"

"They must've just gone ahead with whatever they were going to do."

"Probably. Come on. Get yourself together. I'm going to go see your father."

"Don't leave me here."

"I don't intend to. That's why I want you looking less frazzled."

"Oh." The merry hoyden reappeared briefly. Fright chased it away again. "What do you think is happening?"

"I can't even guess. I hoped Stockwell would help us out."

"Stockwell?"

"The one who got away. I've run into him before. His name was Carter Stockwell."

"Do I still look like we just crawled out of the hayloft?"

"Not quite."

"Darn." The hoyden was back. "I kind of hoped somebody would think I got lucky."

"Lucky for you now would mean deep slop for me later, girl."

She'd changed a lot in the last few years. "I won't tell if you don't." She was a little bit forward now.

I'll bet, I thought. She seemed like a girl who would want to celebrate her conquests publicly.

# 36

Despite Alyx's efforts at self-reassembly, she drew a hard look from Belinda after we invited ourselves into Weider's study. Belinda was head to head with Marengo North English when we arrived. Their discussion seemed very amicable. Marengo's niece was not in evidence.

The dark side always did get along well with the business community.

Weider rumbled, "Garrett! Perfect timing! We were just talking about you."

"We've got problems, boss," I said. "They just tried to kidnap Tom."

"They *did*," Alyx reminded me.

"She's right." I told it quickly. Then I asked North English, "You know anything about this Black Dragon freecorps or its commander, Colonel Norton?"

Marengo made an effort to be egalitarian but only because he was a guest where I was held in high regard. I doubt that he would have spoken to me ordinarily. "I've never heard of either one before. But I'm no student of the war. I put it behind me when I came home. Norton and his Black Dragons may have operated without my permission."

You sarky rascal. "They didn't get mine, either, but I wasn't in the army. I didn't spend much time in the Cantard proper. I'm not up on all the unit names."

Weider beamed like a cherub. He was so pleased to see us kids getting along. He told us, "There'll be a bunch of generals in here later, Garrett. I'll ask questions."

I noted, "You don't seem much worried about Tom."

"How likely is it that anybody could carry someone out of here unnoticed tonight?"

"I don't know. They got in. They have a plan. They must have a getaway scoped. All the suicide commandos got used up in the Cantard."

Weider was not alone there with Belinda and North English. Staying quiet but handy were several men from the brewery docks. Weider told them, "You boys spread the word about what you just heard. And tell Gilbey to come up."

"Tell everybody to watch for Kittyjo, too," I told them. "I haven't been able to find her. Max, these people have some kind of sorcery going. If you take your eyes off them even for a second, they disappear."

That angle was scary. It could mean Black Dragon Valsung had dangerous connections on the Hill.

"Weirder and weirder," Weider grumbled. "Why me? I don't know three people in the sorcery racket and none of them by their first names. They wouldn't pussyfoot, either. They'd stomp me like a bug."

Fire danced in the fireplace. Weider went to stare into the flames. He crooked a finger, calling me away from the others. He murmured, "Am I going to get hurt again?" At the moment he seemed lost, storm-tossed, without compass or anchor.

"Not if I can help it," I promised. I gave North English a hard look. He didn't melt. Somebody probably looked at him hard before. He was all tempered up.

Alyx hugged her father. "Don't worry, Daddy. Garrett will take care of everything."

Which Garrett was that? I wondered. This one hadn't shown me a lot so far.

Weider settled into a comfortable chair. He looked befuddled, unable to keep up with events. I didn't blame him, though that was a side of him new to me.

North English said, "I gather you're not in sympathy with the aims of The Call, Mr. Garrett."

That was a leading remark if ever I heard one. "But I *am* in sympathy. Very much so. I just have trouble with some of the individuals involved. Some of your biggest big mouths. Are they really the kind of guys we want telling us how to run our lives? Not to mention that most of them aren't really interested in rights at all. They just think they can grab something for themselves."

North English eyed me warily, as though he'd opened his breadbox and found a snake smiling back. "The most heartfelt cause will accumulate fanatics and exploiters, Mr. Garrett. That's human nature. It's unfortunate but it's difficult to recruit calm, rational activists like yourself."

Now who was shitting who? "Us calm, rational activists should keep the wild-eyed, wooly-haired types under control. They alienate more people than they convert."

North English's eyes narrowed. He didn't like being lectured by one of the unwashed. In his secret heart he approved of The Call's excesses.

It doesn't take long for any of us to weave elaborate webs of justification and self-deception.

I didn't think much of North English but he was Max Weider's friend and Relway did hope I could slide inside the movement. "I suppose I'm still bitter about my run-in with some of your rogue nutcases a while back."

North English's negotiations mask came out. "Yes. I heard about that. We do try to weed that sort out—which is why so many splinter groups form. Those men were weeds already scheduled to be pulled."

I entertained a suspicion that Marengo had misspoken but refrained from making myself less ingratiating than my history and social standing rendered me already. Relway wouldn't do me any favors if I wasn't in a position where I could help him.

"Please excuse me." I said. "I'm just cranky. I've been trying to help Mr. Weider and things haven't gone well."

"I understand. See me when you're in a better mood. The Call is looking for men like you, men who have been south and who have seen the worst and have given their best and have returned to face indifference, ingratitude, or outright disdain. Men who came home to find everything they fought for controlled by creatures who did nothing to defend it. . . . Pardon me. Without my niece to restrain me I tend to rant. Unfortunately, ranting isn't a good way to attract worthwhile new friends, either."

Marengo North English was one of the richest men of Karenta. Wealth is a superb insulator. Why did he find it emotionally fulfilling to involve himself in a working-class movement?

Guys at his level didn't come home to find there was no work.
They never worked anyway. "Garrett."

"Mr. Weider?"

"Time is passing."

"Yes, sir." That was as close as ever he came to telling me how
to do my job.

# 37

I was lost. I didn't know how to attack the thing. And the complications would increase as more guests arrived. These invaders—if they were around still—could be anybody in a waiter's outfit. And if they had applied half a brain while planning, they would have arranged not to be handicapped by that. The costume was just a way to get past the door.

I had a horrible thought. An awful recollection, really. Carter and Trace had been inside my house, within yards of the Dead Man, but he hadn't caught a whiff of their villainy.

Another horrible thought trotted in right behind the first. It scarred my brain with its little cloven hooves. The boys knew how to get around the Weider house entirely too well.

Alyx followed me. "What're we going to do now?" I stood at the head of the stair that led down to all the excitement.

"Good question. Find yourself a safe place. They might try to grab you or Kittyjo. Or Ty." Ty couldn't run and Lance was no fighter.

"Won't I be safe if I stay with you?"

"The problem is I might not be safe with you."

"Oh, Garrett! You say the sweetest things."

"Let's find Gilbey."

Gilbey was swamped. The mob was arriving faster than the majordomo could holler. Genord would have a sore throat come morning.

"What?" Gilbey demanded, peckish.

"They've grabbed Tom. At least three men were involved,

probably four. They used the back stairs. Tom was alive but out cold when I tried to take him back. Also, I can't find Kittyjo."

"I saw her a minute ago, coming down the main stairs. She's hard to miss. She's wearing bright vermillion. Damn. Another one who'll want to see Max privately." He turned to greet a spear shaft of an elderly gent I recognized belatedly as a retired cavalry brigadier. Gilbey continued, "I'll get word to the men watching the doors."

"The old man sent word already."

"Won't hurt them to hear it twice. Keep looking. They can't get out."

"I'm on the job, boss," I muttered. I moved off as Gilbey offered a slight bow to the brigadier. The old soldier's gaze tracked me. Looked like he thought he ought to know me. Maybe he had me confused with somebody else.

Alyx stayed a step behind as I headed for the service area. Gresser pounced on me. "What am I going to do? I no longer have enough men to cover—"

"Misplace some more troops?"

His cheeks reddened. A vein in his temple throbbed. "Your name is Garrett?"

"I haven't had a chance to change it."

"I don't want to apologize for my failings again, Garrett. If you'd like to discuss something positive that might be done, let's do. Recrimination wastes both our time."

"Point taken. Here's the problem. The guys who sneaked in with your crew have grabbed Tom Weider. I don't know why and it doesn't really matter. I have this urge to mess them up, though. Any ideas about how they might get out?"

I didn't expect any help. Cynical in my old age, I figured Gresser was in on it somehow, around the edge.

"They might grab one of the catering vans."

"The which?"

"The specialty baked goods, the pastries and sweetmeats, all come in from outside. The delivery vehicles are in the back court. The kitchen help brings stuff in so we can replace what the guests consume."

"Mr. Gresser, I take back every wicked thought I ever had about you. I'll put in a good word with Mr. Weider."

"That might help. But what can I do about being shorthanded?"

"Have everybody use two hands instead of one? I don't know. It's your area of expertise."

Alyx tugged my sleeve. "Garrett, they might be taking Tom away right now."

I let myself be led away.

Alyx told me, "You looked like you needed rescuing."

"I don't know—"

"Sometimes you just have to be rude."

"My mom insisted on good manners toward everyone."

"This way." Alyx's manners were good only when that wasn't inconvenient.

Her route wasn't very direct. I spied Tinnie in the distance, headed our way. Would Alyx be trying to avoid her? I waved when the blond wouldn't notice. Tinnie waved back. So did a handsome woman much older than me who seemed thrilled because she'd caught the eye of such a good-looking fellow.

Alyx said sometimes you got to be rude to rescue yourself but I can't, especially when I'm near a beautiful woman.

# 38

"I thought you were worried about Tom." At the moment Alyx just wanted to be friends. *Good* friends, right here, right now. My well-known unshakable resolve was wobbling like gelatin and my capacious capacity for withstanding torture was approaching its limit. If I didn't get out of that unused pantry fast, I was going to become the closest friend Alyx had.

That pantry had missed spring cleaning for years. I started sneezing. Then Alyx started. I staggered into the passageway outside.

Tinnie materialized, coming from the rear of the house, whither we had been headed. "There you are. I was beginning to think you got lost."

"We're looking for Tom," Alyx said from behind me, not the least embarrassed. She was surprisingly presentable considering what she'd been trying to do seconds ago. "Those men took him from his room. Garrett stopped them once but they sneaked up behind us and got Tom away again. Manvil says they couldn't have gotten out of the house yet so we were looking in all the out-of-the-way places, only Mr. Gresser said maybe they could've—"

Tinnie wasn't fooled. Her glance said we were going to talk later. She asked, "Why would they want your brother?"

Alyx shrugged, reverting to the shy, naive child she used to be, pulling it around her like a cloak of invisibility. I wondered if she hadn't been faking when she was younger. Old Man Weider might not be as much in control as he thought.

He for sure fooled himself about Kittyjo, back when. Kittyjo had been more determined than Alyx. And in those days there were fewer interruptions.

I wasn't eager to renew our acquaintance. Kittyjo was a little past neurotic. She was one of those people who hide it well initially.

I said, "Gresser might've been right about the vans. There's so much dust around here we'd know right away if anybody got dragged through."

Alyx snapped, "Somebody is going to explain how come it built up like this, too."

It was a short way to a rear exit. Tinnie had to have come in through it to have approached from the direction she had. "You see anything out there, Red?" I opened the door and leaned outside.

"Exactly what you see right now."

What I saw was two cook's helpers lugging trays. None of the wagons were big enough to require more than one horse. "Let's look them over."

Alyx announced, "I'm not getting horse dukey all over my new shoes."

"Tate's best shoes, too, I would hope." Moments ago she was willing to get anything all over her new dress. I didn't mention it. That would be "different."

Tinnie wondered, "Why don't you go back to the ballroom, Alyx? Ty can't handle it all forever. And Nicks is in no mood to carry him."

Alyx didn't want to entertain. Alyx didn't want to do anything that Alyx didn't want to do. Alyx had to do some growing up yet. But that was something else she wouldn't want to do.

I stepped into the yard while the ladies chatted.

There were five wagons. I dismissed two right away. They couldn't carry anybody away. I considered the others. Maybe one would tell me it was more than it pretended.

They were all seedy. That don't mean much today. You don't see anything new anymore. I can't recall the last time I saw a building under construction. Before I went to war. Maybe when I was a kid.

People fix what they can and make do with the rest.

I checked the dray animals. The great villains of this world, horses, have most humans fooled. The bad guys' animal might be as blackhearted as its masters and give itself away.

One was sound asleep. A second was trying to get there. The beast between those two, though, watched me sidelong from under lowered lashes with way too much malevolent interest. A gelding, it had a notion to get even by avenging its disappointment on me. And, cautious though I am around those monsters, I got a step too close. It snapped at me. I dodged nimbly, suffering only the loss of a few decorative buttons from my left sleeve.

"You're the one," I grumped. "Got to be the one." The beast wore hobbles. That said plenty. Dray animals don't usually need hobbling. Not in the city.

It watched as I moved to check its wagon, showing me big, ugly horse teeth in a huge equine sneer.

"Why not just snooze in the traces like your pals?"

Another horsey sneer, filled with contempt for all old-timers and their slave mentalities.

The wagon's side was made to fold out and lift up. It was secured by a wooden pin on a leather thong. I pulled the pin, grabbed a pair of thoughtfully placed handles, and lifted.

Somebody whacked my bean with a gunnysack full of horseshoes. I fluttered down into the darkness like a spinning maple seed. I don't recall hitting bottom. Or the cobblestones, whichever came first.

# 39

I groaned and cracked an eyelid. Couldn't be morning already, could it? Damn! Not another hangover. There'd been too many of those lately.

An angel drifted into view. She whispered. I didn't understand but I had some good ideas about what I wanted her to say. I'd take her up on it just as soon as I learned how to breathe again.

I mumbled, "I must've died and gone to heaven." That's the way things went in my mother's religion.

The angel continued talking. I began to catch her words. "Don't feed me any of your mouth manure, Garrett. I've known you too long."

"Oh. It's the other place. I always suspected you demons were gorgeous redheaded wenches. Or maybe the other way around."

"Flattery will get you everywhere, Garrett."

"Promises, promises. What hit me?" I patted the top of my bean. I found no unusual number of soft spots. "Couldn't have been a bird taking target practice." Unless maybe it was *my* bird.

"I don't know. When I finally talked Alyx into letting up on you I came out and found you right there. A man was getting set to hit you again. I yelled. The kitchen help came out so he ran away."

"What about the wagon?"

"Which wagon?"

"The one that was sitting here. I was just going to check it out when that chunk of sky bounced off my noggin." There was no reason she should have noticed that particular wagon. "I think we've got a problem." A big problem, if my fears were on the mark.

I managed a feeble, shuffling jog to the tradesman's gate. I recognized the sleepy guard only by subspecies. Very big, very strong, very stupid. Gate-crashers wouldn't get past him, no sir. "Did a wagon just leave?"

He checked me from beneath brows like overhanging cliffs. I was startled by the fact that they were hairless. "Who're you?" he growled, disgruntled because his nap had been interrupted.

"Name's Garrett. Chief of Security for the Weider breweries." So I exaggerated a little. Couldn't hurt.

It didn't. "Oh. Yeah. I heard about you. Yeah. The Simon the Pieman wagon went out. That's cute, ain't it?"

"What's cute?"

"The name. Like how it rhymes. Kind of cute and catchy, ain't it?"

"Sure. I get you. Nifty. Keen. Next question. How come you let it go? Didn't you hear we had bad guys in the house and we didn't want them to leave?"

"No." The man looked baffled. "I ain't seen nobody but that driver since I come on. The bakers and stuff was already here."

"Oh, hell," I said, without much volume or any real feeling. "All right. But don't let anyone else leave till you hear from me. All right? How many bad guys went out with that wagon?"

"I told you. Just the guy driving." He was beginning to resent my attention.

I grunted. I hadn't thought that all my bad boys would clear off that easily. They had a mission.

I turned to stomp away.

Tinnie caught my arm. She looked up with big fake moon eyes. "You're so forceful, Mr. Garrett." Her pearly whites looked particularly wicked in the torchlight.

"What I am is irritated. I had stitches on my head the other day. I ought to wear an iron hat. Maybe one of those ugly-officer things with the big spike on top. I bet I could get one of those cheap these days."

"They'd just hit you somewhere else. Then you might get hurt."

"You always see the bright side, darling."

"I try. You could find some other way to waste your life. I bet there're all kinds of careers where you don't have to deal with people who try to break your bones."

Oh-oh. "I'd better see the old man again. Tom might've been on that wagon."

Oh, did she give me a scary look. What a lowlife, subject-changing sewer rat that Garrett is!

Some things we'll never resolve.

# 40

I didn't think before I burst into Weider's study. I'd never encountered any reason to excuse myself around the Weider place before, little time though I spent there.

I plunged into a silence so sudden it was like the stillness after a thunderclap. Numerous pairs of eyes measured me. Marengo North English appeared to be conducting a summit of the chiefs of every nut group in TunFaire. Every rightsist nut group. I didn't see any democrats or round-earthers.

Belinda sat slightly behind North English and to his right, partially shadowed. The flicker of the fire in the fireplace lent her face a diabolic cast. Even that freecorps psycho thug Bondurant Altoona appeared to be intimidated.

Until you experienced it you wouldn't believe that a woman this young and attractive could come across so threatening. But no one in that room doubted her capacity for launching major mayhem.

I glanced around. "Where's Max?" Cool. Like I butted in on these things all the time. "It's critical."

I could manage without him. But his son was in deep sludge. He ought to know. He needed a say.

After a startled moment North English pasted on his paternalistic smile, told me, "Max just stepped out to confer with Manvil. Gentlemen. This is the Garrett fellow Miss Contague recommended. Mr. Garrett, won't you join us now that you're here? I'm sure Max will return directly."

I engaged in a brief internal debate, decided I ought to find out what gave. It was too late to run that wagon down now, anyway. It could be anywhere in any direction.

I moved a couple of steps into the room, studied the men studying me. A prime lot of political blackguards. Not one was in any danger from the nonhuman side of the community. Those who weren't wealthy, like Arnes Mingle and Bondurant Altoona, had large bands of armed rowdies at their beck. Cynical me, I wondered if The Call wasn't just a device meant to separate my nonhuman countrymen from their wealth and community standing.

North English said, "Garrett, these gentlemen and I, though separated by points of doctrine, all reside in the same ideological camp. Inasmuch as we were all here we thought it might be provident to pool our thoughts concerning these puzzles that have arisen."

Why tell me?

"We've discovered that none of us is responsible for the attempts to embarrass the Weiders. Max may not support our views but he's a friend to every man here." Before I could suppress my cynicism and respond, he continued, "Earlier you observed that none of us can be sure we know about everything happening in our organizations. That's true. But we're agreed that none of us would ever turn on Max."

Belinda's nod was barely perceptible. She had witnessed the discussion.

North English forged ahead. "You said the villains responsible call themselves Black Dragon Valsung." That was not a question so I didn't respond. "None of us knows of any such group. Nor of a Colonel Norton. We've agreed to start looking into that immediately. The group could give our movement a bad name."

I kept my expression bland. "They aren't imaginary," I said. "Several are in the house right now. I came to tell Max that they've kidnapped his son Tom."

Murmurs. "Looney" and "mad" stood out. They knew about Tom.

I offered a sketch of my collisions with Carter, Trace, and the guys in the stable. I avoided sounding antipathetic toward rightsist philosophy.

Weider and a bodyguard blew into the room. The sounds of the revels below came with them. The festivities were in full swing.

"Garrett! Damn! There you are! We found Tom."

"How did you know?"

"Alyx. He's all right. He was wandering around in the kitchen, getting in everybody's way."

I frowned, stared at Weider. He was so obviously relieved.

I wasn't. Something wasn't right.

Something hadn't been right from the beginning but I couldn't pin it down. "Are Ty and Kittyjo all right?"

"Ty's still holding court. I haven't seen Kittyjo. She's sneaking around like a commando. Nobody sees her for more than a few seconds at a time."

Why did somebody knock me over the head?

Gilbey pushed through the doorway. He had Tom Weider in tow. Tinnie was a few steps behind them. Gilbey said, "I have him under control now, Max. I'll take him upstairs. Luke will stay with him."

Something odd . . . "When did he change clothes?"

Everyone stared at me. I said, "He was wearing different clothes a little while ago."

For an instant Tom raised his eyes to look at me, something he'd never done before. It was so fleeting I wasn't sure he'd actually done it. Might've been just a twitch.

"You sure?"

"Yes." And Alyx could back me up.

"I'll check it out when we get upstairs," Gilbey said.

I started to leave so I could help him. I was sure the baddies were still around and still had plans. Marengo North English said, "Would you stay with us a moment more, Mr. Garrett?"

How could I resist when he offered the honorific to a man of my low station?

# 41

I shut the door behind Weider reluctantly. Old Max left me a meaningful look as he departed. I turned to the assembled barons of bug-fuckery. They stared like they expected me to begin belching green fire. I stared like I expected them to spout something incredibly bigoted and stupid. Finally, North English said, "Max tells me that you're very good at what you do."

"I try hard, anyway."

"He also insists that you're sympathetic to our goals."

Remotely. "I believe I've mentioned that myself." I inclined my head slightly so I couldn't be convicted when times changed later.

"Then why haven't you joined one of the rights groups?"

"I'm not a joiner. Unless you count the Marine Corps. And I wasn't offered my preference that time. When I do have a choice I make my own. That's why I'm in the racket I'm in. It lets me be my own boss."

"Exactly."

"Huh?" Often I hide my razor wits so guys like North English will underestimate me.

This wasn't one of those times.

"You appear to be the perfect man to winkle out the truth about these Black Dragon people."

Why not? I was working for everybody but the Crown Prince of Venageta already. Maybe I could get in with Black Dragon, convince Carter and Trace that I regretted my past transgressions and they ought to hire me to find out what that guy Garrett was up to. I knew a guy once, Pokey Pigotta, who used so many disguises and aliases that he did get hired to investigate himself.

"Garrett?"

"Uh? Oh. Yeah. Sounds good, we can work out the financial details. I've got some bones to pick with those guys." I caressed the back of my head. I've been getting bopped way too often lately.

"Financial details?"

"Even us idealists don't get much nutritional value out of serving a righteous cause."

North English scowled and muttered. He was a notorious skinflint.

Bondurant Altoona suggested, "Pay the man and get on with it. You pinch sceats till the King squeals but put out his ransom in silver for—"

"You're right, of course!" North English barked, silencing Altoona. "It would be petty of me to quibble over a few coppers." He yanked a purse from inside his waistband, tossed it at me.

I snatched it out of the air deftly. A few coppers, eh? I started to tuck the bag into an inside pocket of my waistcoat.

North English squawked. The Goddamn Parrot would have complimented him on his accent. His companions grinned. It didn't look like he had many close friends among his own kind. He grouched, "I expect you to take only what you need to compensate yourself for your labors."

"A guy's got to try." The grins got bigger when I opened the purse.

My eyes got bigger, too. What I'd assumed to be a rich man's walking-around sack of coppers, which might include a silver piece or two in case he ran into something really exciting, turned out to be all silver salted with a few pieces of gold. Swiftly I calculated ten days' fees and likely expenses, tripled them and applied my special unpleasant crackpot counter-discount. North English didn't see what I took but he danced like a kid with a desperate need to pee. Silver still isn't cheap, despite our triumph in the Cantard.

There were whispers among the others, some intentionally loud. Bets were laid as to whether or not North English would follow through.

To make sure I added several silver groats in case I ran into some big meal expenses, like, say, with a particular redhead while we were doing research, then passed the bag back. Eyes watched eagerly, hoping North English would open it up and reintroduce himself to all the survivors and mourn the departed.

He resisted temptation. "I'll leave your name with my gateman, Mr. Garrett. He'll have you brought to me immediately if you have anything to report."

Just a glance at the rest of the room told me North English had numerous "friends" perfectly willing to pay nicely for an opportunity to learn what I discovered before I reported it to the man who had hired me.

North English told me, "That should be all for now, Mr. Garrett." Embarrassed, he didn't take time to offer specific instructions. Fine. I like it like that. Means they haven't told me what *not* to do, where *not* to poke.

Excellent.

I backed out of there.

Weider and his bodyguard were waiting. The old man asked, "What're they up to in there?"

"You'd know better than me. They're your friends."

"Only a few. North English and Clive. Faudie and Slink. They asked me to invite the others. They subsidized expenses. They wanted to get all the names in the rights movement together where they wouldn't attract much attention. I get along where I can. It oils the hinges when I want something myself."

"Favor for a favor. I understand."

"Exactly." He nodded toward Tinnie. "I'm all right. We'll all be all right now. You and your friend go have fun."

"Thank you." I headed for Tinnie. But I wasn't about to take time off now.

# 42

Let me sip a few pints of Weider dark reserve and I turn into a dancing fool. I made all the girls unhappy. I danced with them all. Tinnie got the most attention but simmered when I took a turn with Alyx or Nicks or Kittyjo—once, guardedly. I even spun a couple with the matron who had fallen in lust with me earlier. She told me she was Dame Tinstall. That rang no bells. Dame Tinstall had outstanding legs for a woman of her maturity. She made sure I noticed them, too.

Alyx was less pleased than Tinnie. Nicks was too friendly for a girl getting engaged, though she didn't mention her feelings about that. Kittyjo, who looked like a shopworn version of Alyx, had little to say—good, bad, or indifferent. She did seem willing to let bygones be bygones. And Dame Tinstall left me in no doubt that she wanted to tuck me under her arm and take me home. I didn't ask what her husband would think of her plan.

I took the occasional timeout to nurture my relationship with the boss's product. I'm a very loyal kind of guy.

I wondered what had become of the Goddamn Parrot.

"What's the matter?" Tinnie asked.

"Something's wrong with me. I'm worrying about that damned talking ostrich of mine. Have you seen him?"

"Yes. I wouldn't claim him right now. If I were you." She had her devil smile on.

"How come?"

"He got thrown out of the house. You're lucky nobody remembers who he arrived with."

"I hope the owls get him." He'd asked for it.

The majordomo, Genord, who hadn't had a chance to yell much lately, approached us. He bypassed Alyx and Kittyjo. Alyx appeared incapable of harboring a kind thought about her big sister. Kittyjo, though, seemed only about half-alive and was completely indifferent to Alyx.

The majordomo handed me a folded scrap of paper. It had been used and reused. "A gentleman sent this in," he husked. "He said it was important."

Tinnie scowled, sensing more trouble. I feared she was psychic. Just when the evening was starting to roll, too. But that was my kind of luck. Wasn't it? "Thank you, Gerris."

The note said: *Must see you now. Critical. R.* The handwriting was primitive.

R? Who or what might R be? Who would know where to find me tonight? Relway? Who else? And didn't that stir up the mixed feelings?

"Now what?" Tinnie demanded, her psychic side simmering.

"I don't know. But I can't ignore it."

"Right now?"

"Maybe sooner." It would be significant. I didn't doubt that. Relway wouldn't contact me unless it really did matter.

"You're going to ditch your date?"

"What? Oh. Damn. No. I shouldn't be gone long. And she isn't a date, Tinnie."

"Maybe not. But I see how she looks at you when you're not paying attention. Like she wants to devour you."

"Kind of like I look at you even when you are paying attention?"

The ghost of a smile twitched the corners of Tinnie's mouth. "Right, Garrett. Try that line when I have time to notice. All right. I'll tell her why you ran out."

"Huh?" That didn't sound promising.

"I know you. You'll go out there and either get yourself knocked over the head and dragged off or you'll get interested in something and forget everything else or there'll be a pretty girl and your pig-dog nature will take over and—"

"You wound me, woman. Now that you acknowledge my existence again how can I possibly stay away more than minutes at a time?"

"I'm wearing new shoes, Garrett. Specially made. Don't pile it up too deep."

"And they're the most amazing shade of green I've ever seen. They set off your eyes perfectly." Maybe I didn't need to find out what Relway wanted. Not tonight, anyway.

I looked into Tinnie's eyes for a few long seconds. No. I definitely didn't *want* to find out what Relway had.

Her devil smile wakened. "Go on. Take care of it. Then get your big goofy self back in here. We'll see if maybe this threat to the Weiders doesn't require you to stay all night so everybody is protected."

Whoo-hoo! I moved out with a real bounce to my step.

"Mr. Garrett! Mr. Garrett!"

"Yes, Mr. Gresser?"

"Two more of my men have deserted. What am I supposed to do? How can I manage?"

Why me? Maybe Gilbey and Genord were fleeter of foot. "I'm here to handle gate-crashers and bad boys, Gresser, not to make sure Mr. Weider's guests are well served. You're the professional. Surely you know your business better than I. Why not grab a tray yourself?" I pushed past him.

I almost made it before Alyx caught up. She pushed up close, radiating availability. "Where're you going, Garrett?" She looked so damned kissable I had to bite my tongue. Why is it always feast when I can't do anything about it and famine when I can?

"I've had an emergency message, kid. I've got to go out for a few minutes. But I'll be right back." I glanced back to see if Tinnie was scowling. I didn't see her.

I did see Kittyjo watching from a shadow thirty feet away. She didn't look nostalgic for the good old days when we'd been very close friends till she changed her mind. She did look troubled. I winked at Alyx and headed for the door.

Maybe Kittyjo would warn her off me. That would be useful. I don't deal well with temptation.

Morley has a personal rule he recommends often: Yield to temptation whenever you can because every opportunity might be your last. I don't subscribe to that completely. Yielding could bring on the lastness. But I'm weak when blonds, brunettes, or redheads are part of the temptation.

On the other hand, a good rule of thumb would be: Never get involved with a woman crazier than you are. The trick there is to recognize the craziness before you get pulled in. Some hide it well. Kittyjo did.

As I departed a raw-throated Gerris Genord began to croak for attention. It was time Ty and Nicks made their announcement.

# 43

I stopped to see the security guys out front. They knew me. I told them I'd be right back. I stepped into the street, watching for the Goddamn Parrot as well as whoever wanted to see me. I didn't expect Relway himself. Relway prefers to stay out of sight. But the little guy emerged from the darkness like a whispering ghost. I squeaked, "You startled me."

"Sorry." Like hell. He smirked. "Sorry about interrupting your evening, too. But you have to see this."

"It's big enough to bring you out personally?"

"I'm here because every player in the rights game is here. That's significant. Something I have to look over with my very own eyes."

I wondered if he had people inside. I wondered again, aloud, as we walked. I got only silence in response. Which was answer enough for me. It was likely that several of Gresser's workers were secret police. Poor Mr. Gresser.

"It's quiet tonight," I observed. That wasn't a good sign, really. Not in TunFaire, where, by day or by night, completely quiet streets generally mean big trouble.

"Very."

The silence deepened as we walked.

The flicker of torchlight shone around a corner. We had walked only a few blocks, to the far side of the brewery. The torchlight had no noise attached. No excitement. We weren't headed toward a street party or toward a riot.

We turned a corner.

There was my missing wagon. There was my venomous new equine acquaintance. Four men surrounded them. Three carried torches. The fourth held a short spear to the spine of a man lying facedown in the street. Two of the torchbearers wore Gresser's corporate livery. How did they get away unnoticed? . . . Hell. They didn't. Gresser did complain. But the guys covering the front hadn't mentioned them. . . . Were they Relway's people, too? Of course they were. Which meant they were everywhere. Too bad I couldn't con them into doing my job for me.

The wagon was open on the side I'd been about to investigate when somebody decided to put me away for the night. Or a slab of sky had fallen on my noodle.

Relway told me, "These guys saw you get knocked down. They thought it might be interesting to trail the wagon and see what was going on."

I forbore complaint. I now had a notion about one guard who might be in with Relway.

The fellow with the spear forced the captive to keep his head turned away. Relway didn't want his face seen.

These four would be among his best and most trusted men, then. I tried to memorize their faces without being obvious.

"Shit!" I said softly when I looked inside the wagon. "This is what I was afraid of when—" Three corpses had been stuffed in there. Two were naked. Tom Weider still wore the dirty nightwear he'd had on when I was wrestling Carter and Trace. "Aw, shit," I said again. I couldn't express my despair any more articulately. This would crush the old man.

"You know them?"

"These two are Weider's kids, Tom and Kittyjo. The other one worked on the brewery's shipping dock. His name was Luke. He was helping tonight because he liked his boss. I don't think he was getting paid. He had four kids. We got a major problem here, friend. An enigma compounded by a mystery, as they say."

"Please be a little more specific."

"I saw all of these people in obvious good health inside the Weider place after this wagon left. I saw Kittyjo as I was coming out the door to meet you."

Relway grunted. "That doesn't sound good."

"Listen. We had gate-crashers who kept disappearing into the crowd whenever you weren't looking. But we never came up short on a head count."

Relway had to say the nasty word first. "Shapeshifters?"

"I'm willing to bet. Or, at least, somebody who always has some pretty tricky little spells handy."

"Changers have never been a problem here. But—"

"But?"

"The colonel got a letter. Off the Hill. Out of the blue. He didn't share all of it but it had to do with shapeshifters."

"We've got all these outsiders coming in. Some might be shapeshifters. Some up there would be interested." Traditionally, shapeshifters have preferred to play their deadly games where there are no sorceresses or wizards to winkle them out. They aren't a beloved breed. As they do with vampires, most races murder shifters as soon as they give themselves away.

"I didn't want to entertain the possibility until now," I continued. "You never want to see anything this ugly."

Shapeshifters have murdered people and replaced them for a lifetime, but not often. They prefer to hit and run, impersonating someone they've gotten to know well, briefly, without killing anyone. Even when they do commit murder they change guises frequently. Few have the ability to hold a shape and age it. And fewer can fool families and lovers for very long.

Their ultimate provenance is uncertain. They appear to be human most of the time. Maybe, like vampirism, their malleability is the result of some bizarre disease. What does seem to be true, or at least what everyone believes to be true, is that shapeshifters can't survive very long as themselves. They have to mimic. Maybe they even have to kill occasionally in order to appropriate a new soul.

They don't appear to be related to werewolves—though I expect they could become werewolves if they had one to pattern from.

"Anybody got any silver?" Relway asked. That made sense. As vampires and werewolves do, shapeshifters supposedly find silver poisonous. Relway wanted to run a test.

Nobody volunteered so I fished out one of Marengo North English's groats, the smallest silver coin I had. You've got to minimize your risks.

"Looks like your racket pays better than mine does," Relway chided. He knelt beside the captive. I repeated my morality tale about the nutritional value of idealism. Relway laughed. His life must be more fulfilled nowadays. He didn't use to have a sense of humor.

Relway slit the prisoner's shirt down it back. "I'll open his skin and flay it back so you can tuck the coin underneath." He tapped the captive's back in the spot you and I can't reach without a stick. "If they really don't like silver, we'll just let him hurt till he offers to help us find out what we want to know."

He never spoke to the captive directly. He carved with no more emotion than a battlefield surgeon.

The silver hurt the changer from the instant it touched him. He twitched, spasmed, shook, fought back a scream with every gasping breath.

Relway said, "Stay alert. That letter was right, this could attract more of them. They supposedly touch one another mind to mind."

I noted shadows moving in the surrounding shadows. "Did you bring a whole army?"

"Enough so I could handle any rightsist trouble if it happened."

Shapechanger minds were like a Loghyr's? Might that explain why the Dead Man hadn't seen what Trace and Carter were? "I've never heard that about them being mind readers. That could mean real trouble."

"Not like your roomie. They can only read other shifters. And only for general emotion, not specific thoughts."

"You sure?"

"No, Garrett. I'm not. Somebody told the colonel. He told me. Just in case. He didn't tell me why. He likes to pretend the Hill doesn't really influence him. Did anything interesting happen in the Weider place? Did you get a chance to spy on the big meeting?"

"I was mostly too busy. I got in once. By accident. Nobody gave anything away. But while I was there they asked me to investigate the Black Dragon bunch."

"You accepted that commission, I hope."

"That's what I said, did I? That groat you're abusing came out of North English's own purse."

"No. I thought he squeezed them till they squealed." The prisoner groaned. He would've screamed if he'd had any breath left. Relway covered his mouth and nose with a hand, just to make life more difficult. "Let me know when you're ready to talk."

A scuffle broke out in the darkness. It lasted for several seconds. I still marvelled at the absence of witnesses. TunFairens always scatter at the first hint of trouble but, once they feel safe personally, they usually come back looking to be entertained. Maybe the changers were radiating some stay-away emotion so potent even humans felt it.

But then why would I be hanging around?

"Damn!" I said. "If these things really do read each other from a distance, the ones at the house will realize that they've been found out."

"Not necessarily. Not if they just feel emotions."

"How did you know they were out here tonight? Block?"

"No. I didn't know anything till I stopped the wagon. Which I did because I thought it might have something to do with what the rights people are scheming. I wasn't looking for what I found."

"Seems like a lot of trouble just to keep an eye on the rights guys." I gestured at the surrounding night.

"They're dangerous people, Garrett. Until I caught this thing here I would've said that rightsists are the biggest danger Karenta faces. They get people hurt and killed and businesses destroyed and it's only going to get worse. I can't just let that happen. But the danger posed by these things might be even darker."

"I think he passed out." I indicated the changer.

"So he did." Relway let the thing breathe. "You know anything about shapeshifters, Garrett?"

"No. I ran into one once. A Venageti spy who'd replaced a Karentine counterintelligence officer. That's it."

Relway sat down on the changer, ready to use his hand. "I was afraid of that."

"Of what?"

"Not yet. Maybe this thing can confirm my suspicions."

Relway's men dragged someone over. This one shifted slowly between several sets of features. I recognized none of them. Relway searched it after making sure the other one would remain unconscious.

"This is interesting." He showed me a tattoo on the new captive's right forearm. It was black. It resembled a dragon, though the light could have been better. It incorporated a simple Karentine army crest.

"That *is* interesting."

"I do believe I'll have to do some digging. I suspect an untold story has begun to surface."

The changer recovered. His features became fixed. The tattoo faded. We pretended not to have noticed it.

I glanced at the wagon. "I need to go break the news. And grab the villains still inside. Bring the bodies back. The old man will want them."

"You need help?"

"Send your waiters back. Mr. Gresser will be infinitely grateful."

Relway grinned. He had an all-new and challenging bunch of bad boys to eradicate.

I told him, "Let me know what you get from those two."

"Goes without saying. Long as you let me know about the crowd in there."

"They're dividing turf, making peace with the Outfit and making rules about who they can and can't push around. They don't want to irritate anybody who can send troops out and they don't want to waste time fighting each other."

"Ah. Too bad about that."

"Belinda Contague is there. Speaking for her father."

"A genuinely hard woman. And so young. Out of a privileged houschold. Makes you wonder. You're a friend of the family. How come we see so much of her now and so little of her father?"

"Chodo had a stroke. He doesn't want people to see him until he recovers. They might think he's getting weak. But he's as hard as ever and getting mean-spirited besides. Anything new on Crask and Sadler?"

"No. But they're out there."

Those two were worth worrying about. They were nightmares.

# 44

"I'll take these three to the Al-Khar," Relway told me. "Drop by and find out what they had to say."

His people would wait outside the Weider shack while I rounded up the changers inside.

"I want these bodies," I reminded.

"Go ahead. Take them."

I folded the door shut before he changed his mind, pinned it, climbed to the driver's seat. I gathered the reins like they were covered with slime, told Relway's thugs, "You guys want to make sure this monster stays headed in the right direction?"

Monster and thugs eyeballed me. The horse smirked. One of the thugs—their names were Ritter and Abend but their attitudes left them undeserving of remembrance—said, "You can't drive a cart? Get down from there."

"I can drive a cart," I muttered. "If I really want to, I can drive a cart. But I'm going to let you do it this time." I *can* drive a cart. I learned in the Corps. But watching the south end of a northbound beast, knowing the critter is looking for a chance to visit disaster upon me, isn't my idea of fun.

The big bruno on the back gate was on the job now. He had let this very wagon scoot out—along with Relway's guys, whom he'd forgotten to mention, which you just naturally had to wonder about—but now nothing was going to get past him. "What's my name?" I demanded.

"You're Garrett."

"And what's my job?"

"You're in charge of—"

"Bingo! I'm in charge. And I'm telling you to let us in."

"But you never said nothing about—"

"I'm saying it now. I gave you some hard road about letting this wagon get away. Then I went and got it back. Open the gate."

"But—"

Relway's men ran out of patience. They vaulted the low wall and opened the gate. The guard raised a loud fuss. Gilbey arrived before I finished proving I could drive a wagon and got it parked. Of course, it might be sunrise before I got the best out of the damned four-legged snake pulling the vehicle.

Gilbey said, "I thought you went home with Dame Tinstall, Garrett. Your friend is fit to be tied."

"Which friend is that?"

"The one who came with you. What have you got here?"

I opened the side door. There was light enough from the house. Gilbey threw his right forearm up against the side of the wagon, closed his eyes, froze that way. He controlled himself before he asked, "What's going on?"

"Shapechangers." I told him what I'd been doing.

"It explains a few things. I just saw Kittyjo. Now I see why she was staying out of the way tonight when she was so excited about everything this afternoon."

"Any idea why a shapeshifter gang would want to take over the Weider family?"

"Because they like beer? Because they want a brewery?"

That wasn't some attempt at black humor. Gilbey meant it. "I'll bite. Why would they want a brewery? Why right now?"

"Better ask them, Garrett. Anyway, the brewery might not have anything to do with it. What now?"

"Much as I hate to, we have to tell the boss."

He seemed exasperated. "Of course we do. I mean, what do we do about these monsters? We need to catch them, don't we?"

"Sure. And we need to move fast. Before they get the word, change appearance, and get away. I *think* there are only three still here. The others took the corpses away."

Undetected and unchecked, I was sure the changers still in the house would have brought in more of their own. The Weider place would have become a changer fortress and haven.

But why the Weiders? There were other families as wealthy, others more iconoclastic, others better forted up.

But suppose the presence of the leaders of the rights movement had something to do with it. Suppose the changers had come in because of the guest list. Suppose Marengo North English and Bondurant Altoona got replaced? They were goofy already. Would anybody notice?

Whatever, it couldn't be meant long-term. Shapechanger schemes get found out. We liked to think, anyway. In TunFaire some real heavyweights would trample all over them once the news got around. By tomorrow there ought to be a hue and cry. The rightsists would be in deep clover.

Shapechangers scare everybody. Alienists make fortunes proving to losers that their loved ones haven't been possessed by demons or replaced by shifters. Or the other way around if that's where the profit is.

Alienists are like lawyers. Right, wrong, justice, the facts of the case, none of that matters. Results are what count. That's usually somebody else with empty pockets and a dazed expression.

The alienist's client doesn't want to believe his beloved no longer loves somebody as wonderful as him. The explanation has to be supernatural and sinister.

Changers have served as excuses for murder, too, though it seems the corpses never change after death. No murderer ever got off using that excuse.

I told Gilbey, "We won't make anything happen standing around trying not to cry."

# 45

Belinda was in the hallway outside Weider's study, standing delightfully hip-shot, listening to Marengo North English. The man had to have a side I'd overlooked. She seemed enthralled.

He seemed to have forgotten his niece.

Belinda spotted me. Her expression went colder than arctic stone. Then she recognized the damp around my eyes. "What happened, Garrett?"

"You two come with us. Max is there, isn't he?"

North English nodded. "He hasn't made it downstairs yet. Too many visitors." So Marengo and Belinda had been standing around chatting for a while. Interesting.

Gilbey remarked, "Ty will be getting cranky. He dislikes taking second priority."

I opened the study door slowly. Max was seated in front of his fireplace, deep in a comfortable chair. He'd built the fire high. The heat beat out in waves. He stared into the flames as though he saw through them into an age when the world knew no suffering.

"Back again, Garrett?"

"Yes, sir."

"Your friend was furious because you left."

"She gets that way." My friend winced. "I had to see about something outside."

"What's the news, then? How bad is it?"

"As bad as it gets. Tom and Kittyjo have been murdered. So has Luke."

Gilbey said, "That's the man we asked to look out for Tom."

I said, "The change happened before that."

"Change?" Weider muttered.

"They were replaced by shapeshifters," Gilbey said.

I added, "It looks like Black Dragon is a shapeshifter cover. It claims to be a rights group but it's really something else." Nonhumans wouldn't be interested in human rights. Not quite the way The Call is.

Weider sighed. "I'm tired, Garrett," he told me. He *sounded* tired to the marrow. "Sit down, Manvil. Garrett." He indicated chairs. "I just want to put my burdens down. I want to take a long, long rest. I don't have any fight left. If there was anybody to surrender to, I'd let destiny make me a prisoner of war."

"You did your share, Max," Gilbey said. "Take it easy. Garrett and I will handle it." Gilbey glanced at me. I nodded. He asked, "Should we enlist Lance?"

"Lance strikes me as more the executive sort."

Gilbey smiled. "Not far from wrong, Garrett. Though the man can surprise you sometimes." He twisted, looked beyond me. His eyes gleamed for an instant.

"I'll help," Belinda said. I'd almost forgotten she was back there, listening.

I didn't argue. Neither did Gilbey. I was beginning to develop a suspicion that Gilbey would be incapable of arguing with Belinda. He told us, "That junk in the corner there was mostly for decoration but there was a time when all of that was real weapons. Help yourselves."

Without hesitating Belinda selected a wicked fourteen-inch blade, examined it with a professional eye. Gilbey chose a bronze gladius sort of thing and added a small, coordinated buckler for the left wrist. "Stylish," I observed, sighing. Now that I was sitting down I didn't want to get back up.

Gilbey didn't smile. Except for Miss Contague he was all smiled out for the century. Nobody else smiled, either.

I miss the old days. Nobody grins into the face of the darkness anymore.

You need a sense of humor when the going gets grim.

Seldom do I lug lethal hardware but I couldn't find a simple headknocker anywhere. At least nothing sure to stand up to harsh commercial-grade use. A small crossbow, intended for use by cavalrymen or centaurs, caught my eye. I used to be pretty good with one of those things, though I hadn't had one in hand for a while.

Marengo North English considered the choices. Gilbey suggested, "Why don't you stay with Max? He's a little distracted."

North English relaxed visibly.

Obviously the great champion of humanity volunteered only because of Belinda. Oh, what to do when the delicate flower chose danger without thought?

Gilbey picked up a light, thin-bladed antique. "I've heard you were well regarded as a fencer." He extended the weapon to North English.

"When I was young."

"Good," I said. "Then we won't have to worry about Max while we're gone." I gave his shoulder a comradely pat. He puffed up like he'd been handed the key role in the mission. Maybe, in his mind, that's what happened. He seemed incapable of seeing himself anywhere very far off center.

# 46

We slipped into the back stairs. I told Belinda, "You don't have to do this."

"I know. And you didn't have to warn me. Don't waste your breath."

I wasted no breath. I'd argued with her before. And the stairs were steep.

I was shaky when we reached the fourth floor. I'd been pushing my luck a lot lately and Fate wouldn't give me time off for bad behavior. It was one damned thing after another, too often involving me getting hit over the head.

You can't roll the bones with the sickle-toting guy without crapping out sometime.

I controlled the shakes. I learned that trick in the Corps. The hard way. I took a deep breath, held it a moment, asked Gilbey, "Is there more than one way out of Tom's suite?"

"Possibly. There're servants' passages all through the house. But if we hurry, that shouldn't be a worry."

Indeed. And maybe I should have had Relway's guys stick with me, just in case.

Belinda said, "If I knew where we were going, I'd leave you behind just to make you stop thinking, Garrett."

All my life I've been told I think too much. Except at girl time, when I'm told I don't think enough.

So it goes. You can't win.

I stepped into the hallway.

The Luke replacement was standing guard right where Luke was supposed to be. His eyes narrowed suspiciously. I pasted on a big grin. Belinda and Gilbey marched along behind me. I said, "Hey, Luke. The Old Man says bring Tom down. He wants the whole family there for the announcement."

Whoever Luke was really, he couldn't argue without giving himself away. He couldn't let Tom out without courting disaster. And I didn't give him time to consider his options.

A crossbow isn't a customary accessory when you're just going to escort somebody somewhere inside his own home. *Faux-*Luke figured that out almost quickly.

He flung himself back just as I started to pop him with my free hand. He tried to run into Tom's suite. We didn't let him. But he did make a big racket not getting there.

He went down. Belinda had a knife pricking his throat before he stopped bouncing.

Gilbey and I burst into the suite.

And I said, "Well, there *is* more than one way out." It stood open.

There was no light behind the panel except what ambled in from Tom's apartment. That was just enough to show us that the shapeshifter could only head downstairs. This almost qualified as a secret passageway. It was barely wide enough for a grown-up my size. The stairwell was just slightly less steep than a ladder. I thundered down to the floor below. Another door stood open, exiting through a broom closet. The main hall lay beyond it. Gilbey stayed with me. We couldn't let the shifter get a big lead. It would change faces on us again.

A door stood open down the hall, still moving. My mother would have been all over this guy. He was a wonderful bad example. We blew into the room—and froze.

It was Hannah Weider's bedroom. It smelled of sickness and despair. The dying woman had been confined there for ages. Her face brightened when she saw us. She tried to say something.

Hannah Weider was so withered and liver-spotted she looked more like Max's grandmother than his wife.

Words wouldn't come. She wiggled a finger.

Gilbey got it. "It's under the bed."

Trace Wendover scooted out. He headed for the door, realized that I could get there first, flung himself back at the bed. He snagged Hannah, dragged her in front of him as a shield. A knife appeared. He didn't need to voice the threat.

Alyx appeared in the doorway. "Mama, I brought you some of Ty's—Shit! What the hell?"

Trace turned, startled.

Mama tried to admonish her baby about her language.

I shot Wendover in the forehead.

I used to be pretty good with one of those things. Evidently I still had the knack.

# 47

"She's gone!" Alyx wailed. "It was too much for her." There was no vinegar in her now. She was about to fall apart. She shook her mother like that might bring her back.

Belinda arrived. She had her changer under control. She looked at Alyx, shrugged, gave me a don't-look-at-me stare.

I didn't expect her to do any comforting. She wouldn't know how. I doubt that anyone ever comforted her.

"Get Tinnie," I suggested. She knew Tinnie. "Or Nicks."

Trace had a bolt in his head but he remained active. His shape shifted continuously until the bolt popped out. It clunked on the floor.

"There's a neat trick," I muttered. "Sure like to learn that one."

Alyx jumped on the thing.

It tossed her across the room.

I shot it as it got up. This time I followed up. I pushed a silver groat into its new wound.

The changer lost control of its muscles.

I asked, "Gilbey, you want I should tell the Old Man this one?"

"Still my place, Garrett. But this time might be the one too much. Hannah was the reason he kept going."

Belinda's changer kept sliding out of his restraints. He oozed like a slug. By trial and error I found that a whack on the side of the head would do to them what it did to me. "A few yards of silver wire would come in handy about now."

Nicks appeared on cue. "Here, Garrett." She shed silver chain necklaces. "Tinnie will be here in a minute. Alyx? You all right?"

Then Nicks realized that Hannah really was dead. The look she
gave the changer made me glad she was on my side.

I asked, "How come you're here?"

"Your vampire girlfriend told me to come." She had a sharp
tongue on her, Nicks did.

I used her chains to bind the guy I'd bashed. He started shaking and flopping. I thought he'd break the chains easily but he
didn't.

Gilbey knelt beside me. "Gag them. We don't want to upset
anybody downstairs."

Tinnie marched in. Belinda was right behind her. The redhead
said, "Ty will be here as soon as Lance gets somebody to help."

Gilbey shook his head. "He doesn't need to do that. Better he
should meet us in his father's study. If you ladies will see to Hannah's dignity? Garrett. Let's drag this garbage downstairs."

"We have another one running loose still," I said as I gathered
my share.

"I know. I know. We'll deal with it."

I wondered. If Relway was right, that one would know that
something had gone wrong.

# 48

Max surprised us all. Horrible news piled atop horrible news prodded him back to life instead of finishing him. Maybe the pain was just too big to encompass. Or maybe he was too long in the habit of meeting Fate head-on. He glared at our captives but did not touch. He would take a practical, businesslike approach to revenge.

Both changers still twitched and flopped. They would've screamed if not for their gags.

Gilbey left to divert Ty and Lance.

Marengo North English, Belinda, and Nicks had been asked to step out. Max didn't want to share this with them.

Lance followed Ty into the study. Ty was on crutches. You didn't see that much. He was pale and angry. "Fuck up again, Garrett?"

"Be quiet," Max said. His voice was calm and flat and cold. Ty responded instantly. "Sit down."

Ty sat. Likely he hadn't heard that voice in a decade.

"This isn't Garrett's fault. He wanted me to be more careful. Somebody meant to murder us all tonight. Who knows why? We've stymied them. Because we let Garrett do a little. Blame the mess on me. We did capture five shapeshifters." He hadn't been surprised to hear that the secret police were watching the house. "Manvil. What about the other one?"

Gilbey nodded. He must have been up to something.

"Five?" Ty croaked. He stared at the two squirming in front of the fire. That had burned down some now but still put out a lot of heat. The changers didn't like that.

"Garrett dealt with three more outside the house." He didn't mention Tom or Kittyjo. Yet. He looked at me. "We'll get their story?"

"If it can be gotten."

"There's another one here in the house, Ty," Weider said. "I expect to deal with it momentarily."

So Gilbey *had* been up to something. I should've warned him that the creatures could feel one another's distress.

"That we know about," I reminded. "Changers are almost mythical around here. We don't know anything about them. We see the giant meat-eating thunder lizards more often." It was a bad time for thunder lizards, though. "Worst case I know of, and that's probably a fairy tale, involved a family of changers that operated in the forest north of town during the last century. I didn't figure out what was going on here just because changers are so rare. I wouldn't have thought of them at all if weird stuff didn't happen to me all the time."

I headed for the door. Weider frowned but understood when I leaned against the wall where I'd be out of sight when the door opened.

My timing was impeccable. The pseudo-Kittyjo walked in barely a minute later, insufficiently suspicious of a summons from the Old Man. That surprised me.

She didn't seem to sense the distress of the two we had collected already. Was the silver responsible?

Gilbey stepped over to hold the door. When it swung shut there were two of us behind her. She didn't understand till she got a look at me.

Ty broke the hard silence. "What's going on, Dad?"

"This isn't your sister. It's something that murdered her and took her shape."

"Dad?"

"Kittyjo is dead, Ty. Believe it. Tom is dead. Lucas Vloclaw is dead. They were murdered. They were replaced by these monsters." He indicated the roasting shapechangers.

I had my little crossbow ready. I let the changer have a look.

"What did you things want?" Weider demanded.

Ty didn't get it. "Jo, what is this crap?" He did see that there was something strange about her, though.

She seemed stranger by the second.

She was changing! She was maintaining the outward appearance of Kittyjo Weider but inside she was doing something that would, probably, improve her chance of escape. Or, if she was

"This is too big for us to squabble amongst ourselves."

"I'll buy that."

Ty nodded. He scanned the crowd. "That spine shot was all that stopped it."

Worth remembering. "Still only looks temporary." This looked like one of those nightmares where the monster keeps getting up and coming.

Ty said, "Lance, Giorgi went up to Mother's room. Alyx is up there, too. They'll need some support."

I added, "Tinnie should be there, too." I wondered where Belinda was. And somebody needed to watch the changers in Weider's study.

bloody-minded enough, she was becoming something fast and deadly.

I said, "It's changing, people."

The Kittyjo thing glared at me. Gilbey moved. The changer turned his way. I poked it. Felt like I'd slammed my fist into a leather bag full of rocks, too.

The shapechanger didn't go down. It just turned on me. Evidence was accumulating: Shapeshifters were not overly endowed with intelligence.

I ducked a blow like a lightning bolt. Gilbey applied a couple of kidney punches. Neither had much effect. He barked in pain. His knuckles leaked blood.

Ty hollered something about leaving Jo alone.

I plinked the thing with my crossbow, in the throat. My bolt penetrated barely an inch. The changer stopped to fiddle with it.

Gilbey was nearer the weapons collection. He seized a ferocious antique mace, topped the changer a few times. I readied another quarrel. The shifter decided it didn't want to play anymore. It left. Without bothering to open the door.

I loosed another bolt. It struck the small of the creature's back, right in its spine.

The changer sprawled forward, fingertips dangling over the brink of the grand stair. I told Gilbey, "I used to be pretty good with one of these things."

"So I see."

The shifter couldn't get up. It tried pulling itself forward. That worked. It tumbled ass over appetite all the way to the ballroom floor.

I galloped after it.

It looked nothing like Kittyjo now. In fact, it had a distinct thunder-lizard look. Developing armor plates clashed with Kittyjo's dress. A nub of a tail wiggled under the red cloth.

People shrieked. The orchestra stopped playing. A crowd collected. Lance joined me over the changer, shaking. I told him, "She was probably the first one replaced. She would have been the easiest."

Ty joined us, having come down by clinging to the stair rail. He wanted to hurt somebody. He stared at the thing that had replaced his sister and maybe grew up a little. He put his anger aside, found the hidden Weider steel. "I apologize, Garrett. I was out of line."

"That's all right. It's tough."

# 49

Max joined us. "Am I presentable?" He was in control, but barely.

"You look fine, Dad," Ty replied.

"Then let's get our guests calmed down."

I hefted the little crossbow. I had a pocket filled with bolts. Guests backed away.

Presumably the shifter could become its nasty old self with a little effort.

I dug out another coin. These things were going to break me.

The shifter expelled my bolt but its legs still refused to work. Nothing human illuminated its face now. The creature was incapable of emotion in this form.

Max stayed with me. "Just a minor problem with a would-be assassin. It's over. No need to concern yourselves. Go ahead. Enjoy."

Marengo North English materialized among us, over the changer. Sword in hand, handsome, posing, he looked brave as hell. He registered no claim that could be challenged but his stance made it seem that *he* must have been the target of a bizarre murder plot.

My opinion wasn't improving as I learned more about the man. I hadn't seen any proof that he believed what he preached— except that he did put cash where his mouth was. I had a problem picturing a famous skinflint gushing coin without believing.

Maybe Tama Montezuma knew the truth. She appeared more stunning than ever when she rushed up to see if Uncle Marengo was all right, despite being rattled in the extreme. There seemed to be a certain ghastly hollowness to her.

*Doink!* I let the changer have it between the shoulder blades.

"Cut its shirt open," I told North English. "I need to get to that wound." The changer flopped, again eager to go somewhere far from guys with crossbows, knives, and silver.

The guests backed away again but continued to watch. Even the musicians and servants wanted to gawk. There wasn't an ounce of compassion in the house.

What does that say about the human folk of TunFaire?

Valiant Marengo stepped forward heroically. With an elegant flick of his blade he slit the changer's stolen dress. The creature kept trying to wriggle away. Its limbs refused to cooperate.

I yanked the bolt out and pushed my coin in before the wound closed. "This's the last one. I hope." Six was more shapeshifters in one place than I'd ever heard tell of. A few more wouldn't be a real surprise now.

Weider stared at the changer. He shook his head. "I don't get it, Garrett." He was fighting the shakes.

He had a better chance of understanding than I did. It was his house, his family, his brewery. What I understood was, he was my friend. "We'll find out."

Ty agreed. "Whatever it takes, Garrett." He was shaking, too. "No prisoners. No quarter." He refused to sit down.

"I'll need help dragging these things out of here." On cue, Relway's thugs materialized. They must have been listening. They slipped through the crowd like they were greased. "Where were you guys when I needed some backup?" I grumbled. "This needs taking away. I have two more upstairs. I'll show you where."

Weider addressed his guests again. "Please, people. Celebrate. Be joyful." He couldn't fake any joy himself. His despair shone through.

My admiration grew. Max was like those old-time aristocrats who had built the empire. He soldiered on with what had to be done despite any personal pain. He would not yet yield before his duties were satisfied.

I led Relway's men to the study.

One prisoner had slipped his bonds. We got there just in time. It cost me another groat to get it under control again. I was grumbling like Marengo before we finished.

Ritter said, "We'll take them out the back way. You'll hear from the chief."

"Remind him. He promised."

Belinda was waiting when I went back downstairs. She asked, "Are we ready to go now?"

I watched North English entertain a gaggle of hangers-on, flourishing the borrowed sword. He seemed particularly animated. I must have missed the most exciting part of the adventure.

A frown darkened his face when he saw me watching—but he was too pleased with himself to worry.

Miss Montezuma offered me a speculative, enigmatic, almost frightened glance. She looked like a woman who had found a snake in the breadbox. Though I doubted she would know what a breadbox was.

Again Belinda asked, "Can we go now?"

"I can't. Not while there are guests still here." And then there was Tinnie.

Belinda scowled. "There was a time, not that long ago, when you would've dropped everything . . ." It wasn't true. We both knew it.

"Go if you need to, Belinda. I'll get in touch. If you'll let me."

She nodded unhappily.

Belinda Contague was powerful and deadly—and a sad little girl. Not to mention dangerously willful.

Sometimes I'd like to choke Chodo for whatever he did to her.

"I'll go, then." She glanced at Tinnie. "Don't forget me." Damn! She wouldn't get into a killer Contague mood, would she?

Chodo got rid of Belinda's mother because *he* couldn't stand competition.

"Belinda . . ."

She stalked away. She muttered something I didn't hear as she passed Tinnie and Alyx. She paused to say something to Marengo North English. He seemed startled, pleased, frightened all at the same time. He looked at me speculatively. Belinda swept up the stairs to the outside door and Gerris Genord. She and the *major-domo* were gone before I got my thoughts organized. Events had Genord looking bleaker than they did Max or Gilbey.

# 50

Nothing else happened. The do was not the ball of the season. Too much crude excitement for people of refinement. Our sort don't let these things happen. The bigger-name guests shortened their visits. They began leaving soon after Belinda. Those who stayed on were almost exclusively rightsists nabobs and men who wanted a private word with Max Weider. I'm sure Max wasn't much help.

Tinnie didn't stray far the rest of the evening. Alyx tagged along gamely, never grasping the truism that there is no outstubborning a redhead. I should have told her. I have some experience in the field.

Even diehard friends of the Weider and Nicholas clans packed it up before the orchestra finished playing. Ty was unhappy. Nicks was outright depressed. I caught the glimmer of a tear more than one time.

"This is sad," Tinnie mused. We were surveying the grand hall from the vantage of the front entrance. Gerris Genord nodded as though she had spoken to him. The man looked like he was fighting an ulcer. "I feel for Nicks, Garrett. If you make a huge sacrifice just to make your family happy, it shouldn't turn to shit around you the way this has."

"Woman! Such language for such a delicate—"

"Stick it in your ear, Garrett. I mean it. She didn't get any joy out of tonight. I don't think that would be too much to ask in exchange for the rest of her life."

"There's got to be a curse on Max Weider. On the whole damned family. It rubbed off as soon as Nicks decided to join up." I was beginning to wonder if such a curse could actually be managed. It seemed unreasonable that a man's only luck ever had to be bad.

Without really seeing him I watched Gresser bustle around frantically, as though his depleted crew had work to catch up.

Tinnie said good-bye to some straggler she knew, not bothering to introduce me. I asked, "You going to stash me in the flour pantry and only take me out when you want to play?"

"There's an idea." She gave me an arch look. "If I could keep the Alyxes of the world out of there. Are you going to stay?"

That was my secret plan. "Coy doesn't become you."

"Me? Coy? Since when?"

"You're trying to fake it. I don't think Dean would ground me if I didn't come home tonight. Especially if I make up a story that has your name in it somewhere." Tinnie remains one of Dean's favorite people.

One of mine, too.

"What I love about you is your wild enthusiasm when you decide to do—"

"Excuse me, sir." Genord was back from escorting the straggler to his coach. He looked grave. "There's someone to see you."

Again? "Not a gentleman?"

"Definitely not a gentleman."

Tinnie hissed angrily. "I knew something would happen."

I went out. It was Relway. Again.

Of course. Who else knew where to find me? Certainly not my least favorite pigeon. There'd been no sign of the little vulture since he got himself evicted.

Maybe the vampire bats got him. Or maybe he was just lying up somewhere, waiting for the light. He wasn't like the parrots in the islands who stayed up all night, mimicking the cries of the frightened or wounded.

Relway again. Definitely not a gentleman. Gerris Genord would have messed his smallclothes had he known who this runt was.

Relway looked beat. "It wearing you down?" I asked.

"Not yet."

"What's up?"

"I need you to look at something again."

"Not something happy, I assume."

"No, nothing. It's not a happy night."

# 51

It wasn't happy at all.

It wasn't far from where he'd overtaken the murder wagon.

This time it was Belinda's ugly black coach. Empty. One horse lay dead in the traces. A crossbow had caught it in the throat. The other beast was psychotic.

"Poisoned bolt," Relway explained.

One coach door dangled off a broken hinge. A man I didn't recognize sat in the doorway. He held his right arm and rocked slowly. He was in pain.

Two corpses lay in the street. I did know them. Again, spectators were noteworthy for their absence.

"This is Peckwood," Relway told me, indicating the guy with the broken arm. "He saw it happen."

Peckwood didn't look like he'd been content to watch.

Relway told him, "Tell it again for my friend."

Friend? Oh-oh. Keep an eye on that hand patting your back, Garrett. Watch for a glint of steel.

Peckwood spoke stiffly. "The coach came from back that way, not in no hurry. Then I see two guys come from up yonder, running hard." Up yonder meant northward, the direction Belinda should've headed if she was going home. "I figure they meant to do this someplace else, only whoever was in the coach crossed them up."

I'm sure Relway knew who was in the rig even if his man didn't.

Why would Belinda head west instead of north? Curious.

Peckwood continued, "They didn't look like they was up to no good. I tracked them. One guy tried to plink the driver. He missed. He was puffing too hard to shoot straight. The driver started whipping his team. The villain didn't have no choice but to shoot a horse or let the coach get away. I figure originally they planned to croak the driver and grab the whole rig."

A sensible strategy. And the whole rig would've included the beautiful Miss Contague, a lady with several deadly enemies.

One of the dead men was Two Toes Harker. He'd been cut hastily and deeply and repeatedly. His knife lay not far away. He'd had a chance to use it, too. It was bloody.

Peckwood got his wind back. "Soon as the coach stopped, the driver jumped down and that other guy jumped out and the blood started flying. Everybody was surprised to see each other. And the bad guys wasn't expecting a real fight."

"Know them?" Relway asked, meaning the corpses.

I indicated the smaller one. "Cleland Justin Carlyle. Usually called CeeJay. Chodo's current number one cutter of throats and stabber of backs." Carlyle had done some cutting tonight. A nasty blood trail led away from him. "Two men did this?" Carlyle was a pro, hard to take.

Peckwood nodded.

"And they took Miss Contague?"

"A woman. I don't know who she was."

"Tell him who they were," Relway said. "I know. You don't know. But I'll bet Garrett can guess."

"Crask and Sadler," I said.

"The very ones. And even all sliced up they worked Peckwood over when he tried to stop them from taking the girl."

"I got in my licks," Peckwood insisted, gritting his teeth. "They'll carry some extra scars."

"Belinda left the Weider place a while ago. Why was she hanging around?" And where did Carlyle come from? Was he shadowing us before? I hadn't noticed.

Belinda would know.

Crask and Sadler had Belinda.

I was tired. I didn't want to face those two even if CeeJay, Two Toes, and Peckwood had torn a leg off each one. They'd still bite. With poison fangs. "Got any idea where they went?"

"No," Relway said. "My people have orders not to leave a crime site if they're alone. Peckwood carried out his orders."

"Shit."

"I should encourage more innovation?"

"What good would it do if he'd followed them? We still wouldn't know anything happened. And he'd probably get killed for his trouble."

"Glad you see that, Garrett. Most people would argue."

"I want to argue. I just can't. I'm in over my head here. I don't know anybody inside the Outfit well enough to approach. Maybe none of them *would* help. Well, I could go to her father's place but by the time I went out there and got back it would be tomorrow night."

"I'll bet they were in too bad a shape to worry about covering their trail."

There was plenty of blood in the street. But nobody is filled with enough to leave a trail all the way to the sort of neighborhood where Crask and Sadler would hide.

"I don't like ratmen."

"Did I ask you to like them?" Relway smirked. "You need a good tracker, Garrett. When you need a good tracker you have to deal with ratmen."

Some races are just naturally better at some things. Ogres, trolls, humans, elves, dwarves, none of us are much good at tracking in the city. Ratmen with the talent can sniff out a trail through the worst alleys better than any hound.

Favorite trail-covering devices, among those who can afford them, include little sorcerous traps that crisp the nose and whiskers.

Still smiling, cognizant of my aversion, Relway said, "Never be a better time than now, Garrett. It's the middle of the night."

Absolutely. The ratpeople live on the underbelly of the night city. We were at the peak, or depth, of their day. "Any notion who or where?"

"I don't use ratpeople."

"And you sneer at my prejudice?"

"The problem is their prejudice. I don't use them because they start wailing when they find out who wants to hire them. They think we're the death squad branch of The Call, or something."

Ratpeople are timid. They've learned the hard way. I lug around a burden of prejudice but I'm nicer to them than most. I make an effort to control my bigotry.

I sighed. I'd wanted to stay away from Morley, as much for his sake as mine. Now that choice had been taken away.

Relway asked, "You'll let me know how it goes?"

Like he would not as soon as I did. "Why not?" I started walking.

Tinnie was going to promote me back to the top of her hate list. Who did I think I was, running off to save some woman in trouble? Some *other* woman. Especially *that* woman.

It was all right when I saved *her* sweet patootie.

# 52

The Goddamn Parrot plopped onto my shoulder seconds after I parted with Relway. He was shivering. It was cool out now. Or maybe he was scared. There were a lot of night predators around. They snacked on one another when nothing tastier presented itself. The small nocturnal flying lizards will attack anything smaller than themselves, including cats and dogs and the little people. And they are too stupid to figure out that doing the latter is suicidal.

The price of thunder-lizard leather and parchment might plummet.

"My luck ain't never gonna turn," I grouched. "I thought sure you were catfood by now."

Mr. Big had nothing to say.

"Cat got your tongue?" Snicker. What a joker.

Still nary a word. Apparently the Dead Man had no minds left over for me.

Nevertheless, I talked to the bird all the way to The Palms. Night people of all stripes watched nervously from the edges of their eyes. They gave me room. You had to be careful about humans who talked to themselves. Some conversed with ghosts or got messages inside their heads that resulted in attacks on imaginary foes with too-real weapons.

A ploy worth remembering, I told myself. Though with my luck nobody would be impressed the day I tried it. Or somebody would be rounding up recruits for the looney ward at the Bledsoe.

I ran into a new waiter three steps into The Palms. He demanded, "Can I help you, sir?" He eyed me as though I suffered from some grotesque skin condition—though his nose was so high in the air he must have checked me out with mirrors. Maybe I had bloodstains on me somewhere.

"No." I kept going.

I spied a familiar face. Dang me. Tama Montezuma looked better than she had at Weider's. She seemed recovered from her distress. She smiled like she wished we could be pals.

The fellow with her had a back that looked familiar, too. Aha! Marengo North English, brave and bold. Of course. Surprise!

I had my comradely smile on before he turned to see who his niece was ogling.

I nodded to both and kept moving. I noticed others who had been at the Weider mansion. Celebration becomes social disaster when people start dying. That stuff is entertaining only when it goes on between the families of the bride and groom.

"Well, at least ya tried ta dress decent oncet," Puddle grumbled. "Goes ta show. Anyting can happen, ya wait long enough."

"What?"

He ignored that. "What happent? Gang a pansies work ya over an' make ya play dress-up?" He whistled into the speaking tube. I didn't hear a response but one must have come. He said, "It's dat guy wit' da pet parrot. Yeah. Dat one. Agin, I don't know what he wants. I never axed. Garrett. What da hell ya want?"

"Plug your ears."

Puddle gaped.

"I mean it. Plug them up." Once he did shove beefy, grubby fingertips into his furry ear canals I leaned to the tube. "Crask and Sadler just snatched Belinda." That would get Morley's attention. "I need a tracker fast."

Dotes was still buttoning buttons and hooking hooks when he hit the bottom of the stairs. A plaintive call pursued him. He ignored his startled customers, eyed my apparel in mock astonishment. "What happened? They knock you out and dress you up before they made the snatch?"

"Snatch? What snatch?" Puddle demanded. "It was pansies done it, boss. I got dat on good authority."

"His own," I said. "He makes it up as he goes along. I wasn't there. CeeJay was. Got himself dead for his trouble. So did Two Toes Harker."

"Harker was a good man. Dog loyal."

"No virtue goes unpunished. They did hurt Crask and Sadler before they bought it. Maybe pretty bad. And so did one of Relway's guys who showed up during the excitement but couldn't keep them from getting away."

"They left a trail?"

"They were bleeding."

"Puddle. Run tell Reliance I want his best tracker right now. Tell him Garrett will pay top marks." He showed me sharp teeth, dared me to argue. I didn't. Ratpeople are venal.

Someday Morley will get his ass in a sling again and come to me. And I'll get even. And then I'll pile on the expense charges till I've got a lien on his soul. Then I'll shop around and see if I can't get a couple brass tokens for that.

I didn't warn him. If it comes as a surprise, it'll be more exciting for all of us.

Puddle took off.

"That shouldn't take long," Morley said. "Reliance is desperate for cash. Was it smart, you coming here? Being involved with rightsists?"

"My pal Marengo North English is right over there. With the gorgeous brown beast. Supposedly his niece. Incest is best. He's seen me already. I'll worry about that after Belinda is safe."

"That would be the infamous Tama Montezuma?"

"The very child. Which you should know, soaring at your new heights."

"I ignore gossip, Garrett. She's outstanding. And completely wasted on a sour old fart like that."

"Absolutely. So why don't one of us go over and offer to carry her away from her life of luxury and popular envy? Bet you she'll jump at a chance to elope with a guy who's poor but handsome." Then I stunned Dotes by going to squat beside North English's table.

I pretended to speak to the lady while telling North English, "Belinda Contague was abducted after she left the Weider place. Several men were killed. I know who did it. I'm collecting specialists to go after them. Would you care to join me?"

North English eyed me coolly. He glanced at his companion, who seemed very distressed by the news, then at the shadows to the rear of The Palms. It was hard to make out anything back there but he was, without doubt, cognizant of the management's background. He was the sort of man who would have found occasional uses for a Morley Dotes. He nodded graciously. "I appreciate the information, Mr. Garrett. And I wish I *could* join you. The young lady was quite charming. But, as you can see, I have preclusive obligations. Do let me know how this tragedy plays out, though, won't you?"

The preclusive obligation wasn't fooled. I winked. Miss Tama Montezuma awarded me a very friendly twitch of her lip. She seemed to be in a strange mood, feeling no affection at all for her uncle. North English seemed pretty cool toward her, too.

Montezuma was no bimbo, whatever her reputation.

When I rejoined him I told Morley, "I have a suspicion that that could be one very interesting woman."

"Darn! And here you are already up to your ugly, unpointed ears in interesting women. What a pity." He eyed the Goddamn Parrot. "What did you do to Mr. Big? He doesn't look right. Narciscio will be brokenhearted if you—"

"Nothing." Morley's vain nephew had a place on my list only a couple of slots below his uncle and the talking buzzard.

"He isn't talking. Not that I mind that right now, right here, understand." Like he feared that I would cozen that ugly jungle crow into being himself for a few minutes. Right here in front of the paying customers.

"This's where he learned to talk, isn't it? He really shouldn't hold back in familiar surroundings. Find him a cracker."

"Garrett!"

"Heh-heh. Come on, pretty boy. Say something for Uncle Morley."

The little vulture persisted in his silence. If there was a way to disappoint me, he was sure to find it.

Morley's anxienty faded. He put on a smug smile, offered me another fine look at all his pearly whites. He had more of those than two predators deserved. Made me wish I was a ventriloquist after all.

"Ultimate justice does exist, Morley. My hour will come."

"All things are possible. But it isn't going to happen tonight." Quietly, he had begun flirting with Tama Montezuma. Already.

"Don't you have something going upstairs?"

"When I have a friend in desperate need? I couldn't let myself be distracted by trivia."

"I could." And so could he when it suited him. Which was most anytime there was a Tama Montezuma type in the equation.

Puddle joined us. I indulged in silk purse and sow's ear anatomical reflections. However Morley dressed him Puddle couldn't look like anything but what he was. Morley takes care of his friends, which keeps them fiercely loyal. They go along with his every mad scheme. Even unto managing upscale vegetarian watering holes.

Personal loyalty tells you more about most individuals than any surface glitter or grime.

Puddle whispered to Morley. The name Reliance occurred several times. I knew it only by reputation. Reliance was a ratman getting just enough above himself to have become feared and respected within his own community. He was part civic leader, part gangster, but as yet not in any way big enough to arouse the ire of humans. Ratfolk respect Reliance because he has enough nerve to deal with other species. They respect any of their own who are strong, good or bad.

Morley beckoned, headed for the kitchen. Puddle oozed along behind us. I glanced back past him. Several people seemed interested in us, North English and his lovely niece in particular.

Could there be a connection between The Call and Belinda's predicament? Possibly, but it seemed unlikely. North English had thugs of his own by the battalion.

doesn't happen much anymore. The Cantard wasn't as kind to him as it was to me.

"It would," I told Reliance. Chodo's friendships are unpredictable but legendary. He did well by me. I owe him, really. But how do you repay a debt to a human vegetable? Take care of his family? I was doing that now.

Reliance eyed us intently. Most ratfolk aren't bright. They fall between a brilliant dog and a slow human. This guy was a genius for a ratman. He indicated Morley, then me. "I have heard of you. You worked with Shote. Your reputations are sound." He spoke slowly, carefully, so that we could follow him. He knew neither of us ever did his people any willful harm. Shote was another tracker I'd employed. "I will help you. And Chodo Contague will owe me."

"Absolutely." He didn't want money? Ratmen always want money—despite being weak on the cause-and-effect relationship between wages and work. They can make dwarves look fiscally indifferent, though only at the pettiest level.

Reliance looked at me sharply. He suspected I'd committed Chodo too fast, too glibly. Tell the rat anything to get what you want. But he knew Chodo's reputation, too. Chodo always paid his debts. He nodded. "This is Pular Singe." All ratman sibilants tend to stretch out into syllables of their own while r and l sounds get confused. "She is young but very talented."

I checked his smaller companion. She? That wasn't obvious. Her apparel didn't differentiate her. Unlike most human girls she didn't have obvious female attributes. I guess if you're ratpeople you can tell. Or there wouldn't be any ratpeople.

A youngish ratman moved closer, bristling feebly. I said, "If you say she's the best, then she is and I owe you special thanks."

The ratgirl eyed me shyly, unaccustomed to the company of humans. I gave her a wink and a glimpse of one raised eyebrow. Gets them every time. "What do I call you? Pular or Singe?" Depending on the clan—and I have only the vaguest notion how you tell that, though it has to do with which sorcerer created their particular line—surnames can come front or back.

"She is hard of hearing," Reliance told me. "Her talent is a divine compensation. She does not speak human well. Her cousin Fenibro must translate for you."

Fenibro dipped his muzzle. "She prefers Singe."

"Thank you." Singe, I noted, followed every word, maybe reading lips. Easier done with humans, of course.

# 53

Three ratpeople awaited us behind The Palms. One was Reliance himself. He was bigger than most ratmen and had gray in his fur. He had survived longer than most ratmen did. He was dressed better than any ratman I'd run into before, colorfully, including a pair of tall black pirate boots and an ugly purple-and-white thing flopped on top of his head. He was unusually confident for a ratman.

He needed something to complement the red-and-yellow shirt and the green trousers. Mr. Big really belonged on one of those skinny, sloping shoulders.

Morley introduced me. Reliance produced a pair of specially designed TenHagen spectacles and examined me. Dotes suggested I state my case myself. I did so.

"Belinda Contague, Chodo Contague's daughter, has been kidnapped. The men who did it are notoriously vicious." I didn't name names because Crask and Sadler *were* so notorious. I didn't want to scare anybody off. "I need to track them so I can rescue Belinda."

Reliance glanced at his companions. Light escaping from The Palms made his eyes turn red at the right angle.

"Would be valuable to have the friendship of Chodo Contague," Reliance hissed. His Karentine lay just this side of intelligibility. Rat throats don't handle human speech well. They use a polyglot mess of their own.

Their speech, like most dialects, becomes intelligible if you're exposed continuously. Like my brother's speech impediment. I never noticed except when other people asked about it. Which

Time was getting away. I asked Reliance, "Will you join us yourself?" I meant the question only as a courtesy. It would be hard enough working with the other two. This one might think he had something to contribute.

"I do not think so. I am far too old and slow."

"I'll tag along, Garrett," Morley announced. "Come here, Puddle."

"You will? I thought you wanted out of this stuff."

"You can't go after those two alone." The ratpeople would scoot at the first sign of trouble. That was a given. "You think too much. You'd get your candle snuffed. I need you. You're such a wonderful negative example."

He could be right. Or maybe I owed him money I'd forgotten about. "We'd best go. They're getting farther ahead all the time." He couldn't possibly want to tag along just on account of being my friend.

Morley whispered to Puddle. Puddle nodded. He went back into The Palms. Morley pointed a finger at the sky, the moon, and said, "I'm ready."

I told Reliance, "Thank you again, sir. Singe? Fenibro? Ready?" I started jogging. Nobody had trouble keeping up despite ratmen not being built to run on their hind legs. When they get in a big hurry they bounce off their hands sort of like a gorilla. They move fast when they're scared.

The Goddamn Parrot remained dumb, which was a blessing. He roused only once, just long enough to emit a sort of puzzled interrogative squeak. If I'd had time, I would've been worried about the Dead Man.

# 54

"Took you long enough," Relway grumbled. He didn't look much like the Relway I'd left though the changes were cosmetic and subtle. He'd acquired a drooping shoulder and a slight dragging limp, a lisp and a marked preference for shadows. I doubted even Morley would recognize him later, changed and in a different light. The runt even smelled different. The ratpeople wouldn't recognize him later, either.

"Took a while to set it up."

"In the middle of the night?"

"I got the best."

Relway eyed the ratpeople. They were sniffing around and muttering. All the violence upset them. "The best is Pular Singe."

"That's her. You know her?"

"Only by reputation."

Good for Morley and Reliance. Maybe not so good for me. Now I might actually find Belinda fast, which could mean a big fight with TunFaire's two ugliest bad boys.

They would be like wounded animals, even nastier now they were hurt. Like cornered rats. Snicker.

Crask and Sadler were like a malevolent force of nature, beyond control, subject only to laws they created themselves.

I gave the ratgirl another reassuring wink. That seemed to calm her. She responded with the wedge-toothed grimace her kind thinks constitutes a smile.

There's a certain pathos to the ratpeople. Most of them desperately want to be just like the race that created them. Poor deluded beasts.

\* \* \*

Trackers amaze me. Singe amazed me doubly. And she wasn't full-grown. She was going to be a legend. Once on the trail she was limited only by her ability to walk fast and mine to keep up. Fenibro kept giving me the ratman equivalent of a big shit-eating grin. You'd have thought *he* was running the trail. Pular Singe kept looking to me for approval. Boy, did I give her plenty. Evidently she didn't get much at home. Ratmen don't treat their young or females well.

Everybody needs somebody to look down on and treat bad. You wonder who's left for the young ratwomen, though.

Later I grumbled, "These guys must be headed for the arctic." We had covered several miles, leaving downtown's seething heart for a neighborhood called the Plain of Cavalry. Centuries ago, when the citizen militia was TunFaire's only army, the mounted troops assembled there to practice up for scrimmages with neighboring city-states. In those days the plain was outside the wall. Later the wall was extended to enclose the plain so it could be used as a bivouac in times of siege. They started burying dead soldiers there. Eventually it became a vast graveyard. It's not much used anymore. It's become the object of endless dispute. Those who want to build there insist that land inside the wall is too precious to waste on dead folks already forgotten by their own descendants. The descendants disagree. The traditional position has prevailed only because many of the dead are old-time heroes and imperials. But adequate bribes might silence the opposition.

The cemetery is a bivouac again, filled with shanties and crude tents slapped together by refugees. This isn't popular with the neighbors, who have to suffer more than their share of victimizations. The Call is popular around the plain.

Wary tension filled the cemetery air. There was very little light. There's no free fuel to be had anymore. I was uneasy because I hadn't thought to bring a lantern. The moon wasn't much help—though it gave Singe all the light she needed.

Squatter villages appear wherever there's open ground. They're unclean. They stink. It's only a matter of time till some plague gets started. It can't be long before the street conflicts engulf the camps.

"Hold up," I told Pular Singe. I gestured, too. She stopped, waited, watched me with a disquieting intelligence. I suspected her hearing problem was less severe than Reliance thought, more a convenience than a handicap. She got my deaf-and-dumb sign language right away, too, though I was rusty. It was a shame Singe had trouble with the common speech. I got the impression she had a real sense of humor.

She had to be some kind of mutant.

"Morley, wouldn't this pest-hole camp be perfect to disappear in?"

People were moving around us, despite the hour, looking for nothing they could have articulated if asked. Movement itself was the destination.

The squatter population was a volatile mix including every type of refugee. I saw people so exotic they had to be weird to themselves.

"Absolutely," Morley said. "You'd have to be a woolly mammoth to get noticed around here."

"Is the tracking getting harder?" I asked Singe.

She shook her head, a human thing, not natural for ratpeople. Pular Singe tried hard to emulate human ways.

Fenibro told me, "It is difficult but she can single it out."

"She's amazing."

"She is. There is blood in it still."

No blood had been visible for miles.

I observed, "She sure says a lot with a headshake."

Morley murmured, "The boyfriend likes to show off his talent, too."

"Which is?"

"Human speech."

"Oh. Think we're being led?"

"You asking me if I think Crask and Sadler grabbed Belinda hoping that you, personally, would try to rescue her?"

"It's possible, isn't it? They might even have counted on you coming with me."

"*I* might calculate a scheme like that, Garrett. Not those two. They aren't complicated thinkers. They saw a chance to grab Belinda. They grabbed her. They probably expected you to be with her. Things didn't go the way they anticipated."

Yeah? How did they know where to find Belinda? How did they know who she was supposed to be with? "You think they expect to be trailed here?" Morley wasn't giving Crask and Sadler enough credit. They weren't just mountains of muscle. They had brains. That's what made them scary.

"Once they have time to think. They left a heavy trail. But they shouldn't expect trouble this soon."

I glanced around. As a group we presented an unusual look but out there the unusual was the norm—and inquisitive noses tended to get broken. "Figure Relway had us followed?"

"Is the moon made of green cheese?"

"That's what I thought." The tail wasn't obvious, though. "Go ahead, Singe. You're doing wonderfully. But please be careful."

Fenibro looked at me like I wanted to teach granny to suck eggs. But Pular Singe practically purred. Whereupon Fenibro suffered a case of the sullens.

# 55

The change in our surroundings was minuscule but real. Surprisingly, I sensed it before Morley or Singe. I didn't need to prompt Dotes, though. Still, I gestured to point out the fact that the refugee hovels shrank back from one particular mausoleum.

It was an antique from imperial times, a family thing that had been used for centuries. It would be as big as a house inside with several levels below ground. The family must have fallen on hard times. All families do eventually. The mausoleum needed restoration though it remained sound enough for someone to have set up housekeeping inside.

Pular Singe sniffed, pointed, gestured uncertainly. She dashed off. She circled back before I figured out what she was doing.

She whispered to Fenibro but looked at me from beneath lowered lashes, eager for more approval. Fenibro told me, "The devils you seek are in there." He was scared. He wanted to get paid and go. His speech was barely intelligible. I understood Singe's rattalk almost as well. "They have bad odors, sir. They are evil. Even my blind nose tastes them now." He fidgeted, eager to go but afraid to ask for money.

Morley squatted on his haunches. I don't bend that way. I dropped to one knee. Dotes murmured, "Seems like we've done this thing before."

"The vampire thing?" I stared at the mausoleum door. It stood open just wide enough to admit a bulk the size of a Crask or a Sadler. It seemed to sneer.

Dotes asked me, "Do you have anything in case we prance into an ambush?"

"I was thinking about throwing you in there to see what happens."

Fenibro squeaked like one of his ancestors getting tromped. He suffered a sudden, sad suspicion that our natural inclination would be to elect him our tossee. Unlike Singe, he did not grasp the concept of humor.

Singe spoke rapidly in rat polyglot. I caught just enough to understand that she was telling Fenibro to control himself, then that their part of the adventure was over and it was time for them to take off. I started mining my pockets for coins.

Fenibro argued with Singe. He puffed his chest out, male demonstrating dominance. Singe hissed. Fenibro wilted. That left no doubt where real dominance resided. He whined, "Singe says to tell you Reliance requires no payment. Someday he will ask a favor in return."

I groaned. That arrangement always gets me into trouble eventually.

Morley ignored the ratpeople. He persisted, "I thought you might have something up your sleeve. You often do."

"Not this time. I wish, though."

"A light, then. Surely we can come up with a light."

A glance around suggested otherwise. The refugees and squatters had stripped the cemetery of everything burnable.

I nodded to Singe. "Go home now, darling. It might get hairy around here. And be careful."

She took off instantly, practically abandoning Fenibro. He whined as he tried to catch up. There was no doubt that Singe was his girlfriend only inside his own head.

Morley grouched, "You never put any forethought into anything you do, do you?"

"This was your idea. *You* should've thought about bringing a lantern."

"My idea? You're stalling, Garrett."

Yes, I was. In a good cause, too. I'm really fond of my skin. It's rough and it's scarred but it's the only one I've got. Crask and Sadler might decide to use it to make wallets or belts.

Morley heard the sound first but I caught it an instant later. Somebody was sneaking our way.

There was enough moonlight to show me Morley. He gestured. I waved. We sank down behind antique tombstones.

Fate handed me a wonderful opportunity to look goofy. Yet one more time.

I jumped out at the sneaker, expecting Crask, Sadler, one of Relway's goons, a squatter determined to share my wealth, anything but a terrified Pular Singe, who should've been miles away already. We bumped snoots. She squeaked and started to run. I caught her arm. "I'm sorry," I whispered. "I thought you'd gone home."

Her fright faded as quickly as it had come. She looked at my hand. If she'd been human, she would've blushed. She did shiver. I let go but stayed ready to grab again if she bolted.

"What is it?" I used my gentlest voice. And wondered where Morley was.

"I brought . . ." Those words were perfectly clear, if few. And she'd heard me just fine. She seemed too embarrassed to continue. She couldn't meet my gaze. She lifted a shuttered lantern and offered it.

"You're a dream come true, Pular Singe. I might just steal you away from Reliance."

She was painfully embarrassed. She had a sense of humor but didn't understand teasing. She was brilliant for her own people only.

I didn't want her expiring from a stroke of shyness. "Thank you, Singe. You know I didn't think about needing a light. I owe you. Not Reliance or Fenibro or anybody else. You. Personally. You understand?"

Still avoiding my gaze, she reached for the Goddamn Parrot. That critter remained deadweight. Maybe when I wasn't looking somebody did stuff him and nail him to my shoulder. Maybe some wicked sorcerer cast a spell on him. Thank you very much. "Pretty," Singe said.

"You want him?"

She looked at the ground, shook her head in quick little rolling jerks, then scooted away. Mr. Big has to be the most unwanted creature in this whole wide world. I can't get anybody to take him.

Singe made less sound departing than her unaltered cousins might have. The noise she'd made approaching must have been deliberate.

Morley materialized. "Another Garrett conquest."

"What?"

"Maybe it was just an illusion cast by that devil moonlight but these elven eyes saw Miss Pular Singe, brilliant young ratwoman, acting as smitten as any other teenager with a crush." He giggled. "You'd make a great team."

The curse again? I shook my head vigorously. No rat would find anything redeeming in me. Or vice versa.

Morley kept right on snickering. This was delicious. He lingered over wedding plans and what to name the children. "Or would you call them pups?"

"Let's get on with this," I grumped. "Before we're all too old to keep up."

"This is rich, Garrett. Now I remember why I liked being part of your adventures. They create so many memories for those lonely winter nights."

He exaggerated. I think. Elves—even breeds like him—just don't think the way us humans do.

# 56

"Whenever you stop snickering," I said.

"You armed?"

"Only with my wits. Never mind the cracks." I wished I hadn't left that little crossbow back at the Weider place.

"Take this." He offered me a small, flat-handled dagger I hadn't seen on him anywhere. No doubt he was lugging a whole arsenal not evident to the naked eye. He was such a prankster. He'd have a trebuchet on him somewhere. "Don't it seem awfully quiet in there?"

It sure did. Crask and Sadler really had it in for Belinda. A scream or two would have been reassuring. There'd still be somebody to rescue. "Think they killed her already?"

"Maybe. But let's be careful anyway."

"Good plan. After you."

He didn't argue. I had him at a disadvantage now. His night vision was better than mine. He had no sound tactical argument against leading the way—if we had to go at all.

Once we were close enough to make out details it was obvious that the mausoleum's builders had belonged to one of our more bizarre early religions. The doorway was surrounded by carvings of fabulous creatures who glorified ugly. I plucked the Goddamn Parrot off my shoulder, planted him on an outcrop. Maybe he could go for help.

"But for the color he fits right in." And the breathing part. I didn't clue him in, though. He might pick this exact moment to express one of his vulgar opinions.

Dotes grinned, revealing a lot of sharp white teeth.

Enough moonlight leaked into the mausoleum for Morley to see that no one lurked immediately beyond the doorway. He reached back, touched me, found the lantern, tapped it. I cracked the shutter. We'd stirred up a little dust already. The wedge of light swept around like a flaming sword.

It revealed nothing startling.

Morley pointed downward. There was evidence of recent traffic in the leaves and trash that had blown in over the years.

I fought back a sneeze.

Dotes kept moving. I kept a glimmer of light splashing out to probe the way. Even Morley can't see in complete darkness. Again I wondered if Crask and Sadler hadn't set me up. They knew I was a white knight dumb enough to roll the dice with death over a damsel in distress.

The trail in the rubbish ran straight to a wall. "Damn!" I muttered. "Not another secret door. How come people think they can pull that off?"

But it wasn't one of those. The builder hadn't been trying to fool anybody. This door was a massive wooden job. I stabbed its huge hinges with my sword of light. Our friends hadn't oiled them. They wouldn't operate quietly.

Morley shrugged, bounced into place beside the door, whispered, "Let's go."

What the hell. Might as well. It was only Crask and Sadler on the other side of that damned thing. Only a couple of superhuman, demi-demon, stone killers. A pair of walking nightmares. No big deal at all. Did it all the time.

I grabbed the rusty ring and heaved.

A slab of human meat the size of a small barn tipped out and crashed at my feet. One of the villains. I had no time to find out which.

Morley slugged him in the temple with the pommel of a dagger cousin to the one he'd loaned me. Air left the huge killer in a sigh, like he'd never wanted anything more than he wanted to lie down and sleep right now.

"Garrett?" The voice was weak but definitely Belinda's.

"I'm here."

A piglike grunt from the darkness preceded the wobbly rush of a pallid behemoth bigger than the leviathan snoring at my feet. A hand like a ham floated out of the darkness, grabbed me, flung me at the voice just starting to tell me to look out. There were grunts behind me, slaps and thumps and a growl of pain. Morley is

good but he didn't get the best of this exchange. Brute force sometimes smothers style. Dotes cursed as he flew my way, apparently
in the feet superior mode. He crashed into the mess on the floor
before I could get my own feet under me again. The door slammed
a moment later. I hit it with my shoulder an instant after that.

There can't be any nightmare worse than mine about being
buried alive.

The door gave a little. I let out a mad-sorcerer cackle and hit it
again. Something bashed it from the other side. The shock shot
from my shoulder down to my toes and back. Crask cussed me
and Sadler at the same time. "Get up! Get up!" he raged at his
sidekick. His voice was feeble. Between them Two Toes, Carlyle,
and Peckwood had dinged him badly and hurt Sadler even worse.

I shoved. Crask shoved back. "Give me a hand, Morley!" The
lantern's shutter was all the way open, shining on the ceiling and
showing me Morley making points with Belinda by asking if she
was all right.

"Of course I'm not all right, you moron!" she snarled. "I'm
lucky. They passed out before they could torture me much. Help
Garrett. Unless you want to spend the rest of your life here, eating
raw mice." Her voice was feeble but her will remained unflagging.
She was a razor-edged chip off the old Contague flint.

Crask wedged something against the door. We banged into it
until my shoulder ached. We moved it a fraction of an inch each
time, till Morley was able to weasel through. He muttered continuously. This adventure was playing hell with his outfit.

He flung the blockage aside. I stalked out. Belinda clung to my
left arm. She had no choice. She had no strength left. She grunted
with every step. Crask and Sadler had given her a taste of joys to
come.

We hit the moonlight. "What now, dauntless sidekick?" Morley asked. "We don't have a tracker anymore. You should have
kissed her. She would've hung around forever."

"I did what I wanted to do. I got Belinda back." It was time to
head home. Only, what were the chances I would run into Crask and
Sadler in such reduced circumstances ever again? Less than zip. I
grabbed the Goddamn Parrot. "Which way did they go, bird?"

His Highness did not deign to speak.

A silent bird wasn't a problem I'd ever expected to face.

I was worried about the Dead Man. I'd heard nothing for too
long. He should have been nagging me mercilessly.

He'd shown that he couldn't read shapechangers close up.

Maybe they got to him while I was busy at Weider's. If one could pretend to be me long enough to get Dean to open the door . . .

Morley whispered, "Didn't we decide that Relway would have a man watching?"

"I counted on it when we went in there." Sort of.

"Then wouldn't you guess that Relway will know where those two went?"

Probably, come to think. But would he let me know if I asked? Relway just might discover that he had some use for Crask and Sadler no one else could appreciate. I said, "They'll never be weaker. And you know they never forgive and forget."

Morley patted my arm. "Good to see my wisdom finally taking root. But Belinda is in no shape to chase anybody."

Belinda snapped, "Belinda will keep up! Belinda is in better shape than either of them. And Belinda's got another score to settle." Whereupon her legs melted and she had to grab a handy tombstone. "I don't want to hear a word, Garrett." Her voice didn't waver.

Something stirred out in the darkness. It trailed the faintest whisper of disturbed grass. It headed the direction Crask and Sadler must have gone. Dotes and I exchanged glances. I asked Belinda, "Where were you headed when they grabbed you? They meant to catch you on your way home, only you—"

"No. They were waiting on the way to your house. Originally. They were really pissed off because you didn't take me home. They wanted us both."

"Lucky for both of us I had to work, then. Eh?"

"Yeah? Isn't it?" Belinda didn't sound like she believed that in her heart, though.

"Where were you going?" I asked again.

She hesitated, then admitted, "To The Palms. People from the reception were going to meet there."

"Oh." Neutrally, recalling that she had spoken to Marengo North English in parting and he had seemed surprised. None of my business, though. Except that later the same gentleman had seemed quite unhappy about being at The Palms with his delectable niece. I asked Morley, "You want to take her back to your place?" She would be safe there, if she wanted to be.

"You're not going after them alone?" Morley's tone told me nothing I did would ever surprise him. Maybe because this wouldn't be stupider than anything I'd ever done before.

"I'm not going after them. They're Relway's now." For now.

I was very worried about the Dead Man.

# 57

There was no deadly silence in my neighborhood. The night people were out in force and they were busy. Commerce was king. No political dialogue was under way. I exchanged greetings with those I knew. There was no tension in the air. Nobody seemed interested in my movements. A stroll around the area didn't uncover anyone watching my house.

Even Mrs. Cardonlos was otherwise occupied.

I got a strange feeling as I climbed my steps. Not like something was wrong. No. It was more like something was missing. An emptiness I hadn't felt for years. "What's the story here?" I asked the Goddamn Parrot. This close he had no excuse for being out of touch.

The bird was stubborn. He still refused to talk.

"Old Bones?" I tried my key. Miracle of miracles, Dean didn't have any bolts bolted or chains chained. I shoved the door, cocked an ear to the silent darkness.

The house didn't feel right.

It was darker than a priest's heart in there. Dean hadn't refilled the feeble lamp we leave burning in the hallway. I hoped he had a fire in the stove so I could light it again. I'm not big on flint and steel, though I manage if I have to. It was way too late to go mooching from the neighbors.

I felt the wall till I found the lamp. I took it and headed for the kitchen, carefully. There was no knowing what Dean would leave lying around.

I completed my pilgrimage without getting hurt.

The stove was warm. I dug in, found some live coals, got a

kitchen lamp burning so I could find the oil to fill the hall lamp. Its wick needed trimming but I was bone-tired. I would mention it to Dean tomorrow.

Tinnie would be cussing me big-time now, I figured. I ought to start rehearsing my apologies.

Once I had a light I took the Goddamn Parrot to the small front room. He was just aware enough to move to his perch. Maybe he was worn-out, too.

I put the hall lamp in its bracket and shoved into the Dead Man's room. "All right, Chuckles. What's the story? If you've gone to sleep on me I'm gonna . . ."

He hadn't gone to sleep on me. Not this time. No way.

What he'd done was, he'd gone missing.

For a while I stood there with my mouth open. Then I retrieved the hall lamp and prowled the Dead Man's room like maybe a quarter ton of moth-eaten corpse might have gotten lost amongst the dust bunnies. I faced the unusual and weird as a matter of course but this was beyond comprehension.

The Dead Man was gone? How? He couldn't have gotten up and walked. Nor could Dean have carried him.

There were no signs of a struggle. There would've been had he been abducted.

He was just gone.

Dean was going to get rousted out after all.

No, Dean wasn't.

He didn't respond to my knock. "You awake, Dean? I need to talk." I pushed his door open hoping I didn't get him started cranking.

His room was empty.

It wasn't just untenanted or deserted, it was barren. Not one scrap of clothing or stick of furniture remained.

"My gods! They've eloped!" I didn't imagine Dean. When I imagine people I pick them put together like Tinnie or Nicks or Tama Montezuma.

I petitioned the air with the intensity of an actor in a passion play, "What the hell is going on?" A waste of time. I'd asked already and hadn't gotten an answer.

I went back down to the kitchen. A hasty inventory left me baffled. I made something to eat, drew a beer off the keg in the cold well, shuffled around the ground floor balancing food, drink, and lamp while I searched for messages or clues.

I found nothing. Not even a *Dear Garrett* note.

"Hell with it," I grumbled. "Hell with them. Hell with everybody." I dragged myself up to bed, enumerating the names of everyone who ought to join the infernal pilgrimage.

I don't recall lying down.

# 58

I don't recall getting up. My first clear thought surfaced when somebody groaned in pain. A moment later I realized that the groaner was right there in my bedroom and he was making those noises with my dried-out mouth. Then it dawned: The pain was caused by sunburn of the backs of the eyeballs. I was staring out at a morning where the gods, or devils, of daylight were putting on one of the great sunshine shows of all time.

It was almost noon. The sun seemed to span half the sky.

That information developed, I tried to reason out why I wanted to stare into that unholy furnace.

The proximate cause made itself apparent instantly. Which is to say that there were hundreds of idiots out there holding another political discussion. Sticks and stones and broken bones.

Hundreds of guys in brown, wearing a variety of rightsist armbands, showing colorful standards and banners, were proclaiming their message with enthusiasm, not only to the fey but to any handy humans who had a foreign look on them or maybe just parted their hair a little strange.

Maybe my mom didn't raise me right after all. I don't quite grasp politics. Despite claims to the contrary substance has no relevance. Apparently conflicts are decided by whoever shouts the loudest and whacks away with the biggest stick.

Why did they keep doing it in Macunado Street? Why couldn't they take it into the countryside? Nobody but farmers or mammoths or woods elves would be bothered out there. I wanted to grab a big megaphone and yell, "People, we got folks trying to sleep around here!"

I dropped the curtain. After a minute I felt fine. I didn't have a hangover. What did I drink? One beer? Good. Still, maybe I should ease up on the health food for a while.

As I descended to the kitchen I recalled my housemate shortage. I'd have to build my own breakfast. Boy. Life just ain't fair.

The Goddamn Parrot heard me moving around and squawked. He started the thing where he pretends to be a small child begging not to be abused.

He was back to his old self. I'd feed him if I started feeling generous and forgiving. Which could not possibly come anytime but later.

I got some bacon frying and some water heating for tea, then went over the ground floor one last time, hoping I'd find something I was too tired to notice last night. I came up with the same big batch of nothing. No getting around it. Dean and the Dead Man were gone. There was no suggestion of foul play. They'd gotten up and gone because they'd wanted to get up and go.

I sipped tea and nibbled bacon and snacked on halfway stale bread dipped in bacon drippings while I tried to get my mind wrapped around the notion that the Dead Man had moved voluntarily. That would make twice in my lifetime. Last time was when I moved him in here.

Give him another generation and he'd be dancing in the streets.

I glanced at the keg in the cold well. Tempting. But it was too early. And I had work to do.

I shivered. Events had left me a mighty hill to climb.

"Shut up in there!" I barked at Mr. Big, who was singing the marching song of ten thousand verses, each of which begins, "I don't know but I've been told . . ."

I poured tea, stirred in a spoon of honey, found a muffin young enough not to scar the hardwood if I dropped it, migrated to my office. "Good morning, Eleanor."

The lady in the painting smiled enigmatically, bemused by my morning dishabille. She didn't surprise me when she didn't have anything to say.

The Goddamn Parrot was stuck on a verse about ratgirls. It didn't flatter them. He must not have been completely comatose last night.

Me, I thought better of ratgirls since meeting Pular Singe. Hers was an acquaintance worth nurturing.

"So, darling. Did the Dead Man take off so he wouldn't complicate my life now that I'm involved with rightists? Or did he feel unfulfilled and had to find himself and realize his potential?" That was a chuckle. Without continuous nagging Old Bones has the potential of an iceberg. He'll slide downhill if he isn't at the bottom already. If you give him a push.

I finished my muffin and tea, went for another cup. I took the scenic route back to the office. The Goddamn Parrot shut up as soon as I gave him some breakfast. Nestled in my chair again, I told Eleanor, "Listen to this and tell me what you think." I started where I thought it began, did Black Dragon, Crask and Sadler, Belinda, Relway, shapeshifters, the Weiders, Marengo North English, Tama Montezuma.

"So what do you think? Is it all connected? Or have I stumbled into several things all going on at the same time?" Occasionally it helps to bounce the facts off Eleanor or the Dead Man even though neither is inclined to respond. Sometimes the pieces fall into place.

I twisted and kicked and whacked away at the facts with a big faded steel hammer to conjure the mess into a couple of complete scenarios. I was sure neither had much to do with reality. Neither made sense of what was happening.

"I prefer the chaos theory," I told Eleanor. "Shit's flying everywhere and it's by chance a lot is raining down where I'm standing. I'm what ties the whole mess together. . . . Oh. Right. Isn't this exactly what I've been waiting for?"

Eleanor's smile turned more teasing than enigmatic. She knows how thrilled I am when somebody pounds on my door.

I don't always hear them, though. The door, replaced often lately, is heavy. I'm thinking about getting one of those mechanical bells so I can be sure there's somebody out there to ignore.

# 59

"Gods, Garrett," Colonel Block growled. "You been on a three-day bender?"

"You're looking good yourself. We saw one another just yesterday. Remember?"

"You really go to hell overnight, don't you?"

Maybe I did look a little ragged. "All right. So maybe I need a shave." I let Block come inside.

He doesn't come around unless he has something on his mind. "That would be a start."

"Want a cup of tea?"

The Goddamn Parrot broke off crunching sunflower seeds long enough to excoriate the head of the Guard, then the head of the household.

"Can I drown that thing in it?"

"I'll brew you a bucket if you'll do it and take the rap. What's up?" I shepherded him into my office. He helped himself to a chair.

"I wanted you to know what Relway got from the prisoners. And your thoughts about last night. Relway's devotion colors what he sees."

"It was pretty straightforward." I told him what I knew. Once I would've held out just because he was the law. I'm mellowing with age and accumulated head lumps. I concluded, "What I don't have is a clue what it adds up to."

"I find it productive to forget the big question while I root out little answers."

"Uhm?"

"Instead of worrying about what it all adds up to, work on why the shapeshifters chose the Weiders. There are a hundred questions you could ask. You can paint the big picture one brushstroke at a time."

He wasn't offering advice that was new. But there was a subtext, an unspoken message. He was reminding me that collecting brushstrokes would involve me in my least favorite pastime.

What I need to find is a way to cruise through life without having to work.

"So what's the word? Did Relway collect any brushstrokes?" He must have tormented up some random flecks of color.

"He's got a bunch of words for you, Garrett. But there ain't many of them ones you want to hear. The big thing is, we didn't get anything out of the shapechangers."

I must have looked doubtful. I don't know why. Maybe I'm getting cynical. If you can't believe the secret police, whom can you trust?

"Really, Garrett. Before Relway got back to the Al-Khar the prisoners tried to escape."

"The place is a sewer any sane person would want to get away from, but how—"

"They're shapeshifters, Garrett. They can't turn into mice or roaches or anything that's not as heavy as they are but they can turn skinny or plastic enough to slide between bars and—"

"I get the picture. Damn! We should've seen that coming." I selected a quiver of choice expletives, used them up. This could turn real bad if those things could turn into furniture or the carpet underfoot. "So they're all loose again—"

"Not all. Three got away. And they were hurt. The others died trying. Relway says you can study the bodies if you want to."

"Did they all have tattoos?"

"How did you know?"

"Wild and lucky guess. Let me guess some more. The tattoo was a dragon with a Karentine military seal worked in. It was hard to see even when they weren't trying to hide it."

"You've seen them before." He was squinting now, suddenly troubled.

"I have. Relway told me he'd try to find out what the tattoo means."

"He probably hasn't had time."

"My guess is that they're some special ops mercs left over from the war."

"That would be my guess, too. Which means that I made this walk mostly for the exercise. I'm not telling you anything new."

"Exercise never hurt anybody. I'm told. Come on in the kitchen. We'll get that tea." I was sure he had more to say. But maybe it was something he didn't want to tell me. I asked him to come along because in my house we try not to leave visitors unattended. Especially not Winger or officers of the law. Both are almost certain to get into stuff I'd really rather they didn't.

I poured. Block communed with his inner demons. I asked, "Do you prefer the uniform?" He wore a slightly fancy version of the vaguely military, undyed linen outfit recently adopted by the Guard. It did little for the dignity of his office. Most rightsists street thugs dressed better.

Block accepted tea. "We don't have much of a budget. So it's become a point of pride. Shows people we're dedicated."

Maybe. "*Anything* useful come from those changers?"

"No. Except that someone from the Hill, names I can't mention, wants the dead ones." And there it was, his secret burden.

"And I thought you were saving them just for me."

Block sneered. "A bunch of shifters turning up stirred a *lot* of curiosity."

"Think someone knew about the tattoos?"

Block shrugged. "I haven't mentioned them. Yet."

"How come?"

"I wanted to see what happened when they figured it out. I'm just a dumb lawman. I wouldn't notice, anyway."

And what might he be holding out on me? "You'll let me know if anything comes of it?"

He nodded. My coconspirator. "Some big-toothed hounds are going to be on this trail before long." Which was maybe as much as he dared tell me.

That didn't excite me. I don't like sorcerers. They're dangerous. And they're unpredictable. Like lawyers. You don't want to turn your back on one of them. Most of them aren't even kind to their mothers. Still, it would be stupid not to hear what Block was trying to say. "You guys have been awful nice to me lately."

Block shrugged again. "That's because you can help us. We need to make you want to cooperate."

He sounded like Chodo Contague about to offer an infernal deal. "It might be easier to leave town. My mother has cousins upcountry."

"Then you'd be stuck wearing scratchy homespun and

couldn't indulge yourself in all this elegant luxury." He indicated my clothing. "I can't see you as a peasant, anyway."

"They raise sheep."

"That's different. You'd never have trouble finding a girlfriend."

"I liked you better when you were worried about hanging on to your job. You were crabby all the time, but . . ."

He smiled. "I'm a much better person now."

"All right, much better. Where're you headed on this? Let's not duplicate each other's work."

"Then concentrate on infiltrating The Call."

"My loyalty is to Max Weider. The Call isn't going anywhere. The Weiders might. I've lost three of them already, when I *was* paying attention."

"Can't fault your logic."

"Yeah? Relway mention that we caught up with Crask and Sadler?"

"You fishing?" Block isn't as dim as he pretends.

"I'd like to know."

"He did. You rescued the fair maiden."

Interesting. Relway apparently kept his boss informed.

Relway's boss continued, "You let them get away, Garrett. What kind of hero are you?"

"The living kind. I *thought* somebody was watching us."

"Lucky for you."

"We got out of the tomb without help."

"Not what I meant. You came home instead of running after the bad guys. Your unsavory friend also chose to abandon the hunt. We can only assume that he was concerned for Miss Contague." Looking out for Belinda was, of course, looking out for himself.

"You have a point?" I asked.

"Yes. Somebody did stick to the bad guys."

Came the dawn. "You know where they are."

"Sure do. And we wondered if you'd want that information."

"I took them on last night. With help and with them hurt. They still might've gotten the best of it."

"Did I say we'll stand around and watch? These are famous villains. And they don't have any friends now that Chodo don't love them anymore. That gives the Guard a chance to put on a big show for some very important observers. With the invaluable assistance of a certain public-spirited subject. You want to be the public-spirited subject?"

"That why you're here?"

"I want to be visible when the Guard is doing its job right. Let's walk up there and see what happens."

"Let me get myself organized. I wouldn't want your reputation bruised because of the company you keep."

"If that could hurt me, I'd have been exiled ages ago."

"You got a point. I won't be long. Go settle in my office. Try not to poke around."

I knew the Dead Man couldn't keep an eye on Block but Block didn't.

# 60

I was beginning to like Tad Weider's sense of style. I selected an outfit that he might have worn to the horse races. It included a lot of yellow and red and brown. There were ruffles at wrist and throat. I spiffied myself, considered the result in my little mirror. "Oh! The elf girls are gonna carry me off and make me their love slave." I stepped back. "But if I'm going to dress like this, I'd better get a new pair of shoes."

My ragged old cobblehoppers sported memorabilia of a thousand city adventures. They didn't complement the look.

"What happened to you?" Block demanded when I got back. He looked me up and down.

"The Weiders felt I should upgrade my wardrobe."

"People been telling you that for years. But . . . You really need new shoes. Those clogs look like you wore them in the service."

"That's on my list. I thought we had a riot to attend. I'm ready," I said.

"New door?" Block asked as I locked up.

"Yeah. Somebody busted the old one."

"There's still snow piled up here and there. You sure you didn't have anything to do with that? I hear rumors with your name in them."

"How could I make it snow in the summertime? Even if, according to Tinnie, everything is my fault."

"You put in a key lock? You must be doing pretty well."

I'd been doing very well lately but he didn't need to know that. He might let something slip around crooks or tax collectors. Or crooked tax collectors. Or is that redundant? Doesn't it take a unique breed of psychopath to prey upon his fellows that way?

The street was quiet except for the moans of stragglers nursing injuries sustained during the earlier debate. "This is better," I said. "You should've seen it here a while ago."

"I did. I'd have been here an hour ago if it wasn't for that damned parade."

We walked. I didn't like the direction he chose. If he kept on, we would stroll right into the Bustee, the ultimate slum and the most dangerous neighborhood in a city famous for bad neighborhoods. The only law in the Bustee is the law you make yourself. Outsiders won't go in except in big gangs. "I hope we aren't headed where I think we're headed."

"North side of the Bustee."

"I was afraid of that. Another reason to make a show?"

"Yes. To show that the Guard won't back off."

Relway I could see playing to the Bustee audience. Relway doesn't have sense enough to be scared. I was surprised he got anybody to go in with him, though, let alone the sort of highlifes he and Block would want to impress. Maybe I was out of touch.

When we arrived it was evident immediately that the Guard had impressed both the locals and the observers already. They had a dozen prisoners in chains, none of them the great villains Crask or Sadler.

I'd expected troops or something. But Relway had brought only the dozen Guards he would have assembled for the same job anywhere else. Observers outnumbered working lawmen even after we arrived. Block introduced me around. I knew several of the witnesses, though none well. You run into people in my racket. Some are friendly. Some aren't. You rub some the wrong way if you're determined to do your job.

I was overdressed. The most foppish dude there wasn't showing any lace. They all wore grubbies.

I faded away from the Names, joining Relway. Sullen neighborhood brats watched from a safe distance, as friendly as feral cats, waiting to spring their friends in chains. Or maybe to murder somebody from a rival gang. They were filthy. None wore clothing fancier than a loincloth. Several weren't that dressy.

In the Bustee sanitation is the exception rather than the rule. The quarter doesn't have even the rudimentary street-center sewage channels found elsewhere. There are few streets as we know them, just stringers of space where there are no buildings. The Bustee has its own unique aroma, and plenty of it.

"Figure Crask and Sadler know something's up?"

Relway glanced at his prisoners, then at me like he'd suddenly discovered that I was retarded. "Probably. We've been standing around here way too long, waiting to get started."

"I'm sorry. But—"

"This's going to be a blow, I know. But, as important as you are, we weren't waiting on your account."

"I'm crushed. So what *is* the holdup?"

"A dashing young gentleman sorcerer who uses the business name Dreamstalker Doomscrye. Or maybe Doomstalker Dreamscrye. He wants in. We don't tell those people no. He was supposed to be here hours ago. Evidently as an apprentice he wasn't taught to tell time."

Relway's sarcasm was quite daring. I was beginning to think the man had no sense. In TunFaire we restrain our opinions concerning the lords and ladies of the Hill. They can do worse than turn you into a frog if you irritate them.

"Ulp!"

"What?" Relway asked.

"I forgot my bird."

"Then go fetch the prima donna chicken."

"Too late. Might as well enjoy myself." I didn't miss the fancypants crow at all.

Relway's man Ritter was headed our way. A kid maybe fourteen blistered out of a dark chink between tenements. He held a rusty knife extended ahead. I knew the tactic. He was a cutpurse. He just wanted to steal and run before his victim could react. It happened every day, everywhere in TunFaire, though elsewhere cutpurses usually selected more promising targets. This kid had to be counting coup.

His pals were all set to cheer when Ritter sidestepped, snagged the thief's long hair, slashed him several times with a knife that appeared as though by magic. The whimpering boy collapsed into the muck. Ritter came on as though he'd done nothing more significant than stomp a bug.

That kind of cold demonstration was why the Guard was becoming feared.

They were nasty, these new lawmen.

Believers so often are.

"Doomscrye is here," Ritter announced. "What a jerk. He's already complaining about us wasting his valuable time."

These secret policemen were *too* daring.

"He's young," Relway told me. "He'll learn."

Did he mean Doomscrye or Ritter?

# 61

As a place to squat the object of our interest was a long slide downhill from a tomb. It was an ugly little lean-to shanty hugging the hip of a three-story frame tenement that tilted ten degrees sideways while twisting around its own waist. "Good thing we don't have to go in there," I observed. "Our weight would bring it down."

"It's tougher than it looks," Ritter told me. "Ninety-two people live there."

That was probably a short estimate. The occupants might use the place in shifts. I asked Relway, "If the manpower shortage was so awful we let whole tribes of nonhumans immigrate, how come people down here didn't take advantage?"

"Some did. And some are unemployable in any circumstance." Relway's bitterness sounded personal.

He hailed from the underbelly of society. *He* had been able to get somewhere. He was outraged because so many people wouldn't even try.

Plenty willingly made the effort to be unpleasant, though. We were attracting more watchers the age of the kid Ritter had hurt. I saw sticks and chains and broken bricks, the weapons of the very poor.

My companions remained unconcerned.

Ritter pretended to be in charge so Relway wouldn't attract attention. A donkey cart appeared, headed our way.

The observers were getting nervous. Doomscrye complained incessantly. He was very young for a sorcerer. He hadn't seen military service. He might be the harbinger of a generation never to get its rough edges knocked off where *nobody* was special when the Reaper was on the prowl.

Doomscrye did not understand that real trouble could climb all over him any second. Likely he'd never faced even minor trouble.

Fate handed him the opportunity to discover that nobody thought as well of him as he thought of himself.

A hunk of brick got him in the chest. Block snagged him and dragged him behind the cart.

Ritter and several others struck back contemptuously, bashing heads. Other Guards shackled captives with chains from the donkey cart. The only kid to get in a solid blow died swiftly, his throat cut.

"Oh, shit!" I muttered. "We're in for it now." There was a lot of racket. I expected a riot.

I was wrong. The locals *were* intimidated by ruthlessness—particularly once Doomscrye set the brickthrower on fire. The kid was still screaming when we ripped Crask and Sadler's hovel apart and learned that all the buildup had come to an undramatic, anticlimactic conclusion.

There was no epic battle, no ferocious last stand by cornered baddies. Crask was delirious with fever. Sadler was unconscious. It took four Guardsmen to hoist the villains into the cart. Nobody insisted they be treated gently.

Me neither. Though I did recall times when we were less unfriendly.

Crask's delirium faded briefly. He recognized me. I said, "Good morning, Bright Eyes." But looking into them was like looking down a dark well at a remote mountain of ice.

Maybe The Call ought to work on the problem of humans who have no humanity in them.

Crask wasn't afraid. Fear to him was a tool used to manage others.

"You going to question them?" I asked.

"We're a little slower than we like to pretend, aren't we?" Relway sneered. "Would this exercise have a point otherwise?"

"I'd sure like to know why they jumped Belinda when they did."

Relway smiled. "I'll bet you would."

"What's that mean?"

"I expect *she* has some questions. Like how they knew where to find her."

"Is this all there is, then?"

"I expected more excitement myself, Garrett. But I'm pleased there wasn't. They don't seem so terrible now, do they?"

"Neither does a saber-tooth tiger when he's sick on his ass. You guys be careful. They won't be completely harmless even if you hang them."

"I'm always careful, Garrett."

That I believed. But was he careful enough?

I stuck with the gang only till we cleared the Bustee. Wouldn't do to be seen with them by my patriotic friends.

The chained kids would get five years in the Cantard. They would be aboard prison barges before the end of the day. The mines always needed a few good men. Or whoever else they could get. Already they were the catch-all sentence for any crime not a capital offense.

The mines would constitute a death sentence for many, anyway.

So what's changed since I was young? These guys would get shovels instead of swords—and worse odds of getting home alive.

# 62

My favorite venue for exotic research is the Karentine Royal Library, over where all the midtown government buildings cluster, clinging to the petticoats of the Hill. There are lots of books—and no wizards to make them a high-risk objective.

The most interesting books in town are, of course, squirreled away, under lock and key and deadly spell, up the Hill, behind imputed BEWARE OF THE WIZARD signs. Only brawn-for-brains barbarians try to reach them. Which supplies the wizards with leather for bookbinding.

The Royal Library is a Crown indulgence. It isn't supposed to be open to walk-in traffic. I get around that. I have a friend inside.

Linda Lee is a treasure. And cute, too. Especially when she's mad, which she always seems to be whenever I drop by.

"You're full of it up to your ears, Garrett," she snapped. "How did you get in this time? And how come you still have that trash-beak penguin parked on your shoulder?" I'd stopped by the house. Just in case my peripatetic sidekick had chosen not to cover up the fact that we were partners anymore. "You're one slow learner." She was no fan of the parrot. And was always very admiring of the way I put words into his beak without moving my lips. Even from another room.

The secret of getting into the library is you slide in through a small side door that has escaped the notice of most of the world. As a rule, though, most of the world would be more interested in getting out of a library than getting in. Books are *dangerous*.

The library guards are so poorly paid that none of them really gives a rat's butt who comes or goes. And the most indifferent guards get the side entrance. Young or old, the man on duty will be drunk or asleep. Or drunk and asleep. Or maybe not even there because he's gotten dry and had to go out looking for a drink.

I still have to go in on tippytoe. The guards have their pride. You don't make the effort, they are going to yell. You don't make the effort, they can't cover themselves with the gargoyle who rules the place.

Today's steadfast guardian of the priceless tomes was both drunk and snoring and had a huge, smouldering weed banger dangling from his left hand. Which would burn down to bare skin any moment. . . .

"Ye-ow!" echoed through the building.

A screech demanded, "What was that?" That was the head librarian, a wicked old witch with a temper so foul that on her best days she was like a troll with very bad teeth. She began to shift toward the guardroom in a streaking shuffle. She'd lost all sympathy for youth in recent centuries. Her sworn mission was to get in life's way.

I whispered, "She must've been sneaking up on us."

"You keep those hands to yourself, Garrett." Which is all that I had done. So far. Sooner or later she would have her way. "I always give in and give you whatever you want when you start that stuff so you just stop it."

I didn't argue. We both knew she never did a thing she hadn't made up her mind to do. But she's a last-word kind of gal.

"Wouldn't think of it, darling. According to Morley I'm practically engaged to a pretty ratgirl named Pular Singe, anyway."

"Is that thug going to be your best man?"

"Uh?"

"I came by your place last night. To see that Dead Man." They're pals, sort of, him and her. He's never explained how he overlooks the fact that she's a woman. "A neighbor told me Dean and the Dead Man moved out. That they just couldn't take it anymore. And that you were out whoring around with some trollop in black."

It took no genius to figure out which neighbor that would be. "You need to pick who you gossip with more carefully, darling."

"I try. But you just keep coming back."

"*You* went to *my* house." Me forgetting who the last-word kind of gal was.

"I enjoy those conversations with your partner." She gripped my arm, looked up. Her eyes were huge pools of mischief. "Sometimes I *do* just want to sit around and talk. He's so interesting. He's seen everything."

"Now whose hands are—"

"This is different."

Funny. I was breathing just as hard.

"What do you want, Garrett?"

"Huh?"

"The Dead Man doesn't get distracted."

"Uh . . . He's dead. Even then you'd probably . . . Shapeshifters. I need to know about shapeshifters."

"Why?" Always direct, Linda Lee.

"Shapeshifters murdered some people I know. We caught them and sent them to the Al-Khar but some got away before we could question them. The rest died. I need to find out whatever I can about them." Pant pant.

"I can't help much. The information we have here probably wouldn't be reliable." Linda Lee cocked her head. The head librarian was just warping into the guardroom, from the sound. Our whispers hadn't reached her. "What you want you'd probably only find in a specialized library."

"What's that?" I had a feeling I didn't want to know.

"A private library. On the Hill."

Sorcerers. "I'm psychic." I didn't like that answer.

"You don't know anybody up there?"

"I know people. Met another one today. They ain't our kind of people."

"You wouldn't know anybody in The Call?"

"Uh . . . Why?"

"You could try to get into the library at their Institute For Racial Purity. Where they research racial issues. They came here trying to hire a librarian. They have a lot of stuff from private sources. They wanted it catalogued and organized so they could use it to support their theories."

"Linda Lee, you're a treasure."

"I know. What made *you* realize it?"

"I do know somebody in The Call."

"Aha!" the chief librarian shrieked in the distance. "I've caught you, my pretty!" But she crowed too soon. She always declares before she has me in sight. I moved with trained silence and deliberate speed to the end of a stack. I could remain unseen there till the old woman committed to a particular path. Linda Lee would signal me, I'd take a different route and once again the old woman would be scratching her head and wondering what she'd really heard.

It's unnatural that anyone her age would hear so well.

Linda Lee whispered, "I'll see what I can find out." Then she glommed on and kissed me. Linda Lee knows kissing better than she knows books. I didn't start it but after about four seconds I was plenty ready to continue. Weider who? Shapeshifter what? I don't know no Relway.

The chief librarian cackled.

"I've got you for sure this time, my proud beauty! I'll teach you to tryst with your leman in a holy place!" She stomped and clomped her way closer.

I slipped away from Linda Lee, who winked and made noise heading another direction while I sneaked between stacks on little mouse feet. We'd played this game before. Linda Lee probably more times than me.

"Awk! Shit!" said the Goddamn Parrot, with impeccable timing. "Help!" He started flapping.

I'd kill him for sure this time.

A vise closed on my right shoulder. It turned me. I gaped at the ugly grin of a foul-breathed ogre I hadn't seen before and whom I hadn't heard coming. He was twice my size and twice as stupid. I had a notion he wouldn't ask me to recommend a good book.

In fact, I suspected he was the kind who liked to hit people and watch them bounce. Exhibit number one: He had a gargantuan green fist pulled back three yards, all set to whistle my way.

The old lady had foxed me.

I kicked the ogre hard where a sharp knock will drop any reasonably constructed critter, puking. The ogre just showed me more green teeth and put some moxie into his punch. Only trolls and zombies are less vulnerable there.

I never got a shot at his ears.

Ogres drop like stones if you slap both ears at the same time. So I'm told. Nobody I know ever got close enough to try. The source is always a friend of a friend of a friend, but, "It's gospel, Garrett. It really happens that way."

Before the lights went out I had the satisfaction of knowing the old woman would need weeks to pick up all the books that scattered while I was flying through the stacks.

Might be wise not to visit Linda Lee at work for a while.

                              *    *    *

If anybody robbed me while I was splashed all over the alley behind the library, they sure overlooked the one thing I wouldn't mind losing. I came around to find the Goddamn Parrot muttering like one of those psycho guys who stomp around shaking their heads and arguing with ghosts. I hurt everywhere. I had book burns. That ogre had pounded me good after I couldn't see to make a getaway.

There'd been way too much of this stuff lately. I never recovered from one thumping before I stumbled into the next.

Was I nurturing some kind of death wish?

# 63

Time to tap an *old* resource.

Time to drop in on the Cranky Old Men.

I didn't look forward to it. It wouldn't be pleasant. But with my aches and pains and premature cynicism I'd fit right in.

They say there's more than one way to skin a cat. Undoubtedly true, but why would you want to? Whoever the first *they* was. Somebody with strange habits. Who needs to flay felines? I hear they keep right on shedding after they're tanned.

Maybe the saying was started by the guy who knocks out ogres with his bare hands.

The Cranky Old Men are an ongoing crew of antiques who pooled resources to purchase, maintain, and staff an abandoned abbey where they await the Reaper, many because they're so unpleasant their relatives don't want them around home. Somebody in a black humor named the place Heaven's Gate.

In its prime the abbey housed fifty monks in luxurious little apartments. More than two hundred Cranky Old Men live in the same space, three to the apartment and who's got any use for even one chapel let alone the three of the original setup?

The place is cramped and smelly and almost as depressing as the Bledsoe and makes me hope that in my declining years some twenty-year-old lovely with an obsession for chubby old bald guys who smell bad takes me in so I don't have to buy into anything like Heaven's Gate. Of course, with my luck and the way things have gone lately I shouldn't worry about getting old.

The abbey was constructed in a square around an inner court,

two stories high, filling a larger than normal city block. Not an uncommon layout in TunFaire. Tinnie's clan resides in a similar
though larger compound, which includes their tanning and manu-
facturing facilities. In a display of misplaced faith in their fellow-
man the monks had included ground-floor windows around the
street faces. The Cranky Old Men had adapted to modern times by
installing wrought-iron bars. Most people just brick them up.

There are two entrances, front and rear. Each is just wide
enough to permit passage of a donkey cart. Both are blocked by
double sets of iron gates. The place looks more like a prison than
the Al-Khar does.

Somebody's grandson was on some scaffolding, installing
bars on a second-floor window. The deeper poverty arriving with
the immigrants might make the place attractive after all.

I eased around the scaffolding to the gate. It was comfortable
in the shadows there.

"Eh! You! Move along!" a creaky voice insisted. "No loiter-
ing." A sharp stick jabbed between the bars too slowly to hurt
anyone.

Everyone got this treatment, including favorite sons.

"I came to see Medford Shale." Not strictly true, but you do
need to offer a name and I knew that one. The hard way.

"Ain't no Medford Shale here. Go away."

"That's him back there under the olive tree. On the cot."
Which was true. And handy. So maybe my luck wasn't all bad.

The sharp stick jabbed again. I didn't go away. The old man
on the other end came out of the shadows. I said, "Hello, Herrick."

The old man squinted. He scowled. He tried to stand up
straight. "I ain't Herrick. Herrick passed. I'm his kid brother,
Victor."

"Sorry to hear about Herrick, Victor. He was good people. I
need to see Shale."

Victor's eyes narrowed again. "You ain't been around lately,
have you?"

"It's been a while." Medford doesn't make you want to hurry
back.

"Herrick passed two years ago."

All right. It had been a big while. "I'm really sorry, Victor. I
need to see Shale."

"You got a name, boy?"

"Garrett. We go way back."

Victor sneered. "Shale goes way back. You're just a pup." He started to shuffle off, thought better of it. Maybe he decided he'd given in too easily. "What you got there?"

I didn't think he'd miss the bundle. "Little something for Shale." There was more on the way. These sour old flies would need a lot of sweetening.

"Bigger than a breadbox," Victor muttered. He considered the Goddamn Parrot. "You better not be carrying no birdcage there, boy. We got no truck with useless mouths."

I patted the bundle. "It's edible." The best bribes are the wonderful things the Cranky Old Men know they shouldn't eat. Or stuff they shouldn't drink.

"Got a creme horn?"

"I do believe. If Shale will share."

Victor fumbled with the inner gate. He muttered to himself. He didn't sound optimistic about Shale sharing. He had reason to be pessimistic. Great-granduncle Medford is a cranky old man's cranky old man. Maybe he had a little ogre or Loghyr in him somewhere, way back. He hasn't aged obviously since I was a kid and my Great-grandaunt Alisa was still alive. He's one really nasty old man.

But he's got a soft spot for me.

As long as I come armed with molasses cookies.

Victor opened the outer gate.

The instant it opened wide enough so Victor couldn't stop me the Goddamn Parrot revealed his secret relationship with a lady pig.

The old boy just stood there, poleaxed, as I started toward Shale. I said, "Bird, these codgers don't get a lot of meat in their diet. Costs too much. A buzzard in the pot might put smiles on all their faces."

I could see the little monster only from the corner of my eye but, I swear, he sneered. Somewhere, somehow, he'd gotten the idea that he was invulnerable.

Probably my fault.

"Hey, you!"

I sighed, stopped, turned. "Yes, Victor?"

"Whyn't you say you was one of them ventriloquisitors? A guy with a good and raunchy routine would be a big sell around this dump."

"I'll think about that." Might be a good career change. I never saw a ventriloquist with his head bandaged or his arm in a sling. "Let's see what Shale thinks." I just can't seem to get by without people thinking I'm flooding the dodo's beak with nonsense.

How come his big silence couldn't last?

Was some petty little god still carrying a grudge?

# 64

Shale appeared to be asleep. Or maybe dead. His chest wasn't moving. Maybe he was hibernating. Maybe that explained why he never got any older. I hear you don't age when you're sleeping.

He'd been in the same place so long the olive tree no longer protected him from the sun. He was all wrinkles and liver spots and if all his fine white hairs were tied end to end, they might reach his knobbly ankles. His clothing was threadbare but clean. Medford Shale had a thing about cleanliness.

"Shale thinks you're a no-talent little peckerwood and it's probably that mallard doing the actual talking and putting words into mouths." Shale's withered lips scarcely moved. Maybe somebody from the great beyond was ventriloquising him. "You found yourself a wife yet?"

"Good to see you well, Uncle Medford. Nope. Still playing the field."

Any other old boy in the place would've done a wink and nudge and boy-do-I-envy-you number. Medford Shale snapped, "You some kind of nancy boy? Ain't gonna be none of that in this family. What the hell you doing, coming around here dressed like that?"

No relative of Shale's ever did anything that didn't embarrass him. The more sensitive sort never visit him. Generally, that includes even those of us with hides like trolls.

"Your life is so full you don't have a minute to come ease an old man's last years?"

"That's right, Uncle. Given a choice between watching grass grow and listening to you bitch there ain't no contest." I'd always wanted to say that. When I was a kid my mother stopped me. Later, respect held me back—though I think respect should run both ways. Shale is too self-engrossed to respect anything. Right now, with a fresh crop of ogre-inflicted bruises atop the other aches I'd collected recently, I was crabby myself.

"That's no way to talk to—"

"You want to be treated right, you treat people right. If I want to be pissed on and cut down, I don't need to trudge all the way over here."

Shale's eyes widened. He sat up more spryly than you'd expect from a guy three times my age. "That parrot has become confused about what words to put into your mouth. No kin of mine would talk to me that way."

"All right. I'm no kin. And the buzzard is quacking. He says, you want things easier here, help me. I know where to find a baker's dozen of those molasses cookies you like." I gave him a glimpse of the bundle.

Medford Shale wasn't stupid. He wasn't the kind of character who didn't look out for number one, either. I learned to deal with him when I was a toddler, before Aunt Alisa died and he bought into Heaven's Gate thinking the staff would cater to him the way his wife had. And they did. Almost. But he could begrudge the most reasonable request. Human nature made paybacks inevitable.

One of the staff heard me mention cookies. She was wide and ugly and tough, neither tall nor entirely human, probably a war veteran despite her sex. She had the air. Female combat nurses did visit the Cantard.

"Nothing sweet for him, you. Nothing spicy. They make him cranky."

"Really. All my life I've thought he was just a nasty old man."

"No shit. You fambly?" She was so solid she recalled things I'd seen in foreign temples, the sort of wide, steadfast, imperturbable creatures that guard doors and windows and roofs.

I nodded.

"I see the resemblance."

Shale observed, "A cookie never hurt nobody, you ugly witch. Don't listen to a word she barks, boy. She tortures us. She comes around in the middle of the night . . ." He thought better of continuing his rant. Possibly she did visit the troublesome ones in the night.

"What do you want?" she asked me.

"Why?"

She was surprised. "I'm in charge. I need—"

"The residents are in charge. You work for them."

"Very definitely a fambly resemblance."

"I didn't come to see you. Unless you know something about shapeshifters. Then your company would be very welcome."

I was cranky not because the endemic crabbiness there was catching, nor entirely because of all my pains. I was going to have to pan a ton of fool's gold to get any useful information here. But gather a few nuggets I would if I persevered. It never failed. Between them Shale and his cronies knew something about everything. And they'd lived most of it.

"Boy," Shale growled at me, "you can't talk to Miss Trim like . . ."

# 65

You bark at some people, you make nice over others, you spring for a barrel of beer, suddenly you're an honored guest at Heaven's Gate. Even Medford Shale mellowed for six minutes before he passed out.

"Lay him out on his bunk like it's for his wake," I told Miss Trim. She did say she was in charge, didn't she?

Her given name was Quipo, she said. I could keep a straight face when I used it.

It turned into that kind of evening.

"That old fart is so mean he'll outlive me and any children I might father so I might as well enjoy a fake wake."

Miss Trim was all right once she got some beer inside her. But she'd never be a cheap date. She put it away by the pitcher. She chuckled a manly chuckle, slapped me on the back hard enough to crack a few vertebrae. "I like a man wit' a sense of humor, Garrett."

"Me, too. There's a guy I know, name of Puddle, you really got to meet."

One of Quipo's henchwomen appeared. She hadn't acquired her job through sex appeal. Few of the staff had. "The new barrel is here."

I groaned. I hadn't ordered up this latest soldier but I knew who would pay for it. And I hadn't gotten much out of anyone yet, though I'd been offered the impression that I'd learn plenty if I just hung on.

"Have them bring it right over here where I can keep an eye on it. Some of them are indulging a little too much."

The old men were doing their damnedest to get ripped. The

staff were one scant stride behind. Boys and girls alike tried to light lanterns and swat bugs in the courtyard. They did more harm than good but laughter filled the air.

"This is a good thing you're doing, Garrett." Quipo waved vaguely. "These men need a party."

"It's an expensive thing that I'm doing." Not that my employer—employers—couldn't afford it. I would bill them. If ever I rooted out anything useful. "They're lubricated now. I really do need to find out something about shapeshifters."

For a moment Miss Trim looked like she might contribute something. Then she asked, "Isn't that kind of an exotic concern?" Her hand brushed my leg. The Goddamn Parrot noticed, stirred restlessly, muttered under his breath. How steep was the bill here likely to be?

Word was out that I wanted information. Shale had said plenty, most of it untrue, wrong, or just plain libelous, and nowhere near the subject.

Old or young, rich or poor, saint or sinner, the human males of TunFaire have one thing in common. We're all veterans. The tie binds us. Once invoked it can, however briefly, shove aside most other concerns.

One peculiar geezer named Wright Settling, who never recovered from having been a career Marine, drew himself a sputter off the dead barrel. He grumbled because the new one wasn't ready. I told him, "Jarhead, I really need to talk about—"

"Yeah. Yeah. You kids. Always in a hurry. After all these years it can wait a minute."

"What can wait?"

"Hold your horses. Trail and Storey, they'll tell you all about it. Endlessly." Evidently hearing all about it was one of the more painful costs of sharing Heaven's Gate. He glanced at Miss Trim and snickered. "Maybe somebody else's got something for you, too. In more ways than one."

Ever notice how some older people stop caring if they're rude? Jarhead was a case in point, often less politic than Medford Shale, without complaining as much.

"People's lives do depend on me solving this." Solving what? I had only a shadowy notion what was going on.

"That's Storey right there. I'll get him soon as I get my beer."

I fooled Jarhead. I didn't play his game. I broke Quipo's heart by abandoning her, too. Me and my delinquent feather duster went to Storey.

"Mr. Storey? Mr. Settling says you're the one man here who can really help me." Never hurts to mention their importance.

"He did, did he? Jarhead? Why the hell is that old fool putting it on me? Who the hell are you?"

"I'm Shale's great-grandnephew."

"I'm sorry."

"More significantly, I'm the guy who bought the beer. And I may not tap the new barrel. I seem to be wasting my time. Why waste my money, too?" I turned toward the newcomer.

"Me and Trail was in the army together," Storey said, not missing a beat. I had a feeling I was about to hear one of those stories that define a lifetime. "During the Myzhod campaigns we saw more shapeshifters than you'd think could exist."

Myzhod campaigns? Could've been the bloodiest phase of the war but that didn't mean anything to me today. "A little before my time, Mr. Storey."

"I didn't expect you to know." He smiled resignedly. We all learn to do that. "There must have been a hundred huge campaigns that nobody remembers now but them that survived them."

"Yeah." Don't I know it? Most times I mention what it was like in the islands, guys who weren't there just yawn and come back with a story about the really deep shit they got into. "So you ran into shapeshifters down there? Were they Venageti?"

"They was supposed to be ours. Folks forget that they worked for us first."

"Special ops?"

"They wouldn't waste them as infantry, would they?"

"I wouldn't. But I'm not the brass. You never know with them."

Storey chuckled. "You got that right. I recollect one time—"

"So what about these changers back then?" I didn't expect much. "Anything might help."

"They took the point on the Myzhod offensive." Storey seemed a little dry. I made sure he got first crack at the new barrel. He sipped, saluted me by hoisting his mug, continued, "The Myzhod is a dried-up river. The Venageti had a string of bases on the south side. They used them as jump offs in a bunch of different operations. Those bases were tough. They'd stocd up to some heavy attacks. Some big names were getting embarrassed. High Command was pushing hard. They come up with a plan where shapeshifters would infiltrate a base and open the way for us commandos. We'd bust everything open for the regulars following on behind.

"First night us guys carried off the bodies of the guys the changers replaced. Second night, after those things wormed deeper inside, where they would cause confusion and grab the inner gates, we were supposed to attack where they'd prepared the way. We'd rip the belly of the base open before the Venageti knew what was happening."

Storey paused for a long drink. A tear dribbled down his cheek.

Another old man joined us. "This the Myzhod massacre, Will?"

"Yeah. Garrett, this's Trail."

"Glad to meet you, Trail."

Trail said, "Will an' me was almost the onliest ones what got away. That's on account of we smelled a rat because things was going too slick. We'd already switched livery with some dead Venageti so we just ran around like a lot of other scared crazy idiots till we figure it out. Then we cut out soon as we got a chance."

"It was a setup," Storey explained. "The whole thing was from the beginning. The Venageti line troops wasn't told up front they was part of a trap so they didn't give it away. The fact is, them shapeshifters sold us out. They led the whole damned army in there and got most of Karenta's best soldiers killed. Which probably made the war last forty years longer."

I guess the powers that be wouldn't brag about a defeat so severe it took two generations to recover.

I knew I'd learned something interesting but didn't see a connection with my situation now. This was the first I'd heard about shapeshifters serving on our side. Except for what was implied by the dragon tattoos with their Karentine motif, of course.

"When was this, Storey?"

"Forty-one or forty-two."

"Forty-two," Trail said. "It was the year my mother died and my brother was killed. That was forty-two. You remember, Will. The news was waiting when we finally got back to friendly territory."

"Yeah. Would you believe they wanted to charge us with desertion?" Storey grumbled.

Trail grumped, "We demanded a truthsayer. Even then they didn't want to believe us because a disaster that big would ruin lots of careers. But eventually enough others got back that they had to believe a story everybody told."

"We won a kind of battle, just getting back with the truth," Storey said. "The gods smiled on us. We had to cross two hundred miles of desert without getting caught by the Venageti or the natives. If we didn't get back, them shapeshifters could've pretended to stay with Karenta and led even more troops into the cauldron."

"It was bad," Trail told me. "I still get nightmares about that desert. I wake up and try to convince myself it was worth it 'cause if'n Will an' me didn't make it back, maybe there wouldn't have been any war for you kids to win."

"Most of us try to think that way, Mr. Trail." I shuddered, recalling the islands. Mostly we'd just wanted to stay alive but there'd been a flavor of hanging on so somebody else could bring the slaughter to a favorable conclusion someday.

In forty-two, eh? Over fifty years ago. And these old friends were still scrapping with the darkness. Maybe there was one more trick they could play on the nightmares.

"You ever see those shifters up close?"

"Up close?" Storey growled. "Shit. We practically slept together the three months before the attack. I reckon we saw them up close. One I'll never forget. We called him Pinhead. Pinhead sounded something like his name in his own language. And it fit. None of them was really bright. It made him really mad when we called him that."

Trail said, "They were so dumb we figured the gods made them that way to balance off how they could turn into something else when you wasn't looking. Like they had to be too stupid to take complete advantage."

Storey said, "I don't think they had the ability to appreciate the blessing. Some of it they couldn't control. Some of it they had to do whether they wanted or not."

"Yeah," Trail said. "There was this one called Stockwell. He made a chicken look smart. He was only a kid by their standards. The rest of them rode him—"

"Whoa! Stockwell? For sure?"

"He was another one that got called what his name sounded like. Most of them did. We turned this one into Carter Stockwell. It was kind of a joke, too, on account of—"

Couldn't be the same clown. Could it? After all these years? "I've been butting heads with a bunch of shifters. Believe it or not, one of them calls himself Carter Stockwell."

"Really?" Trail asked. For the first time he seemed completely interested. "Ain't that interesting, Will?"

"Sure is. I'd like to run into Carter Stockwell again some time. When I have a sack full of hot irons and silver knives. You know it's almost impossible to hurt them unless you use something silver?"

I nodded. "I noticed."

Trail said, "Always been my pet theory that silver is the reason they got involved in the war in the first place. That they never was on nobody's side but their own. If they could glom onto the silver mines, they'd control the best weapon that could be used against them."

"You could be right," I said, though that sounded like a stretch to me. "Interesting. Have some beer, gents. Keep talking. Name some more names." Not that I believed their Carter Stockwell was mine. He might be a grandson, though. "Talk to me about tattoos."

That drew blank looks and puzzled grunts.

"The changers I'm running into all have a dragon tattoo right here. It's about six inches long but hard to see when they're alive."

Storey shook his head. "I don't remember nothing like that."

"Me neither," Trail said.

"I do," Miss Trim told me. She was well sloshed now, sliding out of focus. She wore a lopsided, trollish leer. Was she making it up to get my attention? "It's a dragon squeezing the commando insignia in its claws."

I grunted. "We're onto something, Quipo."

"They were commandos. Mercenaries. I didn't know they were shapechangers, though. They called themselves the Black Dragon Gang. Said they came from Framanagt."

"Which is an island so far east of nowhere that nobody would ever check. Was anybody named Norton involved?"

"Colonel Norton was their commander. But he was Karentine."

Stockwell and his pal had expected me to know something about their crew. "What did Black Dragon do to get famous?"

"Nothing. It was the other way around. They did everything they could to hang around Full Harbor. They only went out when they couldn't avoid it. You don't make a name doing that."

"That's where you were? Full Harbor?"

"For nine wonderfully miserable years."

Full Harbor was where I'd had my only previous encounter with a shapeshifter, a Venageti agent masquerading as a Karentine spymaster. Was there a connection? Should I have made one? "When did you separate?"

"Six years ago." Quipo didn't want to talk anymore. She wanted to act but the only guy around young enough wasn't interested.

Six years was long before my own encounter.

I reminisced silently, trying to discover if I knew something I didn't know I knew. Apparently I did. Or Black Dragon didn't realize that I didn't know. "Was there ever any suspicion that the Black Dragon Gang might not be trustworthy?"

"Uh?"

The beer was hard at work now. I was about to lose Quipo. "Is there any chance those guys were really working for Venageta?"

Miss Trim's eyes focused momentarily. She gave it a good try. "Uhm? 'Dwould 'splain a lot. Never fought a dat."

Plop! She melted on the spot.

The Cranky Old Men became excited. Only the fact that Quipo had a few sober sisters chaperoning saved her from a catalog of minor indignities and vengeances.

I became the crowd favorite. I was an ear that would listen. Every old man wanted to tell his life story. None of those had anything to do with shapeshifters.

Part of the cost of doing business. I might have to come back someday.

I hung in there bravely, almost as long as the moon did, but eventually the beer ran out and I fell asleep.

# 66

I had a hangover. Again. Surprise.

It was not yet a classic. It was just an infant. But it had potential. This was practically the middle of the night still. Dawn was only a hint of color in the east.

Victor nudged me with a toe in a spot that the ogre had thumped yesterday. I woke up sprawled under an olive tree, supported by cold, damp stone. The Goddamn Parrot was on a branch overhead, muttering. He made no sense but occasionally my name entered the mix. "Get up, Garrett," Victor insisted. Pain blazed through my side. Oh, no! Not another cracked rib. "Some guy is looking for you."

Some guy? That didn't sound good. I hadn't mentioned Heaven's Gate to anybody, ever. Nor had I noticed anybody following me. Not that I'd made much effort to keep track. Crask and Sadler were in the tank. The shifters ought to be licking their wounds. Nobody else should be interested.

"Get up, damn you!" Victor let me have it again, in the identical spot, harder. He knew what he was doing.

Victor was a teetotaller, a member of TunFaire's smallest and most viciously bizarre cult. He was the only born-again alcohol hater at Heaven's Gate. He'd let me know again and again what he thought of me dispensing the devil's sweat.

"Victor, you do that again, you'll need to get fitted for a wooden leg."

Victor chose discretion. "Your party is outside the front gate."

My party was Ritter from Relway's deck of jokers. Brother Relway was looking like a mojo man who sees all and knows all. I asked, "Don't you guys ever sleep?"

"Sleep? What's that? Wait! Yeah! I remember. They used to let me do that when I was in the army. Once a week whether I needed it or not. Don't have time to waste on it anymore, though. This is Card." Somebody unclear, clinging to a shadow, lifted a hand but didn't speak.

I told Ritter, "I always knew you groundpounders had it sweet but you're the first one who ever admitted it. What's happening?"

"Boss wants you back at the Weider place."

"That doesn't sound promising. How come?"

"There's been another killing."

"Shit. Who was it this time?" I should've gotten Saucerhead in there.

"I couldn't say. Nobody told me. I'm just supposed to get you."

"How'd you know where to find me?"

He looked at the thing on my shoulder. "Followed the parrot droppings."

"No, really."

"The boss told me you were here. I don't know how he knew. I didn't ask." That cut me off quick. "I'm just a messenger, Garrett. He picked me because you'd recognize me."

"You guys bring any transport?" Besides being hungover and achy from the ogre's handiwork I was stiff from sleeping on cold, damp stone.

"You kidding, Garrett? You know what kind of budget we've got?"

"Can't blame a guy for hoping. Though I expected the worst. You do that and you're never disappointed. Sometimes you're even pleasantly surprised."

"It isn't that far, you know. Just a couple miles."

"More like four. And I have a hangover and fresh bruises."

"That ogre thumped you pretty good, eh?"

Relway's crew seemed to know every breath I took. Relway had to want me to know that, too. Ritter was hardly so dumb he'd give it away if it was supposed to be a secret.

"Just don't get in any hurry. I'll hike as fast as I can. I gotta do one thing before we go, though."

I limped over to Shale's apartment. He lived alone. His personality guaranteed his privacy. I slipped the packet of cookies into the crook of his arm. He was a nasty old thing but he was family. The closest I had anymore.

# 67

Colonel Block met us on the Weider front steps. "Good morning, Garrett." He was in uniform. He dismissed Ritter and Card, eyed me as though he had developed major reservations. A large, muscular, nameless bruno lurked close by in case Block needed a ton of muscle in a hurry.

The mansion looked deserted from the outside. I saw no light and heard no morning bustle. People should have been stirring.

"You came yourself?" I asked.

"This is getting big. A definite high-level interest has developed. Things are going on that we can't see from down here in the bushes." I got the impression that he was understating—and was not about to go into detail why.

"I didn't want to hear that. Where's Relway?"

"Good question. I haven't seen him since yesterday."

"He sent for me."

"I sent for you, Garrett. Because you know these people. They need to deal with somebody familiar. They're like trapped animals right now."

"Ritter told me there's been another murder."

"Yeah. Guy name of Lancelyn Mac. He had a head-on with somebody who tried to force his way into the house. The cripple was there but didn't see that part happen."

"Ty."

"Ty, then. Talk to him. I can't tell you anything he can't."

"Where is he?"

"Everyone in the house is in the family dining hall. Anybody who leaves has to go with someone else. That rule applies to

everybody. My people included. Nobody should be alone, ever."
Which explained the muscular behemoth attached to him like a
shadow, jabbering like a stone.

"You think changers killed Lance?"

"Maybe. Nobody else is interested in the Weiders. Are they?"

I shrugged, sketched what I'd learned at Heaven's Gate. Block
listened without interrupting.

"Interesting," he said. "The same name cropping up, then and
now. You could cobble together some weird hypotheses if you
made a few assumptions about shapeshifter thinking."

You sure could. I had one notion I wanted to bounce off the
Dead Man. It regarded his hero Glory Mooncalled and plans the
man might have regarding TunFaire. "They have a strategy. They
have a goal. If we knew what that was, we could figure out what
they'll probably do next."

"Next time we catch one I'll be sure to be more careful about
keeping it caught. They're in here."

"Here" was the family dining room that had served as Mr.
Gresser's staging area during the ill-starred engagement gala.

Tinnie ambushed me at the door. "Where the hell have you
been?"

"Out white-knighting around. I rescued a maiden, then I
rushed to the bedside of an old man who doesn't have long to live.
I took him some cookies to ease the pain."

"We heard about Belinda Contague. I want to talk to you
about . . ."

Alyx materialized. Her bounce and deviltry had gone missing.
She was a kid who needed somebody to tell her everything was
going to be all right.

The whole crowd seemed possessed by a universal despair.

"Hi, Alyx. Hang in there, kid. We're going to turn it around.
Gilbey. Max. Nicks. Ty. Can we get right to it?" Ty was in his
wheelchair. Nicks sat nearby at a long rosewood table. Earlier that
table had been shoved against the wall and piled with the goodies
Gresser's people had been serving to the rest of us. Nicks was
nowhere nearby mentally although she did grunt in response to
my greeting.

I needed to hone my charm skills.

"Ty," I said. "Come walk me through what happened." All
business is my middle name—even when I have a beautiful
woman hanging on both arms. In my dreams.

Block wanted to see a re-creation. Ty had refused to do it for him.

Ty pushed his wheelchair away from the table. "I guess." His voice was flat. He was ready to give up but was going on because he was expected to go on. I'd seen it before. It might armor his soul till he passed through the dark fire.

Nicks positioned herself behind Ty's chair. She moved like a sleepwalker.

The remnants of this family would need a lot of help. Though if I didn't get somewhere soon, there might not be a family much longer.

I followed Nicks into the great hall. Block followed me. I heard feet shuffle. Well. Max had invited himself along. Gilbey paced him, ready to help. Max looked like he'd aged thirty years.

"This way," Ty murmured weakly.

Alyx trotted along. She might be up for a fight before long.

Ty directed Nicks to the foot of the steps to the front door. He beckoned me. "I couldn't sleep, Garrett. My back was aching and my leg was burning. I decided I'd get some work done if I was going to be awake anyway. I dragged poor Lance out and made him come down here with me to talk about how we were going to bring the furnishings back. I was in the chair, right here, looking back along the hall, when Gerris said something from up there. I was surprised to see him. He said someone was at the door. He wanted instructions. He seemed rattled. Lance said he'd take care of it."

"Nicks," I asked, "would you walk through Lance's role? Alyx, scoot up there and be Genord."

A snooty voice suggested, "Why not let Genord be Genord?" Genord stepped out of the gallery, which continued to grow behind Max and Gilbey.

"Perfect. You be Genord, then. And we'll walk through it."

Nicks positioned Ty according to his instructions. He told me, "I was saying something to the effect that I hoped Dad wouldn't insist on putting that ugly rust-bucket suit of armor back by the green colonnade when Gerris spoke."

Genord, now at his post, stepped into sight and announced, "Sir, there's a very abusive young man here who insists on being allowed inside."

"That's not quite right. I think he used the word obnoxious," Ty told me. "What's he want, Gerris?"

Genord replied, "He just wants in, sir."

Ty said, "That's when Lance said he'd take care of it. He was exhausted. He didn't want to be awake. He was in a mood to be very rude to somebody. I told him, 'Kick his butt down the stairs if you have to.' He went straight to the door."

I looked up at Genord. He told me, "I stayed with him. Just in case. I wasn't alert enough. Something did happen. And it was over before I could react."

I nodded. "Go ahead. Nicks?"

Genord moved Nicks into position at the door, returned to his own place.

"Freeze," I told them. "Genord. Is this where everybody was? Exactly. Ty? Were you still looking up the hall?"

Genord nodded. Ty told me, "No. I was looking over my shoulder like this. But I couldn't see anything. Lance or Gerris."

I didn't have to bend or squat to see that he was right. You had to be two giant steps to his right even to spot the tail of Nicks' skirts.

"But you saw it all?" I asked Genord. I was down to the unexpected eyewitness.

He nodded. "The man was in shadow, though. And I was turned toward Master Ty when Lancelyn squawked."

"But you got a look at the visitor when you answered the door, didn't you?"

"I'd recognize him if I ever saw him again."

"Did you recognize him then?"

"Excuse me?"

"I'm wondering if he might not have been here for the betrothal party. Possibly as one of Gresser's serving crew."

"I see where you're going. I don't think that's possible. Though if you assume that the assassin was a shapechanger, he could have been here before in a different guise. But didn't you lock all of them up?" Genord seemed to be enjoying himself now. Was he fond of being the center of attention?

Block observed, "Evidently the guy wasn't out to kill just anybody. Otherwise, he would've sliced you up when you opened the door. And he must not have wanted in all that badly or he would've just made his entrance over you and Ty. He's already made one kill. He'd have nothing to lose by another."

I snapped, "He say anything to you?"

Genord appeared rattled again. "Uh. Yeah. Let's see." Genord's snooty accent evaporated. He closed his eyes. After a deep breath he uncorked a string of rude demands for the return of a missing girlfriend. I frowned. So did everyone else. Genord stumbled. "Uh. That's what it sounded like to me. I was puzzled. That was one reason I deferred to Lancelyn. I couldn't imagine that the man had come to the wrong house." There is no other residence near the Weider mansion.

I exchanged glances with Block. The puzzle was growing bigger. I said, "I mean did he say anything after he hit Lance. But before you answer that, tell me, are you saying that this killer was accusing Lance of stealing his woman?"

"No." Genord appeared to be surprised by the question. "Not exactly. Well, he didn't use any names. But he must've meant Lancelyn because he kept accusing Lancelyn directly. Then he did what he did and I think he was completely stricken by it afterward. I think he panicked and ran away."

Ty said, "There couldn't have been any girl, Genord. And you know it. I didn't hear what was said but I know a girl couldn't possibly have been the real problem. Lance told you why himself, Garrett."

"Yeah. His thing for Kittyjo." Not to mention that only a psychic killer could have counted on Lance answering the door if he had a quarrel with Lance. "What was this guy wearing, Genord?"

"What?"

"He wasn't naked, was he? Give me an overall impression. Upscale? Down? Neat? Rumpled? Threadbare? How was his grooming?"

Genord paused. He didn't seem to have thought about this much. "Uh. . . . Almost military? Yeah. That's what I'd call it. His manner was crisp. Like the training sergeants we all recall so fondly."

He could have been describing himself.

He was recovering fast, turning almost cocky again. A changeable guy, Gerris Genord.

Block asked, "Did you notice an armband? Or medals. Or anything else that might connect him to a freecorps or a rightsist group?"

"I didn't see anything to connect him to anybody or anything but death. But he stayed in the shadows."

I took a couple of steps to the side, looked up toward the door. I told Block, "Colonel, let's you and me walk through this ourselves."

Block looked puzzled but his instincts had been right when he had asked for a re-creation.

Genord frowned, troubled again.

I said, "I'll play the killer. You go to be Genord. Genord, get out of the way. Nicks, you be Lance again. Ty, don't move at all. All right?"

"Not a muscle."

"Ahem," Tinnie said. "What're you trying to prove?"

"I'm trying to understand what happened. Something isn't right. This doesn't make sense."

Genord glowered.

I checked the layout. The players were in place. I stepped out-side—without closing the door, so the bogeyman couldn't get me without somebody noticing—then walked through the murder with Gerris Genord directing. Reluctantly. Then we did it again so I could see things from Lance's viewpoint. Then I told everybody, "Go back to the dining room."

Tinnie tarried. I winked. She went but not without a frown.

Block asked, "You got something?"

"Maybe. It all may hinge on what could turn out to be a stupid question."

"Seemed to me . . . I had a gut feeling . . . But a lot of times murder just doesn't make sense."

This one might not make sense even if it was right. "I think it happened pretty much the way we walked through. Nobody con-tradicted anybody."

"But?"

"The question. What was Gerris Genord doing awake and an-swering the door in the middle of the night?"

"Shit. You're right. I never thought of that."

"You felt it. Or you wouldn't have had a hunch. You didn't see it because Genord is supposed to answer the door."

# 68

"Sorry. Just family right now," I told Tinnie. "Nicks, you qualify." I considered before telling Gilbey, "And you."

He was irked because I'd thought about it.

"Let's go to yonder corner. Drag over some chairs." I dragged one for myself. I gathered them in a circle, knee to knee.

"What is it, Garrett?" Max Weider was experiencing a resurrection of will. Maybe he thought something was getting accomplished. I hoped I could maintain the illusion.

"Some of you may think this is a stupid question. But the answer could be critical. Can anybody tell me why Genord would be answering the door in the middle of the night? Even I'm not superhuman enough to stay on the job all day and all night, too."

Ty chuckled weakly. He said nothing. In normal times he would've spoken just to remind us he was there.

His eyes went cold when the substance of my question connected. "I didn't think of that. Gerris is always just there."

"You don't have a night porter? Somebody like that?"

"No."

"Let's take it a step further, then. How do we know there was anybody at the door? We just have Genord's word."

"Shit," Ty growled. "I never thought of that even when I was there. But Genord wouldn't—"

Max snapped, "Why *was* Genord up in the middle of the night?"

Nobody told me maybe I was good at what I do. Nobody said, hey, Garrett, maybe you're onto something. I suggested, "Why don't we ask Genord?"

Gilbey muttered, "I'd hate to pick which one I didn't like the most, Lance or Genord, but under the circumstances—"

"Take it easy. We don't know Genord is telling stories." I didn't want to lynch the majordomo. Yet. But I sure didn't buy the tale he'd told.

Max raised a hand, glaring. Hard Max was back. "Get him, Garrett."

"I'll do it," Gilbey said. He was right. In normal times he'd summon Genord.

Manvil stayed a step behind Genord as they approached. Genord looked worried. He felt the string running out.

I said, "I've got a problem with this thing, Genord. It goes right back to that guy at the door. Nobody saw him but you. Ty says he never heard the guy. But you said he was shouting."

"Maybe I was so scared it just seemed like he was shouting." Genord shrugged. "I can't tell you anything else."

"Sure you can. You can tell us what you were doing up in the middle of the night. You can tell us why you were at the front door when Ty and Lance came into the great hall."

Genord shuffled his feet. He looked for a way out. He didn't answer me.

"They took you by surprise, didn't they? They couldn't help but notice you. Sooner or later somebody would ask you what you were doing. You panicked. You didn't think. You just did the first damned thing that popped into your head. And that was something really stupid. Which you compounded by making up an incredibly stupid story."

"I just answered the damned door!"

"Sure. You heard the knock all the way up to your room on the fourth floor. Come on, Genord. You're not that clever. It's obvious you were sneaking in after being someplace you shouldn't have been. Unless you were waiting for somebody. Or maybe you really were squabbling with somebody. Somebody who didn't get out of the way fast enough when Lance came up and maybe recognized him . . ." That couldn't be quite right. But it might be close. "Colonel Block."

"Uhm?"

"You did have somebody watching the house, didn't you?"

"The shithead supposed to be out there wasn't. He sneaked off, he claims to get something to eat."

"But don't your men operate in pairs?"

"The other now former Guardsman wandered away even earlier. He hasn't turned up yet."

"You kept a few too many Watchmen on the payroll."

"Evidently. Though the first shithead did yell as soon as he found out something happened. Give him that. He did the right thing even though he knew his butt was in a sling."

Genord relaxed visibly while Block delivered his bad news. Not a soul missed that. I asked, "Anybody got a silver coin? And a knife?"

# 69

Gerris Genord was no shapeshifter. But he was a villain. I had no doubt about that. He refused to talk, though. Block predicted, "He will. Eventually." A regular sibyl, he was.

I suggested, "Check his room, Gilbey. See if there's anything there to tell why he'd blow such a cush job."

Block's men took Genord away. He went silently but with defiant pride. I asked, "Anybody know that man well?"

Young, old, male, female, human, or otherwise, none of the staff knew a thing. That this betrayal came hard on the heels of the other tragedies suggested treacheries of incalculable depths.

"Did he have any particular friends?"

Nobody even heard of Gerris Genord, suddenly. He'd never had a friend. Gerris Genord? Is that some tropical disease?

Gilbey returned. "I've got something I want you to see, Garrett."

"What?"

"We didn't know Gerris well at all."

"The man was a pig—" I started, but then intuited, "He was fanatically neat, wasn't he?"

"He was." Gilbey offered me a scrap of burnt wool. I saw nothing remarkable.

"What about it?"

"Would you burn your clothing?"

According to some I should. "Oh." Genord's room contained no fireplace. There was a small charcoal brazier, though, that had seen use lately, despite the season. It contained curled fragments of burned paper mixed with shredded wool remnants and crumbled charcoal. The air still stank of burnt wool.

I said, "Genord had some time to himself before the Guard arrived."

"Obviously. And there were comments about the smoke when we gathered everyone downstairs. I didn't think anything of it at the time. The chimneys do need work."

I stirred clothing with a toe. "He didn't have a lot of time."

"Only a few minutes, really."

"Then we might still find something."

"And look here." Gilbey indicated a large sack in a corner.

"Looks like an army duffel bag."

"And it is." Gilbey upended the sack. Clothing, small personal items, and trinkets cascaded to the floor. "Well. It looks like Brother Genord meant to leave his position without giving proper notice. And in a hurry. This explains why we've had so many valuables turn up missing lately."

It did look like Genord had tried to provide himself with a handsome separation bonus. "He didn't wear jewelry, did he?" He never seemed the type.

"No, Garrett. It's obvious he expected to have to run someday. Soon." Gilbey extracted a heavy gold pendant from the pile. "This was Kittyjo's. It was a gift from Lancelyn."

I glimpsed something blue beneath a tattered shirt, pointed. "Bingo."

"A rightsist armband. I never suspected that. Genord came across as a political eunuch. What group?"

I plucked it out. "This's freecorps. Brotherhood Of The Wolf."

Gilbey frowned. "Isn't that? . . ."

"An armed branch of The Call. With a really serious, hardcore reputation. This gets interestinger and interestinger." Not to mention scarier and scarier.

We turned up nothing else. Genord had found time to do everything but get away. Which made me wonder if the armband wasn't a plant. Or if it hadn't been so special to Genord that he kept it nearby even though discovery would deepen his troubles.

As we went back downstairs I told Gilbey, "Let's don't tell anybody but Max. If everybody knows one of The Call's people got himself arrested here, some of the goofier members of the movement might decide they have to give the Weiders lessons in how to treat their betters."

We didn't know that could happen. Genord might have kept

his work and his politics compartmented. But I didn't believe that. Not with the family and its brewery attracting so much attention lately. Not with the hard-core reputation of the Wolves.

"Good idea. But it won't stay quiet forever."

"Probably not." Which suggested that my next move, inevitable but one I didn't want to make, had to be undertaken soon or the opportunity would evaporate.

I pulled Block aside as soon as we got back to the dining room. "More trouble." I slipped him the armband. "That came out of a duffel bag Genord packed after the murder. Looks like he meant to take off but didn't move fast enough."

"The Wolves were tough, Garrett. Commando types. Genord don't fit the part."

"Maybe he's honorary. Or he's a good actor. You never know about a guy who managed to survive the Cantard. He sure didn't stop to agonize over the morality of killing Lance even though ultimately it was a stupid thing to do."

"There is that. But people do do stupid things when they panic. What do you think?"

"I don't know what to think. I don't want to but I'm going to try to get inside the movement. Maybe I can find some answers there. I want you to take care of these people. Whoever's been trying to hurt them isn't finished. He hasn't gotten whatever it is he wants."

"I'll keep this armband. I'll discuss it with Genord. You shouldn't know anything about the connection if you're going to get close to his friends."

Good point.

"And you might clean up a little. You'll do better if you're presentable. Consider stashing the wonder buzzard, too. Some of those people have fairly refined sensibilities."

"They even hate parrots?"

"They especially hate parrots with an attitude problem. You see what's happening on the streets. Call people don't believe in self-restraint. And the more they get away with the harder they push."

Worth remembering.

"You be careful what stories you tell about yourself, too," Block told me. "They'll know when you're stretching the truth."

"Uhm?"

"Relway isn't the only one watching you."

"Really? Shit!" I have my pride. And one thing I'm proud of is that I'm good at working a tail or detecting one set on me. I hadn't noticed anyone.

There aren't many guys that good.

I had a bad feeling. I asked Block. He told me, "I don't know how they're doing it. Relway hasn't figure it out yet, either. You know it's a trick he'd like to have in his bag."

I'll bet. "How bad is it?"

"Sometimes you have an entourage."

More agony for my bruised pride. Time for a subject change. "What do you know about the Institute for Racial Purity?"

"I've never heard of it. What's it supposed to be?"

I told him.

"Something else to check in my spare time. You be careful, Garrett."

"I'm not leaving yet." I was ready, though. But not for the place I had to go. I preferred a destination where the beds weren't stone, where I could sleep off my residual hangover without fear of interruption.

# 70

I plopped into a chair, told Max what I knew, what I was doing and thinking and suspecting. He was attentive. His anger burned hot enough to heat-treat steel. He didn't blame me for his pain, as a lesser man might have done.

I started awake as an arm snaked around my neck. A taut bottom began making itself comfortable in my lap. "Ulp!" I said.

The Goddamn Parrot chortled. He was watching from the chandelier.

The behind belonged to Tinnie Tate. She was in a snuggly mood. "You fell asleep. Mr. Weider said to leave you alone because you've been working so hard." She leaned back to let me see an expression saying she thought I had him fooled.

"And now?"

"Go home and get some rest?" She wiggled.

My head was so cluttered with sleep I missed her point. "I'll just find a spare room and grab a nap before I hit the road." Then, belatedly, the message soaked in. "On the other hand, there're some mysteries at home that need solving. If I have the help of an amenable assistant."

The Goddamn Parrot snickered.

I did need to be seen around there once in a while or some bad boy from the neighborhood would try his luck against the fear the Dead Man had woven so powerfully around our place.

Tinnie growled. She was tired. So was I. I said so. But, like everyone who didn't have to be somewhere else, I didn't want to abandon the dining room's relative security. Block had left several men on guard there. For what good their presence might do.

Alyx heard me talking. She decided to come over. "Want me to show you a safe place to nap, Garrett?" The devilment was back, if weakly. The stay-together-in-pairs rule remained in effect.

"No thanks." I winked.

Tinnie shifted to a less uncomfortable position. My reward for saying the right thing. She murmured, "How about I show you *my* guest room?"

"A man's gotta do what a man's gotta do."

# 71

Tinnie followed me to the Weider front door. She was dressed for travel in a peasant frock and sensible shoes. Stupid me, I asked, "Where do you think you're going?" Stupid me should have started discouraging her about an hour ago. Not that I could have gotten anything through all that red hair successfully.

"With you. You need somebody with you. That's the rule."

"I've got my talking feather duster."

"What good is he in a fight?"

"He squawks a lot and—"

"Be careful how you answer this one, Garrett."

Oh-oh. Time to make that extra effort. I had to remember my lines just right. Only I hadn't seen a copy of the playscript yet.

Redheads will do that to you.

So will blonds and brunettes and all the lovely ladies of every other hue.

"All right, then. You're in. That'll cure you of wanting in. Real quick." What could happen? I was just going to visit one of Karenta's most beloved subjects at his big, safe country estate.

I learned quickly that the countryside is still infested with country. It isn't my favorite part of the world. I prefer domesticated bugs, cockroaches and fleas and bedbugs. They don't get greedy if they bite at all. They don't rip off an arm and hang it in a tree to come back to later.

It was well-groomed out there, close to town, but still way too green. "You getting tired?" I asked Tinnie. She didn't look tired.

She looked fresh, sexy, full of vitality and likely to be all of those still when I collapsed.

"You trying to get rid of me again?"

"Again? I never . . ." One foot starting to swing out over the abyss, I shut up.

Maybe I was learning.

"Oh, look!" Tinnie took off running, frisky as a fifteen-year-old. She leaped into a patch of cornflowers.

I told her, "The blue detracts from your eyes."

"I like them anyway. Yikes!" She jumped higher and farther than you would have believed possible for such a trim slip of a gel.

A tiny face peered up out of the flower patch. It belonged to a grinning miniature man. Or boy, actually. He was a pint-sized teen. His grin was humorless. It was a conditioned response to the presence of big people. He was terrified. The grin was supposed to buy time while he figured out what to do.

Flower stalks swayed behind him. I glimpsed brown-and-green homespun in motion, a flicker of golden hair tossing, tiny heels flying. Well. I chuckled. The Goddamn Parrot chuckled. I took Tinnie's hand, pulled. "Let the kids have their privacy."

"What? You mean? . . ."

"Yeah."

"Oh. Actually, that's not such a bad idea, Garrett. When you think about it."

I do that a lot. "Well, if you really . . ."

"All this fresh air is getting me giddy. There's a wonderful big patch of cornflowers over there in that pasture."

"Not to mention cows and horses."

"I didn't know any little people still lived outside the wall. Because of the thunder lizards. You're worried about a few cows?"

No. There were horses over there. Eventually they would recognize me.

But the company went to my head. "I didn't want you worrying about the livestock."

"If they bought bullshit by the pound, you'd be the richest man in TunFaire."

"I'll never be anything but a poor second," I replied. "While Morley Dotes is alive."

Tinnie hiked her skirts with one hand. She ducked between the rails of the split log fence. "I'm only giving in because you keep pressuring me." She showed me a couple of hundred taunting pearly whites.

This was my Tinnie. The argumentative evil twin her family doesn't see. Very often.

I leaned on a fence post, the tip of my nose an inch from hers. "I just had a thought." I glanced back toward TunFaire.

We'd passed through a small wood a while ago. The top of the Hill, a few towers, and the general miasma of evil air hanging above everything were all that could be seen of the city.

"A naughty one, I hope."

"Actually, it's more a troublesome one."

"There you go getting serious again."

"Sometimes I don't have any choice."

"All right. What is it?"

"Colonel Block warned me that I'm being followed around, all the time, by some very clever tails. Which would mean that somebody might be following me now."

"Doesn't that just mean somebody takes you serious? Aren't you always complaining because people don't take you serious?"

"Right. It's great for the ego. But it occurs to me that if I yield to temptation and vanish into a flower patch with the most stunning redhead north of the Cantard—and I can't think of anything I'd rather do—I might get trampled by watchers running to find out where I went."

That tree line back there offered the last good cover for someone tracking me.

Tinnie leaned a little closer. Her eyes were only halfway open. Her lips were parted. She breathed, "Most stunning?"

"You witch."

She laughed. "See? You forgot all about—" She stopped, stared to her right.

Somebody had left the wood. Somebody who was in no hurry. Somebody who whistled while he scuffed along the dusty road.

Staying close, Tinnie whispered, "It's still a good idea, Garrett. Maybe on the way home."

"Sooner or later."

A rumble like the stir of remote thunder came from up ahead. We would reach another tree line in half a mile. The rumble came from beyond that. "Now what?" Tinnie asked.

"Horsemen. A whole bunch."

The stroller behind us caught the sound. He vaulted the fence and disappeared into tall pasture grass on the other side of the road. Hmm.

I got myself over on Tinnie's side fast. "Head for those tall weeds."

"Why?"

"Because we don't know who's making that racket. It could be somebody we don't really want to know."

"Oh."

The war taught me to suffer inconveniences and discomfort stoically, so I only grumbled a little about the thistles in the weed patch. Tinnie was more vocal. Poor spoiled city girl. But she did clam up, bug-eyed, when a squadron of centaurs hove into sight. They were all males with the hard look of campaign veterans. They maintained a warlike traveling formation. They were armed and alert. The army wouldn't like this. I didn't count them but there had to be at least sixteen.

They might have been looking for something. They didn't see it in the pastures, though. They moved on quickly.

"What was that about?" Tinnie asked when the coast was clear. "What are they doing all the way up here?"

We had watched centaurs from hiding together before, a while back, in the Cantard, which is where centaurs properly belong.

"I don't know. But those guys weren't your everyday refugees."

"I don't like it."

"It isn't far now. North English's dump is just past the next bunch of trees." I hoped. I'd never been invited out.

# 72

Marengo North English's digs were typical of Karenta's ultra-wealthy gentry. The centerpiece was a huge red-brick manor house that crowned a knoll half a mile behind a tall hedge of some plant consisting mostly of thorns. There was a lot of green grass, numerous well-groomed trees, sheep, cattle and neat military squares of tents. An illustration of the place would have overlooked the livestock and bivouac. Workaday aspects of the rural idyll always get overlooked.

"You ever been here?" I should've asked earlier.

"No. I always heard he's kind of reclusive." She indicated the tents. "Lot of relatives visiting. You been here?"

"My folks never moved in these circles." Tinnie started putting on her shoes. She'd been going barefoot, claiming she wanted to feel the dust squish between her toes. They were very nice toes, even dusty-dirty. But I decided to study the hoofprints outside the gate instead. Numerous oddly shod hooves had milled around there recently. Or maybe it was just a trick of the light. The day was getting on.

"Why isn't anybody on guard?" Tinnie asked, between shoes. She danced on one foot while she tried getting a shoe onto the other, tucked up behind her. Her effort had its moments.

I'd been wondering myself. Was North English that confident? I didn't believe it. Not in this world. Not this near TunFaire. The gods themselves aren't that confident. I kicked at hoofprints. "It worries me, too." Those centaurs hadn't looked like they'd been in a fight.

"Should we head back?"

"It's late. It'd be dark before we got to the gate." In darkness, outside the wall, is nowhere I want to be. Call it prejudice. The owners and workers of manors, farms, orchards, and vinyards get by just fine. Those without stout walls just dive into deep cellars via twisty, tight tunnels if the big thunder lizards come calling. Anything else they kill before it kills them.

I don't take risks if I don't have to.

The night can hold things worse than death in the jaws of a hungry beast.

"You scared, Garrett?"

"Sure. You understand what I'm doing? If you don't, you'd better start—"

"We're a team, big boy. You and me and our ugly baby."

The Goddamn Parrot lifted his head long enough to give her a baleful look. I looked balefully at our surroundings. The spread seemed almost lifeless.

"Something I can do for you folks?"

Here came the missing guard, out of a cluster of evergreens not far inside the gate, next to the road. He was buttoning his trousers. He had trouble concentrating on his fingerwork. He was stunned by Tinnie.

I know the feeling. I get it all the time.

"Name's Garrett. I'm doing some work for Marengo. He was supposed to leave word—"

"I guess he did. I recognize the name." His nose wrinkled. "But he's not here. There's a big rally tonight." He checked Tinnie again, probably wondering if she'd like to change her luck in men.

Things are bad when groat-a-dozen brunos take on airs. Maybe belonging to The Call boosts your self-confidence.

He said, "Go on up to the house. Front door only. Someone will be waiting."

I lifted an eyebrow, started walking. Tinnie grabbed my arm. The gateman looked sad, soulful, constipated. Life just isn't fair.

"You little heartbreaker," I told my little heartbreaker.

"What?"

"You completely destroyed that man just by walking away with me."

"What are you talking about?" She never noticed.

Then she bumped me with her hip.

Devil woman.

# 73

Somebody was waiting. She was long and lean and looked surprisingly regal observing our approach from above. She also looked like she had a sudden toothache come on. I don't think she was glad to see me.

Tinnie offered me another solid hip bump. "That's for what you're thinking."

The woman must be half Loghyr.

Miss Montezuma seemed less than thrilled to see Miss Tate, too, but put her disappointment aside. She was cool, elegant, imperial. This lady was always in control. "Welcome to The Pipes, Mr. Garrett. Miss Tate. You've chosen an inopportune time to visit. Everyone's gone to town. Tonight is supposed to be important for the movement."

We joined Miss Montezuma on the porch. I considered the manor, which dated from the middle of the last century and was supposed to be a minor fortress. Some tightwad had been skimping on the maintenance. It needed a lot of exterior work. The surrounding protective ditch hadn't been cleared out in a generation. If I had friends like Marengo's, I'd keep it filled with acid and alligators.

I surveyed the vast lawns. Or pastures. They were pretty enough. One frazzled kid was trying to convince some sheep that they wanted to head back to their paddocks. "Everybody went? Even Marengo?" North English never included himself in The Call's public exercises. "What happened out there?" One area of lawn was torn up, as though cavalry had fought there. Maybe the livestock had been folkdancing.

Tama Montezuma frowned. "The cattle or sheep must have done it. Tollie has no help at all."

"Why did everybody go?"

"Marengo doesn't tell me everything. But he did say tonight will be a turning point for The Call and Karenta."

"It's a shame I missed him."

Miss Montezuma's gaze brushed Miss Tate. "Isn't it?"

My luck turns fantastic when there's no possibility of benefiting.

Tinnie kicked my ankle. I glanced at her. She had a flower petal in her hair.

The Goddamn Parrot snickered.

"So what do I do now?"

" 'Come in. Have supper. I was about to start my own. Then I'll find you rooms. It's too late to go back to town. And you might not want to be there anyway. We could talk about why you came out. Maybe I can help."

I said, "Ouch!"

"Sorry." Miss Busyfeet took her heel off my big toe. "I'm so clumsy today." The Goddamn Parrot snickered again.

Who am I to argue with a beautiful woman?

She could've left her shoes off, though.

The Goddamn Parrot began to dance on my shoulder. He had not yet eaten today. He said something. It was just a mumble, garbled, along the usual lines but intelligible only to me.

I hoped.

The impact of the presence of two beautiful women must have weakened the spell binding his beak. Or we were too far away from the Dead Man for him to control that beak completely. Or His Nibs had become too distracted to stay on that job—or maybe he had turned routine buzzard management over to one of his less attentive subsidiary minds. None of those were very bright.

Certainly he would not have taken his attempt to mislead rightsist observers so far as to abandon completely his ability to spy on me. That would deprive him of so many opportunities to gather ammunition for future nag sessions.

Yes, Old Bones was still out there somewhere, playing his own hand, involved in some way, whatever appearance he tried to project. This case touched upon too many of his fascinations for his defection to be complete and real.

"You're so sweet," Tinnie said. She scratched the quacking

feather duster's head. "How come you never say things like that, Garrett?"

Tama Montezuma offered me a dose of my own medicine. She raised one eyebrow and smiled a thin little smile that *dared* me to open my yap.

I took that dare. "Shut your beak, you perverted vulture." To the multitalented Miss Montezuma, I said, "Besides reporting in I hoped to do some research on shapeshifters."

She jumped. "Research? On shapeshifters? Here?" Ha! I'd blindsided her with that.

"The Royal Library referred me to The Call's Institute For Racial Purity. Which is supposed to have a library chock-full of books about nonhumans."

"Oh. That. I'm amazed any outsiders take it seriously. The books are piled all over the old dining hall. They keep collecting books without knowing what to do with them. They can't get anybody who knows anything to come out here. I suspect because they think a librarian should work out of conviction instead of for a salary."

"They" probably meant Marengo North English, well-known skinflint.

Tinnie said, "Sounds like a job for Garrett. He can read and everything."

"I'm no good at organizing." Which was why I hired Dean, way back when. The old boy started out part-time. Next thing I knew he'd moved in.

"You hungry?" Miss Montezuma asked.

"Famished," Tinnie chirped. I didn't doubt it. The woman could eat a whole roast pig and never gain an ounce.

I smiled over her shoulder, nodded. I didn't want Miss Montezuma thinking my friend did all my talking for me.

Tama was amused. "I'll take you past the library on our way to the kitchen. You can poke around there after we eat."

"Marengo won't mind?"

"Marengo isn't here."

"Doesn't seem to be anybody here." There was no sign of staff although Marengo's shanty dwarfed the Weider hovel. "Though how you can tell in all this gloom . . ." Hardly a candle was evident.

"There aren't any servants anymore," Miss Montezuma replied. "And we're frugal with all consumables. If we need light to work, we'd better get the job done in the daytime. Though I suppose I could find a lamp for *you*."

They just fall at my feet, willing to do anything.

"There aren't any windows in the old dinner hall."

The Goddamn Parrot snickered.

"You better do something about that sneeze, bird." I asked Miss Montezuma, "What's going on? They say Marengo is tight, but . . ."

"The Cause is a vampire. Its hunger never goes away. He has to cut back somewhere."

Did North English start out less rich than everybody thought? The impedimenta of great wealth seemed plentiful enough, if old and mostly threadbare. "At least he hasn't had to sell the candlesticks to make ends meet."

"Don't be cynical. Marengo believes he has a divine mission."

I doubted that, being a cynic. "What about Miss Tama Montezuma?"

"It doesn't matter what Miss Montezuma thinks. She's just Marengo's fancy woman."

"If I buy that, will you try to sell me maps to hoards of fairy gold? Bargain-priced?"

"I'm sure Miss Tate is far too alert and levelheaded to let me take advantage of you."

I didn't look at Miss Tate. I had a feeling Miss Tate would be hard at work restraining her redhead's temper. My smirk might overtilt the load.

"I'm curious," Tinnie said, reasonably enough. "If you have no servants, how do you eat?"

"I cook better than I do what I'm famous for."

Whew!

Miss Montezuma cooked very well indeed. With Tinnie and I following her instructions we collaborated in constructing a meal featuring a wild rabbit Tama claimed to have caught herself. "A woman of many talents," Tinnie observed.

"Yeah." I made a mental note to check Miss Montezuma's background. Street legend didn't dwell on her antecedents, which was unusual. Everybody loves a scandal.

# 74

During supper I was ordered to call Miss Montezuma Tama and learned that North English's place really was deserted.

The man from the gate was named Stucker. He avoided conversation with a passion. Tollie was a Montezuma-stricken fourteen-year-old who managed the livestock. There was a silent old man who had one eye and a hook for a right hand. Venable constituted security at The Pipes. Venable thought thunder lizards were the most wonderful things the gods ever created. He couldn't understand why they were unpopular. He could go on about them forever. He kept a pack of his own as pets and security associates. They would have the run of the estate tonight. Venable claimed his babies only ate strangers.

I suspected that, if you got yourself eaten, Venable's position would be that you couldn't possibly have been friendly.

An advantage of thunder lizards as guards is their stupidity. You can't bullshit them. But stupid is exploitable, too. They'll forget everything and go for the snack if you toss them something like, say, a squawking parrot with his wings clipped.

Tama discouraged table talk, though Venable wanted to bring me up-to-date on things to do with thunder lizard fandom. Tollie couldn't stand to look at Tinnie or do much more than croak if he tried to talk to Tama.

After supper we headed for the library. I insisted. Marengo might say no if we waited. His racist treasures might be damaged by eyetracks.

Long ago I learned that nobody wants to share information that looks like a resource.

The room set aside for the library was huge and cluttered. Most of the stuff there had to predate any notion of a specialized library. Some, I'd bet, predated any notion of Marengo North English.

Tama said, "Marengo wants to set up his research center here. But he's never found time to get started."

I got the impression she'd heard talk till she didn't listen anymore. "It's not like he's short on manpower. He could drag in a bunch of true believers and set up in a day."

"He's too paranoid."

"Yeah?" I set my lamp on a dusty side table, assayed the job ahead. Books were jumbled into small wooden crates in no obvious pattern. Scrolls were tied in bundles of four or five. I selected a bundle. "How do you feel about what he's trying to do?"

"My thoughts aren't consulted." She wasn't going to offer an opinion.

Did she know anyone well enough to take that risk?

Tinnie prowled the room slowly. She used her lamp to illuminate books where they lay, maybe hoping to luck onto something. Luck did seem as sensible a strategy as any. She harrumphed.

I said, "Miss Montezuma, you're being disingenuous. I asked your personal opinion, not if you're a consultant to the Inner Council of The Call."

"Tama, Garrett. Tama. Listen to me. I'm Marengo's companion. His mistress. Strictly utilitarian. What I think doesn't matter any more than what the chamber pot thinks. Unless one of us actually says something. I like my life here." *Most of the time,* her eyes said.

"And when the bloom begins to fade?"

She understood. She'd thought about that. That was obvious immediately.

I recalled how North English had slobbered over Belinda.

Uncle Marengo was in a mood to expand his horizons.

I dropped the subject.

Tinnie exercised uncharacteristic self-restraint. "Here's something." Her timing was flawless. The volume she handed me looked like it might actually be useful. It was *Werebeasts: The Monsters That Walk Like Men.*

The title turned out to be the most interesting part of the book. It dealt only with people who turn into wolves or bears or big cats or critters of a more mythological conviction. Those gods or devils who turn into eagles or snakes or whatnot, with no problems in the weight differential department, were the only self-directed changers mentioned. The creatures I wanted to demystify were anything but divine.

Tama neither dug in nor read over my shoulder. Was she illiterate? Probably. A pity but common enough, especially among women. I learned to read and write because that was a good way to kill time in the long, dull intervals between war's storms of high terror. A lot of guys did. It was encouraged. Written communications get less garbled over time and distance. Karenta's more literate forces proved marginally more efficient and effective than Venageta's over the war's final generation.

Now Karenta's masters are troubled. They have begun to suspect that allowing commoners access to books may have been a grave mistake. Literacy puts crazy ideas into heads more useful when empty. Books let guys who have been dead for a hundred years pass on the one original notion they ever had, which meant immortality for countless social insanities.

There was scarc talk about the mob possibly teaching their young to read, too, thereby perpetuating the abomination. Today's freethinking insanity might continue for generations. It might destabilize the natural order.

Few girls get much education. Tinnie is an exception because amongst the Tates everybody produces. The Tates are more like dwarves than people, some ways. Tinnie manages their bookkeeping.

In time, Tama said, "I'm no night person, Garrett. And I've been up late a lot recently. I need to get to bed."

I missed her point. She reiterated, more directly.

"I need to hit the sack, Garrett. Marengo will strangle me if I leave you unsupervised."

"Oh."

"I'll show you your rooms. I'll trust you not to sneak off with the North English family treasure during the night."

Without light, tippytoeing between the thunder-lizard pups? Wouldn't Venable be pleased?

I didn't run with Tama's straight line. Tinnie waited for it, watching me with smouldering eyes.

Tinnie noted Tama's mention of rooms, plural, as in closed doors for everybody, maybe with nobody knowing where anybody was.

I got assigned first, presumably on the assumption that Tinnie was less likely to go rambling.

It was very dark in my room, beyond the circle cast by Tama's lamp. "There's your bed," she told me. "The chamber pot is underneath. I'll see you and the bird tomorrow." She took off with Tinnie.

I had returned to the door without killing myself on stealthy furniture, leaned into a hallway filled with darkness. The women were out of sight already. Tinnie hadn't left a trail of bread crumbs covered with foxfire. Bad girl. Or maybe not bad enough.

The Goddamn Parrot chuckled softly.

I was beginning to wonder if having the old gutter-beak version of the bird back might not be preferable.

"There are things in the dark," I told him. "Beware!" I shuffled to the bed, undressed.

# 75

The bed was a fine great mass of down that gulped me whole. I was asleep in seconds, too exhausted to be long disappointed by my solitude.

Nor was I disappointed when, later, I wakened to discover solitude's end. "Did you use a ball of string to mark the way?"

Tinnie hissed, "How did you know it was me?"

"Who else?"

"How about that gaunt witch Montezuma? Or has she been here already?"

I know it's you because I know the scent of your hair and the shape and feel of the rest of you, I didn't say out loud. Also, you are less bony than, not to mention shorter than, the aforementioned gaunt witch. "Not yet, she hasn't. I find it hard to believe myself but not everybody finds me as irresistible as you do."

"Oh? *I'm* the weak one? You want me to show you just how resistible you really are?"

"Hold it down, will you? You'll wake the parrot up."

"Now you're trying to shush me up?"

I knew just the thing to shush her up. But it didn't take for very long. It never does, partly because Tinnie really likes being shushed up.

Two unpleasant things happened at the same time. The Goddamn Parrot broke out in some kind of sea chanty about swords and silver and dead men while someone else gave me a quick, savage finger poke with a nail probably specially sharpened for the task. A soreness upon my ribs suggested that the offending digit had struck several times previously. A whisper accompanied the pain. "Garrett! Somebody's in here with us!" It was not a quiet whisper. The woman was not ashamed.

I groaned, "You're evil. Let me rest."

The bird shrieked like his just deserts were trying to get hold of him. Tinnie snarled, "Garrett! There's somebody in here, dammit!" Which pronouncement was followed immediately by a racket as somebody tripped over some sly and belligerent bit of furniture.

The Goddamn Parrot screamed rape. Tinnie screamed fire, presumably on the assumption that that was more likely to get attention. I yelled, "Be quiet!"

As I climbed out of bed, feeling around for something suitable for bashing undesirable visitors, furniture crashed nearer and nearer the door. Said door opened. For an instant a hunched shape shown in silhouette against a ghostly light from the corridor. Before the door closed I had taken advantage of that light to navigate past two pieces of furniture that would have ambushed me otherwise because they did not seem to be where I remembered them. A third piece, more patient than the others, waited till the door closed to move into position.

The impact of plunging headfirst into a wall—even with my arms thrown forward to absorb it—was enough to leave me groggy and seeing double. Which I was doing when I opened the door and leaned out cautiously.

My night visitor was moving away fast, vaguely illuminated by a weak lantern trailing from her left hand. Her? The figure looked something like Tama, and also a little like the herd boy Tollie, yet distorted. Perhaps by the crack taken by my noggin. So maybe the sweet thing had considered offering some special hospitality and been panicked by hearing Tinnie speak as she was sneaking up on me. Maybe. It could happen.

I could not think of a reason why the kid would want to sneak in on me. Unless he thought he was entering Tinnie's room.

Whichever, how come the wannabe visitor's other hand was hanging on to a hatchet or cleaver or some such large, heavy, sharp piece of metal?

"Who was it?" Tinnie whispered from behind me.

"I don't know."

"I'll bet I can guess."

"No doubt you can. To the bleakest possibility. And make it all my fault."

"Hey, that's your place, lover. In the wrong. You think we should barricade the door? Just in case?"

"I think we should barricade the door." If what I thought I saw was real, that was one nasty piece of iron. "Just in case. But you'd better hope they don't hold bed check over to your room."

"I sleepwalk."

Right. We moved some furniture. Then we went back to bed. Then, somehow, I got distracted and ended up falling asleep before I had a chance to spend any time figuring out what had just happened.

# 76

If Tama Montezuma knew anything about or had had anything to do with or had any feelings about the previous night's events, she gave no sign at breakfast. "Good morning, Garrett. I would've wakened you earlier but Tinnie told me you haven't been getting much sleep lately."

Damn! I never warned Tinnie. But she was all right so it didn't matter.

"He seldom gets up before the crack of noon, anyway," Tinnie said. "This's way early for him."

"Hey!" I protested. Then, "Never mind. Tama, Tinnie tells me you've had word that Marengo is headed home."

"A messenger came a few hours ago. Said Marengo is on his way. And that he won't be in a good mood." For just an instant her eyes seemed shifty, evasive, troubled. "Last night didn't work out for him."

"How come he left you here?" I had been thinking about that and, not being a major aficionado of Marengo North English, had developed some suspicions concerning Marengo and his interest in female persons who were not his wife or niece. I refused to believe that North English was so devoted to his convictions that he had gone off to help bully TunFaire's nonhuman population.

"A dangerous level of confrontation was anticipated." That sounded like a quote from Marengo. "But before you jump to any conclusions, I chose to remain here." And that sounded like the truest thing she had said for a while.

I glanced at Tinnie. Her thoughts had taken her elsewhere.

I hadn't seen anything yesterday to suggest that something dramatic was going happen. On the other hand, I had spent the whole day distracted. Tinnie's presence seldom left me with attention to spare.

Still, you tend not to overlook big gangs of guys all dressed in brown marching back and forth singing and busting heads wherever they find somebody not dressed in brown and marching and singing their favorite songs.

I didn't pursue my question. Tama volunteered, "He said it would be too dangerous." Her mask of control had begun to show cracks.

The missing mob began returning.

First to appear were a dozen freecorps types who roared through the house demanding food. They were ragged. I observed, "The other guys must really look bad." Slings and head bandages were plentiful. Smiles and laughter were not.

Maybe the other guys never got their hands dirty.

Rightsists kept turning up, alone, in pairs, in small bands. Many were injured. The mood was grim. I suspected some wouldn't return at all.

They paid me no attention. They even ignored Tinnie.

"What's with those guys?" I asked Tama, back in the library at last. She'd spent some time helping feed them. "They don't act human."

"They got their butts kicked. Their big show turned on them."

Damn! TunFaire had long dreaded some huge demonstration by The Call. And I missed it. Out of town. Gone fishing.

Was I lucky, or what?

"How come they don't notice you or Tinnie? None of those guys is over a hundred."

"Marengo is inflexible when it comes to what he considers correct behavior. He has made it clear he considers correct behavior a hallmark of the superior being. These men are all superior beings. Therefore, they must conform to the highest standards. Your friend and I are spoken for. It would be incorrect behavior for them to surrender to their natural inclinations. They must show themselves to be the superior creatures they claim to be. Marengo insists. And Marengo pays the bills." Tama said every word with a face so straight you knew she wanted to explode in giggles. She whispered, "I'll tell you a secret, though. When they're in the city, surrounded by persons of other stations and Other Races, they act their ages and classes."

"You can take the boy out of life but you can't take the life out of the boy."

"I'll bet you know what you're talking about, too. Tut-tut."

I had tried to talk to several men, in passing. I'd gotten nothing but grunts and scowls for my trouble. It didn't seem politic to press. "Did they get into it with centaurs?"

"Centaurs?" Tama seemed startled. She recovered quickly. "I don't think so. It just seems all the Other Races were ready to fight. The rioting grew bad enough that troops were sent in, some places."

Bet that didn't do much good. Short-timers who thought just like The Call weren't going to be fanatics about defending nonhumans. Their real mission would be to ensure the sanctity of the property of wealthy friends of The Call, anyway, probably.

Call me cynical.

The Call's strategy was no secret. They'd been pursuing it on a small scale for weeks. They wanted to terrorize nonhumans and destroy their property so they would flee TunFaire. Last night's riots would've been intended to become so intense and widespread that the Crown could do nothing but let them run their course.

The Inner Council of The Call had expected the night to be a watershed. They'd counted on the fire of human resentment to flare out of control everywhere.

It hadn't happened. They'd gotten limited support and unlimited resistance.

The fire had blown back into their faces. The most militant nonhumans had been ready for them. Somebody had snitched on The Call.

It wasn't an ignominious defeat, though. It was just an acute embarrassment.

# 77

Tinnie and I—ever chaperoned by Tama—worked out a system for identifying and reviewing books of potential interest. She sorted and identified. I read. Nothing turned up quickly. I fell behind Tinnie, normally an intriguing place to be.

She asked, "All right if I start a separate pile for stuff that's not in Karentine?"

"I guess." We'd need translators, too? I sneezed. "Wish we could do something about this dust."

The door opened. "Miss Montezuma? Are you? . . . Ah. There you are." The speaker was an old man with a bad artificial leg. His trip to town must have been hell. "The chief is expected soon. He's probably wounded."

"Probably?" Tama was moving already.

"Reports vary. Sometimes he's in critical condition. Sometimes he's only scuffed up a little.

"But he *is* hurt? Garrett. Tinnie. I have to go."

"Have fun." I was sure that the direst reports about North English's condition would originate closest to him. I'd seen him in action.

"Come on, Garrett. You know I can't leave you alone."

I let another great line slide.

As we strolled the hallway in Tama's wake Tinnie remarked, "You're learning."

"Huh?" Wasn't I?

"You've stopped sticking your foot in every time somebody opens a door a crack."

"Did I miss something?"

"I doubt it. But if you did, so much the better."

Pain is a great teacher, darling.

Tama went out onto the same high porch where she'd awaited us. We joined her in time to see Marengo North English's coach arrive. Armed horsemen accompanied it. They were ragged. Bandages were common.

Somebody loved Marengo. A military-style honor guard turned out. So did a haphazard medical team.

How bad had it gotten? There was no smoke over the city so folks hadn't started burning each other out yet, but if there were many casualties, it could turn nastier fast.

Clearly, the fun had gone out of dressing up and bullying the neighbors.

An ugly little devil-worm of a word wriggled through the muck in the pit of my mind. I hoped it didn't get out and infect these guys. They were in a mood to embrace the demon.

Its name was War.

On Marengo's estate, where there were no pesky nonhumans to make them look bad, the members of several Call freecorps sparkled, though guys with different armbands seemed to have scant patience with one another. Did they fight each other when nobody else was handy?

The medical crew whisked North English out of his coach, onto a stretcher, headed for the house fast. From where I stood Marengo looked like a genuine casualty.

Up close he was grimly pale, like he'd lost a lot of blood. He was still leaking. His clothing had been destroyed by people eager to patch him up.

He was awake and aware. He frowned blackly when he saw me. His gaze jerked to Tama suspiciously. Tinnie joined me. North English's suspicion faded. He knew about us.

What was his problem?

Tama fussed over North English. Sounded like she meant it, too.

It wasn't necessary to fake everything in the deal she had.

She moved with the litter, spewing orders. She knew what she was doing. She'd had practical medical experience sometime.

The Pipes crowd seemed accustomed to the presence of mysterious strangers. Nobody questioned us. We were with the boss's woman. He'd seen us himself and hadn't had a stroke. We must be all right.

I did have to field questions about my shoulder ornament. Fortunately, the Goddamn Parrot kept his beak shut. I didn't have to explain how I'd become a ventriloquist. Unfortunately, none of those bold young warriors were in the market for a pet. "Think what a wonderful mascot he'd make," I said. "Put him on your standard and have him squawk insults at dwarves . . ."

The bird squawked an insult at me. It was incoherent but it was there.

Few of the returnees were alert. Mostly they just flopped down somewhere and closed their eyes, safe for the moment.

I remembered that from the islands. After a long, hard, emotionally draining fight, the moment we felt safe we surrendered to exhaustion by collapsing on the spot.

I picked a guy who didn't look as beat as some. "What happened?"

He focused on me momentarily, remembered seeing me with Tama. He shrugged. "Somebody tipped them off. I thought it was gonna be the great big ole hairy-assed mother first night of the Cleansing. I thought we was going to hit the skells and skuggs everywhere, all at the same time. Not just The Call and Theverly but all the groups and freecorps."

That's what they were doing at Weider's the other night. Slapping the last coat of paint on their plan. Using a joyous occasion to mask the stir of darkness. "So somebody leaked it, eh?"

"They was waiting." Like that said everything that needed saying. Misfortune hadn't robbed him of his sense of humor, though. He observed, "Ogres is bad in a street fight."

"They are hard to dent. I speak from joyless experience."

A blond character, shorter and younger than me, born with a board strapped to his back and a chip on his shoulder, stalked into the morning light. He spotted Tinnie, used her as a landmark by which to locate me, came over. "You Garrett?"

I confessed.

"The commander wants to see you."

"North English?"

"Is there another?"

"I'm new at this. I thought maybe Colonel Theverly—"

"Follow me, please."

I did. I caught Tinnie's hand as I passed her.

# 78

Tama was working on North English when we joined them in a room reminiscent of Max Weider's study—though this was much larger. If the weather turned bad, the freecorps goofs could hold their maneuvers indoors. A world of plotting could be managed from there. The gloomy nether reaches contained maps hung above sand tables boasting miniature structures that looked familiar.

Two guys with spears for spines and no imaginations were camped between us and the tables, I guess in case I suffered one of my outbreaks of curiosity.

Good to see they trusted me as much as I would've had I been the old boy getting mummified. "Sir," I said as the officer and I approached, "you wanted me?" He looked less determinedly antagonistic now.

"Tama says you came to see me." His voice was weak and high but stronger than I'd expected. He winced as Tama swabbed an abrasion. Naked to the waist, he was a pasty, doughy sort of man.

Also a lucky sort. He hadn't been treated kindly. He had suffered cuts and stab wounds and bad abrasions most men couldn't have survived.

I said, "I wanted to bring you up-to-date." He lacked enthusiasm. In his position it would be hard to be enthusiastic about anything less than life itself.

I edited my story only slightly. If I was being followed, my movements were no secret. Anything I'd learned, if I'd learned anything, could be learned by others. There was little point holding out. And none to revealing that I was reporting to Block and Relway, too.

I was up to the centaurs. "They were a military unit. Disguised but definitely veterans."

North English waved a hand. "Wait a minute." He pushed Tama away.

I waited while he ordered his thoughts. That took a while.

"Let me get something straight. You had no idea The Call would begin the Cleansing last night?"

"Not a glimmer. But you're the only one I know who'd know about it. You didn't warn me."

"But you're generally well informed and a keen observer. You would have noticed anything obvious." He seemed to be having trouble thinking.

"I thought so myself."

"If you didn't notice, then it wasn't something we did that gave us away." My guess was, he'd just realized that he had a rat in his walls. "Tama. Miss Tate. I want to chat with Mr. Garrett privately. Ed. You and your men step out with the ladies."

Ed was the officer who had delivered me. Apparently bodyguarding was among his duties. He was scandalized. "Sir, I wouldn't recommend—"

"Do it, Ed."

Ed stopped arguing.

Tinnie didn't want to leave, either. Tama didn't want to leave. They did not argue. Marengo North English was in charge.

I chuckled. "You got Ed worried, boss."

North English frowned at my familiarity. "Possibly. And that's my fault. He took the same attitude yesterday, I told him to go away—and I ended up lucky to be alive."

"How bad is it?"

"I told you, I was lucky. Damned lucky. They meant to kill me but a gang of dwarves looking for rightsists to fight popped up and attacked them."

"I'm confused," I confessed. "Maybe you started in the middle. Dwarves saved you? From human attackers? Why would they do that?" It was interesting that terror and pain would put him into such a talkative mood. But why with me?

"They didn't recognize me. And the men who attacked me were disguised as members of the movement."

"Maybe they were."

"Possibly. That's not a thought I cherish. But I do have rivals. Although I don't think any of these men were that because I didn't recognize any of them. Even so, I did want Ed and the others out of here so we could speak freely."

"About what?"

"You must look into what happened while you're doing whatever else it is that you're doing. I'm particularly interested in knowing who those men were. I am confident that they were specifically committed to the extinction of Marengo North English and my survival is due only to an ironic twist of fate."

"I still feel like we're going sideways."

"I'll start from the beginning. Last night was a big night for The Call. We'd planned for months. We put it off several times because we thought we could make a bigger splash later. But now we were coming up on the dwarfish New Year. We had to move before all their rustic cousins came to town for the holidays."

North English composed his thoughts carefully before he continued. He was much more businesslike than he had been at Weider's.

"As you may suspect, like you, I have a taste for toothsome ladies. Not long ago I met someone new and intriguing. She seemed equally interested. Last night presented a perfect opportunity to pursue the possibilities. The Cleansing provided a reason to be away from The Pipes. And there was nothing I could contribute to actual operations short of getting out in the street throwing brickbats with the others."

I listened for hints of hypocrisy. I still had trouble picturing Marengo North English as a true believer.

Maybe the insincerity existed only in my imagination.

"So you had a date. Rough trade, too, looks like."

"I walked into an ambush. I couldn't have been much stupider. Ed warned me but I wouldn't listen. It's the way men get."

"Sometimes," I admitted, having been there.

"It's only sheer fool luck that I'm here now." He snuck a glance to see if I was conscious of the irony.

I eschewed any observation about fools and drunks. "Are you heading somewhere?"

"I am. Yes." Pause. Deep breath. "Eight of the most influential men in the movement were murdered last night. Somebody tried to kill Bondurant Altoona. Burned his house down. But he wasn't inside." Did I hear disappointment? "Ladora Ankeny was hurt worse than I was, poor woman. I was attacked, of course. Set up and attacked."

"Thought you and old Bondurant didn't get along."

"We don't. He's not well liked. We left him out of our plans. But he did hear somehow and left home—to get in the way, if I know the man at all—just before the fires started."

Maybe. "Were the attacks coordinated?"

"I believe they were."

"Why?" I meant why did he think that but that wasn't what he heard.

"The assassins were all human. I can't believe that there's that kind of opposition among our own people. There're only two kinds of humans." Eyes calculating, he paused to read my expression. "Those who're with us and those who're with us but haven't yet awakened."

You might be surprised, boss. "You know who got killed, right? Who they were could tell you why. What did they have in common?"

Evidently North English didn't want to face that question. He had an answer already that didn't please him.

"So?" I asked, noting that he was still trying to read me.

"Everyone attacked was involved in fund-raising. Or made decisions concerning raising funds. I think I might be the only one who could see that connection. So maybe *that* was why *I* was targeted."

Which offered us both an answer he didn't want to face— along with a reason why.

He'd slipped off to meet Belinda, jumping right into a honey trap. And now his ego hurt worse than his body because he feared he'd been set up from the beginning.

Belinda was her father's daughter, with extra weapons. She could blind men with their natural weakness. And she had no concept of mercy.

I said, "If you play on their ground, you obey their law. Only the strong survive. You mess with their money, they kill you. Unless you kill them. They don't think like kings and generals. Or like you. They don't send soldiers to attack your soldiers. They'll kill your men only if they get in the way. They want you. Once you're dead your soldiers are no longer a problem."

That seemed the obvious way to operate, too. I've never understood why, when we caught a big-time Venageti wizard or general or noble, we'd always ransom him. Or even just let him go if he promised not to fight anymore.

I wondered what Belinda would say about last night. Not that I'd ask. I try to separate business and friendship. If a friendship is what we have.

I told North English, "I've known these people a long time. I'm surprised they've been as tolerant as they have."

That startled Marengo. "Tolerant?"

"By their standards."

"It wasn't my intent to engage in criminal activities, Mr. Garrett. I'm the most visible Call leader but not the only one. Not even the supreme one. Other groups started raising money that way a long time ago. I opposed the plan when the Council proposed it. I reminded them that The Call wasn't founded as a criminal conspiracy. I reminded them that one of our missions is to set an example. We can't cut corners because our cause is just. If we do, we're no better than the Other Races. And it sets a precedent we'll pay for later."

The man was heated up for a speech. Maybe he *was* a true believer. I cut him off. "Looks to me like you've got a good counter-argument now."

"Possibly. But I doubt it." He paused. I had nothing to say so that's what I said. He continued, "It's all out of control, Garrett. It's like riding a lion. The beast answers the reins if the mood takes it. And the gods help me if I try to get off." And again with the calculating look.

"What do you want from me? Looks like the Outfit sent a message. Emphatically. You were lucky. You survived it. They'll let you alone if it looks like it took. I say don't aggravate them. Chodo is way less friendly than Belinda."

"Did she set me up?"

"Probably." My guess was, Belinda just thought on her feet and improvised. "Maybe that was why she wanted to meet you."

His pride was bruised more deeply than his flesh. Marengo North English thought well of himself. What kind of world was it where a woman could use him as knife fodder? "You know Belinda. Talk to her."

Was he going to whine? "If you've checked me out, you know I know Chodo better than I know Belinda." Unless she'd developed a true-confession habit.

North English smiled enigmatically. Maybe he knew more than I thought he could. He winced, closed his eyes. His wounds still hurt badly.

# 79

"What actually happened last night?" I asked North English, after we took time for him to rest and take a painkiller.

"I'd arranged to meet Belinda at a rooming house on the far north side. She said the place belonged to her family."

"Remember the name of the street?"

"I don't. That was the driver's responsibility." When I frowned, he said, "I don't think it had one." He colored slightly.

"You went into an elven neighborhood?" Elves don't get excited about frills like street names or house numbers.

"Just the edge. Nobody would expect to find me there."

"No. But somebody did."

"Yes." North English proceeded to describe the attack on his coach, which occurred soon after it entered that street. It mimicked the attack on Belinda's coach.

Was that coincidence?

Quite possibly he'd had an earlier close call and didn't yet realize it. Belinda had asked him to meet her at The Palms. And CeeJay Carlyle had been with Belinda when she headed for her postparty rendezvous. Did Crask and Sadler mess everything up?

I asked, "Should I talk to your coachman?"

"If you know a good necromancer, you might. I'm the only survivor. They didn't get me dragged out of the coach fast enough."

There'd be no way of double-checking details short of consulting the men who had tried to kill him. I had a suspicion that was a long-shot daydream.

The details didn't matter. Had to be Belinda's doing. And

Marengo knew that. But I wondered if she might not have had more than one motive.

Her attack had been extremely vigorous, even for her. If, indeed, she had ordered the attack. It risked warfare now and persecution later if The Call enjoyed any enduring political success.

She must've decided that the Outfit had to make a clear, definitive statement incapable of being misunderstood by anybody. Which might mean she hadn't just been responding to business encroachments.

Just suppose Marengo had had some remote connection with the attack on Belinda . . .

I decided that he must have had. Based upon no evidence whatsoever.

Poor Marengo! That made him a zombie, dead but still walking toward the knife.

Somebody had brought Crask and Sadler back. Those two were fearless but they weren't stupid and were only marginally crazy. They knew lots of people wanted to carve them up.

They must have been sure they could do their work quick and dirty and profitably and be gone before death could pick up their trail.

So somehow North English got word to them when Belinda showed up with me, cleverly grasping the moment. He might not have known that those two thought they owed me. But would he have cared?

I didn't think so, either.

Then Belinda made a date, probably hoping to let North English meet Carlyle for an exercise in comparative knife techniques. And North English agreed, probably thinking he'd have fun with Belinda if his hitters missed.

No proof. None whatsoever. All speculation. But I thought the Dead Man would agree. And he'd looked inside Belinda's head, where the snakes and spiders lurk.

I can conclusion-hop with the best. I've run with villains for years, people who play those kinds of games. You can smell them out if you know the stakes and luck onto a few hints up front.

These scenarios fit the facts neatly.

They didn't toss light into the shadows surrounding the shapeshifters and the Weiders, though. They gave me no mention whether or not The Call was trying to strong-arm the Weiders, or was connected to the shapeshifters somehow.

Damn it. The one thing I'd figured out didn't help much. Belinda and The Call could work out their differences, with bloody steel or rattling jaws. That wouldn't touch me.

Belinda might have let the nonhumans know about the advent of the Cleansing. The Outfit had tentacles reaching inside shadows Relway only dreamed of penetrating. Everybody owes them something, somewhere, somehow. Though in this case Marengo was, probably, the leak himself.

I asked, "Any way you can bully your council into backing off?"

"Backing off?" He got that air of struggling to concentrate again.

"To quit trying to horn in on the rackets."

"I can try. If I had a good reason. If they're really doing that."

"How about staying alive? Is that a good reason?"

"They wouldn't do anything just on my say-so, Garrett. Again, if they're really involved."

Why did he keep pretending? "Here's a reason they can understand. If you get in a war with the Outfit, it won't just be Marengo North English who gets dead. They can get to anybody. Eventually. They'll find somebody close willing to be corrupted. They won't be impressed by who you are, who your parents were, how much you're worth, or who you know. You should've gotten that message last night."

"Last night is why I hope you'll find us a basis for negotiation."

I was puzzled. It showed.

"What?" North English demanded.

"What's to negotiate? They'll tell you to go away or get dead. Then they'll kill as many of you as it takes to make you understand."

I exaggerated a little. The Outfit is no monolith and the people inside are as venal as any other. It could be tamed by somebody who wanted to focus a lot of energy and resources. Somebody like Relway, someday, when he doesn't have to deal with all the other distractions.

Assuming Belinda didn't get to him first.

"Why go for the rackets, anyway?" I asked. "The Call is festering with rich people."

"Not many of whom want to open their purses for the Cause. They're investing their leadership skills." Yes, he was sarcastic. And bitter. "I've financed almost everything. I've fed and armed and clothed a thousand men for Colonel Theverly. Before Theverly it was the Brotherhood Of The Wolf."

"What became of those guys?" I still wanted to figure out where Gerris Genord fit.

"They wouldn't be controlled. They were disbanded when Colonel Theverly came aboard. Some joined the new corps. The hardheads dropped out, went somewhere else." North English waved a hand weakly, dismissing the Brotherhood. It was old news. He had a hobbyhorse to ride. "Do you have any idea how much weapons cost when you have to buy them from dwarves?"

Wouldn't it be something if the dwarves used this crisis to strip humans of their wealth?

Wouldn't it be something if the dwarfish weapons were used to exterminate the dwarfish race?

Life gets funny that way.

I grunted. He could take that as thoughtful commiseration if he wanted.

He changed the subject. "Have you found anything in the library?"

"No. And I really hoped I could root out something about shapeshifters. That bunch at Weider's were part of something big. If I can learn more about the race I might be able to guess what."

North English didn't get excited. "Tama says you're sorting as you go. I appreciate that. I know gathering information and studying it is important but somehow we just never get around to the library. How did you know about it?"

"I went to the Royal Library. They said I'd do better here or in some wizard's private library. I don't know any friendly wizards."

"Does anybody?"

"You kidding?" But he was talking to himself, bitterly. Maybe he had had an unhappy experience.

I must have risen in his consideration. He was treating me like an old retainer now. Almost with respect. But with cautious lack of trust.

"Did you have a problem with one of our sorcerers?" Wouldn't exactly be unique if he had.

North English realized he had given something away. He didn't like that. "Didn't everyone who visited the Cantard?" Quick shift of subject. "Tama overstepped herself by allowing you into the library without consulting me but it was a good idea. Let me know if you find anything interesting. Max Weider is my friend, too."

I was dismissed. He accentuated the point by closing his eyes. He wanted to rest. He wanted to think, to conjure some way he could take his special breed of liberty to TunFaire with better effect.

I left the room.

I found a crowd outside, frowns prevalent, everybody afraid they'd missed something important. Lost in thought, I ignored them.

Marengo had a connection with a wizard? Should that surprise me? He was a powerful man. Wizards prefer the company of powerful men to that of slobs like me. Why? I can be charming.

Did it even matter?

# 80

Tinnie and Tama eyed me expectantly. I told Tama, "He'll live. And he's in a more charitable mood than I'd have thought. It must have been love at first sight, Tinnie. He wants to adopt you. Offered me three shiny new groats if he could have you for a niece."

"That's not funny, Garrett."

"That's what I told him. I said you don't have any sense of humor. He said, 'Just wait till I tickle her fancy.' "

Tinnie snapped, "Why're you laughing, Tama?"

"I'm trying to visualize those words coming out of Marengo's mouth. It isn't a pretty picture."

I said, "He told me to go ahead with the library. And let him know if we found anything."

Tama said, "Since you have his blessing, you and the niece-apparent go to it. I have work to do." Tama pushed through the crowd. Even mistresses have responsibilities. Freecorps officers continued to gather. Maybe they were worried they might have to look for work.

Tama did what none of them dared. She entered Marengo's sanctuary.

Tinnie murmured, "I don't know what to make of that relationship. Most of the time she acts like she doesn't care."

"She can't afford to, too much," I said. "And she probably wonders about you and me, too."

"What's that supposed to mean?"

"That I don't understand, either, but my New Year's resolution was to stop trying to figure out relationships. I'll deal with what people show me."

Tinnie paused to think. She's bright but she sometimes forgets to wake her brain up before she lets her mouth take off. Two of us doing that at once causes problems.

Dean says we were made for each other.

Dean has said the same thing about me and several bright, picturesque young ladies. He's even said it about me and take my pick of his platoon of homely nieces. Real nieces. Dean believes I need more stability. He doesn't like the way I live.

"Now you're drifting off on me?"

"Didn't get enough sleep last night."

"Bragging or complaining?"

"I was thinking about Dean."

"Why?"

"He's gone. They both are."

"Really?" The news startled Tinnie. "I never thought—"

"It's the times."

"Uhm?" She became very quiet. She didn't say anything until we were back among the books. "Is it permanent, Garrett?"

"What?"

"The split with your partner."

I glanced around. I tapped my ear. You couldn't be sure who was listening. The Call were paranoid by nature. After last night they would be doubly so. "It had to happen. My sympathies aren't what they used to be. Dean wouldn't see things my way. He wouldn't listen to reason."

"And?"

"So they sneaked out."

The facts awed me whenever I recalled that the Dead Man actually let himself be moved. Maybe even *asked* to be moved.

Ah. I could find him. If I could unearth Saucerhead. Tharpe must have been in on it. He was one of very few people the Dead Man would trust to help.

I'd be expected to figure that out for myself. Far be it from my pet fruit bat to speak up.

"If the split is permanent . . ." There was an edge to Tinnie's voice. She had something in mind. Maybe something risky.

The Goddamn Parrot shuddered and twitched, fell off his perch. He flopped around amongst the books. Dust flew. Inarticulate noises spewed from his beak.

"I don't know." I stared. Had something happened to the Dead Man? The bird seemed to be trying to talk. Maybe His Nibs was making a desperate effort to get through.

Or maybe darkness was overtaking him at last.

Maybe, before he checked out, he would be kind enough to share his thoughts about what he'd overheard.

If he'd been paying attention. Chances were he'd fallen asleep and this was one of his nightmares leaking.

Tinnie said, "He's been acting strange for a long time."

I opened a book. "How would you know what's strange for that runt condor? You weren't in on getting me stuck with him, were you?" Her sense of humor could include a prank like the Goddamn Parrot. Especially if she thought I deserved it.

"No. But I think Morley showed a lot of flair, finding him."

"That Morley is a piece of work, isn't he?" I grumped.

"Are we going to move in out here?" Tinnie asked. "I haven't been home for days. I imagine Uncle Willard is starting to steam."

"He'll boil over when he finds out you were with me."

"He likes you, Garrett."

"Sure. From a distance."

"He's not blind or stupid."

In a minute we'd be back to me moving into the Tate compound. "You want me to take you home?"

"I don't think my cute new uncle can do it for a while. Besides, he tickles."

I looked around. We'd been through scores of books. That didn't amount to ten percent of the heap. Less if some of the drifts had formed atop dunes of documents not immediately evident.

I didn't want to leave. The library was a great excuse to hang around the heart of The Call. Just being at the North English place would put me next to a lot of interesting stuff. Nobody would notice me after a while. I would become part of the furniture.

"This is a great opportunity . . ." No sense letting Tinnie in on everything. What she didn't know she couldn't share with friends whose politics were suspect.

"I understand that. I don't want you to waste it. But Uncle Willard will be foaming at the mouth."

"Especially when he hears what you've been doing."

She grinned. Those devils wakened in her eyes. "We could give him one more reason for—"

"Wicked, wicked woman. Right here?"

"Look around. Nobody ever comes in here—"

*Click!* The door opened. "Excuse me. I hate to interrupt, but—"

"That's all right, Ed," I told the stiff-backed officer.

He winced. "The old man asked me to include you in our response to a problem that's just come up. He told me I'd find you here."

"He was right again. What kind of problem?"

"Murder."

"Ah, shit. Not again." I shed some dust and the book I was pretending to skim. "What can I do?"

"The old man says you're the expert." Ed looked Tinnie over. He had no trouble with his sexual identity and was one hundred percent in favor of redheads.

The guy might be all right after all.

"Let's go."

# 81

As we descended the front steps, I said, "Ed, I need to take Miss Tate home sometime today. She's overdue. Her folks will be worried."

"Why tell me?"

"I didn't think Venable and his lovable lizards would care and you've got the next closest interest in security here, right? I thought you'd want to know who's coming and going and why."

"If you want to do me a courtesy, I'd prefer you called me Lieutenant, not Ed." His voice was brittle.

I was supposed to be cowed. "All right, Ed. I won't call you Ed no more. But don't look for any military crap. I'm out of that. I don't need it, don't appreciate it, don't like it. If it helps, think of me as a civilian contractor."

He didn't warm to that idea. Civilians are not to be trusted. You don't have enough control. But he said, "All right, Mr. Garrett. On that basis. Call me Mr. Nagit."

"Or Lieutenant?"

"Or Lieutenant. Yes."

Tinnie was tagging along. The Goddamn Parrot had adopted her shoulder for the time being. One of them snickered. I have my suspicions which though both my trials showed straight faces. I asked, "You interested in a parrot, Mr. Nagit?"

"I don't think so."

"He can talk."

"Then definitely not, Mr. Garrett. But when you decide to get rid of the other one . . ." He chuckled.

"Make me an offer." I chuckled, too.

"Garrett!"

"Sorry, darling."

Mr. Nagit smiled. We'd made peace. For the moment.

Mr. Nagit led us toward the front gate. A crowd had gathered out there. More men were headed that way. I said, "These guys need something to do."

"The old man said give them a day to recuperate. But you're right. Uhn! What's this mess?"

We had come to the torn-up part of the lawn. I said, "I noticed this yesterday. I asked Miss Montezuma about it. She didn't know what happened."

Mr. Nagit eyeballed the hoofprints. He moved a few steps this way, a few steps that. I tagged along. He observed, "There were at least a dozen animals involved. Pretty light. And poorly shod. Came this way from the gate, swung around there, then went back. They were galloping when they came up to the turn but they walked back down."

I agreed. "They were chasing somebody."

"This may connect with our murder." Nagit started toward the gate, reconsidered the battered ground. "Sure made a mess."

A mess. Bane of the military mind. "Maybe they were playing with their prey."

"What kind of people would? . . ."

"Tinnie and I saw a band of centaurs when we were coming out here." I described the circumstances. No point being secretive. I'd told North English already and suspected he might have said a word to Mr. Nagit.

"Centaurs? Hmm."

Meanwhile Tinnie tried to shush the Goddamn Parrot. That clown rooster was having a mild fit. I asked, "Do birds behave strangely around here, Mr. Nagit?"

"Not that I've noticed."

"That buzzard's had two seizures this morning. I thought he might've picked up something."

"Not here."

We soldiered on. Toward, it developed, the cluster of evergreens just inside the gate.

I observed, "These people shouldn't be tracking all over the murder scene."

"I understand that. I told everyone to stay out of the trees."

"The body in there?"

"See for yourself."

# 82

I saw for myself.

Mr. Nagit bullied the freecorps thugs into moving back. I did admire their discipline.

There wasn't much smell yet but the flies were plentiful. They're always the first to know. I heard them before I saw anything.

The first dead thing wasn't human. It used to be a wild dog. Before something left nothing but a head and some feet and fur and odd bits of bone scattered amongst the well-tossed pine needles.

I heard a little "Tee-hee." I looked over my shoulder and wasn't surprised to see my one-eyed, lizard-loving buddy Venable checking another savaged remnant of wild Rover.

"Did your babies do this?"

He tittered. "Killed the wild dogs and ate them, they did, yes. And never laid a claw on Stucker. He was dead already. They won't touch carrion unless they're absolutely starving. Even then, sometimes, the strong males will eat the weak ones before they touch cold meat. Hee."

The dining preferences of his pets didn't interest me. Mr. Nagit was less intrigued than I. I asked, "What's this about Stucker? He looked pretty healthy when I saw him a few minutes ago."

Venable looked baffled.

Soon I saw why.

Stucker's corpse was naked. It was dirty and far from fresh. The wild dogs had been at him during the night, long before my glimpse of him in the house a while ago.

There was no doubt he'd been dead half a day before the dogs found him. I muttered, "But he was at supper with us last night."

The pine needles were well stirred. Here and there, in the soft soil beneath, were clear hoofprints.

"Why didn't they bury him?" I wondered aloud.

"They did. Over there," Venable told me. "Just not deep enough. The dogs dug him up. We pulled him over here and brushed him off before we sent for the lieutenant."

I wanted to scream and give Venable a good throttling. But that would do no good now.

I reminded Mr. Nagit that, "We saw centaurs on the road just north of here yesterday. And nobody was on the gate when we got here. We were talking about that when Stucker came out of here still pulling up his pants. I figured he'd gone off to take a dump. But . . ."

Mr. Nagit looked puzzled.

"The boss will understand. It's a matter of shapeshifters. Killer shapeshifters."

The light dawned. "He told us how he handled a couple of those at the Weider masque. I thought they'd all been captured."

"Some were. And used their abilities to get away. There seem to be an awful lot of them around. They keep turning up."

"We'd better grab the Stucker back at the house."

"Good idea. Only I'll bet we don't find him."

"Why not?"

"If you were him up there and saw this mob down here, what would you think?"

"That we found the body." Mr. Nagit showed me his comradely smile.

It wasn't that endearing. Venable's pets smiled that way while they waited for your friendly status to evaporate.

"Exactly. What else strange has happened the past few weeks? Any assaults? Unexplained deaths? Mysterious thefts? People supposedly seen two places at the same time?" The shifters seemed to have the solution to that difficulty worked out, though.

"No." Mr. Nagit barked at the freecorps fighters gradually pushing into the grove, wanting to sneak a peek at disaster. He fingerpointed half a dozen. "You men go up to the house. Grab Stucker."

"But—"

"If you see Stucker it won't *be* Stucker. Stucker's right there. Already starting to ferment. Get moving."

I observed, "That'll teach those guys to get so close an officer notices them."

Nagit smiled again. This had to be a record day. "I suppose it will." He glared around like he was thinking of something else that had to be done. Men backed away.

There was a lot of soldier in those guys still.

"Settle down!" I snapped at the Goddamn Parrot. Having decided he didn't love Tinnie anymore, he had jumped to my shoulder where he was practicing some weird tribal fertility dance.

Lieutenant Nagit said, "Looks like he's trying to see the body but you keep moving."

He was taking up for the bird? "Maybe he's hungry. He's a vulture in disguise. Venable. Think he could play with your pets?"

No?

That wonder buzzard is so damned useless I can't even turn him into lizard bait.

# 83

There was no sign of pseudo-Stucker. Surprise, surprise. The shifter was somebody else now.

So I was not surprised when I spied one Carter Stockwell, known shapechanger, drifting behind the crowd, moving toward the front gate. Evidently it never occurred to anyone else to wonder why an unfamiliar fellow would be wearing the same clothes Stucker had had on for the past two days.

"There's our man," I told Nagit. "Right there. That face is the one he wears whenever he's not replacing someone."

Nagit looked at me narrowly, briefly—then gestured several men closer. "How do you know that, Mr. Garrett?"

"I've run into this shifter before. He always collapses into this shape." Did that make sense?

It did to me.

The creatures really did have to be psychic when it came to threats. Carter looked at me suddenly, as though responding to my interest. He lengthened his stride immediately.

"He knows I've made him, Mr. Nagit."

The lieutenant gave orders quickly, softly. Everyone hurried to execute them. These freecorps boys took their military stuff seriously.

The mob took off after Stockwell, determined little turtles vainly coursing a hare. Stockwell changed as we watched, his legs lengthening until a foot of calf showed below each cuff. He bounded away, gaining ground fast. He circled the tent city and disappeared into the woods beyond.

"Wow," Mr. Nagit said. "That's what I call putting on a burst of speed." He kept a straight face.

Stockwell dwindled into the distance. What was his connection with the centaurs?

There had to be one. Tinnie and I had run into centaurs just up the road. Minutes later the Stucker look-alike, still buttoning his trousers, comes out of the very copse where later we find what's left of the real Stucker. Just downhill from a lot of ruined pasture. "The torn-up turf. The way it was torn up. Those centaurs helped catch the real Stucker for the changer." Which meant that there must be a common mission between the centaurs and shapeshifters. Which I thought the Dead Man, with his special interest in things and personalities out of the Cantard, would find very intriguing indeed. I might even tell him about it. Someday.

The Goddamn Parrot took flight. That little traitor would give the news away first chance he got. For free. Apparently out of practice flying, he had trouble staying straight and level getting across to Tinnie.

"How do I spot one of those things if they come back? Or if there're more of them around?"

"I'm trying to find out. That's why I was in the library. But I hadn't found anything yet. I do know they don't like silver. Not even a little. You could whap everybody with a solid silver ugly stick every once in a while. Why would they replace a low-level guy like Stucker?"

Nagit looked at me like he had sudden doubts about my smarts. "He was on the gate eighteen hours a day. He saw everyone who came and went. Valuable information to a lot of people, I'd think. Plus he had the run of the house in his free time. He could've dug around in there whenever he wanted."

"The perfect spy. He was good, too. I didn't know him so he had no trouble with me but he did fool Miss Montezuma at dinner last night."

"Stucker was the perfect target. He was a loner. Nobody knew him very well. Everybody knew he was totally committed to the movement, though. He did everything possible, in spite of his social handicaps. So the boss always said. You'd never suspect him."

Unless the replacement Stucker never got a chance to bury the man he replaced deeply enough. On account of that meddlesome Garrett turning up. I shivered, thinking a dark wing had brushed my soul. In Stockwell's place I might have paid me a deadly visit during the night.

I assumed the boss was right about the original Stucker. "You had doubts?"

"About Stucker? Never. The man had a minor job. He did it well. I notice people only when they don't do their jobs well."

"I see." I also saw that Tinnie was headed our way, oblivious to the moon-eyes around her. The woman put a definite strain upon these superior beings' commitment to correct behavior.

Every man in sight hated my bones the instant she slipped her arm inside mine.

She purred, "How much longer are you going to be?"

"I don't know, darling. This's another shapeshifter incident. The gatekeeper was a changeling."

"Too bad. He seemed nice."

"We only met the shifter. The real gatekeeper was dead before we got here."

Tinnie glanced that way. She flushed.

I said, "It isn't pretty. Wild dogs got after him. Then Venable's little pals got after the wild dogs."

"I know that, Garrett. What about you being much longer?"

I wasn't looking forward to facing Uncle Willard. "Mr. Nagit, I'm going to take the lady home. I'll be back."

Mr. Nagit wasn't completely thrilled. "Do what you need to do. I'll leave word to let you in."

In parting I suggested, "Venable might try to set his pets on that shifter's trail. If you do catch him, I definitely want to talk to him."

Nagit scowled. "I suppose—Now what?"

The soldiers had begun to stir.

"Looks like somebody's coming."

Yes, indeed. And it was somebody who liked his ceremony. He had outriders out, fore and aft, in numbers sufficient to stave off small armies. A guy who didn't look old enough to be a veteran hobbled up. "It's Colonel Theverly, Lieutenant. He's coming."

And he'd be in a bad mood after last night, too, I expected.

Tinnie scrunched up close. "This looks like a real good time to start hiking, boyfriend."

"Probably."

"Uncle Willard won't be the only one mad at you if these people suddenly get all paranoid about us." Which, on reflection, seemed entirely possible. The returning freecorps people we were about to encounter had no way of knowing that we were accepted guests. And good old Colonel Theverly always had been one to leave a lot of unfamiliar bodies around for the gods to sort out.

Renewing acquaintance with Theverly could wait. I expected to be back before nightfall. We could get together then.

Tinnie and I got out of the gateway to The Pipes only moments before the leading horsemen turned in. We stood across the road and gawked at the cavalcade. Quite a few cavaliers gawked right back at the redhead. Me, I just stood there wrapped in my cloak of invisibility.

Once we did start toward town the Goddamn Parrot began to get excited. He sounded like he was trying to talk again. What language wasn't clear, however.

"He can't stand country life," I explained to Tinnie. "Heh-heh. Maybe I can lose him in the woods."

# 84

"Speaking of woods," Tinnie said. She gestured to indicate the last copse we'd traversed before we'd gotten to The Pipes coming out. "What became of all those people you said were following us?" She'd seen the feather of smoke leaning above the treetops.

"A question definitely worth consideration, my dear," I said. "Perhaps I should've offered to borrow something sharp before we left your new uncle's establishment."

"You sure should've. It's obvious we can't rely on your rapier wit."

"How sharper than a frog's tooth. I shouldn't have run so fast when that goddess wanted to be my girlfriend."

"You? Run from anything female?"

"She was green and had four arms. And teeth like one of Mr. Venable's pets. But she was affectionate."

"I'll bet. There's somebody in those trees."

Her eyes were better than mine. I didn't see anything. But I took her word. She wouldn't joke about danger. Much. I picked up a stick. "This would be handy if it wasn't rotten." It would shatter the first time I knighted somebody. But if I carried it maybe folks would be discouraged from getting close enough to find out that it was mostly decorative. I mused, "I need to stop by the house and arm up."

"I'd help but I really need to go home. Uncle Willard's proba-bly going crazy."

I told the Goddamn Parrot, "The lady's a gold seam of straight lines but I'm a gentleman." I spotted movement at the wood's edge. Someone wasn't good at sitting still. Then I spotted more movement elsewhere. "I hope those people aren't all working together."

They weren't, apparently, but they were aware of one another and wanted to stay out of each other's way. Which made for a lot of rustle and scurry as Tinnie and I strolled through the wood.

"These are the people you never noticed before?"

"They're city boys. They don't do quite as well when they're surrounded by a whole lot of country."

"A not uncommon problem, evidently."

"Hey!"

"I'm starting to think that you've been telling tall tales about you and the Marines. Tell the truth. You were really the guy who mopped the floors at expeditionary headquarters, weren't you?"

"You found me out. Don't tell anybody. They'll kick me out of The Call. Then what would I do for entertainment?"

"You could always harass yourself."

"Wouldn't want to horn in on your only hobby."

Tinnie took my hand. We ambled. We strolled. She didn't appear to be in a real hurry to ease Uncle Willard's anxiety.

Those following me didn't intrude. Guess they just wanted to play follow the leader.

# 85

"It's a different city."

Tinnie felt it, too, though nothing was immediately obvious to the eye. There were ample crowds of all ethnic persuasions working hard doing the things that need doing to keep a city going. "Nobody's talking to anybody."

She was right. And it wasn't just that. People were being careful to give one another room and especially careful not to expose their backs to anyone not of a like ethnic conviction.

It was a wary city. Everybody expected something big to happen. Probably sometime soon.

The Call's adventure hadn't been quite the disaster the boys at The Pipes imagined. The world was waiting for the other shoe to fall. When Marengo figured that out . . .

I was alert, yet not paying close attention. If you can figure that. I ran everything through my head again, trying to find a thread of sense to pick at. But it wouldn't hang together in one big, stinky lump no matter how much I twisted and shoehorned and ignored the usual rules. I could only get it going if I assumed two or more things were going on at the same time. But something down inside me wanted it to be just one big thing that I wasn't seeing right.

"You're the common factor," Tinnie said.

"Huh?" I looked around. We were approaching the Tate compound.

"You were muttering. Doing pretty good, too. You might have a future as a street character. You've already got the wardrobe."

The Goddamn Parrot released a startled blat more like crow

slang than the king's parrotese. He flung himself into the air and flapped away. I barked, "What the hell?" Couldn't be my luck turning good.

Tinnie asked, "How did you wake him up?"

"I don't know." But I had a suspicion what was behind his excitement. What's big and sits in the dark and doesn't breathe a lot? "I'm a common thread but I came in after the fact." The Goddamn Parrot disappeared between buildings. "The way my luck runs nothing will get him."

"You going to come inside?" Tinnie asked. She grinned. She knew I didn't want to deal with Uncle Willard.

"I have to get back into that library." We crossed the street. I noted that most people moved around in large groups and that more weapons than usual were in evidence, some of them quite illegal.

"Can't stay away from Tama Montezuma's bony butt, eh?"

"Has she got a bony behind? I never noticed. I see no one else but you." I damaged my case by noticing a devastating set of twins exiting the Tate retail outlet.

"When you stop shaking and get your heels off your tongue you might try for something a little more convincing."

"Damn." Right behind the twins, chattering at them, came Tinnie's cousin Rose. Rose is a brunette as gorgeous as her cousin but she's got snakes and spiders for brains. Her face lit up like a bonfire when she saw me. "Here comes trouble," I said.

"She's not bad if you understand her," Tinnie said. "She'll try to make something out of me being with you but Uncle Willard will say, 'So what?' and she'll go off and have a good pout." She planted a long, unsisterly kiss on me. "Be careful. Come see me. And stay away from strange women."

"Make up your mind." I kissed her back. Rose was scandalized and excited. "I won't be gone long." I hoped circumstance wouldn't make a liar of me. It did have a habit of doing so.

# 86

I moved carefully homeward. I hadn't spotted a tail since we left that woods, but I was getting used to the idea that I could be followed without being able to catch somebody doing it. I didn't like it, though.

I was more concerned about the new malice in the streets. Trouble has a way of finding people who look like they're vulnerable.

I spent a little concern on the Goddamn Parrot, too, but because I had no control over that situation I did not let it interfere with business.

Approaching the house cautiously is ancient habit. It felt justified today, though I saw nothing indicating trouble—unless the absence of Mrs. Cardonlos constituted a harbinger. Nor did I note any damage to the house itself. Clearly, the bad boys had not yet worked up the nerve to give it a try.

I let myself inside—and froze before I shut the door all the way. Something was wrong. I smelled an odor that didn't belong.

Somebody had been inside. Somebody who wore lilac water to disguise the fact that he found bathing an unhappy chore. Maybe Saucerhead? Tharpe wasn't a stickler when it came to personal hygiene. Or maybe Winger?

Not Winger. Nothing was disturbed. Winger couldn't keep her hands off stuff.

I moved along the hall slowly, avoiding the creaky boards. I don't know what cues there were, other than odor, but I knew I wasn't alone. Which meant somebody had gotten past the wonderfully expensive lock that Dean had had installed.

I told him that damned thing was a waste of money.

I slipped sideways, not into my office but into the Dead Man's room. Amongst the memorabilia were tools useful for removing uninvited guests. I returned to the hallway prepared to repel boarders. I had everything but my eye patch and my parrot.

A mountain of blubber wobbled out of the kitchen, a platter in each hand. "Puddle!" I barked.

"Hey! Garrett! I was just havin' a snack while I was waitin'. How the hell did ya get in wit'out me hearin'?"

"How the hell did you get into my house? And why? To swipe my food?"

"I come in tru' da door. Ya got to get ya a better lock, Garrett. Dem Hameways ain't shit, ya know what ye're doin'. Ya get out an get yaself a Piggleton combernation with da t'ree tumblers . . ." As he nattered Puddle eased into my office. It was obvious that he'd made himself at home there and that he'd been around for a while. And that he was used to having busboys there to pick up after him. He plopped the platters onto my desk, atop the abandoned battle-fields of previous snacks. My personal chair groaned as his ample behind settled.

"Make yourself at home, Puddle."

"T'anks."

"To what do I owe the honor?" I wondered where the food had come from. Puddle definitely wasn't thoughtful enough to have brought his own supplies. Dean must have taken pity. Obviously, I couldn't take care of myself. Well, the whole move-out thing was just for show. For the benefit of my new political pals. I hoped.

"Boss wants ya, Garrett. Sent people out wherever ya might turn up."

"What's the story?" I snagged a chicken drumstick I knew hadn't been in the house last time I was home. I supposed I could hunt up Mrs. Cardonlos and sweet-talk her into telling me what I'd been missing.

Was that a gang of pigs oinking as they fluttered around my chimney?

"Boss'll tell ya all about it." Puddle had his mouth full. Maybe it was him making the porker noises.

"Give me a few minutes, then we'll do it." I headed upstairs. There's a linen closet in the second-floor hall that has no linens in it. I spent a few minutes filling my sleeves and pockets and shoe-tops with assorted instruments of mayhem. I should think about buying a couple of eggs from Venable when I got back to The Pipes. I could hatch them and keep pets around the place if the

Dead Man decided not to come back. If I kept them a little hungry, even wizards off the Hill would have trouble sneaking in.

When I got back downstairs Puddle was digging around in the kitchen again. He had no shame. "I don't get much a dis tasty stuff 'round Da Palms."

"You could've picked a boss with fewer quirks."

Puddle grunted. "Ya ready ta go?" He shoved a couple of pieces of chicken into his pockets.

"Not quite." I needed to get outside some food myself. It had been a long time since breakfast.

# 87

Sometimes I've got an edge like a brick. We must've traveled half a mile before I realized, "Hey! We're not headed for The Palms."

"An' I tole da boss ya'd never notice. Dey's people followin' ya, ya know? An' dey's maybe not all da kind what ya want to know ya got da boss for a fren'."

"There's times I wonder about that myself," I grumbled, having noticed a green and red and yellow and blue ringer amongst the nearest gang of eaves-perching pigeons. A puff of cooler wind raced down the street, which seemed unnaturally calm for late afternoon in a city mad for bickering. Autumn would be along soon. Maybe, if I got lucky, the Goddamn Parrot would have a little goose in him and would head north for the winter.

I suspected we were headed for Playmate's stables, though, as a gods-fearing, righteous man Playmate doesn't have much use for Morley. Any tail who knew much about me probably developed the suspicion before I did. I wasn't concentrating. I had found a thread to worry.

We rounded a corner, turning left. Puddle was street side of me. Two steps later he leaned into me. Hard. I staggered through an open doorway. Before I could growl Puddle started pushing. I just glimpsed an old woman squinting at something she was sewing and a homely youngster probably of the female calling who shut the door behind the fat man. Then we reached the end of the narrow, almost barren tailor shop. I looked down steep steps. A light burned a long way below. "Go," Puddle urged.

I went.

A door closed behind us. It hung crookedly. The stairs had no business surviving our combined weight. Puddle picked up the light off the earthen cellar floor once we got down. It consisted of a cracked teacup half-filled with oil. The wick was a floating glob of lint. Puddle could carry the damned thing. It looked hot. And he knew where we were headed.

"Morley really this concerned?"

"Bad tings goin' on out dere, Garrett. It don't hurt none ta be careful."

Everybody in town was more paranoid than me. Maybe I should get a little crazy myself. "It'll all work out. History's drama has got a way of doing that." But it sure can get rough on the cast and crew.

"Ya ever go ta da plays? Dey's a great new one at da Strand, I been ta see it t'ree times already. Called *Atterbohns da Toid* on account of it's about King Atterbohns, one a da ones from way back."

I was surprised. The Strand doesn't put on the kind of show I'd associate with a mind like Puddle's. Hardly anybody would take their clothes off.

The more excited he grew the denser his speech became. "Dat's da Atterbohns what murdered his brodder and married his sister an' had a baby by her dat grew up ta help his gran'ma raise dis army against his fodder . . ." He whooped off and gave me every detail, half of which were historically inaccurate. Not having seen the drama myself I couldn't tell if the fault was his or the playwright's. The historical Atterbohns married his brother's widow, his sister-in-law, a perfectly respectable thing for the time, though murder was a bit of a gaffe. Less respectable was the fact that the sister-in-law orchestrated everything, including numerous other murders and the revolt of the son—who perished, along with his grandmother, in questionable circumstances later, to be followed to the throne by a six-year-old brother whose paternity was somewhat dubious.

A play about Atterbohns III would have to be one of the new tragedies. Its moral would be too dark and heavy for a passion play or traditional comedy. "I might go see it just to see how much license the playwright took with history. Who wrote it?"

"I dunno. We get ta da end a dis tunnel, ya gotta be quiet. It runs inta anudder one dat ain't ours. We don't wanna attrack no attention."

TunFaire has a million secrets. They probably extend two miles down into the earth and two up into the air. Were there enough overlapping tunnels for me to sneak all the way downtown to the brewery caverns? That sent me into a tumult of speculation. If all the tunnels and caverns under TunFaire *were* connected, control of them would be a major asset.

There were rumors and legends about people and things supposedly living underground. One beaut involved a king of the rat-people who was a sort of cross between a high priest and Chodo Contague, a ratman wish-fantasy, something a Reliance would be if he had a whole lot of brains and guts and luck.

Surprisingly, none of the legends featured dwarves.

Puddle made a right turn when the tunnel ended. I stayed quiet, as instructed. Eventually we found a stairway from the same litter as the one leading down from the seamtress's shop. A door stood ajar at the top. A gray light outlined it. I let Puddle get all the way up before I risked the steps myself. Having survived him I knew they would support me.

I stepped into the entry foyer of a tenement that decades ago had entertained middle-class pretensions. Not a soul was around. The place even lacked the usual squallings of infants, yellings of husbands and fathers, shriekings of wives and mothers, whimpers of despair that characterize such places. But you could almost feel the tenants holding their breaths behind their curtained doorways. The cellar door standing ajar must be an omen of dreadful portent.

Puddle was puffing so hard I thought he'd collapse. He wasted no energy. He used his gasps to extinguish the light, which he left on the step behind the cellar door. He closed that.

We hit the street. Five blocks later we joined Morley in a dwarfish hole-in-the-wall. None of the hairy folk seemed to mind his elven blood.

"What was that all about?" I asked. "Other than the obvious."

"The people following you have a supernatural knack for keeping track. I wanted to test its limits."

"That's all?"

"There's more. In back." He nodded. I preceded him past a dwarfish staff who saw nothing. We were ghosts.

The quest for profit makes for strange bedfellows.

# 88

Spooky people were waiting in a back room. Belinda Contague and Pular Singe sat beside a crippled table with rags piled on top. "What's this?"

Morley let me have it behind the ear with a sap.

I said, "Wha de grungle frunz ya? . . . ." It made perfect sense to me but apparently not to anyone else. At least nobody tried to answer me.

The darkness never really came. Not entirely. I remained vaguely aware of being manhandled and womanhandled and rathandled and half-elf handled around till I was the vain wearer of a tonsorial array fit to embarrass most guys who haunt alleys for a living. Puddle stuffed everything in a bag—including my proud tools of mayhem—and vanished. Morley and Belinda tied me to the rickety chair formerly occupied by Pular Singe. Singe said something apologetic and drifted off after Puddle.

The scow of consciousness pitched and rolled across heavy seas. The thump had reawakened every headache I'd enjoyed lately. I talked some more but only a drunk would have understood. Or maybe Singe. I'd understood her.

Morley said something about if I was the real thing, he'd treat me to the gourmet best of The Palms. I could not express my joy.

Belinda's apologies sounded more promising.

The two of them rubbed me all over with silver.

A dwarfish voice gobbled something. Morley responded in the same tongue. Belinda began letting me loose. I tried to turn her over my knee but had barely strength enough to raise a hand. I said something in a tongue that sounded sufficiently dwarfish to me but drew no response from anyone else.

I understood Belinda when she said, "You hit him too hard."

"I hit him just right. Too hard and he wouldn't be breathing."

"I think you scrambled his brains."

"Be a little hard to mix them up more than they already are. He'll come out of it."

Bless him for his optimism. I would take it into account when I got even for all his abuses.

"Sorry," he told me, not sounding the least bit contrite. "We had to make sure Puddle got the real you. Been several Garrett sightings lately and I'm sure that, talented as you are, you're not yet able to be two places at once."

"I'm gonna work on it, though," I promised. "I'm gonna be having dinner with Relway and Colonel Block while I'm stuffing that talking vulture down your throat. Sideways."

Some of that dribbled out in comprehensible Karentine. Morley seemed surprised by my attitude. But he didn't let it get in his way. "Something that looked like you turned up at The Palms last night asking for Belinda."

I glanced at Belinda. She was still hanging out there? "Not what you think, Garrett," she said. "Crask and Sadler did such a good job I can still barely move."

Morley continued, "We knew it wasn't you right away."

"Uhn?" So a shapeshifter went there pretending to be me. If there was an easy way to recognize one, I wanted to know. Later. After my head stopped hurting.

"Sarge offered you a mixed pepper platter. One of his little jokes. But you took it and dug right in."

"Now I know they're completely stupid." Even a hog has more sense than to eat peppers. Morley's pepper platter is a gorgeous mix of colors and shapes. Kind of like parrot on a plate. Just the stench, though, would've had me gagging—if I'd been into self-abuse far enough to let Sarge shove something that nasty under my nose in the first place. "What did you do with it?" In a few hours one of those critters could destroy a reputation I've worked on for years.

"We caught him but he got away as soon as we turned our backs. Those things don't have bones, apparently. It got out through a crack barely big enough for a cat."

My brain was up to about half speed. And I had a cup in hand, brought by the dwarf, which smelled strongly of boiled willow bark. I'd only have to suffer the headache another hour, then make sure I never ranged too far from a chamber pot. "Let me see. It was after Belinda. With harm in mind?"

"We took more hardware off it than we did off you just now."

"Stranger and stranger. We have shapeshifters attacking the Weiders. We have them attacking The Call. We have them going after Belinda. . . ." I stopped. My mouth hung open. A small but significant fact had caught up. "Belinda. You've been at Morley's place since we dug you out of that tomb?"

"Mostly sleeping."

"But you've been in touch with your people."

"As much as necessary."

"How about with Marengo North English?"

"North English? Why would I? . . ."

I raised a paw. "Wait." I let the brain limp along for a minute. "The Call tried to bring on their season of Cleansing last night."

"It fizzled," Morley said. He showed lots of pointy teeth in a wicked grin. He wasn't disappointed.

"While the rest of his gang were having a good time bopping heads and busting shop doors Marengo North English was up north on the edge of Elf Town expecting to meet Belinda for a night's indulgence in the labors of love."

"What?" she barked. "How could? . . ."

"He got a message. It told him to meet you up there. He believed it was real." I'd believed it was real when he told me. "Men sometimes surrender to wishful thinking." If I'd thought about her condition, I'd have been suspicious as soon as North English mentioned getting the message. Her family owned tenements in the area. It seemed a handy trysting place if you thought in sneakaround terms. Obviously, Marengo did. "When he got there a gang dressed up as rightsists tried to murder him. They got interrupted by a gang of dwarves looking for rightsists to pound."

"A marvelous irony," Morley observed, absolutely straight of face.

"I thought so myself." I managed a feeble smile. The first weak efforts of the tea had begun to make my fingertips tingle and my headache less assertive. "There is a common thread in everything," I said. "However confusing. Shapeshifters. All evidently members of a group of commando mercenaries once known as Black Dragon Valsung."

"What about Crask and Sadler?" Belinda asked. "They aren't shapechangers."

"Maybe I'm not thinking as clearly as I imagined." My headache gave a particularly unpleasant throb. Probably Crask and Sadler wishing me evil from their cell, if they were still healthy enough to entertain wishes. "They were hired by shapeshifters." Just to keep my theory alive.

"Or by somebody who hired the shifters, too," Morley said, knowing that would put a twist on the evidence that I wouldn't like.

I grunted. "Keep in mind that Glory Mooncalled has got to be shoehorned in here somehow, too. I'm pretty sure." Seeing those centaurs had convinced me. Organized, disciplined, military centaurs always have something to do with Glory Mooncalled. No other commander had ever been able to to hold their attention long enough to sell them on the military virtues. No other captain ever got them to fight for ideas instead of money or plunder.

Pular Singe eased into the room diffidently. I wondered what had become of Fenibro. Maybe she'd decided she could get along without the boyfriend. I had yet to see her affliction handicap her very much. "The watchers have followed the parcel of clothing." She spoke slowly and carefully. Her diction was the equal of Fenibro's. She was proud of herself. "I will have no trouble tracking any but one. One leaves no trail at all."

I frowned at Morley. He shrugged. Belinda said, "It shouldn't take them long to figure out that Puddle doesn't have Garrett's bones in that sack."

"Point taken. Can you walk, Garrett?"

"In circles."

Pular Singe said, "The one who leaves no trail is like the one who pretended to be . . ." She pointed at me. "That one had no scent, either."

Interesting. Could that be a way to detect changers? Add a rat-man to your bodyguard?

# 89

"Who had a chance to plant something on you?" Morley asked. We were headed toward Playmate's for real. Dotes was the only one of us walking normally. At a glance we must have looked like beggars. I was dressed the part.

The clothes I'd been wearing lately all came from the Weider place. All Tad's stuff. Could have been anyone there though the list of suspects that occurred to me was very short. And it had to be somebody at the Weider mansion. Nowhere else had anyone had a chance to get to all the clothes. And only a few people there had known I was getting them.

The actual mechanics did not interest me much. Somewhere in each pair of trousers, perhaps, would be a scrap of paper or a loose button with a spell attached. I could round up a dozen half-baked hedge wizards in an hour who would sell me something similar for enough to buy a bottle of wine. There would be some gimmick like an enchanted tuning fork or a feather floating in a bowl of mineral oil that would point at me all the time.

"It's starting to come together," I said. "I don't know who or why but I'm beginning to sniff out a how."

"Well?" Morley asked after I failed to go on.

I turned to Pular Singe. "Singe. The parade following me . . . following Puddle and my stuff. Was the shapeshifter the one who was actually on my trail, with everyone else following him?"

Singe had to think about it. Although she was intensely interested, she hadn't been included in on everything so wasn't sure what mattered. Also, some of what she had was human stuff that made little sense to ratfolk, anyway.

"The one who had no scent. Yes."

Morley asked, "What's that look mean, Garrett?"

"It means the haze is clearing. The clothes were marked so I could be tracked and watched. By shapeshifters. The clothes were delivered straight from the Weider place. Before the engagement party. But there were no shapeshifters inside the house before the party preparations began. Belinda. You promise me you didn't have anything to do with the attack on Marengo North English?"

"I promise, darling. Cross my heart and hope to die. Though I would've done it if it needed doing."

"Does that extend to all his crackpot pals? The human rights movement lost several big names."

"I'd reached an understanding with those people. They would stay off our turf. They hadn't had time to violate it. I'm sure they would've gotten around to it, though."

"Not even using Crask and Sadler?"

"I'm not as hotheaded as you think, Garrett. I considered that. I decided that the Marengo I met thought too much of himself and his prejudices to have hired those two. He'd use his own people. I suspect that argument holds for other rightsists chieftains as well. First try, at least."

I recalled Tama telling me they were having trouble finding a librarian because Marengo and the other big fish were reluctant to pay actual wages. I muttered, "That fits."

"What does?"

"Singe. How would you go about tracking the one who leaves no scent?" I added deaf sign so we were sure to meet on a common border between our languages.

Pular Singe was a serious young woman, determined to get the most out of the abilities she had. She would go far if she remained motivated. Desire and determination do seem as important as raw talent in this world. She thought hard. "I would track those who follow it. The sight-hunters. If they do not give up that when they discover that you have outwitted it."

I hadn't outwitted anybody but myself lately. Didn't seem to be much point in reminding Singe, though.

Morley and Belinda both sneered at me when Singe was looking the other way. Friends always have to get those little digs in, just to let you know they love you. The evidence suggests that the whole world loves me.

"No point me hiding out at Playmate's," I said. "If they've done any digging into my background, they'll know we're friends.

I'll go to the Weider place." I'd abandoned hope of getting back to The Pipes. It was getting dark. "Singe . . . Where'd she go?"

"Off to tail your tail, probably," Morley said.

"She's infatuated, Garrett," Belinda chided. "It happens to a lot of women when they first meet you. This one's still at that stage where she'll do any damn fool thing to make you like her back. Give her a week. Reality will catch up."

They both had a good snicker. So did something on a windowsill two stories overhead. Morley failed to catch the flash of green and yellow and blue and red as the little buzzard took off, but I did. Possibly I was supposed to, now that it knew where I could be found later.

# 90

"Pardon the expression but you look like shit on a stick," Max told me. "I've seen better-dressed bums. What happened to the clothes we gave you?"

Gilbey said, "That's what he's come about." Manvil was a little cool.

"I didn't turn up here sometime in the last twenty hours and do something unpleasant, did I?"

"No. Why?" Gilbey was just tired.

"There was a copy of me running around trying to do naughty things. And you seem a little standoffish."

"Excuse me. Unintentional. Possibly it's because you haven't gotten anywhere. Or because bad things happen when you're around."

I took it like a man. It was true. "I think that's about to change. It's coming together. What I want to know right now is who handled the clothing you sent me. Because somebody tagged them all with a tracking spell that let the shapeshifters stick to me wherever I went." Too bad I couldn't be two places at once. That would be a really useful skill in my racket.

"Genord," Max said. "Gerris Genord handled the clothing." And as soon as he said that I recalled Genord being mentioned at the time. The evidence was there. Maybe I'd gotten bopped on the noggin a time too many. Maybe I ought to stick to working for the brewery.

The news relieved me some. I hadn't wanted to suspect Gilbey. I liked the guy. "Maybe a connection with the shifters is why Genord overreacted when Lance and Ty caught him sneaking in. Maybe there really was somebody at the door, somebody he didn't want to be seen with . . . *How* would he be connected with them? We know *he* wasn't a shifter."

I'd already recognized one commonality between Genord and Black Dragon. The commando connection. Whether or not he seemed the type Genord had had an armband that was worn by a small freecorps made up of former commandos. Once the fair-haired thugs of The Call, the Brotherhood Of The Wolf had fallen out of favor since Colonel Theverly's arrival. But I was willing to bet they were still in business, still associated with Marengo North English. And a shapeshifter had been flushed at The Pipes. "Uhm?"

Gilbey repeated, "I said, 'Why not ask Genord?' The Guard do have him in custody, don't they?"

I couldn't imagine why they wouldn't. But I didn't feel like walking back up to the Al-Khar. I'd put too many miles on me already today. "Can my friends and I get space to rest for a while?" The willow-bark tea was wearing off. I hurt. And I needed a nap.

"Find them a place, Manvil," Weider said. His tone suggested he'd begun to grow disappointed in me, too. I didn't blame him. I was disappointed in me myself.

Carefully failing to alert the staff to our presence Gilbey installed all three of us in a guest room probably reserved for visiting tradesmen. Belinda he failed to recognize. Morley he knew only by distasteful type. He remained rigorously polite throughout.

Gentlemen that we are, Morley and I let Belinda have the one narrow bed. I took the bedclothes to make a pallet for me. Dotes wasn't in a napping mood. He kept muttering about how trying to do a small favor had become a career. I asked, "You want to make yourself useful while I'm snoring, work this out. What could you do with a brewery? Besides make beer?"

"Why?"

"That's where this mess started. The shapeshifters wanted to replace the Weiders. Which makes sense only if they wanted control of the brewery." I snuggled down and went to sleep. The floor was softer than the most yielding cobblestone.

A toe ground into my ribs. I didn't have to open my eyes to know it belonged to Belinda. Only a woman would use a toe like a forefinger. A man would just kick you.

I grunted.

"That's four hours, Garrett. Dotes and I don't have a life to devote to your snoring, entertaining as it is. If I'm out of touch much longer I'm going to find myself out of touch permanently."

I sat up, groggy and disoriented. But I remembered, "I wanted up sooner than this."

"You needed the sleep," Morley said. "You really ought to go home and stay till you're completely recovered. You look a little ragged."

Maybe I did. People kept mentioning it.

I pulled myself together. Belinda looked ragged, too. I felt a twinge of guilt. She needed rest worse than I did. But here she was chasing wild geese with me. "There something going on that you guys forgot to mention?"

Morley looked at me askance. Belinda ignored me. Mostly.

"I appreciate you ambushing me and getting me loose from whoever was following me." I rubbed the back of my head. "I think. But I don't see why you bothered."

Morley shrugged. Belinda, without looking me in the eye, said, "The ratgirl insisted. She was scared those people might do something bad to you."

I smelled a scheme. Some kind of three-cornered deal between the Outfit, Reliance, and Morley Dotes, that would put me right in the middle. I hoped their little hearts weren't broken when I wouldn't go along.

Morley sneered. "I don't know how you do it, Garrett. That Singe would gleefully follow you into Hell. And be your love slave besides."

Sourly, putting herself together for travel, Belinda said, "And that blond bimbo walked right in here a while ago. She was really put out because you weren't alone."

"Alyx? Alyx is just a spoiled kid."

Morley grinned at me and flashed me his own version of the raised eyebrow trick.

"Maybe," Belinda begrudged. "She did come back with some food."

"And we didn't even eat it all," Morley said. "Your share is in that sack over there."

We saw no one as we left the house. The place was a mausoleum infected by despair. Maybe that spread from Tom's room. I felt a sudden fear that more evil might be headed the family's way. "This would be a good time for the shifters to come back." Unless Block's troops were on the job and alert.

# 91

The city was darker than usual, the night people fewer than normal. We drew unfriendly looks but never a challenge. I did see evidence that some fainthearts, especially among the refugees, were getting ready to move on. The Call's botched Cleansing had had an impact.

I didn't need to talk to anybody to sense the tension. TunFaire's population is half nonhuman, most of whom operate nocturnally. But numbers won't mean much if we humans gang up. Most of the other races don't get along with each other any better than they do with humans. For some, like dwarves and elves, the enmity goes back millennia.

I said, "The Call didn't splatter a lot of blood around but they won anyway. You can smell the fear."

"That's true. But what you don't see is the people who aren't running."

Morley probably knew something he couldn't share with me. Though he wouldn't be involved directly in anything, of course. Neutrality was a commodity he'd marketed most of his life.

Belinda said, "If Marengo has half the brains I think he's hiding, he won't do anything for a while. Allegruan and Dryzkaksghul Gnarrisson and the others really sucked up their pride to hold it together long enough to face the Cleansing." Allegruan and Gnarrisson were what you might call the urban elven and dwarfish war chieftains. "That'll all fall apart now if The Call gives them time to remember old feuds."

"You're right," Morley said. "There's talk about that already. One of Allegruan's brothers got into a shouting match with

Dryzkaksghul's uncle *during* the rioting because Gnarrisson's great-grandmother was a sister of the Burli Burlisson who ambushed the elves in Zhenda Canyon when they were headed home after attacking the dwarf caves in Wrightwight Mountain."

"Nerve of them, hitting back like that." I didn't know the incident. The history of the Karentine kingdom and its imperial predecessor is more than I can encompass and there's not nearly so many centuries of that. Nor does it carry such a burden of treachery and betrayal. Among fundamentalist, rustic-type elves, treachery and betrayal are high art forms.

"The brother's point exactly. If nothing else Burli and all his get forever are guilty of boorish manners."

I guess history sometimes is one of those you-had-to-be-there things. "I've always treasured your ability to see the absurd, Morley."

"It's only absurd by modern Karentine standards, Garrett. By those of the time, dwarfish and elvish alike, Burli showed very bad form. He didn't even take prisoners. He killed all the raiders and cut off their heads and set those up on stakes outside the entrance to the forest Thromdredril, supposedly all because he spent a few years in old-time TunFaire and contracted human insanity. And this is where we part ways. Enjoy the Al-Khar."

He and Belinda scooted, deaf to my questions.

# 92

"Don't do it!" I barked as somebody wound up to bop me from behind, right after I asked to see Colonel Block. "It's the real me. Rub me all over with silver. Make me walk around with a crown under my tongue. Just don't hit me on the head anymore."

In seconds I was surrounded. Relway's was the only face I recognized till Block wandered in. He took me at my word. His troops held me down while a guy with a silver dagger tested me for a tendency toward morphism.

Nobody apologized. Block said, "You've turned up here once already today. But the first time you weren't you."

"No shit. But how'd you know?"

"We knew you were out at North English's manor. I can picture you being guilty of a lot but not of screwing up in two places at the same time."

Relway demanded, "You learn anything?"

"I had a long, private talk with North English this morning. I could tell you word for word but I don't think you'd learn anything you don't already know. That bunch aren't as secret as they pretend." I told Relway everything anyway, almost, figuring that would save time. Then I asked Block, "What was this other me up to?"

"Tried to get the duty jailer to release Crask and Sadler in his custody. He sold his cockamamie story, too. We'd have lost them if they'd been able to travel. But the jailer came to me to try to arrange transportation. I understood you were out of town. I went down to check it out personally. The shifter knew trouble when he saw it coming. He took off before we could close in on him."

"So the bad boys are still here?"

"We have a full house. But there's pressure from the Hill to re-lease everybody being held for being public pains in the ass yes-terday night."

"What about Gerris Genord? Gotten anything out of him yet? I just turned up evidence that he might be tied in with the shapeshifters." Or to somebody in between, which is more the way I thought it would be. I didn't think Genord deliberately hurt the Weiders. I suspected he hadn't been knowingly involved in the infiltration of the shapeshifters. I thought he was a pawn moved so that bad things happened around him. His belated recognition of that fact might have caused the irrational state he was in the night Ty and Lance caught him sneaking around.

Relway said, "We haven't talked to him yet. There hasn't been time. Too much excitement to cover outside."

Though, I noted, he did have the resources to keep track of me. "Can I talk to him?"

"I'll collect a team and we'll visit him together."

"I don't want to pull his toes off. I just want to ask a few questions."

"He'll be more eager to answer if I'm behind you with a bunch of rusty tools. I'll keep quiet."

Relway, being Relway. He would be as interested in watching me ask as he would be interested in hearing Genord answer.

That wouldn't cost me. "Let's do it."

Genord was asleep when we got there but he woke up fast. He looked around wildly. He was confined in a cell every bit as evil as imagination could make one. The only positive was that he didn't have to share. Elsewhere captured rioters were piled in on top of one another.

"Comfy down here?" I asked. "I stopped in to see if they're taking good care of you." There'd been a change in Genord and it wasn't what you'd expect of a guy who found himself buried in the Al-Khar. He'd hardened. His eyes had gone cold. He looked like a commando after all. He *was* a shapeshifter but only inside his head.

He didn't respond.

"I've had a thought," I told Relway. "About the changers and our friend here. You think they know we've got him?"

"They do now. If they didn't before. The one who pretended to be you saw him when he came down to visit Crask and Sadler."

"Meaning if Genord does know anything, they'll want to get him out or shut him up."

Relway and Genord both thought they saw the direction I was headed. I took a quick turn on them. "Suppose we cut him loose? What will they figure happened?"

"That he ratted them out," Block replied. "I like it. Turning him out would solve a problem for me, too. It'd free up a cell that wouldn't have to be a single anymore. And if we do hang on to him and his own buddies get in to cut his throat, we're spared having to feed him till a judge lets us hang him."

Relway stage-whispered, "We got a budget. We don't got to account for what we don't use."

That was bullshit. I'd heard a little about the Guard's finances from Block.

I told Genord, "Brotherhood Of The Wolf is made up of elite-forces types. These shapeshifters operated as Black Dragon Valsung in the Cantard. A mercenary commando group. Is there a connection from the war?" Then I floated the suspicion I'd had for some time. "Is there a connection to Glory Mooncalled?"

Not that Genord knew of. That notion startled him momentarily. Then he nodded. "Yeah. Mooncalled's behind everything."

"He's lying," Relway said.

"He thinks he's lying. Thought he was when he said that. He's already wondering, though." You could almost hear Genord pondering the question of whether or not he'd been duped.

He chose silence as the safest route. He hadn't been in charge. He had to have faith that his superiors knew what they were doing. That they would come to his rescue.

Commandos are like Marines that way. They don't leave their own behind.

I mentioned that to Block. He growled, "We're prepared!" like how stupid did I think he was.

I might not have gotten names or a bloody knife but I was now satisfied that there was a connection between Genord's bunch and the shifters. I needed to go back to The Pipes to find out more.

I said, "Hang on to him for a while yet, just so I can get a head start and drop his name a few places. Then go ahead and kick him out." Ty was a vindictive sort. He would find this kind of vengeance particularly satisfying. Provided, of course, Genord couldn't talk his way out of the deep shit.

He hadn't shown much talent for that yet.

*   *   *

Block left a man with Genord in the unlikely event Gerris opened his heart. We were headed for the relative sanity of Block's quarters. Relway had disappeared. Block asked, "You need to check on Crask and Sadler?"

"I don't think so. Long as they're locked up tight I'm happy. They shown any signs of recovering?"

"Unfortunately."

"You be careful with them. And don't forget there's people outside who're worried about them."

"I have some ideas about those two. Assuming somebody really does want them out. Or dead." He gave out a mock-evil laugh.

I suggested, "You're gonna use them as bait in some stunt, don't forget brother Genord." Like he needed reminding again, already.

"He's already moved, I expect." Block played with the evil laughter again. "We're going to get them, Garrett."

"I don't doubt it. I just hope I have some friends alive when it happens."

"They get to Hell before you, they can have the place all fixed up. A keg in every room. Platoons of panting females."

"That's your idea of Hell?"

"Oh. You won't get to touch."

"I don't get to do that now."

Block made like a man playing a funeral flute. "I've heard about your bad fortune."

"My reputation is entirely the product of Mrs. Cardonlos' imagination."

The name seemed to startle Block. He asked, "What's your next step?"

"Back to North English's manor. I'm almost convinced that he isn't behind any of this. Though clever actors have fooled me before. Do you think he's a born-again believer in The Call's mission?"

"I try not to judge the sincerity of his type. Nor that of people off the Hill. I keep an eye on what they actually do."

"You said there was pressure from up there. . . ."

"It'll slack off."

"Thought a lot of Hill types support The Call."

"Only if it's successful. They don't want to be caught out dangling in the wind if North English's gang goes batshit and fucks up completely."

It was getting on toward the hour of the wolf, the coldest, cruelest time of night, when despair rises up and gnaws the bones of even the strong. And also the hour when the worst trolls and ogres are out. When it's plain common sense for a lone human investigator with too many enemies not to be wandering around alone. "You got a cell I can borrow for a couple hours? Just till the sun comes up?" I would nap my way into whichever future successfully conquered the city.

"There's probably one around here with your name on it, reserved. But for now you can use the cot in mine. I won't bother you. I'm up, I might as well work. Maybe interview a few of our clients." Block understood the hour of the wolf, too. There was no better time to question somebody who was chained up in a mass of filthy straw, shivering in the cold, desperately outnumbered by the rats and lice.

"Thanks. Get somebody to waken me at the crack of dawn." Before he could cut me down with a wisecrack, I said, "I ought to see the damned sun come up once before I die."

I found the cot and stretched out. Wow! Two naps in the same night. This was pure luxury. And there wasn't one damned talking bird within miles.

# 93

The somebody who wakened me wasn't one of Block's regularly sanctioned gangsters. The somebody was Pular Singe. I almost whooped as I popped up, startled. "How the hell did you get in here?"

I scared her. I had to calm her down before I could get any sense out of her. She lisped much worse when she was frightened and her hearing went north. In time I learned that she'd just walked into the Al-Khar, following my scent. There'd been nobody on guard. She hadn't thought anything of that.

"Did you see any bodies?"

"No."

"Damn! I hope that means they were ready for an invasion and just ran away." Because that was what a lack of guards meant. Somebody unfriendly had gotten inside but hadn't found anybody to kill. Not right away. I suffered no overwhelming impulse to find out if Block and Relway were all right, though, "Why are you here?" I had myself together now. I started easing her toward the nearest street door. Seemed a stroke of strategic genius to get ourselves far away from whatever big trouble was afoot.

"Reliance sent trackers after everyone following you, Garrett. He believed they would run to their masters as soon as they knew you had shaken the one with no scent. I teamed with two others to follow that thing. It can be done. I learned."

We were at the door. I thought I heard Block's fake evil laughter from deep inside the jail. "How'd you manage that?"

"By sight. This creature is not smart. It does not look back. It does not see those who are not people. That is why others were able to follow it. Even Fenibro is smart enough to look back sometimes. We took turns being closest. It is easy to track one another."

"Hmm." The ratpeople were working real hard to put me in their debt. I had a bad feeling about that. People who do that sort of thing always want something back. Usually something that involves me having to work.

There was enough light out to see. A modest fog had come in off the river. I understand that happens frequently but I'm seldom up early enough to see it.

For some early is late. Singe was uncomfortable being out after daybreak but she stuck with me, valiantly trying to communicate everything Reliance's people had found out about my personal road show. I must say, I appreciated the unflagging interest of all the friends I'd made recently. Even though they were watching one another as much as making sure that they knew every little thing I found interesting.

Only Max Weider wasn't watching me. But Relway was doing Max's share as well as his own. *He* had a whole crew on my backtrail.

Where did he find them all?

That fact that he could round up that many people fanatically devoted to law and order was as scary as the fact that our Marengo North Englishes and Bondurant Altoonas could find all the friends they wanted.

Human folks were flooding the streets now, starting their day. Many were the sort who worshipped Marengo. They did not like what they saw when Singe and I strolled by.

It constituted a little lesson on what it means to be a ratman.

Singe's courage was not up to a prolonged test.

Mine wasn't much less feeble.

Singe told me, "I cannot remain with you."

"I understand. Before you go, though, tell me, did your people track the scentless one to others like it?"

"It went to a place where others of its kind waited."

"Ah! And where might that have been? How many of them were there?"

"Three and the one we followed. We did not understand the language they spoke. Nor could I get very close. They were alert. They were very troubled."

"You did get close enough to listen?"

Singe made a dramatic effort to respond with a nod. "We are often closer than you think."

I hugged her with one arm. She barely came up to my brisket. Somehow, she seemed bigger when we were just walking, talking. "You are the bravest child I've ever met."

Did you know rats purr? I'd heard cats and raccoons do it, but never. . . . Singe did.

I tried to be stern. "You can't take risks like that. These creatures are extremely dangerous. They think nothing of murder. I'd hate myself if you got hurt."

Singe's purr grew louder. I could hear Morley and Belinda mocking me now. I cautioned myself not to let Singe make too much of my praise.

"Where're they hiding?"

She had trouble explaining. Ratpeople don't think in terms of street names and addresses. Not that we have the latter anywhere but on the Hill. Mostly you locate yourself as being so many doors some direction from an outstanding landmark. Like, say, a tavern. Most of those draw their names from signs easily recognized by the illiterate. The Merry Mole. The Gold Seam, for dwarves. The Palms for people overburdened with wealth and self-opinion.

She made me understand. "A lamp, is that it?" She got that across with finger speech when I proved too dense to get it verbally. "Down by the river? There aren't any taverns. . . . The Lamp brewery? That's been closed up and abandoned for twenty . . ."

What a wonderful place to squat. The Lamp brewery was no sprawling monster like the Weider place but in its day it was a leading producer of working-class lager. It went before my time but the old men remember it fondly. I suspect time improves the beer, as it will do. Had the Lamp product been superior, the brewery would still be in business.

"That's interesting, Singe. Very interesting." I'd have to let Relway know. We could give the place a look when I got back from The Pipes.

The shifters had themselves a brewery. But not a functional brewery. Nor one that could be made functional, probably. Anything of any use whatsoever would've been sold or stolen long ago.

I told Singe, "I owe you." She purred some more. "But I really don't want to be indebted to Reliance. I feel like he's up to no good."

The child wasn't completely smitten. Nor wholely thick-witted. I didn't lead her into any verbal ambush. She didn't volunteer anything.

I chuckled. "You're the best. Look, I have to go out to the

country. You go home and rest. You should stop taking risks for that old schemer."

She stopped walking. For a moment she found the courage to look me directly in the eye, which ratpeople are almost constitutionally incapable of doing. Then she extended a paw. I extended my own. She gave me a light, nervous handshake. "Thank you for not being cruel."

"Cruel? What? . . ." Pular Singe vanished into an alley more quietly than one of the creatures from which her race had been wrought.

# 94

Headed toward the city gate I discovered that I was being tailed again. There were three of them, working as a team. They were good. But they didn't have the advantage of having tagged me with a spell. Somebody had to stay close to see me. Which meant I could see him if I paid attention.

One was a Relway thug I'd seen in the background around the Weider place. So my pals at the Al-Khar did have time and manpower to watch me even when there was excitement going on right inside their own house.

Who were the raiders? If the shifters were all holed up at the Lamp brewery, crying in their beer? Could I assume they were Genord's pals?

Relway or Block would let me know. If the mood took them.

Mine was not a comfortable journey, even with the Guard watching over me. I was without defensive resources again. And I was alone. My passage drew concerned or calculating looks everywhere. Already there was a general assumption that a man alone either had reason to be supremely confident or was a complete fool.

I tried to maintain a confident swagger.

I felt a puff of cool air. I hadn't paid much attention to the weather. Clouds were piled up to the south. We might be in for some thunderstorms. This time of year they usually hold off till late afternoon. If I really hustled, I could get back to town ahead of the showers.

By the time I reached The Pipes the temperature had risen and the clouds had become less impressive. They would grow again when the temperature began to fall.

Hey! I don't recall anybody ever paying much attention to that kind of thing. Well, maybe farmers. But you'd have a hell of a racket going if you could predict the weather. Stormwardens make a hell of a racket out of just creating small spots of weather. . . . But that's a tough way to make a living. The magic is harder on the magician than it is on the world around him.

There was steady traffic on the road but I never worried. I didn't draw attention to myself. I was just one more vagabond drifting. Call uniforms and freecorps armbands were plentiful, suggesting a lot of messages moving between The Pipes and Marengo's satraps inside the city. I expected trouble getting past the gate but Marengo and Mr. Nagit had left word. The gate was well-defended now. Still not strongly enough to whip a troop of centaurs but, probably, enough to discourage that crew from attacking in the first place.

What had become of them? Did Block and Relway mention them to their military contacts? Or Mr. Nagit or Colonel Theverly might have done so. It needed doing. We couldn't have random armed bands roving the countryside.

A youngster who reminded me of me six or seven years ago went to the house with me. "You walked all the way out here?" Like he found that hard to believe.

"You must've been cavalry."

"Yeah."

"Figures."

"What's that mean?"

"Nothing personal. I just don't like horses. Anything interesting happened since yesterday?" Probably better change the subject. Cavalry types are goofy about horses. You can't find an ounce of rational paranoia among ten thousand of them.

"Been a campout. Bigwigs been busy, though. The Old Man got mad once he got over having his feelings hurt."

North English let word of his pecadillo get out? I asked.

"Nah, he ain't bragging. But other people know. Word gets around."

Interesting. Marengo told me he was the only survivor of the ambush. I should've been the only one he told the real story. "Just out of curiosity, what story did you hear?"

His story matched Marengo's.

Interestinger and interestinger.

*Why* would he want everyone to know? Most of us prefer to conceal our humiliations and screwups. Marengo North English struck me as very much that sort of man. What was the tactical advantage?

Or had he confided in someone who hadn't kept his secret? Or . . . Might one of his attackers have retailed the story?

# 95

My return must have been portentous for North English. Fifteen minutes after I entered his house I was alone with him in his dimly lighted sanctum. His expression suggested he was unnaturally interested in what I would have to say. Before he could ask me anything I inquired, "Are you aware that every man on the grounds knows what happened the other night? Not the official version but the version you told me?" If the men knew, then Tama must know. Might be a good time to find out if she had formed any opinions.

A darkness stirred behind Marengo's eyes. Perhaps it was veiled anger. He growled, "I didn't tell anyone but you." He watched me intently. I don't know what he expected.

"And I never told a soul," I lied. Then I mused, "You did say that the men who attacked you looked like they belonged to the movement."

North English grunted. He must've thought about that more than he wanted to admit. He must've taken it to heart. The kid who had walked me to the house had told me Marengo was hiding out today, letting no one in to see him but Tama. There were no bodyguards around so maybe he was getting paranoid about everybody.

I told him, "I saw Belinda. She swears she had nothing to do with the attack, nor was she responsible for that invitation. I believe her."

North English's style was becoming plebian. He grunted again, evidently preoccupied with rearranging furniture inside his head. He didn't seem surprised by what I'd just said. Eventually he pulled himself together, and urged, "Tell me what you think."

I offered some ideas that had occurred to me during the walk from town. Marengo continued more attentive than ever before. Somehow he must've come to the conclusion that I was a real person.

"You're convinced there's a connection between Brotherhood Of The Wolf and this Black Dragon gang?"

"There's no absolute proof but the circumstantial evidence looks strong to me."

"And this's something you just came up with on the way out here?"

"Oh, no. The Guard are looking at the possibilities from another angle. There may have been a previous connection during the war. And the shapeshifters may be associated with Glory Mooncalled somehow."

It was obvious that was something Marengo didn't want to hear. "You have a plan?" The North English I wanted to believe in, the one who could contemplate mass extinctions without qualm, seemed about to emerge from behind the mask. Marengo sounded harder and more angry by the minute.

I said, "I have some ideas. There'll be risks. Do you have any men you trust completely? Bearing in mind that the Brotherhood Of The Wolf was practically your bodyguard."

Hard Marengo glared. He didn't like my plan already.

"I can find men on my own. If you prefer." Like he was in whether or not he liked it.

"Talk to me."

I explained. He frowned a lot. He seemed confused by several points, like his memory was a little rocky. He muttered to himself, interrupted himself to ask, "Does this mean you've lost interest in the library?"

"Pretty much." What the hell brought that on? I reviewed briefly, then continued.

Marengo asked, "Will Weider cooperate?"

"I think so." Putting words into the Old Man's mouth.

"I'd guess so, too. He'll want to balance the books. How many men will you want?"

"Say twenty? Enough to put up a fight even if a few aren't trustworthy."

"Good. Good. When do you want to do it?" He seemed eager to cooperate now.

Marengo North English seemed a different man when he wasn't "on" in front of his followers. No sense of conviction came off him at all.

"As soon as we can. Which would be tomorrow night at the earliest, probably. There's a lot to pull together."

"At this end, too. But I think we need to do it. Find Nagit. Don't tell him anything, just send him to me. I'll talk to him, then send him along with you to run messages. So you don't have to ride out here and back every few hours."

"All right. But I wouldn't be riding, I'd be walking."

As I started toward the door he demanded, "Why the hell don't you get a horse?"

I thought he knew. "I need the exercise." They must've done some research on me. That was common sense.

He smiled wickedly. "That's right." And now I got the feeling he did know all about me. I had the feeling that he was taunting me somehow. Or maybe he was just letting me know that I wasn't inside anything here yet and there was no way I was going to get inside. This was a marriage of convenience only.

North English suggested, "Tell Nagit to dredge you up some decent clothing. It'd be a shame if everything went in the shitter because you got dumped into a vagrants' home."

The shitter? Why would he, suddenly, start using language like that? It didn't fit the superior-race image.

# 96

I ran into Tama in the hallway outside. She was carrying tea and rolls for two. The tea smelled good. She seemed delighted to see me, yet infinitely suspicious. "Will you stay a little longer this time?" Her voice husked. My spine quivered. My knees jellied. Boy, could she suggest a lot without saying anything.

Her smile broadened. It told me Tinnie wasn't here to save me this time. I gobbled, "I wish I could." She slithered closer. Long, dark fingers spidered up my chest to my hair, my cheek, then drifted down again. The woman was pure devil.

"Some chances come once in a lifetime. Are you done in there?"

"Uhm." I was done. I was crispy around the edges. "I need to find Mr. Nagit." I gulped. Seemed like I needed an awful lot of air suddenly.

"He went out to the stables. Probably trying to stay out of Colonel Theverley's way. They don't get along. Do take advantage of the *tea* while it's hot."

She stepped very close again. That demon hand . . . Marengo North English was one lucky man. She never stopped smiling and never turned off the raw animal attraction. I took a cup and stared and tried to find my lost breath as she went on to serve Marengo.

I don't know what Tinnie meant. Tama's behind didn't look bony at all. In fact . . .

I found Mr. Nagit out back. He couldn't have been more thrilled to see me if I'd been the old boy with the sickle. But he was a gentleman. He was polite. I told him what I thought he needed to know. "He's going to plug the leak? Wonderful. Then the attack did wake him up."

"Do I detect a tremor of distrust of the high command's wisdom?"

Weak smile. "You *are* a detective. Yes. I've had to stand around in the background, keeping my mouth shut, during an ongoing debate about how much it matters if somebody warns the Other Races that we're coming. I thought the boss had yielded to the majority opinion, that it doesn't."

"The boss might be smarter and tougher than people think. He might be sandbagging."

Nagit grunted. "The one thing they're all forgetting, or just don't want to remember, is that Glory Mooncalled is out there somewhere. Nobody wants to listen when I say he's dealt himself into the game."

"I'll listen. Because you're right. I think he's in the game big. I just don't know how. Yet. But you're right. Marengo didn't like that idea at all when I brought it up."

"He's been a little odd since the attack. More so today. Today he's staying locked up in there, not letting anyone in but the Montezuma woman. You'll want a change of clothes before we go. Right?"

"So many people disapprove of my wardrobe, I just have to assume that that might be appropriate. And I wouldn't mind borrowing a few knives and whatnot, so I'll feel more comfortable while I'm roaming around."

"I expect we can find you a nice outfit and a suite of cutlery." There was something sly about the way he said that. "Pick yourself a horse while you're out here."

"Uh . . ."

"I'm giving up my time to help you, Garrett. You'll make a few accommodations for me, too."

What was this? Did everybody in Karenta know I don't get along with horses?

Probably everybody who's already fallen under the sway of those monsters did. They gossiped behind my back. Those strange people who actually like the beasts probably understand what they're saying, somehow.

I grumbled, "Point me toward the old plodders."

"If that's what you want. Personally, I'd rather have something that could get up some speed if we ran into those centaurs."

"What?"

"There's a large band of centaurs in the area. On the move. Just as you told us. The colonel has patrols out looking for them." Mr. Nagit sounded like he begrudged having to say anything positive about Theverly. "The patrols haven't been able to pin them down. They're doing better watching us than we're doing finding them."

I made masculine noises. "As long as we know where they're not."

"Luck won't love you forever, Garrett. Pick a good horse."

Seemed to me luck wanted a trial separation already. "All right. I'll go to the library and wait when I'm done. Don't forget to see the boss."

"I'd like to. I've got troubles enough without having to hold his hand and run his errands."

Dang me. Sounded like there was disillusionment in paradise. "What's going on?"

"Besides the centaurs? I've got another dead man. I've got a missing man. And I've got a man missing a limb. I've got livestock scattered everywhere. I've got berserk thunder lizards staggering around biting everything that moves—including each other. And I've got a self-proclaimed hero-of-the-soldiers colonel who's completely indifferent to all those problems."

I lifted an eyebrow high. That works differently when you show it to a man. "What happened?" In a tone hopefully dripping empathy.

"The shitstorm started last night when Venable's pets went crazy. They spooked the cattle and sheep, went after each other, tore up Venable's other arm when he tried to get them under control, and killed somebody, apparently an outsider, who's torn up too badly to identify. Tollie was missing this morning but the corpse isn't him because the dead man was shorter, fatter, and older than the kid. I say the dead man must be a stranger because none of the other men are missing."

"And Venable's pets only attack strangers."

"Says Venable."

"Even this morning?"

"Even this morning. He claims they had to be poisoned or ensorcelled. Which is a troubling notion, too. And Theverly could care less about that, either. I'm not a man who swears much, Mr. Garrett, but I do wish this shit would come to an end and we could concentrate on our mission."

I asked several professionally oriented questions, all of which had occurred to Mr. Nagit and none of which had yet generated conclusive answers. He grumbled, "None of that matters anymore because right now I've got no greater mission than to go get orders to join you in your adventures, probably mainly so I can bang you over the head if you manage to irritate the boss or his honey."

"I detect a note of disaffection, perhaps complicated by a dollop of cynicism."

"Not a note, Mr. Garrett. A whole damned opera. I'd leave if there was anywhere better to go. But where? Bondurant Altoona? Arnes Mingle? The sad part is, this, here, is as good as it gets. Parker! I need you."

Mr. Nagit drafted Parker to help me with a mount, then stalked off. I started my search. I looked each beast directly in the eye, hunting for fast and strong but stupid enough to have no intellect left over for malice. Reluctantly, I made a choice and had her prepared.

On my way I encountered Mr. Nagit's favorite colonel, Moches Theverly. Evidently Theverly didn't remember that we'd served together in the islands. At least he didn't seem inclined to drop everything and rehash old times. He didn't seem inclined to acknowledge my existence. And that was fine with me. There might come a moment when I didn't want him to recall who I was.

I noticed that he still surrounded himself with the same cronies he'd had years ago. And still projected the same air of immense competence. And still bore the scars of the wounds that had gotten him pulled out just before the big Venageti hammer came down on those of us who stayed behind.

I studied him while I had the chance and soon decided that he probably didn't signify in anything that was going on with me. He was just somebody who happened to be around, an actor who walked across the stage.

I amused myself sorting books and snatching peeks at anything that sounded intriguing until, after a much longer delay than I expected, Mr. Nagit showed up with a selection of personal weaponry and a change of clothing I didn't find quite suitable. "A uniform?" I complained.

"It's all that's available." That amused Nagit. No doubt he'd conspired to contrive a shortage of more normal apparel.

"Don't get the idea that because I'm wearing the suit I'm one of the troops. Next time I enlist I plan to start my career as a general."

"And work your way to the bottom, I suppose. Listen, Garrett. The Call wouldn't take you in if you did want to join. You're one big old tangle of unanswered questions and nobody wants to bother digging."

And just a few days ago everybody in the rights racket wanted to sign me on, for the full nightmare. When I still had a nonhuman partner and friends of questionable ethnic purity. I must've stopped being the ideal recruit while I was looking the other way.

Maybe Black Dragon Valsung still wanted me. Or Brotherhood Of The Wolf. We could let bygones be bygones. Couldn't we?

As I dressed I chewed on the sour certainty that my position had been marginalized all along, by everyone. They'd all wanted me to poke hornets' nests somewhere else but hadn't wanted me getting intimate with their own schemes. I was a ball bouncing randomly off any number of walls. No more than what Morley would call a finagle or a confusion factor. A bee annoying everybody.

"Not a bad fit," I said, checking over each shoulder. "The styling is a little too army but I do look almost dashing."

"The ladies will swoon." Mr. Nagit fought a smile.

I asked, "You ever see Glory Mooncalled?"

"What?" I'd startled him with the sudden shift. "No, I don't know anybody who has. Why?"

"I just wondered. I used to have a partner. He practically worshipped Glory Mooncalled. Because of his irreverent attitude." Though I couldn't imagine how someone could be more establishmentarian than a Loghyr gone sedentary. For folks like that revolution or change were not Good Things.

"Used to be a lot of that going around. You don't hear much of it anymore. Suppose we get this circus rolling? The sooner we handle it the sooner I come back home."

"I'm ready." I looked myself over again. I wasn't pleased. I looked like one of the boys. I hoped that didn't confuse me or anyone else.

Tama Montezuma was in the hallway talking to somebody when we left the library. The guy scowled at us. Mr. Nagit glared back. I paid the man no mind because Tama turned on the heat and made herself the focus of my existence. "Garrett? Look at you. Why'd they ever let you out of uniform?" The guy she was with sidled off past Mr. Nagit, plainly unhappy that anyone else was getting Miss Montezuma's attention. Men are that way. We can't help it.

Tama's eyes seemed twice as big as normal. What a case! Every woman I ran into seemed determined to fry my brain.

Mr. Nagit said, "Garrett."

"Uh. Yeah." He was Marengo's right hand. "Sorry, Miss Montezuma. Got to run. Work to do."

She smiled a smile both promising and predatory, moved on down the hall.

I just couldn't imagine where Tinnie got the idea that Tama was bony. "Whew!" I said.

Mr. Nagit agreed. "Yeah. What was that all about?"

When Tinnie was with me he'd seemed a normal, red-blooded Karentine sort of guy. "What?"

"That woman doesn't take a deep breath unless it has something to do with her meal ticket. And she just took you over the jumps."

"My ego can't handle it."

"Huh?"

"She wants to throw the boss over for me."

"Exactly. I thought she seemed extremely nervous."

Were we speaking the same language?

When we stepped out of the house I checked to see what the clouds were doing. My earlier expectations wouldn't be disappointed. Rain was coming. A real disappointment stood closer to hand. The horse I'd chosen now looked terribly ferocious for a swaybacked mare almost my own age. And then there were the dozen guys in freecorps outfits all looking like they were headed for the parade ground. I did a quick, paranoid scan of armbands, making sure noboby was dumb enough to wear his Brotherhood Of The Wolf allegiance on his sleeve.

"Is this necessary?"

"Somebody has to run messages. And those unfriendly centaurs are still out there."

Unfriendly to you, fellow.

I felt vulnerable despite having acquired a cutlery sampler.

Something slammed down on my shoulder. For an instant I thought an ogre had jumped me from behind, but when I turned my head I found myself beak to beak with the Goddamn Parrot. "Damn! I thought I lost you for good." I told Mr. Nagit, "You know, these things live a really long time. Someday you're going to want to have a family. Think how much fun your kids could have with their own talking bird."

"I wouldn't deprive your own future scions of the opportunity to enjoy such a wonderful experience." He laughed.

Him and his pals found my plight entertaining. Not one of them wanted his own talking shoulder ornament, no matter how dashing the look. I gathered my dignity and mounted up, getting it right way forward first try. I mouthed the notes of the trumpet call for charge and off we rode. A three-legged centaur would've had no trouble running me down.

# 97

Gilbey didn't like my idea even a little. "We don't want any more trouble here, Max."

The Old Man turned the letter Mr. Nagit had given him, as though Marengo might have scribbled a secret postscript on its blank side. He saw only what I saw, which was the North English seal. "We'll do it, Manvil." He turned the letter again. Whatever North English's message, it made a difference; but it left his old friend Max puzzled. North English's word obviously was gold to Weider. "Clear the great hall again." Wan smile. "Let this young gentleman's friends help." That was a subtle dismissal of Nagit and Gilbey both.

"Will this work, Garrett?"

"I don't know. My record hasn't been outstanding lately."

"No. It hasn't. On the other hand, most of our troubles could've been avoided if we'd listened to you in the first place. I understand that you're handicapped by the head start I allowed evil. But who could believe that such things might happen?" The latter he directed toward himself.

"North English will send in freecorps people he trusts. I assume you trust him. But, even so, I intend to bring in friends of my own."

"Whatever *you* think of the man, Garrett, he's my friend."

I confessed, "I do see him through different eyes. I'll also bring in some Guards people that Colonel Block trusts. Everybody can watch everybody. It'll be like party night at the pickpockets' hall."

Wan smile. "You missed the funerals."

"You had them already?" Of course he had. It was summertime.
"This morning. Early."
"I'm sorry. Nobody told me. I would've been there."
"No matter. You were doing the work of the Lord. I hope."

Max wasn't demonstratively religious but he did belong to one
of the old-time hellfire and brimstone, rip off an arm for a finger
and a head for an eye type of cults. Because of Hannah's incapac-
ity he'd gradually lost interest in the workaday details of brewing
the world's best beers. He remained the grand lord of the brewery
with the final say about everything but he had abandoned the detail management to Ty and the brewmasters. I feared Hannah's
passing might cause him to turn away from the business altogether
and possibly even from life.

"Vengeance is mine."
"Can you pull it together by tomorrow?"
"I can." But I'd be one tired boy when I was done.
"Good. You'd better get started."
Now I was being dismissed.

As I opened the study door, Max said, "Lose the uniform, Garrett. If you're going to be roaming around alone, you don't want to
ask for more trouble."

Max was right.
The comings and goings of freecorps messengers got noticed.
The news spread at the speed of rumor. Tension soon filled the
streets. Tempers grew shorter fast.

I had arrangements of my own to make. I couldn't use Nagit's
men or brewery hands to complete them.

My proud destrier and I put on the miles.

I visited The Palms. Morley told me he could make it and he
suspected that Puddle and Sarge and a few of the boys wouldn't
mind a party, either. I left a message for Belinda, which Dotes
promised to have delivered. Then I dropped in on Playmate, who
not only was available and willing but saved me several hours by
knowing where Saucerhead Tharpe was holed up. I then swooped
down on Heaven's Gate where I talked to Trail and Storey and
Miss Trim and, unfortunately, Medford Shale. Since I didn't have
a keg under either arm or any treats for Shale my welcome was
less than enthusiastic.

Shale could just keep on wondering why nobody came to
visit him.

My weather-prediction skills proved acute. It was late afternoon when I went to see Saucerhead. It was raining. At times the downpour turned unseasonably ferocious.

Through everything the Goddamn Parrot never made a sound. That critter had to be trying to spook me out. Not that I missed the old, foul-beaked Mr. Big. Not even a little.

"Playmate's in. Morley's in," I told Tharpe, who wanted convincing. "The Dead Man might be in. If I can find him. And I particularly need you in. I don't think I can make it all happen without you." Of course I could. But everyone wants to be wanted, Saucerhead more so than most. And I had some special requests, each of which I explained carefully.

The big guy grumbled, "Gonna be a major pain, Garrett. That's a lot of work."

"You got something else going?" In the past he'd always had a good work ethic.

"Not really. Winger had an idea about—"

"You've got to get away from her, man. You ever notice how *she* never gets hurt in any of her schemes?"

"Yeah. I know. It's not real nice but . . . All right, Garrett! Don't start that shit. I really hate it when somebody reminds me that I owe him."

I offered an evil chuckle reminiscent of the one I'd last heard from Colonel Block.

The head Guardsman was next on my list. I hit the street once I finished twisting Saucerhead's . . . uh . . . giving Mr. Tharpe his instructions. With cold water drizzling down the back of my neck. I have to get myself one of those big-ass riding cloaks now that I'm a cavalier.

"That a horse?" Saucerhead called after me, from the tenement doorway. "Are you riding a horse?" He didn't mention the condition of the monster. "I've seen everything now. It really must be important. I better get on this right away." He had a hat on his head already.

How many times have I said he and Winger didn't have sense enough to get in out of the rain? Made me wonder. He did have sense enough to wear a hat while he was out in it.

Pular Singe caught me leaving the Al-Khar, after I made arrangements with Block, who guaranteed Relway's cooperation. The good colonel was in a festive mood. An attempt to rescue Gerris Genord had been crushed without Guard casualties. One invader was dead. Two now shared Genord's cell. A couple of others, whose interest had been Crask and Sadler instead of their old pal Gerris, had gotten out again.

*Very* interesting.

I hated myself for thinking Singe looked like a drowned rat. But I couldn't help it. She did. A drowned rat in a wet shirt. "I hoped your people would notice me running around. . . . Where'd you get the shirt?" It used to be mine. It was Tad Weider's before that.

"From the stuff you threw away. It would be a sin to let that go to waste."

The shirt didn't flatter her. Ratpeople just aren't put together like human people. "You could get trouble from the shapechangers."

She tried to smile. It was an obvious, conscious effort to ape the human expression. "They have been disappointed already. Many times."

The clothes had gotten scattered amongst Reliance's dependents. And they didn't care if the shirts had been tagged.

"I'm glad to hear it. What about my tools?"

"Tools?" She didn't understand. I reminded me to keep it simple and slow. She might be a genius of her kind but she was still ratpeople.

"The weapons I was carrying." That stuff wasn't cheap. Even when you took most of it away from the bad boys you ran into. Still, with a little creative billing amongst my various employers . . . Heh-heh-heh.

"I do not know."

I tried to recall if any could be traced to me or the Weiders if they turned up at the scene of some major villainy. I didn't think so. "Would Reliance let you go out to a party tomorrow night?"

I knew I'd picked the wrong words even before the Goddamn Parrot loosed the first noise to pass his beak in hours. Slow and simple, stupid. Before she leapt too far in her conclusions.

I said, "I'll be working there. I want to hire you to unmask the creatures with no scent. Nobody is as good as you are." I couldn't restrain a grin, which seemed to help. But it was sure misplaced.

What must people think of this rain-bedraggled crew, hatless me, a soggy parrot scrunched on my shoulder, leading a motheaten antique horse, practically hand in hand with a ratgirl who looked like she'd been drowned once then thrown back for good measure?

The thought made me look around for witnesses. By chance I

glimpsed another drowned rat. "Did you know Fenibro is follow-ing you?"

Singe's immediate anger made it clear the wannabe boyfriend hadn't been invited. "I told him not to . . ." I couldn't follow what she said.

"It isn't important. Maybe Reliance sent him to watch out for you."

"One day Reliance will learn that I am not a belonging." I caught that easily enough. She added, "It may take a very painful lesson. I will help you look for the shapechangers." In seconds her enunciation had become nearly flawless.

"Speaking of whom. Are they still holed up in that old brew-ery?"

"Yes." Singe looked over her shoulder. She showed her teeth in an unfeminine threat display. If I'd been Fenibro I'd have got-ten the hell out of there fast.

# 98

Max waved me to a seat. "Lay it out."

"This's only tentative. Subject to change as—"

"Don't bullshit me, Garrett."

The man had exhausted his store of patience. With everything.

"All right. In temporal sequence. Gerris Genord was a plant. Part of a part of this that goes back a few years. And just one of a bunch of plants that put Wolf people inside rich families and businesses. They were after money, plain and simple. It was the Wolves who approached Ty. He or the brewmasters may recognize some of the prisoners.

"Gerris would've known when Alyx decided to bring me in. He would've reported.

"At some point some of the Wolves would've run into some of the Dragons. They'd remember each other from the Cantard. The Wolves asked for help. Or maybe hired the Dragons. But the Dragons had their own agenda. They started using the Wolves when the Wolves thought they were using the Dragons. For their own reasons the Dragons decided to make your family their main target.

"When Genord reported that Alyx was trying to contact me the baddies did some research and decided I could cause trouble. They tried to distract me by involving me in the rights movement. The Dragon crew tried to recruit me. They were recruiting guys at the brewery already. When I showed up there one of those guys reported me and the shifters sent over a team from the Lamp brewery ruins. They failed to discourage me. Genord marked the clothing you gave me so I could be tracked. My part in events since then you know." More or less.

Manvil Gilbey stirred the fire. Max needed a lot of heat to keep going. Weider mused, "Dragons and Wolves using each other. The Wolves after money. What did the changers want?"

"A functional brewery. Don't ask me why. I still have to figure that out. Maybe changers came with a big thirst. But I've got a feeling, supported by not much more than intuition so far, that Glory Mooncalled is in all this right up to his mysterious neck." An implication in part dependent upon my interpretation of my partner's arcane nonbehavior. "I also think that whoever is managing the Wolves has been blackmailed into helping the Dragons. I keep picking up little whiffs of disharmony.

"I have a hunch that that manager brought Crask and Sadler back to deal with the blackmailers. Belinda turning up complicated life. Belinda is dedicated to turning those two good old boys into fish food. So this mystery Wolf decided to uncomplicate life by getting rid of Belinda and me. He gave Crask and Sadler the go-ahead without consulting the allies he planned to ambush later."

Oh what an elegant theorist am I. I was probably off the mark on half of this. But I didn't let a little thing like maybe being wrong slow me down. "After the excitement at the engagement bash Genord began to understand how badly he and his pals were being used. He sneaked away to raise hell about it. He got no satisfaction and, possibly pursued, was in a highly disturbed state when Lance and Ty surprised him at the front door. Since then things have been falling apart fast for the Wolves and Dragons both.

"Meantime, not one person involved in this has dealt with me straight. Everybody, including you, has had an agenda they didn't want to abandon. Although everybody told me a little something here and there so I could have a tool or two to go make things uncomfortable for some other guy. I don't know what your problem was, boss. Maybe you just didn't want a guy with dirt under his nails making the guests nervous by tracking real life all over the place. I'm offended but I'll stipulate that it's your house, your party, your call."

Max's gaze flicked to Gilbey for an instant. Ah. His idea, huh?

Gilbey asked, "You have any idea who this mysterious manipulator is?"

"Just a feeling. No evidence. But if this turns into the pressure situation I want it to become, somebody will point a finger, and say '*He* made me do it.' "

Gilbey stirred the fire again. Max looked thoughtful. I said, "There's more but those are the assumptions I'm working with tonight. We'll see how things come together."

# 99

I stood at the head of the grand staircase, overlooking the Weider great hall. Tinnie wriggled in under my left arm. Morley had reminded me to add her to the guest list, possibly saving me several centuries in Purgatory. Or what she'd make seem like several centuries. Morley's thoughtful effort balanced off about one talon's worth of the Goddamn Parrot.

Tinnie said, "If it wasn't in bad taste, I'd ask who died." There were a lot of people of various persuasions and allegiances below us, mostly gathered in sullen clumps. The main folks circulating, other than Mr. Gresser's serving crew, were hard-eyed men from Theverly's freecorps, the brewery, my friends, and even a few of Belinda's.

"Some parties just never come to life. Damn!"

"What?"

"Saucerhead brought Winger." Winger might decide that being up to her eyeballs in toughs and lawmen represented a challenge. I glanced up. A gaudy glob remained perched on the main chandelier, gawking at the mob. The bird was vitally alert and his beak hadn't gushed an abomination in the past hour. He was way out of character. I was concerned. But even Morley hadn't noticed. If we could just keep it that way . . .

Manvil Gilbey came out of Max's study. "Going to be much longer?"

"Still missing some key faces . . . Speak of the devil. Here come Colonel Block and the secret police." More hard-eyed men, probably *not* Relway's undercover goons because he wouldn't want their faces this exposed, came in through the front door.

Some pulled chains. A few of my guests wouldn't be willing participants. Examples hove into sight: Crask, Sadler, Gerris Genord and his captive friends. Genord seemed particularly unhappy about returning to the scene of his crime.

Him and his buddies got dragged to a bench that was chained to a pillar. They wouldn't be lonely there. The bench already supported eight desolate Brothers Of The Wolf who hadn't scooted fast enough to avoid Lieutenant Nagit's roundup at The Pipes. Apparently Nagit even caught North English by surprise with that. He'd told me that Marengo had been put out in the extreme . . . according to Tama Montezuma, who continued doing most of his talking for him.

Alyx joined us. "That's an awful lot of men who don't like each other crammed in nose-to-nose in one place." She'd dressed. Gorgeously. She looked like she wanted to go down and set the mob at one another's throats. "I'm surprised you got them all to come."

"Hey. We serve the best beer in town. And it's on the house." My gaze drifted to Trail and Storey and Miss Trim. And Medford Shale. Shale had refused to be left at Heaven's Gate. All four were demonstrating an heroic dedication toward making sure they got a fair share of Weider's best.

The real reason most of these people had come was that they were afraid not to. They might miss something critical. It was a tense time in the history of TunFaire. It was a time not to let yourself fall a step behind. It was a time when the future was rewriting itself from minute to minute and you wanted your hands and nose right in the middle of anything that might nudge the pen of destiny.

"Manvil, tell . . ." He was gone. "Oh, good. Better late than never." Saucerhead had completed his mission. Below, Ty had entered the hall from the family dining room. He was on crutches. Nicks was beside him, trying not to look like she was there to catch him if he fell. Ty was directing a crew from the brewery who were dragging one of those huge, thousand-gallon wooden settling tanks where beer sits briefly while the grossest sediments settle out. Later the holy nectar would migrate onward to occupy the kegs and barrels the customer sees. Questions about the tank stirred every little cluster but people were too wary of their neighbors to ask outside their own cliques. Ty gave me a thumbs-up. I blew him a kiss. We were getting along today. I told Alyx, "Go tell your pop. I just dealt myself another ace. Everything's set and we're just waiting for Relway."

"Waiting for Relway. Right."

"He'll understand."

She went. Tinnie asked, "Think she'll remember all the way over there?"

"You're vicious. And she's *your* friend."

"You keep that in mind. All right. You've got everybody that you've ever met gathered in one place. What the devil do you plan to do with them?"

"Oh, I'm going to make them all unhappy. Real unhappy. Unless I manage to make me real unhappy by making a complete fool of myself."

"You think the bookies are giving odds? Is there a point spread?"

"Lift your skirt."

"Right here? I can be conned into a little adventure sometimes, Garrett, but. . . ."

"Three inches will be far enough." Her hemline dragged the carpet. "Ha! I thought so."

"What?"

"You're wearing the green shoes. I don't know if they turn you wicked or you just wear them when you're feeling wicked, but—"

"Somebody's here."

Yes. Somebody was. The boys from the Lamp brewery had arrived. They looked sexy in their shiny new silver-plated chains. I'd expected the logistics to be a problem but Relway had been on the job already, having anticipated having to control shapeshifters again, and better.

"Five . . . six of them. I thought there'd be more. There *should* be more. Hell, there're only five of them." The sixth was a ringer, Relway himself, in disguise and not really part of the coffle. He was pretending to be a little hunchbacked torturer's apprentice, jingling the ends of the chains. Probably no one but Singe and I recognized him.

Singe showed more courage than I'd thought possible. Not only was she on the scene, she was out where people could see her. She stayed close to the walls, though.

The rightsist types were surprised by her presence but it didn't distress them. Not nearly so much as did the presence of Morley Dotes and Belinda's swagging toughs. Ratpeople knew their place.

Everyone I wanted there had arrived. Singe had not yet found any shapeshifters other than those Relway was delivering but she kept on looking. I was counting on surprise visitors of several kinds.

Marengo North English wove his way through the crowd hurriedly, headed my way. He seemed to cringe from the touch of the crowd. He wanted out of the press, fast. His lovely niece trailed a step behind him. Tama seemed uncomfortable and deeply troubled. Maybe that was because there were so many really bad people around, though I couldn't picture her having much difficulty managing in even the direst circumstances. She'd already impressed me as a first-class survivor capable of cool thinking and quick decisions.

While Marengo had been eyeing the Belindas and Tinnies and Wingers and developing an itch, she had been formulating plans of her own, I was sure. Whatever silverware Marengo still had lying around The Pipes might not be there much longer.

Now Colonel Block was whispering with a fawning Relway. Both kept glancing my way. He nodded several times, started toward the stair himself.

Marengo arrived first. He asked, "Are you ready to start?" Oddly, Tama seemed more interested in my answer than he did.

I was, though I hadn't achieved the perfect and optimal mix I'd hoped for. But the crowd was better than the one I'd expected. The front door had been locked. Sarge and Puddle stood between it and the room, looking like some pudgy guardian temple trolls. Them dressed up formal was a vision to behold. Out of a bad dream. Unfortunately, I'd never get joy out of having seen them looking pretty. I was outfitted in Ty Weider's second best get-up. I looked like some limp-wristed, lilac-scented lordlet bent on embarrassing his family publicly. "Yes."

Singe moved around the edge of the room. Marengo glanced down at her frequently, unhappily. Playmate, Saucerhead, and Winger were never far from the ratgirl. Winger cleaned up astonishly well. Marengo's gaze brushed her a time or three. I wouldn't interfere if they decided they were made for each other. They deserved one another. And I had a parrot that would make a wonderful engagement present.

A glance showed me that the future nuptial knickknack was still paying attention.

Singe drifted off to check Mr. Gresser's crew and Neersa Bintor's kitchen gang.

Block puffed his way to the head of the stair. He clung to the rail, sucked in a bunch of air, gasped out, "You've got to stall, Garrett."

"But—"

"Got a good reason?" Max demanded from behind me, as I made a small gesture that brought a colorful lightning bolt down to strike my shoulder. I guess Alyx had gotten all the way there with the message. Her old man sounded darkly suspicious. Which is probably the healthiest attitude if you're dealing with minions of the Crown.

"I think so," Block said. "Though you're free to disagree, of course."

"What?" I asked. I knew it would be ugly. The Goddamn Parrot cocked his head, the better to hear.

"An acquaintance took the liberty of inviting himself down." Slight weight on the last word. I understood perfectly but Max didn't catch it. Block's way-so-mysterious chum from the Hill had decided to stick his nose in. That was wonderful. That was more than I'd hoped for. That made my evening nearly faultless. That was one snake I hadn't really expected to lure in out of the weeds. Now if just one more old shit-disturber, lately of the Cantard republic, couldn't control his curiosity and chose to become a surprise guest, I would've contrived a flawless machination.

Block continued, "He can't make it for a while yet. And I'll tell you, you'll feel more comfortable once he is here." He winked, a very unBlocklike action. "I think." Meaning Block was going to feel more comfortable. His mystery guest must have been riding him hard.

Max clucked his tongue, irked. Max's opinions of folk from the Hill were blacker than mine.

Marengo didn't seem to be disappointed. In fact, he seemed more relaxed. Then I realized he wasn't listening to us, just to the crowd on the floor below.

I asked, "Is your buddy's identity a secret?"

"He's the Stormwarden Perilous Spite."

Never heard of him, I didn't say because Max got in the first word. "Why?" He seemed distinctly unfriendly now. Could this be somebody he knew and disliked? Did everybody know Spite but me? I'm supposed to know things. It's what I do. Know where to make connections. But I couldn't connect this glorified witch doctor to anything.

"Because the stormwarden is extremely knowledgeable in

matters having to do with ranger, commando, special forces, and covert operations inside the Cantard. He was involved. He has un-finished business. He's been following this since he heard about the dragon tattoos."

How did he hear? I wondered. Would Colonel Westman Block be saddled with standing orders to report certain discoveries to certain interested parties? Might such reports be a condition of his appointment? Why, Garrett, how could you be so cynical? You de-veloping a case of creeping realism?

Block surged onward, ingenuously "I don't know why, Gar-rett, but that got his attention in a big way. He's been nagging me like the proverbial fishwife. And seems to know more about what's going on than Deal does . . ." Block decided he was talking too much, which is a liability in his trade. He finished, "Him join-ing us was his idea."

"But he keeps Hill time, of course," I grumbled. Meaning I fig-ured the stormwarden couldn't be bothered catering to the sched-ules of us lesser creatures. But that was all right. I wanted this devil out in the open where I could see him. "Tell me, old buddy, how did this guy hear about my party in the first place?"

Block shrugged. "I don't know. Not from me. I told you. He's well informed."

"Hmm." I glanced at Marengo, there with his old pal Max Weider, being mousy quiet. The very man who was grumbling and muttering about the caprice of sorcerers the other day. "I see."

North English lacked the grace to be embarrassed.

"I see," Max said, too. "So we'll wait, Garrett. Use the delay to build the pressure till these fools blow smoke out their ears. Then let the stormwarden land in their midst like a cat in a mouse nest."

I said, "You're the boss." A little time sweating might indeed make somebody a tad more amenable. "Excuse me." Block had retreated halfway down the stair, then had stopped, looking my way. He had something on his mind.

I went to find out. The colonel whispered, "Relway says to tell you you have to come visit the Lamp brewery."

"He find something interesting?"

"Apparently so. He wouldn't explain. He did say that he didn't understand it but that you might and you probably ought to see it before you go ahead with what you're doing here."

Now? "Maybe he didn't notice but here is just a wee bit busy. And every time he wants me to see something that turns out to be dead bodies. I've seen enough dead people . . . Oh, shit!" Medford

Shale and his Heaven's Gate cronies had been admiring the settling tank like it might be the doorway to paradise. I'd been keeping an eye on them in case they decided to try tapping it, the
results of which were sure to amaze and distress almost everyone.
"Bird, go down there and get those drunks headed in another direction. Go on. Shoo."

The arrival of the talking bird had the desired effect. The old
folks retreated toward the kegs already tapped. But their bickering
orbit around the settling tank brought them face-to-face with the
arriving prisoners.

Storey went berserk. He flailed away at one of the shapeshifters with his walking stick. I murmured, "Apparently it *can* be
the same Carter Stockwell who was involved in the Myzhod campaigns."

"What?"

"Long story. Those old men were soldiers a long time ago.
Some shapeshifter mercenaries sold them out to the Venageti. It
was a big disaster for our side. Looks like these could be the same
shapeshifters. Storey—that's the guy being so stylish with the
walking stick—mentioned the one he's whipping by name."

"I do believe I'm beginning to get an idea of why the stormwarden is interested."

Me, too, if Perilous Spite was what I suspected. "Let's go
calm them down."

"Let's have a whisper with Deal."

# 100

Storey settled down only after, for a moment, it looked like Trail had suffered a stroke. Several shifters bled liberally. The silver fetters took the strength right out of them. Trace whimpered like a whipped puppy. The voice of the guy who'd been in the stable and on the stair to Tom's room said, "We should've killed the sonofabitch when we had the chance." I couldn't tell if he meant me or Storey.

The boys from Brotherhood Of The Wolf were chained to the next pillar over. Several seemed stricken. They saw faces they recognized. Faces that belonged to people who weren't even human. People who had been manipulating them . . . A glance at Gerris Genord told me he'd figured that out already. Maybe while he was in the Al-Khar, maybe even the night he killed Lancelyn Mac. Maybe he knew the key answer, too.

Who.

I had an idea, name of Mooncalled. Only I couldn't make him fit. Going strictly by the available evidence, Marengo North English seemed more likely.

There was no coolness toward Genord on the part of the other Wolves. Block and Relway hadn't told them a thing. They trusted their buddy. Kind of touching, that. These days trust is moribund and fading fast.

It did mean I had guessed wrong about Genord not being the commando type. It takes going through hell with a man to develop that kind of trust. I asked Genord, "You want to put somebody on the spot?"

He looked through me. He wasn't going to tell me jack. If

there was any settlement due, his pals would handle it. We couldn't hold them forever.

That attitude came out of the going through hell together, too. I remember that attitude. I miss it. But all the guys I shared it with are gone. I'm left with just the pale ghost of it in my friendships with Morley and a few others.

An uproar loud enough for all the guests to hear erupted out in the kitchen. Neersa Bintor bellowed like an angry she-elephant. Before I finished making sure everybody didn't rush that way and thereby leave the rest of the mansion unwatched the big woman stormed into the great hall. She had a body over her shoulder, a shifter caught in mid-change, flopping like a crippled snake. In her off hand she carried a kitchen maul that looked like it could be used to drive the stakes that hold up circus tents. She searched the gawking crowd, spotted me, flung the shifter from thirty feet away. It left some skin on the uncarpeted floor.

"I an' I, I be tryin' to manage de kitchen, you Garrett, you. You be gettin' me better help dan dat t'ief, you. You be keepin' you rat out a dere, too, you." Behind her Pular Singe managed to look sheepish and proud at the same time. She'd winkled out the interloper.

It occurred to me that we'd neglected our obligation to inform Neersa Bintor of our full plans. Not an oversight the goddess of the cast iron would easily forgive. In the hierarchy of the Weider mansion Neersa Bintor ranked right behind Max and, just possibly, Manvil Gilbey.

I apologized profusely in front of the mob. A certain gaudily constumed woodpecker had a grand laugh at my expense. "Lend me your cane there, Storey." I whacked the side of the settling tank three or four times. The bird said "Gleep!" and flew back to his perch on the chandelier.

"You listen, you bird-boy, you. I an' I got no room in my kitchen for vermin, be dey talk or no. You unnerstan', you? I will catch my own t'iefs, I an' I." The shifter at my feet stirred. Neersa Bintor raised a prodigious sensible shoe, brought it down hard, then exorcised her venom through a hearty application of her maul. She kept her foot in place while a couple of Guards got the changer fitted with chains.

I whispered to Singe, as though she hadn't understood what had been said, "Maybe you'd better stay out of the kitchen."

She whispered back, "You tink so, you?"

Singe the wonder child. She was being sarcastic. "Yeah.

Scoot." When I turned back to the crowd I saw the Bintor phenomenon withdrawing.

I told the Guards, "You guys better get this thing shackled to its friends before it remembers what kingdom it's in." I suspected the passivity shown by the changers was partly due to their psychic connection, which must be charged with a communal sense of despair.

Block, near Relway, beckoned impatiently.

# 101

Relway is predictable some ways. For example, you can count on him to bring out the melodrama in any situation. He did that at the Lamp brewery, where he had guys with torches creeping around the interior ruins generating wonderfully creepy, dancing, slithering shadows. "It's in worse shape than I thought it would be," I told the little guy. The brick exterior remained sound but the inside walls and floors were falling down and caving in.

"Smells odd, too," Morley said. He drifted over and through rubble and ruin without attracting a speck of dust.

Relway grumbled, "The smell comes from what we're here to see." He wasn't pleased with his pal Garrett. Garrett had let Morley Dotes and Pular Singe tag along. Deal Relway wasn't dim. He knew Morley would try to memorize some identifying detail about him and that Singe, without even realizing it, would accumulate a battery of olfactory clues. I hoped he didn't feel threatened enough to consider some unpleasant form of rectification later.

"Through here." Relway ducked under a sagging floor joist. I had to duckwalk in order to follow him. The dust showed that there had been a lot of traffic before us. "What a glamorous life they lead."

Relway grunted. Block made a small speech about evil always seeming glamorous from a distance but being squalid and ugly when you saw it up close. It was hard to argue with that. I saw proof every day.

On the other hand, the wicked do prosper while the upright perform hopelessly in the theater of their own despair.

"Kind of like my shoulder ornament, you mean?"

The Goddamn Parrot, who hadn't wanted to miss this adventure, made a sneering noise—really! And Morley announced, "I resent that. That avian gem was a gift from me."

"For which you'll never be forgiven. Yech!" The smell was getting stronger fast. Though repellent it had a familiar edge, a malty—

"Here," Relway said, indicating a couple of old copper fermenting kettles that should've been stolen for their scrap value ages ago. "Take a torch and climb up there." He indicated a crude platform fashioned from old crates. "You too, Wes."

I borrowed a torch from a Guard. Colonel Block snagged another. We accomplished the climb with a minimum of injuries, though the wonder buzzard also lost some tailfeathers to a waving torch.

The kettles were full of *stuff*. A big bubble broached the surface of the one nearest me. "Oh! That's foul. Some people shouldn't be allowed to brew their own." That's what they were doing. Badly. That's why the stench seemed familiar.

Relway said, "That's right. Take that paddle and push the scum out of the way."

A six-foot pole with a wide, square end lay across the top of the pot. I followed instructions.

"Shit!" Block exclaimed. "What the hell is *that*?"

I had to keep pushing the surface gunk aside to see it.

It was a slug olive drab thing four feet long and human-shaped. No. Monkey-shaped caught it better. Its limbs were long and skinny and it had a tail. It had a round head with large round lidless lemurlike eyes. And no ears.

There was another in the other kettle, not as completely developed.

"What do you think?" Relway asked. "Think what's in them pots maybe's got something to do with why they'd want to grab control of TunFaire's biggest brewery?"

"They're cooking up baby changers. Damn! Makes you understand their behavior. Some. Makes you kind of sympathize—if that's how they have to reproduce." I smelled ancient sorcery of the same sort that had created Singe's people. "But they're still dangerous monsters from where we stand. I wonder if it'd make any difference to Max that his family didn't die just because of somebody's greed."

"Grief ain't big on caring about why," Block observed.

Singe suddenly squeaked, "Garrett! Danger!" and scooted into the darkness like . . . Well, like a scared rat. Something stirred back the way we'd come. Somebody barked something. Relway started to drag out a black knife. That started everybody else grabbing for weapons.

"Deal!" Block snapped. "Relax."

Relway froze instead.

A wicked vision seemed to materialize slowly from the uncanny shadows, like that mythical breed of vampire that spends part of its unlife as a mist capable of passing through the finest fissure. As it moved into the torchlight I saw that it was someone in black robes with golden lightning bolts embroidered on, his face concealed behind a silver mask. Clearly the aforementioned Stormwarden Perilous Spite, clinging to the traditions of his kind, which have spooky behavior and bad clothes as their foundations.

But people off the Hill dress like they're expected to dress. I sometimes wonder where they find their tailors. I also wondered if I really wanted this guy to turn up after all. Already he felt like clabbered bad humor.

The Goddamn Parrot decided he wanted to go for a fly with Pular Singe. Probably a good idea. I didn't want him attracting attention.

Block caught my eye. He jerked his head. I stepped down. He followed. His pal the wizard took our place. He stirred the kettles and examined their contents.

I call him *he* for convenience. There was a one in three chance that a woman lurked behind that mask. Not that sex made much difference. Those people are all misery on the hoof.

Block tugged my sleeve, gestured with his head. It was time us grunts made ourselves scarce.

I departed still reflecting upon whether or not it was a good thing to have the stormwarden join us. His presence might be enough to guarantee the continued sinister shyness of the specter general from the Cantard, whose appearance would be much preferable to me.

As we strode toward the Weider mansion Relway asked, "You gotten anywhere finding out anything for me, Garrett?"

"Nope. And I'm not going to, either. They've flat out told me I'm not getting inside anything, nor am I getting anywhere near any information they don't already want the whole world to share."

"But you're the perfect recruit."

"I think I was the perfect recruit until I started talking to you."

"Hmm?"

"Just a hunch. But if I was you and Block, I'd keep an eye out for one of your guys who maybe feels as strong about human rights as he does about law and order."

The ugly little man's face turned to cold iron.

Thou shalt have no other gods before me.

# 102

Max stared the length of the hall at the stormwarden. The sorcerer had come inside just far enough to be seen and cause a stir. He'd made himself shadowy and nine feet tall. Teensy lightning bolts slithered through the nimbus surrounding him. He was accompanied by two apparently ordinary men-at-arms who, on closer inspection, showed a slight golden shimmer. Sarge and Puddle were pleased to abandon their posts to the newcomers.

The hall had become a tomb with Spite's advent. Everyone anticipated the moment when he no longer just stood there. The shapeshifters seemed particularly unhappy, which suggested they recognized the sorcerer and knew him well enough to believe they had reason to be unhappy. And Marengo North English seemed to have faded into the very woodwork.

Weider listened closely while I explained what we'd found in the ruined brewery. He nodded occasionally, then observed. "They might've created themselves a small army if they'd gotten hold of my place, then."

"Which was probably their plan."

"But why would they get help from a faction of The Call?"

"We still need to dig that out. But I'm pretty sure the Wolves thought the help was going the other way. We know these shifters are old, now. We saw that when Storey had his fit." Trail and Storey and the Heaven's Gate contingent remained dutifully attentive to the keg they had staked out. "They've had lifetimes to practice telling Karentines what they want to hear and showing them what they want to see."

"Hadn't you better get on with the digging? That spook-wrangler gives me the creeps. He's got a bad feel to him. Try to get him out of here before he starts something I'll regret."

"You heard of him before, boss?"

"Perilous Spite? No. But I don't cross paths with those people much. I'm in trade. A brewer. A brewer doesn't have much contact with anybody but people who buy beer. Even during the worst days of the war the brewery had no intercourse with the war's managers and manipulators. I want to keep it that way. Go to work, Garrett."

"Quit swearing." I surveyed the mob and grimaced. I'm not big on getting up in front of crowds. Not when I have to share the spotlight with a lord from the Hill—especially when that lord is a complete unknown. Block seemed impressed by him, though, and now-invisible Marengo hadn't been too far from being petrified.

"Quiet down!" I bellowed. Immediately every thug from The Call and the brewery and the Guard redoubled the racket by trying to shush everybody else. I would've done better just standing there letting them come to the notion that things were about to ripen. Though tardily, silence did find its way among us.

A sea of ugly faces turned my way. Not a one looked happy. I wasn't overflowing with joy, myself.

I hadn't thought this part through. Get them all together, let it turn into a pressure cooker. Slip a couple cards up my sleeve that nobody but Ty knew about. See what the situation produced. That was the plan.

Should I explain? Some of these people had no idea why they'd been summoned. The rest probably had the wrong idea.

I decided to let the thing unfold.

"Mr. Trail. Mr. Storey. You gentlemen became exercised a while ago. Please explain why to everyone else." I could imagine the rumors that had begun to go around already.

Trail couldn't get a word out while surrounded by so many people who outranked him socially. Storey didn't have that problem, though. He had bolstered his courage mightily at Weider Brewing's expense. He repeated the tale of the Myzhod campaign. I let him ramble and editorialize but he didn't embellish much. The stormwarden demonstrated an intimidating willingness to bestow cruel attention on any member of the audience inclined to become restless. I suspected that a lot of my guests knew more about Spite than I did. I suppose if I'd had one of those posh army sinecures instead of a real job as a Marine, I might have heard something about him, too.

Storey made it clear that he and Trail believed these shifters right here, right now, in this very room, were the same damned treacherous shifters who'd led an entire Karentine army to its destruction fifty years ago.

Once Storey depleted his store of vitriol I announced, "Miss Quipo Trim, lately of His Majesty's Royal Army Medical Corps, is going to tell us whatever she recalls that might be germane."

Quipo told the crowd what she'd told me, adding details she'd remembered since then. Then, in succession, I got statements from everyone else who'd had contact with the shifters. I revealed my own history. I exempted only Relway, who wasn't present anyway, according to official information. Almost everyone had to see that this assembly wasn't about me and the Weiders, as many might have expected. Ultimately, it was about the security of the Karentine Crown.

The stormwarden weighed on my mind when I said, "That establishes the picture. These creatures have pretended to serve the Crown for ages but everywhere they go disaster follows. Rather like Glory Mooncalled. I haven't dug out much more about them. They're a big secret. Their commander in modern times was a Colonel Norton Valsung. Miss Trim tells me Valsung was Karentine but she's the only person I've found who ever met the man. I consider his existence problematical. He may have been a particularly clever shapeshifter."

I was fishing. But somebody might remember something and volunteer it. Heck, somebody might even volunteer to tell me who was behind the Brotherhood Of The Wolf and all The Call's embarrassments. Somebody might, but I wasn't going to bet the family silver that someone would.

The stormwarden moved ever so slightly, over by the front door. A sourceless whisper sounded beside my left ear. Years of practice with the Dead Man kept me from jumping. "Valsung existed. His continued survival is, however, indeed improbable. He was of use to them no longer."

I nodded slightly, letting him know I'd heard. I guessed I was supposed to use the information somehow. I didn't see what use it might be, though. I glanced up at the Goddamn Parrot. The old hen was observing alertly from the chandelier while taking care not to draw attention. Excellent. Remarkable. Bizarre. But excellent. Because if the stormwarden figured out how the wonder dodo was being used, I was going to have one very irritated sorcerer on my hands.

It wasn't possible that anyone would get the blame for me. That's Garrett's law.

I murmured, "I hope you stay very, very quiet and let the wizard carry the load."

The pressure hadn't yet had the effect I'd hoped. Nobody had lost control and started spouting secrets.

I turned to Brotherhood Of The Wolf. With them my footing was speculative and personally dangerous: They remained an enigma despite being subject to human motives. They were in bad odor with The Call but I couldn't question the purity of their politics. Those remained rigorously correct by the strictest standards espoused by the most fanatic of rightsists.

The silence in the hall continued but the overall restlessness quotient kept rising. To hold the crowd's attention I began moving down the stair. As I did so, I said, "There's a circumstantial but evident connection between the Black Dragon creatures and Brotherhood Of The Wolf." The fact that your dialectic might be impeccable and your treason accidental would not impress some true believers, lack of imagination and compassion being leading marks of the beast.

I made no direct accusations. I wanted Genord's friends to come to the light on their own, to decide that they owed amends. Genord himself was hopeless. He had decided to protect somebody.

I hollered back up to the balcony, "Boss, you want to weasel your goofball pal back out of your den?"

Max grunted, nodded to Gilbey. Manvil went. He returned leading a Marengo North English still trying to avoid being noticed by the stormwarden.

I had no mercy. "Tell us about the Wolves. Where did they come from? Why did they go away?"

Marengo didn't want to talk. That sorcerer really had him spooked. North English must have pulled some truly stupid stunt. He spoke only with the greatest reluctance, hastily, stumbling, obviously not always certain of his facts.

Morley materialized beside me. He whispered, "Why do you keep talking? Cut their throats and be done with it." City elves are direct folk. They'll chuck out the baby with the bathwater counting on the gods to look out for the tad if he deserves it.

"Because if I go slicing shifters up, I'll probably piss off about half the people in this zoo. Look around. Every one of these clowns is looking for an angle and trying to figure out how to use this. If they can sneak around the stormwarden—beforehand.

Anyway, we need to find out how widespread this changers cancer really is. Which we can't do using dead men. That being a stormwarden over there, not a necromancer." And I, for my part, being obsessively curious, wanted to ferret out a few whys as well as the whos and whats. And that took getting people's minds into the right frame by asking the right questions so the right answers would float to the surface.

Marengo didn't say much interesting about Brotherhood Of The Wolf. They'd been his first effort to give The Call real muscle, a band of unimpeachable war heroes, accomplished, skilled, and dedicated. But having grown accustomed to deal with the King's enemies unsupervised, for weeks or months at a time, they tended to act without consulting their superiors. When they tried to drive the Inner Council to adopt policies they favored, by means of an unspecified intervention that left the council no other option, said council ordered them disbanded. They would be replaced by less elite, more pliable believers. The new groups grew haphazardly till Colonel Theverly came along. Most of the Wolves joined the new freecorps. A few, like Gerris Genord, dropped out and went elsewhere.

Marengo insisted that the Wolves, disaffected or not, would never knowingly ally themselves with Karenta's enemies.

Only the thickest-witted witness would have failed to understand that just from observing the captive Wolves.

Devotion to the Crown is a foundation stone of the freecorps ethic. We had plenty of evidence that shapeshifters did not share that dedication.

North English said his piece and retreated as fast as he could. His courage was extremely inconstant tonight. Perilous Spite really worried him.

I got the impression that the reverse wasn't true. The sorcerer was indifferent to everyone but the shapeshifters.

# 103

I studied face after face while others spoke. Those not anticipating punishment were growing impatient. Only the stormwarden's presence held them in check.

I went down to Genord, tried one more time. "You meant well but you were conned. And not just by these things." I indicated the shifters. "That's not really your fault. You didn't know they weren't human even though you'd worked with them in the Cantard."

Genord showed me the same blank face he'd worn since he'd come through the door.

I got down on one knee. "Look, guy, I'm trying to give you something to work with. They don't hang you for stupid. But they sure will for stubborn. Who got the Wolves back together? Who got you into this? Who are you covering for? You think maybe he knew about the Dragons? Eh?"

Genord and I both knew that Brotherhood Of The Wolf never disbanded. But we could pretend.

"Who decided to target the Weider family? And why them?"

Genord wouldn't talk but his buddies weren't as single-minded. They'd gotten a grip on the notion that they didn't have to throw themselves on their swords. There might be a way out of their fix. If they'd been tricked into serving evil . . .

"You guys haven't killed anybody, have you? Except Lance?" There wouldn't be any getting out of that for Genord.

Gerris remained donkey stubborn. He believed he was a good man fighting the good fight. Too bad his determination was wasted.

One of the Wolves volunteered, "We haven't killed anyone."

The restlessness around us lessened immediately. People jockeyed for vantage points. They might hear something interesting.

Genord gave the talker a black look. His attitude was shared by none of the other Wolves. The man speaking looked like he was used to being in charge. "We're guilty of nothing but striving to serve the movement and the Crown." He glared at the balcony, at the unseen North English, angry, clearly feeling betrayed.

"Suppose you explain that." I surveyed the audience. I leaned back to check the chandelier. The ugliest bird of the century stared back. Still alert. Good. I glanced at the settling tank. I had hold of a thread, now. Finally. Things might start to unravel. Which could mean some real excitement. "Get away from that tank!" I yelled. Trail, Storey, and Shale were back trying to figure out how to get beer out of the vat. Quipo Trim, though, had established herself permanently beside an active keg of Reserve Dark. She muttered with Winger as she sucked it down. Winger was putting her share away, too, instead of looking out for Singe.

No beer disappears faster than free beer.

With my luck the women were swapping Garrett stories.

I growled. I did not want Winger getting drunk. She loses all sense of caution once she's had a few.

The Goddamn Parrot launched himself off the chandelier, swooped around the room. People ducked. People cursed. The bird landed on Winger's wrist just as she started to take a drink. Beer flew. She glared up at me. I indicated Morley. "Remember, the jungle chicken was his fault." The bird roosted on the chandelier again. I glared at Winger's mug. She began to get the idea. But how long could it stick?

Upstairs, Belinda and Nicks joined Alyx and Tinnie. They must've gotten a cue from Max or Manvil. They had North English surrounded and were keeping him out where he could be seen. If they added Tama Montezuma, they'd create a coven of heart-wreckers of diabolic magnitude.

Where *was* Marengo's favorite niece? I couldn't see her for the surrounding crowd. Hadn't seen her for a while now, come to think.

The Wolf continued his story. "Privately we were told that we weren't disbanding. That the announcement that we were would get that asshole Theverly down off his high horse." The Wolf spokesman seemed determined to stare a hole right through North English. Weider and Gilbey had joined the ladies, now, compelling Marengo to face his critic. Max was extremely unhappy with his friend. "We were told we were going underground to do the stuff we'd trained for. Some of us should take positions in the private world. Openings would be arranged. Some should join Theverly's command and monitor it from inside, taking as much control as we could. Some of us should move over to other rights groups so we could keep track of what they were doing. These were all things we were convinced we should've been doing already."

I gave North English the fish-eye myself. That was exactly the sort of stuff a guy like him would pull. But he called down, "That's not true. I told the Brotherhood to disband because I wanted it disbanded. I agreed with Theverly. They wouldn't be managed. Obviously, time has sustained the wisdom of our decision." Nevertheless, he remained shifty-eyed and kept his face averted from the stormwarden.

The man in chains didn't buy North English's protests. "We got orders from you every day. The last couple of months you've sent word three or four times a day. It got to where you were practically controlling every breath we took."

The man believed what he said. I didn't doubt that a bit.

The Wolf had said, ". . . sent word. . . ." And it hadn't been that long since I'd mentioned the changers' talent for telling Karentines exactly what they wanted to hear. This Wolf had been fed a story exactly suited to his emotional need.

North English looked baffled. Maybe he believed what he said, too.

The Wolf plowed on, "The Call was going broke. They wanted to get ahold of a lot of wealth fast. Two, two and a half weeks ago, not long after we started working with Black Dragon, we got word that the Weider brewing empire would be taken over. We'd worked on that project for a long time. Just in case. The Dragons tried to recruit brewery workers in our name. That was hard for us; you kept us tied up in meetings all the time." The man's conviction began to waver in the face of North English's steadfast head-shaking. North English was getting angry enough to ignore the presence of the sorcerer.

Marengo said, "I haven't spoken to you three times in the last year, fellow."

"You couldn't, could you? Colonel Theverly would throw one of his tantrums. You—"

Pular Singe squealed. Saucerhead Tharpe bellowed. Playmate boomed something. Sarge roared. The Goddamn Parrot shrieked. A sorcerous voice whispered "Beware!" in my ear just as *Look Out*! rumbled inside my head. A woody crash came from the direction of the dining room. Shrieks followed that. Something was headed my way.

That something was a whirlwind of horror that looked like a troll with a bad case of the uglies. It had claws like scimitars. It had fangs like a saber-toothed tiger, top and bottom. It was preceded by breath foul enough to gag a maggot. It bulled straight toward me. Bodies flew and people screamed.

There wasn't a hero in the place. Whatever direction the thing looked it saw flying heels. My first impulse was to show it one more pair. So was my second. I listened to that one.

"Down!" said the little voice in my ear. *Down!* insisted the big voice inside my head. I'm a bright boy. I can take a hint. I flung myself down and clung to cold stone like the gods had announced that they were going to do away with gravity.

Came a sound like somebody slapping a brick wall with the flat side of a big wet board. The sound of big bacon frying followed instantly. The ugly apparition shrieked louder than all the shrieking around it put together. It collapsed upon itself, passing through repeated twisting changes before it assumed the shape like those in the Lamp ruin tanks.

A huge, sourceless voice filled the hall. "Stand back. It's stunned, not dead." The thing began to assume human shape. Evidently young shifters adopt some base form to which they'll revert automatically if they can't maintain a shape they've chosen.

The shifters bound in chains made unhappy noises. Their despair was so strong I felt it—maybe because I'd been exposed to the Dead Man for so long.

Stunned didn't last. An arm grew to an impossible length. One incredibly nasty, sicklelike claw tipped it. That claw slashed at me. I was just fast enough to dodge or the shifter was just slow enough to miss.

A waterlogged blanket slapped a stone floor. Big bacon crackled. The shifter leapt into the air, shrieked, then flopped around like its back was broken. I told Morley, "I think I'll back off a ways."

"Clever fellow. Sign me on as your assistant."

I noted that he wasn't watching the shifter. "Whatcha looking for?"

"Just keeping an eye out." He used his "I've got an idea but I'm not ready to talk about it" tone. I looked around, too.

Block and Relway were busy making sure men kept guarding every entrance. I looked up at Tinnie and the girls. They hadn't

fled. But they had let Marengo get away again. Two large gentlemen from the shipping dock had joined the ladies. Max, Manvil,
and Ty now formed a glowering knot at the foot of the grand staircase, evidently concerned that my new playmate might develop a
taste for toothsome wench. A taste I can't say I begrudge almost
anyone.

I limped over to Genord. I'd banged my hip good getting
down onto the floor. "Here we go again. Want to tell me anything
now?"

Gerris *still* wasn't talking.

"Live a fool, die a fool—Now what?"

Another racket from the kitchen, that's what. Neersa Bintor
was *very* upset about something. Had Singe? . . . No, Singe was
there by the dining-room door, just steps away from Relway, shaking like a last autumn leaf, looking at me, in a stance that begged
forgiveness for failing to expose the changer in time.

Still looking around, Morley asked, "You want some bad
news?"

"No. I'd cherish some *good* news, though. Just for the novelty.
What?"

"Crask and Sadler went missing during that excitement."

Gah! "You're shitting me."

Sure enough, their fetters were empty. How the hell? . . .
They'd been out of the way and everybody had been distracted,
but . . . I stormed toward Relway. "You want to tell me how Crask
and Sadler could do a disappearing act in the middle of a hundred
people?"

"What? They couldn't. I've got the only key . . ." A twisted
hand came out of a pocket empty. "Hunh?" He was flabbergasted.
It's a memory I'll cherish. Relway is seldom at a loss. "Somebody
picked my pocket." He started growling at his own people, forgetting, for the moment, that he didn't want to reveal himself.

I went to Pular Singe, told her, "You did just fine. You couldn't
be everywhere at once. Once the shifters understood that you
could identify them they just stayed out of your way. Are you all
right? You think you can work? I might need you to track those
bad men again."

"Never mind the bad men," Morley said from behind me. "She
turned them loose strictly for their diversion value."

Slap and bacon crackle happened again. People who
should've been concentrating on that last shifter had let themselves be distracted by trying to keep track of me. That changer

was off the floor again. It lurched toward its brethren, sprouting scissorlike claws capable of snipping silver. It seemed to be developing an immunity to the stormwarden's sorcery. A double application was needed to put it down this time.

"Someone would have to know me pretty good to think I'd drop everything if they . . ." Of course. Somebody who controlled the resources of Brotherhood Of The Wolf and Black Dragon Valsung could find out all about me. Somebody who'd had me dogged since before I knew I was getting into this mess. Somebody who . . . Who? I could look around me and see everybody involved in the case except Crask and Sadler. But they were pawns. Of the rest only Marengo remotely fit. Like the lead Wolf said.

North English might be one hell of an actor. But he had been behaving strangely ever since he'd gotten hurt. A fact which left me squinty-eyed with suspicion.

# 104

Wait! What about the redoubtable Lieutenant Nagit? Mr. Nagit was an excellent candidate. He probably felt underappreciated. . . . Then I recalled something he'd said. Something I hadn't taken the trouble to hear at the time.

An evil globule of bright feathers hit my shoulder hard. "Goddammit! . . ."

"Do not be willfully stupid, Garrett. Do not be willfully blind."

People stared. Only Morley Dotes grasped the full significance right away. He turned, stared at the settling tank briefly, said, "You're one sneaky bastard, Garrett." He showed about a hundred pointy teeth in a grin. "I've taught you well, my disciple."

I ignored him. I told the bird, "No. I'm not being blind on purpose. I really just got it. Block! Colonel Block." He was close enough that I didn't really need to yell. "Find the woman. The mistress. Montezuma. It's her that ties everything together." Stupid, Garrett. Stupid. It was right there in front of you all the time. But she was gorgeous so you just didn't think she could be anything else. If she'd gotten lucky with you, you might have ended up as thick as Gerris Genord. Or well nicked by a meat cleaver.

How did she know Crask and Sadler? From her old days, before she got her hooks into Marengo?

We didn't know much about her. Nobody bothered to find out, no matter what we'd discussed. Why back-check a whore, however remarkable she might be?

She might have grown up with the nightmare twins.

Above, Marengo had found nerve enough to show himself. His mouth was open but nothing came out.

Mr. Nagit had told me the woman never did anything that didn't relate to her meal ticket. That explained why she had hooked up with Marengo in the first place. It explained why she'd work all the angles against the day Marengo lost interest. She'd started that as soon as she'd arrived at The Pipes, already old enough and wise enough to know that the ride couldn't possibly last.

Tama Montezuma would be one more reason Marengo North English couldn't finance his bigoted revolution. Tama would have found a hundred ways to suck herself a comfortable retirement out of Marengo's and The Call's cash flows.

It was amazing what vistas opened once I embraced the possibility that the luscious Miss Montezuma might be a villain. The probability of a connection with Glory Mooncalled laid itself out as though announced by trumpeters. I already believed that Mooncalled was behind the shapeshifters somewhere. I had hoped tonight's festivities would somehow lure him to the Weider mansion, too, probably in deep disguise. But no disguise would help as long as he came within a hundred feet of that settling tank.

Mooncalled would've gotten his claws into Tama the instant the Brotherhood Of The Wolf included Black Dragon Valsung in their plans. How she'd manipulated the Wolves was clear enough, based on the testimony of our witnesses. She'd pretended to be Marengo's go-between. Which the Wolf acknowledged when asked directly.

Tama wanted to be rich. She had only one thing to sell. The shifters wanted a brewery. They had nothing to market but their talent for infiltration. Glory Mooncalled wanted . . . what? Where Mooncalled came from and where he was going never had been clear. Even my partner, who made a hobby of studying the man, no longer understood what he was about. And the rest of the world knew only that Mooncalled traveled his own road and was a real pain in the ass about letting himself get pushed off of it.

The vistas stretched but I still had questions. Lots of questions. How did Tama get them to attack Marengo that night? Why try to eliminate all the main leaders of the rights movement? Or was that all staging? Where was Glory Mooncalled now? Why hadn't I pulled him in? Because of Perilous Spite? Or had he sensed the trap? And where was Tama Montezuma? Had she worked her magic on Mooncalled? That would be a real marvel, those two getting all tangled up in each other.

And: Where were Crask and Sadler?

The noise volume rose as everybody decided to do something. They teach that in leadership school. *Do* something, even if it's wrong. Karenta might have been a lot better off for a little more inertia in recent decades.

I have to confess some admiration and sympathy for Tama. She might not have lost me if people hadn't died. I understood what moved her. But she was too selfish and too sloppy.

All the despair now haunting the Weider mansion could be laid directly at her feet.

*Mooncalled is in the area, Garrett,* said the voice inside my head. *He is upset. I sense that he had plans for tonight, too, but nothing has gone his way. There may be trouble.*

We didn't have trouble already?

"Let's don't just stand around, Garrett," Block said. "We've got people on the run."

Morley chuckled. "I don't think anybody will get very far. Right, Garrett?"

"I'm not that optimistic, old buddy. Something will go wrong. It always does. Singe!" I couldn't mention Mooncalled. That would spark too many questions. I waved but Pular Singe didn't have courage enough to risk the center of the floor. Which wasn't a good idea, anyway. Almost everybody not in chains was now headed somewhere else in a hurry, many with their eyes closed in fear or in sheer determination not to become a witness to anything.

The gang from Heaven's Gate, however, remained preoccupied with their personal hobbies so didn't contribute to the general uproar. Trail and Storey remained determined to tap the settling tank. They wouldn't enjoy that particular vintage if they succeeded, though. It was particularly bitter, well beyond skunky. I headed that way. "Will you two leave that damned tank alone?" Shale, at least, had had the grace to pass out. Or just fall asleep. "There's all the goddamn beer you can possibly suck down over there by Quipo. Miss Trim! You're supposed to keep these antique idiots under control." But Quipo had reached a point where she was having trouble managing herself.

"Garrett. Heard 'bout you from your fren'. Winger." Quipo was speaking fluent drunkenese. "Where'd she go? Winger. Where'djou go?"

"Garrett." Max wanted me.

"What?"

"*Must* these people destroy my home?"

"Block!" I bellowed. "North English! Get your people under control!" Speaking of control, bigger trouble was on its way. Nobody was managing the shifters, especially that last one. It *still* wasn't yet properly shackled in silver.

The stormwarden descended into the chaos. He went among the handful of shapeshifters like a Venageti triage sorcerer, specialists who had used their talents to decide which wounded should go to the surgeons and which should be put out of their misery. Those guys hadn't saved many Karentines.

This guy ended two lives just like that, suddenly, viley, noisily. Shifters never went easily, it seemed.

The survivors evidently tendered an offer of submission. The stormwarden's golden buttboys got them up and moving. They went docilely, chains tinkling. I wondered what would happen if the sorcerer turned his back. I asked Max, "You want I should do something about that?"

"What?" Weider demanded.

"It's your house." I kept my outrage well hidden. Karentines learn to do that when our lords from the Hill are out. People who won't control their emotions will suffer severe humiliations—at the least.

"Let him have them. They deserve him. Tell Marengo to shut up and get his ass down here. He's been acting like a fool."

North English was harassing his own people from the balcony, apparently convinced that by yelling insults he could make them catch Tama sooner. I didn't yield to my urge to give him a swift kick. Nor would I give in to my inclination to let Tama get away.

While I got North English rounded up so Max could calm him down Morley assembled his friends and mine. He beckoned me. "You've got to get Singe on Montezuma's trail, Garrett. If she gets a big lead, we'll never catch her. She was ready for this."

"Why do you care?"

"Ooh, he's thick," Winger observed. "Dumb as a stump, we'd say back home." She had a strong beer flavor even from six feet away.

"I've got a notion I don't want an explanation if you're interested in it." I noted the not-yet-departed stormwarden watching us from near the front door. I shivered.

Morley said, "Garrett, even Saucerhead figured out that Montezuma has to have a cash stash. Possibly a very large one. She's been milking North English for several years."

"Oh." Exactly what I'd expect of the whole gang, barring Playmate and—maybe—Pular Singe. Hustle out there and disappear the stolen riches before the rightful owner could reclaim them. Then look innocent. I'd seen Morley do it before. The problem was, Winger was the sort of accomplice who wouldn't have enough sense not to start spending like a sailor before the sun came up. Dumb luck and brute strength keep that girl alive.

I don't think Saucerhead understood that. Someday he'll be genuinely unhappy about letting her talk him into things.

I glanced up at Marengo. He still didn't want to mix with us peasants on the main floor. All right. Go, Tama. I didn't mind him losing his money. And him being broke wouldn't hurt Max. Or any of those gorgeous ladies up there. In fact, it'd be a better world if Marengo North English couldn't afford to be a shithead. "What do you think, latrine-beak?" I asked my shoulder ornament.

The Goddamn Parrot was out of words again. Which was just as well. He'd given too many people too much to think about already.

I had a few of my own left, though. "Crask and Sadler are out there somewhere."

Morley replied, "Your pal the secret policeman can handle them. If he hasn't caught them already."

Relway had vanished while I was blinking. Many of his people were missing as well. I asked Singe, "You want to be part of this?"

"Double share," Dotes offered generously, which made Winger sputter. "You wouldn't have to kowtow to Reliance anymore." He knew his ratfolk. Or this ratgirl, anyway. But this ratgirl was smart enough to know when somebody was blowing fairy dust, too. She did a credible job of lifting an eyebrow when she looked to me for my opinion. A double share of what, Garrett?

I said, "I can't go. I've got work to do here. You guys catch her, you bring her back to me." I tried warning them with sudden shifts of my eyes toward the sorcerer. But the fire of the hunt was upon them.

"Winger, stuff it. Bring her back here. I know it sounds improbable but there're issues in this world as important as your greed."

"Ohh!" Saucerhead purred. "Listen to the man growl. Shut up, Winger. He's probably right."

"Be careful," I told Singe and she understood that I meant she shouldn't ever trust her present companions completely.

Their expedition never hit the street.

*Garrett. Beware. We are about to enjoy a badly misjudged and mistimed rescue effort.*

"A what?"

A racket broke out up front. A centaur galloped in through the front door, a javelin in each hand. It bowled over the stormwarden's glitzy henchmen while seeming utterly amazed to find them there. Another minute and the collision would have taken place outside. The stormwarden had just given up staring at me suspiciously.

"What's this?" Morley asked.

"Glory Mooncalled's been watching," I said. But evidently not closely enough to have seen the truth because that centaur had come inside with no idea whatsoever what he was charging into. He was astounded by the mob looking his way. After toppling the guards he tried to stop suddenly but shod hooves just won't do that on polished stone. He skidded. He howled. He tumbled. He whooped. He reached floor level traveling chin first. His language was enough to make the Goddamn Parrot cover his ears. It wasn't Karentine but every man in the place had been to the land where that language was spoken.

More centaurs arrived. Each was as surprised as the first. Their faces revealed their determination to free Mooncalled's allies and an equal intent to stifle the man's enemies. But they faced big problems achieving their ends, not the least of which was that they hadn't come prepared to deal with so many enemies. I got the feeling that they'd expected to just prance in and prance back out. I guessed the first wave of people rushing out had lulled them.

None of the later arrivals suffered the full ignominy endured by the first. That fellow started getting thumped before he stopped sliding. Funny, though. At first only my friends and Colonel Block's showed much enthusiasm for the sport. You'd have thought the guys from The Call would be particularly unfond of centaurs. Centaurs are the most treacherous natives of the Cantard.

In a moment the stormwarden had a nebula of slithering lights clutched to his stomach. The ball persisted less than an eyeblink. There was another splat of waterlogged board against stone. The latecomer centaurs got a mighty assist in their efforts to get back out of the house. Sadly, none collided with the doorframe along the way. What must have been sold as an easy massacre had turned into a rout of the killers before they ever got started letting blood.

I looked around. I didn't need outside help to realize that the centaurs had expected to get support from allies already on the ballroom floor. But nobody raised a hand to help. Which suggested that Mooncalled had staged his rescue in near-ignorance, trusting too much in unreliable allies. Which didn't fit his reputation at all.

Did I smell desperation?

*Love is blind stupid.*

"Oh, no!"

*Oh, yes, I fear. Your craziest speculation was correct.*

There were more centaurs outside. The uproar out there made that clear. It sounded like a pitched battle. I grinned. My more noteworthy guests must have brought extra help. Just in case.

It's getting to be a sad old world. People just don't trust each other the way they used to.

# 105

The excitement had ended. The centaurs had fled. The rescue attempt had failed without ever having become clearly identifiable as such to some people. Colonel Block and a badly shaken, poorly focused Marengo North English soon worked out a tentative, fragile alliance. They would work together to catch Tama Montezuma. I suspected that alliance would collapse about as soon as somebody actually caught sight of Tama. Both men had plans.

Both were counting on me, too. If I couldn't get Pular Singe to track Tama, she might never be caught. She might not be anyway. She was a survivor. She'd had a long time to get ready for the inevitable. I figured there was a very good chance we'd find no trace of her.

I told Max, "It didn't go the way I planned. . . ."

"Does anything?"

"Yes. Sometimes. Sort of. We did get to the bottom of it, didn't we? Sort of." And some good might come of it. Suspicion would attach to The Call for a long time. Plenty of people would believe Marengo was behind everything and had sacrificed his mistress to cover his ass. I planned to keep a foot in that camp myself until Tama offered a public confession, no matter what my sidekick claimed. I had a need to demonize North English, to see him as slicker and slimier than he could possibly be.

Perilous Spite departed, leaving echoes of sorcery fading in the street. With him went the surviving Dragons *and* the Wolves. Brief, feeble protests from the rightsists had had no effect. Being a cynic, I suspected the stormwarden's captives might not enjoy the full rigors of justice. A tame shapeshifter would be a handy tool if you were in the sorcery and dark master rackets. Guys like Spite have no interest in justice, anyway. Most are incapable of grasping the concept.

"Why didn't you do something?" I asked the Goddamn Parrot.

*Perhaps because I had no inclination to become a part of the stormwarden's booty, Garrett.*

I knew that but it still seemed he should have done something.

*I am doing something. Rather more interesting than what you would have me waste myself doing. Spite will reap no benefit from those he has taken into his possession. His conscription was far too public.*

That sounded a lot like one of those circuitous mollifications he always claims I'd misunderstood when things went to hell later. I couldn't recall why I'd been worried about him the past few days.

My friends stuck around, still hoping I'd give them the chance to beat everybody else to the bad girl. Miss Trim and the crew from Heaven's Gate wouldn't leave. There was still some beer left. I told Saucerhead, "You and Winger and Playmate take the old guys home. Make sure Winger's pockets are clean before she leaves. After you deliver them come back here and help get rid of that settling tank."

*Garrett!*

"Remove the tank, then."

*Kindly get on with your chores. I am expecting company. It will go much easier if the crowd is smaller.*

I threw up my hands in exasperation. That told me that he had managed his end not so he could be a card up my sleeve but in order to hook a fish of his own.

"Am I going with you?" Morley asked.

"I'm not going anywhere."

"Bullshit, Garrett. I know you. You want to duck out with your furry girlfriend so you can get to Montezuma first. Not so you can grab some money but because you don't want the pretty lady to get hurt."

I'm not as squishy as Morley thinks. I'd done some thinking about that night at The Pipes, about the would-be visitor and the knife or cleaver I might have seen. I wanted to think I'd seen a changer in Montezuma shape. But I was keeping an open mind. My failing to survive that night might have solved several problems for Tama. Particularly if she knew what was supposed to happen to her uncle Marengo up on the edge of Elf Town.

I was sure she'd known, now.

*She almost certainly did. Will you quit dawdling?*

"What do you mean, *almost* certainly? You had plenty of time to dig around inside her head."

*Easier said than done, Garrett. Her thoughts were terribly murky. She had some sort of protection.*

"Well, of course." Was he lying? His motives aren't often clear.

Hell with it.

I turned to Morley. I don't mind him thinking I'm soft. It's an edge. "You figured me out." I turned away again. "I talk to the wind." That left him looking puzzled. "After all this excitement tonight I thought you'd want to run back to your place and snuggle up with your favorite squash. Unless you're romancing an eggplant these days."

Winger was leaving with Saucerhead, shooing the old-timers and Quipo, but she wasn't happy or moving fast. She snarled at Block as she passed him where he was hanging around hoping I'd help him. Marengo North English lurked on the balcony above, nursing the same foolish hope. I'd have to ditch them both without being obvious.

Morley and I had been whispering so Singe hissed, "What do you want me to do?"

Morley offered a show of teeth, amused. I told Singe, "This's your choice. You want to be independent. To do that you have to make your own decisions." That would be tough. Ratwomen are more oppressed than most human women. They never learn to think in terms of self-determination.

A smirking Morley Dotes drifted off to send his henchmen home.

"Do you want me to do it?" Singe asked.

"Of course I want you to do it. That's why I asked you. What I don't want is for you to decide to do it just because I want it. I want you to make a choice that's your own, made in your own interest." Gah! That sounded like one of Tinnie's serpentine evolutions.

It's certainly easier being the kind of guy who just uses people.

A stir at the door saved me any more skiprope. A man who appeared to be in his seventies paused to survey the hall before descending to its floor. The guard who should've kept him out seemed not to notice him. Maybe the old fellow was a ghost. He stood stiffly erect, partially supporting himself with a walking stick carved to resemble a fat black cobra. His skin was dusky but not dark like Playmate's or Tama's. His eyes were gray. He seemed to be going blind. He came downstairs slowly, with a marionette's jerkiness, feeling his way with his stick. He looked nothing like the image I'd carried in my head across the years since he'd started acting up in the Cantard. Dammit, this guy was just too old!

Manvil Gilbey, directing a crew already starting to clean up, asked, "Friend of yours?"

"Not hardly. Friend of a friend. Maybe. He should be harmless and he shouldn't be here long." I said that directly to the Goddamn Parrot. "Try to work around him. Don't bother him unless he misbehaves." Which didn't seem likely. I could recall no instance when that old man hadn't had somebody else do his dirty work for him.

Glory Mooncalled walked stiffly to the beer keg. Jerkily, he drew a drink in a mug formerly used by Trail or Storey. A glimmer of fear burned in the backs of his eyes.

I was sure that a lot of calculation and clever manipulation had gone into making this moment possible. No doubt I'd been played like a cheap fiddle for days just so my pal in the tank could manage a sitdown with his hero. With none of that having any real impact on everything else that I was doing.

He was good, Old Bones was. Or I was getting *too* cynical and suspicious.

It's an occupational disease.

"That who I think it is?" Morley whispered.

"I expect so. But nobody's ever seen him. What do you think, bird? Was the mystery man plooking Tama Montezuma?"

The Goddamn Parrot said, "Pretty boy." With a sneer in his voice.

"That does it. Into the pot. Singe?"

"I will help. Not because you want my help but because by doing so I can help myself."

"Excellent. Makes you just like the rest of the team. Morley!" Damned if he wasn't flirting with Alyx. Or maybe Nicks. Oblivious to the fact that the Weiders, father and son, were looking at him in a way more often seen in rightsists observing nonhuman behavior. "Don't do this to me, Morley."

He grasped the situation instantly. "You're right. Not smart. But it'll be torture holding back."

"Tell me something I haven't had to live with for half of forever." I collected Block and joined North English, who still refused to come down from the second floor. "Singe says she might help track Tama. But she refuses to help either one of you." I doubted that she knew who either man was, really, but neither was beloved of ratpeople and a refusal would be no surprise to them.

"Why is that old man here?" North English asked. I noted he kept his back to the visitor. Did he know the man? Was he afraid he might be recognized?

The old-timer took his mug and settled into a chair he dragged over beside the settling tank. There was a quiver in his drinking hand. I had a distinct feeling that it would be a long time before Glory Mooncalled was again a major factor in Karentine affairs. After this interview it would take him an age to reclaim his confidence and build a new underground, the secrets of which were known only to his friends. He would have no secrets after this interview. And he looked too old to start from scratch.

I hoped the bag of bones inside that damned tank had the gods-given good sense to do like I'd asked and rifle the minds of Marengo North English, Bondurant Altoona, and their like tonight. If we robbed them of all their secrets, we could disarm them, too. In fact, if he hadn't been just too damned lazy, he might've spared a mind to sneak a peek at what was going on inside the heads of Block and Relway and maybe even that scab of clabbered misery off the Hill, Perilous Spite. But I doubted he had the nerve to try the latter. Too much personal risk involved.

"Nobody. Friend of a friend." I went back down to Singe. "Do you have a scent?"

"Yes."

She was a marvel, picking it out of the mess that had to be in that hall.

I was surprised immediately. Instead of heading for any door Tama had marched right into the kitchen, past a flabbergasted Neersa Bintor, into the pantry, and from there had descended to the cellars below the house. Which, I shouldn't have been surprised, connected to the caverns beneath the brewery.

"This woman definitely had everything worked out ahead of time," Morley said.

Absolutely. I hadn't known about this way out. Or in, maybe, if you had connections at the brewery end. Had Tama been through there occasionally, say to visit Gerris Genord? Having someone special to protect certainly would explain his stubborn silence. And Tama knew how to get her hooks into a man.

I wondered what she would've done if Mooncalled's rescue

gang had shown up on time. Would she have pretended there was no connection and have tried to stick with Marengo?

As we dithered trying to get lights for my feeble human eyes the Goddamn Parrot squawked, then abandoned me.

*Garrett. Do not overlook the chance that a great many watchers will be prepared to follow you.*

"A possibility very much on my mind." I ignored the odd looks that remark earned me.

# 106

Morley cursed softly. Somehow, cobwebs had gotten onto the lace of one of his cuffs. Soil was supposed to avoid him. "This isn't the fun it used to be, Garrett."

"Fun? Fun doesn't have anything to do with it. We're the last righteous men, standing with jaws firm in the face of the chaos."

Pular Singe giggled.

Morley cursed again, but conceded, "It is a great way to meet interesting women."

"Can't disagree with that." Strange ones, too. "What is it?" Singe had stopped. She sniffed. I couldn't see a thing. The one lantern I'd come up with hadn't lasted all the way through the underground passage.

We were in the wagon lot behind the brewery loading docks, having exited the brewery through the storage caves. I hadn't been able to stop and share a tankard with Mr. Burkel, who'd been disappointed. But he'd told us we were only minutes behind Tama, who hadn't been able to negotiate the tunnels with our ease.

"She got aboard a wagon," Singe told me.

There were at least twenty of those crowded into the lot, waiting for sunrise. Morley grumped something about have to search them all. Singe said, "No, the wagon left."

I glanced back at the dock. There were two dock wallopers on duty, snoozing on stools under a single feeble lantern. Nights, of course, they only loaded independent haulers.

I woke them up. With sullen cheer they admitted having loaded a small wagon a short time earlier. "One driver," one told me. "Out of Dwarf Fort. They're fixin' to celebrate one of their holidays."

"She's on a cart out of Dwarf Fort," I told Morley.

"Then we'd better move fast." Dwarf Fort wasn't far away.

"She won't be headed there herself. She knows about Singe and she's improvising. She'll get off before the wagon goes inside."

Embarrassed, Singe informed me, "I cannot trail her well if she is riding."

"So how about you follow the wagon? Or the horses, if you can stand the stink? You knew she got into a wagon and there's only been one go out of here lately, seems like you could."

Singe brightened instantly. That hadn't occurred to her. Yet. It would have. She sniff-sniff-sniffed, then headed out.

"Not only brilliant and talented and beautiful but fast as well," Morley whispered. "You don't want to let this one get away."

"Did Marengo North English and Bondurant Altoona rub off on you?" He was ragging me at Singe's expense.

"Whoa!" He started to argue but decided against. "All right. Let's abuse the parrot." Who, conveniently, wasn't around to defend himself. He'd chosen to stay behind. Apparently. I was always the last to know what that overdressed crow was up to. Or even what that critter who figured everything out for him was up to, for that matter. We were in for some headbutting after this mess settled out.

"Wish you'd decided that a year ago. Then maybe held him underwater to see how long he could go without breathing." Singe flinched. She still wasn't used to our banter. It always took her a moment to realize we weren't really about to skin each other. "I'm thinking about spiking your goulash with catnip. Then you'd wake up married to Winger."

"Couldn't. She's already got a husband somewhere. And I'm engaged."

"Really? When did that happen?"

"Oh, back before I was born. I just don't talk about it much. My grandparents arranged it. They were immigrants. They stuck to the old ways. They still try to."

"I'll bet you're a major disappointment."

"They weep human tears at every family gathering."

"When are you supposed to start making this poor woman miserable?"

"Oh, a long time ago. But she never showed up for the ceremony."

"Smart woman."

"She just hadn't met me. If she had . . . I don't know if I could've talked my way out of that. The old folks are stubborn as rocks. They still carry on like it was my fault. They can't blame it on Indalir's family. They have royal blood. As if every elf who ever walked doesn't, the way those people tumble anybody who can't outrun them."

"I'm glad you aren't the kind of lowlife who finds women interesting."

"Definitely one weakness you can't pin on me."

Pular Singe stopped. She turned slowly, nostrils flaring. Morley shut up and began searching the night, too. He loosened his sword-cane. I said, "I hoped they'd lose us because of those tunnels."

Singe said, "No. Not watchers. It is the two evil men who escaped. They met the wagon here." She dropped to all fours, circled, sniffed.

I muttered, "Coincidence? Or prearrangement?"

Morley asked the important question. "How could they know where she'd be? She didn't know. She was just running."

"If she thought tonight might be the end of her run, she might've had somebody waiting outside. Who's going to pay any attention to a dwarf making a beer run?"

"There is the smell of fear," Singe said. "Mostly from the driver but also from the woman. I think she did not expect to encounter the evil men."

"She wouldn't want to run into them," Morley said. "After what they've been through they'd have a few bones to crack with her."

"If they got this far, I'll bet it was because they were allowed to," I said. "There'll be somebody else on this trail real soon, Singe. Probably the little man who tries so hard to hide who he is."

Morley tested his cane again. "You carrying anything?"

"I'm not military but I'm fixed." I did wish that I had my head-knocker. I needed to have some more of those made up.

"Notice the streets are empty."

"They're never busy down here. And there were centaurs around. Maybe there still are." It *was* unusually quiet, though.

Singe squeaked. "Blood. The direction changes. That way."

"I'm blind here," I reminded them. "I'm cursed with human eyes."

"Over there," Singe said.

I went. Morley followed. He confessed, "Her eyes are better than mine, too."

The treasure at the end of this dark rainbow was a broken dwarf. He wasn't dead but that was only because Crask and Sadler hadn't felt any urgent need to kill him. They'd only wanted his wagon. We left him for Master Relway. Singe picked up the trail again. She wasted no time getting on with the hunt.

The cynic in me, or maybe the practical businessman, told me I had to get in good with her now because she was going to be a phenomenon later. All she needed was a little more confidence, a little more experience, and a little more force of personality.

I kept up, puffing. I gasped, "I'm worn-out. These last few days just never made much sense. Everybody I know was mixed up in it, all of them banging off each other and getting in each other's way. . . ."

"Sometimes the world works that way, Garrett," Morley replied. "When everybody heads a different direction nobody gets anywhere."

I understood that but it didn't satisfy my sense of propriety. Everybody jumped into the mud. They all clawed and slashed in squalid pettiness, all the while espousing grand ideals.

I grunted. Morley chuckled, then said, "Here you go launching another clipper of despair because all the humans you know act like human beings."

We really are a tribe of sleazeballs but I don't like being reminded of it. It would be nice to believe that at least some of us are climbing toward the light without pursuing a hidden agenda.

Singe slowed. I took the opportunity to recapture my breath before it got away completely. The ratgirl whispered, "The wagon is just ahead." I knew that. I heard its iron-rimmed wheels banging the cobblestones. "It is a small one drawn by two ponies." Which was no surprise, dwarves not being inclined toward big wagons and plowhorses. "I smell fresh blood."

The coldness that always comes when I think about Crask and Sadler began to engulf me. I was almost superstitious about those guys. I wasn't, strictly speaking, scared of them but I dreaded a confrontation because facing them was like challenging forces of nature.

Morley observed, "They'll still be in bad shape. Their jail time couldn't have been any holiday." In tone more than word he sounded like he wanted to convince himself. So maybe he had his own reservations.

The villians had set a course headed north. Soon they'd leave this quiet neighborhood for one where the night people thronged.

he'd still be there when Relway's crew arrived. "I got mine!" I said.

The Goddamn Parrot offered a pleased squawk from somewhere overhead.

The wagon stopped. Morley said, "Crask's inside. He's unconscious."

"Another anticlimax."

"What're you talking about?"

"For years I've expected this. It was going to be an epic battle. Bodies flying around, knocking down houses, busting holes in the street. Going on for hours. Everybody'd have to bring a lunch. Instead we butt heads with them three times in the last few days and hardly got a scratch for our trouble."

"So we caught them when they were weak. That's the smart way to do it. Hang on. This one's bleeding. Hell. He's got a knife stuck in him! I'm not so sure I want to snuggle up with Tama Montezuma after all."

I used strips torn from Sadler's jail smock to bind his wrists behind him. He made vague gurgling sounds. I asked, "Where is she? She in there?"

"Bad news, Garrett. More bad news. There's nobody in here but me and Crask and ten kegs of Weider's cheapest beer. And the dwarves will come looking for that before long."

"Awk!" Eight pounds of outrage in a three-pound package slammed down onto my shoulder. I lurched toward the wagon.

Morley was right. There was no beautiful woman in there at all, let alone the marvelous Miss Montezuma. "Where did she go? How could we lose her? Singe? Singe, where are you?"

Singe didn't answer me. I scurried around calling her name. Morley started laughing. He gasped, "We've been had, Garrett. You realize that? We've been snookered by a ratgirl."

"Yuck it up, you glorified greengrocer."

He kept laughing. "We can't go anywhere without Pular Singe. Not if we want to get there ahead of Relway or North English or Belinda. Only question left is, did the kid do it on her own or did Reliance put her up to it?"

"You really think it's that hilarious?"

"Well, no, actually. I don't enjoy getting slicked, either. I'd rather it was me doing the slicking. But you and I don't really need the money. We just think it'd be nice to keep North English from getting it back. And you want Montezuma for what she did to the Weiders."

Nobody likes to work with strangers looking over their shoulder
We had to do something soon.

"You go along the right side and grab the driver," Morley said.
"I'll take the left."

"Me?"

"You're taller and heavier. You'll have more leverage."

No point arguing with the obvious. "Now?"

"Without all that stomping. You don't want them to know
you're coming."

Stomping? I wasn't making a sound. All I could hear was the
whisper of Singe's nails on the paving stones.

Now there was enough diffuse light that I could make out
vague shapes and keep from crashing into walls and watering
troughs. Soon I made out the dwarf wagon. Morley loped beside
me, in step. I murmured, "I see it."

"Do it."

My heartbeat increased rapidly. This confrontation had
haunted me for years.

From somewhere came a loud, "Awk!" in distinct parrotese. It
didn't sound like a warning so it must have been only to let me
know there was a friendly witness. Which wasn't much comfort
since it was hardly possible for reinforcements to arrive in time if
I screwed up.

Singe must've been more scared than she let on. She began to
fall behind.

Any noise I made got covered by the curses of the man driving. He couldn't get those stubborn ponies to move faster than a
walk. Dwarf ponies have one speed. Slow. The only alternative
gait is dead stop, inevitably exercised in the event of excessive
brutality.

Funny. Dwarf ponies are a whole lot like dwarves.

I grabbed the driver's right arm, used my momentum to pull
him down. I couldn't tell which man I'd grabbed but that didn't really matter. Crask and Sadler might as well have been twins. I
didn't see the other one. He had to be inside the wagon, probably
in worse shape.

I glimpsed a surprised face as my victim hit the cobblestones.
Foul air blew out of him. He groaned, then lay still. I moved in
warily.

There was no need. The anticlimax was real. Sadler had
bashed the stuffing out of the street with the back of his head.
Shaking with the letdown I tried to decide how to tie him up so

I grunted, grumped. "I think I'll just go home and go to bed now."

"Why?"

"I should've expected this. Nothing in this whole damned mess had gone the way you'd expect it to or made any sense while it was going to hell. So I think I'll just wish Singe good luck, drop out now, and let the loose ends tie themselves up on their own."

"Garrett, there's sure to be a fortune involved."

"You just told me you don't need the money."

"I didn't say it wouldn't be nice to have it."

"Tinnie is still back at the Weider place." So was my some-time partner. But he could look out for himself. I was little peeved with him.

"You want Winger to score on this one?"

"You think she'd ditch the old guys?"

"I think Saucerhead will actually have a thought somewhere along the way, will say it out loud, will get no answer, and will discover that he no longer has one of his companions."

"Playmate . . ."

"Is so honest he's easier to flummox than Saucerhead is. He won't suspect a thing if she tells him she had to step into an alley to get rid of some of that beer. Tharpe would be suspicious, though. He's dim but his light isn't all the way out. And he's had experience with Winger."

Relway's troops began filtering out of the darkness. That put an end to all speculation.

The Goddamn Parrot began swearing his black heart out. Maybe my partner took Singe's coup personally even though it didn't really have much to do with him.

# 107

That really should've been the end of it, I thought. Most of the guilty had been exposed as villains. The whys and some of the where-fores of their crimes had been dragged sniveling into the sunlight. Clever exposure of truths dredged from evil minds and a judicious stimulation of wicked rumor by my sedentary sidekick, mainly behind my back, resulted in an indefinite postponement of the Cleansing. It particularly disarmed Glory Mooncalled by laying waste to his beloved rebel image. The more exciting rumors even stirred a Royal Inquest into the behaviors of Perilous Spite when some of his peers began to wonder if those rumors had substance and Spite might plan to use captured shapeshifters in some wicked scheme of his own.

The Dead Man hadn't dared touch the stormwarden's mind at Weider's but four centuries of observing human misbehavior closely had allowed him to manufacture rumors that got the Hill churning like an overturned anthill. Spite's enemies soon resur-rected old questions about his management of the secret and spe-cial services during the war. Even his friends began to wonder aloud about several mysteries surrounding his tenure.

Working with Ty Weider, whom he liked for some reason, His Nibs even helped fashion a face-saving formula whereby Ty Wei-der and gorgeous Giorgi Nicholas could honorably evade an al-liance not even their parents found particularly desirable anymore. That mostly took exposure of the truth that only inertia was keep-ing any of the principals committed and quiet revelation of the "fact" that Ty would be unable to father an heir.

Life was good for Garrett. I had plenty of time to do what I do best, which is nothing.

But Tama Montezuma was still on the run. And Pular Singe hadn't been seen since she'd deserted me, though Reliance and Fenibro both accused me of having squirreled her away in my harem. Neither Belinda nor Relway eased up on their machinations and malfeasances. Neither gave a rat's whisker if the Dead Man did know what they were doing. The Dead Man, of course, didn't make their mischief public, as he did with The Call, Perilous Spite, and his own personal fallen angel, Glory Mooncalled.

The stormwarden was particularly not happy but didn't get a chance to look for the source of his embarrassment. Odds were he never would. He had to devote all his genius to the manufacture of plausible explanations of how a man with his talents could blunder so often and so egregiously while Karenta's chief spymaster and still have grown filthy rich. Rumor began to speculate about possible past connections with the Dragons.

The day had been saved. I think.

At times I wonder, though, if TunFaire really deserves saving—whether the threat is from our own homegrown monsters or those from outside our experience.

If we didn't have a thousand religions already, I'd get me a black outfit and a big black book, grow a scraggly beard and start squawking about salvation and redemption. I know where I can get a black goat.

Grudgingly, of course, I admit that the Dead Man's efforts had made it possible for life to return to normal at the Garrett homestead. Or as nearly normal as a place can be while infested by a menagerie. It was a good week. Not one wannabe client came pounding on my door.

Dean had the place looking respectable again. Saucerhead and Winger had gotten the Dead Man back onto his wooden throne, not obviously the worse for his adventure. He looked like he'd never left home but certainly didn't think like it. He remained way too excited to fall asleep. Strategically, it would've been a great time to take on another tough case. Old Bones was up for anything that would let him show off. The only downside was that he just would not leave off complaining about having been stuffed into that settling tank. And never mind the fact that the ruse had been his own brainchild entirely. I'd nothing to do with the planning or execution of his scheme. I'd had only the shortest and most ambiguous warning that he intended to come to the party.

Dean complained more than the Dead Man did. He hadn't enjoyed having to move out, even for just a few days, never mind that it had been for appearance's sake. He refused to accept that explanation. He was going to make sure I shared his unhappiness.

Fortunately, Tinnie came around several times to help him clean and to cheer him up and to make him feel guilty about being alive. Her visits offered me blessed respites from both cranksters.

I caught up on my gossip with Eleanor. I scandalized Mrs. Cardonlos by telling her that I knew she was a police spy but I didn't mind that. I'm now convinced that she is Relway's creature. But I don't care. Me telling her I know she is a police spy has her backing off. It's clear she doesn't want such ideas to afflict her less tolerant neighbors.

To my complete and eternal astonishment everyone who had hired me paid all the fees and expenses I claimed. I was boggled because there were so few quibbles. Marengo North English astonished me by not holding a wake for each copper he had to let go. I got the distinct impression that he was in a huge hurry to get me the hell out of his life.

Despite all the good news my life was not very satisfying. A lot of people had gotten hurt and not many of the ones who did had deserved it. I couldn't help feeling there must've been more I could've done to keep evil at bay. Something I should probably be doing still.

Sometimes life may make no sense but you can't give up on it. You've got to soldier on. You probably can't win but if you abandon the struggle the darkness rushes in and swallows everything. But, on the other hand, you do get tired fighting the good fight. Me, Block, even Relway sometimes, we all feel faded, like the steel has gone, leaving no heat.

# 108

I was relaxed. I was comfortable. It was time to go review with old Chuckles. He had to be over his worst grump about how unfair it was that everybody had done things exactly the way he'd told them to.

I strolled across the hallway. Up for'ard Cap'n Beaky rehearsed his lines for his next effort to incite mutiny or mayhem. Once I entered his room I found that His Nibs still hadn't started snoring. "Can we talk now? You've had a week. That's time enough to get over it."

He didn't say no.

"That old man at Weider's the other night. That really was Glory Mooncalled, wasn't it?"

*Yes.*

"He was a big disappointment, eh?"

*Indeed. Time, as ever, is a villain.*

I waited. He added nothing, though, so I had to ask, "What wicked trick did time play you?"

*Time caused change. The fiery idealist of yesteryear has become a cold blooded, cynical, power-seeking opportunist indistinguishable from those he wanted to displace when he was younger. My illusions are dead. My innocence is gone.*

"Pardon me," I gasped once I regained control. My stomach muscles ached, I'd laughed so hard. "That's the best story I've heard since the one about the blind nun and the snake with no teeth. And I was just about convinced that you didn't have a sense of humor."

*Your sophomoric jocularity provides striking evidence in con-*

*demnation of that entire concept. Which is an entirely human con-*
*ceit, I might note, and highly overrated.*

"Humor, you mean? Hell, even ratpeople have a sense of humor, Old Bones." In fact, fewer humans have a good sense of humor than do members of almost any other race.

Speak of the humorless. Dean interrupted before we got going
good. He was carrying two chairs. He dropped them and left. He
was back a minute later with a sawhorse, then left again. Next
time he lugged in a couple of planks.

I asked, "What the devil are you doing?"

"Making a table."

"Why?"

"For a dinner party. This's the only room that's big enough."

"Dinner party? What dinner party?"

*I invited several friends in for the evening.*

"*You* invited several friends? Without bothering to consult
your landlord?" Or even bothering to invite him? "I want to talk
about my friends. You had a couple of hours to burgle brains.
What did you learn? Give!"

*Nothing of significance which you do not already know.*

He seemed unusually reticent. That suggested his ego was involved. Which meant his productivity had disappointed him. "You
didn't get anything? What were you doing? Helping Trail and
Storey suck down the beer?"

Dean brought two more chairs. I hadn't seen them before. He
must've borrowed them somewhere. He reported, "Both Mr. Weiders send their regrets but Mr. Gilbey will attend. Miss Alyx and
Miss Giorgi will accompany him."

*The proximity of the stormwarden made extreme caution nec-*
*essary. And a great deal of attention had to be invested in tracking*
*and, in time, controlling Glory Mooncalled. Likewise, the parrot. I*
*had little attention left for mental espionage.* He wasn't usually so
defensive. His testiness was a clue to his mental state. He couldn't
brag about his efforts that night. Which suggested he had done
very little that I might find useful. Normally, he can discover
something self-aggrandizing in almost anything.

"But you already gave me enough to wreck the stormwarden
and cripple The Call. So what was going on inside North English's head? Did he put Tama up to running the Wolves?"

*I do not know. I was not able to penetrate the man's mind.*

What? "Uh. . . . Not able or didn't try?"

*Some of each. Mainly the latter as it appeared it would be a difficult task. He appeared to possess the same protection that the Montezuma woman did.*

But he had had time to shop through the heads of Nicks and Ty and Max and discover that nobody really wanted the wedding to go on.

Many is the time I have had to remind myself that he isn't human, that his priorities aren't human, and, especially, that what might seem important to me will be trivial to him. "You did dig into Bondurant Altoona's head, didn't you? And Belinda's? And those of other principals?"

*I attended that confabulation, humiliating myself by allowing this once proud flesh to be embalmed within a demeaning, noxious cask, only because by doing so I could at last come face-to-face with Glory Mooncalled. I invested a great deal of effort in making that meeting possible. Anything I did on your behalf was incidental. The appearance of the stormwarden, which I did not anticipate because I had been out of touch with your researches, complicated matters immensely. In any event, you brought the matter to a successful conclusion.*

"But not a satisfying one. And now I have to deal with yet another dark suspicion."

Old Bones simply wasn't interested in my problems. He shifted his attention to Dean, who was back with more lumber and another report. "Mr. Relway won't come. However, Colonel Block has indicated that he will be present. Lieutenant Nagit will attend." The old man never glanced at me. This was between him and the Dead Man and my opinion was irrelevant.

And it was my fault alone that both these vipers resided in my house. Not to mention that bundle of colorful snake snack camped out up front. Though that I could blame on Morley. . . .

He did say Lieutenant Nagit? The Dead Man shouldn't know Nagit from a hitching post. Nor did he know Manvil Gilbey, for that matter. What the hell was he up to?

Lieutenant Nagit, though? We might could have become friends if he wasn't so bigoted. His taste in redheads was impeccable.

I might want to keep an eye on him in that area. Unless a redhead with malicious intent to make me sweat was behind his having received an invitation.

Dean continued, "Marengo North English won't be here."

Now there was a surprise. Would Marengo dine with the hired

help? Who, coincidentally, had become far too familiar with his affairs *and* who had a tame Loghyr on staff? Not likely. Particularly in light of my sudden new suspicion, which shouldn't have been that new, come to think of it.

I had to take a few minutes to settle and reflect upon our interactions.

"Miss Tate will be here." Well, of course she would. Would she ever be far off if Alyx or Nicks were close enough to cause palpitations? Again, not likely.

"What's the point?" I asked. "We can't learn anything new from any of those people."

The Goddamn Parrot's laughter echoed down the hall. The little monster launched a rant almost certainly stimulated from outside.

*Occasionally I have an agenda of my own, Garrett.*

Only occasionally?

"Miss Contague will come as well."

What? Why get Belinda in here amongst the gentler lovelies? She was in one of her manic, deadly phases these days. People who had challenged her rule or who had just irritated her lately were finding themselves dead in alleys or turning up missing all over town—though, to Belinda's credit, she did restrict the mayhem to the realm of business. But when she got into one of these moods where she heard murderous commands in her father's voice inside her head I preferred to avoid tickling her interest in me. I had hopes that interest would fade into complete indifference eventually.

"You left out Shale and his pals?"

*Mr. Tharpe and Miss Winger, too. This is neither a reunion nor a rogue's ball.*

What was it, then? "Is Morley coming?"

*I believe Mr. Dotes is arriving now.*

Somebody banged on the door. Dean responded. Evidently he was so excited by the challenge of managing a real dinner that he was willing to assume his other duties without quarrel.

"Why?" I asked. I wanted the Dead Man's plan. He was up to something.

"Not much to do around The Palms," Morley said from the doorway. "Things are slow. Nobody wants to come out while that's going on." He inclined his head toward the street. The racket raised by a really bad marching band was winkling rotten mortar out of old masonry for half a mile around.

The less disciplined and crazier rightsist gangs were attempting to cash in on recent embarrassments suffered by Marengo North English and The Call. They were everywhere, day and night, often armed, usually in the biggest crowds they could muster, trying to appeal to the disenchantment swamping North English's troops.

In the short run the rightsist movement was on a roll. As the faintest of heart of the Other Races hit the road their stronger cousins became more cautious. Fringe rightsists were making themselves ever more menacing by riding the crest of a wave of fear not ameliorated by the relative restraint characteristic of The Call. But they were just more public, not more numerous. I thought the absence of The Call from the streets would hasten the collapse of the more marginal, radical, crazy factions. Without the image of The Call they couldn't maintain a credible camouflage of respectability, rationality, and patriotism. I was sure their popular support would evaporate.

I expected the whole rightsist mess to collapse within a few months. And I hoped recent emotional shocks were enough to keep Marengo North English from pulling himself together before it was too late to keep his curdle-brained brother idealists from stumbling over the precipice of chaos.

It amazed me that nobody agreed with me. Even the Dead Man seemed convinced that the madness could only feed upon itself and grow worse—instead of eating itself up.

The Other Races—those who hadn't yet run for the boondocks—contributed to the misapprehension with their bickering and finger-pointing. I'd bet Bondurant Altoona and his cronies were feeling pretty cocky about their chances of replacing The Call as the flagship goof troop. But all that would change. If I was right.

Strange thing is, the streets are actually safer today then ever before during my lifetime. Bizarre but true. Only the stupidest, craziest, most desperate crooks try anything with dedicated rightsists everywhere, making sure the rest of us humans live up to their righteous standards.

# 109

"Anybody remember to invite Pular Singe?" Morley asked. He couldn't resist a smirk. Like it was all my fault that the ratgirl had outsmarted us.

"I didn't invite anybody to anything," I grumped. "I don't have anything to do with this. Whatever this might be. It's the chubby guy's shindig. I just live here. I just own the place. I'm going to go up and take a nap while you all party."

*Miss Pular has been invited.*

"That must've been some trick." He was chairbound and could get word to her when I couldn't dig up anybody even willing to admit knowing her name during my infrequent outings? "She wouldn't come here."

"She'll be here," Morley crowed. "Count on it."

Which meant he was in on the Dead Man's scheme. Whatever that was. "She isn't your average rat, Morley. You couldn't trick her that easily. Anyway, we don't know that she had any luck robbing Tama Montezuma." And outstanding luck that would've had to be. Tama Montezuma was older, smarter, stronger, more experienced, harder and deadlier than the baddest ratperson around.

The hunt for the missing mistress was one undertaking The Call had not deferred. Marengo's snoops were everywhere. He had told them Tama had been the spy responsible for the failure of the Cleansing. And I would be amazed in the extreme to learn that he was wrong. Although sabotaging the Cleansing might not have been her primary purpose, she would've had to keep her changer allies posted and they would've jumped at the chance to embarrass The Call.

Morley showed me more pointy teeth than might one of Venable's babies after deciding that I'd make a nice snack. I knew Dotes meant to mention how disappointed Tinnie and Dean would be once I revealed my new infatuation with Singe. But he restrained himself. So I would owe a moment of charity when I got even for the Goddamn Parrot.

Dotes said, "She is smart, Garrett. You're right. And she's as cunning as a rat. But we've both had ample opportunity to discover that brilliance alone won't protect you from what you don't know. And what Pular Singe doesn't know is that the rumors she's been hearing are pure fairy dust."

"What rumors? How's she going to hear any rumors if she's hiding from Reliance?"

"Oh, we're counting on her being underground. If she is, she can't check out the stories."

"What makes me think something has been going on behind my back?"

*Intuition tempered by experience?*

"You're behind this? What're you trying to do to me, Old Bones?"

*Make you rich? Right after we save you from your dread, terminal disease, of course.*

"Ask a foolish question. What disease? I'm healthy as a horse—No, healthy as something decent and sane. A randy thunder lizard, maybe."

*No one outside this house knows that. You have not been seen since the day you bearded Mistress Cardonlos.*

"She'll come because she worships you, Garrett," Morley said, still wrestling with inner mirth. "She'll come because she won't be able to miss the opportunity to say good-bye. She'll come because, despite what she's heard, she doesn't really believe in this glob of carrion you call a partner."

"I don't call him a partner. He does. Far as I'm concerned, he's just—"

In the meantime Morley said, "Gleep!" and leapt into the air, goosed by the glob of carrion. He didn't come down. The glob was not amused.

I grinned some, enjoying his predicament. I wondered if I could get him to take the Goddamn Parrot back in return for my good offices in getting his feet turned back around below his head and maybe even on the ground. "Chuckles, I don't have a clue what you expect to accomplish tonight. Sounds like you've been spreading rumors that I'm dying. If I'm that sick, why do I want a bunch of people cluttering up the place?"

"You want to say good-bye," Morley said. Hanging bottom up from the ceiling like some kind of pretty-boy bat evidently didn't bother him much. "So you've asked some of the important people in your life to come visit one last time."

"The pain and despair must be overwhelming me. I can't remember why I'd invite Marengo North English and Lieutenant Nagit but not Saucerhead and Winger and Playmate."

*All my minds will be employed fully. I will have no attention left to monitor and prevent Miss Winger's miscreances. Nor did it seem likely that invitations to your real friends would attract nearly so much attention.*

"Which maybe tells you something about the crowd you hang with, Garrett."

"A crowd that includes you, old buddy. Speaking of hanging around. Keep him up there, Chuckles. Dean, see if you can find a stick. We'll let Morley be the piñata for this soiree."

Dean had just come in with a disreputable-looking pair of chairs he must have found in an alley. He considered Morley. "I believe I saw something suitable in the cellar while I was recovering these chairs." For once in his cranky old life he agreed with me.

*Dean, our other guests will begin arriving shortly. Garrett, play along for the time being.*

Morley turned over and drifted to the floor. "You should've let him have an extra gallon of beer last night. A hangover might help. Even in this light he doesn't look like he's dying. Though any honest tailor would be overcome by grief after just one glance."

"What will I be going along with if I don't go upstairs? What do you hope to accomplish, anyway?"

*I wish to locate Miss Montezuma. I believe she is still in the city. And I suspect that Pular Singe knows where she is hiding. I believe that because she has broken her ties with Reliance, Miss Pular has been unable to take advantage of her knowledge. I believe we can form an alliance beneficial to all of us if we can draw her close enough for me to initiate negotiations.*

Now I knew just enough to feel completely at sea. And I got to ask no more questions because the Dead Man's guests began to arrive, very nearly in a rush. When Lieutenant Nagit came in, as starched as a parade-ground martinet, he was in animated conversation with the redheaded despair of my life. Tinnie scarcely spared me a glance and a feeble wave. Which was no way to treat a dying man.

Of course, she'd be in on the gag, somehow. She'd been to the house enough to know that my health crisis must be somewhat exaggerated. And since they weren't loading me into a hearse, I was fair game for torment. Which explained Lieutenant Nagit.

Manvil Gilbey managed a timely arrival, accompanied by the expected brace of lovelies. Alyx looked as tasty as ever. But Nicks . . . Miss Giorgi Nicholas had made an effort. Miss Giorgi Nicholas must have left a trail of broken hearts all the way to my humble shanty. Miss Giorgi Nicholas looked like what the devil was dreaming about when he invented Temptation. And she'd thrown an extra log on the flirtation fire.

Tinnie ditched Lieutenant Nagit so fast his hair streamed in the breeze as she headed my way.

*I suggest this as an opportune time to exercise extreme caution, Garrett.*

"Go teach granny to suck eggs, Old Bones." Tinnie arrived. "You look lovely tonight," I managed to croak with one of my last few hundred dying breaths.

"I don't want to see you even looking at that tramp."

"Which tramp would that be, my sweet? The lothario with the epaulets on his shoulders and the board strapped to his back?"

*Exercise extreme caution, Garrett.*

He did have a point. "Nicks does clean up surprisingly nice. But you'll still outshine her on your worst day."

*Much better.*

"I knew I should've worn my hip boots." Peace had been declared. For the moment. "What's this all about, anyway?"

"You'll have to take that up with the resident haunt. I just found out I'm dying and you all are here to help me through it."

"You look pretty healthy to me," Alyx said, striking a little pose meant to test her hypothesis. To my destruction.

"Ladies, please. I've only got a few thousand heartbeats left. Don't make me use them up in the next three minutes."

Tinnie scowled at Alyx. Alyx remained oblivious. Maybe that was how she was getting by these days, by just not seeing anything she didn't want to see.

Belinda made her appearance. She, too, had taken some trouble, though all that black still made her seem a gorgeous beast of prey. After a somewhat cool greeting for me she fell into conversation with Lieutenant Nagit, who had been worshipping Nicks from across the room. . . . Where had *she* gotten to?

Gilbey edged close enough to observe, "You don't appear to be in any immediate danger."

"I'm having one of my good spells. Check me again after the ladies go home and I have nothing more to live for."

That earned me a nail in the ribs from the handiest lady.

Once again I had to explain that I had no idea what was going on. Gilbey nodded but didn't understand. "Should you go into remission Max wants you to oversee our interviews for replacement staff."

"Huh?"

"He decided to fire everyone who had anything to do with the conspiracy. He wants to pick up some trustworthy replacements. To do that we're going to have to go outside and take on people we don't know. Max doesn't want to get stung again. You'll interview and you'll background some of the candidates."

All that time cruising on retainer was back to haunt me again. "How'd Skibber Kessel take it?" His nephew had been one of the villains in the stable, back at the start of it all.

"Thinks we let the boy off easy. Skibber is loyal and he hates politics. He hates anything that might interfere with his art."

"Good for Skibber." Most people should understand that brewmasters are genuine artists. The best brewmasters, anyway.

Dean showed Colonel Block into the room. At that point I discovered Morley missing. That made two of them, one of each persuasion, one of whom was a rake and a rogue and a ruffian. "Not in my house, you tailor's dummy!"

"What?" Block had come over to offer his greetings. "If you're as weak as rumor says, you shouldn't be getting excited."

I didn't need to, anyway. Nicks came through the doorway lugging the Goddamn Parrot. Morley was right behind her but seemed chagrined. Was it possible his charm had failed him? I need to live forever because the wonders never cease.

Nicks had the oversize magpie perched on her left wrist. The bird basked in her attention. He didn't say a thing. Was his behavior one of those projects that would preoccupy the Dead Man tonight?

I told Gilbey, "You tell Max to say when, I'll be there. I don't have anything else on my calendar."

Gilbey glanced at Tinnie, sighed a little sigh to tell me I was hopeless, turned to accept a glass of wine from Dean.

# 110

*There are ratpeople in the neighborhood.*

I jumped. I must have dozed off. I listened. His dinner party certainly hadn't gotten rowdy. Too many people with too many agendas for everybody to relax and have fun—especially since everybody down there assumed that I'd had some sinister purpose for inviting them here. I was confident that not even Morley really believed that the whole thing wasn't my idea.

*I am unable to penetrate a rat mind with sufficient finesse to remain undetected but I do sense at least three such minds out there, all interested in this house. I assume them to belong to Pular Singe and her confederates in defying the ratkind Uncle.*

Some ratfolk call bosses like Reliance Uncle, presumably because the bosses treat everyone like favorite nephews and nieces as long as they behave.

I did not ask the Dead Man why he figured Singe would have accomplices. That seemed self-evident. Somebody had to be helping her stay hidden, had to be bringing her food and news and warnings. Fenibro would head my initial list of suspects. But I suppose he would receive the same honor from Reliance and thus would never be trusted by anyone as smart as Singe.

*It is time for you to stop sulking and rejoin our guests.*

"Whose guests? This ain't my shindig, Chuckles."

*Come down here, Garrett. Your presence is required.*

Well, if he was going to get nasty about it.

I drifted into the Dead Man's room as unobtrusively as a servant who didn't consider himself one of the family. Things

Colonel Block told me, "We could always use your talents. Should you recover."

"Righteousness don't put food on the table. How're my two favorite professional killers?"

"Not real good. They were in such bad shape we had to put them in the Bledsoe. Sadler died from his wounds. Crask passed, too, but he might have had some help." Block looked Belinda's way as he said that. "An interesting family. I'd like to get to know them better."

"No, you wouldn't."

Miss Contague and Lieutenant Nagit seemed to be hitting it off.

The Dead Man, I noted, was not a participant in anything. He seemed to be sleeping. But I'd been around him long enough to sense that he was anything but. Right now he was totally focused.

I said, "I'll be upstairs if anyone needs me. A dying man has to get his rest."

Once I reached my room I lay down on my back, tucked my hands behind my head, and began systematically reviewing every encounter I'd ever had with Marengo North English. And my memory is very good.

seemed to be going fine without me though the merrymaking hadn't turned into a rowdy kegger. On the way I had tested my office door and found it locked. Dean could do good work when he wanted. Following the meal Dean had broken down his makeshift table and left folks free to circulate around the ground floor.

The Dead Man must be a better entertainer than I thought. Nobody had pulled out. Yet.

I stood back and observed, not without company for long. Tinnie wriggled herself in under my arm. "You all right now?"

"I needed to figure something out."

"Did you?"

"No. But that's probably because of my personal prejudices."

Soon afterward Manvil Gilbey developed a strong need to get back to the Weider mansion, dragging two unhappy young women with him. Alyx and Nicks had flourished under the gallantries of Lieutenant Nagit and Morley Dotes. They weren't quite ready for the game to stop. Even Belinda had received some intriguing attention, cautiously from Colonel Block and, much less cautiously, from the amazing Mr. Gilbey, whose inhibitions may have gotten a little assistance looking the other way. So the evening was not a complete disaster despite poor sick old Garrett not having come floating belly up. It could've gone on indefinitely had not the Dead Man lost interest.

Next day the whole lot would be wondering what the hell it had been all about. And their confusion would be all my fault. Of course.

I offered Nicks another opportunity to take the wonder buzzard home but she passed. Again. "But you can bring him over to visit," she suggested with husking voice and smouldering eye and just a hint of a mocking smile because the good ship Tinnie Tate, away momentarily refreshing her teacup, was closing fast, under full-dress sail, cutlasses flashing like lightning.

Morley overheard the part where I offered the Goddamn Parrot. He took the opportunity to remind me that parrots often live longer than human beings do, a fact which amused him greatly.

"I can see it now," I said. "Me and the crow in the clown suit still together fifty years from now, living it up in Heaven's Gate." By then the bird and my so-called friends ought to have made me crankier than Medford Shale on his blackest day. "And a certain contentious old woman would come around every day to bang on the bars of the gate just in case I started to get comfortable or showed signs of beginning to enjoy myself."

"You'd better not be talking about me, Garrett," Tinnie declared. "I'm twenty-six, I like that just fine, and I'm never going to get any older."

I was surprised she confessed she was that long in the tooth. Generally she admitted only to a half decade less. And pulled it off pretty well. "I'm glad to hear it. Maybe you'll keep me young, too. Manvil, I need you to do something. Ask Max if he noticed anything unusual about North English when we saw him. Think about it yourself. Let me know right away if you think of anything."

"What? . . ." Gilbey frowned suspiciously.

"It's probably nothing. I've got a bee in my bonnet that's driving me crazy. I'm eighty percent sure I'm wrong. But I'm just as sure that I shouldn't be. I think that answer is in North English's behavior, but the most unusual thing I can come up with myself is that he paid my fees without complaining. Ever."

Still frowning, Gilbey nodded and resumed the difficult task of herding Alyx and Nicks toward the front door.

I turned to say good night to Lieutenant Nagit. "You overheard what I said. You're around your boss all the time. You notice anything unusual about him lately?"

"I know where you're going. And you're way wrong." But he frowned, a long way from convinced. There was something bothering him. He confessed, "He does seem to have developed a strong spiritual streak since he dodged the reaper."

"I can see how that might happen. Is he more social now that he doesn't have Montezuma to talk for him?"

"No. But I do see more of him because I have to."

"Did you find Tollie? Did you identify that dead man?"

"No. And no. And good night." Nagit went away not happy at all.

Then there was just Morley and Tinnie and Belinda. Belinda was surprised to find herself on the front stoop with me as her coach rolled up, almost as though someone had been reading minds. She offered me a darkly suspicious look.

I turned on the boyish charm. "You knew it would be dangerous when you came here. When you didn't have to come."

That touched her sense of humor. She flashed a quick smile, then swamped me in a brief, impulsive hug that left Tinnie tapping her toe.

"They go off together?" Morley asked as I closed the door.

"No. Nagit might be just smart enough not to swim with the

sharks. I wouldn't be surprised if he didn't volunteer to make sure Gilbey gets home safely, though."

*Garrett, it is time we moved to the final phase. To do so I must have Colonel Block removed from the premises.*

"Damn! I almost forgot he was here." The good Guardsman had been making himself small, perhaps hoping to find out what everyone was up to now. And my brilliant associate would be interested in what the Guard was up to. What Block himself might not know directly he could infer from experience and reference to other sources.

*A modicum of respect at last. The colonel?*

"I'm on it. What about Morley and Tinnie?"

*Mr. Dotes' special skills may prove useful. Pular Singe will not be the only observer in place though I have yet to detect any obvious watchers.*

Of course. Brother Relway would have his eyes anywhere any pair of my guests crossed paths.

"Surely there'll be no need for excitement."

*That will hinge upon how badly the interested parties wish to gain control of Pular Singe or Tama Montezuma. Ah. The ratgirl has summoned her courage and is approaching. I suggest you see her in the kitchen. I will ask Miss Tate and Mr. Dotes to remain out of sight here with me.*

"What about Dean?"

*He will have to answer the door. Singe might bolt if you do and she sees that your ill health has been exaggerated.*

"You set this whole thing up just to pull her in?"

*Not just. It was a tapestry. A work in progress. Pular Singe's arrival is the final thread.*

"You learn anything while you were slithering around inside their heads?" I can figure things out. I'm a skilled detective.

*Enough.*

"Meaning you're not going to share."

*Not unless it becomes necessary. Singe is standing in front of the stoop. She will find enough nerve to knock. Establish yourself in the kitchen.*

"How about the other watchers? Her showing up will excite them."

*Pular Singe is invisible. Go to the kitchen. Try to look sick. Dean! Answer the door.*

Singe knocked as Dean and I passed one another in the hall,

me wondering how much of that exchange Morley and Tinnie
would recall later.

*Not a word. They are enjoying a visit with Mister Big. Go to
the kitchen.*

# 111

I did my best to hunch over and look miserable as the sound of claws on wooden flooring rasped toward me. Dean was talking but the words coming out of his mouth definitely were not Deanish. Damn! That meant I would have to listen for a week while the old man pissed and moaned about the Dead Man taking control without asking.

*I suggest you muster what charm you can, Garrett. This child is more difficult than I anticipated. I cannot examine her thoughts without alerting her to my interest.*

I muttered, "I'm beginning to wonder just how much good you are. Seems everybody's opaque to you lately."

The kitchen door swung toward me. I sipped tea but thought about getting together with some beer. Dean said, "Here's Mr. Garrett. Mr. Garrett, it's long past time I retired. I'll see you in the morning. Please remember to lock up."

I grumbled something uncharitable, turned my head to look at Singe.

I did not see Singe. Not immediately. I saw a bent old woman bundled in layer upon layer of rags the way some street folk do. A huge, ugly hat that could only be of dwarfish provenance cast a shadow deep enough to leave her face indefinite. She must have bound her tail up behind her somehow because it wasn't out where it could be seen. She leaned on a heavy cane, which went a long way toward disguising the strange way ratpeople walk.

"Very good. You amaze me yet again. You're going to conquer the world. Tea? Something else? There's beer."

"You were expecting me?"

"I wasn't. Until a few minutes ago. Take a seat." Ratpeople can sit on their behinds although they find human furniture difficult. "Associates of mine wanted you to come see me."

"You're not dying? This is a trap?" Her Karentine seemed to be improving by the hour. She didn't have much more accent than Winger now, though her sibilants still gave her difficulty.

"I'm not dying. Sorry to disappoint you. On the other hand, this isn't a trap. You have my personal guarantee on that. Whatever anyone else might have had planned. That was a clever trick you pulled on us last week."

"Maybe. But foolish." Her "L" sounds still gave her trouble, too. "I did not think through the consequences. A common failing of my people."

"A common failing of everybody's people. Go ahead. Sit."

She sat. I patted her hand, then poured her a cup of tea, pushed across the pot of honey. She showed manners enough not to gobble the stuff straight from the container. Her hand was unsteady as she drank her tea, which she found difficult with a human cup.

I felt a little guilty even though this encounter was not of my manufacture. She was smart enough to understand that her emotions had been manipulated, which meant that they were no secret to those who had manipulated her. Which, of course, she would find embarrassing. "Why did you want me here?"

I reminded her that this was not of my doing but then admitted, "Tama Montezuma. My associates believe you know where she's hiding."

Singe sighed. "Of course."

I whispered, "Montezuma's money means nothing to me. Except that I don't want it to get back to the kind of people who would use it to finance cruelty toward those they hate."

"I am afraid, you know. Very much afraid. I did not foresee the interest others would show in finding that woman. I thought that once she disappeared they would forget about her."

"Human people have very long memories, Singe. Particularly in regard to grudges. Which is a thought to keep in mind if you're ever about to cross someone."

"That is a thought to keep in mind even if you are going to cross a nonhuman. Reliance, I am told, has been very bitter about my show of independence."

"I'll warn him not to be unreasonable. *Do* you know where Tama Montezuma is hiding?"

She had to think about her answer. It took her several minutes to decide to trust me and nod. I didn't become restless, waiting. Unlike other members of the household, I was willing to accept whatever decision Singe made.

I found it both amusing and a tad disturbing that the Dead Man couldn't snoop around inside her head—at least not subtly, undetected. Maybe she could teach me the trick.

"Yes. I know where she is, Garrett."

"Will you show me?"

"Am I wrong about you? Are you just after the money, too? Like your dark-elf friend up front?" She tapped her nose to tell me how she knew.

"Morley? He's my friend. But you're right. You have to keep an eye on him. He has his own agendas. He's interested in Tama mainly because of the money. I'm interested because the things she did caused a lot of people to die. Some of them were people I was supposed to protect. I can't let that go. Not even if I wanted to. Not even though I understand what made her do what she did."

"She is very unhappy. She has not moved since she entered the place where she is hiding now. It was prepared ahead. She can stay there a long time. She cries a lot."

"She sure can't wander the streets. Somebody would recognize her before she walked two blocks." I had trouble imagining Tama Montezuma in tears. They must be on her own behalf.

"She has disguises. But she is waiting for a time when she is mostly forgotten." My look caused her to add, "She talks to herself. Out loud. I found a way to get close enough to listen. That is where I have been hiding most of the time."

"Fenibro and Reliance himself came here looking for you. Several times. They've been at The Palms nagging Morley, too."

"Uncle will have to accept what he cannot change." She shuddered. "Yes. I will take you there."

"I want Morley to go along. I'll keep his greed under control."

"He will be disappointed, anyway. And the copper-haired woman?"

"Hunh?"

"She is in that room with the dark-elf and the bird and something else with an odor like death buried deep. She was at the mansion where the shapeshifters were caught. What is her part?"

A very neutral response was in order, I suspected. "A friend of long standing who heard the rumors you had and came here the same as the others tonight. She won't join us." I hoped. Tinnie made some strange choices when the mood took her and she was hard to dissuade. "She just hadn't left yet when you came to the door."

No telling what was going on inside Singe's head. She accepted my explanation. For the moment.

*I suggest you be on your way before she changes her mind. Do not dawdle exiting the neighborhood. I will bewilder and confuse any watchers but I can manage that only for a few seconds. Certainly less than a minute.*

I grunted grumpily. Any watchers would want to follow me, not the ragged crone.

Singe made an unhappy noise, too.

"What's the matter?"

"I was dizzy for a second. It was like there was a buzzing inside my head."

"Hunh." She had some slight psychic sense, too? Amazing.

# 112

"Quite a comedown from a manor in the country," Morley observed. The structure before us wasn't abandoned but certainly deserved to be. There was no charitable way to consider it fit for human occupation.

We stood in shadow, waiting while Singe shed her disguise. I mused, "But it's probably the kind of place she lived before she found out what she could do with what nature gave her and went to work in TunFaire."

"Where the streets are paved with gold."

Everyone comes to TunFaire to find their fortune. Mostly the survivors find despair. But there are just enough success stories to keep the gullible coming. "Fool's gold."

"Ready," Singe whispered. "Follow me." She darted from cover to cover, her true nature guiding her. The Goddamn Parrot fluttered across, high enough to be heard only, not seen, scouting from above. Morley and I followed the ratgirl. Dotes continued grumbling about not being allowed to bring along any of his friends from The Palms. I stopped listening.

We practically stumbled over a trio of ogre teenagers, one of each sex, who were way out of their territory and almost certainly up to no good themselves. They never saw Singe. They turned tail quickly once they glimpsed the equipment Morley and I were carrying. I decided I had yet another reason for wringing the Goddamn Parrot's neck. What the hell kind of scouting was he doing? He should've warned us.

The encounter did shut Morley up. Which would've happened

anyway. He shows no lack of concentration when the situation gets tight.

We took the rat route inside. No front door. We wriggled through a huge gap in a broken foundation. That placed us inside a cluttered, stinking cellar so dark even Morley couldn't see and had to be guided to a rickety stair by Singe. She murmured, "Stay close to the wall. Especially you, Garrett. It might not take your weight otherwise." Sounded like she was trying to crack wise. She needed practice. Maybe I'd let her work with the Goddamn Parrot.

The stairs groaned in protest. I sneezed despite a struggle to avoid that. Morley was having trouble with the musty air, too. I wondered why we hadn't just come in using the people route. Maybe I'd ask later. Maybe the simple thing hadn't occurred to Singe. We're all creatures of habit.

Tama Montezuma was multitalented but being a light sleeper didn't appear to be amongst her skills. Moreover, she snored like a drunken boatswain. That seemed way out of character.

The memory of a cloying, sweetish odor hung on the air. As Singe struck a spark to light a lamp for my benefit, I recognized that smell. Burnt opium. Opium smoking is an uncommon vice in TunFaire. It's an expensive, dangerous indulgence in an area where far cheaper, safer substitutes will whack your brain just as far around sideways and leave you drooling and acting even more stupid.

I had seen nothing to suggest she was an addict. But many addicts do function quite well much of the time, if they have money.

The light revealed a woman who had fallen apart, not at all the Tama Montezuma I had encountered at The Pipes. This Tama had fled all the way back to her roots, and beyond, in almost no time. This wasn't the Tama everybody wanted to find. This was a Tama overcome by despair, a Tama who had no more reason to live. This was a Tama who couldn't possibly have a stolen fortune hidden.

"You could have taken her," Morley murmured to Singe. "You didn't need our help." He looked at me. I could see the same thoughts flaring behind his eyes as were exploding behind mine.

"Yes. But it did not seem there was anything to be gained."

Our talk roused Tama. She struggled to sit up. She hadn't been eating well or keeping herself clean. She managed to look up at me. "You finally got here."

"I'm a little slow. Singe had to come fetch me." I didn't tell her hadn't been looking.

She reached for her pipe. Morley pushed it out of reach. If she was addicted, she would cooperate more fully if he kept that carrot dangling just out of reach.

Morley said, "Get a ring on Singe's finger before she gets any older or cleverer, Garrett. She played not just you but the Dead Man this time."

"Wouldn't have a coin on you, would you?"

"She's wearing a silver wristlet. So is the woman."

So was the woman. They weren't shapechangers. "Tama. You want to tell me something?"

"The fortune everyone thinks I got. I didn't. They knew. They found it. It wasn't where it was supposed to be when I got there." Tama's eyes wouldn't focus but her brain seemed sharp enough. "They only left the silver I took and the opium I bought as an investment. They expect me to destroy myself for them."

I had a mind like a razor tonight. I saw the answer she'd give me before I asked but I asked anyway. "And who might 'they' be?"

"The shapeshifters. The Dragons."

Maybe. But I didn't think so. More likely the Wolves hoping Tama would think Dragons and point a finger that way when she got caught.

Why would the Dragons leave opium behind? It has value even it it's not popular. It can be exported. There's a good market in Venageta.

"But you got all of the shifters, didn't you?" Morley asked me, in as close to a whine as I'd ever heard pass his lips.

"No. We missed at least one. For a while I thought that one might be North English. I figured he really did die the night he was attacked." It had taken only a slight adjustment of viewpoint, coupled with recollections of odd behavior, particularly at the Weider place when Marengo steadfastly avoided joining the rest of us on the main floor, to make me intensely suspicious. I'd decided he must've wanted to avoid running into Singe and her marvelous nose. There'd been other indicators, too, but once I cleared my head, lay back, considered nothing else, I'd been forced to conclude that the Marengo who had returned to The Pipes the morning after the aborted Cleansing could not have been a shapeshifter—much as I might want to stick him with something. But I was just as sure that he was supposed to have been killed. That he was supposed to have been replaced after he was attacked, that he was supposed to return home apparently badly injured as a means of covering and explaining the differences betrayed by the replacement as he took control of The Call. I had a feeling he might have gone into seclusion temporarily while Tama Montezuma relayed his orders to everyone exactly as she had done with the Brotherhood Of The Wolf. I had a strong suspicion that Marengo's bacon really did get saved by marauding dwarves, contemplation of which irony, ranged alongside various betrayals by supposed true believers, explained North English's newfound spirituality. Only I couldn't quite buy that, either. Maybe because it didn't satisfy my prejudices. Maybe because there were still loose ends.

I kept telling myself that there are always loose ends. Where there are people involved nothing ever wraps up neatly. Truth becomes more elusive than leprechauns. Hell, I've downed a few beers with leprechauns. Truth, when I run into it, often is dressed up in a cunning disguise.

"This is new," I told Tama, gesturing at her opium paraphernalia, pushing her pipe a little farther when she reached for it again. "Was Marengo supposed to be replaced the night he was attacked? You knew about the shapeshifters, didn't you? You were already working for Glory Mooncalled by then."

She tried to ignore my questions by focusing on her addiction. She continued to try for the pipe. I could almost hear it talking to her. She whined, "They forced me. They knew what I was planning. Gerris must have told them." She showed no contrition as she confirmed my suspicions by adding, "Gerris thought he was going to go with me when I went away."

"It was you outside the Weider front door the night Genord killed Lancelyn Mac." It struck me like a lightning bolt. Of course.

Tama nodded. "Gerris figured it out. He was extremely upset. We were arguing. Then the cripple and the other one appeared and Gerris made up a stupid story to cover himself but the one who came to the door saw me. . . . I didn't take them seriously enough. They did this to me. To get even."

"By 'they' you mean Genord's friends, right? The Brotherhood Of The Wolf?" I intended to take her confession with a twelve-pound grain of salt. The woman was a professional liar and now at that stage where she would try to lay the blame on anyone she could make fit.

"Marengo made up with them after he almost got killed. They were thrilled. They were ready to do anything—"

"Tama, don't bother. Your head's not clear enough. You can't make up believable stories. Marengo couldn't have made up with the Wolves. He was far too angry with them. What they'd done could destroy all his work. It could destroy The Call. He didn't know anything for sure until that last night at the Weider mansion but I'll bet he had some strong suspicions. Not exactly on the mark, because he was terrified by Perilous Spite, but close enough to worry you. When did Glory Mooncalled recruit you? I'm sure you didn't fight hard. Then you got your talons into him exactly the way you had Marengo and Gerris and your other accomplices. Didn't you?"

A spark of honesty. "Men are such idiots, Garrett. Especially older men."

A point. A good point. I propose the thesis that the span of time during which a man can be manipulated via his appreciation of a woman shrinks as he ages, because eventually—when he's been through it a few times—reality sets in ever more swiftly after the initial rush. "You say the Wolves did this to you?"

"Yes." Of course there were Wolves out there who hadn't been captured, who hadn't been sought, and more who had been released when the rest of the Hill turned on Perilous Spite.

"Just minutes ago you said the Dragons took everything."

"They did. Before things fell apart. The Wolves found me and did this to me and then hid me here so Marengo wouldn't find me until it was too late."

Could I believe this any more than her claim that North English and the Wolves had gotten back into bed?

Singe touched my arm lightly. "The opium is their revenge."

Tama began to weep. Her hands wouldn't stay still. "I made a mistake once. Long ago. When life was very cruel. I told Gerris about how'd I'd broken the habit afterward but I still craved it almost every day. When the Wolves came they knew. They forced me. In Gerris' name. It took them very little time to get me going again. But they left me only this much opium. And only this much money. So when the opium runs out and craving gets so bad I start throwing up and suffering cramps and screaming about things coming after me out of my memories, I'll have to go out looking for an opium seller. That time isn't far off now. And I don't know any opium sellers. It will take me a while to find one. It will take Marengo less time to find me. I don't expect him to be in a forgiving mood."

That rang true. But a lot of people were looking for Tama Montezuma, not just Marengo North English. And Tama Montezuma stood out. Somebody would get her.

Avengers try to be as cruel as their imaginations allow. Not many soft-hearted men survive to become the breed who make up groups like the Wolves.

"What about Glory Mooncalled and his friends?"

"I don't know. He must have run away. The Wolves. They're going to destroy Marengo. Because they think he betrayed them. Because the lying weasel really did keep them together and did send them underground. Then he never did anything with them. I was using them when I gave them orders. Singe thought you should know. I don't care anymore. TunFaire can burn to the ground. The world will end when I die anyway."

Morley muttered, "A solipsist in despair. Interesting."

"I still care," Singe told her.

I wondered how much of this the Dead Man knew or had reasoned out without bothering to tell me. I also wondered why so many people had been able to dodge around His Nibs. Was he starting to fail? Or was it just the way the dice had come up? The unlikely does happen.

My life is a testament to that possibility.

"How many of those changers were there?" Morley asked. "Do you have any idea how many are still running around loose?"

Tama shrugged. Her hands remained busy, crawling all over her, but her eyes had glazed over. We weren't going to get anything more from her until she'd smoked a pipe and then had had time to ease back out from behind a veil of dreams that were sweeter than life.

Dotes muttered, "We'll end up all having to wear silver amulets if this doesn't get wrapped up soon."

He had a point. I didn't have to invest much imagination to foresee a future in which—if the shifters reproduced successfully—a silver test would be part of every transaction. Every home that could afford them would have silver and spells worked into its doorways. The price of silver would soar. "We'll find out. I know who'll know." The Dead Man had been inside Glory Mooncalled's head. Mooncalled would've known exactly how many shapeshifters had come to TunFaire. We could work it out from there.

"What shall we do with her?" Morley asked. Singe watched me with big eyes, as though this was some kind of test. I had a feeling I would disappoint her.

"I still owe Max Weider. She chose the targets. She sent the killers."

I considered my first night at The Pines. That night visitor with the knife might have been Carter Stockwell thinking about settling up. Might have been. But it might have been Tama Montezuma with a special surprise for the troublesome fellow who turned up just as she was about to take over The Call completely.

Separate bedrooms, eh? I owed that little sneak Tinnie an extra kiss. No telling what I'd have gotten myself into if she hadn't been there.

Right now Miss Montezuma looked like the ideal gift for a friend in the secret policeman racket. Nor did Morley demur, she no longer having any fiscal capacity for arousing his sympathy. Singe did feel for her, as for a sister in despair, but even she wasn't prepared to excuse the evils Tama had wrought—of which those known to us were likely to be only a fraction.

# 113

I sent a note asking Lieutenant Nagit to visit me when next his duties brought him into the city. I received a polite, formal reply to the effect that he was under instructions to have nothing further to do with me. Insofar as Marengo North English and The Call were concerned we had nothing to say to one another anymore.

I didn't try again. I took it up with Max while I was helping interview prospective employees. Morley tagged along and stood around looking bored. Probably because what I was doing was as dull as watching rocks mate.

Nicks sent Lieutenant Nagit an invitation to dine with the Weiders. To no one's surprise but hers Nagit not only showed up, he arrived early, polished till he shone, reeking of rosewater, a bouquet of posies in hand. He was less than thrilled to discover that he'd share the dinner table with me and my feathered haunt but chose to endure the bad with the good.

The Goddamn Parrot attached himself to Nicks as soon as I went over to the mansion, early in the afternoon. They were made for each other, those two. Why couldn't they see it themselves?

Nagit never scowled once at Tinnie or Alyx. He didn't know what to make of Morley since they'd never been introduced. Morley paid him no attention. Dotes was charming to Alyx and all her male relatives. Nagit had no trouble with Max or Gilbey or Ty, either, so it had to be the way I parted my hair. Or something. But he was coldly courteous to me at best.

The servants brought dinner all at once, instead of in courses, then withdrew, except for Neersa Bintor, who made sure the kitchen door stayed closed. She kept her giant maul in hand.

There was little conversation while we ate, though the lovely ladies all tried to get something going, each in her own unique way.

Max growled, "Get on with it, Garrett." He'd barely nibbled his venison and had touched nothing else at all.

I made a small gesture. Morley excused himself from the table. He and Neersa Bintor left the room. With no apology for tricking him I said, "Mr. Nagit, we have one final problem. One more shapeshifter to expose." Now that he had demonstrated that *he* could eat using real silverware, off real silver plates. "Process of elimination says it's inside The Call now. For a while I thought it had replaced your boss. Then I decided it hadn't. You've just demonstrated that it couldn't be you. . . . Yes, boss." Max had begun to glower. He wanted me to get on with it.

I said, "If it wasn't Marengo, I wouldn't much care—except that having a shapechanger inside The Call means Glory Mooncalled still has a foothold there. A reliable witness tells me that Mooncalled has become an evil old man with terrible plans. This shifter could help Mooncalled do truly wicked things to TunFaire. *Then* I realized that even though Marengo hadn't been replaced by a shifter, the way I'd worked it out at first, back when he was attacked, he still could've been later, at The Pipes, in the last week or so. But why should I care? Marengo is Mr. Weider's friend. They went through the Cantard together. And Max is my friend. So I arranged to get you here so I could fill your head with my suspicions. You can deal with the threat to the friend of my friend. You can find the last shapeshifter. The one who left us wondering what happened to Tollie and the one-mitted thunder-lizard lover."

"Venable."

Morley and Neersa ushered Tama and Singe and a short, incredibly ugly little woman into the room. Montezuma was more frightened than the ratgirl was. She had been in the clutches of the Guard for twenty hours, with nary a whiff of opium. The short woman pretended to be a terrified servant of some sort. Nobody bothered to explain her presence. I stifled a grin.

Relway made one truly repulsive woman. But he'd insisted that he couldn't loan out his prisoner if he couldn't come along himself. I hadn't had the nerve to disappoint the head of the secret police—particularly when I had no good reason to shut him out.

I do believe he nurtured some idea of making a connection and being invited to The Pipes with Lieutenant Nagit.

Nagit never noticed Relway. He blurted, "You found Montezuma. How? We never caught a trace."

"Somebody out your way sure did, Ed. Some of the Wolves. Who'd gotten a word or two from Gerris Genord. Remember, they weren't wiped out, either." Nobody had a big enough grudge. Hell, the Wolves were heroes to a lot of men whose minds followed the same paths theirs did. Good old Bondurant Altoona was publicly very vocal about the treachery of The Call. Altoona might have profited more had he not been blessed with the personality of a toad.

I told Nagit the whole story, the way I saw it now, and added, "Tama says she'll cooperate. Reluctantly." She was a survivor. The only way she might get out of the pit she was in now would be to help save a man who might then hunt her for the rest of his days. I asked Nagit, "How's your status with North English?"

"It's weak. I know too much. He's reminded of that every time he sees me. But he does still talk to me. He doesn't have a choice—until he finds somebody dumb enough to want my job. I don't believe he's been replaced."

"Figure out how we could be alone with him long enough to check his reaction to silver, if we have to. Meantime, tell him whatever he wants to know. And you could isolate your senior officers and check them one at a time. That shouldn't be difficult. The real trick will be dealing with the shifter if you find him."

Nagit shook his head. He didn't want to hear it.

"There is one out there, Ed. Has to be. Otherwise, Tollie would still be chasing sheep and Mr. Venable would only be short the one hand."

Nagit rose. He made appropriate remarks concerning his invitation and the quality of the meal. He bowed in Neersa's direction to let her know he knew who was responsible for the latter. Then he asked, "Can I take Montezuma?"

Weider said, "No." Like it was his call. He was grim. In his heart Max had convicted Marengo of being a changeling already. The wounded Max within was looking for somebody to share his pain.

Nagit didn't argue. He did remark, "The boss will be disappointed."

Max observed, "Mr. Nagit, should you find that your employment with Marengo has become too onerous for your conscience, don't hesitate to contact Manvil. We can find a place for a man of your caliber. Don't you think, Garrett?"

"I can't see any objection to that." Well, except for a sudden sparkle in Alyx's eye and a little smile Nicks failed to keep corralled. And a dig in the ribs, in the same old sore spot, that I got for noticing those responses and maybe turning just the faintest bit dour.

Nagit headed for the street door.

Relway went after him. I didn't hear anything he said, but I assumed he was selling himself somehow, while Nagit was distracted by a headful of horrible possibilities.

"Satisfactory?" I asked Weider.

"Satisfactory. I'm going to turn in now."

As Gilbey rose to help Max, he said, "We'll be continuing those interviews tomorrow, Garrett. You and Ty will need to make yourselves available directly after sunrise." He smirked. He knew well my feelings about that godsforsaken chunk of the day forced in before the sun is sensibly standing directly overhead.

The Goddamn Parrot laughed and laughed.

I just sighed. Nobody promised me the world would be fair. Or even a little sane.

# 114

I thought that would be the end of it, as dramatically unsatisfactory as it seemed. I judged Nagit to be the sort who would save me the trouble I'd set myself up for, just to keep everything inside The Call's goofball family. But life—mine, anyway—doesn't come stocked with a surplus of dramatic unity. I resigned myself to the boredom of posing trick questions to men interested in replacing workers dismissed from the brewery. Everybody in town wanted to work for Max Weider. But halfway through the third day of tedium following that dinner the gloom parted when Giorgi Nicholas stepped forth for no better reason than wanting to see me.

Or maybe just to visit my stylish shoulder accessory, I concluded, when her killer smile and sparking eyes seemed to be aimed off center of what I considered the appropriate target. She extended her hand. I started to take it.

"This came hidden inside a note I got from Ed Nagit. It's addressed to you. It might be important."

The Goddamn Parrot began charming her as she started scratching his head. I made a growling noise. She was getting letters from Nagit now? Brother Ed wasn't wasting any time.

Lieutenant Nagit wanted to meet. He offered suggestions as to how we could manage that without distressing Colonel Theverly, whose influence in The Call had swollen substantially lately. Theverly had strong ideas about how a freecorps should be run. Those included excluding contacts with outsiders as questionable as me, be those business or social. I might be dressed in human flesh but the True Believers could smell the Other hidden inside me.

"I assume you'll be answering your own mail. Tell him I'll meet him there."

It was a nice autumn day. Big hunks of cotton cruised around a deep blue sky. The birds and bees were extravagantly cheerful and the temperature was almost perfectly comfortable. It was almost possible to forget this was morning, that half of the day the gods laid on us as punishment for original sin.

Lieutenant Nagit awaited me in that same pasture where Tinnie and I had hidden from the centaurs—who had been, only yesterday, finally discovered by cavalry supported by several sorcerers off the Hill. Official TunFaire had a big hunt on for the Dead Man's onetime role model, Glory Mooncalled, too. I was sure nothing would come of it. That old man had been running his enemies in circles for decades.

"Thanks for coming," Nagit told me.

"How could I resist?" His note insisted he had identified the last shapeshifter but claimed he couldn't do anything about it without help. And he wouldn't name names. "Why not handle this in-house?" I had an overdressed dwarf turkey riding one shoulder and a full-grown shrike of paranoia nesting on the other.

"Colonel Theverly insists the matter is closed. *Very* pointedly. There's no one else I can ask for help. Out here they all want to believe it's over. They want to get on with the mission. And they especially don't want to catch Theverly's eye by doing something he's forbidden."

"What about you?"

"He's a pain in the ass, not a god." A declarative statement which seemed somehow evasive. Lieutenant Nagit had something on his mind. And didn't want to share.

Gee. I never ran into that phenomenon before. "Why me?"

"Because you could bring her." He indicated Tama Montezuma, whom I had borrowed back from the Guard by sweet-talking Colonel Block and making several promises I have no intention of keeping. "And with her along we can get to the changer before anybody reacts."

He was right about that. He definitely held back on me.

Nobody challenged us at the gateway to The Pipes even though an increase in security had been mounted. Nor did anyone prevent us from entering the house. There was a lot of gawking and whispering and finger pointing because of Tama, though.

Montezuma looked worse than she had when I found her. Winger would've said she looked like death on a stick, well warmed over. Her will had collapsed in the cruel torment of withdrawal. She had little reason to go on. But she'd been lucky, in a way. Relway hadn't been around to abuse her.

I didn't go in there with nerves of steel. I had only Tama and Nagit to count on and no faith that either would stand behind me. I was betting to an inside straight. And Moms Garrett had taught me better over twenty years ago.

Was Lieutenant Nagit conning me? Or worse? The man was a true believer in the raging lunacies of The Call. He shared a domicile with numerous gentlemen who bore me huge grudges. I'd seen several familiar Wolf faces already.

Then came a shock that flipped the old pump. We ran into the ugly little woman who looked so much like Deal Relway's twin sister, scrub scrub scrubbing the hallway floor.

Lieutenant Nagit considered her beneath notice even though it was his fault she was haunting the manor. Apparent inconsequence is Relway's great and frightening strength.

The man guarding Marengo's sanctum didn't quite know what to do when Lieutenant Nagit stomped past without bothering to ask to see North English. The fellow must have been a soldier in his earlier days. Marines are taught to think on their feet.

We were through the doorway before he reacted.

As Lieutenant Nagit had promised as we walked, there were several men cozied up with North English. One was my old skipper, Colonel Theverly, who still didn't remember me. Another was the gent who had spoken for the Wolves at Weider's. What was his name? Tilde? Evidently he was back in good odor. There were others, all elderly. Great. I didn't see a spry bodyguard anywhere around.

Our advent interrupted a heated discussion. A frustrated Theverly wanted North English to approve something operational. North English seemed unable or unwilling to grasp the fact that this was the perfect moment for whatever the colonel had in mind. I did catch the Weider name, though.

There was a lot of anger in the air. It blistered in North English's eyes. He surged out of his chair, about to vent that rage on whatever idiot had dared to enter his sanctum uninvited.

He saw Tama. He froze. There couldn't have been anyone he less expected to see.

We kept moving. Lieutenant Nagit said, "See what Mr. Garrett caught. I was sure you'd want to see her right away."

"Uh . . . Yes." Confused and puzzled as well as angry, North English finished rising. And fear began to drive earlier emotions off his face. That seemed to shimmer momentarily as he gawked at Tama. Maybe that was a trick of flickering bad candlelight. Or of my imagination.

Theverly, Tilde, and the old men gawked, too. They hadn't expected to see Tama Montezuma again. Which effect was exactly what Lieutenant Nagit wanted her to produce. Tilde seemed almost distraught. Was it possible that Tama's hoard hadn't found its way back into the loving embrace of the chieftain who had denied the Wolves repeatedly?

I shoved Tama forward. She fell at North English's feet. He would be target the first. Tama played her role flawlessly. She was a superb actress, her skills honed in a harsh school. I couldn't have pushed her around if she hadn't been willing to cooperate.

Tama lunged into Marengo's legs. He squawked, flung himself backward. Colonel Theverly had an impulse to help North English but he couldn't manage much on one leg. He would be target two, chosen so because of his handicap. I kept an eye on him because, the way I'd worked it out, he was more likely a villain than North English, despite my prejudicial preferences.

Lieutenant Nagit surprised me by slipping a silver-chain noose over Marengo's head. He got behind North English. I grabbed Marengo's right arm. Tama caught his left and held on for dear life, which was about all she could expect to get out of this.

Nagit had scammed me mildly. I hadn't thought he believed his boss was the shifter. But he had started murmuring a mantra of a prayer that he'd figured this correctly. If he hadn't, he was going to wish he was doing his time in Hell already. With me right across the dining pit saying, "Please pass the brimstone." When this was over I was going to kick his scruffy butt. He could've given me a little more to go on if I needed to change my mind again.

As Nagit had hoped, North English's companions remained so stunned they did nothing for the vital few seconds it took him to get Marengo under control. A long moan escaped North English. He shimmered, began to get soft, spongy, loose, and I knew for sure now that Max Weider had yet another loss to mourn. And I had to go back and tell him. And I had to go back and think all the evidence through yet again because I'd been ready to give North English a pass despite his odd behavior.

When did his replacement occur?

The old men began to babble in confusion as it became obvious that their boss not only wasn't Mama North English's beloved son, he was one of *them*. One of the Other Races.

North English gave one violent surge, then just lost control. He strained to change but couldn't manage it in any useful way. Silver poisoning caused his body to grow more and more limp. By the time Tilde managed a lame effort to pull Tama away the arm she held had stretched two feet. Marengo's face had wax-melted into something not human at all. It looked like a giant slug's head.

I used a foot to push Tilde away, said, "Find more silver, soldier. Anything silver." Theverly kept hopping and I kept watching him closely. A glare was enough to control the old men. The paranoia I'd brought with me began to whisper of the possibility that there were still more shifters to be found. I was developing the suspicion that I might spend the remainder of my life as worried about changelings as I was about horses. In a few strange years I could be one of those street prophets who screech doom and despair and weird conspiracy at the most embarrassing times. . . .

The Marengo changer didn't fight with the ferocity and vigor we'd seen from others earlier. Maybe he was young, not yet at his full strength and wickedness. Maybe he'd worn himself out passing as Marengo. Maybe it was because he was alone, the last of his kind, lacking the psychic support of fellow changers. He had sunk to the floor before Tilde and the old men began to jabber about the implications this had for The Call. I held on, shaking, wondering what insanity had put me here. I couldn't imagine myself committing deliberate murder even though that was the custom in these situations. I felt the changer weakening, losing its plasticity. Soon it just lay there shivering.

I kept that eye on Colonel Theverly every second. His gaze locked with mine. I let go the shifter with one hand, plucked my own silver chain from inside my shirt. I'd brought it just in case. I hadn't wanted to reveal it. Theverly's face changed, but only into a slight frown. "I should know you from somewhere, shouldn't I?"

"Yeah. You should. The islands campaign." I couldn't find a "sir" inside me anywhere.

"Ah. I was there only a few—Three Force. Black Pete's bunch. Sergeant Peters. You were the kid who could find a girl anywhere, even in the middle of an uninhabited swamp. Garrith? Garrett."

Shucks. He was embarrassing me.

"Did I pass, Garrett?"

No changer could've learned all that. I nodded.

The door opened. A butler type with a refreshments tray invited himself into the room. "Damn my eyes!" I muttered. What a clever pose for a mastermind.

"The tea you requested, sir. . . ." Mooncalled's eyes bugged as he took in the scene. The tea service crashed and splashed.

Through clenched teeth I told anyone who cared to listen, "Grab him! That's Glory Mooncalled. He's the one behind everything that's gone wrong."

Theverly responded instantly. Unfortunately, the race seldom goes to the one-legged man.

The old man was spry. He was out of there before anyone else made up his mind that I might be right. They were just getting their minds around the fact that Marengo North English wasn't Marengo North English anymore. And Tilde was handicapped by his opinion of Colonel Theverly, who tried to order him to get after Mooncalled.

That old man hit the hallway and vanished into thin air, never to be seen again. Even now I don't quite accept Relway's assurances that the man didn't change shape as soon as he was out of our sight. Relway isn't what I call an unimpeachable witness. But the Dead Man also insists Mooncalled was no shapechanger. However, it hasn't exactly been that long since the world proved that His Nibs can be fooled, too.

No matter. Like Tama Montezuma, Glory Mooncalled is a survivor. But he's definitely out of business now.

We didn't finish strangling the shapeshifter. Once Lieutenant Nagit got a good, controlling choke on the thing and had breath of his own left to gasp out a few words he started lobbying Tilde and Theverly alike. His chatter became a constant in the background, like a ringing in the ear. Eventually, he won his point. His mutiny was excused. But Theverly and the Wolf, having formed an alliance without a word being spoken, insisted on taking possession of the changer.

Both men looked like they had a score or two to settle. Both were wondering just how long this thing had been managing and manipulating the movement. I didn't tell them it couldn't have been more than a few days. Already it was their messiah of misfortune, assuming the blame for every screwup in the last three millennia.

Damn! If they were clever enough, they could gain back everything The Call had lost—and more—by playing the existence of the changer off against rightsist prejudice.

You could see Theverly and Tilde evolving, the way humans do when huge changes in their power ecology occur. I made a small sign to Tama. I let go of the shifter's now-rubbery, flaccid limb. "It's all yours now, Ed."

I grabbed Tama's hand. "Time we made ourselves scarce, darling. Let this family clean its own house. Next time you're in town, Ed, if you've got nothing better to do, come by the house. We'll round up Tinnie and Nicks and go out to this romantic little ethnic place I know." Maybe I could find a place that served stuffed, roast parrot.

"I'll look forward to it."

Tama and I hit the hallway. I pushed hard getting out of the house. Heading across that big pasture out front, I whispered, "Keep moving, woman. Get as big a head start as you can. Nobody else promised you anything." Actually, Nagit had but we'd all known that he was lying.

"You going to keep your promise?"

"I always try to, no matter what. Even if I'd rather not. Because my word is really the only thing I've got to sell." We were moving fast, headed toward the gate. All I'd ever really offered her was a running start. If our paths crossed again, I'd pick up my grudge on behalf of the Weiders instantly. I wouldn't have any overriding obligation to society, as the Dead Man had argued in our discussions of Marengo.

"I'm not much on remorse, Garrett. But I do regret that what happened happened. It wasn't planned. For what that's worth."

"It's not worth much. But I do understand. I'm going to have a regret or six when I look back on all this myself."

"Maybe we'll have better luck in the next life."

"Maybe. See you there."

Tama turned south after we left the estate, broke into a long-legged, ground-eating lope. I turned north. Never the twain to meet. But meet something I did, in just a quarter mile. It looked a whole lot like Deal Relway in drag. He must have been planning a party because he had a whole lot of friends with him. I observed, "I take it you've given up the day job." How had he gotten out here with all these secret police thugs? I hoped he didn't have some dumb idea about trying to raid The Pipes. Those people up there were confused, but they wouldn't be shy about burying a few nosy Guardsmen in the back pasture.

Then my paranoia returned. There were lots of secret policemen and only one Garrett. And I was handicapped by the weight of the world's premier talking chicken. But Relway just wanted to chat.

"Soon as you exposed North English as a changer I knew there wasn't much future in scrubbing his floors. Nobody else in The Call can hold that mob together. I got out and waited out here."

"I never did see what his followers saw."

"That's because you're a cynic and a pessimist functionally incapable of believing in anything bigger than yourself."

The Goddamn Parrot began to snicker like he'd just heard a potent off-color joke.

"Bird, you and me and a roasting pan got a three-way date when we get home."

Relway mused, "Now that it's happened I'm not so sure I'm happy with the outcome. Spared their racial theories The Call would've been good for TunFaire."

He would appreciate their interest in law and order and proper behavior. "Here's a challenge you still need to meet. Glory Mooncalled. He's weak now but he's still out there somewhere. If you don't get him now he'll try to put something back together someday. He can't help himself."

"It's still great day for TunFaire, Garrett. One of pure triumph."

I don't know if he meant that or was being sarcastic. You never quite know anything with Relway. And he wants it that way.

"I liked the way you put it, Garrett. Faded steel heat." I'd mentioned that to him the night he'd discovered the tanks in the old Lamp brewery.

"But the war goes on."

"The war never ends. Tell you what. Send me a note when you do decide to roast that pigeon. I've got dibs on a drumstick."

"Ha! You hear that, bird? Your time's almost up."

"Help! Please don't hurt me anymore. . . ."

Chuckling, Relway said, "Don't forget to pick up your rat friend on your way home."

"Huh?"

"The guys say she's hanging around in those trees over there.

Lurking and skulking. General rodent stuff. Probably worrying about you. Would've been amazing to see her try to rescue you from all those thunder lizards and rat-haters."

The Goddamn Parrot had a good laugh at that. I couldn't think of a thing to say, then or when I did see Singe.

Life's a bitch. But it does go on.